D0058004

THE
MATARESE
COUNTDOWN

A NOVEL

ROBERT LUDLUM

BANTAM BOOKS
NEW YORK

The Matarese Countdown is a work of fiction. Names, characters, places, and incidents either are the product of the author's imagination or are used fictitiously. Any resemblance to actual persons, living or dead, events, or locales is entirely coincidental.

2014 Bantam Books Mass Market Edition

Published in the United States by Bantam Books, an imprint of Random House, a division of Random House LLC, a Penguin Random House Company, New York.

BANTAM BOOKS and the HOUSE colophon are registered trademarks of Random House LLC.

ISBN 978-0-345-53825-3

Cover design: Ray Lundgren

Printed in the United States of America

www.bantamdell.com

9 8 7 6 5 4 3 2

Bantam Books mass market edition: January 2015

For Karen— "Suzie"

She came with laughter when there was none.
And brought joy to life once more.

THE
MATARESE
COUNTDOWN

prologue

In the forests of Chelyabinsk, roughly nine hundred air miles from Moscow, there is a hunting lodge once considered a favorite retreat by the elite rulers of the Soviet Union. It was a *dacha* for all seasons, in spring and summer a festival of gardens and wildflowers on the edge of a mountain lake, in autumn and winter a paradise for hunters. In the years since the collapse of the old Presidium, it was held inviolate by the new rulers, an apolitical resting place of Russia's most venerated scientist, a nuclear physicist named Dimitri Yuri Yurievich, a *man* for all seasons. For he had been assassinated, brutally led into a monstrous trap by killers who held no respect, only fury, for his genius, which he wanted to share with all nations. No matter where the assassins came from, and no one really knew, they were the evil ones, certainly not their target, regardless of the lethal implications of his scholarship.

The white-haired, balding old woman lay on the bed, the huge bay window in front of her revealing the early northern snow. Like her hair and her wrinkled flesh, everything beyond the glass was white, frozen new purity from the skies, bending branches with its weight, a paradise of blinding light. With effort, she reached for the brass bell on the bedside table and shook it.

In moments, a buxom woman in her thirties with brown hair and eyes that were alive and questioning rushed through the door. "Yes, Grandmother, what can I do for you?" she asked.

"You've already done more than you should, my child."

"I'm hardly a child, and there's nothing I *wouldn't* do for you, you know that. May I get you some tea?"

"No, you can get me a priest—doesn't matter which variety. We weren't permitted them for so long."

"You don't need a priest, you need some solid food, Grandmother."

"My God, you sound like your grandfather. Always arguing, forever analyzing—"

"I wasn't analyzing at all," interrupted Anastasia Yuriskaya Solatov. "You eat like a sparrow!"

"They probably eat their weight every day. . . . Not that it matters, but where's your husband?"

"Out hunting. He says one can track animals in the new snow."

"He'll probably shoot his foot off. Also, we don't need provisions. Moscow is generous," the old woman said.

"As they *should* be!" interjected Anastasia Solatov.

"No, my dear. Because they're frightened to be otherwise."

"What are you *saying,* Maria Yuriskaya?"

"Bring me the priest, my child. I'm eighty-five years old, and someone must be told the truth. *Now!*"

The elderly, black-robed Russian Orthodox prelate stood over the bed. He knew the signs; he had seen them too often. The old woman was dying, her breath growing shorter, with each moment more difficult. "Your confession, dear lady?" he intoned.

"Not mine, you *ass!*" replied Maria Yuriskaya. "It was a day not unlike this—the snow on the ground, the hunters ready, their guns strapped over their shoulders. He was killed on such a day as this, his body mauled, torn apart by a crazed wounded bear driven into his path by madmen."

"Yes, yes, we've all heard the story of your tragic loss, Maria."

"They said at first it was the Americans, then that it was my husband's critics in Moscow—even his jealous competitors, but it was *neither*."

"It was so long ago, madame. Stay calm, the Lord is waiting for you. He will take you into his bosom and comfort you—"

"*Guvno,* you fool! The truth must be *told*. I learned later—calls from all over the world, nothing written, only words spoken through the air—that I and my children, and their children, would never live to see another daybreak should I speak of what my husband said to me."

"What was that, Maria?"

"My breath is leaving me, Father, the window grows dark."

"What *was* it, my child of God?"

"A force far more dangerous than what exists between all the warring factions on this earth."

"What 'force,' dear woman?"

"The *Matarese* . . . the consummate evil." The old woman's head fell back. She was dead.

The huge, glistening white yacht, its length over a hundred fifty feet from bow to stern, slowly maneuvered its way into the marina at Estepona, the northern point of Spain's opulent Costa del Sol, a retirement haven for the wealthy of the world.

The gaunt old man in the luxurious master stateroom sat in a velvet-covered chair, attended to by his personal valet of nearly three decades. The aged owner of the ship was being groomed by his servant and friend for the most important conference of his long life, a life that spanned over ninety years, the precise age kept secret, for much of that life was spent in the cutthroat arenas of men much younger. Why give those avaricious turks the advantage of his rumored senility, which in reality amounted to several generations of superior experience? Three cosmetic operations on his features might have left his face partially mask-like, but that was merely superficial, a misleading image to confuse the opportunists who would usurp his financial empire, given half a chance.

An empire that meant nothing any longer. It was a paper colossus worth over seven billion American dollars, seven thousand times a million, built on the manipulations of a long-forgotten entity. It began with a vision of revenge and turned ever more violently satanic, further corrupted by underlings who had no vision beyond themselves.

"How do I look, Antoine?"

"Splendid, *monsieur*," replied the valet, applying a mild aftershave lotion and removing a lap cloth to reveal formal clothes complete with a striped cravat.

"This isn't too much, is it?" asked the elegant employer, gesturing at his finery.

"Not at all. You are the *chairman*, sir, and they must understand that. You can brook no opposition."

"Oh, my old friend, there'll be no opposition. I plan to instruct my various boards to prepare for destructurization. I intend to give generous benefits to all who have devoted their time and energy to enterprises they essentially knew nothing about."

"There will be those who will find your instructions difficult to accept, *mon ami* René."

"Good! You're dropping our pretenses, you're about to tell me something." Both men laughed softly as the old man continued. "If the truth were told, Antoine, I should have put you on some executive committee. I can't remember when your advice was in error."

"I only offered it when you asked and when I thought I understood the circumstances. Never in the areas of business negotiations, of which I understand nothing."

"Only of people, correct?"

"Let's say I'm protective, René. . . . Come, let me help you up and put you in the wheelchair—"

"*No,* Antoine, no wheelchair! Take my arm and I'll walk into the meeting. . . . By the way, what did you mean when you said there'll be those who won't like my instructions? They'll get their benefits. They'll all be more than comfortable."

"Security is not the same as active involvement, *mon ami*. The workers will be grateful, indeed, but your executives may feel otherwise. You are removing them from their fiefdoms of power, of influence. Beware, René, several who'll be at this conference are among that group."

The yacht's large dining room was a low-ceilinged replica of a fashionable Paris restaurant, the impressionistic murals on the walls depicting scenes of the Seine, the Arc de Triomphe, the Eiffel Tower, and various other Parisian sights. The circular mahogany table held five chairs, four occupied, one vacant. Seated were four men in severe business suits, bottles of Evian water in front of each, ashtrays with boxes of Gauloises cigarettes beside them. Only two ashtrays were in use, the others firmly set aside.

The frail old man walked into the room, accompanied by his valet of twenty-eight years, known by all around the table from previous meetings. Salutations were exchanged; the ancient "chairman" was lowered into a middle chair, as his servant sat behind him against the wall. The procedure was accepted, none objected, nor could they, for it was tradition.

"So here are all the attorneys. *Mon avocat* in Paris, *ein Rechtsanwalt* in Berlin, *mio avvocato* in Rome, and, of course, our corporate lawyer in Washington, D.C. It is good to see you again." There were muted acceptances of the greeting; the old man went on. "I can see by your eager reception that you are not enthralled by our meeting. That's a pity, for my instructions *will* be carried out, whether you like it or not."

"If you please, Herr Mouchistine," said the attorney from Germany, "we have all received your coded instructions, now locked away in our vaults, and, frankly, we are appalled! It's not merely your intention to sell your companies and all their assets—"

"Excluding rather extraordinary sums for your professional services, of course," René Mouchistine abruptly, firmly, broke in.

"We're most appreciative of your generosity, René, but that's not our concern," said the lawyer from Washington, D.C. "It's what follows. Certain markets will crash, stocks plummet . . . questions will be asked! There could be investigations . . . all of us compromised."

"Nonsense. Each of you has been following the orders of the elusive René Pierre Mouchistine, sole owner of my enterprises. To do otherwise would result in your dismissal. For once, tell the truth, gentlemen. With the truth, no one can touch you."

"But, *monsignore*," exclaimed the *avvocato* from Italy, "you are selling assets far below market value! For what *purpose*? You delegate millions upon millions to charities everywhere, to nobodies who cannot tell a lira from a deutsche mark! What *are* you, a *socialista* who wants to reform the world while destroying the thousands who believed in you, in *us*?"

"Not at all. You are all part of something that began years before you were born, the vision of the great *padrone,* the Baron of Matarese."

"Who?" asked the French attorney.

"I vaguely remember hearing the name, *mein Herr,*" said the German. "But it has no relevance for me."

"Why should it?" René Mouchistine glanced briefly over his shoulder at his valet, Antoine. "You are all nothing but the webs of spiders that spun out from the source, hired by the source, making its operations appear legitimate, for *you* were legitimate. You say I'm giving back millions to those who lost the games—where do you suppose my riches came from? We became greed gone berserk."

"You cannot *do* this, Mouchistine!" shouted the American, springing to his feet. "I'll be hauled before Congress!"

"And I! The Bundestag will insist on investigating!" yelled the *Rechtsanwalt* from Berlin.

"I will not subject myself to the Chamber of Deputies!" cried the Parisian.

"I'll have our associates in Palermo convince you otherwise," said the man from Rome ominously. "You'll see the logic."

"Why not try it now yourself? Are you afraid of an old man?"

The Italian rose in fury to his feet, his hand reaching under his tailored jacket. It was as far as he got. *Kesitch!* A silenced, single gunshot blew his face apart, fired by Antoine, the valet. The Roman lawyer fell, soiling the parquet floor.

"You're *insane*!" screamed the German. "He was merely showing you a newspaper article in which several of your companies are linked to the Mafia, which is *true*. You are a *monster*!"

"That's sheer irony coming from you, considering Auschwitz and Dachau."

"I wasn't *born* then!"

"Read history. . . . What do you say, Antoine?"

"Self-defense, *monsieur*. As a senior informer to the Sûreté, I will put it in my report. He reached for a weapon."

"Shit!" yelled the lawyer from Washington. "You set us up here, you son of a bitch!"

"Not really. I simply wanted to make sure you would carry out my orders."

"We *can't*! For God's sake, don't you *understand*? It would be the end of *all* of us—"

"One certainly, but we'll get rid of the body, fish for the fish under the sea."

"You *are* insane!"

"We became insane. We were not at the beginning. . . . *Stop! Antoine!* . . . The *portholes*!"

The yacht's small circular windows were suddenly filled with faces covered with rubber masks. One by one, each smashed the glass with his weapon and began firing indiscriminately at every corner and shadow of the room. The valet, Antoine, pulled Mouchistine under a bulkhead armoire, his own shoulder blown apart, his master punctured around the chest. His friend of thirty years would not survive.

"René, *René*!" cried Antoine. "Take deep breaths, keep *breathing*! They've gone! I'll get you to the hospital!"

"No, Antoine, it is too late!" Mouchistine choked. "The

lawyers are gone and I do not regret my end. I lived with evil and I die rejecting it. Perhaps it will mean something somewhere."

"What are you talking about, *mon ami,* the dearest friend of my life?"

"Find Beowulf Agate."

"Who?"

"Ask Washington. They have to know where he is! Vasili Taleniekov was killed, yes, but not Beowulf Agate. He is somewhere and he knows the truth."

"What truth, my closest friend?"

"The *Matarese*! They're back. They knew about this conference, the coded instructions that are meaningless without the ciphers. Whoever's left had to stop me, so you must stop them!"

"How?"

"Fight it with all your heart and soul! Soon it will be everywhere. It was the evil that the archangel of hell prophesied, the good that became the servant of Satan."

"You're not making sense. I'm not a biblical scholar!"

"You don't have to be," whispered the dying Mouchistine. "Ideas are greater monuments than cathedrals. They last millennia beyond the stone."

"What the hell are you saying?"

"Find Beowulf Agate. He's the key."

René Mouchistine spastically lurched forward, then fell back, his head resting against the bulkhead. His last words were so clear they might have been gutturally whispered through an echo chamber. "The Matarese . . . the evil incarnate." The old man with the secrets was dead.

1

Six months earlier

In the rugged Corsican hills above the waters of Porto Vecchio on the Tyrrhenian Sea, there stood the skeletal remains of a once-majestic estate. The exterior stonework, built to stand for centuries, was by and large intact, the insides of the various structures destroyed, gutted by fire decades ago. It was midafternoon, the skies dark, heavy rain imminent as a late-winter storm made its way up the coast from Bonifacio. Soon the air and the earth would be drenched, mud everywhere, the overgrown, barely visible paths around the great house to be slogged through, not walked over.

"I would suggest that we hurry, *padrone*," said the heavyset Corsican in a hooded parka. "The roads back to the Senetosa airfield are difficult enough without the storm," he added in accented English, the language mutually agreed upon.

"Senetosa can wait," replied the slender man in a raincoat, his speech betraying a Netherlands origin. "*Everything* can wait until I'm finished! . . . Let me have the survey map for the north property, if you please." The Corsican reached into his pocket and withdrew a many-folded sheaf of heavy paper. He gave it to the man from Amsterdam, who rapidly unfolded it, placed it against a stone wall, and anxiously studied it. He kept turning his gaze away from the map, looking over at the area that momentarily consumed his attention. The rain began, a drizzle that quickly became a steady shower.

"Over here, *padrone*," cried the guide from Bonifacio, pointing at an archway in the stone wall. It was the entrance to a long-ago garden arbor of sorts, odd insofar as the arch itself was barely four feet wide while its thickness was nearly six feet—tunnel-like, strange. It was overgrown with vines crawling up the sides, strangling the entrance— forbidding. Still, it was a refuge from the sudden downpour.

The *"padrone,"* a man in his early forties, dashed into the small sanctuary, immediately pressing the unfolded map against the spidery foliage; he took out a red felt marker from his raincoat pocket and circled a wide area. "*This* section," he yelled to be heard over the pounding rain hitting the stone, "it must be roped off, *sealed* off, so that no one enters it or disturbs it in any way! Is that *clear*?"

"If that is your order, it is done. But, *padrone,* you're talking about a hundred or so acres."

"Then that is my order. My representatives will check constantly to make sure it's carried out."

"That is not necessary, sir, *I* shall carry it out."

"Good, fine, do so."

"And the rest, *grande signore*?"

"As we discussed in Senetosa. Everything must be precisely duplicated from the original plans as recorded in Bastia two hundred years ago, updated, of course, with modern conveniences. Whatever you need will be supplied by my ships and cargo aircraft in Marseilles. You have the numbers and the codes for my unlisted telephones and fax machines. Accomplish what I ask of you—*demand* from you—and you can retire a wealthy man, your future secure."

"It is a privilege to have been chosen, *padrone*."

"And you understand the need for absolute secrecy?"

"*Naturalmente, padrone!* You are an eccentric Bavarian

man of immense riches who cares to live out his life in the magnificent hills of Porto Vecchio. That is all *anyone* knows!"

"Good, fine."

"But if I may, *grande signore,* we stopped in the village and the old woman who runs that decrepit inn saw you. In truth, she fell to her knees in the kitchen and gave thanks to the Savior that you had come back."

"What?"

"If you recall, when our refreshments were so long in coming, I went into the *cucina* and found her in very loud prayers. She wept as she spoke, saying that she could tell by your face, your eyes. 'The Barone di Matarese has returned,' she repeated over and over again." The Corsican spoke the name as it was in Italian, *Mataresa.* "She thanked the Lord God that you had come back, that greatness and happiness would return to the mountains."

"That incident must be erased from your memory, do you understand me?"

"Of *course,* sir. I heard nothing!"

"To the reconstruction. It must be completed in six months. Spare nothing, just do it."

"I will endeavor to do my best."

"If your best is not good enough, you'll have no retirement, wealthy or otherwise, *capisce*?"

"I do, *padrone,*" said the Corsican, swallowing.

"As to the old woman at the inn—"

"Yes?"

"Kill her."

Six months and twelve hysterical days passed, and the great estate of the Matarese dynasty was restored. The results were remarkable, as only many millions of dollars could ensure. The great house with its massive banquet hall was as the original architect in the early eighteenth century envisioned it, chandeliers replacing the enormous candelabrum, and the modern amenities, such as running water, toilets, air-conditioning, and, naturally, electricity, reproduced throughout.

The grounds were cleared, the sodded grass around the main house allowing for a large croquet course and a challenging putting green. The long entrance from the road to Senetosa had been paved, submerged grass lamps lighting the way at night, and well dressed attendants greeted all vehicles as they approached the marble steps of the entrance. What visitors did not know was that each attendant was a professional guard, in the main, former commandos from various countries. Each palmed an electronic scanner that would detect weapons, cameras, or recorders within three meters; in essence, they could expose such objects from a distance of two feet.

The orders were clear. Should anyone arrive with these items, he or she was to be forcibly detained and taken to an interrogation room where harsh questions would be asked. If the answers were unsatisfactory, there was equipment, both manual and electrical, designed to elicit more favorable responses. The Matarese was back, in all its questionable power and glory.

It was dusk, the hills of Porto Vecchio fired by the setting sun, when the limousines began arriving. The Armani-suited guards greeted the visitors solicitously, helping each from a vehicle courteously with hands that unobtrusively roamed over their clothing. There were seven outsized cars, seven guests; there would be no more. Six men and one woman, ranging in ages from their early thirties to their middle fifties, a mix of nationalities with one thing in common—all were immensely rich. Each was ushered up the marble steps of the Villa Matarese where the individual guards led them to the banquet hall. A long table was in the center of the huge room, place cards in front of the seven chairs, four on the right, three on the left, no one closer than five feet from another guest. At the head of the table was an empty chair; a small lectern stood in front of it. Two uniformed waiters rushed about taking orders for cocktails; delicate crystal bowls of beluga caviar were at each place setting, and the muted strains of a Bach fugue subtly filled the room.

Quiet conversations began haltingly, as though none of

the guests understood the reason for this gathering. Yet, again, there was a common denominator: All spoke English and French, so both languages were employed, finally narrowed down to the former, as the two male Americans were neither especially quick nor sufficiently comfortable with the latter tongue. The badinage was inconsequential, reduced to who knew whom and wasn't the weather glorious in St. Tropez, or the Bahamas, Hawaii, or Hong Kong? None dared to ask the essential question: *Why are we here?* Six men and one woman were frightened people. They had reason to be. There was more in their individual pasts than the present suggested.

Suddenly, the music stopped. The massive chandeliers were dimmed as a small spotlight emerged from the railing of the balcony, growing brighter as it shone down on the lectern at the head of the table. The slender man from Amsterdam walked out of an alcove and moved slowly into light and the lectern. His pleasant if dismissible face looked pale under the glare, but his eyes were not to be dismissed. They were alive and steady, centering briefly on each person as he nodded to each in turn.

"I thank you all for accepting my invitation," he began, his voice an odd mixture of ice and repressed heat. "I trust your traveling accommodations were in the style to which you are accustomed." There was a murmur of affirmatives, although hardly enthusiastic. "I realize," continued the man from Amsterdam, "that I interrupted your lives, both social and professional, but I had no choice."

"You have it now," interrupted the lone woman coldly. She was in her thirties and dressed in an expensive black dress with a string of pearls that bespoke at least fifty thousand dollars, American. "We're here, now tell us why."

"I apologize, madam. I am well aware you were on your way to the Rancho Mirage in Palm Springs for an assignation with your current husband's partner in his extortionist brokerage firm. I'm sure your absence will be overlooked, as there would be no firm had you not financed it."

"I *beg* your pardon!"

"Please, madam, I'm uncomfortable with beggars."

"Speaking for myself," said a middle-aged, balding Portuguese, "I'm here because you implied that I could be in serious difficulty if I did not appear. Your coded allusion was not lost on me."

"My cable merely mentioned the name 'Azores.' Apparently it was enough. The consortium you head is fraught with corruption, the bribes to Lisbon are blatantly criminal. Should you control the Azores, you control not only the incessantly excessive airline fees but the excise taxes of over a million tourists a year. Well thought out, I'd say."

There was an eruption of voices on both sides of the table, some hinting at various questionable activities that might have been the bases of the seven coming to the hidden estate in Porto Vecchio.

"Enough," said the man from Amsterdam, raising his voice. "You mistake why you are here. I know more about each one of you than you know about yourselves. It is my legacy, my inheritance—and you are *all* inheritors. We are the descendants of the *Matarese,* the font from whom all your wealth derives."

The seven visitors were stunned, a number glancing at each other as if an unspeakable thing bonded them to one another.

"That's not a name we use or refer to, I shouldn't think," said an Englishman in the sartorial splendor of Savile Row. "Neither my wife nor my children have ever heard it," he added softly.

"Why bring it up?" asked a Frenchman. "The Matarese is long gone—dead and forgotten, a distant memory to be buried."

"Are you dead?" said the Hollander. "Are *you* buried? I think not. Your riches have enabled you to reach the pinnacle of financial influence. All of you lead, by name or in absentia, major corporations and conglomerates, the very essence of the Matarese philosophy. And each of you was chosen by me to fulfill the Matarese destiny."

"What goddamned destiny?" asked one of the Americans, his accent from the Deep South. "You some kinda Huey Long?"

"Hardly, but your casino interests along the Mississippi River might suggest that you are."

"My operations are as clean as they have to be, buddy-boy!"

"I relish your modifier—"

"*What* destiny?" broke in another American. "The name Matarese never appeared in any legal documentation relative to the real-estate interests bequeathed to my family."

"I'd be appalled if it had, sir. You're the leading attorney at a major bank in Boston, Massachusetts. Harvard Law School, *magna cum laude* . . . and part of the most bribery-prone institution that ever sucked money by way of compromising state and federal officials, both elected *and* appointed. I commend your talents."

"You can't *prove* any such thing."

"Don't tempt me, Counselor—you'd lose. However, I did not bring all of you to Porto Vecchio merely to parade the thoroughness of my inquiries, although I concede they're a part of the whole. The carrot and the stick, as it were. . . . First let me introduce myself. I am Jan van der Meer Matareisen, and I'm sure the last name has meaning for you. I am a direct descendant of the Baron of Matarese; he was, in fact, my grandfather. As you may or may not know, the Baron's liaisons were held secret, and whatever offspring resulted were also kept secret. However, the great man in no way abandoned his responsibilities. His issue was sent to the finest families throughout Italy, France, England, Portugal, America, and, as I can attest, the Netherlands."

The visitors were again dumbstruck. Slowly, gradually, their eyes strayed around the table. All stared at one another briefly, penetratingly, as if some extraordinary secret was about to be revealed.

"What the hell are you gettin' at?" said the large, coarse American from Louisiana. "Spell it out, boy!"

"I agree," added the man from London, "what's your point, old man?"

"I believe several of you are already ahead of me," said Jan van der Meer Matareisen, permitting himself the trace of a smile.

"Then *say* it, Dutchman!" demanded the entrepreneur from Lisbon.

"Very well, I shall. Like myself, you are all children of those children. We are the products of the same loins, as the English bard might have phrased it. Each and every one of you is a blood descendant of the Baron of Matarese."

The audience exploded as one with phrases such as "We've heard of the Matarese, but nothing like *this*!" and "That's *preposterous*! My family was wealthy in its own right!" and "*Look* at me! I'm a natural blond, not a trace of the Mediterranean in me!" The protestations grew in volume until the protestors ran out of breath, finally subsiding as Jan Matareisen raised his hands under the shaft of light.

"I can answer your assaults specifically," he said calmly, "if you will but listen. . . . The Baron's appetites were fierce and varied, as he was. Your grandmothers were brought to him as if they were the whims of an Arabian sheikh; none, however, was defiled, for all accepted him for the extraordinary man he was. But I, and only *I,* was the legitimate child in the eyes of the Church. He married my grandmother."

"What the hell are *we*?" yelled the American from New Orleans. "*Bastards* goin' back two *generations*?"

"Have you ever lacked for funds, sir? For education or investment."

"No . . . can't say that I have."

"And your grandmother was, and is still, an extremely beautiful woman, a model whose face and figure graced such publications as *Vogue* and *Vanity Fair,* is that not so?"

"I reckon, although she doesn't talk about it much."

"She didn't have to. She quickly married an insurance executive whose company expanded to the point where he was made president."

"You're not only suggesting, but you're also actually stating, that we're all *related*!" cried the attorney from Boston. "What proof do you have?"

"Buried six feet in the earth on the northeast acreage of this property was a small vault, an oilcloth packet inside. It took me five months to find it. In the oilcloth were the names of the Baron's children and their new homelands. He was, if nothing else, precise in all things. . . . Yes, my Bostonian guest, we are all related. We are cousins, whether we like it or not. Collectively, we are the inheritors of the Matarese."

"Incredible," said the Englishman, his breath suspended.

"My *Gawd*!" said the American from the Deep South.

"It's *ridiculous*!" shouted the blond woman from Los Angeles.

"Actually, it's rather comical," said a man from Rome in the clerical garb of the Vatican. A cardinal.

"Yes," agreed Matareisen, "I thought you might appreciate the sublime humor. You are a rogue priest, in favor with His Holiness but loathed by the Collegium."

"We must move the Church into the twenty-first century. I make no apologies."

"But you make a great deal of money from banks controlled by the Holy See, is that not so?"

"I recommend, I do not profit personally."

"According to my sources, that's debatable. I refer, of course, to a mansion on the banks of Lake Como."

"It is my *nephew's*."

"From his second marriage, the first having been illegally annulled by you, but let us move on. I really don't care to embarrass anyone. After all, we *are* family. . . . You are all here because you are vulnerable, as I am most certainly vulnerable. If I can uncover your various enterprises, so can others. It's merely a question of provocation, time, and curiosity, isn't it?"

"You talk too damned much without sayin' a damn thing," said the agitated American from the South. "What's your agenda, buddy-boy?"

" 'Agenda,' I like that. It tallies with your background, a Ph.D. in business management, if I'm not mistaken."

"You're not. You can call me a redneck and you wouldn't be far wrong, but I'm not a stupid one. Go on."

"Very well. The agenda—*our* agenda—is to bring to fruition the cause of the Matarese, the vision of our grandfather, Guillaume de Matarese."

All eyes were riveted on the Dutchman. It was apparent that despite reservations, the seven inheritors were intrigued—cautiously. "Since you're far more familiar with this 'vision' than we are, might you be clearer?" asked the subdued, fashionably dressed woman.

"As you're all aware, international finance is now globally integrated. What happens to the American dollar affects the German deutsche mark, the English pound, the Japanese yen, and all the world's currencies, as well as each in turn affecting the others."

"We are well aware," said the Portuguese. "I suspect that many of us profit considerably from the fluctuating exchange rates."

"You've suffered losses, too, haven't you?"

"Minor compared to our winnings, as my 'cousin,' the American, might say of his casinos' profits, as opposed to his players' losses."

"You've got *that* right, Cousin—"

"I believe we stray," interrupted the Englishman. "The agenda, if you please?"

"To control the global markets, to infuse discipline on international finance—that was the cause of the visionary known as the Baron of Matarese. Put money in the hands of those who know how to use it, not governments, who know only how to waste it, pitting one nation against another. The world is already at war, a continuing economic war, yet who are the victors? Remember, whoever controls a nation's economy controls its government."

"And you're saying? . . ." The Portuguese sat forward.

"Yes, I am," the Hollander broke in. "*We* can do it. Our collective assets are over a trillion dollars, sufficiently excessive seed money and spread out geographically to influence the power centers we represent. Influence that will spread across the world as rapidly as the hourly transfers of millions from one financial market to another. Acting in concert, we have the power to create economic chaos, all to our individual and collective benefit."

"That's wild," cried the entrepreneur from New Orleans. "We can't lose 'cause we hold the cards!"

"Except a few," said the Matarese grandson. "As I mentioned before, you were all chosen because I found vulnerabilities that served my purposes, the carrots and sticks, I believe I said. There were others I approached, perhaps giving away more than I should have. They were violently opposed to my supplications, stating that they would instantly expose any moves the inheritors of the Matarese might make. . . . They are three, two men and one woman, for the Baron had ten grandchildren outside of the Church. So we go from the abstract, the global, to the personal. To those three extremely influential individuals who would destroy us. Therefore, we must destroy them first. Here, you can all be of service. . . . Gentlemen and dear lady, they must be eliminated before we make our moves. But killed ingeniously, leaving no traces whatsoever to any of you. There was another, not of our bloodline, an old man but so powerful he could have crippled us the instant we started to rise. He is no longer an obstacle, the others are. They are the only ones left who stand in our way. Shall we get down to basics? Or are there any who care to leave now?"

"Why do I have the feeling that if we did, we'd never reach the road to Senetosa?" mused the woman.

"You ascribe to me more than I ascribe to myself, madam."

"Go ahead, Jan van der Meer Matareisen, visions are my business," said the cardinal.

"Then envision this, Priest," said Matareisen. "We have a schedule, a countdown, if you like. Only a few months away, the beginning of the New Year. That is our target for global control, Matarese control."

2

The Hamptons, New York, August 28

The East End of Long Island is less than an hour from Manhattan, depending upon the type of private aircraft involved. The "Hamps" will forever remain the imaginary province of the novelist F. Scott Fitzgerald, at least certain sections where private aircraft *are* involved. It is rich and pampered, replete with grand mansions, manicured lawns, glittering blue pools, tennis courts, and serrated ranks of English gardens in stunning bloom under the summer sun. The exclusivity of decades past has been swept away by the wealth of the meritocracy. Jews, Italians, idolized blacks and Hispanics—all previously excluded—are now the grandees of the East End, peacefully, even enthusiastically, coexisting with the still-shocked WASP inheritors of ancestral prosperity.

Money is a unique equalizer. The various clubs' dues are reduced by the influx of the pretenders, and their generous contributions to the improvements of the numerous premises gratefully, enthusiastically accepted.

Jay Gatsby forever lives, with or without Daisy—and Nick, the conscience of an era.

The polo match at the Green Meadow Hunt Club was in full fury, ponies and riders drenched in sweat as hooves pounded and mallets swung viciously at the elusive white ball that kept veering dangerously out of reach beneath the stampeding horses and across the flying turf. Suddenly, there was an agonized scream from one of the riders. He had lost his helmet in the heat of the chase. His head was a mass of blood; the skull itself appeared to be cracked open.

Everything came to a halt as the combatants sprang off their mounts and raced to the fallen rider. Among them was a doctor, an Argentinean surgeon who parted the bodies in front of him and knelt beside the unconscious figure. He looked up at the expectant faces. "He's dead," the doctor said.

"How could it have *happened*?" cried the captain of the Red Team, the dead man's team. "A wooden mallet might have knocked him out—we've all experienced that—but not crush his skull, for God's sake!"

"What struck him wasn't wood," said the Argentinean. "I'd say it was far heavier—iron or lead, perhaps." They were in an alcove of the enormous stables, two uniformed patrolmen and the local Emergency Medical Services unit having been summoned. "There should be an autopsy, specifically concentrating on the cranial impact," continued the doctor. "Put that in your report, please."

"Yes, sir," answered one of the patrolmen.

"What are you suggesting, Luis?" asked another rider.

"It's pretty clear," answered a patrolman, writing in his notebook. "He's suggesting that this may not be an accident, am I correct, sir?"

"That's not for me to say, Officer. I'm a doctor, not a policeman. I'm only offering an observation."

"What's the deceased's name, and does he have a wife or relatives in the area?" interrupted the second patrolman, glancing at his companion and nodding at the notebook.

"Giancarlo Tremonte," replied a blond rider, his speech born of the old crowd.

"I've heard that name," said the first policeman.

"Quite possibly," continued the light-haired player. "The Tremonte family of Lake Como and Milan are very well known. They have considerable interests in Italy and France, as well as over here, of course."

"No, I mean the Giancarlo part," broke in the patrolman with the notebook.

"He's frequently in the newspapers," said the captain of the Red Team. "Not always in the more respectable ones, although his own reputation is splendid—was splendid."

"Then why was he in the papers so frequently?" asked the second policeman.

"I suppose because he was terribly wealthy, attended many social and charity events, and liked women." The leader of the Red Team looked pointedly at the patrolman. "That's grist for third-rate journalists, Officer, but hardly a sin. After all, he didn't choose his parentage."

"I guess not, but I think you've answered one of my questions. There's no wife around, and if there were any girlfriends, they got the hell out of here. To avoid those third-rate journalists, of course."

"You have no argument with me."

"I'm not looking for one, Mr. . . . Mr.? . . ."

"Albion, Geoffrey Albion. My summerhouse is in Gull Bay, on the beach. And to the best of my knowledge, Giancarlo has no relatives in the area. It's my understanding that he was here in the States to oversee the Tremonte family's American interests. When he leased the Wellstone estate, we were, of course, delighted to accept him into Green Meadow. He is—was—a very talented polo player. . . . May we please remove his remains?"

"We'll cover him, sir, but he has to stay here until our superiors and the medical examiner arrive. The less he's moved, the better."

"Are you implying that we should have left him out in the field in front of the crowds?" said Albion curtly. "If so, you *will* have an argument with me. It's tasteless enough that you roped off the area where he fell."

"We're just doing our job, sir." The first police officer

replaced the notebook in his pocket. "Insurance companies are very demanding in these cases, especially cases where injury or death is the result. They want to examine everything."

"Speaking of which," added the second patrolman, "we'll need the mallets of both teams, of everyone who was in the match."

"They're all on the wall over there," said the blond player with the precise if slightly nasal speech. The wall referred to held dozens of two-pronged colored racks from which the polo mallets hung like wooden utensils. "Today's players are in the red section, the farthest on the left," he continued. "The grooms hose them down but they're all there."

"Hose them down? . . ." The first policeman took out his notebook.

"Dirt and mud, old boy. It can get messy out there. See, some are still dripping."

"Yes, I can see that," said the second patrolman quietly. "Just water from hoses? No dipping in cleaning solutions or anything like that?"

"No, but it sounds like a fine idea," said yet another rider, shaking, then nodding, his head.

"Just a minute," interrupted the patrolman, walking to the wall and studying the mallets. "How many are supposed to be here in the red section?"

"It varies," replied Albion condescendingly. "There are eight players, four to a team, along with replacements and reserve mallets. There's a movable yellow peg that separates the current match from the members not playing that day. The grooms take care of it all."

"Is this the yellow peg?" asked the patrolman, pointing to a bright, circular, snub-nosed piece of wood.

"It's not purple, is it?"

"No, it's not, Mr. Albion. And it hasn't been moved since the match began this afternoon?"

"Why should it be?"

"Maybe you should ask, why wasn't it? There are two mallets missing."

The celebrity tennis tournament in Monte Carlo drew dozens of recognizable performers from films and television. Most were American and British who played with and against the socialites of Europe—minor royalty and wealthy Greeks, Germans, a few fading French writers, and several Spaniards who claimed long-forgotten titles but insisted that the word *Don* preceded their names. Nobody took much seriously, for the nightly festivities were extravagant, the participants gloried in their brief spotlights—televised, of course—and since everything was sponsored by Monaco's ruling house, a great deal of fun—and publicity—was had by all while charity thrived.

An enormous buffet was held under the stars in the huge courtyard of the palace overlooking the harbor. A talented orchestra held sway, playing in a variety of musical styles, from opera to nostalgic pop, as internationally known singers took turns entertaining the crowd, each receiving an ovation as the elegant audience rose from their elegantly dressed tables under the spill of roving spotlights.

"Manny, I want my gig on *Sixty Minutes,* you *got* that?"

"Got it, babe, it's a natural!"

"Cyril, why am I here? I don't play *tennis*!"

"Because there are studio heads here! Go up and recite something in your dulcet tones, and keep turning right and left. Your *profeel,* chap!"

"That fucking bitch stole my *song*!"

"You didn't copyright it, darling. Do 'Smoke Gets in Your Eyes' or something!"

"I don't know all the words!"

"Then hum and push your tits into their faces. The *record* boys are here!" And so it went; altruism will out.

Among the congregation of great, near-great, non-great, and never-great was a quiet man, a modest man of wealth with little or no pretense. He was a research fellow, a scholar committed to the study of cancers, and was in Monte Carlo as one of the contributing sponsors. He had requested anonymity, but his largess prohibited it in the eyes of the Grand Committee. He had agreed, in the name of his Spanish family, to give a very short speech welcoming the guests.

He stood behind a courtyard screen, prepared to walk out to the podium when his name was called. "I'm quite nervous," he said to a stagehand who stood beside him, ready to tap him on the shoulder when it was his time. "I'm not very good at speaking in public."

"Make it short and thank them, that's all you have to do. . . . Here, have a glass of water, it'll clear your throat."

"Gracias," said the genuinely titled Juan Garcia Guaiardo. He drank, and on his way to the podium he collapsed. By the time he was dead, the stagehand had disappeared.

Alicia Brewster, Dame of the Realm by decree of the Queen, emerged from her Bentley in front of the family residence in London's Belgravia. She was a medium-sized, compact woman, but her stride and the energy it implied made her appear much larger, a force to be reckoned with. She let herself into the colonnaded entrance of the Edwardian house, only to be greeted by her two children, who had been summoned from their respective boarding schools and were waiting for her in the large, polished hall. They were a tall, clean-cut, muscular young man and a shorter, equally attractive girl, he in his late teens, she a little younger, both anxious, concerned, even frightened.

"I'm sorry to have called you home," said the mother after briefly embracing each child. "I simply thought it was better this way."

"It's that serious, then?" asked the older brother.

"That serious, Roger."

"I'd say it's long overdue," said the girl. "I never liked him, you know."

"Oh, *I* did, very much, Angela." Alicia Brewster smiled sadly while nodding her head. "Also, I felt you needed a man around the house—"

"He was hardly tops in that department, Mother," interrupted the boy.

"Well, he had a tough act to follow, as they say. Your father was rather overwhelming, wasn't he? Successful, famous, certainly dynamic."

"You had a lot to do with it, Mum," said the daughter.

"Far less than you think, my dear. Daniel was his own man. I depended a great deal more on him than he depended on me. The saddest part of his passing, I always think, is that it was so prosaic, so banal, really. Dying in his sleep from a stroke. Merely the thought of it would have driven him to his gym, swearing."

"What do you want us to do, Mother?" asked Roger quickly, as if to stem the flow of painful memories.

"I'm not sure. Moral support, I guess. Like most weak men, your stepfather has a vicious temper—"

"He'd better not show it," the strapping young man broke in. "If he even raises his voice, I'll break his neck."

"And Rog can do it, Mum. He won't tell you, but he's the Midlands interscholastic wrestling champ."

"Oh, shut up, Angie, there wasn't any competition."

"I hardly meant in the physical sense," interrupted Alicia. "Gerald's not the sort. It's all just screaming tantrums with him. It'll simply be unpleasant."

"Then why not have your solicitor take care of it, Mother?"

"Because I have to know why."

"Why *what*?" asked Angela.

"To keep him more occupied and, I suppose, to enhance his self-esteem, I put him on the finance committee of our Wildlife Association, made him chairman, in fact. Irregularities began to appear, allocations to nonexistent entities, that sort of thing. . . . The bottom line is that Gerald stole over a million pounds from the association."

"Jesus *Christ*!" exclaimed the son.

"But *why*? He's never been stony since you married him! Why *did* you marry him?"

"He was so charming, so alive—on the surface in many ways like your father, but only on the surface. And, let's face it, I was terribly depressed. I thought he had strength until I learned it was only false bravado. . . . Where is he?"

"In the upstairs library, Mother. I'm afraid he's drunk."

"Yes, I assumed as much. You see, I did use my solicitor,

after a fashion. I'll make up the money, but I can't press charges or anything like that—the publicity could harm the association. He was told to pack his bags and be ready to leave at once after confronting me. I demanded that. I'll go up now."

"I'll go with you."

"No, dear, it's not necessary. When he comes downstairs, put him in his car. If he's too drunk to get behind the wheel, call Coleman and have him drive Gerald wherever he wishes to go. I suspect to his new girl in High Holborn. They're quite thick."

Alicia climbed the circular staircase rapidly, purposefully, a vengeful Valkyrie wanting answers. She approached the door of the upstairs library, Daniel Brewster's defiled personal study, and flung it open.

"Well, *well*!" cried the apparently inebriated Gerald, slumped in a dark leather armchair, a bottle of whiskey on the table beside him, his half-empty glass weaving below his lips. "Lady rich-bitch detective arrives. Sorry about everything, old girl, but you see, you *are* getting old, and you're not terribly inviting any longer."

"Why, Gerry, *why*? I've never denied you a *shilling* when you asked for it! Why did you *do* this?"

"Have you ever lived as nothing more than a useless appendage of a rich bitch who wouldn't even assume my name? No, of course not, because *you're* that rich bitch!"

"I explained why I kept the name Brewster and you agreed," said Lady Alicia, walking over to the chair. "Not only for the children's sake, but I was honored in that name. Also, I never treated you shabbily, and you know it. You're a sick man, Gerald, but I'm still prepared to help you, if you'll seek help. Perhaps it *is* my fault, for you were once so much fun to be with, so concerned with my grief, I can't forget that. You helped me when I needed help, Gerry, and I'll help you now, if you'll let me."

"*Jesus*, I can't stand saints. What can you do for me now? I'll spend years in prison, and then what?"

"No, you won't. I'll replace the money and you'll leave England. Canada or America, perhaps, where you can get counseling, but you cannot stay in this house any longer. Take my offer, Gerald, it's the last I'll give."

Alicia stood over her husband, her eyes pleading, when suddenly he lurched out of the chair, grabbing her skirt and yanking it above her hips. A syringe appeared from beneath his trousers, as he clasped his hand over her mouth, and plunged the needle into her hosed thigh. He held his hand brutally in place until she collapsed. She was dead.

A totally sober killer walked over to the telephone on the library desk. He dialed a coded number in France, which was rerouted to Istanbul, then Switzerland, and finally—lost in the computers—to the Netherlands. "Yes?" answered the man in Amsterdam.

"It's done."

"Good. Now play the distraught husband, the anguished guilty man, and get out of there. *Remember,* do not use your Jaguar. A perfectly normal London taxi is waiting for you. You'll know it by the driver holding a yellow handkerchief out the window."

"You'll *protect* me? You *promised* me that!"

"You will live in luxury for the rest of your life. Beyond the reach of any laws."

"God knows I deserve it, after living with that bitch!"

"You certainly do. Hurry up now."

Lady Alicia's second husband raced out of the library, weeping copiously. He plunged down the circular staircase, nearly losing his footing, his tears apparently blinding him, as he kept wailing, "I'm *sorry,* I'm *sorry*! I should never have *done* it!" He reached the huge polished hall, rushing past the Brewster children, to the front door. He crashed the door open and ran outside.

"Mother must have read him the riot act," said Roger Brewster.

"Mum told you to check on his getting into the Jag. Make sure it's safe for him to drive."

"Fuck him, little sister, I've got the keys. That bastard's *out* of here."

On the curb in Belgravia, the taxi was waiting for Gerald, the yellow handkerchief dangling below the driver's window. He leaped into the backseat, breathing furiously. *"Hurry!"* he shouted, "I can't be *seen* around here!" Suddenly, Gerald was aware of a man sitting next to him.

No words were spoken, only the sound of two silenced gunshots. "Drive to the ironworks north of Heathrow," said the man in shadows. "The fires burn all night."

3

In an off-limits strategy room at the Central Intelligence Agency in Langley, Virginia, two men faced each other over a conference table. The older man was the First Deputy Director of the CIA, the younger an experienced case officer named Cameron Pryce, a veteran of the new Cold Peace, with posts in Moscow, Rome, and London entered into his service report. Pryce was multilingual, fluent in Russian, as well as French, Italian, and, naturally, English. He was a thirty-six-year-old product of Georgetown University, B.A.; Maxwell School of Foreign Service, Syracuse, M.A.; and Princeton University, objective, Ph.D.—the last abandoned in his second year. The doctorate was aborted when Langley recruited him before he could complete his studies.

Why? Because Cameron Pryce, in a predoctoral Honors thesis, recklessly but adamantly predicted the fall of the Soviet Union within four months of its collapse. Such minds were valuable.

"You've read the max-classified file?" asked Deputy Director Frank Shields, a short, overweight former analyst with a high forehead and eyes that seemed perpetually squinted.

"Yes, I have, Frank, and I didn't take any notes, honest," replied Pryce, a large, slender man whose sharp features

could best be described as marginally attractive. He continued, smiling gently. "But, of course, you know that. The
gnomes behind those hideous reproductions on the walls
have been watching me. Did you think I was going to write
a book?"

"Others have, Cam."

"Snepp, Agee, Borstein, and a few other gallant souls
who found some of our procedures less than admirable. . . .
It's not my turf, Frank. I made my pact with the devil when
you paid off my student loans."

"We counted on that."

"Don't count too high. I could have paid them myself in
time."

"On an associate professor's salary? No room for a wife
and kids and a white picket fence on campus."

"Hell, you took care of that, too. My relationships have
been brief and movable, no kids that I'm aware of."

"Let's cut the biographical bullshit," said the deputy director. "What do you make of the file?"

"They're either disconnected events or a great deal more.
One or the other, nothing in between."

"Take an educated guess."

"I can't. Four internationally known very rich folk are
killed along with lesser mortals. The trails lead nowhere and
the killers are out of sight, vanished. There's no cross-
pollination that I can see, no mutual interests or investments
or even any apparent social contact—it would be odd if
there were. We have a titled Englishwoman, who was a philanthropist, a Spanish scholar from a wealthy family in Madrid, an Italian playboy from Milan, and an elderly French
financier with multiple residences and a floating palace he
usually calls home. The only common thread is the unique-
ness of the killings, the absence of leads or follow-ups, and
the fact that they all took place within a time span of forty-
eight hours. August twenty-eighth and twenty-ninth, to be
exact."

"If there's linkage, that's where it could be, isn't it?"

"I just said that, but that's all there is."

"No, there's more," interrupted the deputy director.

"What?"

"Information we deleted from the file."

"For God's sake, *why*? It's maximum classified, you just said so."

"Sometimes those folders get into the wrong hands, don't they?"

"Not if handled properly . . . good Christ, you're serious, *it's* serious."

"Extremely."

"Then you're not playing fair, Frank. You asked me to evaluate data when it's not all there."

"You came up with the right answers. The lack of traceability and the time span."

"So would anybody else."

"I doubt as quickly, but then we're not looking for anyone else, Cam. We want you."

"Flattery, a bonus, and increased contingency funds will get you my undivided attention. What's the missing dirt?"

"Orally delivered, nothing on paper."

"Very, *very* serious—"

"I'm afraid so. . . . First, we have to go back to the natural death of an old woman a thousand miles from Moscow several months ago. The priest, who was with her at the end, finally sent a letter to the Russian authorities after debating with himself for weeks. In it he wrote that the woman, the wife of the Soviet Union's preeminent nuclear physicist, reportedly killed by a crazed bear during a hunt, said her husband had in fact been murdered by unknown men who shot the animal and forced it into the scientist's path. They subsequently disappeared."

"Wait a minute!" Pryce broke in. "I was only a kid then, but I remember reading about it or hearing it on television. 'Yuri' something or other. It was the sort of thing that rivets a kid's imagination—a famous person torn apart by a large animal. Yes, I remember."

"People my age remember it very well," said Shields. "I'd just started with the Agency, but it was common knowledge here at Langley that Yurievich wanted to stop the proliferation of nuclear weapons. We mourned his death; a few of us even questioned the veracity of the reports—there was one rumor that Yurievich had actually been shot, not killed by the bear—but the underlying question was, why would Moscow order the execution of its most brilliant physicist?"

"The answer?" asked the former case officer.

"We didn't have one. We couldn't understand, so we accepted Tass's account."

"And now?"

"A different equation. The old woman, apparently with her last breath, blamed her husband's death, his murder, on an organization called the Matarese, claiming it was—in her words—'the consummate evil.' Ring any bells, Cam?"

"None. Only a pattern of untraceability as it applies to these recent killings."

"Good. That's what I wanted to hear. Now we jump forward to the French financier, René Pierre Mouchistine, who was gunned down on his yacht."

"Along with four attorneys from four different countries," interjected Pryce. "No fingerprints, which assumes the killers wore surgical gloves, no traceable shell casings, because they were all so common, and no witnesses, because the crew was ordered off the boat while the conference was taking place."

"No witnesses, no leads—untraceability."

"That's right."

"Sorry, it's wrong."

"Another surprise, Frank?"

"A beaut," replied the deputy director. "A close friend, later determined to be Mouchistine's personal valet of almost thirty years, knew how to reach our ambassador in Madrid. A meeting was arranged, and this man, one Antoine Lavalle, gave what amounted to a confidential deposition to be forwarded to the major intelligence organization in Washington. Fortunately, despite the Senate, it came to us."

"I would hope so," said Cameron.

"Hope is elusive in D.C.," said Shields. "But thanks to cross-reference computers, we got lucky. The name

Matarese appeared again. Before he died of his wounds, Mouchistine told Lavalle that the 'Matarese was back.' Lavalle said his employer was sure of it because it, or they, knew about the conference and had to stop it."

"Why?"

"Apparently, Mouchistine was divesting himself of his entire financial empire, willing everything to universal charities. With that bequest, he was relinquishing the economic power that goes with his global conglomerates, essentially run under his strict orders by his boards and his attorneys. According to Lavalle, the Matarese could not accept that; they had to stop him so they killed him."

"With Mouchistine dead, who runs the international companies?"

"It's so serpentine, it'll take months, if not years, to unravel."

"But somewhere in the financial caves could be the Matarese, am I reading you?"

"We don't know but we think so. It's so goddamned amorphous, we simply don't know."

"What do you want from me?"

"It was in Mouchistine's last words. 'Find Beowulf Agate.'"

"Who?"

"Beowulf Agate. It was the code name the KGB and the East German Stasi created for Brandon Scofield, our most successful penetrator during the Cold War. The sublime irony was that he eventually teamed up with a man he hated, and who hated him, when they both uncovered the Matarese in Corsica."

"In *Corsica*? That's wild!"

"Vasili Taleniekov was his real name, code name Serpent, an infamous KGB intelligence officer. He had engineered the death of Scofield's wife, and Scofield killed Taleniekov's younger brother. They were sworn enemies until they both faced an enemy far greater than either of them."

"The Matarese?"

"The Matarese. Ultimately, Taleniekov sacrificed himself

to save Beowulf Agate's life as well as Scofield's woman, now his wife."

"*Jesus*, it sounds like a Greek tragedy."

"In many ways, it was."

"*So?*"

"Find Beowulf Agate. Learn the whole story. It's a place to start, and no one knows it better than Scofield."

"Weren't there any debriefings?"

"Scofield wasn't very cooperative. He said it was mission-completed time and there wasn't anything to learn from ancient history. Everyone who mattered was dead. He just wanted out and damned fast."

"That's pretty strange behavior."

"He felt it was justified. You see, at one point he was placed 'beyond salvage.' "

"Targeted for *execution*?" asked the astonished Pryce. "By his own *people*?"

"He was considered dangerous to our personnel everywhere. He knew all the secrets. The President himself had to order the 'salvage' aborted."

"Why was it ever issued in the first place?"

"I just told you, he was a walking time bomb. He had joined the enemy; he and Taleniekov were working together."

"*After* this Matarese!" protested Cameron.

"We learned that later, almost too late."

"Maybe I'd better get to know our President. . . . Okay, I'll try to find him. Where do I start?"

"He's in seclusion in the Caribbean, one of the islands. We've got our feelers operating, but so far no concrete information. We'll give you everything we have."

"Thanks a bunch. It's a pretty wide area with lots and lots of islands."

"Remember, if he's alive, he's in his sixties now, probably a lot different from the ID photographs."

" 'Beowulf Agate,' what a stupid name."

"I don't know, it's no worse than 'Serpent' for Taleniekov. Incidentally, translated, in Tashkent your code was 'Camshaft Pussycat.' "

"Oh, shut up, Frank."

The seaplane landed in the mild waters of the Charlotte Amalie harbor in St. Thomas, U.S. Virgin Islands. It taxied to the Coast Guard patrol station on the left bank of the waterfront, where Cameron Pryce climbed down the unstable steps to the dock. He was met by the young white-uniformed commander of station. "Welcome to Charlotte *Ah-ma-lee*," said the naval officer, shaking his hand, "and if you want to fit in, that's the way it's pronounced."

"I'm on your side, Lieutenant. Where do I start?"

"First, you have a reservation at the Eighteen Sixty-nine House, right up on the hill. Damn good restaurant, and the fellow who owns it was once part of your kind of operations, so he'll keep his mouth shut."

"*Once* doesn't fill me with confidence—"

"Count on it, sir. He was AID in Vientiane and the Agency dumped a pile of aircraft on him. How do you think he bought the hotel?"

"He's golden. Do you have anything for me?"

"Scofield folded up his charter service here several years ago and moved it to British Tortola. He closed that down, too, but still keeps a post office box there."

"Which means he comes back to pick up his mail."

"Or sends someone with a key. He gets his pension check every month and, presumably, whatever inquiries there are for his charters."

"He's still sailing then?"

"Under a new name. 'Tortola Caribbean,' a tax dodge, if you want my opinion, which is kind of stupid since he hasn't paid any taxes for over twenty-five years."

"Some deep-cover boys never change. Where is he now?"

"Who knows?"

"Nobody's seen him?"

"Not for the record, and we've asked around. Discreetly, of course."

"Someone's got to pick up his mail—"

"Look, sir, we just got this inquiry eight days ago, and we have friends in Tortola," said the Coast Guard lieutenant.

"They don't have a clue. Tortola is roughly twenty square miles of island with about ten thousand residents, mostly native and British. Its main post office is in Road Town, where mail comes in erratically and most of the time the clerks are asleep. I can't change the habits of a subtropic environment."

"Don't get irritated, I'm merely asking questions."

"I'm not irritated, I'm frustrated. If I could really help you, it would look good on my record and I might get out of this goddamned place. I simply can't. For all intents and purposes, that son of a bitch Scofield has disappeared."

"Not when he has a mailbox, Lieutenant. It's just a question of watching it."

"You'll forgive me, Mr. Pryce, but I'm not permitted to leave my station and sit on my ass in Tortola."

"Spoken like an officer and a gentleman, young man. But you can hire someone to do just that."

"With *what*? The budget's so tight here I have to rely on volunteer help when lousy catamarans can't get into shore!"

"Sorry, I forgot. Bureaucrats in suits make those decisions. They probably think St. Thomas is a Catholic territory in the Pacific. . . . Cool off, Lieutenant, I'm wired into the suits. You help me, I'll help you."

"How?"

"Get me an interisland flight to Tortola with no identification."

"That's too easy."

"I'm not finished. Send one of your cutters to the harbor in Road Town under my command."

"That's too hard."

"I'll clear it. It'll look good on your record."

"I'll be damned—"

"You will be if you refuse me. Let's go, Lieutenant, let's set up shop. Instant communications and all the rest of that horseshit."

"You're for real, aren't you?"

"Reality is my middle name, youngster. Don't you forget it, especially not now."

"What are you after?"

"Someone who knows the truth about an old story with numerous dimensions, and that's all *you* have to know."

"That doesn't tell me a hell of a lot."

"And I don't know much more, Lieutenant. I won't until I find Scofield. Help me."

"Sure, of course. I can ferry you over to Tortola on our second cutter, if you like."

"No thanks. Marinas are watched, the immigration procedures are pretty thorough—those tax dodges you mentioned. I'm sure you can find me an airstrip or a water touchdown that's off the usual routes."

"As a matter of fact, I can. We both use it to interdict drug smugglers."

"Use it now, please."

It was sundown, the third day of surveillance, and Pryce was in a hammock strung between two sturdy palms on the island beach. Dressed in tropic clothes—docksiders, shorts, and a light guayabera—he was basically indistinguishable from the dozen or so other male tourists lolling about in the early-evening sand. The difference was in the contents of his "beach bag." Whereas others were filled with sunscreen lotion, crumpled magazines, and forgettable paperbacks, his bag held, first, a portable phone, calibrated to put him in immediate contact with St. Thomas as well as the Coast Guard cutter moored in the Tortola harbor and capable of sending and receiving less esoteric communications via satellite. In addition to this vital link, there was a holstered weapon—a .45 Star PD auto pistol with five clips of ammunition—a belt-scabbarded hunting knife, a flashlight, a pair of night-vision binoculars, charts of Tortola and the nearby islands, a first-aid kit, a bottle of flesh antiseptic, and two flasks—one filled with spring water, the other with McKenna sour-mash bourbon. Experience had taught him that each item had its place in the scheme of unpredictable things.

He was about to doze off in the debilitating heat when the low hum of the phone penetrated the lining of his waterproof flight bag. He reached down, unzipped the thin nylon strip, and pulled out the state-of-the-art instrument. "Yes?" he said quietly.

"Finally pay dirt, *mon*!" replied one of the black Tortolans recruited by the lieutenant in St. Thomas for the surveillance team; he was calling from the Road Town post office.

"The mailbox?"

"Not much in it, but she got it all."

"She?"

"A white lady, mon. Middle-aged, mebbe forties or fifties, difficult to tell 'cause she damn near as dark as us from the sun."

"Hair? Height?"

"Half gray, half brown. Pretty tall, mebbe three, four flat hands above five feet."

"It was his wife. Where did she go?"

"She got into a Jeep, mon, no license plate. She's heading toward the Point, I think."

"What *Point*?"

"Got lots of names, only one road. I'll follow her on my moped. Gotta hurry, mon."

"For God's sake, keep in touch!"

"You get to cut-boat. Tell 'em to cruise east to Heavy Rock, they know it."

Cameron Pryce switched channels and spoke to the skipper of the Coast Guard cutter. "Pull into the dock and I'll get on board. Do you know a place, a point, called Heavy Rock?"

"Or 'Lotsa Rock,' or 'Big Stone Point,' or 'Black Rock Angel'? . . . Sure, it depends where you live on Tortola. At night it's a favorite landing site for the *contrabandistas*. The older natives say it's haunted with obeah, that's like voodoo."

"That's where we're going."

The long shadows, created by the orange sun disappearing over the horizon, fell across the Caribbean waters as the cutter slowly, lazily, rounded the coastline. "There it is, sir," said the naval officer, a lieutenant j.g. even younger than the commander of station in St. Thomas. "That's 'Big Stone

Mother,'" he added, pointing to an enormous clifflike rock that seemingly had lurched out of the sea.

"Another name, Lieutenant? 'Big Stone Mother'?"

"We gave it that one, I'm afraid. We don't like to come out here, too many shoals."

"Then stay pretty far from shore. If a boat comes out, we'll spot it."

"A Cigarette on starboard northwest," said the sudden voice over the intercom.

"Shit!" exclaimed the young skipper.

"What the hell is that?" asked Pryce. "'A *cigarette*'?"

"Cigarette boat, sir. We're fast, but no match for one of them."

"Please bring me up to speed, Lieutenant."

"That's what we're talking about. Speed. The Cigarette boat is the favorite of the drug crowd. It can outrun anything on the water. It's why, when we know they're in use, we call in aircraft. But with all our equipment, here and in the air, we're no damned good after dark. The Cigarettes are too small and too fast."

"And I thought it was as simple as our lungs."

"Funny man . . . sir. If your target goes full throttle, we'll lose it. No interdiction, no boarding."

"I don't want to interdict and I certainly don't want to board, Lieutenant."

"Then, if I may, sir, why the *hell* are we here?"

"I want to pinpoint where the target goes. You can do that, can't you?"

"Probably. At least to a landmass, an island maybe. But there are lots of them, and if he pulls into one and we get a radar fix, then he pulls out for another, we've had it!"

"She, Lieutenant, *she*."

"Oh? Wow, I never figured."

"Get your radar fix, I'll take my chances."

The minor island in question was named simply Outer Brass 26 on the charts. Uninhabited; questionable foliage; no long-range human habitation considered. It was barely four square miles of volcanic rock expunged from the depths of the ocean, with several hills that permitted profuse greenery from the generosity of the tropic sun, the afternoon showers, and said greenery spread to the lands below. Although once considered part of the Spanish Caribbean chain, it had never actually been claimed in recent history. It was an orphan in a sea of illegitimate children, nobody cared.

Cameron Pryce stood at midships in a diver's wet suit provided by the Coast Guard. Below him was a ladder that led down to a rubber raft with a small, quiet three-horsepower motor that would take him into the shore. In his left hand was the waterproof flight bag with his items of choice and necessity.

"I feel damned awkward just leaving you here, sir," said the very young skipper of the vessel.

"Don't, Lieutenant, it's what I came for. Besides, I can reach you whenever I want, can't I?"

"Of course. As you instructed, we'll remain out here, roughly five miles from land, beyond visual sighting if the light's right."

"When it's daylight, just stay in the path of the sun. The old cowboys-and-Indians movies were right about that."

"Yes, sir, it's part of our combat-strategies courses. Good luck, Mr. Pryce. Good hunting with whatever you're doing."

"I'll need a little of both." The former CIA case officer descended the ladder to the bobbing PVC craft below.

The engine gurgled, it did not really run, as Pryce steered the rubber raft into shore. He chose what appeared in the moonlight to be a small cove; it was wooded, with overhanging palms roofing the perimeter. He jumped out of the raft and pulled it between the rocks to the sand, securing it to the trunk of a palm. He lifted out his waterproof case and flung the strap over his right shoulder; it was time for the hunt, and hopefully luck would be part of it.

He knew what to look for initially: light. A fire or battery-induced illumination, it had to be one or the other. For two people to live on a deserted island without either was not only uncomfortable, it was dangerous. He started to his right, walking cautiously over the rocky shoreline, constantly peering into the heavy foliage on his left. There were no signs of light *or* life. He trudged for nearly twenty minutes, greeting only darkness, until he saw it. But it was neither light nor life, only small metallic reflections of the moon; numerous short poles were in the ground, mirrors on top, angled toward the sky. He approached them, yanked the flashlight out of his case, and saw the wires, leading to the right and the left, connecting the poles. There were dozens, *scores* of them, forming a semicircle on the rock-hewn shoreline. Photoelectric cells! Catching the rays of the sun from dawn to high noon and beyond. Searching farther, he found a thick, central cable that led into the tropical forest. He started to follow it when he heard the words, spoken clearly, harshly, in English behind him.

"Are you looking for someone?" asked the mid-deep voice. "If you are, you've gone about it amateurishly."

"Mr. Scofield, I presume."

"Since we're not in Africa, and you're not Henry Stanley, you may presume correctly. Keep your hands above your head and walk straight forward. It's our cable path, so use your light, because if you break it, I'll blow your head off. It took me too long to put it together."

"I come in peace, Mr. Scofield, without any intent to divulge your whereabouts," said Pryce, walking carefully ahead. "We want information we think only you can provide."

"Let's wait until we reach the house, Mr. Cameron Pryce."

"You know who I *am*?"

"Certainly. They say you're the best, probably better than I ever was. . . . Put your hands down. The palm leaves get in your face."

"Thank you."

"You're welcome." Scofield suddenly shouted, "It's *okay.* Turn on the lights, Antonia. He was clever enough to find us, so open a bottle of wine."

The clearing in the forest was suddenly illuminated by two floodlights revealing a large one-story cabin of tropical wood, a natural lagoon on the right.

"My *God,* it's beautiful!" cried the CIA agent.

"It took us a long time to find this place and longer to build it."

"You built it yourself?"

"Hell, no. My lady designed it, and I boated in crews from St Kitts and other islands to do the work. Since I paid them half in advance, no one took offense at the blindfolds out of Tortola. Just discretion, young man."

"Young and not so young," broke in Cameron, in awe.

"Depends where you're coming from, fella," said Scofield, walking into the light. His thin, narrow face was framed by a short white beard and longish gray hair, but his eyes were bright, youthful behind his steel-rimmed glasses. "We like it."

"You're so alone—"

"Not really. Toni and I frequently take the 'butt' over to Tortola, grab an interisland to 'Rico, and a flight to Miami or even New York. Like you, if you've got a brain in your head, I have half a dozen passports that get me through."

"I don't have a brain in my head," acknowledged Pryce.

"Get one. Maybe you'll find someday that's all you've got. After you've appropriated a few hundred thousand in contingency funds. Placed in off-shore investments, of course."

"*You* did that?"

"Have you any idea what our pensions allow us? Maybe a condominium in Newark in the lesser part of town. I wasn't going to settle for that. I deserved more."

"The *Matarese*?" said Cameron softly. "It's back."

"That's out of *orbit,* Pryce. An old boy in D.C. called me and said that he heard you were looking for me—yes, I've got the same kind of phones you have, *and* the generators, *and* the security, but you're not going to drag me back into that hell."

"We don't want to drag you back, sir, we only want the truth as you know it."

Scofield did not reply. Instead, as they had reached the short steps to the cabin's entrance, he said, "Come on inside and get out of that outfit. You look like Spider-Man."

"I've got clothes in my bag."

"I used to carry one of those. Change of shorts and a garrote, a lightweight jacket and a couple of weapons, maybe some underwear and a hunting knife. Also whiskey, can't forget the whiskey."

"I've got bourbon—"

"Then the D.C. boys are right. You've got possibilities."

The inside of the cabin—more than a cabin, a medium-sized house, really—was nearly all white, accentuated by several table lamps. White walls, white furniture, white archways that led to other rooms, all to repel the heat of the sun. And standing next to a white wicker armchair was Scofield's wife. As reported by the Tortolan in the Road Town post office, she was tall, full of figure but not obese, and with that mixture of gray and dark hair that bespoke her advancing years. Her face was delicate yet strong; a mind was at work inside that handsome head.

"Congratulations, Mr. Pryce," she said in slightly accented English. "We've been on the alert for you, although I didn't think you could possibly find us. I owe you one dollar, Bray."

"I'll bet another that I never see it."

"Finding you wasn't that difficult, Mrs. Scofield."

"The mailbox, of course," the once and former whiz of deep-cover intelligence broke in. "It's a hell of a flaw but a necessary one. We still sail, we still like the charter business, and it's a way to make a few dollars and socialize a bit. . . . We're not antisocial, you know. We enjoy most people, actually."

"This house, the isolation, wouldn't seem to support that, sir."

"On the surface, I suppose not, but the obvious can be misleading, can't it, young man? We're not hermits, we're here for a very practical reason. You're an example."

"I beg your pardon?"

"Have you any idea, Mr. Pryce," interrupted Antonia Scofield, "how many people have tried to pull my husband back into his former profession? Beyond Washington, there's the British MI-Five and MI-Six, the French Deuxième, the Italian Servizio Segreto, and just about everybody in NATO's intelligence community. He keeps refusing and refusing, but they never 'let up,' as you Americans say."

"He's considered a brilliant man—"

"Was, *was . . . maybe*!" exclaimed Scofield. "But I haven't anything to offer any longer. Good *Christ*, it was damn near twenty-five years ago! The whole world's changed and I haven't the slightest interest in it. Sure, you could find me; if our roles were reversed, it'd take me no more time than it took you to find *me*. But you'd be astonished what a little deterrence, like a mostly uncharted island and a stupidly named mailbox, can do to stop the curious. You want to know why?"

"Yes, I would."

"Because they've got a hundred other problems and they don't want the hassle, it's as simple as that. It's so much easier to say to a superior that I'm seemingly impossible to locate. Think about the funds needed for airline tickets along with experienced personnel; the whole ball of wax becomes so tangled they give up. It's just easier."

"Yet you just said you were told I was coming down looking for you. You could have put up barriers, not used the mailbox. You didn't. You didn't protect yourself."

"You're very perceptive, young man."

"It's almost comical that you use that phrase. That's what I called the lieutenant in St. Thomas."

"He was probably half your age, as you are of mine. So what?"

"Nothing really, but why didn't you? Protect your isolation?"

"It was a joint decision," answered Scofield, looking over at his wife. "More hers than mine, to tell you the truth. We wanted to see if you had the patience, that godforsaken quiescence before you made your move. An hour becomes a day, a day a month; we've all been there. You passed with all the colors; you actually *slept* on the beach. Damn good training!"

"You haven't answered my question, sir."

"No, I haven't, because I knew why you had come. Only one reason, and you said the name. The Matarese."

"Tell him, Bray, tell him everything you know," said Antonia Scofield. "You owe Taleniekov that, we both owe Vasili that."

"I know, my dear, but may we first have a drink? I'll settle for wine, but I'd rather have brandy."

"You may have both, if you like, my darling."

"You see why I keep her around after all these years? A woman who calls you 'my darling' for a quarter of a century is a girl you keep."

4

"We have to go back to the turn of the century, actually before that to be accurate," began Scofield, rocking in his chair on the screened-in, candlelit veranda of the isolated cottage on the presumably deserted island named Outer Brass 26. "The dates are imprecise, as the records were lost, or destroyed, but it can be estimated that Guillaume, Baron of Matarese, was born around 1830. The family was rich by Corsican standards, mostly in property, the baronage and the land being a gift of Napoleon, although that's questionable."

"Why?" asked Pryce, in shorts and a T-shirt, mesmerized by the gray-haired, white-bearded former intelligence officer whose eyes seemed to dance impudently behind the steel-rimmed glasses. "There had to be documents of possession, of inheritance."

"As I mentioned, the original records were lost, new ones found and registered. There were those who claimed they were counterfeits, forgeries commissioned by a very young Guillaume, that the Matarese never even knew a Bonaparte, Third or Second, and certainly not the First. Nevertheless, by the time those doubts arose, the family was too powerful to be questioned."

"How so?"

"Guillaume was a financial genius, nothing less, and like most of that ilk, he knew when and how to cut corners while staying marginally within the laws. Before he was thirty years of age, he was the richest, most powerful landowner in Corsica. The family literally ran the island, and the French government couldn't do anything about it. The Matarese were a law unto themselves, drawing revenues from the major ports, tributes and bribes from the growing industries of agriculture and resort developers who had to use their docking facilities and their roads. It was said that Guillaume was the first Corso, that's the Corsican equivalent of the Black Hand, the Mafia. He made the later godfathers look like wimps, the Capones misguided children. Although there was violence, brutal violence, it was kept to a minimum and used to great effect. The Baron ruled by fear, not unbridled punishment."

"Couldn't Paris simply shut him down or throw him out?" interrupted Pryce.

"What they did was worse than that. They ruined two of the Baron's sons—destroyed them. Both died violently, and after that the Baron was never the same. It was soon after this that Guillaume conceived his so-called vision. An international cartel the likes of which the Rothschilds never dreamed of. Whereas the Rothschilds were an established banking family throughout Europe, Guillaume went in the opposite direction. He recruited powerful men and women to be his satellites. They were people who once possessed enormous wealth—inherited or accumulated—and like him had a taste for revenge. Those initial members stayed out of the spotlight, avoiding all forms of public scrutiny, preferring to handle or manipulate their riches from a distance. They employed fronts, such as lawyers, and speaking of the Bonapartes, they used a tactic proclaimed by Napoleon the First. He said, 'Give me enough medals and I'll win you any war.' So these original Mataresans gave out titles, large offices, and extravagant salaries as if they were Rockefeller dimes. All for a single purpose: They wanted to remain as anonymous as possible. You see, Guillaume understood that his design for a global financial network could only come about if the key players appeared completely clean, above suspicion of corrupt practices."

"I'm afraid that's not consistent with my briefing," said the CIA field officer. "Frankly, it's contradictory."

"Oh, really?"

"Yes, sir. The two sources that revived our interest in the Matarese—the reason I'm here—described it as evil. The first called it consummate evil; the second, evil incarnate. Since these statements were made by two elderly, knowledgeable people facing imminent death, even the courts would consider their words valid. . . . You've described something else."

"You're right and you're wrong," said Scofield. "I described Guillaume's vision as he conceived it, and make no mistake, he wasn't a saint. In terms of control, he wanted it all, but part of his genius was to recognize practical and philosophical imperatives—"

"Fancy language," interrupted Pryce.

"And very real," added the former intelligence officer, "very germane. When you think about it, Matarese was almost a century ahead of his time. He wanted to form what was later to be called a World Bank or an International Monetary Fund, or even a Trilateral Commission. To do that, his disciples had to appear legitimate through and through, squeaky-clean."

"Then something must have happened to them, something changed, assuming that my briefing was accurate."

"Indeed something did happen, because you *are* right in that area. The Matarese became monsters."

"What was it?"

"Guillaume died. Some say he passed away while making love to a woman fifty years younger than he was, and he was roughly in his middle eighties. Others know differently. Regardless, his inheritors—that is what he called them— moved in like a swarm of bees to the honeypot. The machinery was in place, Matarese branches throughout Europe and America, money and, even more important, confidential information flowing back and forth weekly, if not daily. It was an unseen octopus, silently monitoring, efficiently threatening to expose the dirty tricks and the unwarranted excessive profits of scores of industries, national and international."

"Initially, sort of a self-policing apparatus where business is concerned—both national and international?"

"That's as good a description as I've heard. After all, who better than corrupt police to know how to break the laws they enforce? The inheritors seized the moment. The confidential information between the branches was no longer used as a threat, instead it was sold. Profits soared and Guillaume's successors demanded a piece of the action of succeeding profits. By Christ, they covered whole territories and became an underworld cult—I mean a real *cult*. Like the Cosa Nostra, new members of various statuses were ceremoniously sworn in, the upper crowd actually wearing small blue tattoos proclaiming their rank."

"It sounds crazy."

"It *was* crazy, but it was also effective. Once proven, a new Mataresan was guaranteed for life—financially secure, protected from the laws, free from the usual stresses of normal living—as long as he or she obeyed their superiors without questioning *any* order."

"And to question any order was *finito* time," said Pryce, making a statement.

"That was understood."

"So, in essence, you're describing a Mafia or a Corso, as I see it."

"I'm afraid you're wrong again, Mr. Pryce—essentially."

"Since I'm drinking your brandy in your house, hospitality I never figured on, why not call me Cameron, or Cam, as most people do."

"As you gathered from my wife, I'm 'Bray.' My younger sister couldn't say Brandon till she was maybe four, so she called me Bray. It just stuck."

"My kid brother couldn't say Cameron. It came out

'Cramroom,' or worse 'Come around,' so he settled on 'Cam.' It stuck, too."

"Bray and Cam," said Scofield, "sounds like a barnyard legal firm."

"I'd be pleased—no, honored—with any association. I've read your service record."

"Most of which was exaggerated to make my superiors and the analysts look good. You wouldn't be doing your career any favors to be associated with me. Too many in the business consider me a flake or a fluke, or worse. Much worse."

"I'll pass on that. Why am I wrong again? Essentially."

"Because the Matarese never recruited thugs; no one ever climbed up the ladder based on the number of 'hits' he made. Oh, they'd kill if ordered to, but no meat hooks, no shotguns, no chains in the river—usually no corpses, either. If the Matarese council—and it was just that—wanted unmitigated brutality that would be publicized, it secretly paid for terrorists untraceable to itself. But it never employed its members for that sort of work. They were *executives*."

"They were greedy bastards, sucking up to a wild boar."

"And then some." Scofield chuckled softly while sipping his brandy. "They were elitists, Cameron, far above the common people. By and large, they were *summa cum laudes* and *magna cum laudes* from the finest universities both on this side and in Europe, the so-called best and the brightest of industry and government. In their own minds, they assumed they would in time become enormously successful; the Matarese was merely a shortcut. Once in, they were hooked, and the shortcut became a world they could not escape."

"What about accountability? What about right and *wrong*? Are you saying this army of the best and the brightest had no sense of morality?"

"I'm sure a few did, Mr. Pryce . . . Cameron," said Antonia Scofield, who had slipped into the white archway to the candlelit veranda. "And I'm equally sure that if they voiced such reservations, they and their families had terrible things done to them . . . fatal accidents, in the main."

"That's savage."

"That was the way of the reinvented Matarese," added Brandon. "Morality was replaced by having no options. You see, everything came in increments, and before they understood that, there was no way out. They were living abnormally extravagant yet strangely normal lives with wives and children and expensive tastes. Get the picture, Cam?"

"With frightening clarity. . . . I know a little—not much—about how you and Vasili Taleniekov came together and went after the Matarese, but your debriefing wasn't very complete. Would you care to fill me in a bit?"

"Certainly he will," said the wife. "Won't you, my darling?"

"There she goes again," rejoined Scofield, glancing warmly at Antonia. "My debriefing was a nonevent because the Cold War was still pretty hot and there were clowns who wanted to paint Vasili, our Soviet enemy, as one of the evil people. I wasn't having any part of it."

"He chose his own death so that we might live, Cameron," said Antonia, walking to a white wicker chair next to her husband. "In terrible pain he flung himself at our enemies, allowing us to escape. Without his sacrifice we both would have been shot, killed."

"From archenemies to allies, even friends who you give up your life for?"

"I wouldn't go that far, and I've thought about it for years. We never forgot what we did to each other, but I think he decided that his was the greater crime. He killed my wife, I killed his brother. . . . It's in the past; nothing changes it."

"I was told about that," said Pryce. "I was also told you were placed 'beyond salvage.' Do you want to talk about it?"

"What's there to talk about?" answered Scofield quietly. "It happened."

"'What's there to *talk* about'?" repeated the stunned CIA officer. "For Christ's sake, your own agency, your *superiors,* ordered your *execution*!"

"Funny, I never considered them my 'superiors.' Quite the opposite most of the time."

"You know what I mean—"

"I do, indeed," interrupted Bray. "Someone added the numbers but came up with the wrong total, and since I knew who it was, I decided to kill him. Then I reasoned I'd undoubtedly be caught and he wasn't worth it. Instead, I stopped being angry and got even. I dealt my cards, which proved to be reasonably profitable."

"Back to Taleniekov," said Cameron. "How did it begin with you two?"

"You're smart, Cam. The keys are always at the beginning, the first door that has to be unlocked. Without that door you can't reach the others."

"A maze with doors?"

"More than you can count. The beginning . . . It was nuts, but there it was and Taleniekov and I were caught up in it. There were two extraordinary kills, two assassinations. On our side there was General Anthony Blackburn, chairman of the Joint Chiefs, and on the Soviet's, Dimitri Yurievich, their leading nuclear physicist."

"Deputy Director Shields mentioned that one, and I remembered it. A famous Russian torn apart by a crazed bear."

"That was the popular version, yes. A *wounded* bear shot by men who whipped it into Yurievich's trail. There's nothing on earth more ferocious than a huge maimed bear, his nostrils filled with the scent of his own blood. He'll smell out a group of hunters and tear them all to pieces until he's killed. . . . Wait a minute. *Frank* Shields? Old bulldog-face with those creased eyes nobody's ever seen. He's still around?"

"He holds you in high regard—"

"Perhaps in retrospect, not when we were current. Frank's a purist; he never tolerated men like me. However, analysts tend to cloak themselves in contradictory alternatives."

"You were saying," interrupted Pryce, "about the two assassinations?"

"Here I must digress, Cameron. Have you ever heard the phrase 'the banality of evil'?"

"Of course."

"What does it mean to you?"

"I suppose horrible acts repeated with such frequency they become commonplace—banal."

"Very good. That's what happened to Taleniekov and me. You see, the considered wisdom of the times regarding black operations was that Vasili and I were the leading players in those kinds of kills. It was more myth than reality. In truth, except for what we did to each other, between us we were responsible for only fourteen fairly well-publicized assassinations over twenty years, he with eight kills, me with six. Hardly in Carlos the Jackal's league, but myths take on lives of their own, growing rapidly, far too persuasively. They're terrible things, myths."

"I think I see where you're going," said Pryce. "Each side blamed the other's presumed chief assassin—you and Taleniekov."

"Precisely, but neither of us had anything to do with those assassinations. However, they had been set up as if we'd left our calling cards."

"But how did you get together? Surely you didn't pick up phones and call each other."

"It would have been comical. 'Hello, KGB switchboard? This is Beowulf Agate, and if you'll kindly reach the illustrious Comrade Colonel Taleniekov, code name Serpent, and tell him I'm on the line, he'll agree we should have a chat. You see, we're both about to be eliminated for the wrong reasons. Silly, isn't it?'"

"The 'Beowulf Agate' is . . . inspired," noted the CIA officer.

"Yes, I always thought it was rather imaginative," said Scofield. "Even Russian in its way. As you know, they more often than not use a person's first two names and omit the last."

"Brandon Alan . . . Beowulf Agate. You're right. But since you didn't make that phone call to the KGB, how *did* you meet?"

"With extreme caution, each thinking the other would shoot to kill, speaking of banal expressions. Vasili made the first move in our lethal chess game. To begin with, he had to get out of the Soviet Union because he was marked for a firing squad—the reasons are too serpentine to go into; and second, a dying, once all-powerful KGB director told him about the Matarese—"

"I don't get the connection," Pryce broke in.

"Think about it. You've got five seconds."

"Good Lord," said Cameron softly, narrowing his eyes. "The *Matarese*? *They* assassinated both men? Yurievich and Blackburn?"

"On the money, Field Officer Pryce."

"Why?"

"Because their tentacles reached into the war rooms on both sides, and the hotheads on both sides thought each kill was a splendid idea, if it could be accomplished without being traced. The Matarese, letting only a very few know in Washington and Moscow, carried out the assassinations, putting a convincing spin on them that pointed to Vasili and me."

"Just like *that*? But again, *why*?"

"Because they'd been doing it for years. Feeding both superpowers information about their enemies' newest weapons of annihilation, forcing each to produce more and more, until the arms race became gargantuan. All the while the Matarese made billions, its defense-contractor clients happily paying off."

"This is coming too fast. . . . So Taleniekov made the first move?"

"He sent me a message from Brussels. 'We will either kill each other or we will talk.' He got over here somehow, and after a series of rendezvous, during which we damn near blew each other away, we did talk. We assumed that our names, our personas, if you will, had taken each of our countries to the brink, only the intercession of the Soviet Premier and the American President curbing the hotheads. They convinced each other that neither nation was responsible for the kills, that Taleniekov and I were nowhere near the scenes."

"If I may," interrupted Cameron, holding up the palm of

his right hand in the candlelight. "As I said, I remembered the death of Yurievich because it was so macabre, but I don't recall the killing of a General Blackburn; perhaps I was too young. The chairman of the Joint Chiefs doesn't mean an awful lot to a kid of ten or eleven."

"You wouldn't have recalled it if you'd been *twice* that age," replied Scofield. "Anthony Blackburn was reported to have died from cardiac arrest while reading the Scriptures in his library at home. A nice touch considering the truth. He was killed in an expensive New York whorehouse having extremely kinky sex."

"Why was he a target? Just because he was head of the Joint Chiefs?"

"Blackburn wasn't just a figurehead, he was a brilliant tactician. The Soviets in some ways knew him better than we did; they'd studied him in Korea and Vietnam. They knew his primary goal was stability."

"Okay, I understand. So you and Taleniekov talked. How did that lead you to the Matarese?"

"The old KGB director, Krupskova—or some name like that—he'd been shot, the wound was severe, and he called for Vasili. He told Taleniekov that he had analyzed the reports of the kills of Yurievich and Blackburn. He concluded that the assassinations were the work of a secret organization called the Matarese, its origins in Corsica. He explained to Vasili that they were spreading out everywhere, blackmailing high government officials, assuming extraordinary power throughout the Free World and the Eastern bloc countries."

"Had this Krupskova worked with them—with it?" asked Pryce.

"He said we all did, had been for years. Signals would be sent, meetings in fields or forests arranged, away from anyone observing them, men in shadows meeting other shadowed men in darkness. Deals were made in the blackest arts—'kill *him* or kill *her,* we'll pay.'"

"They could get *away* with that?"

"On both sides," answered Scofield. "It was their tentacles, *its* tentacles. They knew what the extremists wanted and they supplied the results, untraceable to their clients."

"There had to be records of disbursements. How were they paid?"

"Off the books, clandestine operations being beyond scrutiny for reasons of national security. That's a necessary euphemism for buy whatever you can when you can't get it legally or morally. The Soviets, of course, had fewer problems in those areas, but we weren't far behind. To put it bluntly, our governments weren't officially at war, but *we* were. It was a goddamned bloody mess, and we were the *messees*—on both sides."

"You're pretty cynical, aren't you?"

"Of course, he is," said Antonia Scofield, lurching forward in her white wicker chair. "Men like my husband and Vasili Taleniekov were killers on the loose, killers who had to take the lives of men and women who they knew would kill them! For what purpose? While the superpowers pretended to get together with parades and marching bands proclaiming *détente,* or whatever they called it, while agents like Brandon Scofield and Vasili Taleniekov were ordered to keep killing? Where was the logic, Cameron Pryce?"

"I don't have an answer, Mrs. Scofield—Antonia. It was a different time."

"What's *your* time, Cam?" asked Beowulf Agate. "What are your orders? Who are you after?"

"Terrorists, I guess. Among the more deadly, perhaps, is this Matarese because it's a new kind of terror, I think."

"Exactly right, young man," agreed Scofield. "They may not massacre people or blow up buildings at this point— they pay for those things to be done or engineer them with unknowing, programmed psychopaths—but they can and they will do everything themselves if it's part of their strategy."

"Strategy for *what*?"

"For a malevolent international cartel, dedicated to raw financial power for itself."

"To get anywhere near that goal they'd have to eliminate competition, neutralize competitors all over the place."

"Now you've got it. Capitalism run amok, derailed. One monolithic Daddy Warbucks pushing all the buttons, price-fixing the order of the day, false competition erected by non-competing partners. Then what comes next, Field Officer Cameron Pryce?"

"I don't know what you mean—"

"I mean what comes *next*? The world's leading financial centers under the patronage of a single authority. What follows?"

"Governments," said Cam quietly, his eyes narrowed again. "Whoever has the major sources of money calls the political shots."

"Go to the head of the class, youngster!" exclaimed Scofield, raising his empty brandy snifter, and looking sheepishly at his wife. "Perhaps, my love?"

"I'll bring the bottle," said Antonia, rising. "You've been a good lad for several months now."

"Not by choice, damn it! It's those lousy doctors in Miami."

"But could it happen?" continued the CIA agent pensively as Antonia left the veranda. "Could it really happen?"

"There are more historical precedents than either of us could enumerate, Cameron. Mergers upon mergers, the swallowing up of corporations by buyouts, hostile and otherwise. Global monopolies, young man. It goes back to the pharaohs of Egypt who overrode their pretending princes, and the Romans who packed the senates so the ruling Caesars ran everything. It's nothing new, it's just modernized, computerized. The bastards who want everything will get everything unless they're stopped."

"Who'll stop them?"

"Not *me,* God knows, I don't care any longer. Perhaps the people—the *unconcerned* people—may wake up and see that at the end of the line their freedoms have been sucked away by the unholy apparatus of financial supremacy. That's what the Matarese is driving for. The results are police states—everywhere. They can't survive otherwise."

"You really think that could happen?"

"It depends on what kind of head start they've got and

THE MATARESE COUNTDOWN   [57]

who's on their board of directors. Frankly, yes, it could happen. When you analyze it, we're talking about boardroom terrorism, international collusion, flaunting all the antitrust laws everywhere. It's as though General Motors, Ford, Chrysler, BMW, Toyota, Porsche, and two or three other manufacturers got together and ran the world's automobile industry. It's not really that far-fetched."

"And once there, they go after the governments," said Pryce.

"Oh, I suspect a number are entrenched already, as they were thirty years ago. One of them nearly became President of the United States. They damn near ran our State Department and the Pentagon as well as having undue influence in the House and Senate. Since they're now so obviously international, suppose they controlled Britain's Foreign Office, France's Quai d'Orsay, Rome, Ottawa, and Bonn, it's a nice unhealthy picture, isn't it? Good heavens, in a few years, with politicians in their pockets, a couple of Matarese-rigged summits and we're all marching to their drums, happy as mindless clams—until we understand that when the drumrolls stop, so do our alternatives. We buy what they want to sell us, we take what they want to give us . . . we believe what they tell us to believe . . . or else."

" 'Boardroom terrorism,' that's a hell of a term."

"And as lethal as any other, Cam. Because once they get their footholds, a monopoly here, a megamerger there, interrelated conglomerates here *and* there, they won't accept any opposition."

"They're apparently not accepting any now," said Pryce. He told Scofield about the four kills: the French financier, the Spanish doctor, the Englishwoman, and the Italian polo player on Long Island.

"We know the Frenchman's connected to the Matarese," Pryce went on. "It's on record, his own words, presumably. Also the financial histories of the others are filled with confusing gaps regarding their money, according to Frank Shields's latest information."

" 'Squint Eyes' would be accurate in that department," conceded Beowulf Agate. "He was always very astute where gaps were concerned. He looked for patterns, and when they weren't there, he looked for something else."

"The something else here is the Matarese. The murders took place within forty-eight hours, the killers disappeared, no traces, no tracks——"

"That's consistent," Scofield interrupted.

"And why is the trail of their wealth so complex?" continued Cameron. "'Amorphous' was the word Frank used; undefined, I guess he meant."

"I'm sure he did." The retired, gray-haired former intelligence officer once more laughed softly, more to himself. "How many millionaires do you know who willingly share their portfolios, especially if their sources of income may have questionable aspects, no matter how long ago?"

"I don't know that many millionaires, not personally."

"You know me now."

"Are *you*——"

"Enough on the subject, not another word. See what I mean?"

"I'd rather not, but in light of your service record, I'll consider it a separation bonus. . . . Where do we start? Where do *I* start?"

"You said it yourself, the money trail," replied Scofield. "Frank Shields is good, but he's an analyst. He crunches numbers, works with paper, with computerized printouts of charts and graphs and dossiers written by both responsible, and irresponsible, and usually untraceable authors of same. You've got to deal with *people,* not electronic reproductions."

"I've done that before," said Pryce, "and I firmly believe in doing it. The new technology can span borders and watch and listen, but it can't talk with the men and the women we have to confront. There's no substitute for that. But this money trail, where do I begin?"

"I'd say," said Beowulf Agate thoughtfully, "since you can't find the killers, you start with the victims themselves. Their families, their attorneys, their bankers, perhaps even their close friends or neighbors. Anyone who might know something of their attitudes, of what they may have mentioned about themselves. It's damnably boring—which is part of your job—but you may find another door to open in the maze."

"Why would any of them talk to me?"

"Hell, that's easy. The Company has connections, *Frank* has connections. They'll get you credentials—good God, we've given *them* enough over here. You're the good guy; you're trying to find out who killed their loved ones, and the combined intelligence communities have given you an open road."

"An 'open road'? What does that mean?"

"We make up our own jargon. It simply means you have the authority to ask questions."

"*What* authority?"

"Who *cares*? You have the credentials."

"It can't be as simple as that—"

"Simplicity is the mother's milk of penetration, young Cameron. I'm sorry I have to remind you of that."

"I both understand, and I don't understand."

"Then think about it some more."

Suddenly, Antonia Scofield rushed through the archway. *"Bray,"* she cried, "I went out to the porch to shut off the lights and there was fire on the horizon, explosions, I think."

"Extinguish the candles!" ordered Scofield. "You, Pryce, you come with me!" Like scrambling infantrymen in a jungle, with Beowulf Agate in the lead, the two men raced through the heavy foliage on the barely discernible path. Cameron had the presence of mind to grab his flight bag when he saw Scofield reach for a square leather-bound object on a table as they left the house. Crashing through succeeding walls of greenery, they came to the rock-hewn beach where the photoelectric cells caught the rays of the Caribbean sun.

"Get down!" said the older man, opening the leather case and removing large night-vision binoculars. Pryce unzipped his flight bag and did the same. Together they scanned the horizon. There was a shimmering glow far out in the water, accompanied by erratic flashes of light. "What do you make of it?" asked Scofield.

"I'll tell you in a minute," replied Cameron, reaching into the bag for his precalibrated telephone, "but right now I've got a sharp pain in the pit of my stomach."

"Sort of hollow, right?"

"Very hollow, Mr. Scofield."

"I've been there. It never changes."

"Oh, *Christ*!" spat out Pryce. "There's *nothing*. Nobody answers!"

"Your boat?"

"The Coast Guard cutter. It was blown out of the water. Those kids . . . they were just kids! All *dead*."

"They may come in here—"

"They? *Who*?"

"Whoever sank the cutter," replied Scofield coldly. "We're part of a very small archipelago, six or seven mini-islands, but they may center on this one."

"Who *are* they? Drug pirates getting rid of their hunters maybe?"

"We should be so lucky, young man, and I say that in profound sorrow for those kids."

"What do you mean? Are you suggesting they're after *me*? If you are, that's crazy! I got off port side—the vessel was heading west—and waited for an extensive cloud cover before I pushed off. No one could have seen me except someone here—which was you."

"No, Cameron Pryce, they're not after you; they followed you but they're not after you. You've managed to do what I honestly believed could never be done: You've roped me back into hell. They have charts, a location. If not tonight, sooner or later."

"I'm sorry! I tried to think out every move so as to *pro-tect* you!"

"Don't blame yourself. As experienced as you are, you're not prepared for them, few are. But if it is tonight, someone who *is* prepared has a surprise in store for them."

"What?"

"I'll explain later. Stay here, I'll be back in five minutes or less." The former deep-cover field officer got to his feet.

"Who's 'them'?" asked Pryce.

"Need I say it?" replied Scofield. "The Matarese, young man."

5

Anguish mixed with fury, Cameron imposed a cold control over himself, his hands steady as he stared through the night-vision binoculars. The pulsating glow of light was diminished in the sporadic darkness; finally it ceased to exist. Fire swallowed up by the sea, what was had disappeared. Pryce slowly moved the binoculars with every break in the cloud cover that intercepted the moonlight—to the left, to the right, above where the drowned fires were, then below in case a vessel had crept forward in the darkness.

There it was! A small, black silhouette, illuminated by the now-dim rays of the moon. It seemed to be on a direct course toward Outer Brass 26—or was it? Where was *Scofield*?

As if on cue, he heard the sound of rustling foliage as Beowulf Agate broke through the palm leaves, his wife, Antonia, behind him. Each carried what appeared to be a heavy object, Scofield's defined first. It was a three-foot, four-inch-bore, shoulder-hoisted rocket launcher. The large canvas duffel bag, half carried, half dragged by his wife, obviously contained the ammunition.

"Anything new?" asked Bray, taking the duffel from Antonia and setting the launcher down on the rocks protruding from the sand.

"Another boat, too far out to get a description, but it looks like it's headed here."

"There are several small land masses, barely islands, on

both its flanks. Whoever's skippering may head to the nearest first—we're like third."

"That's not much consolation—"

"It could be enough," Scofield cut in. "I want to see what kind of equipment it's got on board."

"What difference does it make?"

"Enough to tell me whether to blow it to hell or not. Heavy antennae, satellite dishes, radar grids—oh, it makes a lot of difference, take my word."

"You'll have to destroy it if it weighs anchor off the beach."

"Good God, you've just given me another idea!" cried the older man, turning to his wife.

"If it's what I think, you're crazy," said Antonia Scofield, crouching behind her husband, her words delivered through dry ice.

"Not really," replied Beowulf Agate, "we have the advantage, *all* the advantages! Even now we can determine that it's a relatively small craft. How many crew can there be? Four, five, six?"

"I'll grant you the logic, my dear," answered Antonia reluctantly. "I'll also go back to the house and bring us additional weapons." She rose and ran into the heavy foliage.

"Toni always changes 'my darling' into 'my dear' when she's pissed off at me," said Scofield, grinning. "It means she knows I'm right, but she hates to admit it."

"I hate to admit that I don't know what you're talking about! *Either* of you."

"Sometimes I think you're slow, Cam."

"Get off it! What *are* you talking about?"

"Speaking as an ex-professional, wouldn't it be lovely if we got on board that craft? Commandeered it, actually? We might learn a great deal, no? We can suck 'em in here and take control, reverse the circumstances. *They* become the targets."

"*Hey,* my *God,* I see what you mean!" exclaimed Pryce. "There has to be ship-to-shore communication. We take whoever comes in, show them your rocket blaster aimed at their boat, and make it clear that one hostile move and it's exit-city."

"That's the bottom line."

"What's Mrs. Scofield bringing us?"

"Three MAC-Tens would be my guess. They have longer and straighter ranges. Also, they're very special, they have silencers attached; you hear punctuated spits but no loud fire. Our theory is that if we ever have to actually shoot, we could run away and not reveal our positions."

"She knows about that sort of thing?"

"As much as either of us. She keeps up with the world I left far more than I do. She can't forget how long we were fugitives—she still believes we're fugitives now. I think she could put on a scuba tank and blow up a destroyer, if either of us—or Taleniekov—was threatened."

"That's some lady."

"Some lady," agreed Beowulf Agate softly. "Without her, neither Vasili nor I would have survived. . . . Here she comes!"

"I decided on the Uzi for me," said a breathless Antonia, parting the last low-hanging palms and throwing the weapons down. "It's lighter and best at close range." She then lowered the canvas bag from her shoulder. "I've brought sixty rounds apiece for the MAC's; they're in the red-striped plastic pouches; mine are in the blue. . . . What now, my darling?"

"Ah, she softens!" exclaimed Scofield. "It's like Ajaccio or Bonifacio all over again, isn't it, Toni?"

"It makes me sick, you bastard."

"But you see, Cam, she rises to the occasion. Right, old girl?"

"Old I can accept. Dead, I can't."

"Have you got a flashlight in that bag of tricks of yours, Pryce?"

"Of course."

"Take it out, turn it on, and wave the beam around helter-skelter. Don't zero in on the boat but weave around it. We don't want our victims to miss it."

"I hope you know what you're doing," said Cameron.

"To paraphrase you, my boy, I both do and I don't. I just know it can be a shortcut, and that's what we always look for, isn't it?"

"No argument there," agreed Pryce, turning on the high-powered flashlight and circling the dark sky, finally arcing over the suddenly approaching silhouette in the distance.

"He changed course!" said Scofield. "He was heading for Brass Twenty-four, and he turned! Good work, young fellow."

"What now?" asked Cameron.

"They'll send a skiff in," said Antonia. "I'll head to the right of the beach cul-de-sac, and you go to the left, Cam."

"Then what?" asked the younger man.

"We'll see what scoots in," replied Scofield, his rocket launcher in place between the rocks. "I'll also be zeroing in on the craft itself. Whoever's left on board will be on deck. . . . Then we'll know what the odds are."

"Suppose they have what *you* have?" said Cameron. "Seventy-five millimeters, or something like that. They could blow up your island!"

"If they have it, and I see it, and if I catch anybody running to it, the whole shebang is blown out of the water."

The small ship, a trawler, continued toward Outer Brass 26, and as it came within two hundred yards, a heavy-calibered cannon could be distinguished on its bow, large enough and powerful enough to blow up a Coast Guard cutter. But the few hands on deck—three, to be precise—were more concerned with lowering a power-driven PVC boat into the water. The skipper emerged from the bridge, apparently shouting orders to drop anchor, and then stood there, the binoculars at his eyes, a large holstered weapon strapped around his waist.

"I know that face!" exclaimed Pryce. "He's a Swede, on Stockholm's terrorist list. One of the suspects in Palme's assassination!"

"He's found a home," said Scofield. "Now I really want to get on board."

"Be careful, my dear."

"She's still pissed off. . . . I will, lovey, just get to the right flank. But for Christ's sake, stay low and use our little jungle. Remember, he's got the same night-glasses we do."

"On my way."

"You, too, Pryce, head left. We'll have the bastards in a cross fire. But remember, if you have to shoot, the initial rounds go over their heads. We want captives, not corpses."

"I understand, sir."

"Cut the 'sir' bullshit. I'm not your mentor, I'm an accident."

The PVC lapped its way into the beach no more than two hundred feet from Scofield and the launcher. On the right side of the cove's horseshoe configuration, Antonia stood in the shadows of the island jungle, the Uzi in her strong hands. On the far-left flank, Pryce knelt by a large volcanic boulder, the MAC-10 poised to fire. The first of the three men in the rubber raft leaped over the bow, a weapon in his left hand, a rope in his right. The man in the middle was next, gripping a large repeating automatic rifle in both hands. The skipper at the stern shut off the engine and followed the others; he was equally armed. Their combined firepower was considerable.

In the brief illuminations of moonlight, they appeared to be ordinary fishermen. Two had unkempt beards, attesting to the aversion at sea to wasting warm water and manipulating a razor; the third was clean-shaven. This last member was the skipper of the raft and appeared younger than the others, perhaps in his middle thirties, while his companions—rugged, heavyset—appeared to be in their late forties or slightly beyond. Too, the third man was dressed in what could best be described as casual-expensive. Formfitting white jeans, a loose blue cotton jacket, and a visored sailing cap, as opposed to his associates' tattered shirts and trousers whose only laundering was probably a plunge in the salt water every other day or so. Also, around each neck was a rawhide strap attached to a flashlight.

"*You* there, Jack," shouted the younger man, addressing the intruder in front, "beach the raft and look around over there!" He pointed in Antonia's direction. "And you, Harry, check the other side of the beach." It was Pryce's domain.

"There's someone here, that beam of light didn't appear out of nowhere!" The language the search-party leader spoke was English, but it was not his native tongue. The accent was middle European, Slovak or Baltic.

"I dinno, mate," cried Harry, his speech obviously Australian—Strine, as it was called. "These Carib spots can be ruddy loony. Reflections all over the plyce."

"We saw what we saw. Go on!"

"If we saw wot we think we seen," said the man called Jack, evidently a London cockney, "they weren't bashful about it, now were they?"

"Just look, just *look*!"

"I ayn't paid to get me bloody head whacked off by some cryzy savages."

"You're paid far more than you're worth, Harry, now hurry up!" It was at this moment that the concealed Scofield saw what he hoped to see. The search party's superior officer took out a small walkie-talkie from his jacket pocket and spoke into it. "No sign of anyone on the beach and no visible light beyond the trees and the brush. We'll reconnoiter; keep your radio with you."

The comparatively well-dressed leader of the unit lifted the rawhide strap over his head and, looping the flashlight into his left hand, switched it on and swung the beam around, crisscrossing the area. Scofield ducked as the light shot over his head, behind the rocks and the hidden rocket launcher. Darkness again, except for the erratic moonlight; Beowulf Agate peered over the ragged edge of stone. He was alarmed.

The leader had spotted something and Bray knew exactly what it was: the rows of small sun-absorbing plates that fed the photoelectric cells that were an alternate source of Outer Brass 26's energy. Slowly the man crept forward.

At the far right side of the beach, the slovenly subordinate named Jack cautiously walked through the sand, the beam of his flashlight swinging in all directions. He came within two feet of Antonia, and the moment he did so, she stepped out of the foliage, shoved the short barrel of the Uzi into his back, and whispered, "You utter a sound and you'll sleep with the fishes, I believe is the expression. Drop your gun!"

Over on the left flank, Pryce waited behind the boulder as the Australian approached with his flashlight. When the man came nearer, actually brushing the large rock with his shoulder, Cameron circled the huge stone and stepped out, three feet behind the intruder.

"You raise your voice, you're in kangaroo hell, mate," he said quietly but harshly.

"*What* the—"

"I told you *once*!" interrupted Pryce softly, angrily. "I won't say it again. Instead, you'll be a bloody corpse on the beach."

"Don't you worry about me, mate! I didn't come on board for this kind of shit."

"Why did you come on board . . . *mate*?"

"The screw—the salary. The bastards pay every week what it would take me two months to make!"

"Why are you so far away from home?"

"I worked for 'em in the west territories, way above Perth it was, servicing the Indian Ocean. I'm a good hand and m'morals aren't a priority, if you know what I mean. We're all goin' to that hell anyway."

"Do you know whom you're working for?"

"Haven't the slightest. Never asked, don't care. Contraband, I gather; drugs, I suspect. Meeting tankers and cargos on their way to Durban and Port Elizabeth."

"You're a beautiful man."

"M'children think I am. I bring home the bacon, as you Yanks say."

"Hold your head straight, Aussie, it'll hurt less that way."

"*What? . . .*"

Cameron dropped his MAC-10, walked up to the man, his arms raised above him, then crashed his taut, hard, experienced hands into both sides of the rogue Australian's neck. The carotid vessels were damaged, not severed; he would be unconscious for at least two hours.

Suddenly, out of the darkness of the small cove beach, came the words shouted in accented English. "*Jack, Harry,*

I've *found* it! There are more than I can count. Dozens and dozens of small plates that lead to a central cable! They're here, we've found them; this is their electricity!"

"And I've found *you*," said Scofield, standing up from the dark beach rocks, the silenced automatic rifle in his hand. "I suggest you get rid of the AK-Forty-seven before I become upset and put a bullet in your forehead. I don't approve of those weapons; they kill people."

"My God, it *is* you!"

"What did you say?"

"Beowulf Agate, your code name."

"You can tell in this light?"

"I've listened to your voice on tape."

"Why were you so anxious to find me? Not that I was so hard to find."

"We had no reason until recently. Beowulf was a forgotten relic, a man who had disappeared."

"And now I've reappeared?"

"You know the reason as well as I do. The old woman in Chelyabinsk, René Mouchistine on that yacht."

"I've heard of those people."

"Why else would the Agency's *new* Beowulf Agate, the vaunted Cameron Pryce, come after you?"

"I have no idea. You tell me."

"He's an expert, and you have names going back years."

"If I have, I've forgotten them. That world no longer interests me. And, incidentally, how could you possibly have known about Pryce? It was a Four-Zero search, maximum classified."

"Our methods, too, are maximum classified, but very thorough. More thorough than the Company's."

"'Ours' being the Matarese's, of course."

"It's to be presumed that Officer Pryce revealed that to you."

"Actually, he didn't have to, if that interests you."

"Really?"

"Which means that your sources and my sources come from the same source. Now *that's* interesting, isn't it?"

"It's also immaterial, Mr. Scofield. These names you've

forgotten, and the companies they represented—surely you realize they're meaningless now. Most of the people, if not all, are dead, the corporations swallowed up by others. Meaningless."

"*Ah,* yet some do come back to me, I truly believe, but then they were pretty well buried all those years ago, weren't they? Let's see if I can remember. . . . There was Voroshin in the Soviet city of Leningrad, which gave birth, of course, to Essen's Verachten, not so? Both were owned by their governments but they were beholden to someone—*something*—else. In the American city of Boston, Massachusetts, wasn't it?"

"That is enough, Mr. Scofield."

"Don't be such a killjoy. My memory's activated—it hasn't been for years. There was also the English Waverly Industries; it, too, was irrevocably bound to Boston. And Scozzi-Paravacini, or was it Paravacini-Scozzi? In Milan, wasn't it? However, it also took its orders from Boston—"

"You've made your point—"

"Good heavens, not until we consider the untimely, tragic deaths of such leaders as the brilliant Guillaumo Scozzi, the seductive Odile Verachten, and the stubborn David Waverly. I've always felt that somehow they displeased—dare I say the name—the *Shepherd Boy*?"

"Ashes, Scofield. I repeat, meaningless! And that's nothing but a sobriquet for someone long dead and forgotten."

" 'Sobriquet'? That's a nickname, isn't it?"

"You're not uneducated."

"The Shepherd Boy . . . In some parts of that secret world of yours, that world of constant night, he's a legend going back decades. A legend about whom words were written down by those he ultimately destroyed. If found and pieced together, those writings would change the history of international finance, wouldn't they? . . . Or perhaps describe a blueprint for the future."

"I say it for the last time!" The search-party leader both spat and choked out the words. "Meaningless ramblings!"

"Then why are you here?" asked Bray. "Why were you so anxious to find me?"

"We follow orders."

"Oh, I love that phrase! It certainly covers a lot of exculpatory ground, doesn't it? *Doesn't* it?"

"You finish your statements with too many questions."

"It's the only way you learn anything, *isn't* it?"

"Let me be frank, Mr. Scofield—"

"You mean you *haven't* been?" interrupted Beowulf Agate.

"Please stop that!"

"Sorry, go on."

"We live in a different age from when you left the Service, sir—"

"Are you saying I'm antediluvian, out of *touch*?" again Bray broke in.

"Only in terms of technological relativity," replied the Middle European with marked irritation. "Data banks have been upgraded beyond belief, instruments electronically scan thousands of documents every hour and store them, the *depth* of research has become extraordinary."

"Which means if I happened to mention a few of those names to interested parties, it might lead to new ones now—new names, new companies, is that what you're saying? My word, the entire history of corporate Boston would have to be rewritten."

"What I'm *saying,* Mr. Scofield," said the intruder through clenched teeth, as if addressing a senile idiot, "is that we're prepared to pay you several million dollars to disappear again. South America, the South Pacific islands, anywhere you wish. A mansion, a ranch, the finest that can be purchased for you and your wife."

"We were never really married you know, just sort of our own commitment—"

"I really don't *care*. I'm simply offering you a superb alternative to what you have."

"Then why didn't you just come in here and blow us up with your cannon? You could have smoked us out and killed me—ergo, your problem is solved."

"I remind you that Officer Pryce was tracked here. It

would lead to unacceptable complications. And by the way, where is he?"

"Mrs. Scofield is showing him around our lagoon; it's quite beautiful in the moonlight, what there is of it. . . . So you don't reject the solution, only the consequences."

"Just as you would have done in your younger years. Beowulf Agate was the most pragmatic of deep-cover, black-operations officers. He killed when he believed he had to."

"That's not quite true. He killed when it was necessary— there's a difference. Belief, or conjecture, had nothing to do with it."

"Enough. What is your answer? Live out your days in splendid comfort or stay on this tiny island hovel? And die on it."

"Good Lord, such a *decision*!" said Scofield, lowering his MAC-10 automatic rifle against the rocks, his left hand pensively shading his eyes but still on the intruder. "It would be wonderful for my wife—my common wife, as it were, and perfectly legal—but I'd be constantly thinking . . ." Beowulf Agate watched through his slightly parted fingers the subtle movements of the intruder. The man's right hand was lowered, close to his loose jacket. . . . Suddenly, he ripped up the flap and reached for a gun under his belt. Before he could fire, Bray raised his weapon and sent off a single round. The Mataresan collapsed in the sand, blood trickling from his chest.

"*What was* that?" came the voice from the dead man's radio. "*I heard something! What was it?*"

Scofield raced to the corpse, pulling it into the bushes out of sight and removing the small intercom from the jacket pocket; he switched it off. Then, concealing himself in the shadows, he called out sotto voce, "From your silence, my hidden pigeons, I assume you've completed your assignments. With great caution, please return to Father Christmas."

"My man's asleep," said Pryce, emerging from the palm-engulfed bushes. "He'll be asleep for a couple of hours."

"Here's another on his hands and knees," added Antonia,

crawling with her captive out of the foliage. "Where's the other man?"

"He was most impolite; he tried to kill me. He's doing penance in our jungle."

"What do we do now, my husband?"

"Simplest thing in the world, old girl," replied Scofield, peering through the night-vision binoculars. "We activate the bowels of the captain of that so-called trawler. . . . Cam, have you got any rope in your tricky bag?"

"No, I don't."

"Not too bright, either. Take off your T-shirt, rip it in strips, and bind Toni's prisoner, hands and feet. With what's left, shove it in the bastard's mouth, and, if you wouldn't mind, a little physical anesthesia would be helpful."

"It'll be a pleasure." Pryce went to work, his assignment taking less than ninety seconds.

"And me, Bray?"

"Wait a minute, lovey," answered Scofield, still staring through the binoculars. "There he goes. He's heading below, probably to a radio. He's not watching the shore and obviously there's no one else on board!"

"So?"

"So run back to the house and gather up a few flares, four or five'll be enough. Then dash down the east path, say two or three hundred feet, and send one up."

"Good heavens, why? He'll know we're here!"

"He knows already, dearest. Now we've got to confuse him."

"How?"

"By your racing back to the house and into the *west* path, past the lagoon, and setting off another flare over there. Ignite the first one, say in eight minutes, the second in eleven, give or take. Don't you remember?"

"I'm beginning to see what you mean. . . . Livorno, Italy, to be precise."

"It worked there, didn't it?"

"Yes, it did, my darling. I'm on my way." Antonia disappeared into the brush.

"Since I was never in Livorno—actually, I was, but not

when you two were," protested Cameron, "would you mind telling me what you did there? And, while you're at it, what am *I* supposed to do?"

"Can you swim?"

"Yes. Professional certification in deep-sea down to three hundred feet, and all certificates in scuba."

"Very commendable, but we have no tanks here or the time for you to get into your Spider-Man outfit. I mean, can you just plain *swim*?"

"Of course."

"How far in a breath underwater? Without fins?"

"At least fifty to seventy feet."

"That should do it. Go out there, duck beneath the trawler, come up on the other side, get on deck, and take that soon-to-be-confused son of a bitch. Have you got a knife?"

"Need you ask?"

"Get going while our skipper's still below!"

Pryce reached into his flight bag, pulled out his belted hunting knife, strapped it around his waist, and raced to the lapping waters of the beach. He plunged in and with strong strokes started toward the trawler two hundred yards away, his open eyes constantly on the deck of the boat. The captain emerged from the below cabin, so Cameron went underwater. Twenty, thirty, forty feet, surfacing for breath in the darkness, then under again and again until he reached the hull of the trawler. He surged beneath it, rising to the air on the starboard side.

He raised his hand in the water and looked at his waterproof watch. The radium dial told him it had taken nearly six minutes for him to reach the trawler; the first flare would appear in less than two. Slowly he made his way toward the bow. As the initial flare lit up the eastern sky, the captain would undoubtedly race to the stern of his boat, which faced the east. It was his best and possibly sole chance to get on deck without being seen. Cameron understood that his knife was his only weapon and a blade was no match for the captain's bullets.

There it was! The night sky to the left of the trawler exploded with light. It pulsated as the streak was propelled upward, then, reaching an apex, burst again as it briefly remained still, blinding, until it began its slow descent, swinging back and forth as it fell into the tropic forest.

"Mikhail, Mikhail!" screamed the captain, apparently into his radio, while his feet raced across the deck. "What was *that*? . . . Mikhail, *answer* me! Where *are* you?" Pryce surged up from the water, his arms extended; he reached a lateral rib, merely a small bulge, but it was enough. Fingers gripping the wood, he pulled himself up and flung his right arm above him until his hand grabbed the gunwale; the rest was sheer strength. He crawled over the railing and collapsed onto the deck, his body supine, breathing deeply, his chest heaving. In moments, air was back in his lungs, his excessive heart rate receding. All the while, the Swedish terrorist-captain kept shouting into the unresponsive radio. "*Mikhail,* if you can hear me, I'm going to commence firing! It is your signal to return to the ship immediately! With or without you, I'm getting out of here!"

So much for the Matarese's sense of brotherly concern, say nothing of loyalty, thought Cameron. The superior officer would leave his subordinates to a deadly unknown to save his own skin. Pryce wondered why he was surprised. Scofield had implied just that.

There was the second explosion! Far to the right, the western sky was on fire, the light more intense, more blinding than the first flare—or was it the sudden cloud cover that cut off the competing moonlight? Cam rose swiftly to his feet as the thundering cannon roared so loudly it had to blow a hole in the palm-laden greenery of Outer Brass 26. He edged his way along the wall of the deck cabin; the moonlight reappeared. The now-hysterical captain ran to the stern of the trawler, the night-vision binoculars held to his eyes.

Thank you, thought Pryce as he walked slowly, silently toward the man's back. *It's so much easier when it's easy.* With his left clenched fist, he hammered the Swede's lower spine as his right gripped the holster, unsnapping it and ripping out a large .357 automatic. The captain fell to the deck, screaming in pain. "Come on, Mr. Viking, you're not that hurt, just a little bruise on a vertebra. According to your

Aussie recruit, Harry, you're better off than they are. He's convinced that he, London Jack, and fancy Mikhail are going to be sacrificial meat for hungry savages. . . . Get on your *feet,* you son of a bitch! You blew that CG cutter up, killing all those young men! If I didn't think you could be useful, I'd happily put a bullet in your throat. *Up,* you scum!"

"Who *are* you?" choked the captain cautiously, painfully rising. "How did you get on board?"

"That's for you to wonder about. Maybe I'm the avenging angel come to make you pay for taking the lives of all those youngsters. One thing's certain, you're on your way back to Stockholm."

"No!"

"Oh, yes. I've too many friends there to consider anything else. . . . Your radio, if you please?"

"Never!" The captain lunged forward, his hands like grappling hooks. Cameron sprang back, crashing his right foot into the terrorist's groin. Again the Swede fell to the deck, groaning and grabbing his testicles.

"You people seem to enjoy inflicting pain, but you're not very good at receiving it, are you? Why doesn't that surprise me?" Pryce knelt down and yanked the walkie-talkie out of the captain's jacket pocket. He stood up, studied the various buttons in the moonlight, pressed one, and spoke. "Scofield, are you there, or do I have to yell?"

"Oh, I'm here, laddiebuck, and I've been listening to a hell of a good scene. Your slimebucket had his radio on *Transmit.* I guess he was nervous, or confused."

"You've made your point, *sir.* I'd suggest you get out here and we'll look around."

"Can you believe that's what I was thinking?"

"I can imagine it's possible."

Their two living, securely bound captives in tow, Antonia and Scofield pulled alongside the trawler. "What did you do with the elegant dude named Mikhail?" yelled Pryce.

"He's absolutely disappeared, young fella," replied Beowulf Agate. "It's why we're a bit late."

"What are you talking about? If there's a radio here, they've got our coordinates. They'll find his body!"

"Not likely, Cam," said Scofield. "We stuffed him with chum, pockets and gullet, and dropped him off at Breeding Sharks Bay, where we keep our boat. As I say, that's why we're a little late getting out here."

"What?"

"No one with a brain in his head swims there. Believe me, he's absolute history, bless the Almighty for those ravenous fish."

The below-deck cabin was a panoply of computer equipment, lining both the starboard and port walls. "I'll be hanged if I can understand any of this stuff," said Scofield.

"To me, it's all a total mystery," added Antonia. "Surely one must be a scientist to make them work."

"Not really," said Pryce, sitting down in front of a machine. "There are basic insertions that take you step-by-step to the function you want."

"Would you mind translating that?" asked the older man.

"It'd take too long and bore you to death," replied the CIA field agent. "This particular equipment is still on openline, which means it's recently been used and was expected to be used again very shortly."

"Is that good?"

"More than good, a blessing. We can pull up a recall, see what's been sent out." Pryce began pressing letters and numbers; bright green words instantly appeared on the black screen.

Insert proper code for recall.

"Damn it!" said Cameron under his breath, getting out of the chair and rapidly heading for the steps of the cabin's entrance. "I'll be right back," he added. "I'm bringing down our skipper, who's going to unlock this machine for us or he joins fancy Mikhail in shark heaven!"

Pryce ran up the short steps and looked around on the deck in the progressively elusive moonlight. What he saw paralyzed him—it was *impossible*. The captain of the so-called trawler was not there; he had been roped to a gunwale cleat but he was not *there*! Instead, his two companions were a blood-soaked mess, the London cockney obviously dead, the Australian barely alive, his skull crashed open, his eyes losing focus.

"What happened?" roared Pryce to the Australian, grabbing his blood-soaked shoulders.

"'Eee was a bloody fuckin' bahstard!" whispered the mortally wounded man, "that's what he was. He wriggled his way out of the rope an' said he was goin' to free us. Instead, he picked up a winch handle and bashed us both, one after the other, so fast we didn't know what was . . . happenin'. I'll see him in hell!" The Aussie expelled his last breath; he was dead.

Cameron looked over the gunwale; the motorized life raft was gone. Its new helmsman could be heading to any one of five or six small islands. The immediate trail was ended. Cam raced back into the below-deck cabin. "The son of a bitch got loose, killed the other two, and took the PVC!" he yelled. "I can't break into the computer."

"There's still a telephone over there, young fella," said Scofield. "I realize it's not high tech, but I dialed our house and got the answering machine."

"You're a simplistic genius in a lousy high-tech world," said a relieved Pryce, rushing to the phone next to the computer. He pressed the coded numbers he knew would override satellite traffic and connect him to Langley, Virginia, to the Directorate of Operations, the Company's most sacrosanct of secret projects.

"Yes?" said the neutral voice on the line.

"This is Camshaft, Caribbean, and I have to talk to Deputy Director Frank Shields. This is a Four-Zero priority."

"Director Shields left the grounds hours ago, sir."

"Then patch me through to his home."

"To do that I'll need additional information—"

"Try the name Beowulf Agate!" Cam interrupted harshly.

"Who, sir?"

"I thought that was me," broke in Scofield.

"I'm borrowing it, do you mind?"

"I guess not."

"*Beowulf Agate,*" repeated Pryce anxiously into the telephone. Twelve seconds later, the voice of Frank Shields came on the line.

"It's been a long time, Brandon, over twenty years, I'd say."

"This isn't Brandon, it's me. Camshaft and Caribbean got me nowhere with your robot, so I borrowed the name. The owner didn't object."

"You *found* him?"

"A lot more than that, Frank, but this isn't the time to give you details. I need information fast. Is your Big Guy Eye still working?"

"BGI and its brothers and sisters never stop working, they hum around the clock; it's mostly junk. What do you need?"

"There's been a transmission or transmissions from here to God knows where, either by phone or computer via satellite within the past hour or so. Can you pull up the traffic you've intercepted?"

"Sure, how much material do you want, ten or twenty thousand pages?"

"Funny fellow. I've studied the charts. It or they were sent out from these approximate coordinates: longitude sixty-five degrees west; latitude eighteen degrees, twenty minutes north; the time span between midnight and two A.M."

"I admit that narrows it down considerably. That would be our Mayagüez station in Puerto Rico. What are we looking for?"

"I imagine Beowulf Agate to begin with. Scofield was told they were after him."

"The *Matarese*?"

"Exactly, according to a well-dressed scumbucket who's no longer befouling the planet."

"You *have* been busy."

"So have they. They followed in my footsteps—"

"How *could* they? Everything was under wraps!"

"Because one or more of them are on our payroll."

"Oh, my *God*!"

"No time for supplications. Get to work."

"What's your number?"

"We're on a trawler and the number's been removed. But there's a computer here, screen and all."

"Pull up your equipment line in the confidential mode. I'll have Mayagüez contact you directly if they find something. Or even if they don't. I'll also give them a few more clues to look for."

"Find something, Frank," said Pryce, turning to the computer, touching the keys, and delivering the information Shields needed. "An entire crew of fine young men were killed by those bastards." Cameron hung up and, breathing hard, leaned back in the chair.

"What do we do now?" asked Antonia.

"We wait, my girl," answered Bray. "We wait until the sun comes up if we have to. Mayagüez has to filter out a lot of ozone traffic, *if* they can find *anything*."

"A two-hour time span with fairly accurate coordinates should reduce the difficulty," said Pryce. "Even Shields agreed to that."

"Frank may have an impressive new title," Scofield mumbled, interrupting, "but he's still an analyst. He's comfortably in D.C.; you're in the field. In like situations, he's 'Doctor Feel-good.' Keep the on-scene talent happy."

"You really *are* a cynic."

"I've lived long enough, and outlived too many others, to be anything else."

"We wait then." The minutes went by, all eyes on the computer screen. Nearly an hour passed until the bright letters appeared.

In origin-compul-scrambler mode. No interception possible. Based on 'Beowulf Agate' and additional info from D.C., we've cross-checked and send the following. Two transmissions from estimated coordinates may apply. Both verbatim telephone calls in French: "Expensive hawk arriving at Buenos Aires." *Two:* "Naval observers cooperative, neutral zone. Islands southwest of British Tortola." *End of message. Receiver routing still under relay trace. Euro-Mediterranean stations narrowing down destination.*

"My, oh my!" exclaimed the retired Brandon Scofield, "aren't they cute?"

"What do you mean?" asked his wife.

"They learned how to code from cereal box tops," said Bray.

"It's fairly obvious, I'll say that," agreed Cameron.

"*What* is?" said Antonia.

"'Expensive hawk arriving at Buenos Aires,'" replied Scofield. "Translated, the expensive hawk—the hunter—is our new friend Pryce, spelled with an *i*. Buenos Aires is B.A., undoubtedly Beowulf Agate and that's me."

"Oh, I see what you mean," said the tall, attractive, and formidable Antonia, staring at the green letters on the black screen. "And the rest?"

"I'll answer that," said Cameron angrily. "'Naval observers cooperative' . . . and neutralized. They blew up the Coast Guard cutter. *Goddamn* them!"

"The second transmission said 'Islands southwest of British Tortola,'" swiftly interrupted Scofield, "not a specific island, and outside of the Brasses there are at least another twenty south and southwest of us. Let's head into our Twenty-six, and I'll use my equipment—we can also have a drink, which is profoundly necessary."

"You don't have a computer," objected Pryce.

"I don't need one, lad. I've got a telephone, one of those Comsat mobile-link jobs. Cost me a hell of a lot of money, but if you've got a friend in Hong Kong, you can get him on the line."

Suddenly, far away in the night sky, came the sound of distant thunder, but not a storm, not the weather. It was something else.

"What the hell is *that*?" said Cam.

"On *deck*!" yelled Scofield, grabbing his wife by the hand and pulling her to the short cabin staircase while hammering Pryce's shoulder. "Get *out* of here!"

"What . . . *why*?"

"Because this is probably the tenth sortie, you idiot!" shouted the retired agent. "They're *searching* for us. They see this boat, we're finished! *Move,* both of you. And over the side!"

All three did so, furiously swimming away from the hull as a jet fighter swooped down, dropping two bombs on the trawler, blowing it to the dark sky from which the deadly marauder emerged. It sank within moments.

"Toni, *Toni,* where *are* you?" screamed Scofield in the turbulent waters.

"Over *here,* my darling!" yelled Antonia, farther out in the water.

"*Pryce?* . . . Are you here, are you *alive,* Pryce?"

"You're damned right I am!" replied Cameron. "And I intend to stay that way!"

"Swim to our island," ordered Scofield. "We have to talk."

"What's there to talk about?" asked Pryce, toweling himself off on the porch of the dark cabin.

"They've ruined the life I've come to love, young man. They've taken away our happiness, our freedom."

"I can't do anything about that," said Cam as both naked men dried themselves off. "I told you, I did my best to conceal your whereabouts."

"Your best wasn't good enough, was it?"

"Get out of my *face*. By your own admission, you weren't so damned hard to find."

"For you, no, but I was for them. With an exception I never figured on, but I should have. After all these years, they still have a mole in the Agency. A high-placed son of a bitch. Did you have any idea?"

"No, I didn't. You heard what I said to Frank, that someone was on our payroll. He went ape."

"I believe you and I believe him. So that's why you must spread the word. Beowulf Agate is back. Let them know that Beowulf Agate and Vasili Taleniekov, the Serpent, are back, and we will not stop searching until the Matarese is history."

"What about me, Scofield?"

"You're our enforcer, our point."

"*Our?* . . . Taleniekov is dead. He's gone!"

"Not in my head, Cameron Pryce. He never will be."

6

They sat in the dark screened-in veranda, the only light coming from a Coleman lantern, its wick at the lowest ebb, just enough to illuminate the numbers on Scofield's portable phone. He had pressed the esoteric digits that were their direct link to Langley's clandestine operations. "Get on the other phone," ordered Bray as Pryce felt around the table by his chair for the instrument.

"Yes?" Once more the robotic voice half whispered, half spoke.

"Beowulf Agate again," said Scofield. "Patch me through to Shields."

"Just a minute, sir." The line seemingly went dead, then the disembodied words came back. "I'm afraid you're *not* Beowulf Agate. Your voiceprint doesn't match."

"*Voice* print? . . . For Christ's sake, Cam, get on the phone and tell this praetorian keeper of the keys that I'm Beowulf Agate and you're *not*!"

"I just found it; it was on the floor," said Pryce, reaching for the telephone and getting on the line. "Listen to me, Night Watch, a voiceprint doesn't mean a goddamned thing, it's the code that's important, and more than one person can have it. Now, *move!*"

"Cameron?" said the very awake Frank Shields.

"Hi, Squint Eyes," Scofield broke in.

"Brandon, that *is* you!"

"How'd you guess?"

"'Let me count the ways,' starting with your inevitable insult. How are you, Bray?"

"I was a hell of a lot better before you gargoyles from hell came back into my life!"

"We had to, old friend. I'm sure Pryce made that clear. Incidentally, what do you think of him?"

"I can't really tell you what an asshole he is because he's on the other phone."

"I'm on the other phone," agreed Cameron quietly, his weariness apparent. "Let me bring you quickly up to speed, Frank." Pryce rapidly described the events that led to the island search party and the trawler, the murder of the crew, and the disappearance of the trawler's captain. "He must have reached somebody somewhere nearby because an F-Whatever jet fighter bombed the boat into driftwood. Fortunately, and I'll give him all the credit, your former colleague heard the noise and way outfigured me. I wouldn't be talking to you now if he hadn't, and I still don't know how he did it."

"He knows the Matarese, Cam."

"Indeed I do, Squinty," interrupted Scofield, "and our killer captain didn't have to reach anybody. That fake trawler was tracked and mapped from its first transmission. The wheels were set in motion, and the first expendable item was the trawler itself, along with the crew. The Matarese never leaves loose ends, not even the possibility of loose ends."

"There's your answer, Pryce," said Shields, two thousand miles north of the British Virgin Islands.

"Where the hell did the *plane* come from?" exploded Cameron. "It was a fighter jet, armed, military, which means it had to come from an air base! *Jesus,* have they infiltrated the Air Force? They obviously didn't have much trouble with the Agency."

"We're working on that," said Shields softly, haltingly.

"You could be wrong, Cam," offered Scofield from across the veranda. "The explosions blinded us; it was dark and we were swimming for our lives. We're not sure what we saw."

"Thanks to chivalry," interrupted Antonia beside her husband, "I was farther out than either of you. I tried to watch as the pilot circled to survey his work—"

"I dove under, thinking he was going to strafe," broke in Pryce.

"So did I," said Scofield.

"I'm afraid that thought never struck me—"

"What did you see, love? . . . Can you hear her, Frank?"

"Very clearly," replied the man in Langley.

"It was a jet, certainly, but not a configuration I'm familiar with, and there didn't appear to be any markings. However, there was something odd about the wings, and large protrusions on the underside."

"A Harrier," said Cameron Pryce, disgust in his tone. "Capable of lifting off from a patch of cement or a small backyard."

"An easy purchase for them," added Beowulf Agate. "Five'll get you ten they have dozens of them all over, strategically located."

"So, going back to your statement a few moments ago," interrupted Shields, "when you said that the trawler was 'tracked and mapped,' you were really saying the Harrier was already in place."

"I don't doubt it for a minute. When did you fellas on the top floor decide to send Pryce after me?"

"Six or seven days ago, when the CG station on St. Thomas couldn't come up with anything but a post-office box that nobody ever seemed to check."

"Plenty of time to move a Seven Forty-seven to an island, say nothing of a small Harrier. After all, Squinty, and I say it modestly, I'm apparently something of a prize, wouldn't you say?"

"*You're* a . . . never mind." Shields paused, his breathing audible. "I've got an update on the relay trace from our Euro-Mediterranean stations."

"What the hell is that?" asked Scofield. "Something new?"

"Actually, it's not, Brandon. You yourself used it a number of times—just a different name insofar as satellite communications have encompassed computers as well as radio and telephonic traffic. Do you remember when you used to call one number, say from Prague to London, but you dialed a number in Paris?"

"Sure. We loused up the KGB and the Stasi to the point where they often went nuts. One time they damn near shot up a ballet studio they thought was our MI-Six drop until they didn't have the heart to fire through the whirling tutus! We had to change the trip because the ballet teacher, who we all thought was a skinny *la-la,* if you know what I mean, beat the shit out of the roughest Brit agent we had."

"It's the same thing, only technologically more sophisticated."

"Now I *really* don't . . . *Hold* it, I see what you mean! We called it phone-forwarding trips, you call it relay traces."

"Because we work forward and backward. We don't merely send, we can now trace the receivers through the multiple 'relays.' "

"That's remarkable, Squinty."

"The lesson is over, Frank," said Pryce on the phone. "I'll fill in whatever your curious friend cares to hear. What's your transmission update?"

"It's crazy, Cam. The first call was routed to Paris, relayed to Rome, then to Cairo, back to Athens, next to Istanbul, and finally to the Italian province of Lombardy, specifically Lake Como. From that station it was bifurcated—"

"Split destinations!" interjected Pryce angrily. "They split the *wires*!"

"Into three parts, but the strongest signal was to Groningen in the Netherlands, where it stopped. Our experts believe the final leg, on private wire, was sent to Utrecht, Amsterdam, or Eindhoven."

"Three pretty big cities, Frank."

"Yes, we know. Where do you want to start? I'll alert our agents to give you every cooperation."

"He *won't* start!" yelled Scofield into the phone. "He'll begin when I *tell* him to begin!"

"Come on, Bray," said Frank Shields calmly, "I wouldn't sanction you into the field if my life depended on it. Among other things, my wife of forty years would leave me if I did. She adores you, you know that."

"Give my love to Janie, she was always brighter and much more interesting than you. But if you want me back, you son of a bitch, it's on *my* terms."

"Not in the field!"

"I'll accept that, Squinty. My aim's damn sharp, but I can't leap over fences like I used to."

"Then what do you want?"

"I want to run the operation."

"What?"

"I'm the only one who penetrated the Matarese, I was *there* when they were all blown to hell. But before that Armageddon, it was just Taleniekov and me who unearthed their disciples, how they thought, how warped they were, how fanatic their motives, all cloaked in sweet reason so the entire world would march to their hollow drums. . . . You can't dismiss me, Frank, I won't let you! You *need* me!"

"I repeat, not in the field," said the calm deputy director of the Central Intelligence Agency.

"I'd rather not be—I know the limitations of my age. But I'll not give you an open road."

"What's an 'open road'?"

"Hell, I just explained it to your junior officer here. We make up our own jargon, Frank, you know that."

"I'm afraid I don't, Bray. What do you mean?"

"If the boy gets in trouble, I have the right to intercede."

"Unacceptable. 'Trouble' to you is one thing, it could be something quite different to anyone else."

"Say he gets killed?"

"Oh?" Shields again hesitated. "I hadn't considered that."

"But it must be contemplated, mustn't it?"

"Shut up!" yelled Cameron Pryce into the phone. "I'll take care of myself, Frank!"

"Don't try to be a hero, youngster," said Scofield on the nearby telephone. "They always end up with lots of medals, usually sealed in their coffins."

"All right, Brandon, how do you want to proceed," said Shields from Langley.

"Antonia and I intend to come back to this place if it doesn't get blown up, but in the meantime, I suppose we've got to get up to your territory."

"Whatever you want. Our budgets are loose in that department."

"Good Lord, you sound like the Matarese! They offered me a couple of million and a spread in the South Pacific."

"We can't go that far, but we'll give you some attractive options. All safe houses, of course."

"Then let's get to work, Squinty. Time's of the essence."

"Goddamn it!" yelled Cameron Pryce, keeping the phone so close it orally assaulted the other two on the line. "I may not be your old buddy, *Squint Eyes,* but this is still my operation! I found the son of a bitch, and I *will* not be excluded!"

"Surely you won't, young man," said Brandon Alan Scofield. "You'll do all the things I should never try again, and they'll undoubtedly have to be done. You see, there's a factor in this equation that neither of you nor anybody in Washington understands. The Shepherd Boy was removed from this earth, but the crown was passed. He's the key."

"The Shepherd Boy? What the hell are you talking about?"

"I'll tell you when and if I think the time is right."

The four-story stone house above the waters of the Keizersgracht in Amsterdam was a monument to, if not a remembrance of, the splendor that was the port city's wealthiest years at the turn of the century. The Victorian furniture was sturdy yet delicate in design, heirlooms handed down through generations of a family born to riches. The walls of the high-ceilinged rooms were filled with priceless Flemish and French tapestries, the tall windows bordered by velour drapes, the sunlight filtered through the finest lace. A small

brass-grilled mahogany elevator, self-operated, was centered at the far rear wall of the building; it was capable of
carrying up to five occupants. However, to reach the fourth
and top floor required the insertion of a specific code in the
panel, a code that was altered daily, and programming an
incorrect one would result in the elevator's instant cessation, along with the locking of the brass grill. Whoever at-
tempted to reach the fourth floor without code clearance
was trapped, to be dealt with according to the circumstances.

Further, the main area of each succeeding level had a
general function. The first floor was essentially a large
drawing room, complete with a Steinway grand piano; it
was suitable for afternoon teas, cocktail parties, small recit-
als, and occasional lectures. The second level, easily reached
by the staircase, held a grandiose dining room, seating sixteen comfortably, with a separate library-study, and at the
rear, an immense kitchen. The third floor was basically designed for sleeping quarters. There was a master bedroom
and bath, and three additional guest rooms, each good-sized
and with all the amenities. The fourth level was off-limits.
The staircase stopped at the third; the railing curved into
the hallway with no evidence of another floor, only an ex-
quisitely papered wall.

Should an occupant or a guest possess the elevator code,
however, he would be astonished by what he observed when
he emerged on the fourth floor. It was nothing short of a
military war room. The entire front wall was a detailed map
of the world, eerily illuminated from behind, tiny flashing
lights of various colors pulsating in erratic rhythms. Facing
this global display were six white computer stations, three
on each side of an aisle that led to a huge elevated desk, the
station-throne, as it were, for the monarch of the equipment.

Beyond this display of high technology, so anachronistic
in contrast to the floors below, perhaps the oddest observ-
able fact was the absence of windows. On the outside, they
were there. On the inside, they did not exist. Like the staircase that abruptly ended on the third floor, the windows on
the fourth had been sealed off, the only light emanating

from the overwhelming map of the world and the halogen lamps at each computer station. Lastly, as if to finally compound the macabre atmosphere, the six males operating the computers were far from the image of bright young people with eager faces usually associated with such equipment. Instead, they were, to a man, middle-aged, neither slender nor corpulent, with stern features that bespoke successful business executives, prosperous but not given to frivolity.

It was late afternoon in Amsterdam, confirmed by one of the blue clocks on the map atop the Greenwich-mean-time zone containing the Netherlands. All six white computers on the floor level were quietly humming, the operators' fingers nimbly prancing over their keyboards, their eyes alternately on the global screen, on the small flashing lights, geographically ascertaining the information being sent and received.

From a thick side door, the figure of Jan van der Meer Matareisen emerged; he walked rapidly, purposefully to the elevated desk and sat down, instantly turning to his computer. He pressed a series of keys and studied the screen. Abruptly, he called out, his voice metallic, anxious. "Number Five, what's the latest from the Caribbean?" he asked in Dutch. "There's nothing, absolutely *nothing* that I can bring up!"

"I was about to transfer it, *meneer*," replied the nervous, balding man at Station Five. "There's been considerable confusion and the decoding was laborious, as the message was sent hastily and incomplete."

"What was it? *Quickly!*"

"Our pilot is convinced he was picked up by AWACS radar out of Guantánamo. He took evasive action, shutting down all communications, and headed south."

"Destination?"

"Unknown, sir. He implied—for he was not very clear— that he would make 'unorthodox' contact when he was secure."

"Unorthodox," interrupted Station Six, nearest on the right below Matareisen, "which means he'll probably reach one of our branches and have it make contact with us."

"What are his choices?"

"The nearest is Barranquilla in Colombia," answered Station Two, punching his keys. "Or Nicaragua, or possibly the Bahamas, although that's dangerous. Nassau is cooperating too freely with Washington."

"A moment, *meneer*!" cried Five. "A transmission. From Caracas!"

"Good flying, good thinking," said the leader of the Matarese. "We're entrenched in Venezuela." *Entrenched indeed,* thought Matareisen, *they're on the boards of the major oil companies.* "The message, please."

"I'm decoding it, sir."

"Quickly!"

"Here it is. 'Argonaut with Neptune, no inheritors. Report to follow.'"

"Excellent, *excellent*!" exclaimed Matareisen, getting up from his chair. "Make a note that we must reward our pilot. He sank the trawler with no survivors. . . . And I must make my own report." With this last statement, van der Meer walked back to the heavy side door on the right wall. He pressed his palm against the recessed security pad; there was a click; he reached for the knob and opened the forbidding door, then closed it rapidly.

As one, the six operators appeared to heave sighs of relief. "Do you think we'll ever find out what's in there?" whispered Station Three, smiling.

"We're extremely well paid to accept his explanation," replied One, also whispering. "He says it's his private quarters with equipment superior even to ours, and we have the finest."

"Yet he answers to no one, he's also made that clear," said Two. "Whom could he possibly report to?"

"Who knows?" continued Three. "But if that's a communications annex, it must hold twenty or thirty machines. It may be somewhat narrower than this place, but it has to be every bit as long."

"Dwell not, my friends," said the submissive Station One. "We're richer than we ever were; we believe, and we must accept our regulations. I, for one, would never care to return to my corporate position, for the salary, as extravagant as it was, was no match for *Heer* van der Meer's generosity."

"Nor I," said Four. "I have partnerships in several diamond exchanges, the costs excessive because I am a gentile. Entirely beyond my reach before I joined this firm."

"Then I repeat," said One. "Don't speculate. Let us accept what we have and enjoy it. None of us is terribly young, and in a few years we'll all retire as millionaires several times over."

"I couldn't agree with you more," chimed in Station Five. "A moment! Another transmission. This on my Istanbul routing." All eyes turned, focused on the computer screen.

"Read it," said Four. "We may have to interrupt van der Meer."

"It's from Eagle—"

"That's Washington," Six broke in, "our contact at Langley."

"Read it!"

"Give me several minutes to decode; it's not that long." Ninety-seven seconds passed, the executives' eyes all on Station Five. Finally, he spoke. "I've transposed the cipher eliminating the false names. Thus, it reads as follows. 'Beowulf Agate survives. He and the Hawk—read that as Cameron Pryce—in contact with D-Director Shields. Beowulf and the woman flying to U.S. under Agency protection. The wolf will assume operational command.'"

"Break in on van der Meer," ordered Four.

"We're not supposed to when he's in there—"

"*Do* it!"

"Why don't you?"

"I shall. . . . I'll give him a few minutes in case he returns."

Jan van der Meer Matareisen closed the thick door to his private sanctuary and walked into the last light of the day, streaming through the unsealed windows. The enormous suite was designed for comfort. Gone was any sign of the sophisticated machinery beyond the concrete wall;

instead, there were the appointments of a luxurious living room: brocaded easy chairs, a curving sofa covered with pale yellow Loro Piana vicuna, and again, priceless tapestries. There was a huge entertainment complex consisting of a large television set along with all the audio devices, and a mirrored glass bar with the most expensive whiskeys and brandies. It was the dwelling place of someone who demanded the finest things.

Van der Meer stood immobile in front of a wide, gold-framed mirror. "It is I again, Mr. Guiderone. I bring you great news." The language he spoke was English.

"News you didn't have fifteen minutes ago?" came the crisply spoken amplified words, also in English, the accent American—cultured American, not traceable to any region, the speech of the educated, the wealthy.

"It just arrived."

"How important?"

"Beowulf Agate."

"The brilliant *pig* of the world," said the voice of the unseen man called Guiderone, laughing softly. "I'll be out shortly, I'm on the telephone. . . . Turn on the satellite feed from Belmont Park in New York. I should like to hear great news from there as well. I have horses running in the first and third races."

Matareisen did as he was told. The immense screen was filled with dashing Thoroughbreds breaking from the starting gate, jockeys hunched high, straining, whipping their mounts. And Julian Guiderone came out of a door. He was a fair-sized, well-trimmed man, a shade under six feet, and wearing a paisley print sport shirt of Italian silk above creased gray flannels and Gucci loafers. His age was at first difficult to estimate—although he was certainly not young. His gray hair was subtly streaked with pale yellow, bespeaking its original blond, but it was his sharp-featured face that confounded attempts to guess his years. It was a handsome face, perhaps too perfectly proportioned, too symmetrical, and the tan flesh appeared to be ever so slightly discolored, as frequently happens when northern tourists too eagerly confront a tropic sun. This oddity would probably not be noticed in casual meetings; the tan skin took precedence. But it was there if a person studied the lined, handsome face, just as the minor limp was there in his left leg.

"Incidentally, old sport," he said, "I'll be here for another three days, leaving as I arrived—at four o'clock in the morning. Deactivate the alarms for my exit."

"Will another be arriving shortly?"

"Only with your approval. You have your own schedules, of course, and things are coming to a head, aren't they?"

"Nothing I'd permit to inconvenience you, Mr. Guiderone."

"Don't think like that, van der Meer. You're in command, it's your show. In two years I'll be seventy; younger blood must take over. I'm merely an adviser."

"Whose advice and guidance are treasured," Matareisen hastened to interrupt. "You were here in other days when I was merely a raw young man. You know things I can never know."

"But then, van der Meer, you can *do* things I can no longer do. I'm told that despite your professional demeanor and your less-than-imposing size, your hands and feet are lethal weapons. Actually, that you can dispatch men much larger and heavier than you in a matter of seconds. . . . In the old days I climbed the Matterhorn and the Eiger, but I doubt I could handle a novice ski slope now."

"Whatever physical and intellectual skills I have cannot match the wisdom of your experience."

"I doubt that, but I accept the compliment—"

"Tell me about this Scofield, this 'Beowulf Agate,'" Matareisen broke in politely but firmly. "I've followed your instructions without question, but, if I may say it, with a degree of risk. Naturally, I'm most curious. You called him 'the brilliant pig of the world.' Why?"

"Because he lived with swine, dealt with swine—his own American swine, who tried to kill him. 'Execute for treason' was their legal modus operandi."

"My curiosity now knows no bounds! The Americans wanted to *kill* him?"

"He found out, and rather than taking revenge on those

who gave the order, he reversed the circumstances and became truly the untouchable."

"I beg your pardon?"

"He's blackmailed all the other pigs for lo those twenty-five years."

"How?"

"He told them he had documented proof that we had totally corrupted the major departments of his government and were about to install our own man as President of the United States. It was all true. Except for Beowulf Agate and the Serpent, we would have engineered the greatest coup in the history of the civilized world."

"The Serpent?"

"A Soviet intelligence officer named Taleniekov. . . . That's all you have to know, van der Meer. The Serpent died a most unseemly death, and now we must fulfill the order for the execution of Beowulf Agate prescribed by his own people."

"We have. That is my news. The Alpha trawler was blown up. Scofield was confirmed to be on it. He's dead, Mr. Guiderone."

"Congratulations, van der Meer!" exclaimed the adviser to the chairman of the Matarese. "You truly deserve your ascendancy! I shall proclaim it to the Council in Bahrain. If Scofield left any documents, we're prepared for them. The rantings of a disgraced dead madman are meaningless, we can handle that. Again, fine work, Matareisen! Now you can get on to the next level. How goes it? Where are you *really*?"

"We're ready to move throughout Europe, the Mediterranean, and the United States. We've been in secret negotiations with corporate boards that we've packed with our own people—basically we're unopposed; we have the numbers."

"Sound strategy," said Guiderone. "You need the votes."

"We have them. We will absorb companies with transfers of stock we already own, also through bankruptcy purchases that we'll create with credit defaults through the banks we control, and, naturally, numerous mergers everywhere. Simultaneously, we will inflate, then drastically

THE MATARESE COUNTDOWN   [95]

deflate, alternating currency markets, while downsizing our new corporations for cost and productive efficiencies."

"Bravo," mumbled the adviser, gazing admiringly at the younger man. *"Chaos,"* he added softly.

"Within a short time, overwhelming," agreed Matareisen. "At first, merely thousands upon thousands of jobs will be lost, then millions—"

"Everywhere," interrupted Guiderone. "Regional recessions will precede actual depressions, cutting across the economic and social spectrum. What next?"

"What else? The banks. We control or have close to majority interest in three hundred plus in Europe and sixteen in the U.K., if you separate England. We've made some headway in the Israeli and the Arab institutions by claiming support for their opposing positions, but we have to settle for influence, not control, certainly not with the Saudis or the Emirates. They're all family-controlled."

"And in America?"

"An extraordinary breakthrough. One of our people, a nationally recognized attorney from Boston—your home city, I believe—is brokering the merger of four of the largest banks in New York and Los Angeles with a European conglomerate. With their individual branches, we'll control over eight thousand lending institutions in the United States and Europe."

" 'Lending' being the operative function, am I correct?"

"Of course."

"And then what?"

"The capstone, Mr. Guiderone. Eight thousand branches routinely issuing lines of credit to over ten thousand major corporations in major cities and states alone is maximum leverage."

"The threat of closing down those lines of credit, am I again correct, Matareisen?"

"No, you are not."

"I'm *not*?"

"There'll be no threats, simply boardroom fiat. *All* lines of credit will be terminated. In Los Angeles, studios will shut down, motion pictures and television productions suspended. In Chicago, meat-packing plants, sporting enterprises, and real-estate developers will be in limbo, no hard money available. New York will be hit the hardest. The entire garment industry, which *exists* on credit, will be demolished, as well as the aggressive new owners of hotels with their interests in the nearby casinos in New Jersey. Their enterprises are funded by lines of credit. Cut off, they are nothing."

"There'll be utter madness! Protest rallies in scores of cities—utter madness!"

"I estimate that within six months, governments will face crises, out-of-control unemployment. Parliaments, congresses, presidia, and loose federations all will face catastrophe. Global markets will collapse, the people everywhere screaming for better conditions, demanding them."

"For *change,* van der Meer, that elusive abstraction. And our people are prepared—*everywhere*?"

"Naturally. It is to their benefit, as well as their governments', without whom they cannot exist and continue to thrive."

"You really *are* a genius, van der Meer! To do it all so quickly, so efficiently."

"It's really not that difficult, *meneer.* The wealthy of the world want more riches while those below want the benefits of that wealth to provide jobs. It's historically consistent. All one has to do is penetrate one or the other, or preferably both, and convince each that—as the Americans say— they're being 'screwed.' The old Soviet Union appealed to the workers, who had no expertise. The economic conservatives appeal to the entrepreneurs, who generally have no sense of a social contract. *We* have both."

"So then we have control," agreed Guiderone. "That was the dream, the vision of the Barone di Matarese. It is the only way. Except for the governments—he never envisioned that, only international finance."

"He was of another time, and times have changed. We *must* control governments. The later Matarese understood that, of course. . . . My God, the *President* of the *United States*? You could have *done* that?"

"He would have been swept into office," stated Guiderone quietly, a trancelike tone in his voice. "He was unstoppable—and he was ours. Christ in heaven, he was *ours*!" The older man turned toward the last sunlight streaming through the windows and continued, his voice cold with loathing. "Until he was cut down by the pig of the world."

"Someday, when it's feasible for you, I should like to hear the story of what happened."

"It can never be told, my young friend, even to you, and there is none higher in my regard. For if that story, as you call it, ever saw the light of day, no government anywhere would be trusted by those it must govern. All I'll say to you, van der Meer, is stay your course. It is the right one."

"I prize your words, Mr. Guiderone."

"You should," said the elegant old man, turning back to Matareisen. "For while you are the grandson of the Barone di Matarese, I am the son of the Shepherd Boy."

It was as though van der Meer Matareisen had been struck by a bolt of lightning, the thunder exploding within his skull. "I'm *stunned*!" he gasped, his eyes wide in shock. "It was said that he was killed—"

"He was 'killed,' but he did not die," whispered Guiderone sotto voce, his own eyes dancing with amusement. "But it's a secret you'll take to your grave."

"Of course, of *course*! Still, the Council—in Bahrain—surely they must know."

"Oh, that! Frankly, I exaggerated. I frequently reside in Bahrain, but in truth, I am the Council, the others are avaricious mannequins. Live with it, van der Meer, I'll simply advise you." There was a low hum on an intercom that was placed in the wall. Guiderone was startled; he glared at Matareisen. "I thought you were never to be disturbed while you were in here!" he said, his voice guttural now.

"It must be an emergency. No one knows you are here—my God, these are my private quarters, completely sound-proof. The walls and floors are eight inches thick. I simply don't know—"

"Answer it, you fool!"

"Yes, naturally." Van der Meer, like a man coming out of

a nightmare, rushed to the walled intercom and lifted the receiver. "*Yes*? I told you I'm never to be—" Obviously cut off by the voice on the line, he listened, turning pale. He hung up and stared at Julian Guiderone. "Word from Eagle in Washington," he began, barely audible.

"Yes, that's Langley. What is it?"

"Scofield survived the bombing. He's on his way to the States with the woman and Cameron Pryce."

"*Kill* him, kill them *all*!" ordered the son of the Shepherd Boy between clenched teeth. "If Scofield survived the trawler, he'll come after us like a crazed bear—which is how it all began. He must be silenced; enlist everyone on our American payrolls! Kill him before he stops me again!"

"*Me?* . . ." Matareisen's astonishment was now compounded by a terrible fear. It was in his eyes as he continued to stare at Julian Guiderone. "It was *you* then, you were our ultimate weapon. You were about to become the President of the United States!"

"It was a foregone conclusion, nothing could stop me—except the pig of the world."

"That's why you travel so secretly, with so many passports. Everywhere."

"I'll be forthright with you, van der Meer. We have different approaches to our responsibility. No one looks for a man declared dead nearly thirty years ago, but that man, that myth, remains alive to encourage his legions everywhere. He rises from the grave to propel them forward, a living, breathing human being, a *god* on earth they can feel, touch, and hear."

"Without fear of exposure," said the Dutchman, interrupting, studying the American Guiderone in a suddenly critical light.

"You, on the other hand," continued the son of the Shepherd Boy, "work in darkness, never seen, never touched, never heard. Where are your soldiers? You don't know them, you only give them orders."

"I work internally, not externally," protested Matareisen.

"What the hell does that mean?"

"I formulate, I do not parade myself. I'm not a motion-picture star, I'm the brains behind the stardom. They all know that."

"Why? Because of the money you distribute?"

"It is enough. Without me they are nothing!"

"I beg you, my brilliant young friend, to reconsider. You feed an animal too much, he becomes hostile, it's the law of nature. Stroke the animal, it needs to be touched, felt, and to listen to a voice."

"You do things your way, Mr. Guiderone, I'll do them my way."

"I pray we don't collide, van der Meer."

7

The sterile house on the banks of the Chesapeake Bay was the former estate of one of the wealthiest families on the Eastern Shore of Maryland. It had been leased to the intelligence community for a dollar a year in exchange for the Internal Revenue Service washing away a mountain of unpaid taxes due to loopholes declared blatantly illegitimate. The government won both the battle and the war. It would have cost far more to purchase, legally rent, or even reconstruct such a desirable residence and location.

Beyond the stables and the fields was inhibiting marshland, more swamp than marsh, indigenous to untamed inland waterways. In front of the antebellum mansion was a huge manicured lawn sloping down to a boathouse and a long dock, the pier stretching out over the bay's gentle waters, gentle when the Atlantic was at peace with itself, dangerous when it was not. Secured to the pilings were two crafts, a rowboat and a motorized skiff, each used to reach a thirty-six-foot yawl moored a hundred feet out in the bay.

Unseen, in the boathouse, was a large low-slung Chris-Craft capable of forty knots an hour.

"The yawl's there so you'll have something to sail, if the spirit moves you," Deputy Director Frank Shields had said when he met the Navy jet that had flown Pryce, Scofield, and Antonia to the airfield in Glen Burnie.

"It's a little beauty!" Bray had exclaimed, as later they walked across the lawn. "But is our taking a sail such a good idea?"

"Of course not, but every other estate like this has one or two boats, so it might appear irregular if you didn't."

"It'd also appear pretty irregular if it never left its mooring," said Cameron Pryce.

"We understand that," agreed his superior. "Therefore, it can be used for short outings under certain conditions."

"What are they, Mr. Shields?" asked Antonia.

"The patrols are to be alerted an hour before and advised of your precise sailing route; they'll precede you on the shore. Also, two guards must be with you, everyone wearing protective gear."

"You think of everything, Squinty."

"We want you to be comfortable, Brandon, not careless," said Shields, his creased eyes abruptly pinched at Scofield's use of the pejorative nickname.

"Considering that strip of the Okefenokee that covers the north forty, and the platoon of Agency gorillas, including that Army commando unit, to say nothing of a security system that belongs in Fort Knox, who the hell could get near us?"

"We trust nobody."

"And speaking of security," continued Scofield, "any progress with your mole or moles, courtesy of the Matarese?"

"None. That's why our trust is limited."

Living quarters, patrol schedules, and communications with Langley were all arranged by Shields himself. Whatever by necessity had to be typed out was numbered by copy and recipient, the mercury-layered paper incompatible with any duplicating equipment known. Copies would emerge as smudged straight lines, and should the electrified lens of a camera be employed, those same lines would turn yellow, evidence that a photograph had been taken.

Further, all those furnished with the schedules were ordered to keep them on their persons at all times and be prepared to produce them instantly. In addition, no one was to leave the compound for *any* reason, which partially explained why, to a man—except for command personnel— each was single or unattached. Lastly, it was understood that all telephone calls would be monitored on tape.

Frank Shields was leaving nothing to chance. At the highest security level at the Agency, no progress whatsoever had been made in unearthing the Matarese mole or moles. From the top hierarchy to the lowest clerks and maintenance workers, personnel were scrutinized. Background checks were duplicated and triplicated, bank accounts, lifestyles, even the most insignificant odd habits studied. There would be no Aldrich Ames buried as part of the furniture.

The frustrating aspect of the whole exercise was that those select few doing the unearthing had no idea why they were doing it. There was no Cold War, no centralized Russian enemy, no terrorist organization specifically targeted, no cogent leads—just the order to search for *everything. For what, for Christ's sake? Give us a clue!*

Aberrations! Strange behavior, especially among the better-educated personnel. Pastimes or hobbies that appeared beyond their incomes; clubs or associations they couldn't afford; cars they owned; jewelry their wives or lovers wore; and how was it paid for? If there were children in expensive private schools, who covered the tuitions? Anything, *everything.*

"Give us a *break,*" exclaimed one researcher. "You're talking about half the clowns in the top floors! Some cheat on their wives, what's new? Others make quiet deals on schools, real estate, and cars, 'cause they flash their Langley ID's—those plastic cards are secret persuaders. A number drink too much, and, frankly, I probably do, too, but not so much as to compromise ourselves. What's the end product, or who is it? Give us a name, an objective, *anything.*"

"I can't do that," Deputy Director Shields had said to the chief of the research unit.

"I'll tell you this, Frank. If it were anyone but you, I'd go to the DCI and tell him you were nuts."

"He'd probably agree with you, but he'd also instruct you to follow my orders."

"You realize that you're tainting at least three or four hundred decent people who may not tie their shoes right, don't you?"

"I can't help it."

"It's dirty, Frank."

"So are they, and they're here—*he's* here or *she's* here. Someone who's computer-sophisticated with direct or indirect knowledge of the most secret materials we have—"

"So we're down to maybe a hundred and fifty people," the researcher broke in dryly, "if you don't take the word 'indirect' too seriously. . . . For God's sake, we started there! There's not a soul within a hundred feet of the Directorate that we haven't x-rayed down to the marrow in their bones."

"Then go a step further, try MRI, because they *are* here."

The three-man research unit was stymied; among themselves they seriously debated the state of the deputy director's mental health. They had seen paranoia before and the memories were strong. There was the classic and documented case of J. Edgar Hoover over at the FBI, and later a DCI named Casey, who was in the process of building his own supraintelligence organization accountable to no one, surely not Langley or the President or Congress. The official records had their share of paranoia, but Frank Shields was not paranoid. The very first night they spent at the estate on Maryland's Eastern Shore proved it.

Cameron Pryce whipped his head back and forth across the pillow. His eyes suddenly snapped open; he was not sure what had startled him awake. Then it vaguely came to him—there had been a scratch, a scrape, and a brief flash of light. What was it, *where* was it?

The French doors that led to a short balcony? His room

was on the second floor of the three-storied mansion, Scofield and Antonia directly above him. And he *had* heard something; the inner screen of his eyes *had* been assaulted by a flash of light, a reflection perhaps of a boat's searchlight in the bay . . . perhaps. And perhaps not, but probably. He stretched his arms over his head, yawning. The large mass of water beyond the windows, the dull glow of moonlight, in the main blocked by cloud cover; it was all too reminiscent of the conditions on Outer Brass 26 barely twenty hours ago.

It was funny in a way, he mused, settling back into the comfort of the pillow. To the normal civilian, the life of a covert-operations officer was a constant display of derring-do, of events in which he displayed skills that permitted him to survive. It was accepted as fact, depicted inaccurately by films, television, and novels. A small part was obviously true: One had to be trained to do the work, especially the distasteful aspects, but such incidents were few and far between, and therefore, when they came, they were moments of extreme stress and anxiety. Of fear.

Someone once said that the object of scuba diving was to stay alive. Cam, an experienced diver, had laughed at the simile until the time that he and his lady of the season had been caught beneath a school of hammerhead sharks off the coast of the Costa Brava.

No, the life of a deep-cover was to avoid such incidents as often as was humanly possible while under orders. And if those orders were produced in the imaginative realm of a source-control who had seen too many films or read too many novels, they were to be disregarded. If the results achieved something vital and the risks were feasible, that was okay. A job was a job, like any other. But, as in any other job, fear of overachievement was a factor, in this case, fear for his life. Cam Pryce was not about to die to advance some analyst's career.

Another scratch! A scrape . . . outside the windows of the French doors. He was not dreaming, it was there. But *how*? Guards patrolled the grounds, including the lawns and the terraces below; nothing, *no one,* could approach them.

Grabbing his flashlight and his automatic, both beside him on the bedcover, Pryce slowly got to his feet and approached the slender twin doors to the short balcony. Silently, he pulled the left glass-paned panel open and peered outside, first looking down.

Jesus Christ! He did not need a flashlight to make out the two prone, immobile bodies on the ground, the dark pools of blood still flowing from their necks, necks all but severed from their bodies. For all intents and purposes, they had been beheaded! Pryce switched on his flashlight with the blinding beam, and swung it above him.

A figure in a black latex wet suit had crawled up the smooth stone wall of the mansion, suction cups on his hands and knees. He had reached Scofield's balcony, and seeing the beam of Pryce's flashlight, he threw away his right-hand cup, reached into his belt, pulled out an automatic machine pistol, and began firing. Cameron lunged back into the protection of the bedroom wall as a fusillade of bullets soared past, many ricocheting off the balcony's iron grillwork, spinning off into the room, embedding themselves into the wallpaper. Pryce waited; there was a brief lull. The killer was inserting a fresh magazine into his weapon. *Now.* Cam lurched out onto the balcony and shot repeatedly into the body of the black-encased figure above. In milliseconds he was a corpse, obscenely glued to the wall by the suction cups on his knees and his left hand.

The body was lowered, the remains of the two guards removed to a remote environment. There was no identification found on the killer.

"We'll press his fingerprints," said a patrol dressed in Army combat fatigues. "We'll find out who the son of a bitch is."

"Don't bother, young man," countered Brandon Scofield. "If you'll check his fingers, you'll find smooth, bare skin. The flesh has been burned off, probably with acid."

"You're kidding!"

"Not for a moment. It's the way they operate. You pay for the best, you get the best, including untraceability."

"There are still the teeth—"

"I suspect there are many alterations, as in foreign-made caps and temporary bridges, that are also untraceable. I'm sure the coroner will agree with me."

"Agree with *you*? Who the hell *are* you?" asked the Army officer.

"Someone you were supposed to protect, Colonel. You didn't do much of a job, did you?"

"I don't *understand,* it doesn't make sense! How did this bastard get through us?"

"Superb training, I suspect. We're fortunate that Field Officer Pryce, who's also superbly trained, is a light sleeper. But then that's part of his training, isn't it?"

"Ease off, Bray," said Cameron, walking through the glare of the floodlights to the circle of guards around the corpse. "We were lucky, and that yo-yo wasn't as well-trained as you think. He made enough noise to wake up a drunken deckhand."

"Thanks, buddy," said a grateful colonel softly.

"Forget it," acknowledged Pryce in like manner. "And your question's on the mark. How *did* he get past all of you, especially through the marshes, which is the only way he could?"

"We've got patrols every twenty feet," said an Agency guard, "with overlapping beams, thirty lumens apiece, plus circular barbed wire all around the embankment. In my opinion, *no* way."

"The only other method of entry is the road," said an Army patrol, a woman in her midthirties, dressed in dark jeans and a black leather jacket. Like the others she wore an Army fatigue cap with a brocaded insignia above the visor; wisps of pale hair were evident, pulled back over her temples. "In addition to the electrified main gate," she continued, "we've erected a gatehouse a hundred fifty feet before the main, complete with two armed guards and a steel barrier."

"What's on either side?" asked Cameron.

"The most impassable section of the marsh," she replied. "The road was initially built on compressed landfill with stratums of concrete and wire to the depth of seven feet. Very much like an airport's runway."

"Stratums?"

"Strata, if you prefer. Blocks of high-density cement layered to conform to the configuration of the road."

"I *know* what 'stratums'—'strata' are, Miss . . . Miss—"

"Lieutenant Colonel Montrose, Mr. Pryce."

"Oh, you know my name?"

"On a need-to-know basis, sir. Our job is to secure the compound and protect—" The woman abruptly stopped.

"I understand," said Cameron quickly, defusing the embarrassment.

"Lieutenant Colonel Montrose is my second in command," the full colonel broke in, somewhat haltingly.

"Of a commando unit?" asked Pryce skeptically.

"Commando tactics are intrinsic to our training, but we're not commandos," said the lieutenant colonel, removing her cap and shaking her ash-blond hair. "We're RDF."

"Who?"

"Rapid Deployment Force," answered Scofield. "Even I know that one, youngster."

"It pleases me you're so erudite, old, *old* man. Where's Antonia?"

"She took one of the Agency boys and went hunting."

"What *for?*" asked Montrose, alarmed.

"Don't know. My girl's a pretty independent lady."

"So am *I,* Mr. Scofield! There can be no individual searches unless accompanied by one of our men!"

"Obviously there can be, Miss—Colonel. My wife studied the grounds very thoroughly. She's had to do that kind of thing before."

"I'm aware and appreciative of your backgrounds, sir, but I'm responsible for all personnel escorts."

"Come on, Colonel," interrupted Cam, "our Agency fellows may not wear uniforms but they're pretty damned handy. I know because I'm one of them."

"Your *machismo* doesn't interest me, Mr. Pryce. Military escorts are a priority assigned to us."

"Feisty thing, isn't she?" mumbled Bray.

"A bitch, if you like, Mr. Scofield. I'll accept that, too."

"You said it, lady."

"That's enough!" exclaimed Cameron. "We're supposed to cooperate, not compete, for Christ's sake."

"I was merely trying to clarify our specific training and, not incidentally, our firepower."

"I wouldn't pursue that, Colonel Montrose," said Pryce, nodding ever so gently at the bleeding corpse on the ground.

"I *still* don't understand!" cried the RDF full colonel. "How did he *do* it?"

"Well, son," said Scofield, "we know he wasn't afraid of heights, which usually means a person isn't afraid of depths."

"What the hell does *that* mean?" asked Pryce.

"I'm not sure, but that's what a lot of psychologists claim. Someone who skydives generally feels at home underwater. Something to do with the inverse effects of gravity. I read that somewhere."

"Thanks a bunch, Bray. So what do you suggest?"

"Check the waterfront, maybe?"

"Checked and rechecked and triple-checked constantly," said Montrose firmly. "It was our first consideration. We not only have patrols lining the area for nearly a thousand yards on both sides of the dock, but laser trip beams inland. No one could penetrate those sectors."

"And an assassin would assume that, wouldn't he?" asked Scofield. "I mean kind of naturally."

"Probably," agreed the lieutenant colonel.

"Were there any signs of penetration within the past several hours?" pressed Brandon.

"Actually, there were, all negative," she replied. "Children of neighboring estates camping out on the lawns, several drunks who were turned back after parties, and a couple of fishermen trespassing on private property, again all intercepted."

"Did you inform the other patrols of the activity?"

"Certainly. We might have needed backups."

"So concentrations might have been interrupted, isn't that so? Unintentionally, or perhaps—intentionally."

"That's too general a postulation and, frankly, quite impossible."

"Quite, Colonel Montrose?" said Brandon Scofield. "Not totally."

"What are you saying?"

"I'm not saying, lady, I'm just trying to figure things."

Suddenly, from beyond the blinding wash of the floodlights, came Antonia's voice. "We found them, my darling, we *found* them!" The figures of Scofield's wife and her CIA companion rushed through the diffuse, mist-filled light and ran to the circle of guards. They threw down the objects in their hands: a heavy scuba tank; an underwater, suction-pressed mask; a submersible flashlight, its beam blue; a waterproof walkie-talkie; and a pair of fins. "They were in the mud on the bank of the marsh below the main gate," said Antonia. "It was the only way he could have gotten inside."

"How do you *know* that?" demanded Montrose. "How *did* you know?"

"The waterfront was covered, impenetrable. The marshes were patrolled but still open, subject only to diversion."

"What?"

"Exactly like the time Taleniekov told us about, when he was getting out of Sevastopol, right, luv?" Scofield interrupted pleasantly.

"Your memory's very accurate, my dear."

"Why 'my dear'? What did I do wrong?"

"You didn't think of it. What did Vasili do to pass through the Dardanelles?"

"Diversion, of course. A boat with a false hull designed for detection. The Soviet patrols found it, then went nuts because it was empty!"

"Exactly, Bray. Now, transfer that to land."

"Of course! Divert the obvious to the remote, then activate the obvious within a matter of seconds!"

"That's the radio, my darling."

"Bravo, luv!"

"What are you *talking* about?" demanded Lieutenant Colonel Montrose.

"I'd suggest you find out who the drunks were who

wandered onto this property," said Cameron Pryce, "and probably the two fishermen as well."

"Why?"

"Because one or both or all had handheld radios frequencied into the one down there on the ground. Beside our intruding corpse."

Her name was Leslie Montrose, lieutenant colonel, U.S. Army, daughter of a general, graduate of West Point, and underneath that harsh military exterior, a personable woman. Or so thought Cameron, as he, Montrose, and her superior officer, one Colonel Everett Bracket, sat around the kitchen table drinking coffee and analyzing the events of the night. The lieutenant colonel's background had been supplied by Bracket, who obviously, reluctantly, accepted her as his second in command.

"Don't get me wrong, Pryce, it's not that she's a female," Bracket had said while Montrose was outside giving orders to the Army unit. "I like her—hell, my wife likes her—but I just don't think that women should be part of the RDF."

"What does your wife think?"

"Let's just say she doesn't totally agree. And my seventeen-year-old daughter's worse. But they haven't been in combat when things get rough. I *have*, and it's no place for a woman! Prisoners are taken, it's a realistic aspect of war, and I can't help thinking of my wife and daughter in those circumstances."

"A lot of men agree with you, Colonel."

"Don't *you*?"

"Of course I do, but we've never been attacked on our own ground, our own mainland. The Israelis have and there are a great many women in their military—so have the Arabs, and women are in their active and reserve combat forces, even more prominent in their terrorist cadres. We both might feel differently if the beaches of California or Long Island were invaded."

"I don't think *I* would," said Bracket firmly.

"Maybe the women would change your mind. After all, it was the women, the mothers, who got us all through the Ice

Age. In the animal kingdom, the female is the most vicious in protecting her young."

"Boy, you're weird! How'd you figure that?"

"Rudimentary anthropology, Colonel. . . . Tell me, your lieutenant colonel wears the same kind of cap that you do, but the insignia's different. How come?"

"We allow it, that's why."

"I don't understand. A Yankee baseball player doesn't put on a Boston Red Sox cap."

"It's her husband's squadron. Was her husband's squadron."

"I beg your pardon?"

"Her husband was a fighter pilot in the Air Force. He was shot down in Desert Storm over Basra. They say he ejected, but he was never heard from after the cessation of hostilities—which there *never* should have been!"

"That was years ago," said Pryce reflectively. "And she stayed in the Army?"

"She certainly did, and aggressively so, I might add. My wife and I tried to talk her out of it—find a new life, we told her. With her training there are dozens of companies that would take her in a minute. She's management-trained, computer-smart, all those things the television commercials say about the Army, plus the fact that she was a fast-rising officer—a major at the time. She wouldn't have it."

"That seems strange to me," said Cameron. "She could probably make more in the private sector."

"Try ten, maybe twenty times more. In addition, she'd be in a workplace where there were a lot of civilian guys, and with her class probably rich. She could mix with them, you know what I mean?"

"It's not hard to follow. She rejected the suggestion?"

"Like a shot. Probably because of the kid."

"The kid?"

"She and Jim had a son, exactly eight months and twenty days after they both graduated from West Point, a fact she always referred to, laughing like hell. He's fourteen or fifteen now, and worshiped his father. Our guess is that if she left the Army, she thinks her son would resent her."

"Since she's here—incommunicado—where's the boy?"

"In one of those prep schools in New England—Jim wasn't poor and neither is the general's daughter. And the kid understands the phrase 'Your mother's away on assignment.'"

"A normal military brat."

"I guess so. My kids wouldn't take that, but I suppose he does."

"You're not a dead hero," said Pryce, "so they don't have to worship you."

"Thanks for nothing, spook. You're probably right though."

"Still, she's never found someone here in the military that she might find even passably acceptable? After all, she's a relatively young woman."

"You think my wife and I haven't tried? If you could see all the guys we've paraded. . . . She always says good night, *in* our house, with a firm, polite handshake—no chance for any action with anybody. . . . And if you're sniffing around, Mr. Secret Agent, forget it. She's strictly male-free."

"I wasn't sniffing around, Colonel. I simply have to know the personnel I'm involved with. It's my job to do just that."

"You've got the dossiers of every person on this detail, twenty-seven to be exact."

"Forgive me, but I've just spent five days in the Caribbean without much sleep, and the last two without any. I haven't gotten to your dossiers."

"You'll find them quite acceptable."

"I'm sure I will."

The kitchen door had opened, breaking off the conversation between Pryce and Colonel Bracket as Lieutenant Colonel Montrose walked in. "Everything is secure and I've shifted additional patrols to the waterfront," she stated.

"Why?" asked Cameron.

"Because it was his logical way out, for the killer, I mean."

"Why do you assume that?" continued Cameron pleasantly but firmly.

"Because it's his most logical means of egress from the property."

"'Egress'? I gather you mean escape."

"Certainly. The marshes would be on total watch."

"I disagree. You said before that the beach was lined with trip lights for a thousand yards, laterally and inland, electronically fencing off the property. Do you honestly believe that an assassin wouldn't know that?"

"What's your point, Mr. Pryce?" asked an angry Leslie Montrose. "What other escape could he have?"

"The same way he got in, Colonel. Except that Scofield's wife found the scuba gear. I'd suggest you send a patrol west to the nearest road heading north and south. Keep the vehicle as quiet as possible, and see who's waiting there. Naturally, there'll be no headlights, so we shouldn't have them either."

"That strikes me as ludicrous! The killer can't come out. He's dead."

"He certainly is, Colonel Montrose," agreed Cameron. "But unless we have a traitor here with a radio we don't know about—"

"*Impossible!*" cried Bracket.

"I trust we don't," continued Pryce. "And if we don't, whoever's waiting for our assassin doesn't know he's dead. . . . Get on it, Colonel Montrose, that's an *order.*"

Nearly an hour passed. Bracket, his head on his folded arms, slept at the table. Barely awake, Cameron frequently went to the kitchen sink and doused his face with water until his neck and shirt were drenched. The door opened slowly and Lieutenant Colonel Leslie Montrose walked inside, as exhausted as the man she faced.

"The car was there," she said quietly, "and I wish to God it hadn't been."

"Why?" asked a heavy-lidded Pryce, getting to his feet.

"They killed one of my men—"

"Oh, Christ, no!" Cam's voice jolted Bracket awake.

"Yes. They would have killed me, but my corporal shoved me off the road, exposing himself, and in doing so took the bullets. He was just a boy, the youngest soldier in the detail. He gave his life for me."

"I'm sorry, *so* sorry!"

"Who *are* these people, Mr. *Pryce*?" Leslie Montrose demanded, a frantic edge in her voice.

"Someone called them the evil of the world," replied Cam softly, going to her and briefly, tentatively holding her shoulders as she wept.

"They must be *stopped*!" cried Montrose sharply, her head abruptly straight, erect, her eyes focused, furious as the tears fell down her cheeks.

"I know," said Pryce, releasing her and stepping away as a stunned Colonel Bracket slowly sank back in his chair.

The International Herald Tribune
(FRONT PAGE)

STUNNING MOVE BY AIRCRAFT GIANTS

PARIS, SEPT. 30—The combined announcement from London and Paris that British Aeronauticals and the French Compagnie du Ciel have merged into a single corporate entity has sent shock waves through the aircraft industries in Europe and the United States. The merging of these two giants along with their seemingly unlimited resources, their secure private and government contracts, their manufacturing subsidiaries, as well as their access to economically favorable labor markets, makes this new company the largest and most powerful aircraft manufacturer in the world. Financial analysts on both sides of the Atlantic have concluded that Sky Waverly, the new name, will be the granite pillar of the aircraft industry. In the words of Clive Lawes, business columnist for the London *Times*, "They'll be the drummers all the others will have to march to."

The use of the name Waverly is in honor of Sir

David Waverly, who founded the original company, Waverly Industries, absorbed by Anglo-American interests over a quarter of a century ago.

Unconfirmed details of the merger, including stock transfers and projected moves the combined board of directors might take, appear on page 8. Amalgamations of the vast labor pools and the elimination of duplicating management personnel are examined. One might paraphrase an often-repeated quote from an American film in the fifties: Fasten your seat belts, it'll be a bumpy road ahead.

8

It was midmorning on the Eastern Shore of Maryland, the blazing autumn sun halfway to its noon apex, its rays shimmering across the waters of Chesapeake Bay. Pryce joined Scofield and Antonia on the huge screened-in porch overlooking the shoreline; a breakfast buffet had been set up for those staying at the mansion, the remaining personnel billeted in the three more-than-ample guesthouses.

"Sit down, Cameron," said Scofield's wife. "May I pour you some coffee?"

"No thanks," Pryce replied pleasantly, veering toward the buffet with the coffee urns. "I'll get it."

"Poor move," grumbled Bray. "Don't lead her into bad habits."

"You're not real, you know that?" said Cameron, sleep, or the lack thereof, in his speech. "It's too early for you to be real."

"It's not early at all," protested Scofield, "it's damn near ten o'clock. Where the hell are the others?"

"I don't know. I don't even know who they are."

"The two colonels, major and minor, the CIA fella who went with Toni last night—this morning, and Frank Shields's liaison, who looks at me like I'm diseased."

"Frank no doubt told him all about you." Pryce filled his coffee cup, walked to the table, and sat down. Antonia spoke.

"Colonel Bracket and Lieutenant Colonel Montrose are in rooms in the west wing along with Eugene Denny, Director Shields's man. And my 'fella,' as you call him, darling, is down the hall from us. . . . He and I don't have to travel very far to get together while you're snoring away."

"Hah!" cried Bray, grinning. "Cradles are for snatching whatever's in them, Cam, the younger the better!"

"For that you can get your own eggs, my dear."

"Don't want eggs. You keep saying they're bad for me."

"Who fixed all this stuff?" interrupted Pryce.

"Why, you figure it's poisoned?"

"Not specifically, but geometrically along those lines of possibility."

"You speak funny, youngster."

"I'll tell you," said Antonia, once again with the information. "All food is prepared in the kitchens at Langley, hermetically sealed, wired, and tagged, then flown here by helicopter every morning and evening at six o'clock."

"I've heard the noise," Cam broke in, "but I thought it was airborne surveillance or visiting honchos. . . . How did you find out, Toni? I mean, the food, where people sleep—"

"I ask questions."

"You're very good at it."

"Bray taught me. Once in a seemingly passive situation, a refuge or a sanctuary, you should always ask questions— nicely, innocently, as though you're really curious. He claims women are better at that than men, so I do it."

"He's all heart. It also means you're more likely to get shot."

Scofield chortled. "You must have to think before you chew," he said, then abruptly turned serious. "We heard about the RDF corporal who bought it last night. The bastards!"

"Who'd you hear it from?"

"By way of Colonel Bracket. He came up to give Denny the news and there was a fair amount of confusion—accusations, if you like. Toni and I got up and joined the fray."

"What accusations?"

"Just horseshit, that's all."

"No, it's not all."

"Leave it alone, Cam," said Antonia. "Mr. Denny was 'out of line,' as you Americans say."

"What did he say?"

"He wanted to know on whose authority Montrose left the compound with a vehicle," replied Scofield. "Bracket told him that as second in command of the RDF unit, she didn't need any authority."

"Essentially, he was saying that she had *his* authority," added Bray's wife. "The colonel's."

"That's not true," said Pryce. "I gave her the order on my own authority as an experienced field officer who had made a logical field analysis. Regretfully, I happened to be right. . . . What was Denny *doing*? Who the *hell* does he think he is?"

"I am the compound's liaison to Deputy Director Shields, and in his absence have full responsibility for everything that takes place here." The words came from the figure in the doorway, a medium-sized, slender man with a balding head, a pleasant, youthful face that seemed to contradict his loss of hair, and a voice that might be described as a soft monotone. "With that responsibility," he continued, "comes authority."

"You're not just out of line, Denny," said Cameron, standing up and facing the liaison, "you're way the goddamned hell out of line! You listen to me, hot dog. I didn't hear you make any *authoritative* pronouncements last night when a dead killer was dropped down a wall beside the two guards whose necks he sliced from ear to ear. I don't even remember your *being* there!"

"I was there, Mr. Pryce, although briefly—there was nothing I could add to the current circumstances. Instead, I felt it was necessary to reach Director Shields immediately. We were quite some time on the phone, going over all the possible leaks, including the helicopter crews. . . . He'll be here by noon."

"Researching the chopper crews?" asked Brandon.

"Yes, sir."

"So by what authority, on what *expertise*, do you question an RDF decision or my decision?"

"I think that's obvious. A man was killed."

"It happens, Mr. Denny. I hate it, you hate it—we all hate it. But it *happens*."

"Look, Pryce, maybe I flew off the handle when I shouldn't have—"

"You've got *that* right!" Cameron broke in.

"But I'm here to oversee things, to make sure things go smoothly, and that was the first *night*. I look like a fool, an incompetent."

"You couldn't have prevented it, and I think you know that," said Pryce, quieting down and gesturing for Denny to join them at the table.

"Maybe not the two guards and the assassination attempt, but I probably would have cautioned anyone about leaving the compound for the purpose explained. If I'd known about it."

"You would?" Cam's hostility returned. *"Why?"*

"Because there was a better way—assuming someone was actually waiting for the assassin on the old Chesapeake Road."

"If, for Christ's sake! You want to make the call to the kid's family?"

"I was using a prior-hypothetical—"

"He speaks funnier than you do—" interrupted Scofield.

"So does Shields speak funny, but I've been around these clowns long enough to understand," Cam replied. "What would you have done, Sir Analyst—you *are* an analyst, right?"

"I am, and I would have reached our armed personnel in

a camouflaged vehicle in a field north of the entrance drive. They could have made an external assault."

"*What* personnel?" Pryce, still standing, was shouting now. "What *vehicle*?"

"They're there. In eight-hour shifts."

"Why the ff   the *hell* didn't we know about them?"

"I'm familiar with the F-word, Cameron," said Antonia, quiet anger in her words, "and despite your courtesy, I believe it's truly appropriate here. . . . Mr. Denny, why weren't we told about them?"

"For God's sake, I hadn't gotten around to it! The first night, what could happen on the first *night*? . . ."

"That's when you look for it," replied Scofield, his voice suddenly assuming a tone of command. "It's not your fault, though, it's Shields's—and it's not the first time he's done it. The initial instructions to the field should inform us of all the options we have—that's *primary*. No surprises, no alternatives we don't know about, no horseshit omissions, you got that, boy?"

"There can be variations on that scenario, sir."

"Give me one, you son of a bitch!"

"*Please,* Bray," interrupted his wife, her hand on her husband's arm.

"No, I want to hear his answer! Go ahead, analyst!"

"I think you know, Mr. Scofield," said Denny, in his soft, flat voice. "You go back a long time with Deputy Shields."

"The *L-Factor,* am I right?"

"Yes," replied the liaison, barely audible.

"What in God's name is *that*?" asked Pryce, bewildered.

"You just appropriately used the name of the Lord," said Bray. "The L-Factor is Scripture, according to Saint Shields the Immaculate, scholar of the Bible. The *L* is for Leviticus, as in the Pentateuch, the third book of the Old Testament. That much I remember."

"What *are* you talking about, my husband?"

"Shields always believed that the answers to most human problems or enigmas were found in the Bible. Not necessarily the religious aspects, but in the interpretations of the stories, both myth and history."

"Frank's a *religious* fanatic?" Cameron was stunned.

"I don't know, you'd have to ask him. He surely knows his Bible, though."

"This L-Factor, this Leviticus, what is it?" insisted Pryce.

"In short, don't trust the high priest. He may be a rat."

"Come again?" Cameron sat down slowly, staring at Scofield as if the retired intelligence man were a lunatic.

"I'm not sure I ever got it completely straight, but in Leviticus the high priesthood was confined to the sons of Levi or Aaron, I think. They were the rulers of the temple and gave orders to everybody else. Then a few ambitious brothers who weren't part of this exclusive fraternity mocked up some fake genealogical papers and wormed their way into the club. As a result, they had a real political voice over the vox populi."

"Are you *crazy*?" Pryce, his eyes wide, was beside himself with frustration. "That's biblical claptrap!"

"Not necessarily," interrupted Eugene Denny. "Mr. Scofield essentially has the basic facts, if out of context."

"Forget the redundancy," said Pryce. "What's he talking about?"

"In Leviticus, a few male Levites, the sons of Levi, later as they grew in numbers, the heirs of Aaron, were made the high priests of the Temple of Jerusalem, the seat of power. As in all such power centers, there was corruption—minimal by later standards, I might add—but nevertheless corruption by those who wanted to change the rigid system—frequently justified, I might also add. Ultimately, according to legend alluded to in Numbers or Deuteronomy, a zealot became the leader of the Jerusalem temple until he was exposed as a traitor and no son of Aaron."

"Thanks for the lesson, preacher," said Cameron, his words strained, "but what the hell does it all *mean*?"

"It means," answered Scofield, his fury just below the surface, "that Deputy Director Shields isn't sure he can trust *me*."

"*What*?" Pryce turned angrily to Shields's liaison.

"You see, youngster," continued Bray, "in Squinty's

biblical imagination this compound here is the Chesapeake Temple, and contrary to what you two assholes think, neither of you has the authority of a neutered fly over this operation. Only *I* have. That's my deal with Shields—check it out, Mr. Denny."

"I've been apprised of your agreement, Mr. Scofield, and it's hardly my place to interfere."

"Naturally not. You're Frankie-boy's lackey and I'll bet my left ball you're in contact with your 'camouflaged armed personnel' just in case I decide to take a powder and blow this joint with my wife!"

"What are you *saying,* Bray?" pressed Antonia.

"And I'll bet my right ball," continued Scofield without stopping, "that the gate has instructions to reach you instantly if I go through it, which I'm entitled to do because I *am* the absolute authority here."

"You're not making sense, my dear—"

"The hell I'm not! The L-Factor, the Leviticus horseshit. I'm the high priest of the temple who may just be a rat. Isn't that so, analyst?"

"There were other considerations," replied Denny quietly.

"If there were, why weren't we—why wasn't *I*—told about your unit out there? It's priority that I be informed at the outset just in case decisions have to be made that I wouldn't allow you to make! . . . Oh, no, this is one of Squinty's reverse tricks, goddamn it!"

"There was the possibility of a sudden, massive assault on the compound—"

"And two or three 'armed personnel' were going to *stop* it?" broke in a furious Beowulf Agate. "Jesus on a surfboard, what do you take me for?"

"I can't answer that, sir. I merely follow orders."

"You know, son, that's the second time I've heard that within the past thirty hours, and I'll tell you what I told that son of a bitch who became some shark's antipasto. *I don't buy it!*"

"Hey, slow down, Bray," said Pryce. "Maybe Frank was right—about the second part. An assault, I mean."

"It doesn't wash, kid. If he really felt that way there'd be a small brigade out there and I'd be the first to know about it. No, Squinty was waiting for me to make my unpredictable move. *Christ,* he's a fucking genius!"

"You were about to make *what* unpredictable move?" cried Cameron.

"I really don't understand, my darling—"

"In this high-tech age there's no way to communicate with anyone in here by wire or radio, much less telephone, because everyone goes through a detector. The only way is personal contact, secret contact. After that mess with the bastard who killed the guards and tried to waste me—thank you for cutting him in half, Cam—I came to the same conclusion you did. I was waiting for Toni to fall asleep and then I was going out myself, *my* way, which wasn't through the gate or in a goddamned vehicle. I would have been far more successful."

"He's done it before, gentlemen," said Antonia, now squeezing her husband's arm. "In Europe, when we were running for our lives, I'd wake up in the morning and find Brandon and Taleniekov having coffee. The problem that terrified us—the man or the men who had us in their gunsights—were no longer a threat. That's all they'd say about it, nothing more."

"You equate that sort of thing with what happened last night?" Pryce asked Scofield.

"In a way, of course," agreed the retired intelligence officer. "Only Frank got my objectives backward. I wasn't going out to make a secret accommodation with the Matarese, who, as I told Squinty, offered me millions to disappear, I was going to kill the bastards. Or, if I'd had the patience, to take the fuckers alive."

"Then why did you just call him a genius?" asked an angry, perplexed Cameron.

"Because, given like circumstances, I'd do one *or* the other. Frank always covers his bases."

"But to consider you a turncoat, a traitor," exclaimed Pryce, "that's enough to make you want to put him in a box!"

"No, no, never," said Scofield. "When he gets here at noon, I'll surely tell him off, but nothing more."

"Why not?"

"Let me take you back about thirty years. I was undercover in Prague and my control was a man I considered really brilliant, the best, most elusive deep-contact to Moscow ever on our side. I was scheduled to meet him on the banks of the Moldau River one night, when minutes before I left my flat, an urgent message came from Washington, from Langley—from Frank Shields. I decoded it, and it said, 'Send a decoy, not ours but some drug pusher. Stay above on the perimeter.' . . . That cocaine salesman was riddled with bullets meant for me. Frank Shields had led my control into a reverse trap that exposed him. My brilliant contact was a butcher from the KGB."

"So now he's pulling the same trap on you," said Pryce. "Can you accept that?"

"Why not? All his bases are covered, and he could have been right. All I got from my years of service to *my* government was a bonus to buy a boat and a pension. The Matarese offer might have tempted me."

"But he *knows* you!"

"Nobody knows anybody but himself or herself, Cam. We can get under the skin maybe, but we can't penetrate the mind, or the multiple alternatives it might choose to take. How do you know who I really am, or who Toni is?"

"For God's sake, we've talked for hours, about so many things. I *trust* you!"

"You're young, my new friend. But beware, trust is built on optimism, it's a series of shadows. You can't give them three dimensions, no matter how hard you try."

"You've got to start somewhere," said Pryce, his eyes locked with Scofield's. "This Leviticus nonsense, this high priest who may be a rat—what the hell does it all add up to?"

"Welcome to our world, Cameron. You may think that you've been there, but you've just begun your descent into our hell. It's not a hell our pristine Mr. Denny knows, because he, like Squinty, sits behind a desk with all those computers and makes abstract decisions. Sometimes they're right, often they're wrong, but what their computers can't animate are human confrontations. In the end, machines can't talk to machines."

"I believe we've covered this before," said Pryce. "I'm talking about last night, a night I'll never forget. Where *are* we?"

"Well, I guess that the first lesson is that it's not linear—nothing's in a straight line. The second is that it's got to be geometric—the lines flare out in all directions and you have to narrow down the possibilities."

"I'm talking about last night—this *morning*!"

"Oh, that. I can't tell you. Squinty will be here in an hour or so and we'll ask him."

"I can tell you," said the liaison, Denny. "Director Shields is secretly transferring the entire compound to an estate in North Carolina."

"That is the *one* thing he will *not* do!" exclaimed Scofield.

"But, sir, we've been discovered here—"

"You're goddamned right, and I wish we could publicize it in all the newspapers—no, that's probably wrong, let it remain classified. All those who shouldn't know will find out."

"Really, sir, the deputy insists that we start packing—"

"Then send the *deputy* to me and I'll countermand his orders! What you idiots don't know is that the bees fly to the honeypot. It's an old Corsican expression."

The Wall Street Journal
(FRONT PAGE)

THREE WORLD-CLASS BANKS
FORM ALLIANCE

NEW YORK, OCT. 1—As further proof of the new transnationalization of financial institutions, three of the world's largest banks have, for all intents and purposes, merged. They are the equally well-known Universal Merchants in New York, Los Angeles's Bank of the Pacific, and Madrid's Banco Ibérico, the wealthiest institution in Spain and Portugal with vast interests in the Mediterranean.

Using a complex agenda of international laws, they have structured a lateral order of responsibilities to maximize the productivity in their respective centers of influence. The newest technologies that permit instant global communications, prominent among them financial transactions, will create a whole new system of banking, "factually a near renaissance," according to Benjamin Wahlburg, well-known banker, an elder statesman of the financial world, and spokesman for the new conglomerate to be known as Universal Pacific Iberia. "We are approaching the era of a cashless society, saving billions upon billions the world over," continued Mr. Wahlburg, "when corporate and individual assets will be confirmed by plastic cards, their numbers altered over millions of airwaves, purchases and debits paid electronically. We of Universal Pacific Iberia intend to be at the forefront of this exhilarating economic renaissance and we are investing considerable resources into seeing it develop."

It has been estimated that with the thousands of branches owned by UPI, the new financial conglomerate will be a major lending institution throughout the United States, the Pacific Rim, Southern Europe, and the Mediterranean, from Gibraltar to Istanbul.

What concerns some observers of the international marketplace is the question of controls. When reached by telephone, Mr. Wahlburg stated, "Controls will be intrinsic to the evolution. No responsible economist or banker could think otherwise."

The descending helicopter yackety-yacked its way into the Chesapeake compound's circled touchdown. Deputy Director Frank Shields, his creased, narrow eyes practically shut tight repelling the sunlight, emerged from the glistening white metal door only to be verbally assaulted by Brandon Scofield, Cameron Pryce at his side. Fortunately, much of the former intelligence officer's shouting was obscured by the whirling rotor blades, and by the time the two men walked away from the overpowering sound to join Pryce, Scofield was partially out of breath.

"Since you figured out what I was doing, why did it surprise you, much less make you angry?" asked the abused deputy director.

"That's the dumbest damn question you've ever asked, Squinty!" roared Scofield.

"Why?"

"Stop repeating yourself!"

"Hey, you're the one who practices that habit, Brandon, not me. And look at it this way. As you obviously understood that I might employ the L-Factor and you passed—you're clean and *I* don't have to wonder if I missed something."

"It was the Matarese's offer to me, wasn't it? The millions and the ranch somewhere—"

"That was a throwaway line," interrupted Shields, "but it stuck for a while. *You* yourself made a President of the United States pay you off twenty-five years ago. The answer's yes."

"How do you know I didn't accept?"

"Because you never would have brought it up with Denny, especially with such specificity."

"You're *impossible*!"

"Maybe, but remember Prague. By the way, where *is* Denny?"

"I ordered him to stay away until I was finished with you, since, as we agreed, I'm running this operation. I *do* have that authority, don't I?"

"Are you finished with me, Brandon?" asked the deputy director without answering the question.

"Hell, no! Your idea of shutting down this place and moving to North Carolina is out! We're staying right here."

"You're certifiable. The Matarese know where we are—where you are. They know you survived the trawler, and by flying up here to join us you threw down the gauntlet. They won't stop until they kill you."

"Tell me, Squinty, why do they want to kill me?"

"For the same reason we wanted to find you—for what may or may not be in that concrete head of yours. Years ago your initial debriefing was hardly illuminating, but in your own words, you know more about the Matarese than anyone else on our side does."

"What's to prevent me from giving you everything I know on paper?"

"Not a thing, but there are laws and we're dealing with powerful interests, presumably very rich, very influential people in and out of government."

"So what?"

"So typewritten statements—depositions—from a dead, discredited deep-cover agent with a record of flagrant abuse of conduct, including misinformation, disinformation, and consistent lying to his superiors, isn't the sort of file you present to the courts, much less a congressional hearing."

"Tear up the file, burn it! That was ancient history and has nothing to do with the present circumstances."

"You've been away too long, *Beowulf Agate*. This is the nineties. Files aren't neatly inserted into manila folders, they're computerized, and any senior department head with the proper codes throughout the entire intelligence community can access them. And you may be certain a few already have."

"You're saying that my cold corpse can't be interrogated, and all that's left is a record of necessary actions I took that label me a lying loose cannon."

"That's precisely what I'm saying. You'd be posthumous rotten meat for the Matarese grinders." Shields paused, then gestured for Scofield and Pryce to move with him away from the now-silent aircraft and its bustling crew. "Listen to me, Brandon," he continued out of the crew's earshot, "I know Cameron's put you through an interrogation wringer, and I will too. But before we go any farther, I've got to come clean with you. There can't be any secrets between us."

"Squinty has a confession to make to little old *me*?" said Bray mockingly. "I didn't think we prehistoric dinosaurs had any secrets left worth talking about."

"I'm serious, Brandon. It'll explain how far I got—I think I got—and it may even bring you a degree of relief, if you had any qualms talking about it."

"I can't wait."

"When you left years ago, there were so many questions left unanswered, things you simply refused to clarify—"

"I had a goddamned good reason," broke in Scofield quietly, harshly. "Those debriefing clowns were looking six ways to hell and back to pin the whole mess on Taleniekov. They kept repeating the words 'enemy' and 'Commie bastard' to the point where I could have wasted them. They wanted to paint Vasili as the whole evil empire, all by himself, when nothing could have been farther from the truth."

"Only the hotheads, Brandon, only the hotheads. The rest of us didn't say those things or believe them."

"Then you cooler fellows should have put out the fires! When I told them that Taleniekov had to get out of Moscow because he was under a death sentence, they kept saying 'a setup' and 'a double agent' and other stupid clichés they knew nothing about!"

"But you knew that if you told the whole truth, Taleniekov would go down in history as the madman who brought the superpowers to the edge of nuclear war, possibly over it."

"I'm not sure what you mean, Squinty," said Scofield cautiously.

"Of course you do. You couldn't state for any official record that the United States of America was about to elect a President who was heir to the most vicious organization the world has ever known outside of the Nazis. Only it wasn't a Communist Hitler, it was an elusive man only whispered about in the geopolitical cellars. The son of the Shepherd Boy."

"What the *hell*—" choked Brandon, turning to an astonished Pryce, who shook his head. "How did you *know*?" he said, addressing Shields. "I never mentioned the son of the Shepherd Boy. He was dead, the whole damn bunch was dead! And yes, one of the reasons I kept quiet *was* Taleniekov, but there was another, whether you'll believe it or not. Our country, our whole system of government, would have become the laughingstock of the civilized world. How did you find *out*?"

"The Leviticus Factor, my old friend. Remember what I once told you about the L-Factor?"

"Yes, I do. You said 'Look at the high priest, and wonder whether under his robes he's a rat.' Still, how did you figure it out?"

"We'll continue this discussion out on the water. Somebody here is another form of rat, and I'll take no chances on electronic surveillance. . . . That unit you saw at the helicopter is a team of antiterrorist experts trained and with the instruments to unearth all manner of bugs no matter how well concealed."

"I'll say this, Squinty. After all these years, you've picked up a field trick or two."

"Your approval touches me deeply."

The Albany Times-Union
(BUSINESS SECTION, PAGE 2)

CONSOLIDATION OF UTILITIES IMMINENT

ALBANY, OCT. 2—Due to the ever-increasing demand for energy and the concomitant accelerating costs involved, utility companies from Toronto to Miami are engaged in serious discussions about consolidating their operations. Word of these initial conferences began circulating when Standard Light and Power of Boston experienced what could be termed a consumer revolt over the exploding costs of electricity passed on to municipalities, corporations, and individual families. Pockets of industry, as well as numerous research centers, have threatened to leave the state in an already depressed real-estate market. Conventional wisdom predicts that universities might follow, the aggregate leaving Massachusetts an impoverished state and Boston a deserted ghetto.

When questioned, Jamieson Fowler, CEO of Standard L and P, was succinct. "Energy costs money and it's getting worse, not better. Is there a solution? Sure, it's down the road and it's nuclear. But nobody wants those plants within a hundred miles of their districts, so where are we? I don't believe there are any states with deserts that large. Now, if we could unify the vast network of grids into a single authority, a consortium, costs would plummet as a result of eliminating duplication alone."

Bruce Ebersole, president of Southern Utilities, echoed Mr. Fowler's confidence. "Our stockholders would be happy, and they're mostly elderly folk—our beloved grandmas and granddaddies—the public would be better served 'cause we'd upgrade equipment everywhere, and we could all look forward to a brighter day—from those huge combine machines down to the electric bulb, my friend."

On the issue of the tens of thousands of jobs that would be lost, Ebersole stated, "We'd retrain the trainable, I reckon."

The figure standing in the dark, recessed corner of the boathouse peered around the edge of the open door, the waves below lapping against the sides of the Chris-Craft's slip. The speedboat was cruising slowly toward the center of the bay, the three occupants in casual conversation, Scofield at the helm, turning constantly to the others and speaking.

Lieutenant Colonel Leslie Montrose withdrew a small portable phone from her tunic, dialed a series of thirteen numbers, and raised the instrument to her right ear.

"Circle Vecchio," said the male voice over the line. "Proceed."

"Three major subjects in conference beyond surveillance. Make no moves until situation is clarified."

"Thank you. The information will be forwarded to our people in London. Incidentally, your new equipment will be on the six P.M. flight. It's been cleared for transfer. A package from your son."

9

The Chris-Craft's engine was cut to idle as the speedboat bobbed up and down in the gentle waves of Chesapeake Bay, the motor sputtering at the stern.

"I still don't get it, Frank," said Scofield at the wheel, turning back to Shields. "I never *mentioned* the Shepherd Boy or the son of the Shepherd Boy in those debriefings. They were dead, the whole damn bunch of them were dead!"

"It was in the notes we found after the massacre at the estate called Appleton Hall outside of Boston. The fragments were badly burned, but they were studied under glass in our laboratories and the name, or partial name, of 'Sheph-Boy' kept coming up. Then the Corsican branch of Interpol uncovered the name of Guiderone. It was presumed he was the Shepherd Boy."

"So where did that take you?"

"For me to a logical search. In one of the fragments, barely legible, was the stilted phrase, 'he is the *son*,' repeated twice in two separate memoranda. And in the second, 'we must obey.' . . . Am I reaching you, Brandon?"

"Yes," replied Scofield quietly. "It's what Taleniekov and I followed. But how did you?"

"For months, even years, none of us could figure it out. Then finally I did."

"For Christ's sake *how*?"

"The Leviticus Factor again—the high priest was a rat."

"Come *again*?"

"Among those killed that afternoon was the honored guest at the conference in Appleton Hall. He was a true descendant of the Appleton dynasty, brought back to be applauded by the new owners of the estate."

"You knew who they were then," said Scofield, making a statement.

"I was getting closer. The honored guest was Senator Joshua Appleton the Fourth, the anticipated next President of the United States. No one doubted it; it was a given. He was the most popular figure on the political landscape. He was about to become the most powerful leader of the free world."

"And?"

"In reality, the honored senator wasn't Appleton at all; for years he had been someone else. He was Julian Guiderone, the son of the Shepherd Boy, anointed by Guillaume, the Baron of Matarese."

"I knew it, but how did *you* find out?"

"Your doing, Brandon. Let me take you back, step-by-step, as I believe you took them yourself."

"I'm fascinated," Scofield interrupted. "I wish Toni were here."

"Where is she?" asked Pryce, leaning against the swaying gunwale.

"Asking questions," replied Bray without elaborating. "Go on, Frank, what sort of trail did you follow?"

"First, knowing you, I assumed you'd put together some kind of false identification to get you where you wanted to go—that was basic. As I learned, it was up to your creative standards: Your ID officially proclaimed you to be an 'aide' to Senator Appleton himself. Then, since you were in the dark about so many things, you went to see Appleton's mentally disturbed old mother in Louisburg Square."

"She was an alcoholic, had been for over a decade," added Scofield.

"Yes, I know," said Shields. "She was in the same condition twenty-one months later when I saw her."

"It took you that long?"

"You weren't any help. . . . To begin with, she didn't remember you, but when I was about to leave I got lucky. Out of the blue—I should say the haze—she suddenly said in an eerie singsong, 'At least you didn't insist on seeing Josh's old room.' My first bingo because I knew her other visitor had to be you."

"So you did the same thing."

"I certainly did and it led to bingo two. Especially as she said she hadn't been there since Joshua had allowed my long-ago predecessor inside."

"I thought Appleton was dead," interrupted Pryce.

"Actually, the real Appleton was. The whiskey ghosts had taken over."

"What was bingo two?" pressed Scofield. "That room was nothing more than a fake shrine with useless memorabilia. Photographs, school banners, and sailing trophies. Fake because Appleton never lived in Louisburg Square. He came out of the Korean War with a few wounds, and after the hospital returned to the family estate."

"Don't get ahead of me, Brandon, all that's part of the trail. However, you did mention the magic word—'photographs.' The minute we got inside that room the old girl lurched over to a wall and yelled that one was missing. She started screaming about 'Josh's favorite picture.'"

"Well, well, Squinty, you'd found another spoor, hadn't you? You questioned the poor old dear and learned that it was a photo of Appleton and his closest friend. Two strapping young men in front of a sailboat, pretty much the same size, both with imposing builds, both handsome in the prepschool mold—like they could be cousins, maybe."

"Closer, according to Mrs. Appleton. Brothers. Until one went to war and the other suddenly refused to go and flew to Switzerland." Shields reached into his pocket and withdrew a small notebook; it was wrinkled, the pages yellow with age. "I dug this out of a file cabinet. I wanted to make sure I had the facts and the names straight when we talked. Where were we?"

"A photograph . . ." Cameron, by the gunwale, was engrossed. "*The* photograph."

"Oh, yes," said the deputy director, flipping the pages of his notebook. "It was after Korea; Appleton was in law school when he was in a terrible collision on the Massachusetts Turnpike. He nearly died at Mass General, with multiple fractures, massive internal bleeding, and horrible facial disfiguration. The family had specialists from everywhere working around the clock; it seemed hopeless, but obviously it wasn't. So your next move, Brandon, was fairly obvious. You marched over to Massachusetts General Hospital, directly to the Department of Records and Billing. Although she's now retired, the woman in charge remembers you very clearly."

"I got her into trouble?"

"No, but as the chief aide to Senator Appleton, you promised her a personal thank-you note from the man who was soon to become President. She never got it, that's how she remembered."

"Hell, I didn't have time to write," said Bray. "Go on, you're doing pretty well."

"The hospital's R and B didn't tell you a great deal—most of it was medical mumbo jumbo with eighty-odd pages of procedures, services, and whatnot—and you wanted more. You wanted names. So she sent you up to the Department of Personnel, by then completely computerized, the records going back years."

"There was a black kid on the equipment and without him I'd have been a dead pigeon," broke in Scofield. "He was a student at Tech, making ends meet to stay in school. It's funny, but I can't recall his name."

"You should. He's now Dr. Amos Lafollet—Ph.D.—and a leading authority on nuclear medicine. When I finally tracked him down, he said if I ever saw you, I should ask if you liked the inscription in his first book."

"I didn't know he wrote one."

"Well, I went out and bought it; it's a standard text on nuclear medicine. You want to hear the inscription? I've got it here."

"Sure."

" 'To a generous stranger who asked little and gave a great deal, making possible a young man's career, including this book.' . . . Not bad for a stranger who couldn't elicit those words from his own mother."

"My mother thought I was either a gangster or a professional gambler. Let's get back to Boston."

"Certainly," said Shields, returning to his notebook. "Dr. Lafollet, then a young student working the hospital's computers, discovered that the two surgeons of record for Appleton had been replaced, and to his astonishment, one replacement had died and the name of the other replacement had been deleted from the records."

"Don't forget the nurses, Frank," said Scofield quietly, staring at Shields. "For me they were a significant bingo."

"Indeed they were," agreed the deputy director.

"What about the nurses?" asked Pryce.

"Presumably on orders from the Appleton family, the hospital personnel were replaced by three private nurses, all of whom were killed in a freak boating accident four days before Joshua Appleton was released and taken back to the family estate, which, incidentally, was in the process of being sold. To a very old, very wealthy banker named Guiderone, a friend of the Appletons who knew their money was dwindling."

"Say it, Squinty. To Nicholas Guiderone, the Shepherd Boy."

"You didn't have any real answers then, Brandon, but you saw the pattern of a monstrous conspiracy. All you really had were the names of the original two surgeons of record, one dead, the other forced into retirement. His name was Dr. Nathaniel Crawford. He died about fifteen years ago, but I reached him several years before that. He also remembered you, remembered your very disturbing phone call. He told me it brought back his nightmares."

"He should never have had them. His diagnosis was

accurate, but he was set up. His patient, Joshua Appleton the Fourth, died in the hospital as he predicted."

"In the company of the two replacement surgeons and perhaps one or two of the private nurses," added Shields. "I can't know the sequence or what you were beginning to perceive, but I assume that's when you persuaded the young Amos Lafollet to fly to Washington and pick up a set of old X-rays."

"Everything was happening so fast I can't remember the sequence," said Bray, turning the Chris-Craft into the mild wind. "Taleniekov and Toni were being held hostage; there wasn't time to plan much. I was flying half blind but I couldn't stop."

"Yet you knew the X-rays might prove what you had begun to suspect, no matter how outrageous it seemed."

"Yes," agreed Scofield pensively, his eyes on the water, seeing things and feeling things no one else could. "They were dental X-rays taken so long ago, in such different places, they could not have been tampered with, much less removed."

"But you only had one set and you had to match them against another, isn't that right, Brandon?"

"Obviously," said Bray, again turning back to Shields, "and since you'd gotten this far, you had a pretty good idea who it was, of course."

"Of course, but there was no way I could prove anything because you had the second set. You saw, as I did in that room in Louisburg Square, that Appleton and his closest friend both went to Andover Academy. You drove over there, tracked down the dentist—close friends, especially teenage boys away from home, would certainly go to the same dentist—and persuaded the doctor to give you both boys' X-rays."

"So then you learned the truth," said Scofield, nodding. "Good work, Frank, and I mean that."

"It was your bargaining chip if, indeed, you even had one, to free Antonia and Taleniekov."

"*What* bargaining chip?" asked a perplexed Cameron Pryce.

"The X-rays proved that the guest of honor that day at Appleton Hall was not Senator Joshua Appleton but a fellow student and close friend by the name of Julian Guiderone, the son of the Shepherd Boy who was soon to occupy the White House with all that it implies."

"*Christ,*" exclaimed Cameron, "you weren't bullshitting, were you, Bray?"

"You mean you accept it from Squinty, but not from me, youngster?"

"Well, you must admit Frank filled in a lot of gaps you didn't bother to plug."

"Not all of them." Scofield looked over at Shields. "Did Crawford explain to you who one of the replacing doctors was?"

"He certainly did and he gave me his name, too. He was the most prominent cosmetic surgeon in Switzerland. Only the richest trekked to his clinic. Would you believe he was killed when his car went out of control and plunged over a high precipice in Villefranche? Three days after he left Boston for Europe?"

"I can't understand why the Matarese waited three days."

"And that Julian Guiderone, who left the country for Switzerland to avoid fighting in the Korean War, supposedly died in a skiing accident near the village of Col du Pillon, where he was buried because of his love for the Alps?"

"Yes, I read that twenty-five years ago in the newspaper microfilms. I wonder who was in that coffin, or was it merely empty?"

"There's no point in digging up the grave—if there is one."

"There's no point in dredging up any of this, Frank. The Guiderones are gone. The Shepherd Boy and his son are dead. We have to look elsewhere for the Matarese hierarchy."

"That may not be accurate, Brandon," Shields said softly as Scofield snapped his head away from the wheel. "In your debriefing, what there was of it, you claimed that Senator Appleton—né Guiderone—was killed in the cross fire that day at Appleton Hall—"

"The *hell* I did!" roared Bray. "I shot the son of a bitch *myself*! Through the shattered window, with my weapon!"

"The words didn't come across that way."

"Maybe I fudged, I don't know! You bastards had me beyond salvage and I wasn't about to give you any leverage."

"Regardless, you said he collapsed into the immense fireplace, into the flames—"

"That's *exactly* what he did!"

"The police were on the crime scene within minutes, Brandon. There was no corpse in the fireplace. Rather, there were scuff marks on the slate, as if a body had been dragged out. Burned strands of fabric around the area, the flatness signifying that they had been subjected to pressure, the fire stamped into submission. It's my judgment, as well as our forensic laboratories', that Julian Guiderone survived."

"He couldn't have! . . . Even if he had, which is *impossible,* how could he have gotten away?"

"How did you and Antonia get away? There was so much confusion— the gunfire, the explosions going off in the exterior sewers, which I assume you planted—everything was chaos. I interrogated every police officer, every private guard, and one member of the SWAT team remembered that a Mr. and Mrs. Vickery, a panicked man and a woman, reached the main gate in a speeding car claiming they were guests, *only* guests. They had hidden in a closet, and in a lull in the fire, raced out a back door to their car."

"So?"

"Your sister's married name is Vickery, Brandon."

"You're thorough, I'll say that for you, Squinty."

"I accept the compliment, but it's irrelevant. There was another vehicle, a similar story. A wounded guest in a private ambulance that never reached the hospital. . . . The bottom line is that Julian Guiderone, the son of the Shepherd Boy, is undoubtedly alive, and if there's anyone on this earth he wants in the crosshairs, it's you. It's Beowulf Agate."

"Damned interesting, Frank. He and I are about the same age, two old men from another time, both hungering for what each is being denied. He wants obscene power, which I won't allow him, and I want my personal peace, which he won't permit me." Scofield paused and looked at Cameron Pryce. "I suppose in the long or short run, we'll depend on our commanders, and I have total confidence in mine."

"I hope you know what you're doing," said Cam. "All I will say is that I'll do the best I can."

"Oh, you'll do better than that, son."

Los Angeles Times
(FRONT PAGE)

EURO AND AMERICAN ENTERTAINMENT ENTERPRISES IN ASTONISHING COMBINE

LOS ANGELES, OCT. 9—It is a smaller world, compressed by high technology that permits instant transmission of product via satellite and cable. Where it will end nobody knows, but the four remaining major motion-picture studios, along with their networks and subsidiary cable outlets, announced today that they have joined with Continent-Celestial to provide a consolidated source of informational and entertainment programs. The guilds of actors, writers, producers, and directors applaud the move into the future as it will provide multiple employment opportunities for their members. The performing unions have suggested that their members become multilingual. The benefits resulting from this megamerger are self-evident, but what is not so clear are the directions such an amalgamation might take.

Continued on page 2

It was ten minutes to four in the morning when Julian Guiderone placed his last phone call to Langley, Virginia, from Amsterdam. "We're on total S?" he asked.

"Total," replied the voice in the CIA. "My scrambler is my own, courtesy of the Directorate."

"Good. I'll be leaving here in a few minutes, next contact Cairo."

"Not Bahrain?"

"Not for at least three weeks. I've got work to do with our Arabs—not theirs, *ours*."

"Good fortune," came the words from Langley, Virginia. "We all believe in you."

"You should. And you must also believe in Amsterdam. He's on course."

"Then we shall," replied the mole.

Four days and three nights passed when Cameron Pryce confronted Scofield at the breakfast buffet. "This is getting us nowhere!" Cam exclaimed curtly under his breath while sipping black coffee.

"You seem to be getting somewhere," said Bray, lighting a dark brown cigarillo. "With our lady commando, I mean."

"To tell you the truth, I'm not even trying."

"You're seeing a lot of her—"

"Wrong," interrupted Pryce, "she's seeing *me*. I go out to the gate, she shows up. I walk on the beach, suddenly she's there. I mosey over to the chopper pad to see who might be on the next flight, she's thirty feet behind me."

"Maybe she's got a thing for you, youngster. Toni says you're prime."

"Like in meat? That doesn't sound like Antonia."

"No, like in time. When you can supposedly find the best programs. Perhaps the female colonel is curious about you. In other than a professional way."

"Sorry," said Cam, "no signals, no body language, just barely discernible hostility layered with pleasant inanities. It's as though she's watching me, not sure who or what I am. It doesn't make sense."

"Sure it does," said Scofield, grinning as he exhaled the aromatic smoke. "It matches her latest, very professional request relayed by Colonel Bracket to Shields. She wants your complete, unabridged dossier. Naturally, you're not to be informed."

"I don't get it."

"She either wants to marry you, youngster, or she thinks you're the high-placed leak."

"I'm counting on the second. That lady's military testosterone would blindside a general."

Suddenly, breaking into the hum of the few other diners, there was an ear-shattering scream from across the large, screened-in porch. Frank Shields's liaison, Eugene Denny, had lunged out of his chair, gripping his throat, his body twisting as he crashed to the floor, his legs kicking in spasms. Only seconds later, his breakfast companion, Colonel Everett Bracket, did much the same, his right hand curved around his neck, his left grabbing the table as he shook violently, finally collapsing across the surface, sending plates shattering on the tiles below.

Pryce and Scofield raced through the chairs and tables to the fallen men, joined by an Army patrol on kitchen duty. Cameron leaned down, alternately touching the necks of Bracket and Denny.

"My God, they're *dead*!" Pryce cried, getting to his feet. "It had to be poison."

A young, stunned RDF soldier knelt to examine the plates. "Don't touch those, son!" said Scofield quickly.

Cam and Bray looked down at the broken plates, at the spilled food beside each. Both men had eaten eggs, either poached or lightly fried, since portions of soft, yellow yoke were apparent.

"Who knows you like eggs?" asked Pryce quietly.

"Hell, probably every one of the boys who've worked in here. Toni was pretty outspoken about my eggs, and most of the time I listened to her. Two months ago those medical idiots in Miami said my cholesterol was over three hundred."

"Did you order eggs this morning?"

"Order? This is a buffet, haven't you noticed? Those metal servers on the table hold scrambled with sausages, and the one next to it has poached floating in slow-boiling water."

"But you didn't have eggs today?"

"Had 'em yesterday . . . and I figured Toni might walk in."

"Seal off the kitchen," ordered Pryce to the RDF soldier.

"Seal off? I *am* the kitchen, sir. Everything comes in sealed, including the eggs, and whoever's on duty here follows the regs on how to make 'em."

"Regs?"

"Instructions, sir. By the numbers, although we sure don't need them. I mean, what can you do with eggs?"

"Kill people, my friend," said Scofield. "Seal off the kitchen. *Now!*"

One of the normal two cartons of eggs was still in the mansion's walk-in refrigerator. Otherwise it was bare except for a few quarts of milk, several packages of cheese, and unopened cans of soft drinks.

"What do you make of it?" asked Cam. "Maybe it wasn't the eggs."

"Maybe not," answered Bray, turning to the RDF patrol. "Tell me, soldier, what about these instructions—for the eggs, I mean?"

"They're taped on the wall to the left of the first stove, sir, but I can detail 'em like the ABC's. . . . Mix six in a bowl with a little milk and whip them up in a skillet with some butter—those are the scrambled. Then you break the other six in the big hot-water server over the Sterno on the table and sort of wing it."

" 'Wing it'?"

"Check 'em now and then depending on who shows up. If they get too hard, which is like when they're light yellow, you scoop them out and replace 'em."

"Do you do that often, soldier?"

"Not really, sir. Those who like them that way usually get down here early. *Jesus,* I don't understand!"

"But you understand that you're not to say anything, don't you?" said Scofield pointedly.

"Sure, but that's crazy—I'm sorry but it's *crazy*! The word'll go out all over the compound, you can't stop it!"

"I know that, son, I just want to know who learns about it outside of this compound. So let's try a little containment."

"I still don't understand—sir."

"You don't have to. Now bring that carton of eggs over to the sink and mix up some liquid soap and warm water."

Using the soapsudsy solution, Bray shook each egg, dipped it into the water, and held it up to the light. Each displayed tiny bubbles at the apex of the shell, the opening too minuscule to be seen by the naked eye.

"I'll be a son of a bitch," said Pryce, studying one of the eggs.

"You'd be a dead one if you had eaten that," added Scofield. "This method of killing was developed by the Borgias in the middle of the fifteenth century, only far less sophisticated. They used the hatpins of their ladies' finery and painstakingly allowed the poison to seep in. They also injected tomatoes, squash, plums, and their most-favorite, punctured grapes left soaking for a few days."

"How civilized," said Cameron sardonically.

"These eggs were done by the most-modern, thinnest syringes available. Same trick our lesser magicians employ when they inject supposedly fresh eggs with a substance that makes them instantly solid so they can be smashed without breaking. Amusing, in a horrible sort of way, isn't it?"

"No, not remotely," said Pryce. "What do you want to do now, since you're the honcho of this operation?"

"The obvious. Quarantine the kitchens at Langley and place everyone who works there under total surveillance."

The computer in the Chesapeake compound clacked out the information:

The products in question were purchased from the Rockland Farms in Rockport, Maryland, under contract issued by the Central Intelligence Agency after a full investigation of the company's standards. The CIA personnel in the Langley kitchens are mostly long-

term employees who were subjected to background checks. Reevaluation adds nothing. Intensive scrutiny will continue.

The Baltimore Sun
(BUSINESS SECTION, PAGE 3)

ROCKLAND FARMS SOLD

ROCKPORT, OCT. 10—Rockland Farms, one of the country's leading poultry producers and the largest in the eastern United States, has been purchased by Atlantic Crown, Limited, worldwide distributors of produce with offices around the globe. Jeremy Carlton, spokesman for ACL, issued the following press release.

"With the absorption of Rockland Farms, Atlantic Crown vastly enlarges its markets so as to better serve our clients in many countries. The addition of poultry to our varied exports of produce from America's heartland has long been a dream of Atlantic Crown. The global expansion of fast-food franchises alone justifies the expenditure. With our network of international outlets, we can expedite our products across the world to everyone's benefit.

"This statement would not be complete without expressing our thanks to the Bledso family, the previous owners of Rockland Farms, for its cooperation in negotiations and the wisdom it showed in selecting Atlantic Crown. In all things, we will endeavor to uphold the family's great tradition."

The press release did not disclose the terms of the sale and since both companies are privately held, neither is compelled by law to do so. However, it had to be immense, for the "absorption" of Rockland Farms makes Atlantic Crown the most profitable combine in the food-processing/exporting industry, possibly in the world.

The dimly lit study in the large house on the outskirts of Rockport, Maryland, was not unlike other houses in the three-million-dollar range on the properties of megamillion-dollar "farms" far from the odors of their businesses. Although the cold winds of autumn had barely arrived, the fireplace was roaring, the flames casting shadows that danced against the walls. An angry man in his forties approached an elderly figure in a wheelchair.

"How could you *do* it, Grandfather? I've turned down Atlantic Crown for years! They're vultures, buying up every processing plant in sight until they own it all and can dictate the markets!"

"And *I* own this company, you don't," wheezed the old man, bringing an oxygen mask to his mouth. "When I'm dead, you can do what you want, but until then it's mine."

"But *why*?"

"You all got decent money, didn't you?"

"That's irrelevant and you know it. They're not our sort of people. They're *bloodsuckers*."

"All too true, Grandson. But there was a time over fifty years ago when the money behind what's known now as Atlantic Crown backed a young visionary. With finances that could have come from moneylenders expunged from hell. How do you think a neophyte agronomist could have bought over ten thousand acres of fertile ground without them? By *God,* they were the visionaries, not I."

"Are you saying you couldn't *refuse* them?"

"Nobody can."

The velour-draped boardroom of Atlantic Crown in the penthouse of the ACL building in Wichita, Kansas, was deserted except for two men. The man at the head of the table, appropriately dressed in a subdued dark pin-striped suit, spoke.

"Next shot is the beef industry," he said. "Orders from Amsterdam."

"We'll need an infusion of capital," said the subordinate executive in a navy blue blazer and French cuffs. "I hope that's been made clear."

"We'll have it," answered the CEO of Atlantic Crown. "Incidentally, that minor problem about the eggs in the Chesapeake complex, was it taken care of?"

"Our final investigating negotiators made sure of it. Right down to the sealed crates for the helicopter."

"That's good. We must be precise in all things."

10

The teeming streets of Cairo seemed awash with the odor of sweat as thousands rushed about in the harsh midday sun. The traffic was dense; horns clashed in angry spurts as voices erupted in incessant conflict, pitting languages and dialects against one another. The mass of humanity was as diversified as the vocal tumult; Arabic robes comingled with Western suits, jackets, and blue jeans, while the Muslim headdress vied with bowlers, Stetsons, and baseball caps. In a sense, it was a macrocosm of East and West, the numbers favoring the Arab, as it was his country, his city. Cairo, the font of legends, where myth and reality were inseparable, yet very separate in a land of contradictions.

Julian Guiderone, dressed in an *aba, thobe*, and *ghotra*, and wearing large dark glasses, walked down the crowded Al Barrani Boulevard looking for the sign that would tell him he had reached his destination. There it was! A blue fleur-de-lis on a small white banner hanging in the storefront window of a jewelry shop. The son of the Shepherd Boy paused to light a cigarette in front of the glass; it allowed him to slowly glance up and down the street, his eyes searching for the unusual. A man or a woman whose eyes were on *him*. Such was the danger of the conference that was about to take place on the second floor of the store. No one, *no one* outside of those conferring could know the purpose of the meeting about to begin. Should even a rumor be floated, it could spell disaster.

Satisfied, Guiderone stamped out his cigarette and walked inside, instantly holding up three fingers waist high in front of his robes. The clerk behind the counter nodded twice and gestured with his head to a dark red velvet drape on his right. Julian acknowledged with a slight bow and proceeded through the curtain that concealed a staircase. He climbed the narrow steps, as always annoyed by the impediment of his injured leg, the limp restricting his swiftness. At the top of the stairs he looked around at the three doors on the second floor; he saw the blue dot on a brass doorknob and awkwardly maneuvered his way around the curved railing toward it. He stood still briefly except for his hands, which roamed under his robes checking his two weapons, a small .25-caliber automatic on his right, and a fluted grenadelike missile on the left that when hurled against a wall exploded a gaseous substance lethal to any who inhaled it.

Guiderone reached for the brass knob, twisted it, swung the door open, and remained in the frame, studying the room. There were four men all dressed in bedouin robes around a table, each wearing a desert veil cloth, a protection against sandstorms, here a protection against identity. Julian had no need for such a device. He wanted all to know the face of the son of the Shepherd Boy, for if they disobeyed, that face would haunt them until each took his last breath, which could come any hour or any minute from the moment of disobedience.

"Good morning, gentlemen, or is it now afternoon?" he said, entering and taking the chair nearest the door. "I trust that you, *all* of you, have thoroughly checked the security of our meeting place."

"The room is bare but for our chairs and this table," replied the Arab at the opposite end from Guiderone, the brocaded gold on his *ghotra* signifying a chieftain's status. "The walls have been examined by our subordinates and deemed clear of listening devices."

"And what about yourselves? *Ourselves?* Desert robes can conceal so many things, can't they?"

"Despite the times," said another to the left of Julian, "the ancient rules of that same desert prevail. A traitor's punishment is still decapitation by dagger, excruciatingly slow in its work. None of us would shirk at executing another, and each of us knows it."

"That's succinct, to say the least. So let's proceed. Since nothing can be written down, I believe each of you, as leader of your faction, has an oral report to give me, am I correct?"

"You are," answered a third member of the conference, at the far end of the table. "They may appear to be repetitive as each essentially delivers the same information—"

"Then in the interests of brevity," interrupted the last man, diagonally across the table on Julian's right, "since each of us has a price on his head, and none cares to remain here any longer than necessary, why not state the general information, each following up with geographical specifics?"

"An excellent idea," agreed the son of the Shepherd Boy, "but allow me to compliment all of you on the obvious. You speak my language far better than most of my countrymen."

"You are a polyglot society of vastly undereducated people," said the Arab chieftain at the end of the table. "We are different, far different. I, for one, read law and international jurisprudence at Cambridge—along with many others of my Islamic brothers."

"And I am a physician, University of Chicago's School of Medicine, residence and practice in Stanford—among several hundred other Muslims over the years," added the man on the apparent leader's right.

"I held the chair of medieval studies at a university in Germany several years after my doctorate from Heidelberg," quietly noted the impatient member.

"My credentials are less impressive," said the fourth delegate, "but perhaps more pragmatic. I am an electrical engineer and worked on major projects for firms dealing with governments and private industry. I pray for the day I can return and build in our own homeland."

"Fascinating," mumbled Guiderone, scanning the dark eyes of the four Arabs. "You're the elite of the Middle East, yet they call you terrorists."

"Others prefer the term 'freedom fighters,' which is far more accurate," corrected the chieftain. "The Hagganah and the Stern Group simply had more apologists in the West than we do, and we continue to do what we do, for those who should be our allies constantly make deals with our mutual enemies. It's revolting."

"They'll think twice before entering into such negotiations after we've struck," said the restless man, "so why don't we get down to business?"

"Splendid," agreed the son of the Shepherd Boy, "and since you're eager to do so, why don't you begin with the general information applicable to you all."

"With pleasure, sir," said the impatient former scholar, "especially since you are one of our most generous benefactors. . . . Our units are in training in twenty-four locations, from the true Yemen to the Baaka Valley, all in deserts and waterfronts beyond the scrutiny of enemies and infiltrators. Also, we have learned a lesson from the Jews at Entebbe: Precision is the key to our operations. Thanks in part to your financing, mock installations have been built both on desert sand and in the water. The teams are under the leadership of our most experienced military personnel as well as experts in intelligence, infiltration, and sabotage. When the hour comes to strike, we will operate in unison, a conflagration the world will never forget, never be able to expunge from history."

"Confident words, my friend," said Guiderone, nodding his head slowly. "Now to specifics. Shall we begin with your counterpart across from you?"

"With even greater pleasure," replied the physician trained in Chicago with an enviable residency and practice in California. "My units' targets are in Kuwait, Iraq, and Iran, the absence of prejudice a mark of our universality.

Ten thousand oil wells will be put to flames, making the Kuwait disaster a minuscule campfire."

"My teams are concentrating on the major Saudi fields from Ad-Dawādimī to Ash Shad'ra to the wells north of 'Unayzah," said the electrical engineer. "Then to the tankers in the Persian and Oman gulfs anchored offshore in fueling ports from Al Khiran to Matrah and Muscat—"

"Thus including the Emirates, yes?"

"Of course, all of them; the sultans know nothing."

"And I will oversee the ports in the eastern waters," added the scholar of medieval studies from Germany, his eyes bright above his desert veil. "Descending from Bandar-e Deylam south to Bandar-e 'Abbās in the Strait of Hormuz. As the wells are destroyed, so will be millions upon millions of tons in the ports."

"I save for myself," said the bedouin sheikh at the opposite end of the table from the unmasked son of the Shepherd Boy, "all the exports loaded off the shores of Israel, hundreds of ships in the harbors of Tüilkarm, Tel Aviv, and Rafah, their merchandise—produce, machinery, and illegal armaments—blown up in concert. The monied Zionists will break any treaties to fill their treasuries with shekels. We will put a stop to it, and watch the moneylending banks in Jerusalem and Tel Aviv plummet into chaos!"

"You can assure us of this?" asked Guiderone.

"As my name is Al Khabor Hassin, which you well know, and therefore also know that I am the Protector of the Hassinites, from which you Westerners derive the word *assassin*. Never underestimate our power of death."

"That's very enlightening, as well as quite melodramatic," said Julian softly, his right hand reaching unobtrusively under his robe. "And do you feel, as Protector of the tribe of the Assassins, that you will have lived up to your position?"

"*Naturally!* It is my victory over the despised Israel!"

"And no one can do it but you?"

"My troops are in place. The seas will have no night, for weeks, even months! The fires everywhere, from the gulfs to Cairo, will light up the land like the morning sun. *Everywhere* in the Middle East. It is our *victory*!"

"Whose victory, Al Khabor Hassin?" asked Guiderone quietly.

"*Ours*. All of ours. And *mine*, above all *mine*! For I am the leader!"

"That's what I thought," said the son of the Shepherd Boy as he raised his automatic above the table and fired twice, the shots muted by the caliber, but accurate. Al Khabor Hassin, killed instantly, fell to the floor, blood pouring from two holes in his forehead. The remaining three at the table shot back in their chairs, stunned, their bodies rigid, their dark eyes staring at Guiderone.

"He would have destroyed us all," said Julian, "for his cause was himself. Never trust a leader who proclaims himself a leader before anyone else does. His maniacal ego gives away too much. He cannot control it."

"What should we do with him?" asked the practical engineer.

"Take him out to his desert and let the carrion decide."

"And then what?" said the physician from California.

"Reach his second in command and send him to me. I'll evaluate him and if he's acceptable, I'll explain that the overstressed Al Khabor Hassin suffered cardiac arrest. It's not difficult."

"Nothing else has changed, I trust," said the medieval scholar from Germany.

"Not a thing," answered Guiderone. "Al Khabor was correct. Whole areas of the Mediterranean will not see the dark of night for weeks as the fires burn. It will be a symmetry of horror, all the instruments reaching a crescendo of terror. It will also be the same in the North Sea, oil rigs by the dozens blown up by our personnel in Scotland, Norway, and Denmark. When the fires die, the civilized world as we know it will be in chaos. It will be ours to control . . . on a rational, therapeutic basis. For above all, we are benevolent."

"When do you project that will be?" asked the terrorist scholar.

"The first of the New Year," replied Guiderone. "We begin the countdown tonight."

Cameron Pryce knocked on the door of Scofield's suite in the main house. It was five-thirty in the morning and Antonia, suppressing a yawn, admitted him. She was in flannel pajamas, for which she apologized. "I'll put on a bathrobe and tell the grouch you're here. I'd also better put on some coffee; he's a monster without it."

"That's not necessary, Toni—"

"Of course it is," she interrupted, "maybe not for you, but for him. You wouldn't be here at this hour unless it *was* necessary."

"It is."

"Then come on in, but plug up your ears while I start the coffee and wake him up." Pryce followed her into the tiny kitchen alcove.

"He's that tough?"

"Imagine a gargoyle roaring. He's used to tropical hours, Cam. Ten or ten-thirty is synonymous with the break of day."

"You know, you speak English so terribly well."

"Blame it on Bray. When we decided we should stay together, he flew in dozens of those records, then tapes on *How to Speak,* et cetera, et cetera. He went to Harvard, but now claims my grammar is better than his. Frankly, he's right. He doesn't know a dangling participle from an adverb."

"Neither do I," said Cameron, sitting down at the small table as Antonia manipulated the coffee machine. "But if you'll allow me a moment of curiosity—which you damn well may refuse—how did you decide to 'stay together,' as you put it?"

"I suppose the obvious thing is to say love," answered Antonia, turning away from the white plastic coffee appliance and looking at Pryce. "And certainly there was that, both physically and emotionally, but there was more, so much more. Brandon Scofield was a man in turmoil, hunted by both his superiors and his enemies, each wanting his execution. He could have made—he and *Taleniekov* could have made—numerous compromises that would have eliminated those demands for their deaths. Neither did, for they had found the truth of the Matarese. The *truth,* Cameron. So many in private life and in governments were afraid to follow them, for too many had been corrupted. . . . Bray and Vasili said to hell with them, and they never stopped. Taleniekov died so we could escape the carnage, and I was left with a giant, an unassuming, thinking man, in many ways a gentle man until violence is required, and he was perfectly willing to give his life for me. How could I not love that man, how could I not revere him always?"

"He doesn't strike me as a man who wants reverence. He seems to reject it."

"Of course he does. Because it reminds him of the bad days, as he calls them. The days when the gun was the equalizer—you killed, for if you didn't, one of your own would be killed."

"Those days are in the past, Toni. The Cold War is over. That isn't done anymore."

"In nightmares he still remembers. He cut short the lives of the young and the old with a bullet. It never leaves him."

"If he hadn't, our own would have been killed. He knows that, too."

"I suppose he does. I think it's the young fanatics who have always bothered him. They were too young, too vulnerable, to be responsible for their insane commitments."

"They were killers, Antonia."

"They were children, Cameron."

"I'm not equipped to solve Bray's problems, and incidentally, that's not why I'm here."

"Of course not. Why *are* you here, at this hour?"

"Why don't you get the gargoyle up? It'll save time and I won't have to repeat myself. Frankly, I don't want to stay here too long in case I'm under someone's scope."

"Really?" said Toni, her eyes locked with Cam's.

"Really," replied Pryce softly.

Five minutes later a disheveled Scofield walked into the alcove, followed by Antonia. Both were in bathrobes—

Toni's a neat white terry cloth; Brandon's a relic, clean but torn in several places. "If we'd gone to a decent hotel," he said curtly, "I could have stolen a robe. . . . What the hell is this, son? It better be good or I'll put you on report or whatever these military idiots do—where's some coffee?"

"Sit down, darling, I'm getting it for you."

"So talk, Cam. I haven't willingly gotten up at this hour since a bad night in Stockholm when a young lady had the wrong room but the right key."

"Braggart," said Antonia, bringing two cups of coffee to the table as she sat down.

"None for you?" asked Pryce, nodding at his cup.

"I'm a tea drinker and I'm out—"

"And *I'm* pretty damned curious," Scofield broke in. "Speak, young man."

"You remember my telling you that our Lieutenant Colonel Montrose appeared to be dogging my tracks?"

"Sure, and I recall suggesting she had the hots for you."

"Which I dismissed out of hand, she didn't. Believe it or not, I know the signs and we're not in Stockholm. So when Bracket was killed last week and she was put in command of security, I figured it was a good time to reverse the procedure. She had far more responsibilities and her concentration had to be split tenfold, besides which she's an overachiever and wants to make her mark at the Pentagon."

"So you began tailing her, right?" Brandon leaned forward, his wrinkled eyes over the coffee cup suddenly alive.

"Yes, very carefully and mostly late at night. Twice, the first time at three o'clock in the morning, the second at four-fifteen the next night, she left her quarters and walked down to the boathouse. There's a single, wire-meshed light in the ceiling over the Chris-Craft; both times she turned it on. I crept up to the small right window and looked inside. On each occasion she pulled out her cellular phone and made a call."

"That's goddamned *stupid,*" said Scofield. "Those frequencies can be picked up by anyone with a radio scanner! They're only to be used as communications of last resort."

"That's what I thought," agreed Pryce. "I was also given to understand that only she and Bracket and you and I had those phones."

"Exactly," confirmed Bray. "All other telephones are monitored, courtesy of Frank Shields. I wonder who she was calling."

"That's why, using my authority as the CIA senior officer, I drove into Easton this afternoon, ostensibly to pick up newspapers and magazines."

"Why the hell did you get me *U.S. News and World Report* and those financial rags? You know I don't give a damn about that stuff."

"They didn't have *Penthouse,* the *National Enquirer,* or any comic books. However, the literature notwithstanding, that wasn't why I went into town. I used a pay phone, called Frank in Langley, and asked him if he could trace the numbers called on Montrose's cellular. He said sure, all calls were billed. He told me to hang on, and in a minute or two he was back."

"What did he find out?" asked an impatient Scofield. "Who'd she call?"

"That's the funny thing. No one."

"But you *saw* her," insisted Toni.

"I certainly did, and I was emphatic about it. Shields told me to hold on again, and when he came back, he had some startling information. No calls were listed on Montrose's phone, but three were on Colonel Bracket's."

"Those phones all look alike," said Bray. "She switched them!"

"But *why*?" pressed Antonia.

"Obviously to cover her ass, luv. But she didn't count on Bracket being killed. *His* cellular, at least the one he had with him, went back to Langley with the body, didn't it?"

"Another surprise," said Cameron. "It didn't. Frank assumed that since you and I reached Bracket's and Denny's bodies first, one of us took it."

"But neither of us did. I didn't even think about it."

"Neither did I."

"So there's a loose phone around. Let it stay that way."

"Frank agrees. They're now monitored for conversations."

"So who were the calls to? Montrose's calls?"

"Surprise number three."

"What?"

"The White House. She was calling the White House."

One by one, at intervals of twenty minutes, seven private aircraft flew into Amsterdam's Schiphol Airport. The owners deplaned and one after the other were led to waiting limousines by muscular escorts last seen in the hills of Porto Vecchio above the waters of the Tyrrhenian Sea. They were driven to the elegant four-story house on the Keizersgracht, the canal that flows through the wealthiest parts of the city. Finally, one by one, the seven descendants of the Baron of Matarese were shown up to the huge second-floor dining room.

The setting was remarkably similar to the great hall of the estate in Porto Vecchio. The table was long, the extravagant wood polished to a glistening hue, and the chairs were separated by several feet, as if to give each guest the space to think, to consider, to evaluate. Absent were the delicate crystal bowls of caviar; in their places were small notepads with silver ballpoint pens beside them. All notes were to remain at the table; after the meeting they would be burned.

Once the descendants of the Baron were seated, Jan van der Meer Matareisen entered and took his place at the head of the table. "I'm glad to see that a degree of camaraderie is present at this our second conference." He paused. "There *should* be. You've all done superb work."

"Good Lord, old chap, I dare say we've all profited enormously," said the Englishman. "Our investments have gone through the roof!"

"My brokerage house, with our recent alliances across the country," said the blond woman from California, "hasn't seen such expansion since the eighties. It's terrific."

"It's also on paper," admonished Matareisen. "We'll tell

you when to sell. Do so immediately, for there will be a collapse."

"That's hard to imagine, little buddy," interrupted the American from New Orleans. "My real estate and my casinos are on a thunder roll. Everybody wants in."

"And after all the mergers and downsizing, our bank is leaner—and meaner," added the attorney from the Boston bank. "We're becoming a national, even international, economic force. We cannot be stopped."

"Oh, but you must be," Jan van der Meer broke in. "It's part of the larger plan and there can be no deviations. We'll tell you to whom you sell your major assets; in the main, they will not be to the highest bidders."

"Do you presume to dictate to the Vatican Treasury?" asked the cardinal.

"We certainly do, Your Eminence. For you are in the core of the Matarese first, a priest second."

"Blasphemy," said the cardinal softly, his eyes riveted on Matareisen.

"Reality, priest, merely reality. Or would you rather the Vatican Treasury be informed of your financial peccadillos, the handsome estate at Lake Como, a mere drip in a full bucket, as they say."

"What is this foolishness—'not the highest bidders'? Do you take us for idiots?" the man from Portugal demanded.

"You all will have made considerable profits, perhaps not in the figures you anticipated, but it is necessary."

"You talk in circles, *senhor*!"

"But we *are* a circle, are we not? The Matarese circle."

"Please be clearer! What are you saying?"

"In specific terms, you will be instructed to sell your interests to the buyers who are least experienced, least equipped to manage them."

"Sacrebleu!" erupted the inheritor from Paris. "You are talking nonsense! Why would such people be interested?"

"Ego, *mon ami,*" replied the leader from Amsterdam. "Such people overreach constantly, paying for a prize they covet but cannot control. International finance is rife with examples; the giants in Tokyo first come to mind. They wanted the film industry in Los Angeles, so they paid and paid and paid until they were devoured by the studios because they were not equipped to run them."

"It sounds like muleshit to me!" raged the entrepreneur from New Orleans.

"No, he's right," said the cardinal, his eyes still leveled at the Hollander. "It lends believability to the collapse. It invalidates the system, infuriating the masses who instantly begin looking for solutions, for change."

"Very good, priest. Strategically, you're perceptive."

"Reality, Dutchman, merely reality. Or should I say credibility?"

"They become interchangeable, don't they?"

"Ultimately, of course. The scholastic philosophers had their points. So now that the seeds are sown, when do we harvest?"

"Everything must be coordinated everywhere. One event preceding another, each action leading to another, on the surface seemingly unrelated—except one. The American and the European economies are a catastrophe, and no amount of high technology can cure it, for the advances drastically reduce the labor force. Technology does not produce jobs, it eliminates them."

"Theoretically," asked the frowning Englishman, "what is your—what is *our*—solution, if we have one, if only for public relations?"

"Benevolent consolidation, the ultimate authority given to those who can nurture the enterprises after replacing those who cannot. A meritocracy that will appeal to the rich, the educated, and the ambitious, as well as a controlled system of benefits for those of lesser abilities as long as they willingly, even enthusiastically, join the support substructure."

"What's next?" said the Bostonian. "Four-day workweeks, a television in every house combined with a monitoring system?"

"Sophisticated technology does have its opportunities, doesn't it? But such concepts are far in the future. First, we must come out of the financial chaos with an agenda of our own."

"Which brings me back to my question," the cardinal broke in. "When do we harvest?"

"Less than three months, depending on updated progress reports. And the harvest will take time before all its restricting ramifications are bluntly understood. I'd say eighty days. 'Around the world in eighty days.' It has a nice ring to it."

"Pryce!" roared Scofield, racing across the lawn above the boathouse as fast as his aging legs would permit. Cameron turned; he had been walking around the compound ostensibly aimlessly, but his stroll was not aimless at all. He was looking for someone who might emerge from some concealed place, someone who might have on his person a missing cellular telephone.

"Hey, take it easy," said Pryce as a breathless Scofield approached. "You're not exactly ready for a two-twenty sprint."

"I'm as ready as you are, kid!"

"Then why am I here?"

"Oh, shut up," ordered Bray, breathing deeply and wiping the sweat from his face. "Listen, those magazines you brought back from Easton—I began going through them."

"I apologized for no comic books—"

"Shut *up*! How long has this been going on?"

"How long has what been going on?"

"These mergers, the buyouts, companies absorbing other companies, whole industries and utilities combining?"

"I'd say about twenty or thirty years, probably a lot longer."

"No, you idiot, I mean *now*! Within the past weeks or maybe months?"

"I've no idea," replied Cam. "Those kinds of things aren't a high priority with me."

"Goddamn it, they *should* be! It's pure *Matarese*!"

"What?"

"The style, the strategy! It's Corsica, Rome, Paris, London, Amsterdam—and yes, by God, *Moscow* all over again! It's the trail, the *trails,* Taleniekov and I followed, right back to Boston, Massachusetts. Down in the islands, I suggested that you go after the victims, their families, friends, lawyers, learning whatever you could—"

"I'm working on that. Frank Shields is assigning a couple of researchers to get me backgrounds on the Italian polo player who bought it on Long Island; the Spanish scientist who was poisoned in Monaco; and the woman philanthropist who was killed by her second husband in London. If nothing breaks here in a few days, Frank's getting me military transport to the U.K."

"Then I'm going to make another suggestion," said Scofield. "Put 'em all on a back burner and go after what's in front of your face right here!"

"I beg your pardon?"

"Those magazines, all that financial crap; the wizards of the boardrooms, the money slimes and their profit lines. And while you're at it, put the researchers on those companies, both national and international—the names are there, and I'll bet there's a lot of newsprint we don't know about— with more names, more trails!"

"You're serious, aren't you?"

"You're damn right I am. When I saw the name Waverly, it set me off! I can smell it, smell *them,* and the stench is overpowering, let me tell you."

"If you're right, and I'm not saying you are, but if you are, it could save a lot of time."

"We always look for shortcuts, don't we?"

"That's axiomatic, if they're genuine."

"It's all genuine, Cam. I couldn't be mistaken, not about this. I was there before you learned to write your name in the snow, if you know what I mean."

"I'll reach Frank in Langley, get his reaction."

"The hell you will!" objected Brandon. "I'll call him myself on our secure line. You lack a certain conviction, and I'm still running this operation."

"I thought it was my function to implement it," protested

Pryce. "All those things you didn't care to do—or couldn't do, like running sixty yards across a lawn."

"Don't nitpick. Actually, one good thing is coming out of this," said Scofield, grabbing Cameron's arm and propelling him back toward the main house and a sterile telephone. "Instead of you running helter-skelter all over Europe without direction, I'll be able to keep my eye on you, give you guidance."

"Can I ask for Daffy Duck instead? He'd give me better advice and Lord knows, he'd be easier to live with."

What neither man knew as they walked across the lawn at sundown on Chesapeake Bay was that in an unmapped airstrip on the outskirts of Havre de Grace, Maryland, a Black Hawk SOA helicopter with the identical markings as those that flew north from Langley, Virginia, was preparing to be airborne, heading south. However, instead of a cargo hold filled with the normal supplies for a sequestered, isolated unit on the Chesapeake shoreline, its underside was lined with six one-thousand-pound bombs. It had a mission to accomplish, ordered by a man in Amsterdam.

11

"Now, have you got everything, Squinty—sorry, I forgot we're on tape—Deputy Director Shields, the finest analyst since Gaius Octavius sent Crassus out to find that Spartacus?"

"I've got everything," said Frank Shields over the line from Langley, his voice quiet, tense. "Your dollops of levity are always welcome when we're under stress. May I speak to Officer Pryce, if you please?"

"He can't tell you anything, Frank. He's just beginning to put it together." Scofield sat up in the bed in his and Antonia's suite, looking over at Cameron, who stood by a window. "To tell you the truth," continued Bray, "he seems to have doubts, but I don't."

"I have something to tell him, Brandon. All the material he requested on those three people who were killed will be on the six o'clock chopper."

"How complete is it?"

"Very. Everything we could unearth in the time allowed. Families, friends, neighbors, business associates, assets and debits, three whole balls of wax, thanks mostly to Interpol and our friends in London."

"I'm sure he'll tell you he's grateful, but right now that's all in limbo. Tell your researchers to concentrate on what I just gave you."

"Field Officer Pryce, please?" repeated Shields. Scofield gestured with the phone at Cam, who walked across the room and took it, standing beside the bed.

"Yes, Frank?"

"I just told Brandon that you'll have the backgrounds you wanted. They're on the six o'clock flight, marked for you personally."

"I gathered that when he mentioned the limbo status. Thanks, I'll go through them tonight. Any news about our Colonel Montrose's connection to the White House?"

"They claim she doesn't have one. They say they don't even know who she is."

"They're lying."

"That switchboard doesn't have a pulse, just numbers that connect you with live people. We're working on it. . . . What do you make of Bray's theory about all these mergers?"

"Look, Frank, I can't deny there may be some substance in Bray's speculations, but when you consider the antitrust laws, and the commissions, like Federal Trade and the Securities and Exchange, if there were fishy mergers, or even negotiations, wouldn't they be picked up?"

"Not necessarily," replied Shields. "The big financial

boys have teams of corporate attorneys, any one of whom makes more in an hour than we see in a month. They know what buttons to press, who to buy, where to allocate a company jet. I'm exaggerating, of course. There's undoubtedly less than I'm suggesting, and probably more than I want to believe."

"Boy, have you learned how to straddle a fence," said Pryce.

"It's also called trying to be fair. Shall we give our senior citizen the benefit of the doubt?"

"Senior? Aren't you two about the same age?"

"Actually, I'm a year and a half older but don't tell him. In the old days, when he wasn't calling me Squinty, it was Junior. It makes him feel wiser—and the rotten thing is that you come to realize he usually is."

"Then let's go with him. We still have the Euro-dossiers, and we'll probably use them. Talk to you later, Deputy Augustus Spartacus, or whatever in hell he called you." Cameron handed the phone back to Scofield. "We're going to play in your sandbox, Bray, at least for a while."

"If I'm wrong, I'll apologize, which I always do when I'm wrong. Come to think of it, I can't remember when I last had to apologize, so I couldn't have been wrong very often."

The Central Intelligence Black Hawk helicopter was in midflight on its north-northeast routing to the Chesapeake compound when the flight officer turned to the pilot. "Hey, Jimbo, isn't this airspace corridor supposed to be restricted?"

"You're damned right. Six in the morning and six at night. The word's gone out to all the fields, public and private, with very strict warnings. We're top secret, Lieutenant. Doesn't that make you feel real important?"

"Right now I've got the feeling that someone didn't get the word."

"What do you mean?"

"Look at the radar screen. There's an aircraft closing in on us. It couldn't be more than nine hundred or a thousand feet to the west."

"I don't need the screen. I can *see* it! Where are we? I'll reach Langley."

"Coordinates twelve and eighteen, over water, west of Taylors Island. Time to head north to touchdown."

"This is *nuts*!" exclaimed the pilot, staring out the chopper's side window panel. "It's one of *ours*, an SOA . . . He's heading right for us! Now he's sideslipping—the markings . . . good *Christ,* they're . . . *ours.* Get on the horn, I'm going *evasive*!"

These were the last words spoken. There was a shattering explosion, blowing apart the aircraft. What was left of the helicopter spiraled down to the water below, a fiery ball that disappeared rapidly as it sank.

The radar-tracking operator at Langley frowned at his upper-right screen. He punched several buttons, enlarging the images, then called out to his supervisor. "Bruce, what's going *on*?"

"About what?" asked the middle-aged, bespectacled man at the desk in the center of the large, antiseptic room.

"I lost Silent Horse."

"*What?* The *Chesapeake* run?" The supervisor sprang to his feet when the operator continued.

"It's *okay*!" he went on quickly. "It's back. Must have been a power glitch. Sorry."

"If it happens again, I'll break out with hives. Silent Horse, *Jesus*! The way those bastards in Congress are yelling, we probably haven't paid our electric bill."

Within minutes, and when the excited callers could get through, the police authorities in Prince Frederick, Tilghman, Taylors Island, and the Choptank River received a total of seventy-eight calls concerning a fireball in the early-evening sky, an explosion of sorts, a plane perhaps. Immediate inquiries to major and minor airports and airfields produced no information, much less confirmation of such an event. The police in Prince Frederick reached Andrews Air Force Base, a military/government complex, whose circumspect press-relations officer was duly courteous, sympathetic, and offered no concrete answer to any direct question. He simply was not aware of recent or ongoing atmospheric experimentation but, naturally, he was not in a position to deny the possibility. The American taxpayer was well served by the military's constant search for safety procedures and weather evaluations.

"The PR idiot at Andrews won't stay on or get off the pot," said the chief of police in Prince Frederick to the desk sergeant. "It was probably one of those low-flying reflecting weather balloons is the way I see it. Pass it along to the others and let's get back to work—if we have any."

The slow-moving skiff, its small engine puttering quietly, made its way out of the Choptank River and into Chesapeake Bay. The two elderly fishermen in soiled overalls, one aft, one in the middle of the motorized rowboat, held their poles out on opposite sides of the craft, trawling for the hungry early-evening fish. They would return to the riverbank picnic site where their wives tended to the fired grills, confident their husbands would come back with their supper. They had been doing so twice weekly for a number of years; they were automobile mechanics in the same garage, and their wives were sisters. It was a good life. They worked hard and the Chesapeake rich with their fancy cars provided steady employment. But best of all were these picnics, when the sisters would gab and the guys could diminish the bay's fish with their expertise and a couple of six-packs.

"*Al*," said the man at the helm. "Lookee over there!"

"Where?"

"On my side."

"At what, Sam?" asked Al, turning around.

"That round thing floatin' over yonder."

"Yeah, I see it. And there's another, to the left."

"Yep, I see that, too. I'll head over." The boat careened to the right, approaching both objects. "I'll be schnozzled!" cried Sam. "Them's life preservers."

"You get yours, then swing around and I'll pick up the other." Each did so, pulling both objects into the skiff.

"Wowee!" shouted Sam. "These is real U.S. Air Force

issue. Musta cost mebbe a hundred or even two hundred dollars apiece!"

"Probably three hundred, Sam. Ten bucks to make and the soldier boys buy 'em for three, mebbe four hundred. You heard about them toilet seats and the wrenches, right?"

"Sure did."

"That's why our taxes is so high, right?"

"Right, so let's get a little of our own back. We'll keep 'em, right?"

"Why not? All these years we never had a life preserver." Al held up his solid white ring in the fading light.

"We never needed one," said Sam. "This old thing is as safe as a cement whale."

"A cement whale would sink, buddy."

"Then we'll keep 'em. You know, when we was comin' out of the Choptank, I heard one of those helliocopters headin' upstream. You think he lost 'em?"

"Naw," objected Al. "The soldier boys are trained to get rid of things like this. Then they got to buy more, like the cracked toilet seats and the lousy wrenches. I read some-where it's part of the system."

"Hell, I'm patriotic, goddamn it. I was at Anzio and you was at that place in the Pacific nobody can pronounce."

"Eniwetok, buddy. A piece of crap."

"So we keep these, right?"

"Why not?"

"Good. Now let's catch some more fish before the beer runs out," said Sam.

No one knew what happened; nobody understood; every-thing was madness. The Langley chopper approached touchdown, the ground crew in place, when suddenly the aircraft swung up to the left, automatic weapons blazing from the open supply portal, killing or severely wounding the soldiers gathered below. Then, just as suddenly, the heli-copter veered to the right, sweeping over the compound as if looking for another target. It was swiftly apparent: the es-tate's great house, the mansion that overlooked the enormous lawn and the boathouse. The chopper circled, ascending as it did so, to make its final run of devastation.

Stunned by the thunderous explosions of gunfire, Scofield and Pryce ran to the south windows, the direction from which came the staccato bursts and human screams.

"Good *Christ*!" shouted Brandon. "They're coming in after us!"

"It's too concentrated," disagreed Cam rapidly. "One source—*look*! My God, it's Silent Horse! What the *hell*? . . ."

"Wanna bet, kiddo?" countered Scofield. "It's mocked up to *look* like Silent Horse! It's heading toward us. We're out of here!" Bray started for the door.

"No!" yelled Pryce. "The north balconies!"

"What?"

"There are two drainpipes. We don't know what he's carrying. Can you handle it?"

"Try me, sonny boy. I've got to find Toni!" As one, both men raced to the French doors across the room, flung them open, and stepped out on the small balcony with the wrought-iron railing. The helicopter thundered above, the roar ear-shattering as the aircraft headed north, slipping into a turn.

"Bombs!" yelled Pryce. "It's loaded with bombs!"

"He'll be coming back to blow this place to Jupiter—"

"He's got to get more altitude unless he wants to blow with it. Let's *go*!" Each man climbed over the railing on opposite sides of the balcony. They reached out, half lunging, grabbing on to their respective drainpipes. Like two panicked spiders, hands below descending hands, at moments in sheer slides, they plummeted to the ground as the chopper swung up into its turn to reach a safe altitude for a bombing run. "Stay down and as close to the foundation as you can," ordered Cameron. "He'll make at least two or three passes to unload that junk."

"Even in my senility I figured that out," said Scofield. "When he goes into his first pass, dropping his load, we can get away from here. . . . I've got to find *Toni*!"

"Do you know where she went?"

"She said something about the boathouse—"

"Why not?" Pryce broke in. "If worse comes to a lousy worser, we can zigzag across the bay."

"Your grammar's impeccable," mumbled Bray. "Here *comes* the son of a bitch!"

What followed was nothing short of complete horror. The entire top floors of the great house were demolished, leaving only fires and smoke and debris where once stood architectural grandeur.

"Let's *go*!" repeated Cameron. "Down to the boathouse! We've got at least forty seconds because his second pass will come from the south."

The two figures ran across the descending lawn as the mocked-up Silent Horse continued its reign of terror. Billows of fired smoke curled into the sky as the lethal explosions shook the earth. Breathless, Scofield and Pryce leaned against the wall of the boathouse, watching the devastation.

"Did you *hear* that?" asked a washed-out Brandon.

"I certainly did and *do*!" replied Cam. "And I want that bastard in front of my weapon, preferably at close range in front of his face."

"No, son, the other stuff!"

"What are you talking about?"

"The pops, the automatic fire. Our boys have regrouped and are going after that chopper!"

"Tell that to those who didn't survive."

"Wish I could," said Scofield, his lined features filled with sadness. *"Toni,"* he abruptly yelled. "Let's go inside and see if she's here!"

She was, and the scene under the sloping roof of the boathouse astonished both men. For across the slip where the Chris-Craft bobbed in the water, Antonia held an automatic in her hand. It was aimed at Lieutenant Colonel Leslie Montrose, who was holding a portable telephone, but not the sort issued by the Central Intelligence Agency.

"Remembering what you said about our colonel here and her phoning from the boathouse on two separate occasions, Mr. Pryce, I decided to make her my personal surveillance."

The explanation was interrupted by a series of deafening explosions from outside.

"There goes the rest of the house, Colonel," said Cameron in quiet, ice-cold fury. "Were you running the strike from in here? And how many others were killed, you *bitch*?"

"It will all be explained to you—if necessary," said Montrose calmly, coldly.

"It better be right *now*!" exploded Scofield, reaching into his belt and pulling out a handgun. "Otherwise I'll blow your pretty face apart. You're working for the enemy!"

"If it appears that way," said Montrose, "it's devoutly to be wished."

"You've been calling the White House!" roared Pryce. "Who's your contact, who's the mole, the *traitor* at Sixteen Hundred?"

"No one you'd know."

"I'd better learn now, or I'll tell my friend here to put a bullet in your head."

"I think you would—"

"You're goddamned right I would! You're garbage. *Talk*, bitch!"

"Apparently, I have no choice."

"You *don't*."

"My contact, as you call him, is close to the President, an authority on clandestine activities. I was—*am*—in a unique position to render a service."

"*What* position? What *service*?"

"The enemy, as you called them, kidnapped my son. He was taken from his school in Connecticut. Unless I supposedly do as they ask, they'll kill him."

A final earthshaking explosion shook the boathouse. Three windows were blown out, the fragments of glass showering over the Chris-Craft. Beyond, clearly visible among the debris, was a helium-filled red balloon attached to a destroyed upper window frame. It had miraculously survived, fluttering at the end of a long string.

It was the marker that led the killer aircraft to its target. Someone in the compound had been following Beowulf

Agate, and minutes before the strike knew exactly where he was.

12

The body bags and the wounded were airlifted out of the compound within the hour, the few stunned, uncomprehending local police kept at bay by the federal authorities. The relatively distant neighbors, horrified by the noise but unable to observe the site, which was prohibited, demanded explanations. They were given, in the main, hastily concocted "classified" fictions relative to drug interdiction. Four estates went on the real-estate market immediately, despite assurances that the successful "operation" had been completely shut down.

According to the radar-tracking tapes, it was assumed that the false Silent Horse had maneuvered due east over Delaware's Bethany Beach and out into the Atlantic, where it disappeared off the screen. Supporting confirmation came from the Patuxent River Naval Air Station in Nanticoke, southeast of Taylors Island. Their own interceptor screens showed an unidentified aircraft passing rapidly toward open ocean water when it abruptly was erased.

The professionals were in agreement, for it was known strategy where terrorist acts were concerned. The killer helicopter had headed for an Atlantic rendezvous where the crew bailed out, to be picked up by boat. Also, it could be assumed that prior to abandoning the chopper, a preset explosive was activated, blowing up the aircraft moments later, sending the remains to the bottom of the ocean. The Matarese was precise in all things.

Frank Shields walked with Scofield through the once peaceful, lovely compound. All around were painful sights of the carnage, mainly from the smoking debris of the destroyed great house. Shattered doors, windows, walls, and columns were nothing more than smoldering ruins, some as far away as six hundred feet, the length of two football fields.

"It's like a battlefield after a clash between two armies," said Bray solemnly, "only in this case, we didn't even know we were in combat. The *bastards*! . . . And it's my fault! I could have stopped the whole thing and I'll never forgive myself." Scofield's words trailed off quietly, painfully.

"I don't think you could have stopped it, Brandon—"

"Come on, Frank! You said you wanted us out of here and I said *no*. I'm a stubborn, pigheaded old fool who doesn't realize he should stop giving orders! I've been away too long to have the authority."

"I'm not trying to make you feel better, or even absolve you from all responsibility," Shields broke in. "I'm simply saying you couldn't have stopped it."

"How can you *say* that?"

"Because it would have happened wherever you were. . . . We're riddled, Bray, right up to interagency memoranda, including office codes and confidential instructions to departments."

"How do you know?"

"When the emergency signal came through and we learned what was taking place here, I called External Security and blew my stack. Where the hell was our air cover, our on-site sky patrols? They were always on the parameters of the corridor, six in the morning and six at night."

"So where were they?" asked Scofield angrily. "Goddamn it, we heard them every time the flyboys came in! They woke up Toni in the mornings. Where *were* they?"

"X-Security told me they received an in-house order under the standard emergency code to stand down the Silent Horse escort fighters due to severe chopper maintenance."

"*What?* Who authorized it?"

"Certainly not me, Brandon."

"Your *office*? Who in your office?"

"You don't understand. It could be anyone, but who would *dare*?"

"Rip your personnel apart!" yelled Bray, furious. "Put every son of a bitch and female slime on the racks until they bleed! You can't do any less—they may as well have manned the guns and dropped those bombs themselves. Eight people killed and four more who probably won't make it. *Do* something, Frank! I can't but you can—goddamn it, it's your *turf*!"

"Yes, it's my turf and it'll be done my way because I have both the authority and the responsibility, and my judgment calls aren't based on obstinacy or a desire to stamp my own imprimatur on anything."

"Oh? . . ." Scofield stopped; he reached over and gripped Shields's arm. "All right, Squinty, I deserved that."

"Yes, I think you did."

"I'm angry as hell!"

"So am I, Brandon," said the deputy director, his narrowed eyes steady. "But a putsch at the Agency, such as you suggest, would only drive our enemies farther underground while creating an atmosphere in which they could thrive. Dissension can be a very effective diversion."

"Oh, Jesus," said Bray, releasing Shields's arm as they continued walking. "I guess that's why you're an analyst and I'm not. . . . But what I *can't* understand is that if I'm the one they want deep-dead, why not an assassin's bullet in my head? Simple, clean, and quick, with minimum risk and maximum percentage of a kill. God knows we've got our own mole inside here. That red balloon wasn't put there by one of Santa Claus's elves."

"No, but it answers your question. Whoever it was had to know that you, Antonia, and Pryce were rarely, if ever, out of sight of compound surveillance."

"Is that a fact?"

"Certainly. We tried to consider every contingency we could dream up. We didn't invest all this effort and materials, to say nothing of money, to have you taken out from in here."

"How come I didn't spot it? Or Toni or Cameron? None of us is an amateur."

"It was done mostly by remote, according to sectors. A sergeant might call a corporal on his walkie-talkie and say 'Bomba'—that was you—'is leaving Sector Six, pick him up Seven.' We divided the compound into grids—you know the rest."

"Alternating vehicles," agreed Scofield. " 'Brown sedan turning off Eighth Avenue, tail it Forty-sixth Street.' "

"Precisely. That tactic never loses its efficiency."

"The old ones are usually the best, Frank. . . . What the *hell* are we talking about? We're up to our necks in bullshit and we sound like a couple of trainees!"

"We're talking like this so we can think, Brandon. It's all we've got left."

"We'd better stop thinking and start doing, Junior."

"Really, Bray, I can tolerate the 'Squinty,' but not 'Junior.' Besides, as I told Pryce, I'm older than you."

"You *are*?"

"Eighteen months and eleven days, *boy*. . . . Since you'd rather not think, what've you got in the doing department?"

"First," answered Scofield, "piece together what we have. The young corporal shot on the outside road; the infiltrator who scaled the wall to blow away Toni and me; Bracket and Denny poisoned, killed at a breakfast meant for me; the bombing strike we can't trace with a target marker placed in here by a mole or moles we can't find. Finally, there's the Montrose woman's contact at the White House. What does it all add up to?"

"Now you're back to thinking," said a sad but bemused Shields. "However, as to the Montrose flap, she's clean, even if she did panic. How she can even function is beyond me. She's got to be consumed by what may happen to her son."

"How did she get involved with Sixteen Hundred?"

"Colonel Bracket. He and his wife are—were, in his case of course—close friends of Montrose's. When the kidnapping took place and she was reached by what we can assume to be the Matarese, she was close to a breakdown. She had nowhere to turn, certainly not to the loose-lipped bureaucracy. According to Mrs. Bracket, who's under a great deal of stress herself right now, Montrose confided in her husband, Everett, a military colleague and in some ways a mentor."

"That sounds reasonable," said Bray, nodding as they rounded the tarmac that was the Black Hawk helicopter's touchdown. "She confided in him because he was a friend, a fellow West Pointer, and a confidant; she trusted him. But what about the White House?"

"Bracket was sent to graduate school at Yale and one of his classmates was Thomas Cranston—"

"I *know* that name," interrupted Scofield. "He was one of us, wasn't he?"

"Right up the ladder and damned good. In addition to his natural talents, he was a terrific salesman. If he'd stayed in Langley, he might have been plucked for the directorship, and I would have supported him."

"Squinty, that could have been *your* job! Don't you have any normal, jealous, hate-filled bones in that frail body of yours?"

"Not when I know I'm not qualified and enjoy what I do—which I do well. Cranston left the Agency to head up one of those think tanks funded by international academic wannabees. From there it was a quick jump into the political maelstrom. He's now the President's chief aide for national security."

"So Bracket sent Montrose to him."

"Yes, it seemed logical, and in light of what's happened, it was sound. We have expertise and clout, but we're obviously cancerous. Her son would have been killed if she'd come to us."

"But what can this Thomas Cranston do?"

"I have no idea, but whatever it is, it'll be very back-channel."

"To whom?"

"I don't know."

"Then we should find out."

"I've requested an off-limits meeting with him. Maybe

we'll learn something Sixteen Hundred doesn't want us to know—at this juncture."

"Aren't we on the same goddamned *side*?" asked Bray, raising his voice.

"We sometimes work at cross-purposes."

"That's *crap*!"

"No question about it, but that's the way things are."

"All right, all right. Naturally, I insist on being at that meeting. Also Pryce and Antonia. We're the experts, remember?"

"You'll be included," agreed Shields. "Not, however, Colonel Montrose. Cranston's worried about her anxiety level."

"Understandable . . . Now, about all these financial doings, the mergers, the corporations getting together, and, as I see it, corralling markets. I can help us here. I'm no computer but I remember names, relationships, friends of the Matarese, and the enemies they either swallowed up or destroyed. I just need methods of operation, backgrounds of company lineage—that's important, it's vital. The Matarese's ultimate weakness is that they're incestuous; they always call in their own, going back years, blackmailing or enlisting on greed. It's a pattern, completely secret, but the outlines are there and I'll recognize them."

"Our researchers are working on everything you wanted. You should have it all within a few days. It will be couriered to you in North Carolina."

"Another compound?"

"No, a mountain retreat consisting of a dozen terribly expensive condominiums in the Great Smokies. You should be quite comfortable at the unknowing taxpayers' expense."

"*Hold* it!" cried Scofield, his eyes on a scrap of silver metal on the tarmac. He reached down and picked it up. "It's from the Black Hawk that bombed us to hell," he said, spitting and rubbing the surface with his thumbnail.

"How do you figure?" asked the deputy director of the CIA.

"Our patrols fired back on the second or third pass and

blew apart a small section of the fuselage. It couldn't be anything else."

"So?"

"The paint's relatively new. Send this to Sikorsky. Maybe they can trace it to the original aircraft."

"I'm not sure I understand you, Brandon."

"It's part of a maybe-maybe answer—maybe."

"*What* is?"

"The Black Hawk that bombed and strafed us was a fake, disguised by the Matarese. Find out from Sikorsky who leased or bought an MH-Sixty K Special Operations chopper within the last six weeks."

"I thought you left that world behind."

"Antonia asked questions. One of the RDF gunslingers identified it."

Cameron Pryce and Antonia Scofield had gathered the personal effects of the dead and wounded—a chore the guilt-ridden Scofield could not accept. The unpleasant task finished, they joined Brandon and Frank Shields at the touchdown tarmac, along with Lieutenant Colonel Leslie Montrose.

"We'll be escorted to North Carolina by four F-sixteens, two circling in front, two behind," said the deputy director as the four compounders put what luggage they possessed on board.

The Black Hawk helicopter spiraled off the ground, Shields in the flight deck with the pilot and the flight officer, Scofield seated next to his wife, and Pryce with Montrose. For the latter two, the first airborne moments were awkward, neither knowing what to say to the other. Finally, Cameron spoke.

"I'm sorry, *truly* sorry—about everything."

"So am I," replied the Army officer coolly. "Would you have allowed Mr. Scofield to kill me?"

"That's a tough question. I thought you were responsible for the air strike . . . at the time I probably would have. Men were killed, a lot more wounded. My reaction was pretty violent."

"Mine would have been, too. I can understand that."

"Then why the *hell* didn't you tell us about your situation?"

"I was told not to, ordered not to."

"By whom? A guy named Thomas Cranston?"

"I knew you'd find out. Yes, Tom Cranston, and with the authority of his boss, the President."

"Why?"

"Because Cranston didn't trust the CIA's ability to thoroughly screen the compound. It turns out he was right, wasn't he?"

"A good friend of mine, who's up in the flight deck right now, is agonizing about that. He's in real pain."

"They're everywhere, Mr. Pryce, whoever they are they're *everywhere*! And we can't see them, we can't *find* them!"

"You don't know who they are?"

"I only know the terrible phone calls from places like Cairo and Paris and Istanbul, telling me what will happen to my son! What would you do in my position?"

"Exactly what you did, lady. Go to the top, if you can, not the amorphous, leak-prone middle."

"Cranston told me that there were channels above the intelligence community, or below, if you like, who could make threats no one else could match. I'm a mother, I want my *son* back! His father died in the service of his country, and I'm all he has left. If I can't have him, I'll die trying, which I'm perfectly willing to do. I'm a soldier, and I know the risks, and I'll go to the last extremity to get what's due me. Which is why, thank God, I was able to go to the top. You're part of a flawed organization, Mr. Pryce, and I'll go around you to get my boy back. My husband and I have given enough!"

"May I make a suggestion?" asked Pryce, letting the emotion of the moment subside.

"I'll listen to any suggestion as long as I believe the person making it is on my side."

"I'm on your side, Colonel. So is Frank Shields, so are the Scofields."

"I'm sure you are, as far as you can be."

"I don't know what that means."

"You have your own agendas, and you have to cover your asses—reputations is a gentler way of putting it. I have only one agenda, the safe return of my son."

"Not to contradict you," said Cameron softly, "and I don't mean to, but it seems to me you handled your responsibilities back at the compound extremely well. It was hardly your primary agenda."

"Tom Cranston told Ev Bracket that it might be connected, so between them they got me the assignment."

"*Might* be connected? That's all you know?"

"Beyond the existence of a terrorist organization whose targets are you and the Scofields, especially Mr. Scofield, we aren't on a need-to-know basis regarding specifics."

"You *bought* that shit?" said Pryce angrily. "Excuse my language, but it *is* pure shit—sophistry is the gentler way of putting it."

"I buy that shit, or sophistry, because I believe in the chain of command. I grant you it, too, has its flaws, but it's far more often right than wrong. Information in the hands of the inexpert or inexperienced can be extremely dangerous."

"Give me a specific."

"I think it's encapsulated in that old World War Two poster. 'Loose lips sink ships.' "

"Even among those who're skippering those ships?"

"If they should know, they'll know."

"Has it ever occurred to you that if even one captain of a ship isn't informed, he may crash into another vessel?"

"I'm sure such possibilities are always factored. . . . What *is* your point, Mr. Pryce?"

"You're a major player, Colonel, and you don't have the whole picture—you should have. I'd think you'd demand it, considering Everett Bracket's death, his murder, to be precise. He was your friend, a very close friend. In your place, I'd be terribly sad and angry as hell."

"I mourn in my own way, Mr. Pryce. I lost a husband, remember? As to anger, believe me, it's there. . . . What was your suggestion? I recall you said you had one."

"And you've just reinforced my argument for your taking it."

"I beg your pardon?"

"The chain of command you're so fond of—it's being misused and abused. A meeting's been arranged between me, the Scofields, and Cranston; Shields insisted on it. But you're not going to be there."

"Oh?" Leslie's eyes reflected her instinctive suspicion and her reluctant acceptance.

"I think you should be," Cameron continued quickly. "I repeat, you're a major player with a great deal at stake. You should have the whole picture, not just fragments. Sometimes we carry the need-to-know maxim too damned far until the left hand isn't sure where the right hand is. Take my word for it, I've been there in the cold. You should be at that meeting."

"There's not much I can do about it," said Montrose in a caustic monotone. "Undersecretary Cranston made a decision. I'm sure he had his reasons."

"They're fatuous. He's concerned about your very personal involvement. He thinks you might fold."

"I resent that."

"So do I. What I resent even more is that, de facto, he's eliminating any contributions you might make."

"How could I do that?"

"It would depend on what was said in the calls to you. Were you able to tape any of them?"

"No. The men who spoke to me—different men—said they had equipment that could detect such devices, and if they were activated, the consequences would be severe. However, every conversation was indelibly printed on my mind and in a notebook back in a safe in my house."

"Does Cranston have that notebook, or copies of the pages?"

"No, I simply gave him summaries."

"He was satisfied with that?"

"It's what he asked for."

"He's not only fatuous, he's an idiot," said Pryce.

"I think he's a very brilliant and caring man."

"He may be both, but he's also an idiot. And how can you say that? He's excluded you from an important conference that ultimately, directly affects your son."

"I'll say it again," replied the lieutenant colonel, "he had his reasons. Perhaps he's right; how objective can I be?"

"I'd say your control is outstanding. I can't know what being a parent in your circumstances is like, but I know why I've never told my mother, father, brother, or sister where I'm going or what I'm doing. . . . Don't you *want* to be at the meeting?"

"With all my heart—"

"Then you will be," interrupted Cameron firmly. "And I'll only have to use a little blackmail to get you there."

"You've lost me. Blackmail?"

"Hell, yes. I can threaten Shields with the news that the Scofields and I refuse to attend without you, and he'd better straighten Cranston out."

"Why would he accept that?"

"Number one, they both need us, and far more important, number two, Cranston never asked for that notebook of yours, he settled for summaries. That alone would send Frank, the analyst, and Brandon, the once and former super-deep-cover, into orbit."

"Weren't the summaries sufficient?"

"Never."

"Why not? They conveyed the essential information. What else was there?"

"Word usage, references, strange idioms, anything could lead anywhere," replied Pryce, the total professional. "As I read it," he continued softly, beside Montrose, "Cranston is one hell of a geopolitical strategist, like a Kissinger, but he was never in the field himself. There are the forests and there are the trees. Cranston may be terrific in projecting the greenery, but he doesn't know the difference between a real tree and a plastic stage prop that has a ton of explosives inside it. . . . You'll be at that meeting, lady—excuse me, Colonel."

She was.

———

The military turboprop took off from Andrews Air Force Base at five o'clock in the morning carrying two passengers, Undersecretary Thomas Cranston and Deputy Director Frank Shields of the Central Intelligence Agency. Its destination was a private airfield in Cherokee, North Carolina, seven miles south of a condominium resort development called Peregrine View in the Great Smoky Mountains. As each man respected the confidentiality of the other prior to the meeting that was to take place barely two hours away, the conversation was innocuous, but not without information.

"How did you fellows find this place?" asked the undersecretary.

"The developers extravagantly overbuilt a golf sanctuary that only the wealthiest could afford, but unfortunately the wealthiest were, by and large, too old to take the altitude as well as the difficult paths," replied Shields, chuckling. "The developers went under and we bought it for half the paper."

"I think Congress ought to reevaluate its concerns about your budget. You're damn smart businessmen."

"We can spot a bargain when we see one, Mr. Undersecretary."

"What's it like?"

"Very elegant and very isolated. We keep a minimum crew to maintain it, and use it for a maximum-security sterile area. In the old days, a lot of Soviet defectors learned to play golf there."

"Such a capitalist game—"

"Most took to it like padding their KGB expense accounts in Washington's favorite restaurants."

"Yes, I remember seeing copies of those expense reports. In the old days. . . . Where are we meeting?"

"It's called Estate Four, a golf cart will take us there. It's about a quarter of a mile up the mountain trail."

"Will I need an oxygen mask?"

"Not at your age. Possibly at mine."

They sat in comfortable chairs in the living room of a well-appointed condominium near the base of the Appalachians'

Great Smoky Mountains. Scofield was next to his wife, Pryce and Lieutenant Colonel Montrose to their left, she in civilian clothes, a pleated dark skirt and a white silk blouse. Across the room were the deputy director and Undersecretary Cranston.

Thomas Cranston was a medium-sized man, slightly corpulent, with a face that might have been sculpted by a benign Bernini. Soft in flesh, but aquiline in features, he had the air of a middle-aged don in academia who had heard it all but remained intellectually skeptical. His large eyes, magnified by his tortoiseshell glasses, conveyed a desire to understand, not confront—unless it was necessary. He spoke.

"After your friends from the compound stopped shouting at me, they made clear the error of my ways. Again, I'm sorry."

"Tom, I didn't mean for anything like this to happen—"

"If you didn't, *I* did and do, little girl!" broke in Brandon Scofield angrily.

"My name is Montrose, Leslie, and I'm a lieutenant colonel in the United States Army, *not* a 'little girl'!"

"You're not much of an intelligence officer, either, and neither is Mr. Fancy-pants here. Good *Christ,* you've got verbatim records of those phone calls, or at least close to it, and this clown settles for *summaries*?"

"May I remind you, Mr. Scofield," said Montrose with military authority, "Undersecretary Cranston is an aide to the President of the United States."

"You sure throw around the U.S. of A. a lot, don't you? I'll *bet* he's an *under*secretary, I wouldn't let him be secretary to my cat!"

"That's enough, Brandon." Shields shot up from his chair.

"Knock it off, Bray," said Pryce, leaning forward.

"You've made your point, dear," added Antonia.

"Whoa, hold it," said Cranston, a thin smile creasing his lips. "Agent Scofield has every right to be upset with me. I'm not above learning, and as has been pointed out, I've neither been in a hostile field nor do I have the expertise to advise

those who have been. My work is different, and is of little
help to you in the short run."

"Try a long pass," said Bray under his breath.

"I'll do better, Agent Scofield, I'll try a 'Holy Mary,' if
my football parlance is accurate."

"How so?" asked Cameron.

"I've studied Leslie's—the colonel's—notebook, as well
as placing the pages into a word-processing computer with
its myriad functions. My former and far more knowledgeable colleague, Frank here, told me what to examine, and
since it was easier, with Leslie's consent, that I retrieve the
notebook first, I may have come up with something."

"Do tell," said Scofield sarcastically. "So far your 'Hail
Mary' is heading for a 'Judas trap.'"

"Cut it out, Brandon," Shields interrupted wearily, sitting down.

"Can't help it, Squinty. These types put me beyond salvage."

"I was in my middle teens when that egregious decision
was made, Mr. Scofield, and having read the record, I would
have firmly dissented. You may accept that or not."

"You're convincing, I'll say that," responded Bray. "I
also believe you, although I'm not sure why. What did you
come up with?"

"Two expressions that appear in each of the communications Colonel Montrose received from her son's kidnappers. There are minor variations but the redundancy is there,
that's the best way to say it."

"Then say it more clearly," said Scofield.

"The colonel—"

"'Leslie' is fine, Tom," interrupted Montrose, "they
know we're friends, and right now military titles are a bit
unnerving. They're rather cold, aren't they?"

"We're all going to swear we never heard that," said
Pryce, smiling gently at the lieutenant colonel, who could
not help but laugh softly, embarrassed. "Please go on, Mr.
Undersecretary," continued Cameron.

"All right—Leslie was contacted about her son a total of
seven times, twice from the Netherlands—Wormerveer and

Hilversum; we assume that's Amsterdam—the rest from Paris, Cairo, Istanbul, and over here, Chicago and Sedgwick, Kansas. The geographical—global—spread was basic to their intimidation. Who were they? Where do they come from? It was meant to be terrifying. In each case, the men who called her issued instructions that were to be carried out once she was inside the compound; they were to be followed or else her boy would be killed . . . slowly."

"Good *God*," whispered Antonia, looking at Montrose.

"What were the expressions?" asked Shields. "The two expressions you picked up?"

"The first was in all her instructions. They were to be executed 'with great precision.' The second was in an admonition that was intrinsic to their threat of reprisal."

" 'Reprisal' doesn't say it, Tom," Leslie broke in. "It's the torture and death of my child."

"Yes." Cranston paused, avoiding her stare. "The words were as follows, starting with the first call from Wormerveer in the Netherlands—"

"Which you assumed to be Amsterdam," interrupted Scofield. "Why?"

"I'll get to that later," replied the presidential aide.

"The words, please, from Wormerveer," said Frank Shields, his creased eyes slits of concentration.

" 'Stay cool,' a peculiarly American expression—spoken by a man in the Netherlands."

"African American, to be more accurate," added Pryce, "although it's been incorporated far beyond its origins. Sorry, go on."

"From Hilversum, also Dutch, 'Remember, be cool.' In the Paris and Cairo calls, the words 'stay cool' reappear; then from Istanbul, 'it is imperative to remain cool'—from a *Turkish* intermediary. A remarkable linguistic transliteration, wouldn't you say?"

"Depends who's saying it," answered the current and former Beowulf Agate. "What else?"

"Here in the States, from Chicago and Sedgwick, Kansas: 'Don't lose your cool' and 'Cool it is, Colonel, or the cradle falls.' "

Montrose closed her eyes, the hint of a tear appearing. She inhaled deeply and resumed her military posture in the chair.

"So summarize what we've got," said Scofield harshly, glancing painfully at Leslie, then turning to the White House man. "You're pretty fond of summaries, so summarize."

"The instructions were scripted, written out for the messengers to use regardless of where they were calling from. Leslie described the voices as being diverse, the accents varied, which is perfectly natural. What isn't natural is the consistent use of the terms 'with precision,' and the variations on 'cool.'"

"I think we'd all agree with that, Tom," said Shields. "What's your point?"

"Would you also agree that the word 'cool' is American-oriented?"

"Of course," interrupted an impatient Brandon. "So what?"

"Designed for an American ear, for vernacular emphasis—"

"It would seem so," agreed Pryce. "What else are you suggesting?"

"The obvious," replied Cranston. "The instructions were written by an American, someone in the upper ranks of the Matarese."

Lieutenant Colonel Montrose bolted forward in her chair. "The *who*?" she asked.

"That's their name, Leslie," said the undersecretary of state. "The people who kidnapped your boy are called the Matarese. I've prepared a file for you, everything we have on record, in the main supplied by Mr. Scofield here, known to the Matarese as Beowulf Agate."

Montrose snapped her head toward Bray and started to speak when she was cut off by Frank Shields. "I see where you're going, Tom," he said, oblivious to Leslie's consternation. "The upper ranks, the *hierarchy*."

"Nobody below that level would be permitted the information, or even know who our colonel is."

"And if Brandon's right, somewhere in the Matarese group over here, probably a company or a conglomerate marching to its drum, is a heavy corporate type who wrote out those instructions. . . . Besides Chicago, where was the other call from?"

"Sedgwick, Kansas."

"I'll have the research unit that's compiling all the materials for Bray concentrate on Illinois and Kansas." The CIA deputy director got out of his chair and walked across the room to a telephone.

"It may not lead anywhere but it's a start, Frank," said Cranston, nodding.

"Will *somebody* tell me what's going *on*?" cried Montrose, standing up defiantly. "What materials? And what is this *Matarese*?"

"Read the file, Colonel," replied Scofield, slightly, purposely emphasizing her rank as opposed to the demeaning *little girl*. "When you're finished, Toni and I will add whatever we can, which will be considerable."

"Thank you, but what does it all have to do with my *son*?"

"Everything," said Beowulf Agate.

13

The formerly bankrupt resort known as Peregrine View at the base of the Great Smoky Mountains was as visually different from the Chesapeake compound as its security personnel were from the RDF and CIA patrols; instead of the latter, there was an elite Special Forces undercover Gamma unit from Fort Benning, recently returned from Bosnia. The soldiers were told only that the guests of the government sequestered there were selected embassy officials brought back for debriefing, and since their posts had been sensitive—read borderline dangerous—they were to be guarded from any external interferences—read physical threats. It was enough; these were professional military men used to understanding the unspoken. It was the nature of their Gamma operations: infiltrate and perform, the orders indirect and obfuscated.

Since everything was drastically altered in this area, and everyone in the Chesapeake compound gone but still under surveillance, provisions were brought in from the town of Cherokee, a welcome relief from the twice-daily thunder of the helicopters. However, small planes regularly flew into the Cherokee airstrip carrying the materials requested by Scofield and were driven up to the restricted mountain complex. These ranged from financial reports to all manner of correspondence, from executive speeches to interoffice memoranda where they could be secretly unearthed, whether by expert thieves or bribery. Within a few days the cartons filled the living room of Brandon and Antonia's bi-level condominium, known as Estate 6. Flanking this dwelling were Estates 5 and 7, respectively occupied by Pryce and Lieutenant Colonel Montrose.

Frank Shields and Thomas Cranston had returned to their posts at Langley and the White House, staying in constant touch over sterile telephones and confidential-mode fax machines. The work was laborious, the four of them poring over the materials for hours at a time until spines were stiff and eyes exhausted. The financial reports were the worst: myriad columns of figures followed by addenda of projections and analyses of assets procured or on the table. For instance, "Project M-113" would be briefly described as "undervalued. See Section 17 in this report, then cross-check with Sections 28 and 36 for clarification." To make matters worse, the language was out of a textbook for advanced economics—theoretical and pragmatic, definitely on the doctoral level and the proverbial "Greek" for the layman. But one thing was clear to Brandon Scofield. These abstruse insertions were designed to mystify to the point of unintelligibility, going to the precipice of illegality, but not over the edge.

"M-One Thirteen is never spelled out!" yelled a frustrated Bray. "And the lousy thing is, it doesn't *have* to be."

"I couldn't get through that stuff," said Cameron, "but what do you mean?"

"The precepts of laissez-faire, which beat the hell out of the Malthusian laws of economics."

"Come again?" asked Leslie.

"Competition," answered Scofield. "Until a bid is actually made, opposing interests have no right to know one is projected or even thought about."

"What's that got to do with the Malthusian thing?"

"Iron, bronze, and gold, youngster. Iron wants to become bronze, and bronze would prefer being gold, and gold wants the whole kit and caboodle. Guess who's gold?"

"The Matarese," said Pryce.

"Sweet Jesus, you're filling the hole in your head. . . . Mark this one down. It's a possible Matarese."

"What's the company?" asked Antonia, paper and pencil in hand.

"A global conglomerate all the way. Atlantic Crown, headquarters Wichita, Kansas."

"We need more than a corporate report, Bray," said Cameron.

"This is just the beginning, son. Once we've found a pattern—if we found the pattern—we know what to go for. I'm surprised I have to tell you that."

"Forgive me, darling," Antonia sat forward in her chair, "but I think we should take some time off. We've been at this for hours, and I, for one, am losing my concentration."

"I hate to stop," said Leslie, a sheaf of papers in her hand, "but I agree. I have to continuously reread so the words mean something."

"Wimps," mumbled Scofield, yawning. "Although you may have a point. I could use a drink."

"You could use a nap, my darling. Come, let me take you upstairs."

"An animal," said Bray, winking at Pryce and Montrose. "She's sheer animal. Can't wait to get me into a bedroom."

"Very refreshing," Leslie noted. "It's usually the other way around, isn't it?"

"That's a myth, dear," replied Antonia. "Dogs chase cars, but they can't drive."

"I'm surrounded by pharisees." Scofield rose from the chair, once again yawning as he and Toni walked to the staircase.

"Perhaps I'll scare the hell out of him," said Antonia, wiggling her hips.

"You could be sorry, luv—I think." The couple started up the steps, disappearing behind the staircase wall.

"They're really adorable," said Montrose.

"Love her, hate him," said Cameron quietly.

"You don't mean that for a minute."

"No, I don't," admitted Pryce. "He's got more in two brain cells than I have in my whole head. He's been where few of us will ever go."

"He's also a very troubled man."

"Over events he could never control," added Cam. "He finds guilt where there shouldn't be any."

"That's up to each of us to discover, isn't it? Guilt's intrinsic to all of us, according to certain beliefs."

"None that I subscribe to, Colonel. Doubts, yes, not guilt, unless you're guilty of something rotten you can control."

"That's quite philosophical, Mr. Pryce—"

"Cam or Cameron, remember?" he interrupted. "We agreed on that . . . Leslie."

"Sometimes I choose to forget."

"Why?"

"Frankly, I'm uncomfortable. You're a very nice guy, Cam, and I have other things on my mind—one other thing, to be exact."

"Your son, of course."

"Of course."

"He's on my mind, too, believe that."

Montrose looked at him from the adjacent chair. "I do,"

she said finally, their eyes locked. "It can't be the same, however, can it?"

"Of course not," agreed Pryce, "but that doesn't lessen my concern. So where are we?"

"I'd like to take a walk, get some air. Brandon's little cigars are pleasantly aromatic, but a lot goes a long way."

"Tell him, he'll stop or cut down."

"Good heavens, no. In his way he's as obsessed as I am, and if puffing away helps him, so be it."

"Still, I gather you don't smoke," said Pryce aimlessly as they got out of their chairs.

"You'd be wrong. Jim and I both quit. We monitored each other, in fact, but when he was lost I'm afraid I took it up again. Not heavily and never in front of the troops—that's frowned upon—but there's something to be said for calming the nerves, no matter how dumb."

"Come on, let's go for that walk." They started toward the door.

"I forgot again," said Leslie as Cameron opened the steel-plated sterile house door. "We delicate females aren't supposed to walk around alone. We're to be accompanied by one of you big, strong men, or preferably a Gamma patrol."

"I have an idea that both you delicate females could nail our tails to a wall with one shot."

"How delicately spoken."

"Walk, smart-ass."

Montrose laughed, briefly to be sure, but it was a nice laugh, a genuine laugh.

They came to a fork in the mountain path, contrarily paved with white concrete, which was easier on elderly feet and golf carts. The left side descended gradually to a pond, a challenge on the course fronting the sixteenth tee, a scenic spray of water cascading from a pump in the center. The right path ascended more sharply toward a stretch of woods that separated the first nine holes from the second.

"The fountain of youth or the forest primeval?" said Pryce.

"Oh, the forest, to be sure. There's nothing that recycled grime could do for our youths, what we remember of them."

"Hey, neither was that long ago. I gave up my wheel-chair, and I don't see any gray in your hair."

"There's a strand or ten, believe me. You haven't looked close enough."

"I won't follow that up—"

"*Thank* you," interrupted Leslie, bearing right on the white concrete and immediately continuing. "Have you changed your mind about Tom Cranston?"

"Not entirely," answered Cameron, catching up. "He gets too apologetic, too humble too quickly. That's not normal for such a bright guy. Frankly, I'm not sure I trust him."

"Bunk!" said Montrose. "He's smart enough to realize when he's wrong and to admit it. Like he did with the cell phone in the compound."

"Which phone?"

"The one he sent me on the Black Hawk, ostensibly a package from my son. The handwritten note inside, which I was ordered to burn, said—and I quote verbatim—'My *God,* I forgot the Agency can trace those phones of yours! Use this and I'm sorry.'"

"Still, you switched phones with Bracket."

"The hell I did!"

"Frank traced the White House calls to his phone; there were none on yours."

"Then it must have happened at the beginning of our transfer to Chesapeake. Everett opened the carton with our two phones, checked the batteries and the backups, and simply handed me one."

"Didn't he know each was registered?"

"I don't think he gave à damn. Ev could be impatient with minor details. Anyway, what difference did it make?"

"Blind alleys."

"What?"

"We've got enough blind alleys in this so-called opera-tion," said Pryce. "We don't need false ones. But there's a real one left from the compound. Who's got Bracket's phone? It disappeared."

"I'm sure it's at the bottom of Chesapeake Bay," replied Leslie. "Whoever stole it would get rid of it as soon as possible. It could be traced, even monitored, remember?"

"Why was it stolen in the first place?"

"Perhaps to be deprogrammed and sold, if it could be smuggled out. Or by the mole who was told to steal it for intercepts. If that was the case, he probably got cold feet and deep-sixed it, since everyone's under scrutiny, even after they left the compound."

"If this, if that, and perhaps—blind alleys," he said again.

"To change the subject but not really, do you think Mr. Scofield—Brandon—is on to something?"

"About that conglomerate, Atlantic something?"

"Atlantic Crown," said Montrose. "You see its commercials on television all the time. They're usually very classy and on the better programs."

"They never seem to sell a product," agreed Pryce, "just low-key scientific processes, as I recall. But to answer your question, if Bray smells something, there's usually an odor."

Suddenly, from behind them, a man shouted; it was a Gamma patrol and he was running up the concrete path. "Guests *Three* and *Four*! Guest Number One has been trying to reach you on your phones!"

"Good Lord, I left my purse in the condo."

"And I left my phone on the table."

"He's mad as hell, folks," said the breathless soldier in camouflage fatigues as he approached. "He says he wants you back at . . . the *base* camp, he called it."

"A term from the past," clarified Cameron.

"I *know* what it means, sir, but this isn't a combat-incursion area."

"It is to him."

"Let's go!" said Leslie.

Scofield was pacing back and forth in front of the dark fireplace, Antonia in an easy chair patiently reading from a single fax sheet.

"The reason we have our telephones," said Brandon,

abruptly stopping as Pryce and Montrose walked through the door, "is for immediate communication, or am I wrong?"

"You're not wrong and we're guilty of all charges," replied Cameron. "Now let's forgo the Savonarola bullshit and tell us why you interrupted a very pleasant walk."

"Sorry, Brandon, we were simply careless," said Montrose.

"I hope not in all things—"

"*That* is offensive!" protested Leslie.

"Shut up, my dear," said Antonia, glaring at Scofield, "and get on with it."

"All right, all right! . . . Last week at the compound I told you to forget the overseas connections and concentrate on what we've got here, correct?"

"That's what you said, but I never said I agreed. Only temporarily, along with Frank Shields."

"Well, I take it back, or as the colonel would say, I rescind the order."

"Why?"

"London's MI-Five found a passel of notes in a locked drawer of that Englishwoman's husband, the one who killed her. They refused to fax them for security reasons, but the fax they did send is mighty interesting, whets the appetite. . . . Give it to him, Toni." She did and Cam read the thin, glossy sheet.

Papers found in a locked drawer indicate that Gerald Henshaw, vanished husband of the murdered Lady Alicia Brewster, kept obscure records of his associates. According to Lady Alicia's children, a boy and a girl, both in their teens, now alone and severely troubled, Henshaw was frequently inebriated and blurted out confused and contradictory statements while drunk. Suggest you fly over an experienced field officer as well as an American psychologist, a specialist in adolescent behavior, perhaps, to assist us. And to keep it out of London circles, as it were.

Pryce handed the fax to Leslie. She read it and stated simply, "They don't need a psychologist, they need a mother. And I'm it."

14

The U.S. diplomatic jet landed at Heathrow Airport and taxied to the restricted annex, where Pryce and Montrose were met by Sir Geoffrey Waters, chief of Internal Security, MI-5. The British intelligence officer was a thickset, broad-shouldered man of medium height and in his middle fifties, his full head of brown hair gray at the temples. There was about him an air of quiet humor, his light blue eyes bordering on the mischievous, as if to convey the silent message, *Been there, seen that, so what?* The Air Force crews unloaded their passengers' luggage, which was minimal, one suitcase apiece, and the MI-5 chief instructed the ground personnel to carry them to the open boot of his car, a large Austin.

"Sir Geoffrey Waters, I expect?" said Leslie, emerging from the plane first.

"Mrs. Montrose, welcome to the U.K.! Your luggage is being taken to the car."

"Thank you."

"Sir Geoffrey?" Cameron walked up to Leslie's side, his arm extended. "The name's Pryce, Cameron Pryce." They shook hands.

"*Really,* old boy?" said Waters in mock surprise. "I never would have guessed! Of course, we have a file on you at least a foot thick, but who counts inches, right?"

"Nothing's sacred. . . . Of course, our file on you is probably two feet long, but then we can't count very high."

"Ah, colonial exaggeration, it's why I adore Americans! However, one thing *is* sacred. Drop the 'Sir,' please. It's totally unwarranted and given only to make somebody else look good."

"You sound like someone I know—we both know."

"My, my, how *is* Beowulf Agate?"

"As wolflike as ever."

"Good, we need that. . . . Come along now, we've a ton of work to do, but you'll need the night off after your flight. It's almost six o'clock, barely noon your time; you'll have to adjust a bit. You'll be picked up at eight in the morning."

"From where?" Montrose asked pleasantly.

"The undeserved 'Sir' does have its advantages. I wangled you a suite at the Connaught off Grosvenor Square. Top drawer, in my judgment."

"Top contingency funds," added Pryce.

"A *suite*? . . ." Leslie looked pointedly at Waters.

"Oh, not to be concerned, my dear. Separate rooms, naturally. The reservations are in the names of Mr. John Brooks and Miss Joan Brooks, brother and sister. If anyone should inquire, which is highly unlikely, you're over here to settle an inheritance from a British uncle."

"Who's the attorney?" asked Cameron. "The solicitor, I mean."

"Braintree and Ridge, Oxford Street. We've used them before."

"You're smooth, Geof, I'll say that."

"I should hope, after all these years, the rough edges have been ground down a touch. . . . Come now, into the car."

"May I say something?" Montrose's immobility stopped both men.

"Of course, what is it?"

"The suite's fine, Geoffrey, but our flight was west to east, not the reverse. As you mentioned, it's still around noon for us. I'm not at all tired—"

"It will catch up with you, my dear," interrupted the MI-5 chief.

"Probably, but I *am* extremely anxious to get to work. I think you know why."

"I certainly do. Your child."

"Can't we take an hour to freshen up and start?"

"I have no problem with that," said Pryce.

"Your suggestion is music to my suddenly undeaf ears! Tell you what, chaps, since we can't remove any papers from the office, a car will pick you up, say around seven-thirty. If you're hungry, you'll have time for room service, not the dining room, however."

"Great contingency funds," mumbled Cameron. "Wish you'd talk to a guy named Shields in Washington."

"*Frank* Shields? Old *Squint Eyes*? Is he still around?"

"I think I'm hearing a broken record," said Pryce.

Rome, five o'clock in the afternoon

Julian Guiderone, in a dark silk suit from the Via Condotti, walked down the cobblestoned Due Macelli and up the Spanish Steps toward the canopied entrance of the celebrated Hassler-Villa Medici hotel. As he had done in Cairo's Al Barrani Boulevard, he paused in the narrow cul-de-sac and lit a cigarette with his gold Dunhill, his eyes straying to the top of the famous stone steps glorified by Byron. He stood still and watched for a man or a woman who might quickly emerge, his or her own eyes darting about. None appeared. He could proceed.

Guiderone crossed under the scarlet canopy; the automatic glass doors opened and he entered the opulent marble lobby, immediately heading to the left and the bank of glistening brass elevators. He was aware that several hotel guests, also waiting, glanced at him. It did not concern him; he was used to the attention. He realized that when he cared to, he radiated natural authority, a superiority born of features, breeding, height, and tailoring; it was ever thus, and he knew it, he welcomed it.

The elevator doors opened; he walked in last and pressed the button for the fifth floor. Two stops later he was there, emerging into the heavily carpeted hallway, studying the brass plaque that directed him to the suite he sought. It was at the far end of the corridor, on the right, a small blue circle affixed to the doorknob. He knocked on the center panel four times, a pause of one second between raps; he heard a click and walked inside.

The room was large and ornate, the walls covered with pastel scenes of ancient Rome, the soft velour colors varied but predominantly gold, white, red, and blue. The events depicted ranged from chariot races in the Colosseum to erupting fountains to the more famous statuary from the chisels of Michelangelo and his contemporaries. The central area of the room was filled with four rows of four chairs, all facing a lectern, and all were occupied, the occupants exclusively men. Their ages were as diversified as their nationalities, from early thirties through the forties, the fifties, and the sixties. Their origins covered all of Europe, the United States, and Canada.

Everyone in attendance, in one form or another, was in the profession of journalism. Some were recognized reporters, others editors of repute; a number were controllers or financial consultants, and the remainder were on the boards of several major newspapers.

And each—in one form or another—had been compromised by the son of the Shepherd Boy, the ultimate leader of the Matarese.

Julian Guiderone walked slowly, deliberately to the lectern as the room became silent. He smiled benevolently, then began.

"I fully understand that there are those of you here unwillingly, not of your own volition or commitment, but under duress. I sincerely hope to change your minds so you will come to understand the progressive enlightenment of our objectives. I am no monster, gentlemen. Rather, I am a man extraordinarily blessed with vast wealth, and I can assure you, I'd much prefer tending to my widespread interests—my investments, my horses, my athletic teams, my hotels—than leading what amounts to an economic revolution for the good of us all. But I cannot. . . . Let me ask you a rhetorical question. Who but a man with unlimited resources, a man beholden to no one for his survival or lifestyle, with no responsibility to special interests whatsoever, can objectively discern the financial sickness that pervades our civilized nations? I submit that only such a man *can*, for he has nothing to *gain*. Conversely, he could lose a great deal, but even that would be insignificant in the long run. . . . What I am, gentlemen, is the unfettered, completely neutral referee, an arbiter, if you like. But to fulfill that vision and my destiny, I need your support. I trust I have it, so let me hear your reports. No names are necessary, only your publications. We'll start with the first row on my left."

"I am the principal investments adviser for the Manchester *Guardian,*" said the Englishman, his reluctance evident in his low, hesitant voice. "As scheduled, I've delivered the long-term economic projections relative to the paper's anticipated accelerating losses over the next decade. They call for supplemental capital far beyond anything envisioned by the *Guardian*'s directors. There's no alternative but to seek a massive infusion of external funds . . . or an affiliation with other journalistic publications." The man from the *Guardian* paused, adding quietly, "I've had highly confidential meetings with my counterparts at the *Independent,* the *Daily Express, The Irish Times,* and the Edinburgh *Evening News.*" He abruptly stopped. He was finished, his face set in disgust and defeat.

"*Le Monde,* Paris, Marseilles, Lyon, *et tout de France,*" spoke the Frenchman sitting beside the Britisher. "As our section—this first row—is primarily concerned with structured finance, I echo my English colleague's calculations and have acted accordingly. The projections are self-evident. Along with normal inflation, the dwindling resources of paper accompanied by soaring prices demand economic reassessments, basically consolidation. In this pursuit, I, too, have held very discreet talks with select executives of *France Soir, Le Figaro,* and the Paris *Herald.* They will bear fruit."

"There's no doubt of that," said a balding American in his middle fifties. "The technological advances in computerized, multifeed print operations make it irresistible; one plant can service a minimum of six newspapers, tomorrow a dozen, with totally diversified copy. My contacts at *The New York Times, The Washington Post, Los Angeles Times,* and *The Wall Street Journal* are merely waiting for the first shoe to drop. They call it survival."

"You can add the Toronto *Globe and Mail* and the *Edmonton Journal* to the list," completed the fourth member of the row, a youngish Canadian, his eyes alive with the realization that he was among the elite of his profession. "When I return, I'm heading west to initiate preliminary negotiations with the *Winnipeg Free Press* and the *Vancouver Sun*!"

"Your enthusiasm is to be applauded," said the son of the Shepherd Boy, "but keep in mind the walls of utter secrecy within which you must operate."

"Naturally! Of *course*!"

"Now to our second row," continued Guiderone, "our section devoted to the boards of our leading international publications, namely, again, *The New York Times* and the *Guardian,* as well as Rome's *Il Giornale,* and Germany's *Die Welt.* I understand, gentlemen, that you are all currently subordinate—dare I say lesser?—members of your respective boards, but please accept my word—your statuses will change, both by mortality and forced attrition. Each of you will soon become a major factor, a voice with control. How say you?"

There was not even a murmur of dissent. When in position, they would act in concert. For practical survival.

"Our third row, the basic engines that drive your endeavors, the guts, as we Americans say, of your newspapers— the journalists themselves. These are the men in the streets, in the states, the provinces, and national capitals, those on the front lines who daily report the events enlightening readers across the world."

"You can ease off on the hype," said an elderly American with a husky voice, his creased features bespeaking years of endless nights and too much whiskey. "We've got the message. You issue the 'events,' we'll write 'em up. We haven't got much of a choice, do we, since we prefer our status quos to the alternatives?"

"I agree, *meneer,*" added a Dutch reporter. "As the *English* say, you are too clever by half."

"C'est vrai," said a journalist from Paris.

"All too true—*das stimmt!*" joined in a German reporter.

"Come now, gentlemen, that's such a negative approach," said Guiderone, slowly, charmingly shaking his head. "I know only two of you personally, but all four by reputation. You are the leaders in your fields; your words cross oceans and continents with electronic speed, and when you appear on television screens you are accepted authorities, honored men of the fourth estate."

"I hope to hell we can keep that one," interrupted the cynical American.

"You will, of course, for you will accurately report events as they take place . . . naturally emphasizing the positive aspects and minimizing whatever negative reactions there may be under the blanket of the new century. After all, we must be realistic; we must advance our civilized countries, not let them erode."

"You say a great deal with but a few bromides," said the Hollander, laughing softly. "You are quite the politician, *meneer.*"

"A vocation pressed upon me by others, great minds, to be sure, but not a direction of my own choosing."

"Better yet, *monsieur,*" observed the Parisian, "you are the outsider on the inside. *Très bien.*"

"And you are, each one of you, extraordinarily talented and convincing journalists. Whatever your past indiscretions—and they will never be exploited by me—they pale beside your abilities. . . . Now to our fourth and final row, perhaps the most unique for our purposes. The editorial staffs of the four major publications in the world, and through their chains of ownerships, the editorial flagships for over two hundred important international newspapers in Europe and the Americas. Your influence is vast, gentlemen. You mold opinions throughout the industrial nations, endorsements by you, or the lack of same, can make or break candidates."

"You're too flattering," broke in a corpulent, white-haired German, his heavy legs dwarfing his chair, his lined, splotched face betraying a sedentary existence. "That was before the television," he continued. "Today the challengers and the incumbents *buy* the television! *That* is where opinions are formed."

"Only to a degree, *mein Herr,*" objected the son of the Shepherd Boy. "You put a lightweight cart before a strong horse. When you speak, television reflects on your words and always has. It must, for you have the time for reflection, it doesn't; everything is immediate, instantly processed. The majority of television executives, if only to avoid embarrassment, go back and heed your opinions, even to the extent of distancing themselves from political advertisements."

"He has a point, Gunther," said another American, in counterpoint to his cynical reporter-compatriot, dressed in a conservative business suit. "More and more we hear the words 'The following is a paid commercial' or, conversely, 'That was a political advertisement paid for by the committee for Senator so-and-so, or candidate such-and-such.'"

"*Ach,* so what does it mean? It's all so fast."

"It means we still and will always carry weight," answered a third editor, British, by his accent.

"I trust it will always be so," added the last of the men in the fourth row, an Italian wearing a tailored pin-striped suit.

"I reiterate what I mentioned to our second section, those members of the four boards of directors," said Guiderone, his eyes focusing briefly, staring, at each man in the last row. "I—*we*—realize that you are currently at the lower ends of your editorial staffs, but that will change. Through procedures you need know nothing about, you will be elevated to positions of leadership, your judgments accepted as writ."

"Which means," said the fastidious American in the dark suit and regimental tie, "that we editorially endorse what you suggest we endorse throughout our chains of newspapers."

" 'Suggest' is such a flexible verb, isn't it?" asked the son of the Shepherd Boy. "It's so subject to interpretation. I prefer the word 'advise,' for it limits alternatives, doesn't it?"

There was a momentary silence, far beyond a pause, until the Italian spoke. "Done," he said, nearly choking on the affirmative. "Or we all lose everything."

"I do not make threats. I merely open the windows of possibility. . . . I believe our meeting is over."

It was.

All together, as if to rid themselves of the stench of a communicable disease, the congregation summoned by the Matarese left the room. One of the last to depart was the enthusiastic Canadian.

"Oh, MacAndrew," said Guiderone, his hand touching the young man's elbow. "Now that this dreary business is over, why don't we have a drink in the lounge downstairs? I believe we have mutual acquaintances in Toronto. I'd like to catch up." He mentioned several names.

"*Certainly,* sir! A pleasure."

"Good. I'll meet you there in five minutes. I've got a phone call to make. Grab a table in the rear, if you can."

"I'll be waiting . . . *sir.*"

The "acquaintances" were, except one, only vaguely remembered names to the young MacAndrew, but the fact that they were in Guiderone's memory elated him, especially the one he did recall vividly. His ex-wife.

"I was so sorry to hear of that," said Julian.

"It was probably my fault, sir. I admit I was terribly ambitious, and treated her rather badly where business was concerned. You see, after getting my doctorate in managerial finance from McGill University, I was filled with myself. So many offers coming in, none that well-paying although prestigious, until out of the blue came a position with a Montreal investments firm at a salary I truly believed I wouldn't reach for a decade!"

"I understand. And then one thing led to another."

"Oh, *boy,* did it! I then—"

"Excuse me, young man," interrupted Guiderone. "I'm out of Cuban cigars. Would you please buy me several at the counter in the lobby? Here's a ten-thousand-lira note."

"Of course, sir. A *pleasure,* sir!"

The ambitious Canadian promptly rose from the table and walked rapidly out of the bar. The son of the Shepherd Boy withdrew a small packet from his pocket and emptied its contents into the young man's drink; he gestured for a waiter.

"Tell my friend I had to make a telephone call. I'll be back shortly."

"Sì, signore."

Julian Guiderone did not return, but the young Canadian did. His head turning right and left, anticipating the sight of the most important man in his life, MacAndrew drank from his glass. Thirty-four seconds later he fell across the table, his eyes wide in death.

The son of the Shepherd Boy walked down the Spanish Steps into the Via Due Macelli, and turned right to the American Express office. His coded communiqué to Amsterdam would be deciphered quickly and acted upon. Decoded, it read:

Our Canadian was a threat. In his enthusiasm, he talked too much. Problem solved. Search for another.

Guiderone walked back to the intersection of the Via Condotti, one of the shopping meccas of the world. He would not buy; however, he would stop at a coffee shop and have a slow cappuccino or two, summarizing his thoughts.

He—*they*—the *Matarese*! had accomplished more than any other elite organization on earth ever had. They controlled industries, utilities, global suppliers, motion pictures and television, and finally newspapers the world over. Nothing could *stop* them! Soon they would control the planet, and it was all so simple.

Greed.

Infiltrate and promise, or blackmail, and who could resist? The bottom line keeps rising until it's out of sight, profits are extraordinary, the lower classes stand in line for their share—better the devil you can live with than one you don't know. And what of the underclass, the indigent and the uneducated parasites on society? Do what they did in the eighteenth and nineteenth centuries! Force them to better themselves! It could be done. It's what made *America*!

Was it really? Or was it something else?

The blinds were drawn in the neon-lit room of British intelligence, MI-5. There was no need to block out the bright light of the London day, for it was past ten in the evening. It was merely a precaution held over from the Cold War when telescopic cameras were found in buildings across the wide street.

Pryce and Montrose had been picked up at the Connaught at seven-thirty; they arrived at MI-5 headquarters well before eight o'clock. Coffees in hand, provided by Geoffrey Waters, without-the-Sir, the three of them had pored over the notes found in Gerald Henshaw's locked drawer in the Brewster house on Belgrave Square. In the main they were scraps of paper torn from loose-leaf pads and filled with hastily scribbled, barely legible handwriting. Then, in contradiction, the majority had been neatly folded two and three times over, as if they were secret clues in a treasure hunt, to be shoved under rocks or into the bark of trees.

"What do you make of it all?" asked Waters, returning to the hot plate after refilling Cameron's cup of coffee.

"For starters," said Pryce, "the obvious. Everything's written in random codes, which means there's no basic code whatsoever. No consistency, no meaning to anyone but him, each different, or mostly so, and each probably decipherable in a different way."

"I'm certainly no expert," said Leslie, "but have you tried all the usual decoding methods?"

"To the point of driving our inanimate computers up the walls," replied Geoffrey, heading back to the round oak table and sitting down. "Numbers in arithmetic and geometric sequence; lexical and alphabetical overlaps, synonyms and antonyms, both in plain English and street idiom, as well as the more vulgar applications—Henshaw didn't speak a foreign language."

"How do you know?" asked Cameron.

"The children. It was one of the few times they displayed a touch of humor during our extensive questioning. Like many wealthy youngsters in sophisticated families, they've traveled widely and speak a passable French. So when they wanted to exchange confidences in front of Henshaw, they did so in French. It usually made him furious, which they obviously enjoyed."

"Some of this nonsense is so simplistic it's ridiculous," Pryce noted, holding up the scrap of paper in his hand. "Look here," he added, placing the torn scrap faceup on the table. "*MAST/V/APR/TL/BF*. All in capital letters."

"I don't understand," said Montrose.

"A simple unscrambling of the abbreviated anagram makes it fairly clear. *Amsterdam via Paris telephone in billfold*. That's supported by the way all these pieces of paper are double- and triple-creased, folded methodically to fit in small places."

"Isn't that a bit of a leap?" asked Leslie.

"We don't think so, my dear," answered Waters. "We came up with the same thing on that one. . . . How about this little darling?" The MI-5 veteran picked up another note from the pile on the table. "I'll read it; nothing's in caps, incidentally, all small letters: *ng*-dash-*st*-dash-*oh,* period. It doesn't make a bit of sense. On the other hand, here's one that does: *cy*-dash-*bk*-dash-*nu*-dash-*bf* again, period."

"A bank account," said Cameron, "probably in the Cayman Islands, the number, like the telephone number to reach Amsterdam, also shoved into a billfold."

"Quite, old man, that's what we believe."

"He might as well have written it out, it's so clear."

"That's just it," exclaimed the frustrated Waters. "He jumps from the simplistically ridiculous to the unfathomably sublime. I swear, if the chaps who created Enigma had ciphered this way, our boys at Chequers would still be working on it!"

"Didn't Cam say it was a code he devised only for himself?" said Montrose.

"Indeed, yes," agreed the Englishman. "It's why it's unfathomable. It's only in *his* head."

"Beware the amateurs," said Pryce. "They'll screw you up every time. . . . There's still no clue as to his whereabouts?"

"None at all. It's as though he's vanished from the face of the earth."

"That's a frightening thought." Cameron got out of his chair, stretched, and walked to a window, separating a blind to peer outside. "And one that's not particularly surprising."

"How so?" asked Leslie.

"No corpse, Colonel. Scofield told me that whenever the Matarese killed without hiring killers, its law was to leave no corpse."

"Are you saying that Henshaw was part of the Matarese?"

"A minor part, Geof. From everything we know, he was too stupid to be more than that. But his killer—*if* he was killed—wasn't. Whoever it was is *very* major; 'Make sure it's done, you're accountable, and there can be no traces.' That's the way I read it."

"It makes sense," said Waters. "Where do you suggest we go next?"

"I assume you've covered relatives, friends, neighbors, solicitors, banks, doctors—the whole bag?"

"Most definitely. Lady Alicia and her first husband, Daniel, were paragons of civility, using their wealth and prominence for the benefit of worthy causes. They were, from all reports, a very congenial and generous couple."

"And after her husband's death?" said Montrose. "When Henshaw came on the scene?"

"Quite a different story. At first he was accepted, then progressively he began to lose that acceptance. There were rumors of infidelity and excessive alcohol. Along with the gossip, there were more tangible reports of automobile accidents while under the influence. The bills are quite substantial, as are the verified complaints of numerous pubs and clubs that refused him entrance. Finally and most dastardly, the accounting firm that handles Lady Alicia's Wildlife Association volunteered that Henshaw was suspected of squirreling funds from it. They'll go no further for fear of drying up other sources of revenue, but I'll bet it was true and involved a hell of a lot of money."

"The bank in the Cayman Islands," said Pryce.

"That would be my guess, chap."

"It's more than a guess, Geof. But even if we had the account number, it'd be tough to invade."

"We have our ways, old man. However, we may not need them. Just before she died, Lady Alicia made out a check for two-million-plus pounds to Wildlife. Her children made some mention of it, but did not elaborate. Again, protecting her charity."

"You asked where we should go next, Geoffrey," said Leslie. "I think you just answered that. The children. May we see them?"

"Of course. They're in town rattling around in that old place on Belgrave Square. But I should warn you, they're still terribly upset; they were very close to their mum, and the boy's a veritable tiger. They're besieged by vultures of all stripes—relatives they barely know, solicitors making outrageous claims against Henshaw, streams of reporters from the tuppenny cheap sheets—tabloids, you call them— those horrible papers and magazines obsessed with female mammaries, you know the sort of scum."

"Why is the boy a tiger?" asked Leslie. "He's only, what is it, seventeen, isn't he?"

"Looks more like twenty, with a physique that could match a very tough rugby player's. He's extremely protective of his younger sister, and without assistance bodily ejected three—not one or two, but *three*—slime-type journalists who were questioning her. Our boys were impressed; apparently he wrapped all three together, then booted them out one by one. Two suffered broken arms and the third— how should I put it?—had a groin problem."

"We'll be very gentle," said Cameron, "and I'll wear a steel jockstrap."

"Other than that, he's quite pleasant, if a touch intense. Actually, they're both rather nice, just upset."

"He sounds like a time bomb, Geof."

"Hardly, chap. He's a wrestler, that's all. Gathered a few medals in the Midlands, I'm told."

"I like him already," said Leslie. "My son's a wrestler. He's only fifteen but he's won the Junior Interscholastics two years in a row—"

"I chase butterflies," interrupted Pryce. "The nets are heavy but I manage. . . . When can we see them, Geof?"

"Tomorrow. Name the time, they're expecting you."

15

Roger and Angela Brewster rose as one from their armchairs in the downstairs drawing room in the mansion on Belgrave Square. The morning sun streamed through the large bay windows, highlighting the antique furniture and fine paintings on the walls. The grandeur of the room did not diminish its aura of comfort; instead, it seemed to cry out, *Relax, chill out, this is a friendly place—a chair is still a chair, a sofa just a sofa.*

Geoffrey Waters preceded Leslie and Cameron through the open double doors of the room. His appearance had an immediate effect on the two adolescents.

"Sir Geoffrey!" said the girl enthusiastically as she approached him.

"Morning, Sir Geoffrey," added the boy beside his sister, his hand extended.

"Now, now, haven't I taught you *anything*? . . . No, Roger, I will *not* shake your hand until you change your salutation!"

"Sorry, *Geoffrey*," said the Brewster wrestler, shaking hands.

"And you, child?" Waters looked at the girl. "Also a peck on the cheek, if you'd be so kind."

"All right . . . Geoffrey." She kissed Waters, speaking to the two strangers. "Isn't he a charmer?"

"One can't help getting older, my dear, but one doesn't have to *be* old. May I introduce my two new associates? Lieutenant Colonel Montrose, United States Army, and Special Agent Pryce of the Central Intelligence Agency."

They shook hands, briefly, haltingly. "I don't get it," said Roger Brewster. "What does our mother's death, her *murder,* have to do with the United States Army?"

"Specifically, it doesn't," replied Leslie. "But I'm going to be up front with you two even if my superiors bust me to private or throw me out of the Army. The people responsible for your mother's death have kidnapped my son. They claim they'll kill him if I don't do as they say."

"Good *Lord*!" exclaimed Angela Brewster.

"That's *horrible*!" echoed her brother. "How do they contact you?"

"They haven't for nearly three weeks now. I was given instructions through a third party, which I ostensibly carried out in our last post. In essence, they were testing me: Where were we? What was the security? The firepower? . . . That sort of thing. Since we learned there was a mole, or moles, in the CIA, the information I delivered was accurate but superfluous."

"When do you expect to hear from them *again*?" asked the Brewster daughter.

"Any moment . . . any hour now," replied Leslie, her eyes briefly distant, inward. "Somewhere soon a message will arrive—a telephone number to be dialed from a public phone—where and when to call, and a recorded voice giving me my orders. There was no way they could reach me during the past five days. Our entire security was altered, moleproof, we believe, but this morning we let the word out at Langley. They now know I'm in London."

"Doesn't that *frighten* you?" exclaimed Angela Brewster.

"It would frighten me far, far more if they didn't contact me."

"What can we do?" asked the Brewster son.

"Tell us everything you know about Gerald Henshaw," replied Pryce. "And answer the questions we ask you."

"We've told what we both know to the police and MI-Five—everything."

"Tell *us*, Angela dear," said Montrose.

"Do so, my child," added Waters. "We're all human, therefore imperfect. Perhaps our new friends might pick up on something we've missed."

The litany began with Henshaw's weaknesses: his frequent drunkenness, the womanizing, his flagrant abuse of the money he was both given and stole, his arrogance toward servants when Lady Alicia was out of earshot, the constant lies as to his whereabouts on the occasions when he could not be found—the list was seemingly endless.

"I'm surprised your mother put up with him," said Cameron.

"You'd have to know Gerald Henshaw to understand," answered Angela, her voice soft, as if searching for words. "Mother wasn't stupid, she just didn't see the things other people saw. He hid that side of himself from her."

"He was a bloody genius at it," Roger broke in. "Around her he was all lovable charm. For a few years I actually liked the bastard. Angela didn't but I did."

"We women are brighter in that area, don't you think?"

"That's a myth, little sister, and in the early days he *was* good for her."

"He distracted her, that's all."

"But weren't you two away at school most of the time?" asked Pryce.

"Yes," replied the brother, "for the past six years anyway, but we were home during the summers and the holidays and occasional weekends. Not necessarily together, but we were here enough to see what was happening."

"Enough to change your mind, Roger?" pressed Cameron.

"Definitely, sir."

"What started your conversion?" asked Leslie. "To your sister's way of thinking."

"All the things we've told you."

"Things you learned gradually, I assume. I mean, they weren't all suddenly apparent to you, were they? Something had to start you thinking."

Brother and sister looked at each other. Angela spoke. "It was the automobile-repair shop in St. Albans, wasn't it, Rog? They called to say the Jag was fixed, remember?"

"That's right," agreed the brother. "The owner thought he was speaking to Gerry. He said he wouldn't release the car except for hard cash—no checks, no bills to accountants, just plain money."

"Why was that?" Pryce looked at Geoffrey Waters, who shook his head, signifying bewilderment.

"As I later learned, it was the eleventh time in a year and a half that Gerry took the Jaguar in for repairs. He and Mum were in Brussels for a Wildlife gig, so I drove her Bentley up to St. Albans and talked to the fellow. He told me that Henshaw had him send the first few bills to Mother's accountants, who aren't famous for paying immediately. Also, they apparently haggle a bit."

"That's hardly a reason to demand cash," said Montrose. "Insurance companies commonly question automobile repairs."

"Well, that's just it. Gerry never used our insurance, he didn't report the accidents."

"Some people don't," explained Cameron, "because their premiums go up."

"I've heard that, sir, but there was something else. Why did he have the shop in St. Albans do the repairs in the first place? Why not the Jaguar Motors right here in London? We've been dealing with them for years."

"Probably to keep your mother from learning about the accidents."

"That's what I figured, Mr. Pryce, but Mum wasn't blind, and a missing car is pretty obvious. Especially a bright red Jag that's usually parked out front—Gerald couldn't be bothered to put it in the garage."

"I see what you mean. Then this 'something else,' did you find it?"

"I may have, sir. The bill for the repairs that day was twenty-six hundred and seventy pounds—"

"Twenty-six *hundred* . . . nearly three thousand *pounds*?" exploded Waters of MI-5. "He must have practically totaled the damn car!"

"I'm afraid he didn't, at least nothing on the bill indicated it. There were charges for a fender pounded out and re-painted, also a 'detailing,' which is merely a thorough wash-ing and vacuuming."

"What *else*?" demanded the MI-5 chief. "How did the bugger come up with over twenty-six hundred pounds?"

"The remainder was listed under 'miscellaneous'—"

"What?" said an astonished Pryce. "Did he think he could get away with that?"

"I don't believe he thought about it," replied Roger Brew-ster. "I should explain that when I arrived, he was startled that I wasn't Gerry. I don't think he would have told me the amount over the phone if he knew it was me."

"Did he *justify* the 'miscellaneous'?" pressed Cameron.

"He said to ask my 'old man.' "

"Did you bring the money, the cash?" Leslie inquired.

"Yes, I wanted to get the car back. Since Mother traveled all over the place for Wildlife, she set up emergency ac-counts for Angela and me. I stopped off at the bank, made a withdrawal, and drove to St. Albans, expecting to hire someone to drive the Bentley back here."

"Were you going to tell your mother?" continued Mon-trose.

"Well, I figured I'd confront Gerry first, see if he had any kind of reasonable explanation."

"Did you?" asked Pryce.

"Of course, and he really blew me away. To begin with, he peeled off three thousand pounds—and he *never* had that kind of money—saying that the extra was for the trouble I went to. Then he told me not to say anything to Mum be-cause she was responsible for the Jag's repairs and he didn't want her upset."

"How was she supposedly responsible?" asked Geoffrey Waters.

"He claimed Mother drove it to our country house without oil in the crankcase and with the wrong petrol. That he had to have the whole engine overhauled."

"You accepted that?"

"Hell, *no*! Mother hated that car; it was a present to Gerry, who loved it. It wasn't the fact that it was a Jaguar, it was the color. She said it was ostentatious, stood out like a bleeding thumb. That wasn't her way."

"Why didn't you ever mention this during our interrogations?"

"It never came up, Geoffrey. Nobody asked how we learned about the real Gerald Henshaw."

"How *did* you?" asked Cameron. "An automobile-repair bill, no matter how out of whack, couldn't tell you that much, could it?"

"Rog was angry," answered Angela, interrupting. "He talked to me, which he doesn't always do, and he said something was wrong, *really* wrong. I said of course it was, I always knew it! Then we both remembered, we had a cousin, a barrister in Regent Street. We went to see him and asked him to look into Gerry, find out everything he could."

"That's when the whole ghastly story came to light," added the brother. "The girlfriends, names and addresses included, the drinking, the paid-off accidents, the banishments from restaurants and private clubs—the entire bloody mess, all *confirmed*."

"Did you go to your mother and tell her?" Pryce glanced back and forth between the two children.

"Not at first," replied Roger, "but try to understand why. Gerry was a rogue, a charlatan, but he *did* make our mother happy. When our father died, she was a basket case—for a while Angela and I actually feared she might take her own life."

"And then this marvelous *actor* appeared," said Angela. "Tall, polished, with extraordinary credentials—none of which proved accurate—but he was there for her. How could we destroy that?"

"If I may, chaps?" asked Sir Geoffrey Waters, not answering the question. "We've covered most of this. Where are we heading?"

"It's that 'miscellaneous,'" answered Cameron. "Twenty-six hundred pounds for a fender bender? I think we should drive to St. Albans."

"Two points for the colonials," said the man from MI-5.

The St. Albans Motor Works was a small shop in the industrial part of the city. The hammering and the shrill sounds of multiple drills along with the incessant, wheezing bursts of air from the two-pronged lifts announced its occupational activity. The owner was a portly fellow in grease-laden coveralls, his face that of a man who worked physically hard for a living, the lines around his eyes and creasing his forehead premature, the result of his labors, not from indulgence. He was in his forties and his name was properly Alfred—Alfie Noyes.

"Oh, yes, I remember the young chap as if it was yesterday, I do. Bit of a surprise he wasn't his old man."

"Then you expected Mr. Henshaw, his *stepfather*?" asked Waters, who had displayed his intimidating MI-5 credentials.

"Indeed, I did, sir. Our arrangement was that we was off-limits, if y'know what I mean."

"I don't," said Pryce, introduced obscurely as an American consultant to British intelligence. "Tell me, Mr. Noyes."

"I don't want to get m'self in any trouble, I don't. I didn't do nothin' wrong."

"Then *tell* me. What was this arrangement?"

"Well, it was maybe two or three years ago, somewhere in between, it was, this chap come to me and says he's got a new customer for me, a rich bloke who has some domestical problems. A lot of prominent folk do, y'know—"

"The *arrangement*, please."

"There was nothin' illegal, I wouldn't put up with anything like that, I wouldn't! It was just a professional courtesy for a prominent chap from a very upstandin' family.

That's what it was, and I swear on m'mother's grave that's *all* it was."

"The professional courtesy, Mr. Noyes?"

"Well, it was as simple as ABC, it was. Y'see, whenever he had trouble with the red Jag, he called us and we'd drive a truck down to wherever he was and pick it up."

"These were accidents, am I correct?"

"A few, yes, not all."

"Oh?" Geoffrey Waters's eyebrows shot up. "A *few*?"

"Surely, sir. He's a nervous driver, he is, like a . . . hypochondric—y'get the sniffles, it must be the vapors, y'know what I mean?"

"I'm not sure I do," said the man from MI-5. "Explain, if you will?"

"Well, like he might say there's a knock in the engine when there's nothin' wrong, or he hears a squeak in a window, which wasn't there when we got it—probably a little rain in the rubber rims. I tell you, gentlemen, he could be a pain in the *arse,* but we sent the trucks and he paid the bills."

"Let's get to the bills," said Leslie Montrose, standing deferentially to the left of Cameron. "I gather you had trouble with Henshaw's—the Brewster family's—accounting firm."

"Oh, that would be the Westminster House, but I wouldn't call it trouble, ma'am. They has their job to do and we has ours. They weren't too quick to pay off, but I could live with that, I got a good business, I do. Eventually they'd cough up, so you don't complain too much, not with an account like Mr. Henshaw's."

"What was the name of the man who came to see you two or three years ago?" asked Waters.

"If he gave it, he was so quiet I didn't catch it. He said he represented a private merchant bank that looked after Henshaw's interests."

"Which bank?"

"He never said."

"Didn't it occur to you to ask him why you couldn't send the bills to him, since he was Henshaw's banker?"

"Oh, he was very clear about that, sir. There wasn't to be any public connection between him or the bank and Mr. Henshaw."

"Didn't that strike you as odd, old chap?"

"Indeed, it did, it did. But as he explained, quite clearly in fact, wealthy families have their odd ways where husbands, wives, and kiddies are concerned. . . . Y'know, all them trust funds and inheritance rules, stuff the likes of us wouldn't have a clue about."

"So what were you supposed to do?"

"Whatever Henshaw told me. He was on his own in that department. . . . Sure, I padded a few bills to back up his complaints, but that was only to pay for the trucks and the drivers, I *swear* it! The whole situation was a bit crazy, but we don't usually have customers the likes of Henshaw and the Brewsters. I mean, blimey, you read about 'em all the time in the newspapers—the respectful ones."

"Let's get to the bottom line, Mr. Noyes," said Leslie firmly. "The reason we're here. What's the explanation for the 'miscellaneous' on the bill Roger Brewster paid you in cash? Something over fourteen hundred pounds, I believe."

"*Christ* almighty, I knew that'd come up sooner or later! And I tell you truthful-like, I got really pissed off! Excuse my language, miss. I carried that charge on my books for damn near eighteen months! Henshaw said he'd pay it, but if I sent it to the Westminster people, I'd never see him or his business again. Finally, I was so fuckin' mad—excuse me—"

"Excused, go on."

"I was so angry, I told Henshaw over the phone—I *thought* it was Henshaw—that he either paid it or no red Jaguar!"

"What was it *for*?" continued Montrose.

"Mind you, I swore I'd never say anythin' to anybody."

Geoffrey Waters reached into his pocket and withdrew his MI-5 identification for a second time; he flipped it open and spoke. "I think you should speak now, old boy, or be charged with crimes against the Crown."

"*Crimes,* not *me*! I'm a member of the civil guards!"

"They were disbanded ten years ago."

"Talk," added Pryce.

"Awright, I don't want no trouble with your types. . . . About two years ago Henshaw told me he wanted a first-class safe, a small vault, in fact, hidden under the steel floor of the Jaguar's boot, that looked like part of the undercarriage. It took over a week at full speed, although he said he wanted it in two days. We had to put everything else on hold—I charged him *right,* I did! Especially since he had another garage install the switch for the boot plate. Can't tell where the bloody thing is without it!"

"Did you ever see the man from the merchant bank again?" asked Cameron.

"Not himself, but lots of his associates."

"How so?"

"Whenever the Jag was picked up and fixed, one of the blokes would come in and check our repairs. I tell you, I resented that, just like I took offense about the boot plate. I've got a hell of a good reputation, trustworthy to a fault."

"Were those men ever alone with the car?"

"Have no idea, I was usually busy."

"Thank you, Mr. Noyes," said MI-5's Geoffrey Waters. "You've been most cooperative. The Crown appreciates it."

"Thank heavens!"

The red Jaguar was in the three-car garage at the rear of the house on Belgrave Square. Roger Brewster had dragged out his deceased father's massive tool case, finding an acetylene torch in another section of the workshop area. Pryce held the plans they had taken from Alfred Noyes's files as the Brewster son opened the boot of the red Jaguar.

"I used to sit on the bench watching my dad for hours as he tinkered with his cars," said Roger. "I don't know if he was a good mechanic or not, but he was usually good at whatever he tried because he concentrated so. . . . Here we go," he announced, ripping out the carpeting of the boot down to the metal and reaching for the acetylene torch and the goggles. "Chalk out the section, will you please, Mr. Pryce."

"You sure you don't want me to do that?" said Cameron. He was holding a box of white chalk and the plans from St. Albans.

"No, for a couple of reasons," replied the son. "If there's anything here, I want to nail the son of a bitch myself, and how better to do it than with my father's tools?"

Roger Brewster went to work, the bluish-white flame progressively melting the steel of the boot in a perfect rectangle. When the process was completed, the teenager poured cold water over the area; the sizzling sent small clouds of steam up into the hood of the boot. He then picked up a hammer and tapped the outline; it fell away into the darkness below. With tongs from the tool case, Roger reached in and pulled the metal slab from its recess, dropping it on the floor. Revealed was a small, thick vault with a soiled black-and-white dial in the center. Pryce again studied the plans from St. Albans Motor Works, reading what Gerald Henshaw never remotely considered: the sequence of numbers for the combination lock as printed by the Manchester Vault and Safe Company.

They removed the contents and placed them in a row on the workbench. Included were a short pile of bearer bonds, redeemable on progressive dates, the first negotiable as of seven weeks ago, the morning of the killing of Lady Alicia; four keys for four separate doors, presumably flats for Henshaw's various paramours; a number of post-dated traveler's checks; coded, wrinkled notes that revealed nothing, to be deciphered only by a man who had vanished and could be presumed dead.

"It's a bloody hodgepodge!" cried Waters. "Where can these things really lead us?"

"To begin with," replied Pryce, "this is how they paid him—the people behind the kidnapping and Lady Alicia's murder. An obscure automobile-repair shop far outside of London, owned by a none-too-bright, hard-working guy who's inordinately impressed by his so-called betters."

"Yes, that's rather apparent, old man, but Noyes was quite open with us, cooperative, in fact. I don't think he was concealing anything."

"You didn't give him a choice, Geoffrey," said Montrose.

"So we've unearthed an extremely clever method of communication, but not one we can track down. No identities, no descriptions, no clues whatsoever. They've all gone *ppfft*!"

"I agree with you," interrupted Leslie, "that Mr. Noyes didn't withhold anything consciously, but I was bothered by something."

"What was it?" asked Cameron.

"He repeated several times what a good business he had, what a fine reputation he enjoyed, how, essentially, he wasn't pressed for money—"

"That's not the way *I* heard it," broke in Roger Brewster. "He kept whining about how stony he was and couldn't keep up with his bills and his payrolls. He damned near fell to his knees when I showed him the twenty-six hundred pounds."

"That sounds more like the truth to me," continued Montrose. "I mean, if he was as successful as he led us to believe, why wasn't his garage larger, with more space for more cars? And I only saw two other mechanics inside; that's hardly a staggering payroll."

"So maybe he lied to impress us," said Pryce. "What with Geoffrey's ID, it would fit."

"Granted, but there's a real contradiction here. He talked about the Brewsters' Westminster accountants in almost glowing terms. They had their jobs to do, he had his, so why make a fuss?"

"To keep Henshaw's business," replied Waters rhetorically. "Where's the contradiction?"

"Because that's not the way things are, Geoffrey. Since my husband died, I've had my share of bouts with car repairs. Those people are a pretty aggressive breed, and I can't believe it's much different over here."

"No sexism intended," said Pryce, "but those people, as you call them, tend to be a little rougher on women, figuring your knowledge of their work is limited."

"That's my point, or part of it. When Jim didn't come back, a friend of ours, a CPA with his own accounting firm, took care of all our finances until I could get things together. Because I was transferred several times, the arrangement lasted almost a year—"

"What is your point, Leslie?" asked an impatient Cameron.

"I was in several accidents, one my fault for lack of concentration, the other two fairly minor bashes in parking lots. Joe Gamble—he's our accountant and even he agrees it's a hell of a name for a CPA—told me the worst part of his job was the car-repair bills. Not only were the insurance adjusters impossible, but the shop owners, whose bills were outrageous, dunned for their money, constantly swearing at him like Vikings."

"My dear girl," interjected Geoffrey Waters, "on such a flimsy coincidence you're inferring some parallel *here*?"

"Not a parallel, a contradiction, an inconsistency."

"Which is?"

"Alfred Noyes's benign appreciation of the Brewster accountants. They regularly delayed paying him on time, frequently argued with him over his charges, and all he could say was 'They has their jobs to do'?"

"I restate my opinion that plainspoken old Alfie didn't care to risk losing Henshaw as a customer."

"Alfie may be plainspoken, Geof, but he isn't stupid to the cube," said Pryce. "He was providing a valuable confidential service arranged by a stranger. As long as he followed the rules, he wasn't going to lose Henshaw. I think he was assured of that."

"What are you all *talking* about?" interrupted Angela Brewster. "I don't understand."

"Neither do I," said the brother.

"How well do you two know the accounts people at the Westminster House?" asked Leslie. "Whom do you deal with there?"

Again the Brewster offspring looked at each other, frowning.

"We went down with Mum a couple of years ago to sign some papers," said the sister. "We met the head of the firm, a Mr. Pettifrogge—I remember the name because I thought it was wild—and everyone was very nice and polite, but then people were usually like that around our mother."

"Did Henshaw go with you?" asked Waters.

"No, he didn't," answered the brother, "and I recall that clearly. Don't you remember, Angela? Mum said there was no reason to tell Gerry that we'd all been down there."

"Of course I do. The papers were very confidential."

"What were they?" said Cameron. "If they're not too confidential."

"Something about the disposal of selected properties—in the event of . . . et cetera, et cetera," replied Roger softly. "I didn't read them too carefully."

"Well, I read them more carefully than 'et cetera, et cetera,' " said Angela firmly. "There were several pages of inventory—paintings, tapestries, furniture—that were to remain in the Brewster family and not be removed from the premises without the consent of Rog and me under the supervision of Mum's solicitors."

Pryce whistled quietly. "*Whoa,* one Gerald Henshaw was efficiently locked out."

"No, sir," countered the younger sister, "the inventory was locked in. There was a clause—an order really—that in case our mother's whereabouts couldn't be verified after forty-eight hours of trying to locate her, the house was to be put under guard, nothing was to be removed."

"Parental discretion just got a new definition," said Cam.

"Certainly she began to have her suspicions about Mr. Charm, at least," Angela said.

"However," broke in Geoffrey Waters, "there was no one specific person at the firm that you were to reach in case it was necessary?"

"No, but a number have been around since Mother's death," replied Roger. "Old Pettifrogge came over once, more as a condolence call than anything else; he's so ancient you can picture him with a quill. The man who seemed to be in charge, who kept checking the inventory list, was a fellow named Chadwick. He introduced himself as an assistant managing director whose major duties concerned Mother's accounts as well as the Wildlife's."

"I'd say the Westminster House of Finance should be our next stop, wouldn't you, chaps?" said the man from MI-5.

The Westminster House was exactly what it proclaimed. A narrow, venerated eighteenth-century city dwelling of brownstone, six stories high and lovingly renovated, in Carlisle Place. The tasteful brass plaque to the right of the entrance of thick glass double doors clarified its identity.

WESTMINSTER HOUSE
ESTABLISHED 1902
PRIVATE FINANCIAL SERVICES

The building itself emanated an image of understated strength, and bespoke generations, even dynasties, of the wealthy and the powerful as clients. The Westminster House had enjoyed nearly a century of quiet influence in London's financial circles, justified by its acuity and unquestioned integrity. It had built a near-impenetrable wall of total respectability around itself.

As the MI-5 vehicle with Waters, Pryce, and Montrose sped toward Carlisle Place, that wall was about to experience a crack in its stone, a fissure so wide that Westminster House would be subject to insidious speculation.

Geoffrey Waters turned right on Victoria Street into Carlisle; he and his colleagues were astonished at what they saw. In front of Westminster House were two police cars and an ambulance, their red lights flashing. Together, the two intelligence officers and the U.S. Army colonel leaped out of the car and raced into the crowd in front of the building. The MI-5 chief of security, showing his credentials, bulldozed his way through the onlookers, Leslie and Cameron behind him.

"I.S.—MI-Five!" yelled Waters. "This is Crown business, let me and my two associates *in* there!"

Inside, the pandemonium was electric, all were in a state of shock. Executives, secretaries, file personnel, and maintenance crews were hysterical. Finally, after shoving aside and shoulder-blocking the crowd, Geoffrey Waters confronted a man in a vested dark suit, his superior position apparent. "My name's Waters, MI-Five, in service of the Crown! What *happened*?"

"Oh, *what*? Everything's so confused—"

"What *happened*?" yelled Cameron.

"It's so terrible, so absolutely *terrible*!"

"*What* is?" cried Montrose.

"Brian Chadwick, our first vice president and the chap we all knew would run the firm someday, just committed *suicide*!"

"All police *officers*!" shouted Sir Geoffrey Waters. "Seal off the office of the deceased!"

16

Bahrain, two o'clock in the afternoon

In an alabaster villa on the shores of the Persian Gulf, a young man of fifteen sat at a desk in a white-walled room with bars covering the windows. It was both a cell and not a cell, for he had private toilet facilities, a comfortable bed, a television set, and whatever books and writing materials he requested. His name was James Montrose Jr., his nickname, Jamie.

His schedule, such as it was, was self-imposed within limits. He was free to walk around the grounds of the walled estate as long as he was accompanied by a guard, and he had full use of the swimming pool as well as the tennis backboard—the two courts were useless as there were no other "guests" to play against. Also, he could order the meals he favored. It was an odd sort of captivity, but it was captivity nevertheless. He could not be driven into the capital of Manama or any other area of the independent archipelago. He was confined to the villa, with no communication to the outside world.

Jamie Montrose was a good-looking teenager, large for his years, a meld of his attractive parents. He had that quiet resolve that is so often found in children of the military. It apparently comes from the frequent moves from base to base, at home and in foreign lands, and the constant adjustments from the familiar to the unfamiliar. In the case of Leslie Montrose's son, however, there was a side to him that was often absent in military offspring. Whereas statistics indicate that military offspring often harbor a highly developed sense of resentment toward their parents' way of life, especially toward the father, who was usually the one in uniform, James Montrose Jr. worshiped his father, or more precisely, the memory of him.

His devotion did not manifest itself in aggressive military posturing, nor did he proselytize on the positive aspects, of which there were many, of life in the services. He felt it was a decision to be made by an individual after careful introspection and evaluation of one's weaknesses and strengths. If a single description could outwardly sum up Jamie, it would probably be that he was a quiet observer who studied circumstances before he became a participant. The last few years of sudden adjustments had taught him to be soft-spoken and cautious but not indecisive. Beneath his calm, even laconic, exterior was the strength and determination of a very quick mind.

"James," came the loud voice from beyond the locked door, "it is convenient for me to enter, is it not?"

"Come on in, Amet," replied young Montrose. "I'm still here 'cause I could only bend the iron bars in the windows a few inches. I can't squeeze through them yet."

The door opened and a slender man in a Western business suit but with an Arabic headdress walked inside. "You are always quite amusing, James," said the newcomer, his diction clipped in the manner of those from the Middle East who learn English in British schools. "You can be a delightful guest when you are not . . . sullen, I believe is the word."

"Try angry. You haven't let me phone my mother. I don't know what she knows or doesn't know, what she's been told or hasn't been told. I'm not sullen, Amet, I'm real angry!"

"You have not been abused, have you?"

"What do you call it?" asked a contentious Jamie, rising from the desk. "I'm locked up here in Ali Baba Land, a prisoner in a fancy jail, but my cell is just that, a lousy cell! When are you going to tell me what's going *on*?"

"But you know, James, your mother is assisting her superiors in a highly secret, extremely dangerous assignment. By sequestering you here, you're out of harm's way with no chance of your whereabouts being traced through any means of communication. Believe me, young man, your mother is most grateful. She understands that she could be compromised if anything happened to you."

"Then let *her* tell me that! A call, a letter . . . for God's sake, *anything*!"

"No risks can be taken. She understands that, too."

"You know something, Amet," said the Montrose son, walking around the desk and standing in front of the Bahraini, "you tell me these things and you expect me to believe them. But why should I? When the headmaster at school called me out of class and told me I'd be driven to Kennedy Airport and be met by government officials—all on a national-security priority—I went along figuring it had something to do with my mother. Outside of verifying the ID's of the Washington guys, which looked real enough, I didn't ask any questions."

"Why should you have? You're an Army brat, I believe is the expression. You must comprehend the chain of command where complete security is involved."

"I can accept it when I understand it. But this whole thing is crazy! I know my mother and she doesn't act like you say. She would at least have called me, clued me in."

"There wasn't time, James. She was pulled into the operation at the last minute and on her way beyond recomm before she could even pack. You *do* understand what 'beyond recomm' means, don't you?"

"Yes, I do, because that's what I am. No communication. So now, tell me this. Why is it when I tried calling Colonel Bracket from the airport, the recording said the number was no longer in use? Then when I reached an operator she said the current number was unlisted and she couldn't help me. I repeat, what's going *on*?"

"Substitute 'government' for 'God,' and you'll find the answer in your Bible. It moves in mysterious ways."

"Yeah, but not totally crazy!"

"That's a judgment call, as you Americans say. I cannot answer you."

"Well, somebody better," said James Montrose Jr. firmly, his eyes locked with those of the Arab, a ranking member of the Matarese.

"Or what, young man?"

Jamie Montrose said nothing.

The body of Brian Chadwick was removed from London's Westminster House to the coroner's office. The instructions were for a full autopsy despite the fact that the bullet hole in his right temple and the automatic in his hand would seem to confirm the manner of death by suicide. The question was, *why*? A man in his midforties, with a superb reputation, about to enter the prime of his professional life—what made him *do* it?

The forensic pathologist had the answer.

It was murder.

"There were no traces of potassium chlorate on the skin of his right hand, no powder burns as the telly constantly, though usually erroneously, tells us," said the chief coroner. "Further, there's a massive contusion at the base of his skull, an ecchymosis that had to be inflicted by a skilled killer. He was rendered unconscious, shot, and the weapon forced into his hand."

"That's kind of stupid for a trained killer, isn't it?" asked Pryce, sitting at the table in MI-5 headquarters, where the doctor had come for a confidential meeting.

"If you want a guess, I'll give you one," said the forensic pathologist. "I'd say the man who murdered him was in a great hurry and didn't have time for cover-up niceties. I remind you, that's only a guess."

"You mean he was reached and told to do the job immediately?" asked Leslie.

"If not sooner," added the doctor.

"In other words," said Cameron, "you're saying that whoever it was knew we were on our way over to see Chadwick, right? But the only people who knew were the two Brewster kids." Pryce shook his head. "That doesn't make *sense*!"

"Can't help you there, old man."

"Perhaps I can," Waters broke in. "It's something we hadn't considered, and we should have."

"What's that, Geof?"

"With all our sophistication and high technology, we overlooked the primitive procedure of bugging a house."

Angela Brewster peered through the sliding-glass security slot and opened the front door for Waters, Montrose, and Pryce. "Where's your brother, my dear?"

"He went with Coleman over to the home-alarm company—"

"What *happened*?" asked Leslie sharply.

"Nothing. It was Coleman's idea. He said we should change the system, or at least areas of it."

"Who's *Coleman*?" insisted Cameron.

"I forgot to mention him, chap—"

"Coley's sort of a man for all jobs around here, I guess you'd say," replied Angela. "He's been with us for years, since before I can remember. He was a friend of my father's, a sergeant major under Dad's command during the Emirates skirmishes in the fifties. He and Dad both got the Military Cross."

"What does he do?" pressed Montrose.

"Like I said, just about everything. If we have to be driven, he drives us; if Mum needed something at the shops, he got it. He also oversees the cleaning maids, who come in twice a week, as well as any and all deliveries and maintenance repair people. Many a time I've heard him tell plumbers or electricians that they didn't know what the hell they were doing."

"Sounds like one of your British sergeant majors, Geoffrey."

"They're a breed apart, Cameron. I truly believe they were responsible for most of our victories since the seventeen hundreds, the one exception being the colonial revolution, where they were obviously absent. . . . Coleman's a likable, plainspoken fellow who refuses to admit he's getting on in years. Rugged chap, too, for his age."

"Does he live here, Angela?" asked Pryce.

"Only when nobody's home, sir. When we're away, he stays in one of the guest rooms. His flat is close by with immediate contact to the house. There are special phones in every room; if we need him, we ring and he's here in a mo'."

"Independent guy, isn't he?"

"Yes, and our dad always said we should respect that."

"He was right," agreed Cameron. "He has a life. . . . After your father died, how did he get along with Henshaw?"

"I think he hated him, but out of loyalty to Dad and Mum, he didn't show it much. He mostly stayed to himself when Gerry was around. . . . Let me explain why I'm sure Coley didn't have much use for Mr. Charm. One Sunday morning about six months ago, I was home for the weekend; Roger was at school and Mother was at church when it happened." The young girl paused, as if embarrassed to go on.

"*What* happened, Angela?" asked Leslie gently.

"Gerry walked down the staircase in his undershorts. He had a massive hangover and the upstairs library bar didn't have the whiskey he wanted. He lurched back and forth and I guess I overreacted—I mean, he looked so angry, so unstable . . . so . . . naked. I rang for Coley, pressing the button several times, which is the signal for him to come right over."

"Did he?" said Geoffrey Waters.

"In less than two minutes, it seemed. By this time Gerry was really spaced; he was yelling at me, calling me ugly names because he couldn't find his damned whiskey on the copper bar. Of course, at the sight of Coley, Mr. Charm was stunned; he tried to straighten up and sweet-talk us. But good old Coleman wasn't having any. He walked between us and I'll never forget what he said." Here Angela briefly stopped, and, as teenage girls frequently do, imitated the voice of the one she was describing. In this case, it was a gruff, bass-toned Yorkshire dialect. "'You're not properly dressed for the drawing room, sir, and I'd advise you not to take another step forward. I assure you I have no need of a weapon, but the result could be the same, and it would be one of the greatest pleasures of my retirement.' . . . Wasn't that *amazing*? I tell you, Henshaw ran out of the room, stumbling up the staircase like a drunken scarecrow!"

"Did either you or Mr. Coleman say anything to your mother?" asked the MI-5 chief.

"We talked about it and decided not to. However, Coley made me promise that if I ever saw Gerry like that again, I was to ring him immediately."

"Suppose he wasn't home?" Montrose said.

"He told us he has a device on that phone which transmits the message up to fifty kilometers. And if he ever takes a trip beyond that, he'll make other arrangements."

"Like what?"

"Two chaps here in London who were also in Dad's Oman brigade. Both are retired but Coley said they were really qualified. One's a retired constable, second class, the other worked for Scotland Yard."

"Rather splendid credentials."

"I thought so."

"What changes did Coleman want in the alarm system?" continued Pryce.

"Something about television cameras that could be seen in his flat. He wanted to study the plans with Rog and see what was possible, I think."

"Did he say why?" asked Waters.

"Most of it was mumbo jumbo that I didn't understand, but Rog seemed to, unless he was faking, which he sometimes does."

The front-door chimes rang; the man from MI-5 spoke quickly. "That's probably the team from our office," he said. "I called them from the car and asked them to get here as soon as possible."

"What *team*?" Angela was surprised, anxious. "What's the hurry?"

"We don't want to alarm you, dear," answered Leslie, glancing at both men, who understood, "and it may be nothing, but there's an outside possibility that a bug was placed in your house."

"Oh, my God!"

"I'll let them in."

"Deactivate the alarm," cried the young girl rapidly as Waters approached the door. "The small panel on the right, press *two, one, three,* and wait a few seconds."

"Right." The Englishman did as he was told, admitting three men, two carrying electronic equipment not unlike the materials used by electricians and television-repair people, the third holding a large black bag. "We'll start in the garage," continued Waters, leading the unit toward a door at the far end of the great hall. "It's where a particular conversation took place; there's an entrance back here. . . . Coming along, you three?"

"At your heels, Geof," replied Cameron, escorting Angela Brewster and Montrose.

"How could anybody *do* it?" asked Angela. "Get inside to leave one of those things, a bug, I mean?"

"If there's one, there's probably more than one," said Pryce.

"How *disgusting*! It's worse than reading someone's diary. I keep mine locked up. On my tenth birthday, Dad got me a little wall safe, and I can change the combination anytime I want to."

"When I was your age, I kept a diary, too," said Leslie. "My brother was always trying to find it and read it."

"You had an older brother?"

"Younger, dear, and it's far worse. You have to kind of look after them and they sabotage you at every turn."

Quiet laughter followed all of them down the staircase to the large garage. "I didn't know you had a brother," whispered Cam on the steps.

"I thought you read my dossier."

"I scanned your qualifications, not your life history."

"Thank you for that."

"Does your brother know what's happened?"

"Emory's a dear, a really sweet guy, but he's not the sort of person you run to when you're in trouble."

"Oh?"

"My brother has a short beard and more degrees than a thermometer. He's the youngest tenured professor at Berkeley, and he and his wife backpack through the mountains carrying their tapes of Mozart, Brahms, and English madrigals. Got the picture?"

"He sounds interesting. Any kids?"

"They haven't decided, decisions being a big problem with them, usually resolved by procrastination."

"Now I get the picture."

The three intercept specialists from MI-5 went to work in the garage. Two walked slowly around the space next to the walls under the guidance of the third man, waving what appeared to be miniature telephone poles with dual antennae shooting out from the sides. Dials were attached to the instruments, and the supervisor of the team kept checking the readings and taking notes on a clipboard.

"There's a lot of iodized metal in here, Sir Geoffrey," said the unit's leader as short bursts came and went from the poles. Finally, after eight minutes, there was a rapid, steady stream of beeps from the instrument held close to the back wall of the workbench. It was a Peg-Board panel with numerous tools suspended on the hooks.

"Take the whole thing down, chaps," ordered Waters.

The three men removed the tools, placing them on the bench. They then proceeded to pry the Peg-Board from the wall, where it was anchored at the four corners and the center with heavy Molly bolts. Once it was loose, they propped the panel against the red Jaguar and thoroughly examined the wall beyond. And then examined it again and again.

"There's nothing here, Sir Geoffrey."

"There *has* to be," responded the MI-5 chief. "Your instruments don't lie, do they?"

"No, sir, they don't."

"The tools," said Pryce. "Scan the tools, bless each one."

Within minutes the bug was found. It was embedded in the handle of a large hard-rubber hammer, a tool rarely if ever used, as the jobs that entailed it would be done by a repair shop.

"Ian," said Waters, addressing the supervisor, "did you bring along your magic machine?"

"Certainly, Sir Geoffrey." The team's director knelt down, opened his black bag, and pulled out an electronic instrument the size of a thick book. He placed it on the garage floor, returned to the bag, and withdrew a metal-framed grid divided into squares, tiny lightbulbs in the middle of each square. A thin wire with a small plug attached curled out of the top of the frame.

"What's that?" asked Leslie.

"A tracing instrument, miss," replied the supervisor. "It's not perfected to the point where we would like it to be, but it can be of assistance. You see, this grid here represents roughly twelve hundred square meters, say three blocks circumference, which is the usual range. I plug the frame into the searcher, press the intercept, or bug, into the receptacle, and the lights skim over the areas and settle on where the receivers are located. Not specifically, of course, but within a reasonable distance."

"That's remarkable," said Leslie.

"I'm surprised you don't know about it," said Ian. "We've shared the technology with your intelligence service."

"We run a tight ship," said Cameron quietly. "Sometimes too tight."

"Proceed, please, old chap." The supervisor lifted the machine and the frame to the bench and did so, inserting the small, circular intercept into the orifice and turning on the equipment. The tiny lights flickered clockwise in sequence twice around the grid, finally settling on a square in the upper left-hand corner.

"What does it show us?" asked Montrose, Angela at her side. "How do you read it?"

"It's angled to the four points of the compass," replied Ian, the team leader. "Actually that's a built-in, metal-rejecting compass in the lower center," he added, pointing to a glass-encased floating needle at the six-o'clock spot. "Just picture what's outside as if this were a map."

"You mean the streets, the blocks, around Belgrave Square?" said Angela Brewster.

"That's right, miss," continued Ian, indicating several squares adjacent to the lit one. "That would be Grosvenor Crescent, this Chesham Place, and the one with the lights and presumably the listening post, probably Lowndes Street."

"*Lowndes?*" exclaimed Angela. "That's where Coley lives," she added softly.

The night sky over Bahrain was dark, the last Islamic prayers shouted by the mullahs from the minarets, the hour for sleep and the nocturnal games of the privileged royals about to begin. Jamie Montrose slowly got out of bed and silently put on his clothes. Fully dressed, he turned on the desk lamp, walked to the locked white door, took a deep breath, and suddenly started hammering his fist on the steel panel.

"*Help!*" he screamed. "Somebody *help* me!"

"What is it, Master James?" shouted the voice beyond the door.

"Who are *you*?"

"Kalil, Master James. What *is* it?"

"I don't know, but my stomach's on *fire*! I guess you should call a doctor—I've been doubled up on my bed for almost an hour but the pain won't go *away*!" James Montrose Jr. picked up an iron dumbbell that he had been given for his exercise routine, and stood by the wall next to the door. "For God's sake *hurry*! I feel like I'm going to *die*!"

The door crashed open as the Bahraini rushed inside; seeing no one, he was briefly bewildered. The moment he turned, the teenager smashed the dumbbell into his forehead. The guard fell to the floor unconscious.

"Sorry, Kalil," whispered the youngster, breathless. "My dad would have called it a diversion." Jamie proceeded to search the immobile figure, removing a Colt .45 from its holster, several papers written in Arabic, and a billfold containing what appeared to be a great deal of paper money. He remembered what Amet, the head of the prison-villa, had said to him. *Don't try to bribe our guards with promises, James. By our lights, they are very well paid, quite rich, really.* Young Montrose put the money in his pocket. He then dragged the unconscious body to the bed and ripped the top sheet into shreds; he wound several strips around the guard's mouth, then his hands and feet, pulling the linen tight, and raced back to the desk, switching off the light.

He walked cautiously through the open door and closed it softly, turning the large brass key, then made his way down the corridor he had walked for weeks, toward the arch that led to the open area of the estate. From long nights of looking through the bars of his opposing windows, Jamie knew the grounds were patrolled by two guards with automatic rifles strapped across their shoulders and sidearms holstered at their hips. Dressed in white Arabic robes and headdresses, they walked in casual, quasi-military fashion, meeting at the east and west walls and retracing their steps.

The whitewashed arch that Montrose approached led to the east yard and wall, seen through the dim light shining from the main house. He crouched in the darkness of the stone corridor and waited until the two guards came into view, meeting at the center of the white wall, which was equidistant from the locked, impenetrable north and south gates. The guards paused, maddeningly lighting cigarettes and chatting. Jamie was suddenly alarmed. The blow he had dealt the guard, Kalil, was harsh enough to render him unconscious, but not life-threatening; there was no need for that. Kalil might well regain consciousness any minute, and there were a dozen ways he could make sufficient noise to attract the guards—kicking chairs, shoving plates off tables, smashing the television, so *many* ways.

Young Montrose remained frozen, staring at the two Bahrainis, silently urging them to resume their patrol. Still they did not move, instead laughing quietly at some joke. Jamie Montrose began to sweat, perspiration born of anxiety and fear. It was common knowledge that the laws of the Arab Emirates were as tough as those anywhere in the world, depending upon whom one displeased, and it was the *whom* that determined the punishment. . . . *But what was he worried about?* His "sequestration" was a joint exercise between Bahrain and the United States government!

Or was it? That was the question, for Jamie could not adequately convince himself that he had been told the truth. There was simply too much that was too crazy! His mother would have reached him someway, *somehow,* to let him know—even a *hint*—of what was going on. To think otherwise was nuts, as crazy as everything else that had happened!

It came! A crash from his cell, followed by moans and muted screams at the window. Then the smashing of glass and china dishes, finally the collapsing of wood from a disintegrating table and desk. The two guards raced over to the east window and Jamie held his breath, terrified that the worst would happen. It did *not*! They had no flashlights!

The guards screamed in Arabic, each pointing in opposite directions. One to the north, the other to the arch where Jamie was crouched in the shadows. The second guard raced past him, intent only on reaching his cell. Suddenly, searchlights were flashed on throughout the entire villa and its compound.

There was no one yet on the east wall. It was his only chance! He ran out into the yard and raced to the eight-foot wall, jumping as he had never jumped before, ripping his bleeding fingernails as he gripped whatever crevices of stone he could feel. In sheer panic, he reached the top of the ledge, then, again suddenly, he realized that his hands were drenched with blood. The wall was crowned not only with shattered glass, but also a coil of barbed wire, its points as sharp as razor blades.

Jamie thought for a second, a millisecond—*circumstances. Evaluate. What would* Dad *have done?* The roving search-lights caught him in their beams and converged on his frozen figure. Thinking suspended, instinct his command, he leaped over the top of the wall as a pole-vaulter might, twisting his body in an arc and landing hard on his shoulders on the ground. His right arm was in agony, but he could live with it as long as he was out of his so-civilized prison.

Running wildly, he reached a dirt road, and waited for a car or a truck he could flag down. Several passed, paying no attention, then finally a taxi stopped. The driver spoke in Arabic.

"I don't understand you, sir," said young Montrose, out of breath. "I am an American—"

"Americain?" shouted the driver. "You *Americain*?"

"Yes!" cried Jamie, nodding his head rapidly, grateful that the man understood some English. "Is there a . . . consulate or an American embassy here?"

"H'ambassie Americain!" replied the driver, shouting and grinning and also nodding his head up and down like an excited chicken. "Shalkh Isa . . . in Manama!"

"The *embassy*?"

"Yes, yes—"

"Take me there—*drive* me!" Montrose reached into his pocket, pulled out a fistful of money, and jumped into the backseat.

"Aiyee Americain!" gleefully shouted the Bahraini as his taxi roared off down the road.

Sixteen minutes later, after crossing three bridges, Jamie's blood-soaked hands curled in his shirt, they were in the capital of Manama. The sights and sounds seemed strange to Montrose junior, peering out the window. Sections of the small city were in silent darkness, few people in what appeared to be nearly deserted streets. Yet other areas were brightly lighted, storefronts blazing with exotic wares, and Middle Eastern music emanating from loudspeakers;

these streets were crowded, not raucous at all, but filled with
people. What astonished Montrose junior was the sight of
numerous American sailors and naval officers.

"H'ambassie Americain!" exclaimed the driver, gesturing ahead at a pink-and-white mansion in the Shalkh Isa
Street. Jamie looked outside at the front of the building—
something was *wrong*! There were four men in Arab robes,
two on each side of the ornate entrance of glistening dark
wood. At first glance, it might be presumed they were
guards, but American embassies, without exception, posted
American Marines as guards. And those few embassies that
required external patrols at night would never, *never* use native civilians of the host city for that duty. It was not only
unheard of, it was potentially suicidal. Montrose junior had
been in too many countries to doubt that.

There was only one answer: The four Arabs were from
the alabaster villa on the shores of the Persian Gulf! "Keep
going!" yelled Jamie, gripping the driver's shoulder with the
strength of a young wrestler and jabbing his right index finger back and forth, indicating the street ahead. "Take me
back to the lights, the people . . . the *stores*!"

"Aiyee, shoppees! You buy!"

His hands wrapped in gauze, awkwardly purchased at a
pharmacy, young Montrose wandered into the thick crowds
roving through the shopping area of the Az Zahran district
in Manama. He spotted a naval officer, a lieutenant senior
grade, as denoted by the insignia on his open-shirted
summer-dress collar and the silver wings on his shirt.
Something about the man and the way he handled himself
vaguely reminded Jamie of his father. The black officer was
tall, his features clean-cut, sharp but not aggressively so, his
informal manner conveyed by his humorous handling of
several enlisted sailors who had obviously discovered shops
where illegal liquor could be obtained. He gently mocked
their salutes and conferred with a few, apparently urging
them to get out of the area before they were spotted by the
shore patrols. The advice was taken.

Montrose junior approached the officer. "Lieutenant," he

said, speaking loud enough to be heard over the noise of the crowd, "may I speak with you, sir?"

"You're an American," observed the naval officer. "What the hell happened to your *hands,* kid?"

"It's part of what I have to talk to you about, sir. I think I need help."

17

Cameron Pryce walked aimlessly, anxiously around the stately furniture in the Brewster drawing room while Leslie Montrose sat with Angela on the brocaded sofa.

"We're being *sidetracked,* damn it!" cried the CIA field officer. "We're going around in circles, circles with no tangents, as Scofield would say."

"What are you talking about, Cam?" asked Leslie.

Pryce had no chance to answer as MI-5's ill-humored Geoffrey Waters came bounding down the staircase. "Damn, damn, *damn,*" he exclaimed.

"I already said that," remarked Cameron. "Why now you?"

"The whole bloody place is wired! It could bloody well be an adjunct of the BBC, or one of those penny-dreadful offshore stations in the channel!"

"Clarification, please?" said Pryce.

"Try this, chap. We found the bug in the garage, three in this room, two in the dining room, and one in every other damn room in the house—excuse me, another two in the upstairs library."

"That's so *disgusting*!" cried Angela.

"It had to have taken a long time to install them," said Leslie.

"Without being observed," added Cameron. "A person or persons in here alone without fear of being discovered." He turned to Angela Brewster. "Since your mother's death, you and your brother have been back at your schools, haven't you?"

"We stayed here in London about a fortnight after the funeral—meeting with solicitors and executors and too many relatives, that sort of thing. And, of course, we've come back for a couple of weekends. Rog picks me up and we drive down like we did yesterday."

"What Special Agent Pryce is getting at, my dear," said Geoffrey Waters, "is that when you were *not* here, we must assume that Sergeant Major Coleman was, is that correct?"

"Yes," replied Angela, barely audible, her eyes downcast.

"Then I'd say we have the answer as to who planted the intercepts. He's obviously a candidate for the Old Bailey and I'd be delighted to call Scotland Yard right now." The MI-5 chief started toward a phone.

"*No,* Geof!" objected Cameron, raising his voice. "That's the last thing we do—or with luck, the next-to-last."

"Now, just wait, chap. The only person who could have planted those intercepts is Coleman, and I remind you, it's a crime."

"Then we put him under surveillance, the tightest possible, but we don't lock him up."

"I'm not sure I follow you—"

"It's what I was saying before," interrupted Pryce. "We're being distracted by everything that's happening and not concentrating on the fundamental question, the reason Leslie and I flew over here. *Why* was Angela's mother killed? What's the connection to the Matarese?"

"The *who*?"

"I'll explain later, dear," said Montrose.

"I strongly disagree," Waters broke in. "By pursuing everything that's happened, hopefully we'll find that connection. Have a little patience, old man. What else have we got to go on?"

"We're missing something," continued Cameron, slowly shaking his head. "I don't know what it is but we're *missing* something. . . . Maybe we should go back to what Scofield said on Brass Twenty-six—"

"On what, chap?"

"Oh, sorry. Where I first met Beowulf Agate."

"What a charming ellipsis," said Leslie. "What did Scofield say?"

"Basically, that we needed an in-depth profile of Lady Alicia. Talk to lawyers, bankers, doctors, neighbors; build a psychological dossier; above all, follow any money trails."

"My dear *fellow!*" exclaimed the MI-5 man. "Do you think we've been sitting around sucking our damn *thumbs*? We've put together a rather generous file on Lady Alicia, covering most of those items you just mentioned."

"Why didn't you say something?"

"We had other priorities, if you recall. Priorities we honestly believed would lead to shortcuts on the way to that connection you speak of."

"Shortcuts? You've been talking with Scofield."

"Not in years, but we all look for shortcuts, don't we?"

"And psychological profiles are long shots," said Leslie. "They take a great deal of time, which I'm not sure my son can afford. That may be selfish . . . but I can't help it."

"No one could blame you for that!" said Angela Brewster.

"No one is," said Waters. "You're right, Cameron, we put the bastard Coleman under complete surveillance, personal and electronic. Considering the dynamics of recent events, he could well lead us to others."

"And if he suddenly moves around a lot and your personnel runs thin, *then* we call in Scotland Yard."

There were four rapid beeps from the area beyond the archway. It was the front door. "That would be Rog and Coley," Angela said. "They both have remotes that shut off the alarm. . . . I don't know what to *say,* how to *behave.* What should I do?"

"Just act natural," replied Leslie Montrose. "Don't feel you have to say anything other than perfectly normal greetings. I suspect they'll be doing most of the talking—they'll have to."

Roger Brewster came through the arch carrying two large cardboard cartons, apparently not very heavy. "Hello, everybody," he said, carefully lowering the cartons to the floor.

"How did it go, Rog?" asked Angela haltingly. "Where's Coley?"

"Question two, he's driving the Bentley down into the garage. . . . Question one, just fine. Old Coley's a devious son of a bitch, let me tell you!"

The others in the room exchanged glances. "How so, young fellow?" said Waters.

"Well, he walked into the security company like a lamb, getting our alarm records and plans, asking the questions we wanted answered, and making sure the technology was available to transmit the system to his flat in Lowndes Street. It was, of course."

"So where's the deviousness?" asked Pryce.

"He suddenly turned and became a bloody tiger, a regular Jekyll and Hyde! He'd hinted at some irregularities in the system when we were in the car driving over, but he didn't elaborate so I figured he was just bitching—these systems all have glitches."

"But he wasn't just bitching?"

"Hell no, sir. He held up the computerized-record printout and proceeded to give the firm's owner what-for while referring to his notebook."

"What was he complaining about?" said the MI-5 chief, his outward calm disguising his anxiety.

"He claimed there were errors, quite a few of them, in the entries. You see, our system electronically computes the dates and times when the alarm is turned on, as well as any violations while it's activated."

"*And,* Bro?"

"Coley said that there were occasions when he left the house, noting the times when he turned on the alarm, and they weren't listed on the printouts. And if they weren't listed, how could he believe there weren't any violations."

"What did the owner say?"

"Not an awful lot, Mrs. Montrose, Coley didn't give him a chance. When the owner said that Coley probably didn't insert the correct codes, old Coleman simply told him that wasn't possible."

"One of your classic sergeant majors, Geof," said Pryce softly.

"Indubitably, chap," agreed Waters. "What's in the boxes, Roger?"

"There are two more in the foyer, I'll bring them in."

"What *are* they?"

"I'll let Coley tell you. I'm not sure I understand." Roger dashed into the archway, instantly colliding with an emerging figure carrying two cartons. Oliver Coleman, exsergeant major in the Royal Fusiliers, was a medium-sized plug of a man whose broad chest, thick neck, large shoulders, and erect posture gave away his military background, despite his business suit. His lined face was topped by brush-cut white hair with tinges of its former red, his features set, neither pleasant nor unpleasant, instead noncommittal. The larger Roger Brewster had literally bounced off him.

"Sorry, lad," he said, glancing at the off-balance young man. "Good afternoon, Sir Geoffrey," he continued in his pronounced Yorkshire accent, "I see there's a gray van outside, I figure it's one of yours."

"You're not supposed to. It's unmarked."

"Then I'd suggest you paint a sign on the sides, like Fishmonger or Greengrocers. Those gray vehicles stand out. You might as well be announcing yourselves."

"I'll bear it in mind. . . . May I introduce you to our new associates, Sergeant Major. Lieutenant Colonel Montrose, United States Army, and Special Agent Pryce, CIA."

"Yes, the children told me about the two of you," said Coleman, first approaching Leslie.

"Sergeant Major." Montrose leaned forward on the couch, extending her hand.

"I'd salute, Colonel, but that was quite a few years ago." They shook hands. "It's a pleasure, ma'am, the kids think very highly of you—of both of you." Coleman turned to Cameron; they also clasped hands. "An honor, Special Agent. We don't get to see many of you chaps."

"The name's Pryce, and I'm not 'special.' We don't have

'special agents,' Sergeant Major, but I can't get it through Sir Geoffrey's head."

"And I'm Coley, Mr. Pryce, everybody calls me Coley."

"While we're at it, Coley old man, Roger said you'd explain the paraphernalia in those boxes. Please do so."

"With enthusiasm, sir! Y'see, I kept a record of my exits and entries over the past—"

"*Yes,* old chap, the young fellow explained all that, your notebook, et cetera. What are you *doing*?"

"Well, a week and a half ago I got suspicious, I did. I drove down to Kent one morning—on a rather personal matter—and when I returned late in the afternoon I noticed that the potted azaleas on the front steps had been disturbed, several new buds broken off, actually, as if struck by something. I didn't think much about it; postmen and delivery people often carry large packages, if you see what I mean."

"But you thought enough about it to start keeping a record, is that right?" asked Pryce, studying the old soldier.

"That's it, sir. I wrote down the exact times whenever I left and reentered the house. Sometimes it was only for a few minutes, like down to the market and back, at others I'd wait around the corner for an hour or more to see if any bounder showed up."

"But no one ever did," said Cameron.

"No, sir, and that gave me an idea—in truth, it only struck me the other day. On Thursday, I picked up a phone in here, coughed loudly while pretending to dial, then spoke clearly, saying I'd meet a chap in Regent's Park around noon. I added some nonsense that could be construed as a code and hung up."

"The oldest infantry trick since radios were introduced into combat," said Pryce. "The assumption based on the probability that the enemy had zeroed in on your outer frequency."

"That's *right,* sir!"

"Let me finish your scenario. You drove to Regent's Park, picked up a car on your tail, parked, and waltzed through the paths until you saw who was following you—"

"You're *bloody* right, sir!"

At that moment, the three-man intercept unit from MI-5 came down the staircase carrying their equipment. Ian, the team's leader, spoke while reaching the great hall's floor and glancing at his clipboard. "We found two more in the attic, Sir Geoffrey."

"Coley, *look*!" shouted Roger Brewster.

"What, lad?"

"The equipment they're bringing down! It's like the stuff we picked up at your friend's shop in the Strand."

"So it is, Roger. MI-Five wasn't far behind us. They simply got here before us."

"What do you mean, Coleman?"

"Bugs, Sir Geoffrey. There had to be listening devices all over the house! I damn well proved it."

"You proved it and we found them," said Waters, his voice low and laced with suspicion. "Rather splendid if unusual timing, wouldn't you say?"

"I'm not sure what you said, sir."

"I believe we should have a look-see at your flat, Coleman."

"What for? The new equipment won't be installed for several days."

"We're interested in the existing equipment."

"I beg your pardon?"

"I'll be blunt, old chap. This afternoon may be a brilliant performance on your part but I doubt you're aware of the latest technology in intercept tracking."

"I haven't the foggiest what you're talkin' about," said Coleman, his face beginning to flush with anger.

"The listening post for the devices in this house was determined to be in Lowndes Street. Your flat is in Lowndes Street. Need I say more?"

"If you're suggestin' what I think you're suggestin', your title and rank be damned, I'll tear your throat out!"

"I shouldn't advise that," said Waters as the MI-5 unit stepped forward as one. "Bad form, old man."

"It's a hell of a lot better than yours, y'*scum*! Brigadier Daniel Brewster was the finest commander I ever served under. He was also the greatest friend I ever had, a friendship

I would never have known if he hadn't saved my life in the mountains of Muscat, where the terrorists left me to die! When he passed on, I swore to meself I'd serve the family till m'last day on earth. So how *dare* you come in here spoutin' your *garbage*?"

"Your excellent acting is beginning to annoy me, Coleman."

"And your insinuations have got me blood boilin', *Sir Hogspit*!"

"Cool it, both of you!" ordered Pryce. "We can settle this very quickly. . . . Sergeant Major, have you any objection to Sir Geoffrey's checking your flat?"

"No, of course not. Asked like a gentleman, I would have said so before."

"When were you last home?" pressed a somewhat sub-dued Waters.

"Let's see now," answered Coleman, "the children got here late yesterday, and I've been staying upstairs, so it must have been three or four days ago when I checked on my mail. The computerized alarm records, *if* they're accurate, will show that."

"There. See, it's settled," said Cameron, turning to the MI-5 chief. "Get the entry code and send your team over, Geof."

"Well, I may have been hasty, Coley, old fellow, but the evidence seemed pretty firm, y'know."

"Yes, well, Lowndes is a pretty big street. Also, I may have been a touch hasty m'self—I try to be more disciplined with my superiors. Sorry about that."

"Think nothing of it, old chap. I'd have done the same."

"Hey, Coley," Roger Brewster interrupted. "I like Sir Geoffrey, but he's not your 'superior.' He's a civilian and so are you."

"Right!" Angela chimed in.

"I'm thoroughly chastised," said Waters, a warm gleam in his eyes. "It's hardly the first time. However, except for discovering the bugs, we're back where we started."

"I wouldn't say that, sir," objected Coleman. "I didn't get a chance to finish, but I recognized one of the chaps who was following me in Regent's Park. He works for the alarm company, a repairman, and I think his name is Wally or Waldo, something like that."

"Run with it, Geof!" Pryce cried. "Get your people on it. Find the guy, and dig up his whole enchilada."

As if the impersonal instrument had been privy to the words spoken in Belgrave Square, Waters's cellular phone suddenly erupted from inside his jacket. The MI-5 chief pulled it out, pressed the button that stopped the ringing, and brought the phone to his ear. "Waters," he said, then listened. "You rang me at the right moment, Mark, I was about to call you, although on an entirely different matter." Sir Geoffrey removed a notebook and a ballpoint pen, began writing, and continued. "Repeat that please, chap, and spell the names. . . . Oh, they're bona fides, you've researched them already. Very good, I'll be along in a bit. Now, to the other matter." Waters proceeded to issue his instructions regarding a Wally or a Waldo employed by the Brewsters' alarm company. "Dig deep but in silence." Waters replaced his cellular phone and turned to Cameron. "Hereafter, *Agent* Pryce, this may possibly be in our lexicon 'the day of dual shortcuts.'"

"Speak American English, Geof."

"A linguistic oxymoron, sir. . . . However, a top chap in the Foreign Office, one of the few who has limited knowledge of our operation, called my assistant and said he might have something for me. Do you remember the three others besides Lady Alicia who were killed, and how we looked for a linkage and couldn't find any?"

"Sure," replied Cameron. "The French millionaire on his yacht, the Spanish doctor in Monte Carlo, and the Italian polo player on Long Island. There was no linkage, not even any evidence that they knew one another."

"There is now. The doctor poisoned in Monte Carlo was a research scientist from a wealthy family in Madrid. The university where he had his laboratory was in the process of pulling up data from his computers when out popped several transmissions to Alicia Brewster, Belgravia, off-line, confidential."

"What was his name?" asked Roger quickly.

"Juan Garcia Guaiardo."

"*I* know that name," said Angela.

"How so, my dear?" Waters sat down, his concentration on Lady Alicia's daughter.

"I'm not sure. But every now and then when Rog and I were home and we were having dinner or tea, Mum would mention that she had heard from a Juan, or a Guaiardo, and she would become tense, her eyes kind of funny-like, unfocused, even angry. Once I heard her say something like 'Stop them, they must be stopped,' or words to that effect."

"She never elaborated?" asked Pryce.

"Not really," said Roger Brewster pensively, blinking in thought. "You see, Mother worked very hard, too hard in my opinion, after Dad died. She'd get pretty stretched sometimes, and say things that didn't always make sense."

"What your sister just said makes a great deal of sense," interrupted Cameron. "Where's your mother's computer?"

"Upstairs in her office," answered Angela.

"Are you thinking what I'm thinking, Cam?" said Leslie Montrose.

"It wouldn't surprise me. . . . Where's your mother's office?"

"Come on, we'll show you," said the daughter, getting up and heading for the elegant circular staircase, followed by the others.

Alicia Brewster's home office was a combination of old-fashioned comfort and modern efficiency. Flanking either side of the large bay windows were the room's two distinctly different areas. On the left were floor-to-ceiling bookshelves, a long, soft leather couch and armchairs, and assorted tables and fringed lamps. If a word was applicable for this area, it would be *warm*.

Conversely, the opposite side was a gleaming white nightmare of the most expensive, up-to-the-minute technology. There was a huge computer with an appropriate screen, an outsized printer, two fax machines, and a telephone console/answering machine with at least four separate lines.

The term *ice cold* was far too warm for the right side of the room.

"Geof," said Pryce, once they were all inside the office, "call your friend at the Foreign Office and get the dates of the Guaiardo transmissions to Lady Alicia."

"Right. . . . Can you operate these things, old man?"

"Reasonably well."

"Good, because I'm no expert."

"I am," said Lieutenant Colonel Montrose, her voice a monotone. "The Army sent me to the University of Chicago, Department of Computer Sciences. I trust I'm somewhat more than reasonably proficient."

"Then go to work, Army, I'm not in your league."

"Few are, *Special* Agent Pryce. Let me study the equipment and any manuals I may find." Eight minutes later, a manual perused and the dates of the Madrid transmissions in her hand, Leslie bent over the computer, her fingers literally flying over the keys. "We're in luck," she said. "The search and retrieve function hasn't any blocks. We'll pull up the Madrid transmissions and check for any replies within the time frame."

One by one, each page emerged from the printer, accompanied by a barely audible hum. There were seven pages of varying lengths, four from Madrid to London, three from London to Madrid. Taken all together, they were a barely comprehensible road map, a map where the routes had no numbers, the towns and villages no names, but one that offered so many elusive hints as to form a mosaic of possibilities. In sequence, they were as follows:

Madrid, August 12. My dear cousin. Tracing and employing what medical records I could find of the original members going back to the year 1911, I've come up with numerous surviving issue. This was facilitated by the fact that the members were exclusively from established families, the genealogies available.

London, August 13. Dearest Juan. Thank God you're in research. Move as rapidly as you can. Word from Lake Como, the Scozzi survivors, as in the old Scozzi-Paravacini, pressure is being applied.

Madrid, August 20. Cousin Alicia dear. Using my certainly tainted but very real resources, I've employed highly reputable private investigators, giving them minimal information. As a result, I have eliminated 43 percent of my original list. Perhaps more will follow. Quite simply, they had no cognizance or association whatsoever. Voice-tape analyses confirmed their complete ignorance.

London, August 22. Keep digging, dear heart. Pressure building from Amsterdam, which I have firmly rejected.

London, August 23. Dearest Juan. The pressures from Amsterdam have turned ugly, bordering on threats. The children don't know it but I've hired bodyguards to stay close to them, hopefully without being seen.

Madrid, August 29. Cousin dearest. The slaughter at Estepona killing Mouchistine and his four international attorneys was a disaster. I cannot trace the order, but one thing is certain, it came from the M, for Antoine Lavalle, Mouchistine's confidant, revealed the old man's intentions. The attorneys from Paris, Rome, Berlin, and Washington were merely fronts. But how were they to execute Mouchistine's orders and how can we find out? I'm at a loss.

"*Damn* it!" shouted Roger, after reading the next-to-last transmission. "I *knew* it! There were these three or four blokes. They'd show up at different times, odd times, like in a pub or around the soccer field. I confronted two of them and asked them what they were doing. They were like innocent lambs—claimed to be local lads who liked a pint now and then and rooted for our teams."

"I saw mine, too, Bro," said Angela. "I'm afraid I got one into trouble. I reported him to the prefects as a possible stalker with sexual intentions. Then he wasn't there anymore, but there were others. That's when I figured it out. Mum was worried about us."

"Why didn't you *tell* me?"

"Because you've got a quick temper, Rog, and I figured Mother knew what she was doing."

Monte Carlo, August 29. The murder of Giancarlo Tremonte, the last male descendant and heir to the original Scozzi interests, is proof that the M will stop at nothing. It intends to silence us all. Be careful, my dearest cousin. Trust no one.

"So much for linkage!" exclaimed Waters. "My God, they were *cousins,* very *close* cousins! How did we miss it?"

Once again, Waters's cellular phone sounded its muted ring from inside his jacket. He retrieved it, punched the button, and spoke. "Yes?" he said. What followed could hardly be good news, for the face of the MI-5 officer changed from its usual neutrality to a frown and then a grimace. Finally, he closed his eyes and sighed audibly. "I agree, it's hardly helpful, but keep digging. Find out who his mate was in Regent's Park." Sir Geoffrey turned to the others as he replaced his telephone. "The body of Wallace Esterbrook, also known as Wally Esterbrook, employed by the Trafalgar Guardian Company, was fished out of the Thames this afternoon with two gunshots in the back of his head. The time of death has been temporarily established as within the past forty-eight hours."

"Thursday night or Friday morning," said Coleman. "M'God, it *fits*!"

"What fits?" asked Pryce.

"There was a moment, just a few seconds, it was, when our eyes met. He knew I recognized him."

"What about the guy *with* him?" pressed Cameron.

"I dunno, I really can't say, but I seem to recall that he glanced at both of us."

"Run with it, Geof!"

18

Brandon Alan Scofield, a.k.a. Beowulf Agate, was in the element he knew best, remembered from a quarter of a century ago. He was the stalker once again, the primeval cat who hunted its prey at night, or the two-legged, deep-cover killer who sought out the enemy in darkness, killing as a last resort, for capture was eminently more desirable.

To keep communications intact and Scofield's whereabouts a secret, Antonia remained at Peregrine View in the Great Smoky Mountains. Any calls that came from Cameron Pryce or Leslie Montrose in Europe could be instantly communicated to him through the magic of cellular technology. She demanded only that Bray, once he landed in Wichita, reach her every eight hours, telling her of his progress. If he was more than two hours late, she would call Frank Shields at the Central Intelligence Agency and tell him the truth. Scofield objected but Antonia was adamant. "I want you back whole, you overage idiot! What the hell could I do with Brass Twenty-six without you?"

Beowulf Agate was in Wichita, Kansas, the headquarters of Atlantic Crown, Limited, purveyors to the world. Someone in the upper regions of its executive offices had written the orders to Lieutenant Colonel Leslie Montrose and had them replicated in Amsterdam, Paris, Cairo, Istanbul, and God knew where else. That someone was a member of the Matarese hierarchy, and Brandon intended to find out who it was.

The clock in the rental car read 2:27 A.M. The enormous parking lot of Atlantic Crown was nearly deserted, only the well-lit security cars seen under the floodlights, their white-lettered Patrol Vehicle markings very obvious. Bray smiled to himself. In the old days, the Soviets were much smarter. The last thing they would do was advertise. Taking a hunting knife out of its scabbard, Scofield opened the car door, stepped onto the pavement, and silently closed it. He crept swiftly through the floodlights and proceeded to slash all the tires on the patrol cars. He then weaved through the intermittent shadows to a side door and studied the alarm box, customary for a well-armed complex, but also its weakest point. It was almost primitive, thought Bray. Atlantic Crown, like many overprotected, overindulgent companies, overlooked the essentials of basic series electronics, believing that a security breach could never happen to *them*. Salaried security personnel were a necessary expense, complicated wiring systems were often more trouble than they were worth, a duplicating cost.

Scofield pried open the box with a small crowbar he removed from his belt, pulled out a penlight, and examined the wires. Primitive, hell, these were antediluvian. Another few thousand dollars for each circuit would prohibit overpass throughout the entire complex. *Bless the bean counters,* he mused, as he pointed the beam of light at the various wires. *Red, white, blue, blue, orange, white, blue.* Amateur time. Bray pulled out a pair of small pliers and snipped the three blue wires. He waited for the response. There was none. He had dismantled the east quadrant of the system.

"The old man can now go to work," whispered Beowulf Agate to himself. *"Move, boy!"*

Miniature wire prongs in his hand, Bray manipulated the lock of the side door and walked inside. The corridors were dark, the neon lights at their dimmest, gray upon gray, all muted, dull and shadowless. Bray knew he could not use an elevator, so he looked for a staircase; he found it and began climbing. The Atlantic Crown building was seventeen stories high; he had to reach the sixteenth floor.

He did so.

In an odd way, Scofield felt exhilarated. The fear was there, of course, and that was a good thing; he had been away too long and needed the brakes of caution. But he had recalled the tools of his former profession, starting with the thick crepe-soled shoes that reduced the noise of footsteps; the lock prongs; a blue penlight; a magnetized stethoscopic meter for vaults; a canister of immobilizing gas; a miniature camera; a Heckler & Koch .25-caliber automatic, silenced, of course, and a wire garrote. His hair had been cut, his beard trimmed, and he wore Army-issue combat fatigues with multiple pockets. He delighted in the fact that Frank Shields had paid for his entire outfit by requisitions without being told the truth.

"You're *not* to go into the field!" exploded the CIA analyst. "We agreed to that."

"Of course I'm not, Squinty," Beowulf Agate had replied. "You think I'm as fruit-looped as you are? I know what I can do and what I can't do even though I'm a hell of a lot younger than you."

"Barely a year and a half, Brandon. Then why all these expenditures?"

"Because the lead I've got could be the breakthrough we need over here."

"That doesn't answer my question."

"All right, I'll be upfront, but only to a point, and you'd better accept it. I hired the best rogue agent the Stasi ever had, a cold-blooded son of a bitch wanted by a few governments as well as Interpol representing a few others. He's off the books, off any and all records, with no name and no history. We've done it before, Squinty; we've got to do it again."

"What's his tariff?"

"Two thousand a day plus all expenses, and a bonus of a hundred thousand if he brings back the goods."

"It's outrageous, of course, but if what you say is true and your rogue can pull it off, I guess we can live with it. We've paid more in the past. Pick up the supply funds at the Commercial Bank of Nova Scotia, there's only one and it's in the book. Ask for a vice president named Wister, he's the finance contact. I'll authorize an initial ten thousand."

"There's a financial good side, too, Squinty. Our man says that if he buys a grave, we're off the hook. As he puts it, he hasn't got any relatives he'd leave a deutsche mark to, so the hell with it."

"He's a confident bastard, isn't he?"

"He's both. That's why he's good."

Damn, thought Scofield as he approached the fifteenth-floor landing, out of breath. He should have quoted Squinty Shields five—*ten* times what he had told him! His fictional Stasi agent was such an inspiration he almost believed in the man himself. There was no question about it, mused Beowulf Agate, briefly resting his legs and his lungs, the out-of-sanction agreement with his brilliant German creation had to be restructured. Considerably upward. That was, if anything came from the Wichita operation, which, Scofield considered, he had better start thinking about.

Scanning the data they had gathered from the Atlantic Crown conglomerate, legally and illegally, two names kept surfacing. They were Alistair McDowell, chief executive officer, and Spiro Karastos, treasurer and chief financial officer. Their memoranda to each other, as well as to their subordinate departments, were almost robotically similar, mixing the corporatese with contemporary vernacular. Judging by analysis of isolated words and phrases, either or both could have been responsible for the instructions issued to Lieutenant Colonel Leslie Montrose, mother of the kidnapped James Montrose Jr.

It was a simple matter to learn the whereabouts of each man's office and the schedules of the night cleaning personnel. The offices were on the sixteenth floor, so near to each other that there was a connecting door, and the cleaning crews who divided up their maintenance labors generally reached the sixteenth floor between one and one-fifteen in the morning; their chores took no longer than forty minutes. It was further established that as the stairs beyond the exit

doors had to be mopped and all debris removed, the doors to
the floors' corridors were opened in sequence. A well-
rewarded cleaning woman, convinced that her job would
not be in jeopardy—quite the contrary—agreed to place a
rubber doorstop on the sixteenth-floor landing. She did, a
hundred dollars richer in the cause of a harmless corporate
prank being played by top executives. In addition, and in
the spirit of corporate conviviality, she also agreed to keep
the door to Alistair McDowell's office unlocked. The purpose? So his corporate associates could surreptitiously
place two dozen Happy Birthday balloons, along with a buffet of caviar and champagne, in their colleague's office.
Why not? The elderly corporate big shot, who had made the
request in the parking lot, was such a nice gentleman, and
dressed in one whale of an expensive suit. Pricey enough to
feed her family for six months.

Beowulf Agate had retained a few of his more-persuasive
talents. In other days, older days, he might have opted for
less time-consuming, but riskier, preparations. However,
the advancing years dictated a more carefully thought-out
approach. In retrospect, he wished he had had the wisdom
of such cautionary practices before. Perhaps it would have
eliminated two shoulder wounds, three bullets in his legs,
and a stomach puncture that took weeks to mend. So what?
He couldn't spring over a five-foot fence now, either. Five
feet, hell, three with luck and a sore back!

The muscles of his calves still throbbing from the climb,
he shook his legs one by one rapidly, harshly, and started up
the final flight. As promised, the small rubber stop kept the
crash door open barely an inch, sufficient without being apparent. Again in the arrogance of satisfactory security, there
were no cameras in the hallways; a team of night watchmen
patrolled the corridors, checked the office doors, and
clocked in with their keys at the end of each floor. Scofield
reached the top step, approached the door, and pulled it back
just enough to glance down the hallway. He immediately
shoved it back against the rubber; a guard was walking
toward him, dangling the large metal security key that he

would insert into the watchman's clock at the end of the hall, only feet from the exit staircase.

Suddenly concerned, Bray crouched, removing the doorstop and painfully holding the heavy steel door by his fingertips so that barely a slit of light showed. His right hand in agony, his fingers on fire, he held his breath in an attempt to suppress the pain. At last, he heard the click of the watchman's time clock and the sound of the guard's footsteps retreating toward the elevators. He again pulled the crash door open slightly, plunged his left hand into the tiny space, and removed his right, bringing it to his mouth for warm moisture. The uniformed guard stood by an elevator; he pressed the button and the undisturbed panel instantly opened. The man disappeared and Scofield, perspiration gathering at his hairline, quickly walked into the dim hallway.

The cleaning crew had disappeared, the silence comforting. Bray rapidly made his way down the corridor, checking the nameplates and the titles on the doors.

ALISTAIR MCDOWELL
CHIEF EXECUTIVE OFFICER

It was the center door directly ahead at the far end of the hallway. There were no similar doors on either side, signifying a suite, not a normal corporate office. Scofield reached for the glistening brass knob, hoping his rewarded cleaning lady had duplicated her service at the exit staircase. She had. Slowly Bray turned the knob and cautiously opened the door, prepared to run if an undetected alarm went off. None did, and he swiftly entered, pivoting, and closing the door as he switched on his small, powerful flashlight with the blue beam. He circled the room with it, aiming the light at the floor, then crossed to the four large windows, found the cords, and pulled the heavy drapes across the glass. He was ready to start his search.

Alistair McDowell was a family man and apparently wanted everyone to know it. Emphatically. There were at least two dozen silver-framed photographs placed about his huge polished desk and in the bookshelves between the windows. They depicted three children in varying stages of growing up, from infancy in their mother's arms to teenage status. They were seen with their parents and the accoutrements of the progressing years: cribs, baptismal robes, playpens, swings, tricycles, bicycles, tennis racquets, horses, and Comet sailboats. What was shown was a limited history of the Good Life, deserved by a God-fearing man who was proud of his family, his community, his church, and his country. The fruits of his industriousness were wealth, happiness, and stability. It was the American way; he reveled in it.

And if Beowulf Agate's suspicions were even close to the mark, one Alistair McDowell would be among the first to destroy that way of life by restricting it to a select elite, with its legions of sycophants—read slaves.

The desk drawers, two of which were locked, presented no problem for the prongs but neither did they reveal anything helpful except, perhaps, for an appointments calendar. Scofield removed his miniature camera with the 1,000-ASA film and photographed every page; it took nearly fifteen minutes. He then proceeded to examine the entire suite, starting with the unexpected bedroom beyond the right wall, the interior of the office itself, and ending with a conference room on the left, stern but elegant in its heavy simplicity. The search had uncovered several items that required intensive examination. First among them was a wall safe concealed behind a row of leather-bound legal volumes. They had caught Bray's attention, for regardless of McDowell's vaunted ability in management, he was not an attorney.

The thick tomes were there to impress his visitors, not for practical research. They were also an excellent front for a wall safe. Another discovery was a locked closet that, when manipulated open, revealed an obviously state-of-the-art computer and a curved white plastic chair, the enclosure so small only one person could sit inside. A third object was a four-tiered locked mahogany file cabinet that awkwardly stood below the painting of an old English hunting scene, as if the interior decorator had forgotten to build it into the wall. The last entry in the reevaluation sweepstakes was the most curious: a large freestanding antique music box that was placed above a carved cherry wood cabinet, the price undoubtedly in the neighborhood of thirty thousand dollars, if not a great deal more.

What piqued his curiosity, however, were the unique contents within the locked cabinet, once again subjected to Bray's sophisticated prongs. It was a self-contained electronic unit, but not a computer, for it was designed for a single purpose and nothing else. Beowulf Agate recognized it at once, recognized the typewriter keys and the four succeeding cylinders that rolled forward and in reverse, slowly, as if inexorably, until all were synchronized and came to a halt, its elusive problem having been solved, a cipher broken. It was a decoding unit designed around the principles of the converter that had cracked the famous Enigma, the cipher machine used by the German high command to send encrypted messages in the Second World War.

The one modern addition to this machine was obviously usurped from the computer. Instead of a printed page that emerged from the lowest platen, there was a small television screen mounted on top of the equipment. Scofield recalled his earlier days in London while working with British intelligence and how he had been fascinated by the stories about cracking Enigma. An English colleague had taken him to a branch office in Oxford where an updated version of a decoding machine was in operation, the proximity to the university for purposes of immediate scholarship and research.

"Type in the word 'aardvark,'" the young MI-5 officer named Waters had said. Bray did so and the screen instantly printed out the words *SCREW OFF, ASSHOLE*. "I'm afraid a few of our graduates in training have a warped sense of humor," Geoffrey Waters had continued, chuckling. "Now, spell out the phrase 'The apple rolls far from the tree.'" Again, Scofield did as he was told, but this time the screen went to work in a civilized manner. *MEETING CONFIRMED STUTTGART AS SCHEDULED*. "That was an actual transmission we intercepted from a mole we unearthed last week in the Foreign Office sent to the Stasi in East Berlin."

"What happened?"

"Oh, he went to Stuttgart, all right, but I'm afraid he never came back. One of our lads over the Wall told the Stasi he was a double."

Brandon found the switch and turned on Alistair McDowell's personal decoder. For the hell of it, he typed in *aardvark*. The screen displayed the word *INSUFFI-CIENT*. At least the American product was better mannered. He then inserted the sentence *The apple rolls far from the tree*. The screen faded as the cylinders rolled, finally coming to a stop. The letters appeared: *ADDITIONAL DATA REQUIRED—ZERO SEARCH*. Trees and rolling apples were not in cipherable fashion. Scofield pulled out his camera and took several photographs of the machine in the hope that the manufacturer might be found. Whoever it was would have to be among those contractors for the military and/or the intelligence community dealing in maximum-classified materials. In the parlance of the trade, it was a possible.

Bray returned to the file cabinet, switching on a nearby floor lamp. There were four drawers so he pulled over a straight-backed chair and started at the bottom, beginning with letters *T* through *Z*, seven index dividers, within which were numerous file folders.

The reading was not only laborious, it was also paralyzingly dull. The vast majority of Alistair McDowell's correspondence and memoranda concerned acquisitions, potential acquisitions, marketing strategies, budgets, profit margins and how to improve them. The minority consisted of matters of less import, such as copies of bland speeches made to Rotary Clubs, chambers of commerce, and corporate and trade conventions, as well as letters to politicians, equally bland, and a few to the headmasters of several private schools (apparently the McDowell offspring were not so squeaky-clean after all). Plus an assortment of memos from the chairman involving past and current negotiations, his strong points italicized. Scofield's eyes were glazed, his mind numbed by the banality of the files. Until the letter *Q*—under the inexplicable title of "Quotient Group Equations."

What did it mean? What were "quotient group equations"? There were five folders filled with handwritten pages of numbers and symbols, formulas, or formulae, of one sort or another, but what they signified, Bray hadn't a clue. Yet instincts born in years past came back to him. They meant *something* that Alistair McDowell did not want anyone to understand. Otherwise there would be headings on the pages, descriptions—no matter how brief—of the contents. Instead, there was nothing, no inkling whatsoever.

Scofield knew that *quotient* was a mathematical term, as was *equation,* but where the *group* fit in was beyond him. He looked around the office, hoping to find a dictionary. He did, naturally, on the lower shelf of a bookcase. Carrying it to the desk, he glanced at the windows, making sure the drapes were completely closed, and turned on McDowell's lamp. He opened the dictionary, flipping through the pages until he reached:

Quotient—The result of division; the number of times one quantity is contained in another.

And just below:

Quotient group—A group, the elements of which are intrinsic to a subgroup of a given group.

Beowulf Agate recognized when he had struck a vein of intelligence gold. He photographed every handwritten page in the five folders, beginning to understand the dark, clouded outlines of the obscure material, which could well be leads to the groups and subgroups of the Matarese.

Scofield continued through the file cabinet, finding nothing of interest, but in several folders, items that amused him. Chairman McDowell kept monthly totals of his wife's clothing and household accounts, all annotated as excessive, including liquor bills marked with angry red exclamation points. These pages did not exactly reflect the loving, good-natured family life depicted in the silver-framed photographs. There was turmoil within the house of McDowell.

Brandon closed the top drawer of the file cabinet and returned to the computer closet. He switched on the light and studied the totally unfamiliar equipment. There was nothing else for it. He took out his cellular phone and called Peregrine View in the Great Smokies.

"You're over an hour late!" said an irritated Antonia. "Where are you, you old fool?"

"I'm where none of those amateurs thought I would be."

"Come back here quickly—"

"I'm not finished," interrupted Scofield. "There's a computer and a wall safe—"

"Yes, you *are* finished!" exclaimed Toni. "Something's happened."

"What is it?"

"Frank Shields called a few hours ago. He's not sure what to do."

"That's odd for Squinty. He always knows what to do."

"Not this time. He wants your input."

"I'll be damned, I've been promoted out of grammar school. Well, what *is* it?"

"Naval intelligence reached him. If the information's accurate, Leslie's son escaped and is aboard ship at the American base in Bahrain."

"By Christ, that's *great*! Good for the kid!"

"That's just it, Bray, he *is* a kid, a child, really. Shields thinks it may be a trap."

"For God's sake, *why*?"

"Because according to the naval officer who's with him, the boy won't speak with anyone but his mother. No American government official, no one from intelligence or the White House, not even the President himself. Only his mother, so he'll know if it's really she."

"*Damn!*" exclaimed Scofield, absently striking the nearest object in frustration. In this case, it was the computer's keyboard. At the instant of the blow, ear-shattering alarm bells resonated throughout the entire building. The hidden, off-limits machine was not only sacred, but given to hysterics. Bray yelled into his cellular phone. "I'm getting out of here! Tell Squinty I'll call collect from a pay phone, it's safer than the cell. That's his signal to go on scrambler. Wish me luck, old girl!"

Scofield ran out of the office, closing the door behind him, and raced down the hallway to the staircase exit on the left. He pressed the crash bar, opening the thick fireproof panel, and quickly closed it while reaching down and picking up the small rubber doorstop. Suddenly, he heard the shouts of the guards on the floor inside. Apparently there was some kind of heated argument, and Bray immediately understood. No one had a passkey to the CEO's office. Every other door could probably be unlocked, but not McDowell's, and in all likelihood not Karastos's, the chief financial officer's, which had a door leading to his superior's suite. *Goddamn it!* thought Brandon, he hadn't the time to inspect the latter's room or rooms, much less the safe in the bookshelf. There was no point in dwelling over missed opportunities, he had to get out and reach Shields. Montrose's kid! *Jesus!*

Then he heard the orders yelled by someone who either had the authority or assumed it. "Check the staircases! I'll call the Big Mac and tell the son of a bitch to give us the combination to get his fuckin' key! Suppose there was a fire? Would that asshole rather have his joint burn down than let us get in?"

"Kick the fuckin' door down!"

"It's layered steel, for God's sake. Besides, he'd take it out of my pay, the bastard!"

There was not only turmoil in the house of McDowell, but also in McDowell's fiefdom. The *staircases.* There were two others in this T-shaped section of the building. How many guards were there, and which of the three staircases would be checked first? *Christ,* probably all at once! Brandon plunged down the concrete steps as fast as he could, literally swinging around each landing as he held on to the railing. Breathless, his face drenched with sweat, his legs throbbing, he reached the bottom floor where he had entered.

He paused, gasping for air, and trying to smooth out his Army-issue combat fatigues.

Footsteps! Several floors above on the staircase, perhaps four or five, and descending rapidly. He had no choice; he had to simply walk out, knowing that the guards were undoubtedly running around throughout the building. No time to think!

The guards were, at least one guard was. The blue uniform saw him emerge from the staircase, and ran forward. "Hey, *you*!" shouted the heavy, middle-aged man, pulling his pistol from its holster.

"Not hey *me,* fella!" roared Beowulf Agate in a voice that echoed off the walls like a marching cadence. "It's hey *you*! . . . I'm Colonel Chaucer, National Guard, Special Forces Security, and this company is a max-fax contractor for the government. We're wired into your alarm system."

"You're what—*who*?" asked the perplexed, overwhelmed patrol.

"You *heard* me, fella. We're wired because AC is developing some top-secret chemicals."

"The alarms just went off less than five minutes ago—"

"Our vehicles patrol around the clock. We're never far away."

"Oh, my *God*—"

"My men are scrambling around the whole complex. Now, *hurry*! Check the northeast staircase, this one's clean. I'll rendezvous with my men." Scofield dashed to the exit door, turning at the last second. "Tell everyone to stay inside! My people might shoot."

"Oh, my God!"

Brandon sped out of Wichita over back-country roads until he reached Route 96, the main highway, where he hoped to find a public telephone on the long, nearly deserted stretch of darkness. He found one, a dimly lit plastic shell covered with obscene graffiti. He inserted a coin and dialed an operator, which took what seemed to Bray time enough to fly to Washington, and placed a collect call to Frank Shields's secure home phone.

"Where are you, Brandon?"

"Where no wheat grows nor buffalo roam, Squinty. It's four-something in the morning and all I can see is Kansas flat."

"All right, I'm on scrambler and it's hardly likely you could be intercepted."

"I'd say impossible."

"Still, don't mention names, only I will."

"Gotcha."

"First, did you get anything?"

"What are you talking about?"

"Antonia told me you were 'hunting,' and I didn't have to ask any more, you lying bastard!"

"To answer your question, *sir,* I think I did find something. Now what's this about the missing item?"

"It's crazy, Bray. The boy's with an officer, a pilot assigned to our fleet base in Bahrain."

"And he won't talk to anyone but our Army lady, Toni explained that to me. What's your problem?"

"If I put them in touch, I could be signing both their death warrants. Bahrain is one of the most progressive high-tech places on earth. Its mechanics can pull things from the ether as fast as we can. How can I take the chance of revealing where they both are?"

"Don't do anything until I get back, Squinty, I've got a couple of ideas. Send a military jet for me."

"Where, for *Christ's* sake?"

"How the hell do *I* know? I'm on a highway about ten miles from Wichita."

"Get back to the Wichita airport and call me. I'll tell you whom to contact."

Julian Guiderone, the son of the Shepherd Boy, sat at a table in Rome's Via Veneto, enjoying his morning caffè latte when his cellular phone beeped in his breast pocket. He pulled it out and spoke. "The Shepherd," he said.

"Wichita has been compromised," reported the recognizable voice from Amsterdam. "To what extent we do not know."

"Survivors?"

"Our two people. They weren't on the scene."

"McDowell and Karastos?"

"They were both at home. They were not involved."

"Yes, they were. Kill them, and sweep their offices."

19

The aircraft carrier U.S.S. *Ticonderoga* was immense, a virtual city within itself, with the military equivalents of various stores, pharmacies, restaurants (mess halls), gymnasiums, offices, and rooms—single, double, and dormitory-style. And there were more corridors, alleyways, and abrupt corners than could be found in a *Star Trek* version of San Francisco's Chinatown. The farther one went belowdecks, the less peopled were the drab steel hallways, albeit with more turns and hatchways and cargo holds than those above the waterline. At the moment, two figures were running up a low-ceilinged corridor, both rather conspicuous. One was a tall black officer who had to continually bend his frame so as not to collide with a lateral pipe, the other a young white male, a muscular teenager, his hands bound in fresh surgical gauze.

"Hurry *up!*" cried Lieutenant Luther Considine, his summer uniform unpressed and in need of cleaning.

"Where are we going?" asked an excited Jamie Montrose.

"Where I hope the officer of the watch and his bloodhounds won't find you!"

They came to a heavy metal door marked Authorized Personnel Only. Considine took out a key, unlocked it, and shoved it open. They walked into a small white-walled room with a long Formica table around which were brown-cushioned swivel chairs and a large screen on the right, a mounted slide projector on the left.

"What is this?" said Montrose junior.

"It's a debriefing room for pilots on top-secret runs."

"How'd you get the key, Lieutenant?"

"The security officer was my wing commander until the brass figured he was too smart or too blind to fly. He's still my roommate and thinks I'm having a tête-à-tête with a dark angel of mercy."

"That was very nice of him."

"Nice, *schmice*. I bailed him out of the casino on Rhodes. Take a chair and relax. I flip on this switch and the red letters outside say DO NOT ENTER."

"I don't know how to thank you, sir."

"You don't have to, Jamie. Just fill me in more, and remember, I could be busted to a swab-jockey if you shuffle me."

"Everything I've told you is the truth—"

"I believe you!" interrupted Luther Considine, his black eyes glaring. "I believe you because it's so nuts and you're so young and you're the son of a fighter pilot we considered the best in the business, so why would you *lie*? But the captain, the four-striper driving this floating metropolis, thinks you ran out of my quarters and I can't find you because our intelligence officer ordered you to talk to Washington."

"No *way*!" insisted Montrose junior. "You talk about shuffling, I've been shuffled enough!"

"Okay, okay. Let's go back. What exactly did the two government spook-jocks say to you at Kennedy International?"

"Not very much. . . . Basically that my mother had been assigned to an undercover operation and in case there were any leaks, they wanted me 'out of the loop.' "

"What about their ID's? . . . Forget it, they could easily get fakes. And you accepted what they told you?"

"Well, they seemed like really nice guys, you know? I mean, they were concerned, genuinely sorry about everything, and even got me on board the plane without any hassle over tickets and my passport and that sort of thing."

"Didn't you ask any questions?"

"I asked a *lot* of questions, but they didn't know much more than I did."

"What *did* they tell you?" said Considine, studying the youngster.

"Well, they told me the plane was going to Paris, which, of course, I could read on the signs, but they said I'd be going on, only they didn't know where to. Just that I'd be met at Orly Airport by another two guys who would take over."

"They didn't say anything more about your mother or the operation?"

"They didn't *know* anything. They were really sincere about that. Then I told them I had to make a couple of phone calls and they said go ahead. I called home and there was no answer, not even the machine. Then I called a close friend and fellow officer who often worked with Mom; the operator broke in saying the number was changed, the new one unlisted. That's when I figured whatever they were doing was really undercover. But I've told you all this, Lieutenant."

"Not everything, you left out the phone calls before. Anyway, I may want to hear it again and again. I could be flying over something I can't see yet."

"There's nothing to miss, Lieutenant."

"Drop the 'Lieutenant,' Jamie. It's Luther. The next time you see me I may be Seaman No Class. From a blacktop gun to a swab with a mop. . . . Colin Powell will whip my ass, and I'm a big fella, but he could do it."

"I don't think race enters into any of this . . . Luther."

"Oh, I love you white liberals. Why couldn't you have picked a nice, white naval officer to tell your tale to? There's a prick in my squadron who hates anyone that isn't all spit-and-polish. He'd turn a cook in for having grease on his apron."

"Then he'd turn me in, too."

"You've got a point. So tell me about the phone calls. Specifically the one where the number was changed."

"It was to Colonel Everett Bracket. He was at the Point with Mom, and he and his wife were friends of Mother and Dad. He frequently asked for Mom on certain assignments."

"What's the nature of his assignments?"

"He's an elite hog in Army intelligence. My mother was trained in high technology, like computers and stuff. It's a subdivision of G-Two, and Uncle Ev called upon her a lot, I guess."

"Why did he pick her for a supposedly dangerous undercover operation?"

"Darned if I know. After Dad died he was kind of a surrogate father to me, and the last thing I think he'd ask her to do was to go into a dangerous situation. It doesn't make sense!"

"Now, listen to me carefully, Jamie, and try to remember. When, *exactly,* did you get the word from Washington—through the head of your school—that you were to leave and go to Kennedy Airport in New York?"

"It was a Friday, I don't remember the exact date, but it was before the weekend."

"Now, again, as precisely as you can recall, prior to that Friday, when did you last talk to your mother?"

"A few days before, maybe three or four. Just a regular call, about how my classes were going and stuff like that."

"And you didn't talk to her after that?"

"No, there wasn't any reason to."

"Then can we assume she didn't try to reach you during those three or four days?"

"I know she didn't."

"How so?"

"In Paris, at the airport, I told the two men who met me that I had to call a cousin of mine who lives there because Mom told me to. It kind of threw them, but I got the impression that they didn't want to rock the boat, so they let me, practically breathing down my neck by the phone."

"So?"

"I have one of those phone cards, you know, the kind you can use anywhere, and I sure know the numbers to reach the States and the school—"

"You do?" interrupted Considine.

"Hey, Lieutenant—Luther, I spent a few years as a traveling Army brat, remember? But most of my friends, even when I was a kid, are in Virginia, which is our real home."

"So you were on the phone, and I presume you called your school, not any nonexistent cousin."

"Oh, Kevin exists all right. He's a lot older than me and he goes to graduate school at the Sorbonne."

"A very impressive family. But you *did* reach your school."

"Sure did. Olivia was on the switchboard; she's a scholarship student and we've got kind of a thing going, if you know what I mean."

"I'll try to remember. . . . *And*?"

"Well, she knew it was me, and I asked her if my mother had tried to call me—the switchboard keeps records. She said Mom hadn't, so I pretended I was talking to Cousin Kevin and hung up. I'll have to apologize to Livvie for that."

"Do so," said Considine, his fingers massaging his forehead. "That's also another phone call you didn't tell me about."

"I guess I forgot. But I told you all about that big house over the bridges, and the guards, and how I couldn't call anybody and how I was kept in a room with bars on the windows and everything."

"And how you escaped," agreed the pilot, "which was remarkable in itself. You must be a tough kid; your hands were a mess but you kept going."

"I don't know about tough, I just knew I had to get out of there. The things my warden, Amet—I called him a warden—kept repeating sounded like a broken record and about as convincing. After all those days nobody could figure out how to get my mother and me on the phone together. That's bullshit!"

"And undoubtedly timed down to hours, if not minutes," mused Luther Considine, abruptly standing up.

"What do you mean?"

"If you're straight-arrow, and I'm pretty well convinced you are, the bad guys had to get you out of the country before your momma joined this undercover operation, said operation probably the only truthful thing your kidnappers told you."

"I don't get it, Luther." Jamie frowned in bewilderment.

"It's the only thing that *does* make sense," said the pilot, glancing at his watch. "Whatever your mother's involved in concerns the maggots who snatched you, and it's got to be mighty heavy."

"Come again?"

"Kidnapping's big-time *any*time, and kidnapping the kid of an Army officer attached to government security is executioner's meat. They took you out of the loop and pulled you into another. Theirs."

"But *why*?"

"So they've got a hook into Mother Montrose." Considine walked toward the door. "I'll be back in a few hours. Get some rest, some sleep, if you can. I'll keep the red letters on, no one'll bother you."

"Where are you going?"

"You've described the place where they kept you in damn clear detail, and I've wandered all over the Bahrainian territory. I've got several ideas where it could be; there aren't too many areas where estates like that are built. I'll bring along a Polaroid with a dozen or so cartridges of film. Maybe we'll get lucky."

Julian Guiderone was relaxing alone in his Lear 26 jet on the way to his home in Bahrain, in many ways the seat of his immense financial empire. He always enjoyed Bahrain, its comforts and its lifestyle. Manama was hardly as enticing as Paris or as civilized as London, but if there was ever a place on earth where the term *laissez-faire* was purely applied, it was Bahrain. Noninterference was its credo, and went beyond economics and the marketplace to the soul of the individual, even more so, of course, if he was among the rich.

Julian had friends there, though not close friends—he had no close friends; they were an impediment—and he considered having several small dinner parties, inviting a few royal pretenders, but mainly bankers and oil barons, the true royalty.

His sky pager buzzed, cutting short his reverie. He pulled it out of his pocket, alarmed to see that the party calling him was in the area code 31, the Netherlands. The number itself was meaningless, for it was false. There was only one person who would call. From Amsterdam. Jan van der Meer Matareisen. He reached for the telephone cradled in the console of his air desk.

"I'm afraid I have terrible news, sir."

"Everything's relative. What's terrible one minute can be beneficial the next. What is it?"

"The package we transferred via Paris to the Middle East has disappeared."

"What?" Guiderone bolted forward with such force that the metal buckle on his seat belt dug painfully into his stomach. "You mean the parcel's *lost*?" he choked, wincing as he gripped the buckle, disengaging it. "Have you *looked* for it, really *searched*?"

"We've got our best personnel on it. Not a trace."

"Keep looking—*everywhere*!" The son of the Shepherd Boy gasped, trying to find some measure of control. "In the meantime," he began slowly, collecting his thoughts, "I've leased the *boat,* the *big* boat, so clean it out, completely *out.* Also, release the crew, the *entire* crew, and send them to our marina in Oman, to Muscat. The sheikh who's taking it has his own people."

"I understand, sir. It will all be accomplished before the day is over."

"But for God's sake, keep searching for the package!" Guiderone slammed down the phone and yelled out, *"Pilot?"*

"Yes, *signore*?" came the voice from the flight deck only eight feet away.

"How is our fuel?"

"Plenty. We've only been airborne for twenty-two minutes, *signore.*"

"Enough to fly me to Marseilles?"

"Easily, *signore.*"

"Alter our flight plan and do so."

"Immediately, Signor Paravacini."

Paravacini. A name from the forgotten annals of the Matarese, but for the few who knew, the name struck, if not terror, certainly grave concern. The firm of Scozzi-Paravacini, created through marriage between the two families, had been absorbed by other interests over the years, but Guiderone's use of the name served him well in certain parts of the world. Legends die slowly, especially those born and expanded in fear.

Although Count Scozzi had been among the first of the Barone Guillaume de Matarese's recruits in the early twentieth century, he became a figurehead. With the family's fortune waning, a marriage was arranged between a Scozzi daughter and a son of the rich but brutal Paravacinis.

As the years passed, the once inseparable Scozzis and Paravacinis, who owned estates only several miles from each other on the renowned Lake Como, Italy's *internazionale lago a celebre,* grew so estranged neither acknowledged the other. In time, the estrangement became ugly. Several invaluable executives, known to favor the Scozzis, were murdered, the killers believed to be in the hire of the Paravacinis, although there was no proof. Then an heir of the Scozzi family was found dead, supposedly drowned, his body washed up on the banks of the Como. The police of Bellagio, in fear of the reputedly violent Paravacinis, neglected to report that there was a tiny puncture, as if inflicted by an ice pick, through the chest cavity of the corpse, penetrating the heart. The authorities had good reason to be circumspect, for the Paravacinis had borne male children who grew up to be priests, important priests, *Vaticano* emissaries! One treaded cautiously under the circumstances.

The Scozzis, through their *avvocatos,* their attorneys,

sold their interests to another great Italian consortium, the Tremontes, a family rooted in immense wealth as well as Judeo-Christian ethics. And who would know both better? For the Tremontes began their climb to international fame with the union of a brilliant Italian Jew and an equally astute Roman Catholic. Both church and synagogue frowned, but the largesse that followed to both religions muted their criticism.

Here, *now,* however, Julian Guiderone considered, the legend of the Paravacinis was still operative in the Mediterranean, especially in Italy. One did not play loose with a Paravacini, for one could be dead within hours if he did. *Perception.* That was the key.

As for the Tremontes and their holier-than-thou philosophy, the death of their polo-playing advocate in America might reduce their antipathy to the Matarese. They knew that others could follow, it was the prophecy of the Paravacinis. They had to heed it, for all death ultimately becomes intensely personal.

What bothered Guiderone to the point of paranoia was the emergence of a stench he could not tolerate. The pig of the world, *Beowulf Agate*! He was operating again, as he did a quarter of a century ago! *He* was the mind behind the search, a convoluted brain that looked for the impossible. He had to be stopped, *killed,* as he was supposed to have been at the Chesapeake compound. Julian would issue the order in Marseilles. *Kill* Brandon Alan Scofield. No matter the cost!

The Air Force F-16 flew from Wichita directly to the Cherokee field seven miles north of Peregrine View. A CIA vehicle was waiting for a disheveled Scofield, taking him swiftly to the former resort as the early-morning sun washed over the Great Smoky Mountains. Bray was only mildly surprised when, after greeting Antonia, he heard a familiar voice calling from the kitchen.

"I hope you got some sleep on the plane," yelled Frank Shields, "God knows I didn't! That damned turbo pilot had a talent for steering into every stretch of rotten weather from Andrews to here." The CIA analyst appeared at the kitchen door carrying a mug of coffee. "I suppose you want a cup of this," he added.

"I'll get it, Frank," interrupted Toni. "You just bawl him out, he deserves it." She walked past Shields into the kitchen. "I'll make some eggs for him. He's a mess and I'm an idiot."

"I should, you know," said the analyst, coming into the living room and staring at Scofield's sweat-stained combat fatigues. "Yell at you, I mean. What the hell are you dressed as, an extra in a Rambo movie?"

"It served its purpose, Squinty. If I'd worn a suit, I'd be hanging out in a Kansas jail."

"I'll take your word for it, just don't explain. I'd like a little deniability. . . . I assume you've already depleted the ten thousand I authorized."

"I've only just begun to spend the rest of it. When you see what I've brought home to Mother Goose, my friend from the old Stasi will require his *hundred* thousand."

"Everything's subject to interpretation, Brandon, including reconnoitered materials."

"Such fancy language—"

"However, first things first," broke in Shields in utter seriousness. "What about the Montrose boy? I've stated my reservations and you told me you might have some ideas. What are they?"

"Pretty simple," replied Scofield. "You said the kid was with a naval officer, a pilot, isn't that right?"

"Yes, Leslie's son literally picked him out of a crowd in Manama. He's a fighter pilot on the *Ticonderoga,* a squadron leader, name of Luther Considine, with a hell of a reputation. The brass think he's a real comer, War College candidate, and all that goes with it."

"The boy picked a bright guy."

"Obviously."

"So deal through *him,*" Scofield said.

"What?"

"The kid apparently trusts him, so talk to this Considine. Be honest with him, it's all you've got left. You have to tell

Leslie her son's out of danger and in safe hands, it would be unthinkable not to."

"I agree, but there's a problem. James junior can't be found. He's disappeared—"

"He's *what*?"

"That's the latest word. They can't be sure; they don't think he got off the carrier, but they can't find him."

"Ever been on an aircraft carrier, Squint Eyes?"

"Christ, you're annoying! No, actually, I haven't."

"Visualize most of Georgetown and float it on water, that'll give you an idea. Junior could be anywhere, it could take days, maybe weeks, to find him, if he's mobile, as he obviously is."

"That's ridiculous! He has to eat, sleep, go to the bathroom—eventually somebody will *see* him."

"Not if he's got help, say a naval officer who's befriended him."

"Are you saying—"

"It's worth a try, Frank. I learned years ago that pilots are a breed apart, probably something to do with being encased in a flying warhead miles above the earth, all alone. And Junior's father was a highly decorated fighter pilot . . . posthumously. You have nothing to lose, Squinty. Contact this Considine. Give him a shot."

Nothing is perfect in the world of high technology, mainly due to the fact that once a technology is perfected, a new counterproduct is invented, just as perfect. However, MSTS—Military Satellite Transmission Scrambler—is as close to clandestine perfection as can be expected. Until, perhaps, next week. The key is in the sending and receiving instruments: They have alternating calibrations that both separate and combine the voice patterns on their instantaneous journeys through the airwaves of space. There was a minuscule margin of risk, but it had to be weighed against a mother's sanity and the degree of protection of the parties involved.

Lieutenant Senior Grade Considine was ordered to the carrier's communications complex and put in contact with

Peregrine View, where the proper electronic equipment had been hastily flown down from the Pentagon. It was installed on Clingmans Dome, the highest peak in the Great Smokies. Shortly thereafter, Luther Considine sat in front of a console, earphones in place, on the aircraft carrier U.S.S. *Ticonderoga* in Bahrain.

"Lieutenant Considine," said the disembodied voice eight thousand miles away from the Persian Gulf, "my name is Frank Shields, deputy director of the Central Intelligence Agency. Can you hear me?"

"I read you, Mr. Director."

"I'll be as brief as possible. . . . Your young friend refuses to speak directly with any government official and I can't blame him. He's been lied to enough in the name of the government."

"Then he's been telling me the truth!" interrupted the pilot, not disguising his relief. "I *knew* it."

"He's been telling you the truth," agreed Shields, "but for reasons of personal safety, I don't believe we can put him in touch with the person he insists on talking to. Perhaps in a few days when we can work out the most secure arrangements, but not at the moment."

"I don't think he'll accept that. I don't think I would, if I were he."

"Then you know where he is?"

"For the record, no. Next question, please?"

"It's not a question, Lieutenant, it's a request. Ask him to tell you something, *anything,* that only the person he wants to reach would know. Will you do that?"

"When and if I find him, I'll convey your message, Mr. Director."

"We'll be waiting, Lieutenant. Your senior communications officer has the codes to reach me. They're only numbers; no one else has been privy to our conversation."

"Good-bye, sir. I hope I can help." Considine removed the earphones as a technician switched off the transmission.

"Listen to me, Jamie," said the pilot, sitting across from the wary youngster, both on crates in a storage room below-decks. "The man sounded straight—actually he sounded like he was embalmed, but he made sense. He's an intelligence guru and has to study all aspects of a complicated diagram."

"I don't know what you mean, Luther."

"He's afraid of a trap. He said he understood your position about talking only to your mother because you'd been lied to in the *name* of the government. He mentioned his concern with 'personal safety' and 'secure arrangements' before he puts you two together. He's thinking of both of you."

"In other words, I could be a lure. I might not be *me* at all."

"Very good . . . Where did you learn that?"

"I've heard Uncle Ev and Mother talk. Although they were both G-Two, they would be assigned to other branches for counterintelligence purposes."

"Sweet *Jesus*," muttered Considine, his low voice emphatic. "I said before that your momma must be involved in something heavy, but this is heavier and deeper than anything I've ever thought about. She's dealing undercover with something world-class. Good God, Jamie, do you realize that our intelligence exec has been on the safe-horn with NI in Washington, then was turned over to the DIA, the State Department, and finally to the White House's Thomas Cranston, who is like the President's shadow where national security is concerned? If you recall, he's the guy who guaranteed to get the Big Man himself in touch with you!"

"I don't know the President, I know my mother. No one could imitate her voice to me, or know what she knows."

"That's all this Shields wants from you, what *you* know that only *she* could know. Can't you see that? Once he knows you're for real and she confirms it, he can move. I think that's reasonable, just as I think whatever's going on is rumbling the highest levels of the government. Now, come on, Jamie, give me something."

"All right, let me think." Montrose junior got off the crate and paced the steel floor of the storage room. "Okay," he continued, "when I was a kid, I mean a real little kid, Mom and Dad got me a small stuffed animal, a lamb, the kind a child can't get hurt with. Even the buttons were kidproof. Years later, months after my father was killed, Mother sold our house and we moved—too many memories, stuff like that. While I was helping her clean out the attic she found the little stuffed lamb and said, 'Look, here's Malcomb.' I didn't remember it, and certainly not the name. Mom told me that she and Dad laughed when I called the thing 'Malcomb,' which I could barely pronounce. She said I got it from a cartoon character on television. I couldn't remember, but I took her word for it."

"Then that's it?" asked Luther. "The name of the stuffed animal?"

"It's all I can think of. And I can't think of anybody else who'd know about it."

"Maybe it's enough. By the way, have you studied the Polaroids of the estates?"

"I marked two that could be it. I can't be positive, but I think it's one of those two." The teenager reached awkwardly into his pockets, inhibited by the gauze around his hands, his extended fingers now encased in tape, and handed Considine a dozen-plus photographs.

"I'll look at them after I report upstairs. Incidentally, I'm moving you when I come back."

"Where to?"

"My inside wingman wangled a three-day pass to Paris, where his wife's flying in for the week. She's a fashion editor or something, and his roommate is in sick bay with the measles—can you believe that, the measles? Before you know it, our squadrons will be flown by twelve-year-olds."

"I'm fifteen and I've already taken eleven hours of flying lessons. I'm ready to solo, Luther."

"That gives me great comfort. See you later."

Leslie Montrose was in a glass booth within a large white room filled with electronic equipment that rose to the ceiling. There were green-tinted screens everywhere, replete with dials and digital readouts, and workplaces for ten operatives, men and women, all expert in covert communications.

It was MI-6's international message center, transmissions sent and received to and from all over the world. Leslie sat in front of a computerized telephone console, three phones in cradles across the machine, each in a different color—green, red, and yellow. A female voice came over the booth's unseen speaker.

"Madam, will you please pick up the green telephone? Your call is coming through."

"Thank you." Montrose reached for the phone, a horrible wave of anxiety passing through her. She feared the worst as her trembling hand picked up the instrument. "This is the officer assigned to London—"

"It's okay, Leslie," Frank Shields interrupted, "no obscure litany is required."

"Frank?"

"They say this hardware is as confidential as if we were talking in a broom closet in Alaska."

"I don't know anything about that, but I've been on an emotional roller coaster ever since Geof Waters told me to be here for a call. He didn't even say it was you."

"He doesn't know, and if he's an honorable Etonian, he won't when we're finished, not unless you tell him."

"For God's sake, what *is* it, Frank?" Montrose suddenly lowered her voice to a whispered monotone. "Has anything happened to my son?"

"I may have news for you, Leslie, but first I have to ask you a question."

"A *question*? I don't want a question, I want news of my *child*!"

"Does the name Malcomb mean anything to you?"

"Malcomb—*Malcomb*? I don't know anybody named *Malcomb*! What kind of stupid question is *that*?"

"Calm down, Colonel, take it easy. Just think for a minute—"

"I don't have to *think, goddamn* you!" yelled a near-hysterical Montrose. "What the hell is a *Malcomb* and what does it have to do with my *son*? I don't know anyone—I've *never* known anyone . . ." Abruptly, Leslie stopped; she gasped, pulling the green telephone away from her ear, and staring blankly through the glass at the white wall beyond, her eyes widening. "Oh, my God!" she whispered, bringing the phone back. "That little stuffed sheep, a woolly lamb, a three-year-old's toy *animal*! He called it 'Malcomb' after the cartoon—"

"That's right, Leslie," confirmed Frank Shields, four thousand miles away at the base of the Great Smoky Mountains. "A young child's stuffed toy, long forgotten by both of you until—"

"Until we found it in the attic!" cried Montrose, breaking in. "*I* found it and Jamie couldn't remember, so I told him. It's *Jamie*! You've heard from my *son*!"

"Not directly, but he's safe. He escaped, an extraordinary feat for a young man of his age."

"Hey, he's an extraordinary *kid*!" exclaimed the wildly happy mother. "Maybe not a whiz at biology or Latin, but he's a hell of a wrestler! Did I tell you he's a damn fine wrestler?"

"We know that."

"Oh, Lord, I'm babbling, aren't I?" admitted a tearful Lieutenant Colonel Montrose, U.S. Army. "I'm sorry, Frank, I'm babbling and crying at the same time."

"You're entitled to, Leslie."

"Where *is* he? When can I talk to him?"

"At the moment, he's at a naval base in the Middle East—"

"The *Middle East*?"

"I can't risk putting him in touch with you right now. There's no way we could install the proper equipment that would guarantee complete secrecy of communication. I'm sure you can understand that those he escaped from are searching for him everywhere, and they're no less talented than we are at electronic interception."

"I understand, Frank. I'm a computer girl."

"So I've been told by Pryce."

"He's a dear, incidentally. He insisted on coming over here with me, and I know that he and Sir Geoffrey had other plans. Plans that included a relaxing night of poker at Waters's club. Richly deserved, I might add."

"Have you told him who, or what, you really are? A roving G-Two officer and not a bona fide RDF colonel?"

"No, but he probably suspects, since I worked the computers in Belgrave Square. I'm not sure he'd know the difference, or care."

"He might. He doesn't like anything withheld. He's as rough as Beowulf Agate in that department."

"I don't see a problem. You'll get word to Jamie that I know the situation, won't you?"

"Sure. Give me something like the Malcomb so he knows it's from you."

"All right. . . . Tell him I received a personal note from his biology teacher. He'd better start cracking or he could become ineligible for varsity sports."

Leslie walked out of MI-6's international message center into the long, wide corridor, deserted except for two figures. One was an armed guard seated at a table at midpoint, the other was Cameron Pryce, standing at the far end. Her heart pounding as rapidly as she could ever recall, Leslie nodded to the guard and quickened her pace toward Cameron. Her face ecstatic with joy, her bright smile childlike, she rushed the final ten feet into Pryce's arms, holding him fiercely and whispering into his ear.

"It's *Jamie*! He got away, he's *safe*!"

"That's wonderful, Leslie!" Cam began to shout, quickly lowering his voice. "It's terrific, really *terrific*," he added, holding her as tightly as she held him. "Who reached you?"

"Frank Shields. They got word quite a while ago, but they had to make sure—and they *did*. It's *Jamie*!"

"You must be so relieved—"

"There aren't words!" Abruptly, as if Lieutenant Colonel Montrose was suddenly aware they were in each other's arms, she stammered and said quietly while partially disengaging herself, "I'm—I'm sorry, Cam. I'm behaving like a child—"

"Because *your* child is safe," Pryce rejoined, still holding her gently as he tipped her face up with a soft right hand. "You're crying, Leslie."

"They're not tears of sorrow, my friend, my good friend."

"Great relief will do that."

"Yes, I guess it will. Just as great sadness does." Their faces, their eyes, were barely inches from each other's. Cameron released her and stepped back, his hands on her shoulders. "Thank you, friend," she said.

"For what? For being here? I wouldn't be anywhere else."

"For that, too, but that's not what I meant. A few seconds ago I wanted to kiss you, *so* wanted to."

"You're pretty vulnerable right now, Colonel."

"That's what I'm thanking you for. For knowing it."

Pryce smiled, and removed his hands. "You're off the hook for the time being, but don't trust me. I'm not a thirty-six-year-old monk."

"Nor am I a thirty-six-year-old nun. . . . Well, I suppose I sort of have been for the past few years."

"Let's ponder this conundrum the way we intelligence folk examine a problem."

"I'm afraid that would exclude me—"

"Come on, lady, I've known since the Chesapeake compound."

"Known what?"

"You're top Army G-Two and so was Ev Bracket."

"What?"

"You're an elite unit, what the British call Special Branch. You go from place to place unearthing the evil people—with proper training, naturally."

"How in heaven's name did you *learn* that?"

"You gave yourself away too many times. You think like a spook, often talk like one, and the Army doesn't send a commando or an RDF officer to the University of Chicago's computer-science graduate school so he or she can carry a laptop into combat."

"This is funny, really *funny*!" exclaimed Montrose, her reddish eyes laughing, no denial in them. "Only five minutes ago, Frank asked me if I had told you, and I said I hadn't, but I thought you might have suspected because I used the computer in Belgravia. He doesn't mind, incidentally, but *was* it the computer?"

"No, much simpler. I realize that some people at the Pentagon and in Langley think it's unwise, but we CIA types and you G-Two types often have good reason to work together. The bottom line is that I reached an old friend in Arlington and he researched you and Bracket for me. One or the other of us saved the other's life on a Prospekt in Moscow, can't remember which. He had no choice."

Leslie now laughed out loud, softly but loud enough for the guard at the table to glance over. "Agent Pryce," she said, "or even Special Agent Pryce, do you think we can spin the tape back a bit and start again?"

"I think it's a grand idea, Colonel Montrose. Our tape's clean and I suggest we begin again with a dinner of thanks at a very fine restaurant. Since I play fast and loose with contingency funds, it's on me."

"And I shouldn't trust you?"

"Not for an instant. That should be on the tape."

20

Frank Shields instructed his secretary of nineteen years that he would be "off property" for two days and nobody was to be told his whereabouts. That included anyone and everyone at the Agency, no matter their rank.

"I'll use the Denver connection, if any crises come up," had said the middle-aged woman who was all too familiar with her employer's "disappearances." She went on to say that she would reach Mrs. Shields, reassuring her while preparing her for her husband's absence, and would issue an order for an aircraft to fly the deputy director to Montreal.

This order was to be classified top-secret and subsequently canceled after the plane to Cherokee was early airborne, the pilot instructed to return to Andrews.

"As usual, you've covered all the bases, Margaret," Frank Shields had complimented. "However, perhaps you should run a check on the Denver relay."

"I already have, sir. There've been no invasions. I call Colorado and your pager alerts you, the call itself ending in Denver."

"I think I'll propose you for the directorship."

"It's yours for the asking, Frank."

"I don't want it and you're organizationally better qualified. . . . And, Maggie, tell Alice I'm really sorry I had to leave today. The kids are coming to dinner tonight or tomorrow with all their children; she'll be pretty upset."

"That's not until later this week," corrected the secretary. "You may be back by then."

"How do you know?"

"Alice called and asked me to check your calendar. I'd rather you didn't make a liar out of me, so I hope you *will* be back."

"I'll do my best."

"*Please* do."

"I believe that's an order."

Shields then redoubled his efforts to put the Montroses, mother and son, together, working at the highest levels of security with Geoffrey Waters, MI-5, and MI-6. It was decided that the simplest and perhaps the most obvious method of travel would also be the safest. The *Ticonderoga* was scheduled to patrol the Persian Gulf between Bandar-e Chārak and Al-Wakrah; that was the modus operandi. As the jets swept off the carrier's deck on their reconnaissance runs, one aircraft, its fuel at capacity, would break formation and fly to a Royal Air Force base in the district of Loch Torridon, Scotland. The pilot was Lieutenant Senior Grade Luther Considine, his passenger, James Montrose Jr.

The only comment from an elated Jamie was, "Hey, out of *sight*! Except that biology prick had to write Mom! That sucks!"

The reunion would take place in a small village twelve miles north of Edinburgh. Geoffrey Waters personally made the arrangements for special communications equipment and three armed MI-5 personnel to meet the American aircraft and drive the pilot and the Montrose boy to the country inn on the far outskirts of Edinburgh. The inn was commandeered by the government, no locals or tourists to be in residence for forty-eight hours starting with the arrival of Miss Joan Brooks and her brother John—Leslie Montrose and Cameron Pryce.

Waters remained in London, staying in touch with Frank Shields and Brandon Scofield relative to the new material Beowulf Agate had unearthed.

There was another reason for Cameron Pryce to be on the flight to Scotland. Luther Considine carried on his person photographs of the two Persian Gulf estates Jamie Montrose had identified as similar to the compound where he was held prisoner. The pilot had obtained what backgrounds he could find on the owners of the two mansions. It wasn't easy. Bahrain was highly protective when it came to sheltering finances from taxes. So a clandestine triangle was created from London to the Great Smokies to an obscure village in Scotland. Information could be instantly relayed, and information was the only weapon they had to penetrate the Matarese and the global strategies it had set in motion. And that it had set "things" in motion was becoming more and more apparent.

The Washington Post
(FRONT PAGE)

HOUSE INVESTIGATES ORGANIZED-LABOR TACTICS

WASHINGTON, OCT. 23—In a surprise move, the House Committee on Antitrust has unexpectedly turned its guns on labor, not management. It has called into question the influence major national unions hold over tens of thousands of workers, inhibiting economic expansion.

The Boston Globe
(FRONT PAGE)

ELECTRO-SERVE MERGES WITH MICRO WARE

BOSTON, OCT. 23—Startling the computer industry, the merging of two leaders, Electro-Serve and Micro Ware, will immediately result in the loss of thirty thousand jobs. Wall Street is enthusiastic, other sectors demoralized.

The San Diego Union-Tribune
(PAGE 2)

NAVAL BASE TO DOWNSIZE; THOUSANDS OF EMPLOYEES TO BE LET GO

SAN DIEGO, OCT. 24—The Department of the Navy in Washington has announced that it will drastically reduce operations and facilities at the San Diego naval base, transferring 40 percent of its personnel to other navy installations. The majority of civilian employees will be terminated. As to its extensive Coronado properties, they will be auctioned off to private industry.

Things were happening, but no one in the private or the public sector knew what; or if they did know, they kept silent.

The meeting between Leslie Montrose and her son was predictable. The mother's eyes were filled with tears, the sight of Jamie's bandaged hands nearly unbearable to her. James

Montrose Jr. showed an admixture of relief and exuberance with a touch of embarrassment over his mother's behavior. Cameron Pryce remained at a discreet distance, in the shadows of the deserted inn's publike barroom. After Leslie released her red-faced son, blew her nose, and took several deep breaths, she spoke.

"Jamie, I'd like you to meet Mr. Pryce, Cameron Pryce. He's a field officer in the Central Intelligence Agency."

"Same business, huh, Mom? Nice to meet you, sir." James junior broke away from his mother.

"It's a pleasure to meet you, Jamie," said Cam, walking forward out of the shadows. "I should say honor," he continued. "What you did was extraordinary, and I mean that." They shook hands—cautiously, gently.

"It wasn't really that tough, sir, not after I got over the wall. The top was filled with broken glass and coiled barbed wire."

Leslie Montrose gasped.

"That's where you got the hands?" Cameron said.

"Yes, sir. They're healing pretty well now. Those Navy doctors know their stuff. . . . By the way, where's Luther?"

"In the other room, on the sterile phone with our associates in MI-Five and MI-Six."

"Okay, Mr. Pryce." The teenager hesitated, then the words rushed forward in growing anger. "Will somebody tell me what the hell's going *on*? Why have all these things *happened*? The lies, my being kidnapped, not being able to talk to Mom, telephone numbers suddenly not there or changed and unpublished, all that crap! But especially the *lies*! *Why?*"

"Your mother and I will tell you everything we can. God knows you deserve it."

"Well, I guess the first question I want answered," said Jamie, "no disrespect intended, sir, but where is Uncle Ev— Colonel Everett Bracket?"

"Dear," interrupted Leslie, walking to her son. "I've been trying to think of a way to tell you this, but I honestly don't know how."

"What do you mean, Mom?"

"Everett was part of this operation. Army intelligence was recruited by the CIA for military protection. He wanted me to operate his security computers, he could never get the hang of them. And the phone calls had started. Horrible calls, terrifying calls, from all over the place. You had been kidnapped, and if I didn't do as I was ordered, you would be tortured and then executed. Uncle Ev was sure it was all tied up together."

"Holy *shit*!" exclaimed Jamie under his breath. "What did you do, Mom?"

"Controlled myself in ways I never thought I was capable of. Everett was great. He went to Tom Cranston, an old friend in the White House. Cranston's instructions were explicit. We weren't to say anything to anyone, Tom was going to handle everything at the highest level. Then Chesapeake became a series of horrible incidents, finally a battleground. Everett was killed, how doesn't matter."

"Jesus *Christ, no*!"

"I'm afraid so," said Cameron softly.

"Oh, shit, shit, *shit*! Uncle *Ev*!"

"That was my second exercise in control, Jamie. I couldn't even let Mr. Pryce know how devastated I was. I had to submerge my feelings and deal only through Tom."

"Your mother was very successful," said Cameron, a slight edge in his voice. "If she had been clearer with me sooner, perhaps we might have made more progress."

"About *what*?" shouted Montrose junior.

"That'll be my job to explain," replied Pryce, "and it will take a long time. So I suggest we tackle it in the morning. All of us, especially you, young man, have had a harrowing few days. Let's get some rest, okay?"

"I *am* tired, but I've got so many questions!"

"You haven't gotten any answers for nearly three weeks, Jamie, so what's a few more hours? You need some sleep."

"What do you say, Mom?"

"I think Cam's right, son. We're all so stressed, so exhausted, I'm not sure any of us can think straight."

" 'Cam,' Mother?"

At Peregrine View, Scofield, Frank Shields, and Antonia stood around the condominium's dining-room table, which was littered with photographs. The rolls of film Bray had taken in Wichita had been processed locally on an emergency basis, a Gamma patrol in attendance during the developing and enlarging procedures.

"This batch," said Brandon, pointing to several rows of photographs showing pages of handwritten names and dates, "I took from Alistair McDowell's appointments book."

"I'll photofax them up to my secretary so she can run an in-depth check on everyone. Maybe we'll find a pattern, or a few surprises."

"What are these, Bray?" asked Toni. "They look like formulas. . . . Mathematics or physics, scientific things."

"Damned if I know," answered Scofield. "They were in folders marked 'Quotient Group Equations.' I've always figured that when someone goes to the trouble to dig up obscure, ambiguous words, then writes out even more inscrutable letters and numbers, that means he's trying to hide something—something that he has to have access to, but is afraid to put in a computer."

"Because computers can be permanent," said Shields, picking up several of the quotient photographs. "Even deletions have a nasty way of returning, in the hands of an expert."

"That's exactly the way I figured it," agreed Bray. "You can burn papers, but it's tough to torch a machine."

"These aren't math or physics," continued Deputy Director Shields, "they're chemical formulas, which are in line with McDowell's dossier."

"I think that calls for an explanation, Squinty."

"Alistair McDowell's a chemical engineer, top of his class at MIT, right through to his doctorate. By his middle twenties, his brilliance in the laboratory was nearly legend and Atlantic Crown snapped him up, promising to fund all the research he could handle."

"It's rather a leap from the laboratory to the head of a food company, isn't it, Frank?" posed Toni.

"Certainly, but there was a damn good reason for his fast

climb up the ladder. His smarts were matched by his organizational skills. Given virtually unlimited financing, he reorganized all the research divisions—apparently he was a virtual dictator in the laboratories—until they were more profitable than they had ever been. He was a natural for top management."

"There's information in those letters and numbers and fractions, Squinty. I feel it, I *know* it."

"I think you're right, Brandon. I'll send this off to our chem-analysis unit and see what they come up with."

"There've got to be variations of codes that lead to names, organizations, countries—"

"If they don't," said Shields flatly, "they're the newest products or the latest preservatives. But for the moment, I happen to think you're right."

"What about these pictures?" asked Antonia, gesturing at seven photographs of technical equipment.

"Four are of a decoding machine that was concealed in a music box, and the other three are of the computer. I thought we might find out who the manufacturers are and go from there."

"I'll tell you right now that the computer is from Electro-Serve, who have a covert arrangement with us. If the computer is similar, the company is in violation of *our* contract. It could cost Electro millions."

"In court, Squinty, but you know damn well your people can't go into court."

"There's a degree of truth in that," said Shields disconsolately. "You know it better than most of us. So where do *we* go?"

"Down and dirty, Mr. Deputy Director," replied Beowulf Agate. "No hearings, no courts, no congressional interference from either the House or the Senate. Just down and dirty, way down and dirty. We get the names, the regions, the corporations. We learn who the Medusa is, the cranial temple that produces the snakes. Then we cut off their heads, one by one."

"That's abstract, Brandon."

"No, it isn't, Frank. They're people, just as they were

people a quarter of a century ago. Taleniekov and I broke them then, and Pryce and I will break them now. . . . So go to work, and give us everything you can get."

"You'll do nothing without our approval, first get that straight."

"That's not our agreement, Frank. Remember, you came to me, I didn't show up on your doorstep. You mentioned deniability before. Believe me, I'll give you plenty of it."

The secure red telephone rang; it was on a table nearest Shields. He walked over and picked it up. "Yes?" he said then fell silent and listened. Thirty seconds later, saying, only "Thank you," he hung up and turned to Scofield. "If assumptions can be made, and I think they can be, you have two less snake heads to sever. Alistair McDowell and Spiro Karastos were killed in an automobile accident when they drove home together last night, Karastos at the wheel. They must have been sidewinded by a huge semi because the car was totaled."

"*Must* have been?" exclaimed Brandon. "Don't they know?"

"It was a hit-and-run. The police are—"

"Close their offices!" shouted Scofield. "Shut 'em down and put guards in the hallway. We've got to tear apart that equipment!"

"Too late, Brandon," said Shields quietly. "Within an hour or so after the accident, both offices were stripped clean."

"On whose *authority*!" screamed Bray.

"Company policy. Apparently whenever an important executive at Atlantic Crown dies suddenly, all his office effects are removed immediately."

"Why?" Scofield broke in, still yelling.

"Industrial espionage is rampant, it's common knowledge these days. . . . Heart attacks, seizures, unexpected tumors, they're also common. Highly competitive corporations try to protect themselves under those circumstances."

"That's *crazy,* Squinty! What about the *police*?"

"Where's the crime? It was a backcountry intersection,

no witnesses, only imbedded fragments of metal indicating a possible collision. So far, it's listed as an accident."

"But *you* know and *I* know it wasn't."

"I agree with you completely," acknowledged the deputy director of the CIA, "especially considering the swiftness of the office-cleansing. One might even say the tragic event was anticipated."

"Of course it was, and even the *suspicion* of foul play gives the police the right to seal off all avenues potentially relevant to a crime."

"That's both the irony and our proof of premeditated homicide. Oh, was it *premeditated*?"

"What do you mean, Frank?" asked Toni.

"By the time the police and the paramedics at the scene of the 'accident' had finished their work, the contents of those two offices were history."

"'Within an hour or so,'" said Scofield, repeating Shields's earlier words. "You're right. There's no way Atlantic Crown's directors could have learned so quickly."

"Age is addling your brain, Brandon. Of course we know how they knew."

"Oh, yes, we do, don't we? Then we have to find out where they *took* everything!"

"And who gave the order," suggested Antonia, "and who reached whoever it was that carried it out."

"Three excellent questions," agreed Shields. "We'll start on each immediately."

"It should be interesting," said an angry Scofield.

Sir Geoffrey Waters, OBE, studied the information the American lieutenant Luther Considine had delivered on the secure phone from Scotland. An official fax, sterile transmission, would follow so the pilot could check his words, but as the equipment was temporarily down, the MI-5 officer decided not to wait for confirmation.

To say that the two Bahrainian estates had a convoluted history of ownership, both past and present, would be a gross understatement. The names obtained were the names of attorneys, companies, and international corporations and conglomerates; no specific people were accountable for ownership. It was a maze of obfuscation; even the Middle East lawyers, who wanted to cooperate, could do nothing. Contracts were electronically transmitted, they reported, and the funds for purchase were wired incognito from such diverse cities as Madrid, London, Lisbon, and Bonn. Monies were transferred; there was nothing to question.

There was, however, one extraordinary exception, extraordinary insofar as the Bahrainian attorney brokering the purchase had received an additional one million dollars, American, beyond the purchase price. An additional zero had been innocently punched into a coded financial-transfer computer. The Bahrainian broker, aware of the strict territorial laws regarding fraud, dutifully reported the overcharge to the authorities, as well as to the sender. It was an obscure holding company in Amsterdam.

Amsterdam.

The slender, balding man in the data-processing complex of the Central Intelligence Agency rose from his desk in his assigned cubicle and brought both his hands to his temples. He walked out of his area and staggered to the next station, a cubicle adjacent to his own. "Hey, Jackson," he said to the occupant. "I've got one of my migraines again. *Jesus,* I can't stand it!"

"Go to the lounge, Bobby, I'll switch your machine over to mine and cover. You really ought to see a doctor about those."

"I have, Jackson. He says they're brought on by stress."

"Then get out of here, Bobby. You could grab a better-paying job anywhere."

"I *like* it here."

"That's bullshit. Go on, I'll cover your screen."

Bobby Lindstrom did not go to the employees' lounge, but instead walked outside to one of the pay phones on the concrete walk. He inserted four quarters, one after another, and dialed seven zeros. A series of bell tones sounded, five of them, and then he pressed eight zeros and waited.

"On tape," said the metallic voice over the line. "Go ahead."

"Eagle reporting. Have unscrambled DD Two communications. Targets are in North Carolina, the P.V. complex. Proceed according to Marseilles. Out."

It was night, a dark night, the rays of the moon blurred by the mountain mists that hovered over the ground everywhere. From the ascending approach road to the Peregrine View gatehouse, there came into gradual focus the dual beams of headlights. As it drove nearer to the steel barrier that fell across the road cut out of the forest, a brown sedan was revealed, a government vehicle with two military flags flanking the hood. The insignias proclaimed it to be a general's car, a two-star general officer.

The vehicle came to a stop as a guard emerged from the gatehouse. He peered inside at the four uniformed officers—the driver a major, the general beside him in the front seat, and two captains in the rear.

"General Lawrence Swinborn, young fella," announced the general, holding papers in his hand, which he extended across the driver's chest to the open window. "Here are my clearances from the CIA and the Department of the Army."

"I'm sorry, sir," said the Gamma Force sergeant, "we are to have those clearances at least twelve hours prior to a guest's arrival. No can do, sir. You'll have to turn around in our cul-de-sac to your rear."

"That's a pity, Sergeant," replied the general, angling his head slightly to the left and nodding once. At the signal, the captain in the left rear seat raised a silenced pistol and fired the deadly spit, shooting the man in the forehead. At the sight of his comrade falling, the second guard ran out of the windowed gatehouse only to be met by two rounds fired by the same captain, again head shots, cutting off all sound from the victims.

"Get out," ordered the general officer, "drag the bodies into the woods and raise the barrier."

"Yes, sir!"

"Major, extinguish the headlights."

"Right away! *'Lawrence'*—nice ring to it."

"I trust you'll never have to remember it." In the darkness, the steel bar was raised, the captains returned to their seats, and the sedan slowly started up the road. A third guard appeared through the mist and the shadows; he was obviously bewildered and approached the car.

"What the hell is this?" he asked. "Who are you people?"

"Pentagon security check, soldier," answered the general. "I presume you can see the flags."

"I can hardly see a damn thing, but this isn't in the regs."

"We're cleared, Corporal, we're here, and I'm General Lawrence Swinborn."

"General or not, sir, our instructions are to blow up any vehicle we haven't been told about."

"You obviously missed the roll call, soldier. Now, where are the others concentrated? I don't care to be stopped again."

The muscular, broad-shouldered Gamma Force corporal studied the car and its inhabitants. He slowly backed away, his right hand on his holster, unbuckling it, his left pulling a radio out of a strap on his field jacket. He could see a pistol through the open rear window. "None of your damned business, mister." The guard spun and dove to his left, rolling over and over as the spitlike bullets exploded the earth around him. He shouted into his radio. "Hostile vehicle, *Sector Three! Gunfire.*"

"Phase *B*!" commanded the man who called himself Swinborn, as all four jumped out of the left side of the sedan and began removing their uniforms while the corporal, now wounded in his right leg, struggled to his feet, ran into the cover of the woods, and began returning fire. The four invaders used the protection of the sedan as they shed the last of their outerwear, revealing camouflage garb identical to that worn by the Gamma Force patrols. "Spread *out*!" ordered the false general. "He's in the first structure on the right, about two hundred yards up the road. Use the woods, we'll meet there!"

What followed was violence and chaos born of confusion. The beams of powerful flashlights cut through the ground and forest mist. Uniforms—camouflage combat field jackets—were the first marks of identity, and weapons were lowered at the sight of them. Then those lowering their guns were killed in their legitimate mistakes.

At the sound of the erratic, guerrilla-like gunfire, Scofield turned off all the lights, convincing Antonia and Frank Shields to stay in the darkest shadows of the room. He grabbed two MAC-10 automatic weapons from their small arsenal and handed them to his wife and Frank, instructing them to go on rapid fire should anyone appear through the door or a shattered window.

"What are *you* going to do, Bray?" asked Toni.

"What I'm pretty good at, old girl," replied Scofield, heading for the kitchen and the back door, dressed in his combat fatigues and picking up a standard Colt .45 with six magazines of ammunition. He slipped outside and ran into the surrounding woods. Silently he crept through them, like an angry panther protecting its lair, instinct telling him that he was all-too-possibly the object of execution. His legs and arms ached with the prowling, his bones and muscles and lungs lacking the strength they had years ago. But his eyesight was decent, his hearing still acute, and the hearing was paramount.

He *heard* it! The crack of a dead branch under the weight of a foot. And then the rustle of fallen branches as boots brushed them aside. Beowulf Agate retreated into the underbrush, pulling the forest debris over him. What he saw through the leaves and the sparse particles of small limbs not only puzzled but infuriated him. Three figures, dressed in Gamma Force field jackets, berets, trousers, and boots, had made a mistake! To a man their hair was short, but not the usual crew-cut variety favored by the Gamma guards. Strands fell below their berets at the napes of their necks, unheard of for the patrols at Peregrine View. Hair was clipped so short it was practically invisible, especially at the back of the skull, for that was where sweat formed in moments of heat and stress. A minor physical irritant, but an irritant nevertheless, and the Peregrine forces could not afford it.

A fourth man appeared out of the forest, obviously in an

arranged meeting with the other three. "By shouting that I was 'in pursuit,'" said the ersatz Gamma leader, laughing quietly, "I sent the Boy Scouts over to Sector Seven, the farthest area in the compound. Our targets are inside this fancy place here. . . . Waste them! Let's *go*!"

Scofield raised his automatic and fired twice, bringing down two of the deadly intruders. As he did so, he lurched through the underbrush, scrambling roughly ten yards from where he had pulled the trigger of the Colt. A fusillade of bullets filled the night air, hissing on Bray's right, shattering clumps of forest garbage, and thumping into trees with terrible finality.

"Where *is* the bastard?" yelled the leader hysterically.

"I don't *know*!" roared the other man, "but he just dropped Greg and Willie!"

"*Shut* up! No names! . . . He's somewhere over there—"

"*Where?*"

"Around or behind that cluster of bushes, I think."

"He hasn't fired again . . . maybe he took off."

"Maybe he didn't. Let's blast!"

"If he's there, we'll get the bastard!"

Like crazed animals, the two killers rushed forward, their weapons on automatic fire. After several prolonged bursts, they stopped. Silence. And during that silence, Scofield hurled a heavy rock far to the left of the invaders. The firing instantly began again, and Bray waited for what he knew would happen.

It did. Through the filtered mist he could see that one of the men upturned his weapon; he had stopped shooting for the simple reason that he had run out of rounds and had to insert a second magazine.

So Scofield shot the second man, breaking through the woods as he fell. "Drop the iron!" ordered Bray, confronting the killer who held his weapon in his right hand, a full magazine of shells in his left. "*Drop* it!" repeated Brandon, clicking the hammer of his automatic into the firing position.

"Jesus Christ, you're *him,* aren't you?"

"Your grammar notwithstanding, yes, I'm he. But then, I'm a Harvard man, although nobody wants to believe it."

"Son of a *bitch*!"

"That would be you, I assume. Or should we put it another way? A son of the Matarese." The man slowly, half inch by half inch in the forest mist, moved the magazine toward the automatic weapon. Suddenly, he shook his right leg, lifting it slightly off the ground. *"Easy,"* said Scofield, "you're less than a breath away from being history."

"It's my leg, goddamn it! I've got cramps from all this running."

"I'm *not* going to say it again, *scum*. Drop the gun."

"I will, I *will*!" The killer pressed the automatic rifle against his upper right leg, wincing as he did so. "I gotta separate these muscles, they're climbing all over each other."

"Well, I'll agree with you there, scumbucket. Cramps can be—" The Matarese assassin suddenly whipped around, plunging the loaded magazine into his weapon's chamber and literally spinning in midair, ready to blow Scofield away. Bray fired. The killer collapsed, his body a tangled heap of dead flesh.

"Damn," cried Beowulf Agate. "I wanted you alive, you slime."

An hour later, Peregrine View had been stabilized, the few dead mourned, their parents soon to be notified; no one with a wife or children had been assigned. Scofield sat in a chair, exhausted.

"You could have been *killed*!" shouted Frank Shields.

"Goes with the territory, Squinty. I'm here, aren't I?"

"One day you may *not* be, you gray-haired old fool," exclaimed Antonia; standing beside Bray, holding his tired head.

"So what else is new, Frank?"

"We've heard from Wichita, Brandon. The entire contents of McDowell's and Karastos's offices were shipped on KLM Airlines. Destination, Amsterdam."

Amsterdam.

21

The sleek Citröen limousine rolled slowly through the furious night downpour on the Marseilles waterfront, the swirling mists and the drenching rain reducing visibility to no more than forty hazelike feet. The headlights were almost useless as their beams were swallowed up by the fog rolling off the Mediterranean, the illumination refracted into walls of billowing white. Julian Guiderone peered out the left rear window.

"This is the row of warehouses!" he yelled to the driver over the pounding rain on the vehicle's roof. "Have you a flashlight—a torch?"

"*Oui,* Monsieur Paravacini. Always."

"Shine it over there, on the left. We're looking for number forty-one."

"This is thirty-seven. It cannot be much farther, *monsieur.*"

It wasn't. A small, dim, wire-meshed bulb glowed, barely seen through the mist. "Stop!" ordered the son of the Shepherd Boy, now using the ominous name of Paravacini. "Press your horn, two short blasts."

The driver did so and immediately a large loading door was raised, somewhat brighter lights revealed inside. "Shall I drive in?"

"Only briefly," replied Guiderone, "just long enough for

me to get out. Then back up and wait in the street. When the door opens again, come in for me."

"An honor, *monsieur*."

Julian Guiderone climbed out, standing on the deserted concrete floor, and nodded to his chauffeur. The limousine backed out into the downpour; the loading door slowly descended. Guiderone stood alone, knowing it would not be for long. It wasn't. Out of the shadows walked Jan van der Meer Matareisen, his slender figure and square pale face seemingly dwarfed by the cavernous warehouse.

"Welcome, my superior in all things."

"Mother of *Christ,* man!" exclaimed the son of the Shepherd Boy. "I trust you can justify dragging me here at this hour. It's nearly four o'clock in the morning, and I've had an exhausting two days!"

"It was unavoidable, sir. My information is such that it can only be delivered in person, for we must discuss immediate strategies."

"*Here,* in this cold, damp, cement mausoleum?"

"Please accompany me to my office. Actually, I have offices in every building, for I own all the warehouses on this street. Also six piers, which I frequently lease out. They cover all of my expenses."

"Am I to be impressed?" asked Guiderone, following Matareisen toward a glass-enclosed office thirty feet away.

"Forgive my boastfulness, Mr. Guiderone. It seems I constantly seek approval from you, for you are the guiding star of our movement."

"I *was,* Jan, now you should look upon me as merely a consultant." They entered the office with its abundance of electronic equipment. Guiderone chose a black leather couch; Matareisen sat behind his desk. "Let's discuss this strategy you speak of. I'd like to get back to my hotel as soon as possible."

"I think you should know, sir, that three and a half hours ago I was comfortably asleep in my house on the Keizersgracht in Amsterdam. I felt it necessary to get up, alert my pilot, and fly to Marseilles."

"Now I *am* impressed. Why?"

"We must move up our schedule—"

"*What?* We're not ready—*you're* not ready!"

"Hear me out, please. Events have taken place that we could not have envisioned. There are serious problems."

"*Beowulf Agate,*" whispered Guiderone in a monotone. "Tell me he's *dead*!" roared the son of the Shepherd Boy.

"He did not die. As near as we can determine, the mercenary unit failed, losing their lives in the attempt."

"What are you *saying*?" Julian, his voice chilling, his erect posture in the chair immobile, stared at the younger man.

"I'm saying it as calmly as I can, although I feel the rage you feel. Apparently, Scofield's talents in the field have not deserted him. The word from Eagle is that he took out the entire unit himself."

"The *pig* of the *world*!" Guiderone's voice was guttural and barely audible.

"I'm afraid there's more, which is why we must discuss tactics," said Matareisen quietly yet with a hint of strength. "We know it was Scofield who broke into McDowell's office in Wichita, but we don't know what he learned, if anything. However, the fact that he zeroed in on McDowell tells us a great deal, and combined with the news from London—"

"What happened in London?" asked the son of the Shepherd Boy icily.

"I had the Brewster house in Belgravia wired."

"Was that necessary?" Guiderone interrupted, his voice once again cold.

"Yes, it was. Lady Alicia reacted violently against my entreaties, protesting that the Matarese was no part of her life nor ever would be. She made it clear that there were others who felt the same way, those who devoted their lives and their riches to repay the sins of their ancestral wealth. That statement led us to the heir of the Scozzi-Tremontes, the so-called playboy, Giancarlo, who was actually an international attorney opposed to us."

"He was killed on a polo field in America. So what? No traces."

"So your enemy, Beowulf Agate, was called in by the

Central Intelligence Agency. He knew—*knows*—more about us than anyone on earth. God knows why or how, but he was recruited."

"The *pig* of the *world*!" Guiderone spat out again.

"That's why we had to know what transpired at the Brewster house in Belgravia. We compromised her idiot husband to act as our surveillance, finally ordering him to kill her when the damn fool stole millions. Accidents will happen and he was a disaster, though a temporary one. We took care of him. Again, no trail."

"We stray," said Guiderone curtly. "So you had Belgravia wired—"

"The bugs were discovered."

"Surely that was a given from the start. The people who service the Brewsters are not fools, they're highly paid stewards who can't afford to be careless. One slip and a truckload of debugging paraphernalia would be at the front door—which it obviously was. To our detriment."

"It's more complicated than that, but I assure you, there's no trace ability. The man who did the installation has been eliminated, and his receiving post in Lowndes Street cleaned out, all the tapes removed."

"I commend your efficiency," said the Shepherd Boy's son, who years ago was about to occupy the White House. "But I'm sure there's more. You didn't fly down in the middle of the night from Amsterdam to impress me with your efficiency." Guiderone paused, his hostile glare returning. "You mentioned something about moving up the schedule, which I'm unalterably opposed to. There's far too much to do, too many operations to be refined. There can be no interruptions, no changes!"

"With respect, I disagree. Through your outstanding efforts and my minor contributions, the major chess pieces are in place throughout Europe, North America, and the Mediterranean. We must strike while our machine is primed, before any obstacles suddenly appear."

"What *obstacles*? It's the boy, *isn't* it, the Montrose son!"

"Gone, vanished, disappeared," said the Dutchman quickly. "He's in the past and is irrelevant. What have we lost? The obedience of a mother who's no longer important to us? She's in London now with Scofield's associate, a man named Pryce, deadly by reputation. To stem any conceivable progress they might make, both will be killed within days, perhaps hours, and that *is* important to us."

"Why is it? I have no objection, but there must be things you're not telling me."

"Forgive me, sir, but those 'things' are self-evident."

"Be careful, young Matareisen. Remember whom you're talking to."

"My apology, but with respect, I must make my case clear. . . . How, we don't know, but McDowell was uncovered in Wichita. *How?* How did Scofield know? Everything in McDowell's office was shipped to us; the files under spectrograph indicated recent tampering; the decoder as well, and we know an attempt was made to use the computer because that is what set off the alarms. What did your Beowulf Agate learn, or did he learn anything?"

"What could he learn?" asked Guiderone quietly, pensively. "McDowell was as cautious as he was brilliant. He'd never leave anything in his office pertaining to us. It's unthinkable."

"He may have felt safer in his suite at Atlantic Crown. His marriage was sour, his wife a jealous alcoholic—with good reason. Don't you see, sir, we just don't *know*!"

"Certain lapses granted, it's no reason to alter schedules. To achieve the results we seek, everything's in the timing. It must be flawless, the successive shocks catastrophic. Our progress is sound. There'll be no changes."

"Then I'll try to be clearer," said the frustrated man from Amsterdam. "And you're right, there are things I haven't told you, for they were under control and there was no point in bothering you. However, when the news about Scofield's kills reached me, I knew it was time to meet you face-to-face."

"In order to convince me?"

"In order to convince you," agreed the grandson softly.

"Then try harder, Jan," said Guiderone, alarmed, his concentration now absolute. "You've accomplished a great deal—extraordinary leaps, to be sure. I can't dismiss you. Go ahead, what haven't you told me that you think is so vital?"

"It's not simply one thing, it's when you put them all together. . . . We must go back to the trawler in the Caribbean, the Swedish captain who escaped. He made his way to Puerto Rico by way of Tortola—"

"Yes, yes," interrupted Guiderone impatiently. "You funneled money to him to fly back to Amsterdam, I know all about it."

"He never arrived. He was spotted on the plane by a Swedish businessman, met at Heathrow by the police, and flown back to Stockholm to face charges in the Palme assassination."

"Unfortunate for him, but how does it concern us?"

"He's pleading for his life. We could be part of a deal."

"He doesn't *know* that much."

"He knows enough. He was under orders, no matter how obscured."

"I see. Go on."

"Prior to closing down the Lowndes Street listening post, our informer reached London control with the news that Pryce, the Montrose woman, and an MI-Five officer were on their way to Westminster House—"

"The Brewsters' private bank, for all intents and purposes," broke in the son of the Shepherd Boy. "If you recall, to make a casual inroad or two, I used the same accounts man who serviced her ladyship, a fellow named Chadwick. Had several pleasant lunches, but I didn't learn much."

"That's why he had to be killed," said Matareisen, his voice flat. "We could have no idea what transpired between the two of you, but we understood that there could be no possible linkage. Our control himself took care of the job and removed your file from Chadwick's office. It was fortunate that he did."

"Why is that?"

"Among Mr. Chadwick's comments were, and I quote, 'Mr. Guiderone is inordinately interested in the Brewsters of Belgravia. Another rich American social climber no doubt.'"

"The dirty bastard," said Julian, chuckling; and then he was abruptly serious. "Again, I commend your efficiency, Jan, and I'm sincerely grateful. It was a stupid and unnecessary risk on my part. . . . But you're talking about what-ifs and all-too-*possible* events that do not necessarily lead to the consequences that so disturb you."

"Substitute 'possible' with 'conceivable.' Only a shade of difference, Mr. Guiderone."

"Neither is strong enough to interrupt the operations now being developed and refined. The Persian Gulf, the Mediterranean, the North Sea—progressive strategies that will paralyze the fuel of the financial world, my young friend. Done with the sweep of a Götterdämmerung! Irresistible. . . . You'll have to come up with something much stronger, Jan."

"I think I can, if you'll give me another minute."

"You have it."

"The progressive financial madness in the Euro-American-Mediterranean markets is all to our benefit, exactly as we planned. The current economic analyses project a loss of over eighty million jobs, again to our benefit, for we are prepared to fill the vacuums and restore stability, with us as the mentors—"

"All to the good, Jan, all to the good! Perception is everything, reality only secondary. We shall control the economies, and therefore the governments, of sixty-two countries, including the seven most influential national capitals. Our goal will be reached, the Matarese agenda complete! Everything legal under the laws, or beyond the laws into the spatial continuum of legal theory. We are invincible!"

"You still do not *understand,* Mr. Guiderone," shouted Matareisen. "You do not *see!*"

"See *what*? The fulfillment of a legend as vital as the search for the Arc of the Covenant? The answer for our planet!"

"*Sir,* I implore you, face that reality you consider secondary, for it so easily becomes perception!"

"What are you babbling about?"

"Through my inheritor in Lisbon, a man of enormous influence matched only by his deviousness—"

"The fellow who corralled the Azores, taxes and all?"

"The same, also the man who had our enemy, Dr. Juan Guaiardo, eliminated in Monte Carlo."

"Yes, what about him?"

"He's very close to corruptible elements in the nearby Spanish government, by and large the remnants of the old Franco crowd, including Madrid intelligence. He wasn't sure what it all meant, but it so stunned him that he reached me this afternoon—yesterday afternoon—and faxed me up what materials he could get his hands on. They weren't complete, but they're frightening."

"About *what*? Spit it out, Matareisen!"

"I'm trying to choose my words carefully—"

"Try *quickly*!"

"Apparently, unknown to us, Dr. Guaiardo and the Brewster woman, both of whom violently opposed us, were close cousins, much closer than we knew."

"So the Armada achieved at least something. So what?"

"Dr. Guaiardo, a research scientist, put his medical skills to other endeavors. He was building no less than a genealogical chart of the Matarese organization dating back to the Baron, naming families, companies, corporations, and alliances. It's like a genealogical tree, each entity a marriage or birth that evolves into another entity, until it has to finalize into our major cartels."

"Oh, my *Christ*!" whispered the son of the Shepherd Boy, his fingers harshly massaging his lined forehead. "You say *has to* finalize—*has* it? Is the chart complete?"

"We can't be sure. As I said, our inheritor made clear—"

"Even if it *were*," interrupted Guiderone, breathing deeply, defensively, "such evidence would take months, perhaps years, the complexities overwhelming, each conclusion legally challenged."

"You're too brilliant to know that's not feasible, sir. Even the specter, the *perception*, that such a global enterprise as ours is linked to the economic crises that are spreading across national borders is a blueprint for disaster. Our disaster, Mr. Guiderone."

"The pig of the world!" said the son of the Shepherd Boy quietly, leaning back on the black leather couch. "He killed his assassins and found Wichita. Christ, *how*? He's behind everything. *Again!*"

The Marblethorpe was a small, elegant hotel on New York's Upper East Side, a temporary residence for the movers and shakers of the international scene. These included diplomats, giants of transnational finance, emerging and receding statesmen of consequence, all usually in negotiations best not conducted where the parties might be observed. The Marblethorpe was ideal for such occasions; it had been designed along those general lines, built by a multimillionaire who sought confidentiality as well as comfort above the crowded streets of Manhattan. There were no advertisements beyond the required line in the telephone book's white pages, and no single or double rooms, only suites. Each floor was divided into two large areas across from each other. Eight stories high, sixteen suites; none was ever available, all perpetually "leased."

"There's a side entrance with very little light and a green door," said Frank Shields, sitting in an overstuffed pale red easy chair, as Scofield walked around a Queen Anne desk with a white telephone console on top. Antonia emerged from one of the bedrooms.

"It's all really quite beautiful, Frank," she said, smiling. "When it's midnight, will it turn into a hovel?"

"I hope not. A number of guests might have heart attacks—or *their* guests would."

"Oh, a house of assignations?"

"I'm sure there are and have been, my dear, but that's not its primary function. In truth, the board of directors frowns on that sort of thing."

"Then what?"

"You might say conferences between people who for one reason or another shouldn't be conferring. The security here is the best in the private sector. You don't make a reservation at the front desk, you have to be referred."

"How did *you* get in, Squinty?"

"We're on the board of directors."

"Good work. Still, it strikes me that these digs are out of your league, unless you've become careless with contingency funds."

"We have an arrangement. As part of the board, we research in depth the referrals."

"So you don't pay."

"We also learn who's meeting with whom. It's a splendid quid pro quo and since our service is often invaluable, we couldn't allow the taxpayers to absorb these costs."

"You're a beaut, Frank."

"But why in New York?" asked Toni, interrupting. "If people need secrecy, I'd think there are better places than one of the most famous cities in the world. The countryside, islands like ours, hundreds of places."

"I'm afraid you'd be wrong, Toni. It's easier to be hidden in a bustling, overcrowded city than it is in the boondocks. Ask the mob boys who were in Appalachia—or ourselves in Chesapeake and Peregrine, or even you two on Brass Twenty-six. Pryce found you because there was a trail to follow. Trails can get lost in a frenzied city, and God knows New York is that."

"I'll have to think about it," said the now and always Mrs. Scofield. "But why are *we* here, Frank?"

"Hasn't Brandon told you?"

"Told me what? . . ."

"It struck me as an excellent idea, and knowing that I could commandeer a place here, I went along with him."

"Told me *what*?" Toni demanded.

"I was getting around to it last night at Peregrine, but if you recall, you slept in the other bedroom."

"Because I was furious! An overage fool approaching seventy goes out at night into a shooting gallery. You could have been *killed*."

"I wasn't, now, was I?"

"Please, you two, cut it out."

"I want an explanation! Why are we here, Bray?"

"If you'll calm down, I'll explain, old girl. . . . New York's a major hub of international finance, I think you'll agree with that."

"So?"

"International finance is essential to the Matarese, that's what they're aiming to control, if they haven't already. Now, there's another 'essential' in their operations, and I know it because Taleniekov and I saw it, lived through it, and damned near got killed because we learned it—"

"I was there, too, my husband."

"Thank God you were, old girl. We'd *both* be dead if you weren't. But this was before we found you, how we traced the Matarese to Corsica in the first place."

"What in heaven's name *is* it, Brandon?" exploded Shields.

"Hell, Squinty, I told you."

"Oh, yes, yes, now I recall. It's why we're here. Sorry, Toni, it's just that he's so . . . melodramatic, and I'm so tired."

"Tell *me*!" shouted Antonia.

"The Matarese hierarchy never fully reveals to its branches—its disciples, if you like—the negative things that happen. It's as if they can't admit they're vulnerable in any way, for if they do, fear of exposure might spread."

"And?"

"Well, you see, girl, Wichita is finished, gone, history, a blip on a radar screen. But I'll bet my offshore accounts that the disciples don't know about it."

"Your *what*? . . ."

"Shut up, Squinty. You're so much older than I am you can't remember what I told you yesterday."

"I never heard your last statement. Offshore—oh, *Jesus*! . . ."

"So you see, Toni-mine, I'm going to make like I'm a high muckety-muck in the Matarese—recently from Amsterdam, which apparently plays a large role in the organization. I'm going to tell each and every one I secretly *confer* with that Wichita is finished, out, *finito*."

"Who *are* they? Who are you going to 'confer' with?"

"A few dozen goddamned presidents, CEO's, treasurers, and chairmen of the boards of all those mother-loving companies and corporations that have engineered mergers, buy-outs, and all kinds of funny business. We've got a list of thirty-eight possibles here and in Europe. Someone will blink."

"If you're right, Brandon," Shields broke in, "suppose they *reach* Amsterdam?"

"That's the squeegee on the glass, Squint Eyes. I'll tell 'em that Amsterdam may be the next Wichita and my advice, as the emerging major player, is to stay the hell away from Amsterdam, they've screwed up enough."

"But will they *believe* you, Bray?"

"M'love, Taleniekov and I spent years honing our malignant skills for just such times as this. The words will come from both of us. By *Christ,* they'll come!"

It was morning in Loch Torridon, Scotland; the multipaned window of the inn's small dining room overlooked the dew-drenched fields that led to the Highland hills. The breakfast dishes had been cleared away, two large pots of coffee and tea left for the occupants of the table. They were Leslie Montrose and her son; Cameron Pryce; and Luther Considine, lieutenant senior grade, U.S. Navy. Explanations, as complete as they could be, had been delivered.

"It's *wild*!" said the pilot.

"It's what's happening," countered Pryce.

"Are you sure I should be in the loop on this?" asked Considine.

"Probably not. However, your somewhat unorthodox clearance comes from someone nobody's going to argue with—"

"Oh, I see," the pilot broke in. "That deputy director at the CIA I spoke to. A Mr. Shields, I think."

"No, he's small potatoes."

"Then *who*?"

"Your young friend here, Montrose junior, whom you ran into in Manama."

"Jamie?" Considine looked over at the teenager. "What the hell did you do, kid?"

"Without you, Luther, I'd probably be in a sandpit in Bahrain. You're entitled to know why you risked being a swab-jockey, remember? . . . Also, when you're an admiral, maybe you'll help me get into the Navy or Marine Air Corps like my dad."

"I don't know whether to thank you or run like a chicken out of here! This whole thing is way above my maximum altitude. Great balls of muleshit, a worldwide conspiracy to take over the financial interests of half the globe—"

"The rest to follow, Lieutenant," interrupted Leslie Montrose. "By corruption and fear, that's their agenda. My son and I were only a minor event in an attempt to kill one man who knows the Matarese's history and can possibly point the way to the present."

"Yeah, the Mata-whatever. What does it mean, Colonel?"

"It's based on a name, Luther," answered Pryce, "a Corsican whose original ideas became a blueprint for an international monopoly, far more powerful than the Mafia."

"As I said, way above my max altitude."

"Above all of ours, Lieutenant," said Leslie. "None of us is prepared for it, no training exists to address it. We each do what we can to fight it in our individual spheres, hoping to God that those above *us* are making the right decisions."

Considine shook his head in consternation. "What do we do now?"

"We're waiting for instructions from Frank Shields," replied Cameron.

"In Peregrine?" asked Leslie.

"No, they've moved to New York."

"Why New York?"

"Scofield's created a scenario he thinks might work. It's worth a try. Geof Waters is mounting the same strategy in the U.K. out of London."

"*Hold* it!" exclaimed the black naval officer, his dark eyes on fire. "Am I supposed to understand that, too? . . . Who's Scofield, *what* 'scenario,' and who's Waters in London?"

"You retain specifics extremely well," said Montrose.

"When you've got several dozen printouts at thirty thousand feet, you damn well better, ma'am—Colonel."

"I told you, Mom, he's really gonna be an admiral someday."

"Thanks, Jamie, and you may be consigned to a juvenile detention center."

The telephone rang, the phone on the table installed by MI-5. Cameron Pryce picked it up. "Yes?"

"Waters, here, London. Scrambler both ends. How are you?"

"Bewildered, how are you?"

"Equally so, old chap. We're mounting Beowulf Agate's strategy but it'll take a day or so, if we're not penetrated, that is. However, this transmission can't be."

"Small favors and all that kind of thing," said Cam. "What do you want us to do? Where do you want us to go?"

"Is your American pilot officer within reach?"

"He's sitting next to me."

"Ask him if he's certified in fixed-wing, low-flying propeller aircraft."

Pryce did so. Considine replied. "I'm certified in anything that leaves the ground, with the possible exception of spacecraft, which I could probably handle."

"Did you hear him?"

"Clearly, and that's good. In two hours a vintage but totally refurbished Bristol Freighter, a twin-engined workhorse of a machine, will land at the Loch Torridon airfield. You're all to get on it."

"Where are we going?"

"Your sealed instructions are to be opened once you're airborne, at the precise minute written on the envelope."

"That's *bullshit,* Geof!"

"That's your Beowulf Agate, chap. Something to do with radar."

It was 5:30 A.M. in Marseilles, the sprays of dawn breaking through the sky over the slowly awakening harbor. Teams of dockworkers trudged along the piers and the multiple sounds of erratic machinery began to be heard. Jan van der Meer Matareisen was alone in his office, the relief he had felt with Julian Guiderone's departure suddenly shattered by the news from London. "Do you have an explanation for such incompetence?" he asked sharply over his sterile telephone.

"I doubt if anyone else could have done better," replied the voice in the U.K., a woman's voice, her speech clipped, aristocratic.

"We can't know that, can we?"

"*I* know it and I resent your attitude."

"Resent all you like, although I doubt you're in a position to do so."

"That's hardly civil, Jan. Or fair."

"I'm sorry, Amanda, things are very difficult—"

"Shall I fly over to Amsterdam and try to ease things for you?"

"I'm not in Amsterdam, I'm in Marseilles."

"You do get around, don't you, my dear? Why Marseilles?"

"It was necessary."

"It was *Julian,* wasn't it? I think he considers Marseilles his third or fourth home. It's the one I liked least, the people who came to see him were so gross."

"Please don't remind me of your relationship—"

"*Past* relationship, way past. And why not? I've never hidden anything from you . . . and it's the way we met, darling."

"Perhaps in a day or so—"

"Don't let him bully you, Jan! He's an ugly, horrible man, concerned with no one but himself."

"It's the way he has to be, I understand that. Still, I must have an explanation for him. Two failures in a row are simply intolerable."

"I don't know what you're talking about—"

"You don't have to," broke in Matareisen, his hand beginning to tremble. "I meant what I said before. What *happened*? How did Pryce and the Montrose woman disappear?"

"I didn't say they disappeared, I said they got away."

"How?"

"By plane, obviously. When my source in Tower Street told me they were at an inn in a place called Loch Torridon, north of Edinburgh, I reached the man you call London Control and relayed the information. He thanked me and said it was all he needed."

"He's not permitted to call me, we're in contact only through third and fourth parties. Did he tell you?"

"Of course—"

"Then for God's sake *tell me*!"

"You haven't given me a chance. You've simply shouted—you were quite abusive."

The Dutchman in Marseilles briefly held his breath, calming himself. "All right, Amanda, what did London Control say?"

"He's quite a remarkable man, very resourceful."

"What did he *tell* you?"

"He said that by the time he reached the inn at Loch Torridon, the owner told him that the four people he was looking for had checked out."

"Four people?"

"Four Americans. A brother and sister, both registered as Brooks, a black American naval officer, and a young teenager, neither of whom registered at all, as instructed by Mr. Brooks."

"Mother of Christ, it's the *Montrose* boy! They flew him to Scotland!"

"What *are* you talking about?"

"Never mind. What else?"

"Your London Control learned they had all been taken to the airport. So he drove there and found out that the people he described had boarded a two-engine propeller plane less than an hour before he got there."

"Oh, my *God*!"

"Here's where I think your soft-spoken London fellow was extremely resourceful. He said to tell you, in case you and he hadn't spoken by now, that he found the flight plan for the plane the four Americans boarded."

"What was the destination?" asked Matareisen rapidly, perspiration breaking out on his forehead.

"Mannheim, Germany."

"Unbelievable!" exclaimed the Dutchman, clearly panicked. "They've now zeroed in on the Verachten Works, the Voroshin offspring! Years ago . . . *generations* ago! They're doing it. They're filling out the chart!"

"Jan? . . ."

The Englishwoman was too late. Matareisen had slammed down the phone.

22

The twin-engine, late-forties Bristol Freighter was airborne, heading southeast over the North Sea, when the pilot, Luther Considine, glanced at his watch. He turned to Pryce, seated next to him in the first-officer's position. "I'm not too happy with you in that chair, but it's time, Cam." He handed Pryce a sealed brown manila envelope, the red plastic stripes unbroken, not tampered with.

"Why aren't you happy?" asked Cameron, breaking open the envelope and extracting two smaller ones. "I showered this morning."

"Suppose I get a bad stomachache, or worse. You gonna fly this mother—excuse me, this *grand*mother?"

"I'll hold your head while you throw up, and you can tell Jamie how to do it. Here—" He handed an envelope to the pilot. "That's for you."

Both men opened their instructions. Considine spoke first, as his was the shorter. "My, oh, my!" he mumbled, checking the aircraft's dials, in particular the airspeed, altimeter, and the Greenwich mean time clock. He then glanced at the plastic framed chart above the complex dash-board. "We're going to make a rapid descent, ladies and gentlemen, in about two minutes, thirty seconds!" he said in a loud voice, turning his head so Leslie and her son, in the bulkhead seats, could hear above the engines. "Not to be concerned a bit, but it might be a good idea to clamp your noses and force the air out of your ears. Again, nothing to worry about, a piece of cake."

"Why?" asked Leslie. "I've been on a lot of missions, and outside of hostile gunfire, I've never heard of this. Why the evasive action?"

"Mom, cut it out! Luther knows what he's doing."

"Orders, Colonel, I just read 'em. . . . Secure seat belts—tight, please."

"I'll explain later," cried Pryce as Considine advanced to his arc of descent, the engines roaring. Cameron read his orders; without question they were the words of Brandon Alan Scofield, a.k.a. Beowulf Agate.

```
Sweet young gorilla, this is your
commander speaking. We're now entering
Operation Wolf Pack, forgive the play on
my name.
   Your pilot is going to descend to an
altitude that will avoid the immediate
radar, which is listed on his scope as
Vector 22. Your flight plan lists
Mannheim, Germany, as your destination,
but he will change course and head for
Milan, Italy. Once on the ground, you
and your party will be met by several
friends of mine from the old days.
They're splendid fellows, although they
may not be dressed in apparel
sanctioned by Gentlemen's Quarterly.
They're savvy and know the ways of the
Matarese in and around Bellagio and
Lake Como. The key is the name
```

```
Paravacini, one of the long-forgotten
Scozzi-Paravacini companies.
   Using my old friends and the
information they give you, begin
penetrating the Paravacinis. The
bastards are still there—they have to
be, rotten families always hold on—and
you should find another avenue to the
Matarese. Suggest you do as I'm doing
and Waters's boys in MI-5, that you
speak for Amsterdam, soon to be
discredited.
```

The plane came out of its dive-descent, pilot and passengers breathing deeply as they literally skimmed over the water.

"What happens now?" asked Pryce.

"I stay three to four hundred feet above sea level until I reach the Alps, then take the lowest routes until I reach spaghetti-land. Whoever vectored this flight plan knew what he was doing. He should be employed by the drug meisters."

"*Then* what do you do?"

Considine looked at Cam. "Don't you know? Wasn't it in your orders?"

"No, and no, again."

"I'm temporarily detached from the fleet and assigned to you."

"For what?"

"For whatever you need, I guess. I fly airplanes, maybe that's what the high brass had in mind."

"Welcome aboard, pilot," said Pryce. "You come highly recommended by the younger crowd."

"That's got me troubled." Luther spoke softly, studying his dials. "We go to one hell of a lot of trouble to get the boy out of Bahrain, out of harm's way, and here we are taking him back into a danger zone. I feel kind of responsible. He's a good kid."

"I can't answer you, Lieutenant. I hadn't really thought

about it, which makes me a prime jerk, because you're right, it's stupid. I'll reach Shields and Waters soon after we land."

It was not necessary for Cameron to make the calls to London or New York. A separate set of instructions for the plane was awaiting them in Milan. It was addressed and delivered to Lieutenant Colonel Leslic Montrose. Startled, she thanked the uniformed American Marine who was the courier, and opened the sealed envelope with the markings of Rome's Embassy of the United States of America on the upper left-hand corner.

"I flew up with this an hour ago, Colonel," explained the Marine. "My name's Olsen, captain of the embassy guard detail, and the envelope hasn't left my person."

"Understood, Captain, and thanks again."

"You're welcome." The officer saluted and walked away.

"It's from Tom Cranston," said Leslie, moving across the noisy tarmac with Pryce and her son while Considine made arrangements for the plane.

"That explains the embassy in Rome," said Cam. "Maximum security, White House and State back channels. You've got clout, lady."

"I'm impressed, Mom."

"You may not be for long, Jamie. You're going back on the plane. Arrangements have been made for you to join the Brewster children in France. Tom says that you'll all be completely safe, your whereabouts kept secret."

"Aw, *Mother,* come *on*!" yelled the son, stopping in his tracks. "I don't want to be dumped in France."

"Hey, cool it, Jamie," said Pryce with quiet but firm authority. "It's for your own good, surely you can understand that. I don't think you'd be overjoyed being yanked back to Bahrain, or some place like it."

"Hell, no, but we've got fifty states across the pond, as they call it. Why not somewhere back home? Why with two guys I don't *know*?"

"You won't believe this," answered Cameron, "but you're more vulnerable making such a trip, either alone or with your mother, than you are in protective custody somewhere in Europe."

"That's the thinking regarding the Brewster kids," Leslie broke in. "Fast, private aircraft, short distance, total control. No airports watched, no informers in the Pentagon or the CIA or British intelligence to report covert flights or high-level clandestine orders."

"Who *are* these people you're so afraid of?" demanded Montrose junior. "You're talking like they're some kind of all-powerful crime nuts!"

"You're not far wrong," said Pryce, "except they're very bright nuts, and very, very powerful. But not all-powerful. Not yet."

"Okay, okay," mumbled a disconsolate Jamie, "who are these Brewster guys?"

"Not guys, son. A brother and a sister who may be targets. British intelligence wants to exclude any future hostage-taking. You'll like them, Jamie. I do."

"Yeah, well, sometimes English kids can act kind of superior, you know what I mean?"

"Not an English kid who was obviously number one in his welding and blow-torching class," replied Cameron.

"*What* class?"

"Welding. You mean your expensive prep school in Connecticut doesn't have such a course?"

"No, why should they?"

"Roger Brewster said he should learn a trade, like those who didn't have his advantages."

"Wow, no kidding?"

"No kidding, Jamie," confirmed his mother. "He's also a wrestler, like you."

"That's all I need, to get pinned by a Brit."

Luther Considine was seen walking rapidly across the tarmac. "We'll be ready to get upstairs in five minutes, Junior," he said, approaching the trio. "I gather you've got the scoop by now."

"You *knew* about this, Luther?" asked Jamie.

"I had to, kid, I'm the driver, remember? We're refueled and we've got a weird flight plan, but it'll be interesting. I bought you one of those throwaway cameras at a spaghetti booth so you can take pictures. You're never gonna see this kind of travel again!"

"It's *safe,* isn't it, Lieutenant?" Leslie's eyes were wide with anxiety.

"A milk run, Colonel. Even if both props stopped spinning, we're low enough to glide our grandmother down into a field or a highway."

"Where are you going?" said Pryce.

"Would you believe, Cam, I'm not even permitted to tell *you*?"

"Who says?"

"The White House. You want to argue?"

"I don't think I'd win."

"You wouldn't, spook. By the way, your suitcases are in baggage. Come on, Junior, we've got to get over to Runway Seven, and we're not even allowed field transport. We're nonexistent, you might say."

Mother and son embraced briefly, with emotion, and James Montrose Jr. ran to catch up with the Navy pilot, racing across the field to their plane.

Brandon Scofield's "several friends from the old days" turned out to be one elderly man in his midseventies. The journey to reach him was circuitous. It began when Pryce and Montrose approached the Milan terminal. Suddenly a hoarse voice called out.

"Signore, signora!" Out of the shadows of a cargo door a scruffily dressed youngster, perhaps eighteen or a year older, walked toward them. His demeanor telegraphed his anxiety as well as a fair degree of furtiveness.

"Che cosa?" asked Cameron.

"Capisce italiano, signore?"

"Not very well, I haven't in years."

"I speak some English—*abbastanza.*"

"'Enough'? That's good. What is it?"

"I take you to Don Silvio. Hurry!"

"Who?"

"Signor Togazzi. *Rapido!* Follow!"

"Our luggage, Cam."

"It'll wait. . . . So can you, *ragazzo. Attesa!*"

"*Che?*"

"Who is this Togazzi, this Don Silvio? And why should we follow you? *Perchè?*"

"You see him."

"*Quali nuove?*"

"I am to say—*Bay . . . ohh—lupo? . . .*"

"*Lupo,* 'wolf.' Bay . . . ohh—*wolf*? You're to say *Beowulf*?"

"*Sì. Vero!*"

"Let's go, Colonel."

At the far end of the airport's parking lot, the young man held open the door of a small Fiat, gesturing for Pryce and Montrose to quickly climb into the backseat, a cramped area once they were inside.

"Are you okay?" asked Cameron, somewhat out of breath from the rapid pace across the crowded lot. They were interrupted by having to dodge several cars that seemed to have exploded out of their spaces.

"How can Italians *build* such tiny automobiles? Haven't they seen all those pictures of heavy *mamma mias* dancing tarantellas? To answer your question, you're crushing me."

"I find it rather pleasant. Think I'll buy one while I'm here, then hire a chauffeur to drive us around."

"That's all we'd be doing—driving around." Suddenly, the scroungily dressed driver whipped into a series of turns through the streets of Milan, streets filled with traffic. "I think I just broke two ribs."

"Want me to check?"

"No, I want you to tell that idiot to slow down."

"*Lento, ragazzo, piacere lento!*"

"*Impossibile, signore. Don Silvio impaziente.* . . . You change *macchina* little soon."

"What did he say?"

"He said he couldn't slow down because this Don Silvio is impatient. Also, we're going to change cars."

"That should be a blessing," noted Leslie.

It was and it wasn't. The automobile was larger with far

more room in the backseat, but the next driver, middle-aged, wearing dark glasses, and with long black hair that fell to his shoulders, was far wilder behind the wheel than the teenager. Once the transfer was made, no greetings were exchanged, no names used; the driver simply careened through the streets to the second entrance of the city's main highway. It headed north, the arrows on the signs reading Legnano, Castellanza, and Gallarate. Cameron recognized the route; it led to Bellagio, on the shore of Lacus Larius, internationally known as Lake Como.

Thirty-eight minutes later, they reached the ancient village that over the centuries had grown into a town, yet still retained its postmedieval flavor. The streets were narrow and winding, with abrupt ascents and sudden descents, reminding one that in distant times past they were dirt thoroughfares traversed by merchants and peasants, their carts and wagons pulled by mules through the fields and hills overlooking the majestic lake. And in those narrow streets, on both sides, so close together they might as well have been attached, were rows of dwellings, half-stone, half-wood, most if not all rising three and four stories high. They were like miniature fortresses, one on top of another, akin to the Pueblo caves or the earliest condominiums, perhaps. However, the effect was startlingly different from either, for there was no space for light, only wide alleys of shadows, the stone and the wood blocking the sun.

"At least this is a tad more comfortable, if no less terrifying," said Montrose, leaning into Pryce's shoulder as the car raced up the highway. "It's a strange automobile, isn't it?"

"Yes, it is," answered Cam, glancing around. "It's like the outside is denying the inside."

Pryce's remark summed it up. The large car was first seen as an old, nondescript gray sedan with multiple scratches across the paint and numerous dents, from the fenders to the trunk. An observer would judge it to be an abused relic; that is, until he stepped inside. For within, the seats were covered with the softest and most expensive wine-colored leather, and facing those in back was a well-equipped mahogany bar. There was a telephone mounted on the side, its panel also mahogany. Coupled with the tinted windows, it was apparent that the owner of the vehicle insisted on the amenities but had no desire to call attention to the car itself.

The equally strange and silent driver sped up an inclining street, emerging from the dark, tunnel-like environs below into the bright afternoon sunlight. On one side there was a succession of grazing fields, cows and sheep comingling; on the other, a scattering of houses and barns, these quite separate, even isolated from one another. They turned right and rushed along a road that paralleled the immense Lake Como, eliciting from Leslie an appropriate comment.

"It's all absolutely breathtaking!" she said, studying the panorama. "It's one of the few places that lives up to the postcards."

"Good observation," agreed Cameron. "It does."

And then it happened. Once again the blinding Italian sun was shredded into erratic shafts of light and shadows. They had turned off the scenic route onto a wide dirt road cut out of a forest, huge trees flanking them, eliminating any view but thick trunks, climbing vines, and dense foliage, an underbrush that seemed impenetrable. They began to slow down, the reason obvious: There was a small concrete structure ahead; a heavy steel barrier extended across the primitive access. A thick-bodied plug of a man wandered out, a shotgun strapped over his shoulder. Sicilian-style, thought Pryce.

The guard nodded at the chauffeur, the barrier was raised, and the nondescript gray sedan proceeded up the road. Suddenly, the outlines of a huge one-level house could be seen, almost at one with its forest surroundings. It appeared to extend so far into the woods that the end of the building could not be estimated, much less discerned. Once more, heavy wood and dark stone, the traditional materials of Bellagio, repelled the sunlight, preferring the shadows.

Leslie and Cameron got out of the car, only to be met by another guard with a shotgun hanging from his shoulder.

"Coma wis me," he said in barely understood English, the salutation obviously tutored. They followed the armed man up a graveled path, both glancing above, marveling at the roof of dark green that did not merely shelter the lair of Don Silvio Togazzi, but essentially concealed it.

The second guard waved his head, instructing the Americans to walk up the short flight of steps that led to a pair of immense double doors while he removed a small instrument from his trousers pocket. Whatever it was, he activated it, and the panel on the right opened, revealing a third man. This guard had no shotgun hanging from his shoulder; instead, an extremely large holster was on his right hip, held in place by a wide leather belt that creased his hill-country clothing. He was a large man, taller than Pryce, with a massive chest below a thick neck and a swarthy, impassive face in the middle of an outsized head. Studying the man, Cameron concluded that he was the don's number one protector. But a protector from *what*?

And why the series of intricate, elusive moves apparently designed to hide any connection between Togazzi and his guests? Caution, yes; a degree of secrecy, of course; but to go to these lengths—who *was* Togazzi? Scofield's backchannel instructions had said "several friends from the old days," with the gratuitous observation that they were probably a crew of unwashed antiques who had survived the brutal times and knew the Matarese. Instead, there appeared to be only one man, whose actions so far were more like those of a member of the Matarese than of someone sworn to destroy it.

Cam and Leslie were led across the huge, dark, windowless room decorated with simple furniture, a large fireplace, and paneled walls with two archways on the right leading to other areas. It was the interior of a basic elongated log cabin in the mountains—no frills, only necessities. The third guard pointed to a screen door at the rear of the room. *"Avanti,"* he said.

Pryce opened the screen for Montrose and they walked through, both stunned. The first sight that awed them was the open porch itself. It was barely seven feet wide, but its length had to be twenty times that. The framed opening, from the waist-high railing to the ceiling, was filled with panels of green venetian blinds, a number drawn, once more creating shifting shadows. Through the open spaces one saw the scenic splendor of Lake Como, the mountains rising in the distance beyond the blue lake, the trees of the forest having been topped to afford the view. And, as if in counterpoint to the overwhelming natural beauty, there was a row of red telescopes spaced twenty feet apart, the most modern wide-lensed telescopes high technology had developed.

All this was absorbed in a breathless few moments, then came the second shock. It was the figure of an old man seated in semidarkness in front of two drawn venetian blinds. He was in a cushioned white-wicker armchair—all the porch furniture was white wicker—and his attire ended once and for all Cameron's expectations of Scofield's unkempt friends.

Don Silvio Togazzi was dressed in a pale yellow linen suit, white patent-leather shoes, and a blue paisley ascot, the combination undoubtedly custom-made at the most expensive emporium in the Via Condotti. The don may not have lived up to the current ideal of *Gentlemen's Quarterly,* but he certainly would have qualified if the magazine had been published in the late twenties or early thirties.

"Forgive me, young people," said the still ruggedly attractive old man, his tanned, leathery face lit with a smile below his flowing white hair. "But a long-ago injury to my spine has caught up with this ancient body. An injury, by the way, caused by Bayohlupo—that's what we called him, Bayohlupo—because he did not properly catch me when I escaped over a balcony."

"Bayohlupo . . . Beo*wulf,* am I correct, sir?" asked Pryce.

"Exactly. The English Beowulf made absolutely no sense to us. I am an educated man but . . . it wasn't even English."

Leslie stepped forward to shake the Italian's hand; instead, he took hers and kissed it. "You're very kind to see us, Mr. Togazzi," she said.

"And I thank you for not saying Don Silvio. I'm sick of it. Your American films and television have so denigrated the term 'don' that anyone whose peers believe he deserves it must perforce be a Mafioso, or fill his face with so much pasta he drools while ordering executions. *Pazzo!*"

"I think we're going to get along." Cameron leaned forward and shook the old man's hand. "May we sit down?"

"You don't have to ask. Sit."

White-wicker chairs adjusted, they sat opposite Togazzi on the narrow porch—narrow, close, and filled with shadows and shafts of light. Bellagio. "What did Brandon Scofield tell you, sir? To be up-front, he sent me a message saying that you could help us."

"I can help, Signor Pryce. I flew to Rome, to your embassy. Brandon spoke to me at length over one of those nonintercepting channels—"

"We hope," interrupted Cameron.

"Neither Signor Scofield nor I are fools, young man. As you Americans say, we've been around the block. We spoke elliptically, substituting codes and metaphors as we used to do long ago. But we each understood the other perfectly clearly, as few others would."

"Officer Pryce told me there would be several others, sir," said Montrose. "Are we waiting for them?"

"There would be no point, Signora Colonel, they will not come. They are two men, very old men who have given me everything they know, but will not meet you face-to-face."

"Why not?" Leslie asked.

"As I said, they are very old, *signora,* older than I, and do not care to be involved in past wars that caused them so much pain. However, everything's been written down for you."

"Yet you're willing to help us," Cameron said.

"I have their memories, and I also have other reasons."

"May we know what they are?" asked Leslie.

"It's not necessary. Bayohlupo knows."

"*He's* not here," said Cam. "We are."

"I see. I have treated you in a most unusual and inconvenient manner. You are no doubt thinking we could have met anywhere, say in a park or a hotel room in Milan."

"Yes, we could have."

"You don't know me, so I can say anything I like, and because I use Scofield's name, you think *I* believe you'll accept my words."

"Something like that," agreed Pryce.

"But now you ask yourself . . . who *is* this man?"

"I've already asked myself that."

"Rightly so. You now consider that I might not be what I appear to be, but, instead, a false courier with access to specific information, certain names."

"I can't help thinking what I think, no matter how out of line it is."

"Of course you can't. You cannot deny your years of training. As Brandon said, you're very good, perhaps the best the Agency has."

"Are you sure that was the Scofield I know?" asked Cameron, suppressing a laugh, then continuing. "You understand where I'm coming from. Tell us your reasons for helping us. Give us something that'll make us believe you."

"I can only tell you the truth," replied the old Italian, struggling out of his chair and walking slowly out from the shadows toward an open space, to one of the red telescopes. It was different from the others, as there was a black circular instrument above the thick red tube. He stopped and patted it, turning back to Pryce and Montrose. "You've heard of the two families, the Scozzis and the Paravacinis?"

"Yes," answered Cameron, "together they owned the Scozzi-Paravacini Industries until there was bad blood and they split."

"Not merely 'bad blood,' Signor Pryce, but *real* blood, murderously spilled by the Paravacinis to force out the Scozzis. Force them out so they could ascend in the deadly Mataresa. Brothers and sons were murdered, executives bought and blackmailed, directors manipulated into compromising incidents that cost them their directorships. Scozzi-Paravacini was diseased, poisoned from within, and the disease won."

"I think I see where you're heading," said Leslie softly. "You were very close to the Scozzis, the Scozzi family."

The old man laughed, a quiet, sad laugh. "Quite perceptive, Colonel, although 'close' is not the word I would choose. I *am* a Scozzi, the last living member of the Scozzi family."

"But your name's Togazzi," protested Cameron.

"'What's in a name?' as the lady said. You can call a rose a tulip but it remains a rose. . . . We must go back several decades—before the killings began. The killers would never be found, of course, for the Paravacinis had great influence in Milan and Rome, as well as the Vatican. Because my mother despised and feared them, I was sent to Sicily, to the home of a *cugino* of my mother's, for my own protection. In the early years I was tutored, then sent to Rome for advanced education, using the *cugino*'s name, Togazzi, again for my protection."

"Is that where you met Mr. Scofield?" said Montrose.

"My dear Colonel, you reveal your *youth*!" Don Silvio chuckled as he slapped the telescope. "That was many years later, after my *universitario* days."

"By then you were with Italian intelligence?" asked Pryce.

"Yes, the Servizio Segreto. I was accepted as soon as my studies were complete, courtesy of a few well-connected friends in Palermo. Outside of my normal duties, I entered the Servizio with only one thought in mind, one obsession. To bore into the Paravacini interests, the whole sordid landscape, which led, naturally, to the Mataresa. That is when I encountered Scofield and Taleniekov. Our concerns were the same, but to gain their confidence, I told them my story, as I tell it to you now. You may, of course, confirm everything with Brandon, but you'll have to do it elsewhere. There is no equipment here that would guarantee confidentiality."

"It won't be necessary," said Cameron.

"I agree," added Montrose.

"And no one here in Bellagio knows who you are?"

"*Mio Dio,* no. I'm an immensely wealthy *siciliano,* whose once-blond hair and riches buy him respectability in the northern provinces." Again, the old man touched—

caressed—the red telescope. "Here, I want to show you something. Come, come, both of you look through this."

Leslie and Cam did so, marveling at the magnification. What each saw was a mansion on the banks of Lake Como, complete with manicured lawns, a pier, an immense yacht moored in the water, and fountains everywhere. Figures of men and women strolled around the grounds, so enlarged in the lens they could be thirty yards away, not several miles.

"Nice spread," said Pryce, backing away and turning to Togazzi. "Whose is it?"

"It is the Paravacini estate, and even the harshest mountain winds will not move this telescope. It is bolted in place. I can see, and if need be, photograph, everyone who comes and goes."

"You're a special piece of work, Don Silvio," added Cameron. "By the way, can your new name be traced?"

"Silvio Togazzi is duly registered—or should I say inserted—in the proper records of birth in Palermo, as is his baptism at the Church of the Blessed Savior, a country church south of Cafala. These documents are beautifully executed, as 'authentic' as any in the ledgers."

"Who bestowed the title of 'Don'?" asked a bemused Pryce.

"When one hires scores of men to clear the land and build, is extremely generous with the local families, pays for several festivals, and funds a new church or two or three, the 'don' comes naturally. Enough, however, about me. Come inside and I shall deliver everything we've put together for you. I think you'll be pleased."

"Forgive my curiosity," said Colonel Montrose, "but you mentioned that the injury to your spine was a result of Agent Scofield's failure to break your fall from a balcony. Was the incident related to your combined hunt for the Matarese?"

"Hardly, my dear Colonel, although my escape was mandatory. The woman in question was married to a fanatic *comunista,* such a slave to his work that he paid little attention to his wife. I merely tried to fill a void. . . . Come now, to the information we have compiled for you."

23

It was a drenching rain in New York City, both cleansing and an inconvenience for the noonday traffic. On a busy street that intersected Madison Avenue, three police officers removed the temporary No Parking signs. The instant they were taken away, cars swung into the spaces, the first a limousine within feet of a pale green door belonging to the Hotel Marblethorpe, the other two across the street directly opposite the luxury vehicle. Inside the three automobiles were armed men, their concentration on the man who emerged from the car near the pale green door, accompanied by an apparent bodyguard who kept his right hand under his raincoat. As if timed down to seconds, the hotel door was opened by another police officer; he nodded and the two hotel guests were admitted. The New York police, under orders from command, knew who the VIP's were, if not by name, by connections.

The man under protection was of medium height, in his late forties, and when he removed his canvas hat and raincoat in the short hallway, he appeared to be an expensively dressed business executive. His face was pale, his eyes darting back and forth in fear.

"Where the hell do we go?" he asked gruffly.

"The elevator is down the hall on the left, sir," replied the policeman.

"Thank you, young man, and my regards to the commissioner."

"I'll tell him myself, sir. We're on special detail and report only to him."

"You'll have a long and rewarding career, fella. What's your name?"

"O'Shaughnessy, sir."

"Another wop, right?" The three men laughed as the VIP and his bodyguard walked down the hall to the elevator. "I can't believe I'm *doing* this!" continued the businessman, his breath short. "Some nobody flies in, supposedly from Amsterdam, and I'm *summoned* to meet him, and that's exactly what it was, a goddamned *summons*! Who the hell does he think he *is*?"

"The others say he knows the words, Albert," replied the man acting as bodyguard, removing his hand from under his raincoat. "*All* the words."

"It could be a fishing expedition," said the shorter man, the one called Albert.

"If it is, he knows where certain fish are. The banking and the utility boys want to meet you after you've seen this William Clayton—"

"No doubt a false name," interrupted the executive. "There's no one by that name on any list I've got."

"You hardly have an inclusive list, Al, none of us do. Just listen to his words and don't volunteer a damn thing. Do as the others did, act innocent and shocked."

"You know, just because you're a lawyer you don't have to remind me of the obvious." The elevator door opened; both men walked in, and the armed attorney pressed the four-digit code for the floor as it had been given. "Take off your coat and hat, Stuart," added Albert Whitehead, CEO of Wall Street's Swanson and Schwartz, a major brokerage firm.

"I will now," agreed the lawyer named Stuart Nichols, removing his Burberry and Irish walking cap. "I didn't care to before. I wanted to make sure those cops were on our side."

"That's paranoid."

"No, memories of things past. I was a military prosecutor in Saigon, where a lot of uniforms wanted to see me dead. A couple nearly did and they were dressed as MP's. . . . You're still going to introduce me as your attorney?"

"You're goddamned right. I'll add that you know every-thing—*everything*—about me. I'm an open book to you—*only* you."

"He still may ask me to leave."

"Give him reasons why you shouldn't. You're good at that."

"I'll try, but if he insists, I'm not going to argue."

"Glad to meet you, Mr. Nichols, and delighted you're here," said "William Clayton," a.k.a. Brandon Scofield, a.k.a. Beowulf Agate, convivially addressing the attorney and shaking hands. Scofield was dressed in a conservative dark blue business suit that came off a very high-priced rack ser-viced by tailors. He led his guests to their appropriate chairs, each with a side table, and rang a silver bell. Antonia, dressed in a starched black-and-white maid's uniform, her graying hair pulled back into a severe bun, emerged from a door. She was an imposing sight.

"Coffee, tea, a drink? . . ." asked Brandon. "By the way, this is Constantina, from the hotel, and she doesn't speak a word of English. It was a request I made; she and I converse in Italian."

"Sorry it's not French," said Stuart Nichols, the lawyer. "I took several years at prep school and it served me well in Saigon."

"Let's see. . . . Constantina, *vous parlez français?*"

"*Che cosa, signore?*"

"*Capisce francese?*"

"*Non, signore. Linguaggio volgare!*"

"I'm afraid she can't join us. She says it's a vulgar tongue. When will they make peace with each other?" No one cared for anything, so Antonia, nodding professionally, was dismissed. "I know your time is limited, as is mine," said Scofield, "so shall we get down to business?"

"I'd like to know what our business *is,* Mr. Clayton," insisted Whitehead.

"Our *mutual* business, sir," replied Beowulf Agate. "Stocks, bonds, debentures, loans—corporate and transnational, in the main—initial stock offerings, naturally, but, most vitally, your servicing the intricacies of mergers and buyouts. Inestimable contributions."

"You're covering an enormous range of activities," said the CEO of Swanson and Schwartz, "and the majority are of a highly confidential nature."

"As they are in the Exchange in London, the Bourse in Paris, the Borsa in Rome, and the Börse in Berlin, all are highly confidential. But certainly not regarding Amsterdam."

"Would you clarify that, please," broke in Nichols.

"If I have to, perhaps you don't know your client, or his firm, as well as you think you do," answered Brandon.

"I'm the *firm's* attorney, Mr. Clayton. It is my sole client. There isn't anything I'm *not* aware of."

"Does that include Mr. Whitehead here? Because if it doesn't, I suggest you leave us."

"He's already told you it does."

"Then I can't imagine your not knowing about Amsterdam. . . . Twelve years ago, a Randall Swanson, now deceased, and a Seymour Schwartz, currently retired and living in Switzerland, combined to start a new brokerage house in the most competitive few blocks in the capitalistic world. Wonder of wonders, within a few years they blossomed into an important player, growing so rapidly they soon were on the edge of becoming a major force rivaling Kravis and the former Milken. Then, more wonderful still, during the last year Swanson and Schwartz engineered the most impressive mergers in recent memory—number one on the charts, my friends. Simply remarkable, but how was it *done*?"

"Talent pays, Mr. Clayton," said the lawyer, in complete control. "Mr. Whitehead is considered a brilliant, if not *the* most brilliant, managing director in current financial circles."

"Oh, he's good, very, very good, but can anybody really be *that* good? Talent without the resources to exercise that talent is a terrible waste, isn't it? But perhaps I've said enough, for if I'm wrong, I've frittered away your time, as well as my own, and that is unforgivable. Time *is* money, isn't it, gentlemen?"

"Just what do you mean by resources?" asked a nervous Whitehead, unable to stop himself despite the subtle shaking of his attorney's head.

"Just what I said," replied Scofield. "Investments in your talents, specifically foreign investment, if you like."

"There's nothing remotely illegal about that, Mr. Clayton," said Stuart Nichols. "Surely, you realize that."

"I never implied that it was. . . . Look, my time is short and so is yours. All I wish to say—and if it does not apply to you, forget I ever said it—is this: Do *not* deal with Amsterdam. Amsterdam is finished, kaput, banished out of the league, for it wants to control everything and that cannot be permitted. Amsterdam can't be trusted any longer, it has turned, for its own short-term advantage, ultimately to self-destruct. For that reason I left—fled to be precise."

"Could you be clearer, please?" asked the attorney.

"No, I can't," answered Beowulf Agate, "for the records are buried in a maze of complexity. I'm not at liberty to discuss them. However, if you should care to reach me, call this hotel, ask for the manager, and he'll tell you the number and the code. However, again, if anything I've said does make sense, take my word, do *not* call Amsterdam. Should you do so, you could be on its death list. . . . I think this is good afternoon, gentlemen."

Scofield showed his bewildered guests out and firmly, loudly, closed the door on their backs. He then turned and walked into the living room as Antonia came out of the kitchen; she was still in her black-and-white uniform, but her hair had been freed from its confinement.

"They're lying from jib to jigger," said Bray, lighting a small, thin cigar. "By the way, luv, you were damned convincing."

"It wasn't difficult, darling, the role fit, no acting required. You, on the other hand, gave a grand performance, extremely imaginative."

"Why thank you, my sweet, how so?"

"I read your notes on everyone you've already met with. With the others I could follow you, for there were too many coincidences, too much convergence of similar interests leading to collusion. You genuinely frightened a few of them, and they hid their fear with silence and abstract denials; the rest were completely confused. But when you mentioned foreign investments to these two, their silence was very loud, the mention of Amsterdam frightening, or so it seemed."

"Yeah, I kinda dragged that one out of my butt. It paid off, though, didn't it? They couldn't deny it fast enough, or at least justify it."

"How did you figure it, Bray? I'm simply curious."

"Part of the truth, Toni, part of the essential truth. We called them gaps in the old days, spaces that weren't filled. . . . Why would an up-and-coming brokerage house named Swanson and Schwartz sell out when their best years were ahead of them? Swanson died of a coronary when he had no history of heart trouble, and Schwartz left the States and became a citizen of Switzerland, both in their middle forties. For me, it was a classic Matarese pattern of manipulation. Both of those boys are Matarese down to their Gucci shoes."

"Sometimes you really revert to Beowulf Agate, don't you?"

"If the Serpent were still with us, I hope he'd agree. We owe a great deal to Taleniekov."

"Our lives, Bray, only our lives."

"So let's get on with it, luv," said Brandon, walking to the telephone console on the desk. He pressed a series of numbers and reached Frank Shields in an unmarked federal car nearby. "Everything under control, Squinty?" he asked.

"Would you mind not using that offensive name over government communications?"

"Sorry, Frank, it's meant only as a supreme compliment.

You see what others can't see 'cause you narrow things down."

"Bullshit isn't required. . . . We're tailing the two subjects; they're turning onto Central Park South."

"What do you figure?"

"Well, he's not heading back to his office, which tells us something. This was the last one, wasn't it?"

"Two as it turned out. Yes, they were. Stay in touch and if anything develops, call me. Toni and I are going to relax and order our way through the room-service menu, which, of course, the taxpayers don't have to cough up a dime for."

"*Please,* Brandon!"

"He *knows*!" cried a terrified Albert Whitehead in the limousine. "He knows *everything*!"

"Possibly," said the attorney, Nichols, coolly, "and just as possibly, he may not."

"How can you *say* that?" protested the CEO of Swanson and Schwartz. "You heard him, the stock offerings, the loans, the mergers and buyouts, for Christ's sake! Our entire schedule!"

"All easily discovered and confirmed by legal research. A first-year law student could do it."

"Then answer me this, Clarence Darrow! What about the foreign investment? How do you explain *that*?"

"That may be where he slipped up. The monies were funneled through a Texas consortium of venture capitalists, done orally through Amsterdam, and left no paper trail whatsoever."

"You can't be sure of that, Stuart."

"No, I can't be," admitted Nichols, turning and gazing absently at Whitehead. "It's what bothers me, I'll be honest with you. This Clayton is obviously tuned in to Amsterdam, which says a great deal . . . and he claims it's now off-limits, *really* off-limits."

"Dangerously so! He mentioned a death list—that's not an unknown calculation among our silent partners. They'll stop at nothing. We can't risk calling Amsterdam."

"So we can't learn the truth, if there's another truth, and we're not scheduled to report for another eight days. If we violate that schedule, which is timed for sterile satellite transmission, Amsterdam will know we think something's wrong."

"We could make *up* something, you're good at that!"

"Nothing I can think of. We're on time with everything, not a glitch in the agenda. Perhaps the others will have an idea, a reason to call the Keizersgracht."

"One of them *must*," insisted a panicked Whitehead. "We're all in this together and we've made millions!"

"You do realize, don't you, Albert, that this Clayton may be employing an enormous bluff?"

"Yes, I do, Stuart. But who's going to call it?"

The room-service table was filled with the remains of a devoured porterhouse steak, veal piccata, assorted vegetables, iced goblets of Iranian caviar (for Antonia), and three chocolate eclairs (for Scofield). They were now enjoying espresso coffee with ponies of Courvoisier VSOP brandy. "I could get used to this, m'luv," said Scofield, wiping his mouth with an enormous pink napkin.

"You could also die, old man," said Antonia. "If we ever get out of this, I want you back on the fish we catch and the fresh vegetables we grow."

"They're all so dull."

"They keep you alive, you old goat."

The telephone rang, and as if the sound were a relief, Scofield jumped out of his chair and walked rapidly to the console. "Yes?"

"It's Frank, Brandon. You're proving to have a fine batting average. The two big shots from Swanson and Schwartz ended up at one of those little unadvertised garden restaurants in the Village, the kind where you've got to have a financial pedigree to make a reservation."

"Not in my frame of reference, Mr. Director."

"Think of those clam houses in Brooklyn and Jersey, where the clientele are descendants of the old Moustache Petes and they can ice-pick anyone they like because they own them. These new ones are way upscale; the suits and the speech are different, but the meetings aren't."

"Get to the point, Frank."

"Your two honchos left your hotel and met with the banker Benjamin Wahlburg of that new banking conglomerate, and both Jamieson Fowler, head of Boston's Standard L and P, and Bruce Ebersole, president of Southern Utilities. They represent the mergers of the major electric and bicoastal banking institutions with a heavy arm in the Mediterranean. We have photographs. You had ten candidates and four proved out. Congratulations, Beowulf Agate, you're batting four hundred."

"Thanks, Squinty. What have you heard from London?"

"Find them, find *him*!" screamed Julian Guiderone over his satellite telephone on board his private jet en route to London from Marseilles. "We pay millions to gnomes who have lifestyles far beyond anything they could possibly earn, who exist only to *service* us! Why are they failing, why are *you* failing?"

"We're all working around the clock, I assure you," replied Jan van der Meer Matareisen from his sanctum sanctorum above the Keizersgracht in Amsterdam. "It's as if an unseen, unexpected blanket had descended over our sources."

"Then remove it, blow it apart! Kill several dozen on your payrolls—send out the word that they were suspected of betrayals. Spread terror through the ranks, create your own inquisition. As the bodies fall, traitors will be exposed; fear is the catalyst. Have you learned *nothing,* 'Grandson'?"

"I've learned to have patience, sir, and do *not* shout at me. While you fly around the world engineering crises, *I* have to hold the entire operation together. And may I remind you, sir, that while you are the son of the Shepherd Boy, *I* am the legitimate grandson of the Barone di Matarese, who *created* the Shepherd Boy. You have many, many millions, but *I* have billions. I respect you, sir, for what you nearly achieved—my God, the *White House*—however, I beg you, do not fight me."

"For God's sake, I'm not fighting you, I'm trying to *teach* you. Your heart and your intellect convince you that you're right, but you must have the stomach to follow through with those convictions! Where you find weakness, you root it out, the weed as well as its offshoots. Destroy everything in your path, no matter how appealing the wildflowers!"

"I've understood that for years," said Matareisen, "and don't try to insinuate that I haven't. I have no emotions where the work of the Matarese is involved; our disciples live or die by their actions."

"Then do as I say, start the killing, create the panic. Someone out there will know—or will force himself to *learn*—where Scofield is! Especially if failure may well cost him his life. *Beowulf Agate!* He's the one behind these interruptions, I told you that!"

"Our sources cannot tell us what they don't know, Mr. Guiderone."

"How do *you* know that, 'Grandson'?" asked the son of the Shepherd Boy caustically. "For all your brilliance, Jan van der Meer, you have a flaw common to genius. You believe that what you have created is infallible, for the creator cannot be faulted. *Nonsense!* You don't have the vaguest idea what Scofield is doing, what attack strategies he's mounted, or with whom. He neutralized Atlantic Crown . . . how many others are walking—no, goddamn it, probably *running*—into his nets? Once confirmed, how many of those may break?"

"No one will be broken," answered the Dutchman quietly. "Not only do they understand the consequences, but there are numerous fallback positions designed by our attorneys that completely legitimatize everything we've done. We're legally immaculate, free to continue until everything's in place. I also created that."

"You think you have—"

"I *know* I have, *old* man!" broke in Matareisen, suddenly shouting. "The only near catastrophe was because of *you* and your foolishness at Westminster House in London," went on Jan van der Meer, abruptly lowering his voice, "but you've apologized so we'll say no more about it."

"Well, well," mused Guiderone out loud, "the young lion really wants to dominate the pride."

"I do dominate it, through your appointment, if you recall. Do you regret it?"

"Good heavens, no. I could never do what you've done. However, I doubt I was the only catastrophe. Something happened in Wichita, and I don't believe I've ever been there, nor did I know the gentlemen involved."

"And they knew no one but a code and an answering machine in Amsterdam, buried in the Department of Canals."

"An inscrutable bureaucracy," conceded the son of the Shepherd Boy. "You are truly a genius, Jan van der Meer, but you're missing something, and that something is a someone. *Beowulf Agate.* If you do not find him, *kill* him, he will discover more flaws—and bring your house down. He did it before and we thought—we *knew*—we were invincible. Don't let it happen again. . . . You were correct, of course. I'm an old man, and so is Scofield. The difference between us is that he can move with the quick and the dead, I can only move with the dead and the near dead. You, on the other hand, can move with the quick and the dead *and,* above *all,* those filled with greed. They're the most powerful army on earth, an unstoppable battalion. *Use* it, use them! Do not disappoint me."

Guiderone slammed down the telephone, annoyed that the sudden turbulence had caused his glass of Château Beychevelle Médoc to spill over his table.

Sir Geoffrey Waters signed for the top-secret envelope delivered to his house in Kensington by an MI-5 officer. He began to open it as he walked back through the narrow hallway to his breakfast in the dining room. His wife, Gwyneth, a gray-haired woman of delicate features and wide, intelligent brown eyes, looked up from the London *Times* and spoke.

"Communiqués at this hour, Geoffrey? Couldn't it have waited till you got to the office?"

"I don't know, Gwyn, I'm as surprised as you are."

"Open it, darling."

"I'm trying to, but these damn black plastic tapes require scissors, I think."

"Use the steak knife."

"Yes, rather. Nice of you to have Cook get me a small fillet with my eggs."

"Well, you've obviously been under considerable pressure these past few weeks. Better to send you off with a satisfied stomach."

"Much appreciated," said the MI-5 chief of Internal Security as he slashed the crisscrossing tapes and opened the large manila envelope. He scanned its contents and plummeted down into his chair. "Oh, my *God*," he exclaimed.

"Is it something I'm permitted to know?" asked Gwyneth Waters. "Or one of those things I'm not supposed to?"

"You'd bloody well better! It's your brother, Clive—"

"Oh, yes, dear Clivey. He's doing so well now, isn't he?"

"Perhaps too well, my dear. He's on the board of directors of the new Sky Waverly consortium."

"Yes, I know, he phoned me last week. Quite a stipend, I gather."

"Or quite a mess, Gwyn. Sky Waverly is under an intensive investigation concerning matters I can't discuss with you—once again for your own well-being."

"Yes, we've been through this before, Geof, but after all, you're talking about my *brother*."

"Let's be honest, dearest. I enjoy Clive, I like him; he's a charmer with a wonderful sense of humor, but I don't think either of us considers him among the better barristers in London."

"He does have his shortcomings, I'll grant you that."

"He's gone from firm to firm, never rising to a partnership," continued Waters, "usually hired on the strength of *your* name. Bentley-Smythe is an honored name in English law."

"He's a decent man," interrupted the sister, "and he had too much to live up to, which he couldn't. Is that a crime?"

"Of course not, but why was he plucked from a minor

legal firm in which he was a downscale member to the board of directors of Sky Waverly?"

"I've no idea, but I'll call him this morning and ask him."

"That's the one thing you must *not* do," said Waters, softly but firmly. "Leave this to me, Gwyn. In my opinion, your brother's being used. Let me handle it."

"You won't hurt Clive, will you?"

"Not unless he's hurt himself, my dear, I promise you that. . . . Thank the cook for me, but I haven't time for breakfast." Geoffrey Waters left the table and walked rapidly to the hallway and the front door.

The twenty-minute drive to his office was a time of painful reflection for the British intelligence officer. The reason was Clive Bentley-Smythe and what Geoffrey's wife perceived about her brother as opposed to a harsher reality. Waters did, indeed, like his brother-in-law; he *was* a charming fellow with a quick, if shallow, wit and a generous nature, generous to a fault, if he had any faults. And *that* was his glaring fault. Clive Bentley-Smythe was as close to being a cipher as a human being could be, the living personification of the phrase *his reach exceeds his grasp*.

He had been born into a wealthy family of barristers and solicitors going back for generations—so established that there were those who said they probably framed the Magna Carta—for a price—and others who claimed that Shakespeare's "let's kill all the lawyers" in his play *King Henry VI* was inspired by the ancestors of Bentley-Smythe. Clive floated through life, the attractive addition to very social functions, adding little but his presence, and, in seeming contradiction, a devoted husband to a wife who had no regard whatsoever for the marriage covenant. It was common, if concealed, knowledge that she slept in some of the wealthiest beds in England, Scotland, the Netherlands, and Paris. The joke in certain circles was that if Clive ever found out, he would probably forgive her and ask if she'd had a good time.

Geoffrey Waters was aware of this dossier material, which he never shared with his wife, for she was the eternal big sister, protective of her younger brother to the walls of the proverbial barricades. There was no point in upsetting her. But now there was another equation, and the MI-5 chief of Internal Security knew he had to face it, analyze it, and act upon it. The French phrase *cherchez la femme* kept repeating itself in his mind, his imagination.

"Sorry I felt the need to send you the information, Geoffrey," said the MI-5 director of Operations, "but I felt you might want to talk to your wife about it."

"I did to a minimal degree, and I do mean minimal. There are many things she doesn't know about her brother, and I don't care to worry her. I'll act upon it myself. Are there any other possible breakthroughs?"

"Several, old man, but nothing certified," answered Waters's superior, a gray-haired, corpulent man in his sixties. "First, there are rumors out of Fleet Street that some sort of amalgamation, I guess you'd call it, is in the works."

"A Murdoch enterprise?"

"No, it's not his style. Whatever he is, he's usually up-front with his intentions. He buys and sells, profit his first consideration, editorial positions secondary, although he certainly respects them."

"Anything else?"

"I said several, not one," corrected the director. "There are movements in a number of banking institutions, centralization they call it, but I'm not convinced that the mergers are financially motivated."

"You're going against the economic stream. Why not?"

"Because all the institutions are profitable in their own right, all very independent. Why should they give up their fiefdoms?"

"Someone's forcing them to," replied Waters softly.

"Precisely my opinion. I've prepared a list of all their boards of directors, as well as the major journalists who appear to be part of this rumored amalgamation of newspapers."

"We'll work on every one, I assure you."

"There's a last entry, and it's a beauty. A directive was funneled to us from a newspaper in Toronto, Canada, a duplicate sent to the Servizio Segreto in Rome. It seems a reporter of theirs who flew to Italy called his paper from Rome, telling his editor that he would have the journalistic scoop of the century. He's since disappeared, no further word from him."

"We'll follow up," said Geoffrey Waters, writing in his notebook. "That's it, then?"

"One final thing, and I'm afraid it concerns your brother-in-law's wife, Amanda."

"I had an idea it might come to this."

24

While his subordinates redoubled their efforts at peeling away the layers of the Sky Waverly conglomerate and its French partners, as well as digging into the newspaper rumors and the apparently massive bank mergers, Geoffrey Waters began building a dossier on Amanda Bentley-Smythe. It was not a personal history based on gossip; the MI-5 officer was not interested in his sister-in-law's promiscuities except where there was a specific pattern. Then one emerged, and it concerned him deeply.

Amanda Reilly was the daughter of a respectable Irish couple who owned a prosperous pub in Dublin known for its friendly atmosphere, steady customers, and, oddly enough, its limited kitchen. The attractive child grew into a lovely-looking, red-haired teenager, then into a ravishing young woman whose presence caused drinkers to stop the passage of glasses to lips as she waited on their tables. According to the available information, a magazine photographer on assignment in Dublin walked into the pub, saw her, and asked her very Catholic parents if he could take photographs of their daughter.

"No smarmy stuff or I'll break your face!" was the oft-reported reply of the father. The rest was fairy-tale legend, as the tabloids would write. Amanda was brought to London, schooled in the social graces while climbing the ladder of modeling prominence. Through the process, she lost much of her Irish dialect, except for the attractive lilt, and whether because of her upbringing or her parents' stern guidance, she appeared only in classic attire, by and large adorned with terribly expensive jewelry. She became a star of her profession.

Then something happened to the adorable Irish lass, thought Geoffrey Waters, as he added data upon data. Amanda Reilly moved into the social circuit of the famous, the would-be famous, the established wealthy, and the pretenders. She was photographed on the arms of the recognizable—minor royalty, film stars, divorced financiers, and finally one Clive Bentley-Smythe, whom she chose to marry. It simply did not make sense to the MI-5 chief. With all the giants in her sea to choose from, she picked an innocuous blowfish for her crown prince.

There followed the inevitable: the gossip, which provoked an intelligence search of both airline tickets and private aircraft with their destinations and flight plans. The computers narrowed down the comparative frequencies of the total and the presumed recipients of her favors, based on previous, confirmed information, along with photographs. Among the London and Scottish elite were youngish and middle-aged barons of industry, inheritors of well-known estates and castles with hunting grounds familiar to the Crown, and dashing yachtsmen rich enough to enter international racing. Paris included numerous heterosexual haute-couture designers, as well as the Parisian gay crowd, who adored her. The only void was one of her most frequent destinations during the past year: the Netherlands, especially the flights to Amsterdam. No one ever appeared to meet her usually private aircraft, no one was reported as having escorted her to a car or a limousine. Nobody. The internationally famous model had taken taxis into the center of the city and, for all intents and purposes, had disappeared.

Amsterdam.

And then Sir Geoffrey Waters began to understand, and it was as if he had been shot in the stomach. Was *he* the reason for the blowfish? Although his picture never appeared in the newspapers, among the government-oriented, he was known as the powerful MI-5 chief of Internal Security. What better connection for the Matarese? And the outrageous assumption—or was it merely a presumption?—did answer a few questions that had been lurking in the shadows of Sir Geoffrey's mind. Clive and Amanda had within recent months become so damned friendly with Gwyneth and him, inviting them to dinner parties that Waters found both irrelevant and annoying, although he said nothing because he knew his wife adored her brother. However, in a fit of irritation, he did pose a question.

"My dear Gwyn, why this sudden rush of affection? Are there rumors of our sudden demise? Good God, they'll inherit your money—what you haven't already given him—and I'm small stakes in that department. It seems they're on the phone or our doorstep several times a week. Please, old girl, I still have to work for a living."

"Not if you'd let me pay the bills, dear heart."

"Wouldn't hear of it. Also, I'm rather good at what I do."

"Please, Geof, Clive worships you, you know that, and Amanda dotes on you. She always insists on sitting next to you. Don't tell me any man, even one approaching sixty, isn't thrilled to sit next to one of the most beautiful women in the world. If you did, I wouldn't believe you."

"She asks too many foolish questions. She thinks I'm an overage James Bond, which I definitely am not—and neither was the original Bond. He was a stringer, more interested in his bloody gardens than in his work for us."

Yet, *damn* it, Amanda Bentley-Smythe *had* asked too many questions. Nothing Waters could not handle with a wave of his hand, but still—he wondered. As several of those awful dinner parties went on, his glass constantly filled by the glamorous, seductive Amanda, had he unconsciously revealed something, or someone, he should not have? He did not think so; he was too experienced for that, but anything was possible insofar as he had always considered his seatmate to have an IQ in double digits. Had she learned something she should not have, something he mentioned innocently, something that was common knowledge, but that she zeroed in on? Was her unknown contact in Amsterdam really part of the Matarese? Geoffrey Waters had to confront his own personal doubts.

His red intercom buzzed softly, it never rang. It was his sterile link to the all-powerful director of Operations. "Waters here," he said.

"I'm afraid it's rotten news, Geof. Prepare yourself."

"My *wife*?"

"No, the subject you've been researching, your sister-in-law, Amanda Bentley-Smythe."

"She's disappeared, right?"

"Hardly, she's dead. She was garroted, her body thrown into the Thames. It was recovered an hour ago by a river patrol."

"Oh, my *God*!"

"There's more, old boy. Three major executives of banks in Scotland, Liverpool, and West London have been shot, all through the head. None survived. Underworld-style executions."

"It's a *purge*!" exclaimed Waters. "Seal off all of their offices!"

"There's nothing to seal. Everything's been removed."

"You must *think,* Clive," pressed Geoffrey Waters, staring into the tear-stained eyes of his shattered brother-in-law. "God knows I feel for you, but this terrible thing that's happened has implications far beyond anything you can imagine. Now, these past few days—"

"I *can't* think, Geof! Every time I try, I hear her voice and realize she's gone. That's *all* I can think about!"

"Where do you keep your brandy, old boy?" asked Waters, glancing about the Bentley-Smythe library that led through French doors to a bright sunlit garden in Surrey. "Oh, yes, the cabinet over there. I believe a drink will help."

"I'm not sure," said Clive, wiping his eyes and cheeks. "I'm not good with the stuff, and the phone keeps ringing off the hook—"

"It hasn't for quite some time now," interrupted Sir Geoffrey, "because in a way it *is* off the hook."

"What?"

"I've had all your calls switched to an answering machine in my office. When you like, if you like, you may hear the messages yourself."

"You can do that?"

"Yes, chap, I can, I have." Waters pulled a bottle out of the cabinet, poured a short glass of brandy, and carried it to his stricken brother-in-law. "Here, drink this."

"What about the reporters outside in the street? They're surrounding the house and sooner or later I've got to face them."

"They're not surrounding anything. The police have dispersed them."

"You can? . . . Of course you can. You have." Bentley-Smythe drank, wincing as he did so, a man not comfortable with alcohol. "Have you heard the terrible things they've been saying on the radio and the telly? How Amanda was suspected of having lovers, affairs—too many to count? They're painting her as an upper-class tramp. . . . She *wasn't,* Geof! She loved me and I loved her!"

"I'm sorry, Clive, but Amanda wasn't a candidate for Sunnybrook Farm."

"Good God, you think I didn't *know* that? I'm not blind! My wife was a vibrant, exciting, and very beautiful woman. Unfortunately, she was married to a passably handsome dullard from an illustrious family who possessed very little talent. I know that, too, because it's me and she needed *more* than me!"

"Then you turned a blind eye to her . . . shall we say, her indulgences?"

"Of course I did! I was her anchor, her calm between the

storms of publicity and celebrity, the steady refuge when she was hurt and exhausted."

"You're a most remarkable husband," observed Sir Geoffrey.

"What else could I *do*?" pleaded the remarkable husband. "I loved her more than life itself. I couldn't let her leave me over irrelevant social moralities. She was above all that to me!"

"All right, Clive, all right," said Waters. "But you must permit me to do my job, old man."

"She was *murdered,* for Christ's sake! Why aren't the police or Scotland Yard questioning me? Why *you*?"

"I hope to make that clear to you. The fact that I am questioning you should provide an answer. MI-Five supersedes any police or Scotland Yard investigations. We all work together, naturally, but in circumstances like this, we're the forerunners."

"What are you *saying*?" Bentley-Smythe, his mouth parted in bewilderment, glared at his brother-in-law. "You're like the Secret Service; you catch spies and traitors, that sort of thing. What has Amanda got to do with you? She was *killed,* damn it! Catching the killer is police work."

"May I ask a few questions?" said Waters, gently overlooking Clive's protestations.

"Why not?" replied a confused, disconsolate Bentley-Smythe. "You've shut down the phone, chased away the reporters; you couldn't do those things unless you were serious. Ask away."

"These past few days, even weeks, did Amanda show any signs of strain or stress? What I mean to say is, did her behavior change? Was she abnormally upset, or touchy?"

"No more than usual. She was furious at the photographer over her last shoot, claiming he was dressing her in 'matronly' clothing. She acknowledged that she was no longer a twentyish model but she wasn't ready for 'dotty granny outfits' was the way she put it. She did have a rather fierce ego, you know."

"I mean beyond that, Clive, beyond the ego. Did she receive any phone calls that obviously disturbed her, or visitors that she didn't care to see?"

"I wouldn't know. I'm at the office during the day and she was usually out. She kept a flat in town for when her schedule was too full to make the trek out here."

"I didn't know that," said Sir Geoffrey. "What's the address?"

"Somewhere in Bayswater, in the two hundreds, I think."

"You think? Haven't you been there?"

"Frankly, no. But I have a telephone number. It's not published, of course, quite private."

"Give it to me, please." Clive did so and Waters walked swiftly to a telephone on the desk. He dialed, listened intently with a frown, then hung up, looking over at Bentley-Smythe. "The number's been disconnected," he said.

"How could that *be*?" shouted Clive. "She wasn't going anywhere and even if she was, she always kept her answering machine on. Good God, it was her secret lifeline!" Realizing that his words could be misinterpreted, the dead woman's husband was abruptly silent.

"Why was it secret, old boy?"

"That's probably not the right word," replied the lawyer in Bentley-Smythe. "It's just that when she went on her continental locations, I asked her several times if I might relay her messages—you see, she'd call me almost every day."

"I thought you said you'd never been to her London flat."

"I haven't. She had one of those machines that gives you your messages whenever you call in. I suggested she give me the numerical code to collect her calls, but she refused—rather adamantly. . . . I understood."

"*Most* remarkable," mumbled the MI-5 chief, turning back to the telephone. He picked it up and called his office, giving an aide the phone number on Bayswater Road. "Use official channels, get the address, and send over a search team, including a forensic. Lift all the fingerprints you can find and call me back here." He hung up.

"For Christ's sake, Geof, what's going *on*? You're behaving as if this weren't the horrible murder of my wife but some sort of international incident."

"I couldn't have said it better, Clive, because that's what it well may be. Three other people were killed here in England within hours of Amanda's murder, and each was suspected of being part of a financial conspiracy affecting many countries and millions upon millions of people."

"Dear God, what are you *saying*? My wife had her weaknesses, I concede that, but what you're suggesting is so far beyond her comprehension it's ludicrous! I even convinced her to hire an accounting firm to handle the money she made. She couldn't balance a checkbook! How could such a financially naive woman be part of a *financial* conspiracy?"

"One has nothing to do with the other, dear boy. Amanda loved the fast lane, the international jet-set circus with all its superficial trappings. Money was never a consideration, merely an inconvenience."

"She loved *me*!" screamed an increasingly hysterical Bentley-Smythe. "She *needed* me—I was her home and hearth! She told me so over and over again."

"I'm sure she did, and I'm sure she meant it, Clive, but celebrity can do strange things to people. They frequently become *two* people, the public and the private person, often so different."

"What more do you want from me, Geof? I'm out of explanations."

"Only what you can remember of the past few weeks. Start from perhaps a month ago, especially around the time that you were told you were being considered for the board of Sky Waverly."

"Oh, that's easy, I heard it first from Amanda. She returned from a photo session in Amsterdam—you know, grand ladies in gorgeous clothes touring the canals—and said she met a man involved with Sky Waverly who told her they were looking for a prestigious name for its board. She suggested me, and they jumped at it. Quite a marvelous extra income, I might add."

Amsterdam.

"Did she tell you who the man was?" asked Sir Geoffrey casually.

"She couldn't remember his name, and I didn't pursue it.

When the call came from Paris, I was exhilarated and accepted, naturally."

"Who called you?"

"A man called Monsieur Lacoste, I believe, like the sportswear."

"Let's return to the last weeks, Clive, your days with Amanda. I'll ask questions and you simply answer with whatever comes to mind."

"I'm rather used to this," said Bentley-Smythe. "I've been in therapy, you know."

They spoke for nearly two hours, Waters writing sporadic notes on his pad while prompting his brother-in-law to expand on certain memories, certain conversations. The scenario, as it evolved, described a most unusual marriage, indeed. There was complete trust on the part of the husband, along with total infidelity on the part of the wife. It was apparently a La Rochefoucauld union, one of absolute convenience, tilted extravagantly toward the woman. Amanda Reilly had married Clive Bentley-Smythe for what she and others could gain from the name, not the man. Further, considering her attributes of beauty and fame, she had been ordered to do so. By whom?

Amsterdam?

The telephone rang and Waters picked it up. "What have you got?" he asked.

"What you don't want to hear, sir," said an MI-5 subordinate. "The entire flat was stripped, the walls everywhere covered several times with new thick paint, all the furniture surfaces destroyed with acid. Nothing, Sir Geof."

"The telephone records?"

"All erased."

"Who the hell could manage *that*?"

"Roughly five hundred underground-line technicians who know how to do it."

"So we're back to square one—"

"Not necessarily, sir. While we were there our man in the street spotted a chap who approached the building, obviously saw several of our search team through the windows, and quickly turned and rushed away."

"Did our man follow him, and if not, *why* not?"

"There wasn't time, sir, the suspect disappeared around a corner and there was traffic in the street. However, he did the next-best thing. He grabbed his high-speed camera and took a series of rapid exposures. He told me that most were of the fellow's back, but not all, as the man turned several times, apparently to see if anybody *was* following him."

"Well done. Have the film developed immediately at our laboratory and bring the photos to my office under seal. No one is to see them until I do. It'll take me roughly forty minutes to get back to London. I'll expect them to be on my desk."

John and Joan Brooks, brother and sister, stayed in adjoining suites at the famous and famously expensive Villa d'Este hotel on Lake Como. The normal credit search revealed that the siblings were wealthy Americans from the Midwest who had recently inherited additional millions as the only heirs of a childless uncle in Great Britain. Neither was currently married, he having divorced two wives, and she one husband. All the information was confirmed by the American State Department, the British authorities, and the law firm of Braintree and Ridge of Oxford Street, London.

Frank Shields, analyst extraordinaire, along with Sir Geoffrey Waters of MI-5, had done their jobs well. Cameron Pryce and Leslie Montrose could have entered into negotiations to buy Credit Suisse and been taken seriously.

Rumors spread throughout the great houses on the shores of Como that brother and sister had furthered the careers of international celebrities—motion-picture and television stars, singers, au courant artists, and fledgling opera companies. It simply was their wont to do. How much money did one need? Spend a little!

Don Silvio Togazzi initiated the flotilla of misinformation throughout the Bellagio community, knowing it would reach those who counted. And, indeed, it did. He chuckled when told invitations began to arrive at the Villa d'Este for the two Americans with such rapidity that the concierge exclaimed, "*Pazzo!* These people are more trouble than the

Saudis and their dreadful rugs!" Finally, the one invitation that they were waiting for, hoping for, was delivered. It was to a midafternoon "Buffet and Croquet" with drinks on the yacht following the strenuous lawn exercises. The concierge himself brought up the invitation, delighted to see that since Miss Brooks was visiting her brother, he could express his approval to both at once.

"I urge you to accept, *signore* and *signora*. The Paravacini estate is the most glorious on the lake, and the family is so inventive, don't you think?"

"In what way?" asked Cameron.

"Buffet and croquet, *signore*! No dull, boring dinner dances or crushing cocktail parties for the Paravacinis, no indeed. Exquisite food, laughter on the croquet course, drinks at sundown aboard the finest yacht on the lake, it's so imaginative."

"It sounds delightful!" exclaimed Lieutenant Colonel Montrose.

"It will be, but I warn you, the Paravacinis are masters with the mallet and the ball, especially the cardinal. Keep your wagers reasonable, for I assure you, you'll lose."

"They bet on croquet?"

"*Sì, signore,* everything for charity, of course. Cardinal Rudolfo, a most charming and erudite priest, frequently says he enlarges the Vatican's coffers more from his mallet than from his sermons. He has a wonderful sense of humor, you'll like him."

"How formal is the dress, *monsieur le concierge*? Most of our luggage is still in London."

"Oh, extremely *informal, signora*. The *padrone,* Don Carlo Paravacini, claims that starched shirts and tight clothing make for less amusement."

"An unusual opinion for an old man," said Pryce.

"Don Carlo is hardly old. He's thirty-eight, I believe."

"That's pretty young for a 'don,' isn't it?"

"It is the position, not the age, *signore.* Carlo Paravacini is an important financier with assets and properties throughout all Europe. He's very . . . how do you say it? . . . *astuto.*"

"In international finance, I gather."

"*Sì,* but these things are beyond me. You will enjoy yourselves, and if it is not an inconvenience, do send my best regards to Don Carlo."

"We certainly will," said Leslie, nudging Cam. "Are your shops still open?"

"For guests of the Paravacinis, I will personally send up whatever you care to see."

"That won't be necessary. I'll browse around myself."

"Whatever you wish. *Arrivederci,* then."

The concierge left and Montrose turned to Pryce. "How much money do you have?"

"Unlimited," replied Cam. "Geof Waters gave me six credit cards, three for you and three for me. No limit on the charges."

"That's nice, but what about hard cash?"

"I'm not sure. About three or four thousand pounds—"

"Less than six thousand dollars, American. Suppose the Paravacinis gamble with real money, Italian-style?"

"I hadn't thought about it."

"Think about it now, Cam. Mr. and *Miss* Brooks can't arrive with credit cards."

"We don't know how much they bet—"

"I was posted in Abu Dhabi once and ran up a tab of eight thousand dollars," interrupted Montrose. "I had to wake up the embassy to get me out of there alive!"

"*Wow,* you've led a much more exciting life than I have, Colonel."

"I doubt that, Officer Pryce, but get on the phone to London and have Geof wire Mr. Brooks at least twenty thousand, credited to the hotel by the Bank of England."

"You're very sharp, Colonel. This is my territory and you're thinking ahead of me."

"No, I'm not, my dear. I'm a woman, and women try to predict when mad money may be required. It's a universal conundrum."

Cameron held her shoulders, their faces close, their lips inches apart. "You know what my conundrum is, don't you?"

"I was waiting for you to wake up, you damn fool."

"I was afraid—your son, your husband, Ev Bracket. . . . They were too much a part of you, and I wasn't convinced I could break through all that."

"You have, Cam, you have, although I never thought it was possible. Do you know why?"

"No, I don't."

"I'm almost afraid to tell you because you may not like it."

"Now you have to tell me."

"You read my dossier, and you must certainly understand that I got yours."

"I suppose I'm flattered you wanted it but furious that it was given to you."

"I, too, have friends in the bureaucracy."

"Obviously. What's your point?"

"Cutting through the nonsense, you're basically a self-made man, no generals in your background like me, nor a great deal of money, again like me."

"Hey, we weren't on welfare, lady," said Pryce, amused and releasing her shoulders, but not moving away from her. "My father and mother were teachers, and they both were damned good. They made sure I was able to go beyond a master's, which they could never afford to do themselves."

"When the CIA picked you out of Princeton," completed Leslie, "why did you accept?"

"Frankly, I thought it was exciting . . . and I was running up so many student loans it would take half a professor's career to pay them off."

"You were also an athlete," interjected Leslie, her face still close to his.

"I was all-state in high school, mainly—as I often said—because I hated the idea of being tackled."

"You were prime meat, my darling—"

"Would you say that again, please?"

"Yes, I will. . . . My darling, my totally unexpected darling."

They kissed, long and with growing excitement, until Leslie moved back and looked into Cam's eyes. "I haven't told you why you broke down my barriers."

"Is it important?"

"It is to me, my dearest. I'm not a one-night stand and I trust you know it as well as I do. I'm not a whore."

"Goddamn it, I could never think of you like that!"

"Lighten up, Officer Pryce. Some of my best friends have been unfairly categorized that way. You have no idea what marriage is like in the military. Months and months of separations, your own natural longing, the attractive men who hit on you in the officers' clubs, including your husband's superiors."

"That *stinks*," said Cameron.

"It certainly does," agreed the lieutenant colonel, "but it happens."

"Did it happen to you?"

"No. Fortunately I had Jamie, the reputation of a general's daughter, and Bracket's crazy assignments. Without them, I don't know."

"I do," said Pryce, holding her in his arms, and then kissing her again, longer than before, their initial intensity undeniable, needed by both.

The hotel telephone rang and Leslie pulled back. "You'd better answer it," she suggested.

"We're not here," replied Cameron softly, still holding her.

"Please . . . I haven't heard from Jamie—"

"Sure," said Pryce, releasing her, "but you won't, you know. Waters told you that."

"I could hear about him, couldn't I?"

"Yes, of course." Cam crossed to a table and picked up the phone, cutting off a third ring. "Hello?"

"We're on scrambler here, but limited on your side," said Geoffrey Waters from London. "Speak in kind, please."

"I understand."

"Are you making any progress?"

"I was until you called."

"I beg your pardon?"

"Nothing, forget it. Yes, we are. Some native jewelry and one particularly exquisite tapestry will make wonderful additions to our collection."

"Excellent. A solid connection, then?"

"We believe so, we'll know later tonight. Incidentally, my sister wants money."

"Charge anything you need."

"The natives won't accept credit cards."

"I see. Beyond what I've sent?"

"Sent where?"

"The Villa d'Este cashier's office."

"They left a message earlier but I haven't called back."

"I wired ten thousand pounds," said Waters.

"What's that in American dollars?"

"I'm not sure, around seventeen or eighteen thousand."

"I guess that's close enough. She mentioned twenty."

"Good heavens, what for?"

"Maybe the tapestry."

"I see. I'll send another ten."

"Anything on your side that might add to our collection?"

"Very definitely. A major purchase right here in London. A painting I'm convinced is an early, unsigned Goya during the days of betrayal, as he called them. I'd wire you a photograph but it wouldn't do the work justice. You'll see it when you return here on your way to the States."

"That's wonderful news. We'll keep in touch."

"Do call if the connection works out."

"Naturally." Pryce hung up the phone and turned to Leslie. "We can pick up a lot of cash downstairs and Geof will send more."

"I loved that 'my sister wants money.' "

"Better you're greedy than me. It's more logical for a rich woman."

"Sexist."

"Quite true." Cameron approached her. "Now where were we?"

"I want you to come down with me to the shops, help me pick out some attractive casual clothes. But first tell me what the 'wonderful news' was."

"The way I interpreted it, they got a photograph of a mole in London, a Goya betrayal, he called it."

"A *what*?"

"Goya's obsession with the Spanish executions."

"I *know* who the painter was, what are you talking about?"

"I think they found the Matarese spy in London. And he's very high up."

"That *is* progress. Now, let's do some of our own."

"I'd rather do some of our very own—isn't that okay?"

"Not now, my dear. I want to as much as you do, but we've only got three hours to get to the Paravacini place."

"What's an hour or so?"

"To begin with, it's at least forty-five minutes around the lake, and we've both got to be properly dressed."

"Why do I have to go down to the shops with you?"

"Because men know what they find attractive in a woman. I've been in uniforms so long, I haven't kept up. You'll know when you see it."

"What about me?"

"I'll know when I dress you."

"Sexist!"

"To a degree, I'll accept that. . . . And since we've cooled off a bit, I'll tell you why you broke down my barriers. Do you want to hear?"

"I'm not sure. But yes, I guess I do."

"You're a uniquely decent man, Cameron Pryce. You felt the vibes between us, as I did, but you kept your distance—you respected me when others might not have. I like that."

"I didn't think there was any other way. Sure, the vibes were there, but you had your own problems—your husband, your son, the terrible things you've gone through. How could a stranger get past all that?"

"You did, kindly and gently, yet in your work you're neither kind nor gentle. . . . Yes, Cam, I've read all about you. You're essentially a black-operations officer, no quarter given, none taken. You've killed twelve terrorist leaders on record, and probably a dozen or so unrecorded. You infiltrated them and you assassinated them."

"It was my job, Leslie. If I hadn't, they would have killed

hundreds more—perhaps thousands with their insurrections."

"I believe you, my dear, I'm only trying to say that there's another side of Officer Pryce that he's shown to me. Am I allowed that?"

"Certainly, but let's limit the circulation, okay?"

"Oh, I will, I *will*. Do you know why? Never mind, I'll answer that. . . . I don't know what will happen next week or next month, or God knows, next year, but at the moment I don't want to lose you, Cameron Pryce. I lost one decent man, I can't lose another."

They fell into the bed, each holding the other fiercely.

A string quartet played under the roof of a sculpted gazebo on the far right of the croquet course. By the time John and Joan Brooks arrived, the now well-publicized brother-and-sister philanthropists of American culture, most of the guests were already there in their casual finery. A large green blackboard had been set up on a stanchion behind the goal wicket; a pairing of players had begun in bracketed colored chalk. Several buffet tables with the finest linen and silver were scattered about the immense manicured lawn by the lake.

The huge, imposing yacht was moored at the end of the long dock, a sturdy gangplank with chrome railings leading to the lower deck; a canopied veranda capable of holding sixty-odd people overlooking the northern waters of Lake Como was an awesome sight.

The mansion itself had only been hinted at under the magnification of Togazzi's telescope. It was a contemporary "castle" of flagstone and teakwood, rising four stories high with flagged open-air turrets. The only thing missing was a moat. The Villa d'Este concierge was accurate when he extolled the Paravacini estate as the most glorious on the lake.

"We paid roughly a month's salary for each of these outfits," said Montrose as they walked along a brick path that rounded the great house and led to the lakeside carnival, "but I have an idea that we look like the poorest people here."

"You're crazy," protested Pryce. "I think we both look terrific, especially you."

"That's another thing. Stop gazing at me like that. We're supposed to be brother and sister, but not incestuous."

"Sorry, it comes kind of naturally."

"Don't look over, just laugh and tilt your head to the right. There's a man staring at us. He's in blue slacks and a bright yellow shirt."

"I caught a glimpse of him. Never saw him before."

"He's coming over—*John*."

"Gotcha—*Joan*."

"You must be the Brookses!" said the dark-haired, extremely handsome man enthusiastically, his English laced with a deep Italian accent. "I can see the family resemblance."

"We hear that frequently," said Leslie, extending her hand. "And who are you?"

"Your obedient host, Carlo Paravacini, grateful that you accepted my invitation," replied the don, kissing Montrose's hand. "Or as my American friends call me, Charlie," he continued, shaking hands with Cameron.

"Then I'll be presumptuous," said Pryce, "and say it's a pleasure to meet you, Charlie."

"I like that, I like it. . . . A libation, perhaps, a fine Chablis, or a rare Scotch?"

"Someone's been tattling on us," interrupted Leslie, laughing. "Those are our favorite drinks."

"But always in moderation, I've learned that, too. And I like that, I like it."

"Then it's the moment to tell you that Villa d'Este's concierge sends you his regards," added Cameron.

"I accept them gratefully," said the attractive host, "but for God's sake, don't tell him that I stole his first sous-chef to cater this little afternoon party. That scoundrel steals all of his superior's recipes, and after all, it's his day off."

"Our lips are sealed, Carlo—*Charlie*," said Montrose charmingly as Pryce glanced at his lover, not entirely pleasantly.

Paravacini, taking Leslie's elbow, led them through the

strolling crowds toward a bar table and ordered drinks. While he did so a relatively tall, elegant figure, dressed in tan trousers and a black short-sleeved shirt, topped with a clerical collar and graying hair, approached them. Carlo turned at the sight of the priest and introduced him.

"His Eminence is my uncle, Cardinal Rudolfo Paravacini, but here in Como we call him Papa Rudy. Isn't that right, holy Cardinal?"

"I grew up here, why not?" replied the exalted priest of the Catholic Church. "I ran in these fields chasing goats and rabbits like everyone else. I was chosen, I did not seek. My nephew's generosity allows me moments of luxury that my commitments do not."

"Nice to meet you," said Cameron, shaking hands.

"A pleasure," said Leslie, doing the same.

"Thank God for American Protestants," replied the cardinal. "My Italian, French, and Spanish flocks kiss my ring and think I can guarantee them a place in heaven when I cannot guarantee it for myself. . . . Welcome to Lacus Larius."

"I hear you're a . . . heck . . . of a croquet player, Cardinal," said Pryce.

"I'm one *hell* of a player. Care to go against me?"

"I'd rather be on your side. My sister's a better player than I am."

"Set it up, Carlo," ordered the priest. "My partner will be Signor—*Brooks*."

"As you wish," said Don Carlo Paravacini, looking strangely at the cardinal.

The time passed on the croquet course, the yelps of a successfully entered wicket accompanied by the desolate groans of those who missed. And during the succeeding games, servants rushed out with iced tea and lemonade to refresh the players, alcohol absent by design. After three hours, the winners were awarded sterling silver croquet mallets, instantly monogrammed, and everyone began to repair to the yacht's canopied veranda.

"I'm really sorry," said Pryce to his partner, Cardinal Paravacini. "I loused us up."

"Although the Lord forgiveth, I find it hard to do so, John

Brooks," said the priest, smiling. "You were a disaster. However, your sister, Miss Joan, teamed with my nephew, Carlo, won the whole damned *thing*! They make a lovely couple, don't they? So handsome together, so intelligent. Things could go further, not so?"

"Well, my sister's not Catholic—"

"There's always conversion," interrupted the prince of the Church. "We annulled his first marriage, and his second wife died not long ago."

"I don't know what to say," said a totally confused Cameron Pryce, staring at Lieutenant Colonel Montrose, who was laughing and walking off the croquet course gripping Carlo Paravacini's arm.

Half an hour later, still in the presence of the cardinal, Cam had met dozens of other guests who flocked around both men as the curious might at the arrival of two celebrities. In a sense, both were; the priest had celebrated influence inside the Vatican, and the fine-looking American's vast wealth was enough to gain him instant celebrity status. Finally, feigning social exhaustion, Cardinal Paravacini insisted they sit down at a relatively isolated table on the captain's-wheel perch, easily seen but not easy to reach. Pryce's eyes roamed over the crowd looking for Leslie.

She was not there. She had disappeared.

25

"Excuse me, Cardinal, but my sister's not here. I can't see her anywhere."

"No doubt, my nephew is showing her around the estate," said the priest. "It's really quite beautiful, and his art collection is among the finest in Italy."

"Art collection? Where is it?"

"In the main house, of course." At the mention of the mansion, Cardinal Paravacini apparently saw the sudden alarm in Pryce's eyes. "Oh, I can assure you, Mr. Brooks, you've nothing to be concerned about. Carlo is the most honorable of men, he would never take advantage of a guest. In truth, he doesn't have to, the ladies have always seemed to line up for his affections."

"You don't understand," Cameron interrupted, "my sister and I have an agreement between us whenever we're out together, especially where there are a great many people. Each lets the other know when he's leaving, for whatever reason."

"That sounds positively suffocating, Mr. Brooks," observed the priest.

"Not really, it's just common sense," replied Pryce, thinking quickly and doing his best not to show it. "When we're out separately, which is most of the time, we each have an armed escort."

"Now you sound insulting, sir."

"You wouldn't think so, Your Eminence, if you knew the number of kidnapping threats we've received. Last year alone, our security firm in America thwarted four attempts against me and five against my sister."

"I had no *idea*—"

"It's not something you make public," said Cameron with a grim smile. "The idea could be planted in too many demented minds."

"Naturally, such crimes have been committed here in Europe, but the idea, as you call it, is still shocking to an aging cleric like myself."

"So you see," continued Cam, "your nephew, Carlo, doesn't worry me at all. I'll be relieved if she's with him, so if you'll pardon me, I'm going to see if I can find them. The art collection, right?"

"Yes, the gallery's on the main floor, west wing. I understand you have a superb family collection yourself, along with priceless tapestries."

That's it! thought Pryce as he rose from his chair. In all the misinformation circulated about the American Brookses, there was no mention of an art collection or tapestries. John and Joan Brooks were reported to be self-indulgent dilettantes, socialites who loved the spotlight, especially show business, not serious collectors of paintings and tapestries. . . . Cameron's telephone conversation with Geoffrey Waters in London had been tapped, and this attractive prince of the Church was sadly part of the conspiracy.

"Main floor, west wing," said Pryce, glancing down at the cardinal. "Thanks. See you later." As he entered the brick walk that led to the mansion, Cam was grateful that his false concerns about his "sister" were an acceptable reason for him to get into the Paravacini house. However, except for a minor twinge of adolescent jealousy, he had no worries about Leslie. Lieutenant Colonel Montrose was perfectly capable of taking care of herself, probably with a crushing knee to the groin. Also, it was likely that the extrovert Don Carlo was simply impressing her with the extraordinary beauty of the Paravacini estate with its numerous fountains, its ancient and modern statuary, and the rows of gardens, exploding with color. Cameron had no idea what he might learn inside the castlelike structure, but an axiom of his profession was that to infiltrate any property was to make progress.

He was wrong on all counts, *all* counts.

Cameron walked through massive doors of the mansion into the marble hall of the great house. It was deserted, the silence disturbing as opposed to the distant, muted laughter outside. The door closed automatically, the silence now complete. He casually strode forward toward a high-ceilinged central room preceded by another intersecting marble corridor that extended both east and west. He turned right into the west wing where there were scores of exquisite paintings covering the walls, many recognizable from art books and magazines devoted to the masters.

Suddenly, along with his own, other footsteps echoed off the walls; they were behind him. He stopped and turned around. A heavyset man in nondescript dark clothing stood immobile, a trace of a smile on his lips. "*Buona sera, si-*

gnore, please keep walking," he said, the last three words in relatively cultured English.

"Who are you?" asked Pryce sharply.

"I am an aide to Don Carlo."

"That's nice. What do you aid?"

"I'm not required to answer questions. Now, *piacere,* walk to the end of the gallery. There is a door on the left."

"Why should I? I'm not used to being given orders."

"Do try, *signore.*" The Paravacini aide reached behind his loose black silk shirt and pulled an automatic from his belt. "Follow this order, *piacere,* to the door, *signore.*"

The armed, heavyset man opened the thick, carved door. It led to what could best be described as a very high-ceilinged aviary: birds in scores of cages hanging from the beams, all sizes, from the lesser parrots to mature macaws, to large falcons, and huge vultures, their wired prisons commensurate with their sizes. It was the immense personal collection of an eccentric. And behind a long polished table in front of a wide-paneled window that overlooked the manicured lawn at sundown was Carlo Paravacini. On his left, Leslie Montrose sat stiffly in a chair, her face impassive.

"Welcome, Officer Cameron Pryce," intoned the don of Lake Como in a flat, courteous voice. "I wondered how long it would take you to come here."

"Papa Rudy suggested I do so, as I expect you know."

"Yes, he's such a lovely man, so committed to his faith."

"When did you find out?"

"About the cardinal's faith?"

"You know what I mean—"

"Oh, you're referring to Agent Pryce of the American CIA, and Colonel Montrose, United States Army Intelligence." Paravacini leaned forward on the table, his eyes leveled at Cameron. "Would you believe less than an hour ago?"

"How?"

"Please, I'm sure you understand the necessity of confidentiality; after all, you live with it every day. You're living with it now."

"Speaking of now—what now?"

"Obviously, it can't be very attractive for you." Don Carlo rose from his chair and walked around the glistening table, heading toward the cluster of cages, hanging in varying heights, none lower than seven feet from the floor. "How do you like my airborne friends, Colonel Montrose and Officer Pryce? Are they not magnificent?"

"Birds aren't my favorite animals," answered Leslie coldly from the chair. "I told you that when you brought me in here."

"How come they're so quiet?" asked Pryce.

"Because there's peace in here, nothing to upset them, nothing to provoke them," replied Paravacini, picking up a small wooden instrument from a low mahogany stand. He raised it to his lips and blew into the mouthpiece. For a half second there was only silence, then suddenly, without warning, the room was filled with screams and shrieks as if some obscene hell beyond human understanding had broken loose. Wings flapped and feathers flew; panic showed in the riveting large eyes of several dozen caged, furious birds. Carlo reversed the instrument and blew again; within three or four seconds, the ear-shattering, thunderous clamor stopped. "Rather amazing, isn't it?" the host said.

"That was the most horrible sound I've ever heard in my life!" cried Montrose, removing her hands from her ears. "It was bestial!"

"Yes, indeed it was," said Don Carlo, "because they're truly beasts, you see. In one way or another, they're all attack birds, some carnivorous, others so protective of their nests they are willing to go to their deaths."

"What's your point, *Charlie*?" asked Cameron, glancing at the heavyset armed guard still holding his weapon on the two prisoners.

"It goes back years ago," answered the young don of Lacus Larius, "when I became obsessed with the medieval sport of falconry. Such an ingenious exercise of man's control over the flying beast. It started, perhaps, with the ancient training of simple pigeons to return to their nests, having been smuggled miles away to bring back messages to their pharaoh owners. They were the original spies before the wireless and the radio. But my studies taught me something: All birds can be trained, from the pretty household parakeets to the larger avaricious falcons, to the immense lethal vultures. It came down to an anatomical and chemical combination of inbred sight and acute smell."

"You're not impressing me, Charlie," said Pryce. "All of us have esoteric methods, some anatomical, others chemical, and a lot brutal. Why are you so different?"

"Because I'm more clever than you are."

"Why? Because your Matarese moles in Washington and London let you know who we are?"

"Washington gave us nothing because they didn't *know* anything! Beowulf Agate is a genius, I'll grant you that. However, our man in London put it together, and his immediate target is your British ally, Sir Geoffrey Waters. He'll be dead within twenty-four hours."

"You're the Italian branch of the Matarese, aren't you?"

"Of course I am! We are the answer to the global economy, as our predecessors were. We will put the world on a stable basis, no one else can do it!"

"As long as everyone goes along with you, buys what you sell, *only* what you sell. Collusion is the order of the day, mergers and buyouts eliminating competition until you run the whole goddamned thing."

"It's far better than the economic cycles of a warped capitalistic system. We will eliminate recessions and depressions."

"You'll also eliminate *choice*."

"I've had enough of your sophomoric abstractions, Mr. Pryce. Neither you nor Colonel Montrose will survive this day."

"What if I told you that MI-Five and our Italian branch of the CIA know that we're here right now?"

"I'd have to say you were lying. On pure speculation, all your calls have been monitored from the Villa d'Este."

"Hell, I knew that when your lousy *prince* of the Church told me about our tapestries! You think that when our bodies are found with bullets in our heads, you're off the hook, *Charlie*?"

"There'll be no such thing. Let me show you." Paravacini crossed back to his table and pressed a button on the right. The huge window behind him slid back, its opening at least twenty feet by twelve. He then pressed a second button and blew into his wooden instrument; the cages opened and at least forty screeching birds of all sizes and shapes flew out into the sundown, circling in the orange sky. The don blew into the opposite end, the signal for the birds to return. "By the time they come back, next time, you'll be dead," said Don Carlo as his guard began spraying Pryce and Montrose with an aerosol can.

"Why?" asked Cameron.

"Because you're dead meat, I believe is the phrase. The smell on you guarantees it. Dogs can be immobilized with darts and bullets, but my birds devour corpses until there's nothing left."

"It's time for a *McAuliffe,* Colonel!" yelled Pryce as the maniacal birds flew back through the window, screeching and screaming their horrific caws. As the deadly flock flew in, Montrose, yelling "*Nuts,*" crashed herself into Carlo Paravacini, rubbing her dress around his own clothes as Cameron sent a deadly *chi sai* chop into the startled guard, grabbed the aerosol can and sprayed it over him, then aimed it at Paravacini.

"*Leslie,* let's go!" shouted Pryce.

"I want his *weapon*!" yelled Montrose as the birds circled around her.

"He probably doesn't have one, you idiot! Come *on*!"

"Yes, he does, you moron! It's a small twenty-two. Get these goddamned birds *off* me!"

Pryce fired two shots with the guard's automatic. The vicious birds flew in circles, collisions everywhere, as he grabbed Leslie's hand. They raced out the door and down the marble hallway.

"Are you all *right*?" asked Cam as they ran to the grass parking area.

"I've got pecks all over my neck—"

"We'll call Togazzi and get you to a doctor."

They reached their rental car. It would not start. "They must have pulled out the plugs," said Leslie, exhausted.

"There's a Rolls," said Pryce. "Do you mind going first class? I know how to hot-wire a Rolls. Come *on*!"

"This soon-to-be-middle-aged mother," cried Montrose, chasing after Cam to the elegant brown-and-tan automobile, "is not going to question a maniac who says he can hot-wire a car while I'm running for my life from a bunch of flesh-eating birds! My *God*!"

They opened the doors and jumped in, Pryce behind the wheel. "I love the rich!" he exclaimed. "They leave their keys in their fancy automobiles. What's a Rolls or two? We're *out* of here!" The powerful engine roared as Cameron shifted into gear and sped over the lawn and out to the lake road, tires screeching and grass flying.

"Where to?" asked Leslie. "I don't think the hotel is a very good idea."

"It couldn't be worse. We'll head for Togazzi's, if I can find it."

"There's a phone," said Montrose, pointing it out below the dashboard.

"Only if I really get us lost. Those things are sieves."

After several wrong turns in the narrow streets of Bellagio, Pryce found the steep hill that led to the long mountain road paralleling the lake far below. Twice they missed the hidden entrance to Silvio Togazzi's equally concealed house. Finally, the orderly pavane at the guardhouse over with, the exhausted, still-in-shock Cameron and Leslie sat with the don on his screened-in balcony overlooking the lake. Stiff drinks were brought to the couple; they were gratefully received.

"It was all so *horrible*!" said Montrose, shuddering. "Those dreadful, screaming birds, *augh*!"

"Many have believed that Carlo Paravacini's obsession with his creatures would one day be his death," said the old man. "And so it was this day."

"What?" interrupted Pryce.

"You haven't heard then?" asked Togazzi. "You didn't turn on that lovely automobile's radio?"

"Hell, no, I didn't want to touch anything more than I had to."

"All Bellagio knows, tomorrow all Italy."

"Knows *what*?" insisted Leslie.

"I shall relay it as delicately as possible," continued Don Silvio. "The door to Carlo's aviary had been left open and soon the guests began to notice many different birds soaring in the sky. At first it amused them until strips and pieces of human flesh began falling over the lawns and the yacht. Apparently, there was pandemonium and servants rushed into the mansion. What they found caused many to vomit, others to faint, and all to wail and shriek in horror."

"The bodies," said Cameron, making a quiet statement.

"What was left of them," agreed Togazzi. "The shredded clothing was the principal means of immediate identification. As with the seagulls over beached fish, the eyes were the first to go."

"I think I'm going to be sick," mumbled Montrose, turning away.

"What do we do now?" asked Pryce.

"You stay here, of course."

"What clothes we have, and a great deal of money, are at the hotel."

"I will take care of the Villa d'Este, the concierge is in my employ."

"He *is*?"

"As well as the ambitious sous-chef, a thoroughly dislikable fellow but invaluable to me in so many ways."

"Such as?"

"Powders in a wine, if I care to have my people interrogate an individual—or poison to a Paravacini slave who has killed once too often. Remember, I am a Scozzi."

"You're really something—"

"I was a brother of the best. He's called Beowulf Agate, and I learned so very much from him."

"So I hear," said Cameron. "But back to my first question. What do we do next?"

"I have a scrambler code to Scofield, and I should be

hearing from him shortly, unless he's had too much to drink. Even so, the lovely Antonia will shake him up."

"If he's *drunk*?" yelled Pryce. "What the hell are you *talking* about?"

"Beowulf Agate is far more perceptive, drunk or sober, than any intelligence officer who hasn't touched liquor in twenty years."

"I don't *believe* this!"

Togazzi's telephone rang. He picked it up from his white wicker table. "You old scoundrel!" he cried. "We were just talking about you."

"What in blazes has that kid been *doing*?" yelled the voice from New York.

"Forgive me, Brandon, but I'm going to put you on speakerphone, so you may address us all." Togazzi pressed a button on his white telephone.

"Pryce, are you there?" shouted Scofield over the amplified instrument.

"I'm here, Bray. What do you know?"

"*State*—the State Department, in case you've forgotten—tries to keep its rotten ears to our activities."

"I remember all too well. So what?"

"Their man in Rome called Washington, and State called Shields, asking if we had a black operation going in northern Italy. Naturally, Squinty denied any involvement. Is that true?"

"No, it isn't. We were at ground zero."

"Oh, *shit*! How come?"

"Because we were about to be killed."

"That's a good answer. How's Leslie?"

"Still shaking, Brandon," said Montrose. "Did you know that our associate, Officer Pryce, can hot-wire a Rolls-Royce?"

"That thief could probably wire a tank."

"What do we do now?" Cameron broke in.

"Get out of Italy, and *fast*! . . . Silvio, can you arrange it with Rome?"

"Of course, Brandon. And what is my reward?"

"If and when this is over, Toni and I will grab a plane and buy you the biggest dinner on the Via Veneto."

"I probably own most of the restaurants, you *bastardo*."

"I'm glad neither of us has changed, you son of a bitch!"

"Grazie!" roared Togazzi, laughing.

"Prego!" shouted Beowulf Agate, doing the same.

"Where do you wish to go?" asked the don of the Bellagio hills, hanging up the phone.

"Back to the States," replied Pryce. "We might have enough now to strike."

"Please, Cam, an hour or so with my son? He's so young and he's been through so much," pleaded Leslie.

"I'll check with London," said Pryce, gripping her hand. "And I have to warn Geoffrey!"

Luther Considine banked the renovated Bristol Freighter to the left in his final approach to the private field near Lake Maggiore, twenty-eight miles from Bellagio. Waiting on the ground at the far end of the designated airstrip were Pryce and Montrose; they were in Togazzi's shabby-looking limousine. It was four o'clock in the morning, the night sky made darker by the cloud cover, the landing lights on the single strip the only illumination. As the plane landed and taxied to within thirty yards of the car, Leslie and Cameron got out of the backseat, nodded to the driver-guard, and ran to the aircraft. Pryce carried their two suitcases, retrieved by one of Don Silvio's staff from the Villa d'Este. Luther flipped a switch and the side loading door snapped up. Cameron threw in the luggage and helped Leslie inside, jumping in after her.

"Lieutenant," shouted Montrose over the roar of the engines, "you'll never know how happy I am to see you!"

"Good to see you, too, Colonel," replied Considine, closing the door and reversing the aircraft to taxi back for take-off. "How's the spook business, Cam?"

"A little hairy—or I guess I should say feathery."

"What does that mean?"

"Let's call it a lot of birdshit."

"Must have been a ton of it, the way the Brits want you

back. I've flown routes, and I've flown *routes,* but these F-plans were constructed by high-wire tightropers who don't care for nets."

"To avoid tracking?" asked Pryce.

"Has to be, but not the ordinary national-security variety. Not any nation I've flown over."

"These people *aren't* normal, Luther," interjected Montrose, "not normal at all."

"They must have pretty swell equipment, then."

"They can have anything they want," said Cameron. "They buy it or bribe it."

"You know what the rad-station in Chamonix said? The head trackboy said, 'What do we need the Stealths for when we got Black Beauty up there?' Nice, huh?"

"Black Beauty?"

"Hell, Cam, I can get sunburned but it doesn't exactly show. . . . Hang on, folks, we're going upstairs with Grandmother!"

Once airborne and leveled, Leslie spoke. "Luther," she said, "you mentioned how much the Brits want us back, and I assume that's London."

"That's right."

"I thought we were cleared for a stop in France!" Montrose added angrily.

"Indeed we are, Colonel. Normally, it'd take me about an hour to get there, but with our flight plan, it'll be nearer two. It'll be light out, dawn's on its way. Incidentally, there's coffee in what passes for a galley back there."

"By the way, Luther," said Pryce, "how's this new assignment treating you?"

"*Man,* it's so cool, it's ice cream! Except for the cat who's trying to take over my squadron on the carrier, it's a hoot. I live in nice hotels, have breakfast in bed by picking up a phone, go to conferences with the spook planners, and get to fry some of the new RAF jets."

"No negatives?"

"Yeah, one, and it's heavy. I've got a shadow on me twenty-four hours a day. I go out, he goes out; I have dinner, he's at a nearby table; I stop at a pub, he's right down the bar."

"It's all for your own protection, Lieutenant."

"That's another thing. That Sir Geoffrey dude keeps telling me he's sure the Navy will 'look favorably' on a promotion for me. I told him to lay off any intervention; he doesn't know that our admirals aren't usually wild about their admirals."

"Geof could do it for you, Luther."

"Then I'll take it back and apologize. I've been going with a doctor in Pensacola off and on for a couple of years. We could merge, I figure, but she's a full commander, and I'd like to be a little closer in rank."

"Then listen to Sir Geoffrey. Washington owes him, and with any luck, will owe him big."

"Heard and acknowledged."

"Incidentally, where are we going in France?" asked Leslie.

"I'm flying you there, Colonel, but I'm not permitted to tell you where 'there' is. Hope you understand."

"I do."

As dawn broke over the eastern horizon, both Pryce and Montrose were astonished at the plane's low altitude over water and land. *"Jesus,"* cried Cameron, "I could jump out and go for a swim!"

"I wouldn't advise it," said the pilot, "especially since we're about to skim over Mont Blanc. Lots of deep snow and ice down there."

Considine landed the Bristol at the alternate airport at Le Mayet-de-Montagne reserved for private aircraft, the ultimate destination still unknown to his passengers. The morning sun swept over the fertile Loire Valley, the early colors magnified by the moisture of the enveloping dew.

"There's your car over there!" announced Luther, taxiing toward a nondescript gray sedan parked off the runway. "I'll refuel here, and subject to orders from London, I may be airborne for a while, but I'll be back in ninety minutes and that's our airborne time. It's absolute, no later."

"A car, yes," said Leslie, "but how long will it take for us to reach the children?"

"Perhaps ten or twelve minutes."

"That doesn't leave much time, for God's sake!"

"It's what's permitted, Colonel. You're military, you know the regs."

"Yes, I do, Lieutenant. Reluctantly, I do."

The side windows of the automobile were so darkly tinted that neither Pryce nor Montrose could see outside. Also, the driver's front window had sheets of dark film on both extremes of his windshield; the only thing they could see clearly was the road.

"What the hell *is* this?" yelled Leslie. "We have no idea where we're going."

"It's designed to protect the kids," said Cameron. "What you can't see, you can't tell."

"For God's sake, it's my *son*! Who would I tell?"

"Maybe that's where we're a little more experienced than you. Under chemicals you could describe what you saw on the way to him."

"Assuming I'd be captured?"

"We always have to assume that, Colonel. You know it, and you know the procedures."

"Again, reluctantly. My two cyanide tablets are in my uniform, with the luggage."

"I don't think anything like that is part of our current scenario," said Pryce. "Our security is total."

The road ahead came to a gatehouse, the civilian guards all recruited from the Deuxième Bureau, the most secret of France's covert operations. The French driver, also Deuxième, spoke briefly and the car was admitted beyond a now-seen stone wall. They entered a large compound; at its center was a long one-story farmhouse, surrounded by pastures with cattle and a fenced-in corral holding a half dozen horses.

Suddenly, it was apparent that there was mass confusion throughout the complex. All around there were French Army vehicles as well as local police cars, men racing in various directions, the constant wail of ear-shattering sirens.

·"What the hell's going on?" yelled Cameron.

"I don't *know, monsieur*!" cried the driver. "The gate only told me to drive slowly, that there was a crisis!"

Military vehicles raced out of the gate, along with the local police and scores of men on foot, running in different directions, spreading out everywhere.

"What *happened*?" shouted Pryce, jumping out of the Deuxième car, grabbing the first man he could intercept.

"The young *Englishman*!" answered the patrol. "He's escaped!"

"What?" yelled Leslie Montrose. "I'm Colonel Montrose, where is my *son*?"

"Inside, madame, as bewildered as all of us!"

Cameron and Leslie raced into the farmhouse and found young Angela Brewster, her arms around James Montrose Jr., who was crying uncontrollably on a couch. "It's not your fault, Jamie! You didn't do it, you didn't *do* it!" she kept repeating.

"Yes, I *did*!" cried Montrose junior between his tears.

"*Stop* it, Jamie!" roared his mother, rushing to the couch and grabbing her son's shoulders, releasing Angela's hands. "What *happened*?"

"Oh, *Christ,* Mom!" answered Jamie, reaching for his mother, holding her as if she were a lifeline and an abyss yawned below. "I told him!"

"What did you tell him, Jamie?" asked Pryce gently, kneeling in front of the mother and son by the couch. "What exactly did you tell him?"

"He kept asking me over and over again how I got out of Bahrain, how I got over the wall and into the city—and how I found Luther."

"The circumstances here are very different," said Cam, his palm on Jamie's trembling shoulder. "He must have told you how he could do the same."

"He never told me *anything*! He just did it. Over the wall and *out*!"

"But he had no resources," interrupted Leslie, "no money."

"Oh, Roger has money," interjected Angela Brewster.

"As you probably know, our mail is flown to us twice weekly so we can reply to those we think we should. The replies are sent back to London for mailing. Roger requested a thousand-pound bank draft; he got it two days ago. He laughed when he opened the envelope."

"So *simple*?" asked Colonel Montrose.

"His signature was enough, Leslie. I think Mum had a controlling interest in the bank."

"The rich *are* different," said Pryce. "But *why,* Angela, why would he want to leave this place?"

"You'd have to know my brother, sir, really know him. He's a terrific guy, I mean *terrific*. But in some ways he's like our father. When something's wrong, *really* wrong, he can go into a rage. I think he wants to find Gerald Henshaw and send him to hell. He feels he has to kill Gerry for murdering our mother."

"Get Geof Waters on the phone!" ordered Leslie.

"Right away," said Cameron, rising and running to the nearest telephone.

26

Sir Geoffrey Waters leaped out of his chair, stretching the cord and pulling the telephone half across his desk. "We're getting bits and pieces of information from Rome and Milan, but the picture isn't clear yet. It was *you* who killed him?"

"No, it wasn't us, it was him, *Paravacini*! His own birds ate him alive. We were caught and damn near lost the whole ball of wax until we got the hell out of there. Listen, Geof, Leslie and I will fill you in when we reach London in a couple of hours, but right now we've got two large problems, and one of them is you."

"The threat against me? I got your warning but—"

"You have to take this seriously. Paravacini said you were going to be killed within the next twenty-four hours. Those were his exact words, 'twenty-four hours.' Watch your flanks, Geof, he wasn't kidding, he meant it!"

"I'll bear it in mind. What's the second problem?"

"The Brewster kid. He flew the coop."

"Good God! *How? . . . Why?*"

"Over the wall when it was dark. His sister says he's going after Gerald Henshaw, the once and former stepfather who killed their mother."

"What does that cheeky whippersnapper think he can do that all of us haven't *done*? Henshaw's disappeared from the face of the earth. He's either somewhere in an African or Asian city, living well but isolated, or more likely, as I understand the Matarese, at the bottom of the Channel in a weighted body bag."

"I agree with you, but we're not him."

"Where would he go? Where would he *start*? An angry teenager asking foolish questions in the shabbier parts of the city is a target with or without the Matarese."

"He's angry, sure, but he's not stupid, Geof. He's smart enough to know he needs help. He won't go to you because he figures you'd pull him in and lock him up someplace—"

"It's what we should have done with all three of them," interrupted Waters.

"It's what you thought you *did* do, only none of us factored in the rage of a youngster who lost a father he worshiped and saw the murder of a mother he deeply loved."

"*So?*" asked the MI-5 chief defensively.

"I think he'll go straight to a man he trusts, a sergeant major who was so devoted to his brigadier that he'd follow him to hell and back, as you people say."

"*Coleman,*" exclaimed Waters. "Sergeant Major Coleman! . . . Only I believe the expression originated in the States, not the U.K. It's not our style, old chap."

"Whatever. If I were you, I'd check him out. By the way, the kid has money on him. A thousand pounds."

"It's certainly enough to get him here anonymously, if he's as smart as you believe."

"He is."

"I'm on my way to see our sergeant major. I won't bother to call."

Roger Brewster boarded the train at Valence. He had planned everything out, down to the last detail except one. He had pored over maps, centering on locations within hours north of where he assumed they were, and as he spoke French fluently, he had narrowed down the area reasonably well from the Deuxième guards. He had gone over the wall much in the way his new friend, Jamie Montrose, had described his own escape from Bahrain. Searchlights were in constant use; one had to wait for the absence of the light. One also had to elude the guards, who were positioned to protect their "guests" from external assault. It was a simple matter to convince a Deuxième patrol that his sister, in the room next to his, complained incessantly when he had a cigarette. She had the nostrils of a wolf.

The patrol was a smoker; he laughingly understood. Once over the wall in relative darkness, Roger ran through the fields to what appeared to be a main road. He waited on the side, using the normally accepted raised hand and thumb, as cars and trucks went by. Finally, a produce truck stopped; he explained in French that he was a student who had to return to his *pensionnat* before daylight or he might be expelled. He had spent the night with his girlfriend.

Toujours l'amour. The driver understood, displaying a degree of envy, and drove the student to the train station.

Roger had learned from his maps and various other pamphlets that there was a flying school in Villeurbanne. As Jamie Montrose had done, he had to find a pilot, but unlike Jamie, his could not be an accident in the street. Since there was such a school, there were pilots, and if there were pilots, one could be bought, and if he could find that one, he had a thousand pounds. *England.* London and Belgravia. And the one detail he left to last. Old *Coley*. He would call him from the airfield.

Former Sergeant Major Oliver Coleman disabled the alarm and opened the heavy door of the Brewster house in Belgravia. "Good morning, Sir Geoffrey," he said, admitting the MI-5 officer.

"You knew it was I?"

"I've installed microcameras in the two pillars, sir. It seemed to be the proper thing to do for the children when they return. You see, there's the camera mounted on the wall above the door."

"Rather costly, I'd say," mumbled Waters.

"Not at all, sir. I made clear to the security firm that my concern over their gross negligence in permitting their own personnel to install bugs in the house could well lead to the courts—and a great deal of publicity. They were happy to oblige me at no cost."

"May we talk, Mr. Coleman?"

"Of course, Sir Geoffrey. I was just having some mid-morning tea. Would you care to join me?"

"No, thank you. I have to get back to the office, and we can speak right here."

"Very well. What should we speak about?"

"Roger Brewster broke out of the hideaway where we placed him, his sister, and the Montrose boy—"

"Bloody-good show," interrupted Coleman, "he's a fine lad and you can't confine him."

"For *God's* sake, Sergeant Major! We're *protecting* him, can't you understand that?"

"Surely, I do, sir. But the boy has other things on his mind. As *I* do. Where is that fiend, Gerald Henshaw? We've heard nothing from you people."

"Hasn't it occurred to you that he was undoubtedly killed?"

"If so, we'd like proof of that."

"There are so many ways, Coleman. We may not learn for months, even years."

"But you don't know now, do you? Roger's as obsessed

as I am with finding that bastard. If I get to him first, I'll end his miserable life in ways no barbarian ever thought of."

"Listen to me, Coleman. Alone, searching blind, the boy's a goner. If he contacts you, for heaven's sake, *call* me!"

"He's not a goner if I'm around," said the former sergeant major. "His father risked his life for me, and I'd willingly give my life for his son."

"*Goddamn it,* you can't do what *we* can do! If he reaches you, call me. If you don't, his death could be on your head."

Roger Brewster got off the train at Villeurbanne. The early-morning light began to emerge, too early to head for the airfield. He walked from the station into the streets; he realized he was terribly tired and the wrestler in him told him that his body needed fuel. Food. He found a bakery, walked inside, and spoke with the sleepy owner in French.

"*Bonjour.* I'm supposed to meet my father at your airport, but the only train from Valence was at this hour. Your bread smells great."

"It should. It's the best in the province. What would you like?"

"Whatever you suggest that comes out of your oven. And milk, if you have some, and a mug of coffee perhaps."

"I can do all that. Can you pay?"

"Certainly. I would not ask if I couldn't." Refueled and enlivened by the strong coffee, Roger paid, including an impressive tip, and asked, "Where exactly is the airfield?"

"A mile or so north, but there are no taxis available at this hour."

"That's all right. North, you say? Any particular road?"

"Four streets down," replied the baker, pointing to his right, "turn left into the highway. It leads directly to the airfield and that terrible flying academy."

"You don't like it, the flying school?"

"You wouldn't either if you lived here. Crazy students buzzing all over the place. You watch, one day there'll be a horrible crash, followed by more crashes and citizens killed! Then *poof,* the stupid academy will be gone. Good riddance!"

"I hope that doesn't happen, the crashes, I mean. Well, I'll be off. Thank you, sir."

"You're a nice young fellow. Good luck . . . and your French is very understandable, if perhaps too Parisian." Both laughed, and Roger headed for the door.

The trek to the airport was relieved by the sounds of engines, then the sight of small planes pitching up into the early-morning sky. These reminded the Brewster son that when he was a tyke he would frequently accompany his father, who was determined to earn his pilot's license, to the practice field in Cheltenham. Daniel Brewster claimed there was nothing so exhilarating as flying with the first light of day. He would often wake up Roger to make the trip, stopping for breakfast only after their forty-five minutes in the air. Those were the good days; they would never be again.

The telephone rang in Belgravia and Oliver Coleman picked it up from his chair in the huge Brewster library. He dramatically altered his voice, as he had done scores of times in the Arab Emirates over the headquarters radio, speaking in a tight, high register very unlike a sergeant major's. (Orders for the British forces from various emirs and Emirates leaders were often best lost in the pipeline.)

"Good morning, this is the housekeeper. To whom do you wish to speak?"

"Oh, perhaps I have the wrong number—"

"*Ahem!*" Coleman coughed loudly, clearing his throat. "Sorry, sir, a horse in the gullet, if you know what I mean. But I recognize your voice, young man, you're the Aldrich lad, Nicholas Aldrich, a school chum of Master Roger's."

"That's right," said Roger Brewster from a pay phone in Villeurbanne, France, instantly understanding. "And you must be Coleman, *Mister* Coleman, sorry."

"Quite all right, lad. I'm afraid Roger's not here. He and Angela are off visiting relatives somewhere in Scotland—or is it Dublin, I'm not really sure."

"Do you know when Rog will be back, Mr. Coleman?" asked young Brewster, listening carefully.

"Quite soon, I imagine. He called the other night from a

boring, overly jovial cousin's house, where all they talked about was grouse hunting, and said he'd trade the *full moon* outside his window for a pint in Windsor. He hoped to be home this afternoon around three o'clock, but he couldn't promise. Why don't you call around then?"

"All right, sir, I shall. And thank you *very* much."

Brewster hung up the pay phone in Villeurbanne knowing the information he needed was to be found in old Coley's words and phrases. The "full moon" was first; it was familiar but he couldn't place it. Then there was "a pint," and that did not make sense, therefore there was meaning in it. Roger wasn't a drinker; he did not disapprove, he simply didn't like the taste. And then "Windsor" and an "overly jovial cousin"—what did they mean? Also, the "shooting of grouse," where did it fit?

He went inside to the airfield's waiting room, where there was a coffee machine. He poured himself a cup, sat at a table, and from a notepad, the flying school's logo on top, tore off a page and wrote out Coleman's words. It took him a while, but finally it came together.

The "full moon" and the "overly jovial cousin" were matched with "Windsor." And it wasn't "shooting of grouse," it was "grouse hunting." And "a pint" meant where a pint could be purchased. The Jolly Hunter's Moon in Windsor! It was a pub roughly a half hour from Belgravia that catered in great measure to veterans of the armed forces, mainly commandos and airmen, therefore the "hunter's moon." Every month or so Coley and Roger's father had gone there to see old comrades. Several times, when their mother was on a Wildlife trip, they took young Roger and Angela with them, seated in a separate room with games to play. On the condition, of course, that they never tell their mother. That was *it*! The Jolly Hunter's Moon at three o'clock in the afternoon!

The recruiting of a pilot and a plane to England, a negotiation Roger was totally unprepared for, proved to be easier than deciphering Coley's code. The pilot, a major in France's *armée de l'aire*, who made extra money teaching students at the flying school, was more than happy to oblige. When the Brewster son opened with an offer of five hundred English pounds, the man's eyes widened above his moustache and slightly reddish nose, and when Roger consented to a body search for drugs, as well as agreeing to pay fuel costs and any landing fees required, the major said, "*Monsieur,* you shall have a most pleasant flight! And the fields near Windsor are familiar to me."

In the communications room at MI-5 headquarters, the woman in the telephone complex covering the Brewster phone in Belgravia removed her earphones and turned to an associate in the adjacent station. "That sergeant major at the Brewster house could have been trained by us."

"How so?" asked the man next to her.

"The way he handles inquiries. He invents ambiguous locations, details fictitious circumstances, and implies a quick return without any guarantees."

"Very professional," agreed the associate tapper. "He allays any suspicions with the expectation of a relatively soon contact. Excellent. There's nothing, then?"

"Nothing at all. I'll send the tape upstairs, but on a low priority."

Oliver Coleman needed the hours to make sure Sir Geoffrey had not put him under surveillance, which, naturally, he had. The former sergeant major picked up the MI-5 vehicle less than a mile from Belgravia, a shabby Austin sedan that turned corners too rapidly. He drove around London, traversing the city from Knightsbridge to Kensington Gardens, from Soho to Regent's Park and Hampstead, finally losing the MI-5 surveillance in the traffic of Piccadilly Circus.

He sped out of London on the north road to Windsor, hoping all his racing around made sense. Had Roger figured out his message? Would he show up around three o'clock at The Jolly Hunter's Moon? Or had everything been for naught? Coley was cautiously optimistic, however, insofar as young Brewster had so quickly understood their charade on the telephone, instantly assuming the role of Nicholas Aldrich, actually the name of a school friend he had brought home on several occasions. Roger was a bright lad with a quick mind and a sense of purpose very much like his father's: A sense of purpose that carried a great deal of impatience. But what was his purpose *now*? Was it really to hunt down Gerald Henshaw? Coleman knew that Roger had continuously badgered Sir Geoffrey, trying to learn what progress had been made in unearthing Henshaw; there had been none. Had the legendary Brewster impatience surfaced, overriding reason?

Coleman realized that his own hostile attitude toward Sir Geoffrey had been unreasonable; even now his actions lacked logic. MI-5, along with the other cooperating services, all were far more equipped to search for Lady Alicia's killer than a retired old soldier and an angry teenager. Still, the former sergeant major had to make clear his loyalties. The son of Brigadier Daniel Brewster—officer, scholar, sportsman, and entrepreneur—took precedence over all things, including the government. If Roger wished to make contact with his father's aged comrade in arms, contact would be made.

But what purpose would be served? What help could *he* provide? Unless Roger Brewster knew something, or remembered something, that others had overlooked. Coleman would learn the answers to his questions soon—if the lad showed up.

He did, at six minutes past three in the afternoon.

"Thanks, Coley, thanks so much for seeing me," said Roger Brewster, having spotted Coleman in a back booth of the pub, and sitting down quickly across from him.

"I wouldn't have it any other way. I'm pleased you understood my message."

"It was confusing at first, but not when I thought about it."

"I was counting on that, you think clearly. I'm convinced our telephones are tapped, and Sir Geoffrey has already come to see me, threaten me actually, about what to do if you reached me."

"Oh, *Christ,* I don't want to get you into trouble!"

"Not to worry, I lost his bloody tail back in Piccadilly. However, young man, I must ask you. Why, Roger, *why*? Sir Geoffrey and his troops were *protecting* you, I'll grant him that. Why did you do this to him? Is it Henshaw?"

"Yes, Coley."

"Can't you understand that MI-Five and its highly professional associates are doing everything they can to find him, if, indeed, he's alive?"

"Yes, I know that, but I also understand that there are moles in the services. Sir Geoffrey said as much to Mr. Pryce and Colonel Montrose, I heard him! I didn't want to take the chance that the information I had could be intercepted."

"What information, lad?"

"I think I know where Henshaw may be hiding, or at least the person who can tell us where he is."

"What?"

"Outside of the whores and the call girls, Gerry had a special girlfriend in High Holborn. Mother knew it but never said anything outside the family, and precious little to us. One night, however, around eleven o'clock, I passed their bedroom door; Henshaw was drunk and they were fighting—nothing new. Then he announced that he was going out for some 'comfort and relaxation.' That pissed me off, so I followed him in the Bentley and saw where he went."

"For God's sake, why didn't you say anything about this *before*?"

"I'm not sure. Mum hated any sort of scandal, you know that, and I guess I just put it out of my mind. Then a few days ago, I remembered Mother's words to Angie and me as she was going upstairs to confront Gerry, the night he killed her. 'Call Coley, don't let him drive the Jaguar. He'll probably go over to see his girlfriend in High Holborn,' or words to that effect."

"Then we must go to Sir Geoffrey with your information—"

"No," broke in Roger. "I'm going there first! If he's there, I want him to myself."

"For *what*? To kill him? You'd throw your life away by killing a worthless scoundrel like Gerald Henshaw?"

"Wouldn't you, Coley, if you were me? He murdered my mother."

"I'm *not* you, lad!"

"That doesn't answer my question."

"In a way it does, my boy," replied Oliver Coleman quietly. "To answer your question directly, yes, *I* would kill Gerald Henshaw with my bare hands, as I freely admitted to Sir Geoffrey. It would be a slow death of excruciating pain, but it would be done by me, *not* you. I am an old soldier without much time left on this earth. You, on the other hand, have your whole life in front of you. You're the son of the finest man I ever knew, and I couldn't permit you to throw that life away."

"Suppose, dear friend," said Roger, looking sheepishly up and locking his eyes with the once and always sergeant major, "I simply beat the living crap out of the bastard, and *then* turned him over to Sir Geof?"

"In that case," replied Coleman, "as they say in those insufferable American television programs, let's roll, young man."

The Bentley slowed down in the street in High Holborn, stopping at a parking place nearest the apartment house Roger pointed out. "I remember he pressed the top button on the left," said Brewster as they got out of the car.

They walked up the steps, entered the glass-enclosed foyer, and stood in front of the panel of buttons. Roger pressed the top button on the left. There was no response. He pressed it again and again, still nothing.

"Here," said Coleman, studying the names opposite the numbers. "We'll try something else," he added, pressing the button marked Management.

"Yes?" said the gruff voice over the intercom.

"Sir Geoffrey Waters, sir, Crown Military Intelligence. We're in a dreadful hurry, but if you care to check the MI-Five Index, you'll find that I *am* who I say." Coleman's authority was absolute. "We must talk immediately."

"Good heavens, of course!" cried the obviously frightened

manager of the building. "Come right in," the man continued as the entrance buzzer sounded, "I'll meet you in the hall. I'm on this floor."

The former sergeant major flashed an old Royal Fusiliers ID card in front of the startled manager and spoke—again with enormous authority. "Flat Eight-A, there's no response. Is the lessee, Symond, not in?"

"Hasn't been for days, your . . . sir."

"We have to check the premises, it's most urgent."

"Yes, certainly—sure!" The shabbily dressed manager led them to an elevator at the end of the hall. "Here's a master key," he said. "You can let yourselves in."

"The Crown thanks you." Coley accepted the key with a cold nod.

The Symond flat was a well-appointed, attractive apartment with upscale decor and expensive furniture. Roger and Oliver Coleman began their search. There were three rooms, two baths, and a kitchen. A bedroom, the living room, and what appeared to be a library/study, the shelves minimally filled with books, but papers scattered across the desk. Coleman started with the papers, a hodgepodge of bills, magazines, memos reminding the writer of various engagements—initials taking the place of names—and numerous personal letters, many sent from the Continent. The postmarks read like the itinerary of wealthy fun-seekers and shopping aficionados: Paris, Nice, Côte d'Azur, Rome, Baden-Baden, Lake Como, the watering and purchasing centers of Europe.

The letters themselves were chatty, innocuous, the wish-you-were-here variety—in a word, boring. Coleman would, of course, turn everything over to Sir Geoffrey; it was his duty to do so, but the woman named Symond would remain an enigma unless she could be found.

"Coley!" shouted Roger Brewster from another room. "Come *look* at this!"

"Where are you, lad?"

"The kitchen!"

Coleman ran out of the study, glanced around the living

room, then dashed into the white-tiled kitchen. "What is it, Roger?"

"Here," replied young Brewster, standing by a wall phone with a notepad beside it, a ballpoint pen hanging from a small brass chain on the right. "There, see that? There are puncture marks on the pad and they were made by someone angry, I mean really pissed-off. So much so he—or I guess she—stabbed the pad."

"What? All I can see are parts of two letters and three numbers. The rest are only indentations."

"That's because this kind of pen doesn't write well on the side, you know, on the horizontal. We have one in our dorm at school—most of the time we substitute pencils, but they don't last—"

"What are you driving at, lad?"

"Well, if we're in a hurry, say a girl's giving us a number, we just keep writing *heavy,* then figure it out later."

"We've all done that," said Coleman, ripping off the page, "and you've got a point. The Symond woman must have been in a dreadful hurry. Otherwise, she would have put the caller on hold and gotten a decent writing instrument." The retired old soldier carried the page to a counter, took a mechanical pencil from his inside jacket pocket, and began lightly drawing the lead back and forth over the indentations. "What do you make of it, Roger?"

"NU Three Five Zero." Young Brewster read the emerging white lettering. *"Amst. K-Gr. Conf. Tues. Surrey A.P. . . .* I can figure out the first and the last parts. The 'NU Three Five Zero' are the tail numbers of a private plane. I know that because Mother often had to hire one for Wildlife trips. And the 'Surrey A.P.' is obviously an airport in Surrey."

"Perhaps I can fill in the obvious parts of the rest. The 'Amst.' is Amsterdam, 'Conf.' and 'Tues.' undoubtedly a conference on Tuesday. The 'K-Gr.' is apparently a location in Amsterdam, and since we can assume the 'Gr.' is 'Gracht,' which in Dutch is 'canal,' it's probably the address of some place on a canal with the letter 'K' in it. There are probably dozens of canals with a prominent 'K,' and hundreds and hundreds of such offices or residences."

"What do you think it all means?" asked Roger.

"I think it means we should march right over and deliver this information to Sir Geoffrey Waters."

"Come *on,* Coley. He'll lock me up again in France!"

"That, young man, would not make me unhappy. Now, we'll tear this flat apart, looking for any evidence of Henshaw's whereabouts, but if none can be found, you've accomplished your mission, won't you agree?"

"Suppose she comes back?"

"We'll make an agreement with Waters and MI-Five. In writing, if you like. He'll have this place covered as if there's a skin around the street. Should Symond or Henshaw return, you'll be instantly notified and flown back to London."

"Let's start *looking*!" exclaimed Roger Brewster.

Sir Geoffrey Waters did his very best to control his nearly uncontrollable temper. Called by Coleman to come to the Brewster house in Belgravia, his face flushed with anger at the sight of Roger Brewster.

"I trust you realize, Roger, that you've caused this organization, *and* others, a great deal of aggravation, to say the least, as well as placing the lives of Angela and James Montrose in extreme jeopardy."

"The boy has also brought you what I believe to be extraordinary information," said Oliver Coleman firmly, in defense of young Brewster. "None of us knew about the Symond woman until he remembered her. *He* did it, I didn't, and he should be given credit for doing so. By your own admission, he couldn't trust your—"

"*Myra* Symond?" interrupted Waters. "My God, it's *incredible*!"

"Yes, I believe that was the first name on the letters sent to her," said Coleman. "Why is it incredible?"

"She was *one* of us, damn it! A member of our associate branch, *MI-Six*! She was one of the most successful operatives in foreign penetrations."

"Yet she was obviously a traitor, a mole," continued Coleman. "So our young friend has brought you information you knew nothing about."

"How could we?" protested Waters. "She retired a year ago, claiming burnout, which is not unusual."

"She wasn't too burned out to work for somebody else, was she?" said Roger. "Gerald Henshaw killed my mother because she stood up against this Matarese, her computer messages to and from Madrid damn well proved it. Suddenly, this Symond woman is tight with Gerry and Mum's murdered. *Jesus,* sir, it doesn't take a rocket scientist to see the connection!"

"Yes, yes, it's quite apparent," Waters spoke quietly and nodded his head in understatement, "and your knowledge of that, should it ever be suspected, would mark you for a Matarese bullet or a knife. And as someone recently said, 'They're everywhere, we just can't see them.'"

"I understand, sir, I'll go back to France, no argument from me."

"No France, either, Roger," said Waters. "We closed that place down within minutes after you were found missing. I wasn't joking, young man, you seriously risked the lives of the others by the chaos you created. People talk and other people listen; word spreads swiftly when a secret government operation is uncovered in a foreign country."

"I'm truly sorry, sir."

"Well, don't be *too* hard on yourself. The sergeant major is right, you have brought us extraordinarily helpful information. More than you realize, perhaps. . . . I'll tell you this much. We believe we've identified a Matarese agent here in London. Combined with what you've discovered, we may be a step closer."

"To what, sir?"

"The soul of the serpent, I dearly hope. It's still beyond our reach, but a step is a step."

"Where will I be going?" asked the Brewster son.

"South is all you have to know."

"How will I get there?"

"We use only one pilot and one plane. Come to think of it, it's been a rather exhausting day for the poor chap. Oh, well, he's young and strong."

"Luther's a gas, sir."

"Yes, he's refueled a number of times today. Petrol, I mean."

27

Lieutenant Senior Grade Luther Considine, U.S. Navy, once again swept left for yet another final approach, this in to an alternate diplomatic airstrip at Heathrow Airport. "You've got to be *kidding*," he roared into the mouthpiece of his radio headgear. "I've been ferrying this relic since four o'clock this morning, and it's now almost five o'clock in the afternoon! Give me a break, like lunch maybe?"

"Sorry, Leftenant, those are the orders."

"It's not *leftenant,* it's *lootenant,* and I'm hungry."

"Apologies again, old sport I'm simply relaying the orders, I don't make them. The flight plan will be delivered to you by an officer of MI-Five."

"Okay, okay, Brit. Tell the refueling truck to get out here fast, and bring the passenger with it. I'd like to get back to London by midnight. I've got a heavy date with a single bed and a large meal."

"What's the matter?" asked Cameron Pryce, sitting with Leslie in the bulkhead seats.

"I drop you cats off here at Heathrow and pick up an anonymous requiring full fuel tanks. Where to, I've got twenty minutes to figure out."

"You're the best, Luther," said Montrose, raising her voice above the engines. "That's why they chose you."

"Yeah, I've heard that before. 'Many are called but few are chosen.' Why the hell did it have to be *me*?"

"The colonel just told you," yelled Cameron as the pilot reversed thrust upon landing. "You're the best!"

"I'd rather have lunch," said Considine, proceeding down the runway.

The movement on the ground was choreographed. Luther taxied down the airstrip to a predetermined, isolated area. A refueling truck raced from a hangar, and as two uniformed mechanics reeled out hoses for the dual-wing tanks, a third man in civilian clothes approached the plane. Considine opened the fuselage panel of the Bristol Freighter; the man spoke. "Here's your flight plan, Lieutenant. Study it and if you've any questions, you know whom to call."

"Thanks a bunch," said Luther, reaching out and taking the manila envelope. "Here's your cargo," he added, gesturing at Pryce and Montrose.

"Yes, I assumed that. If the two of you will please accompany me, our car is directly behind the truck."

"We have luggage," Cameron broke in, "give me a minute to get it together."

"Lieutenant," said the MI-5 officer, "perhaps you could assist us."

Luther Considine, U.S.N., looked imperiously down at the stranger. "I do not do windows," he said with quiet authority, "and I do not do laundry, and for your information, Cipher Head, I'm not a redcap in one of those old movies."

"I *beg* your pardon?"

"Never mind, fella," interrupted Pryce, "our friend is a little stressed. I've got the suitcases."

"Thank you, Chicken Little."

"What *are* you chaps talking about?"

"It's colonial code," answered Cameron. "Our pilot is brewing tea to throw into the Southampton harbor."

"I don't understand a word you're *saying*."

"They're both stressed," broke in Leslie, her voice flat and insistent. "Let's go, *kiddies*."

As Pryce, Montrose, and the intelligence agent walked rapidly toward the MI-5 vehicle, a second car, its windows shaded from the late-afternoon sunlight, sped out on the field to the Bristol aircraft.

"That must be Mr. or Mrs. Anonymous," said Leslie.

"Unless you've short-circuited my perceptions," observed Cameron, "it's a young mister."

"Roger *Brewster*?" whispered Montrose, as they were in the backseat. "But why and where are they flying him?"

"To the south of Spain, a bull ranch owned by a colleague of ours during the Basque rebellions, and you were right, Cameron," said Geoffrey Waters, addressing Pryce and Montrose in his office at MI-5. "He reached old Coleman in Belgravia because, as you correctly assumed, he had no one else to turn to."

"Good Lord, you *are* good," interjected Leslie, looking at Cam.

"Not really, I just tried to narrow down his options. What could he do alone, without help? But he had to have a substantive reason for breaking out and coming back here."

"He did, indeed," agreed Waters, his voice rising. "A woman in High Holborn we knew nothing about."

Sir Geoffrey Waters described the revelations as they had been told him by young Roger Brewster and Oliver Coleman. He then produced the letters and, most notably, the deciphered notepad from Myra Symond's flat. "*Amsterdam,* Pryce! The head of the snake has got to be in *Amsterdam*!"

"It looks that way, doesn't it? But whoever it is in Amsterdam that's running this whole obscene thing is a manager, a bureaucrat, not the total power. There's someone else behind him or her."

"Why do you say that, Cam?" asked Leslie.

"I know you'll think I'm stupid, or something, but when I was in college, I really loved reading and listening to recordings of Shakespeare. Silly, isn't it? But one phrase always stuck with me—I can't even remember the play."

"What was it?"

"'Between the acting of a dreadful thing and the first motion, all the interim is like a phantasma or a hideous dream.'"

"I believe it's *Julius Caesar*," said Waters. "What's the application here?"

"The 'phantasma,' I think. I had to look it up to get the context. The specter, the hidden phantom. There's someone or something beyond Amsterdam."

"But Amsterdam is certainly our first priority, isn't it?"

"Of course, Geof. Definitely. But would you do me a favor? Fly Scofield over here. I think we need Beowulf Agate."

The New York Times

MEDICAL COMMUNITY STUNNED

Over Nine Hundred Formerly Nonprofit Hospitals Sold to Consortium

NEW YORK, OCT. 26—In what can only be described as a move that has stunned the medical community, 942 formerly nonprofit hospitals in the United States, Canada, Mexico, France, the Netherlands, and Great Britain have been sold to Carnation Cross International, a medical group whose headquarters are in Paris. The consortium's spokesman, Dr. Pierre Froisard, issued the following statement.

"At last the medical dream of the century, Project Universal, as we call it, has become a reality. In private hands, and with instantaneous global communications so readily available, we shall upgrade the quality of hospital care wherever we have the authority. By pooling our resources, information, and expertise, we can and will provide the best. Again, Project Universal, to which we have devoted quiet years and extraordinary sums of money, is now a reality, and the civilised world will be better for it."

In response to Dr. Froisard's statement, Dr. Kenneth Burns, a noted New England oncological surgeon, had this reply. "It depends on where they go. If words were actions, we'd all be living in utopia. What bothers me is so much authority in so few hands. Suppose they take another tack and say, 'You do it this way, or we *don't* share.' I think we've seen enough of that with the insurance companies. Choice is obliterated."

Another opposition voice came from the plain-spoken Senator Thurston Blair of Wyoming. "How the [expletive deleted] did this ever happen? We've got antitrust laws, foreign-intervention laws, all kinds of laws that prohibit this kind of thing. Were the [expletive deleted] idiots on the watch asleep at the switch?"

The answer to Senator Blair is quite simple. International conglomerates only have to satisfy the laws of the specific countries in which they operate. The laws vary and none prohibits subsidiaries. Therefore, Ford is Ford U.K. in England; the Dutch Phillips is Phillips, USA; and Standard Oil is all over the world as Standard Oil—wherever it is. By and large, these international corporations benefit the economies of their host locations. Therefore, it may be assumed that Carnation Cross will be C.C. USA, C.C. U.K., C.C. France, et cetera.

Continued on Page D2

Brandon Scofield and Antonia had settled into their suite at the Savoy, Bray exhausted by the trip on the Air Force jet, Toni exhilarated by the fact that they were back in London. "I'm just going to go out and wander around," said Antonia, hanging up the last of their clothes.

"Give all the pubs my best wishes," said Scofield, shoes off and supine on the bed. "I'll try to touch base with the best of them."

"They're not on this tourist's agenda."

"I forgot, you're the reincarnation of that bitch Carry Nation."

"A little of *her* agenda wouldn't hurt you." The telephone rang. "I'll get it." Toni crossed to the bedside phone. "Hello?"

"*Antonia,* it's Geoffrey! It's been a thousand years, old girl."

"At least twenty or so, Geof. I understand you're now Sir Geoffrey Waters."

"Accidents happen, luv, even in this business. Is the reprobate there?"

"He is and he isn't. He hates the time zones, but here he is." She handed the phone to Brandon.

"Hello, Sir Asshole, would you mind if I got a couple of hours' sleep?"

"Normally, I'd be loath to interrupt your much-needed rest, old chap, but what we have to discuss is extremely important. Cameron and Leslie are with me."

"So important we can't talk about it over the phone while I'm lying down?"

"You know the answer to that, Bray."

"I do now," said Scofield, wearily moving his legs over the side of the bed and sitting up. "You still at the same place?"

"You won't recognize the insides, that's where the money went, but the outside hasn't changed in several hundred years."

"Better architecture back then."

"Yes, the prince keeps reminding us of that, and I happen to applaud him for it."

"He needs all the applause he can get. We'll be there in twenty minutes plus. By the way, dò I have to call you 'Sir' to your face?"

"Only when there are people around. If you don't, they'll behead you."

The reunion was brief, warm, and overlaid with a sense of urgency. The initial greetings over, the five sat down around a table in a secure conference room at MI-5 headquarters. Waters brought them all up to date regarding recent events in general, including the actions of the Brewster son but saving the London specifics for later. He then turned the chair over to Pryce and Montrose, who related their experiences in Lake Como, including Don Silvio Togazzi's assistance and the horrible deaths of Paravacini and his aide.

"My *God*," broke in Scofield, "Togazzi's a 'Don' and

Geof's a goddamned 'Sir'! Next, Silvio will probably be King of Italy, and Butterball here, no doubt, Prime Minister. The world's gone crazy!"

"You're too kind," said Waters, chuckling. " . . . So, from Como we can assume the collapse of a major force in the Italian Matarese, and a Paravacini cardinal at the Vatican."

"Collapse may be too strong," suggested Leslie. " 'Charlie' Paravacini undoubtedly built a strong, efficient organization."

"We don't know that," Brandon interrupted, "and even if we assume it, he was a real power, the only power in the whole sector. According to Togazzi, he didn't delegate a hell of a lot."

"If that's the case," said the MI-5 chief, "the organization may not have collapsed but it's certainly in disarray and quite vulnerable."

"Agreed," added Cameron, "and that's what we're looking for, vulnerability. When we have enough facts, evidence of a near-global conspiracy within the industrial countries, we can strike back."

"By *exposing* it?" asked Scofield quizzically, his eyebrows raised in doubt.

"It's one way," replied Sir Geoffrey, "but perhaps not the most profitable."

"What do you mean?" said Antonia.

"We want to eliminate the Matarese from international finance, not plunge the world's industries into chaos."

"How do you do that without exposing it?"

"Down and dirty, Toni," answered Pryce. "We cut off the heads of the multiple snakes, leaving the extended bodies to whip around and strangle one another."

"Why, Cam, that's real poetic, kid," said Scofield. "You could have taken a lit course at Harvard."

"I didn't know it had one."

"May we ask the children to stop playing in their sandbox," Leslie Montrose said firmly, turning to the MI-5 intelligence officer. "Geof, I think Toni has a point. How do we short-circuit the Matarese without exposing it?"

"I'll answer that, Leslie, after we hear from Brandon. Go

on, you relic. Outside of Atlantic Crown, which we all know about and for which we grant you reluctant praise, what other progress?"

"You tell 'em, luv," said Bray, turning to Antonia. "She keeps score, and I really shouldn't indulge my lessers."

"Even I was impressed," Toni admitted. "From the materials he found and photographed in the Atlantic Crown files, combined with a computer-reduced summary of outstanding mergers, buyouts, and hostile takeovers, he narrowed it all down and set up what you call a sting operation at the hotel in New York, along with Frank Shields." Antonia Scofield explained that her husband had confronted fourteen Matarese candidates from the most influential areas of American business. "Four of the major players, who supposedly did not know one another, got together after meeting with Bray at an out-of-the-way restaurant in New York. Frank Shields's people took photographs from a distance. It's now on record."

"Well done, Brandon!" exclaimed Waters. " . . . Now, I'll bring you au courant here in London." Sir Geoffrey walked to the windows and closed the venetian blinds, although the early-evening light was not an impediment. He crossed to a slide projector at the head of the table and switched it on; a white square appeared on a screen at the end of the room. Waters pressed a button for the first slide. It was a photograph of a man running down a London street, his head turned as he looked behind him. He was a relatively tall, slender man, his legs disproportionately longer than his upper body, and dressed in a conservative business suit. The expression on his lean, high-cheekboned face was one of surprise and fear. Additional slides showed him obviously gathering speed, twice more looking around, his features pinched, now close to panic. The slides ended with the subject rounding a corner; the screen went white, then dark, as Waters turned on the overhead neon lights. Sir Geoffrey, walking and standing by his chair, spoke.

"This was the man running from the flat of Amanda Bentley-Smythe, now established as an operative of the Matarese, just before her death was made public. We have identified him as Leonard Fredericks, an upper-level attaché in the Foreign Office. His phone is tapped and he is currently under total surveillance by SIS, who coordinates with us. To date, since that day in Bayswater, he's not been in formal contact with anyone of consequence, he's merely a piece of furniture at the Foreign Office. Yet we're convinced he's the prime contact with the Matarese."

"Why not bring him in and *break* him?" said Pryce angrily.

"Because it would send a message we don't want to send, *goddamn it*!" exclaimed Scofield.

"Why, Your *Holiness*?"

"We're not close enough!" insisted Brandon. "If there's a big snake in Amsterdam, we have to zero in on him first. By destroying the contact, you cut off the road to practicality."

"I may be crazy," said Colonel Montrose, "but I think I know what he means."

"So do I, and I really hate to admit it," agreed Cameron Pryce. "It's like altering an electronic compass for a pilot lost in the mountains."

"You could find a cleaner metaphor, youngster, but essentially you're right. Let the unseen designer, who may not be as powerful as he thinks he is, continue to believe he has total control. Once his link to reality is shattered, he— or she—is isolated. That's when you break the Matarese circle. A key may be in the 'K-Gracht' found in the Symond flat."

"I believe I hear Beowulf Agate speaking," said Geoffrey Waters quietly.

"Come on, Geof, there's nothing mythical about it. You work from the large boulders down to the rocks, then even stones and pebbles, if you have to. Human behavior everywhere is pretty much the same, Taleniekov and I agreed about that."

"Beowulf Agate really has a vision," said Cameron Pryce quietly, almost to himself, staring at Scofield. "Let's talk about the stones and the pebbles. What do we do, Bray?"

"Oh, that's simple," Scofield replied. "I'm going to become a dedicated member of the Matarese."

"What?" The other four looked at one another, per-plexed.

"Relax everybody, it's really very easy. Our Matarese mole, Leonard Fredericks, will encounter an emissary from Amsterdam—God knows I have enough information to make me believable."

"The guy's just a stringer, a damned good one but a stringer nevertheless," said Cameron. "What do you think he can tell you?"

"I have no idea. It depends on the cards I'm dealt. I make statements, he reacts; I ask questions, he answers. One thing usually leads to another, the other to something else. It's sort of like instant mental tennis."

"How in heaven's name do you think you can get away with it?" asked Sir Geoffrey, astonished.

"He doesn't know me, and the only photographs of my handsome face are twenty-nine years old and were once in the Agency files. I haven't been over here in, let's see, at least twenty-five years, so he won't have a clue."

"I hate to add to that ego of yours," said Cameron, "but your reputation has definitely preceded you. Even Parava-cini, while damning your soul to hell, acknowledged your talents. If he, an Italian, spoke so generously of you, you'd better believe that all of Matarese Europe knows who you are and what you're capable of."

"And certainly it wouldn't be difficult for their people to hunt down any number of men who were at Chesapeake or Peregrine," added Leslie. "They could pick up clear descrip-tions of you."

"Also, Bray," said Antonia firmly, "Frank Shields freely admitted there was a covert Matarese inside the CIA!"

"To answer the lieutenant colonel first"—Brandon nodded, smiling at Montrose—"I'll just have to be a little more inventive, won't I? As to you, m'luv, the matter's eas-ily disposed of. The minute Squinty heard from Cam that he had found me on Brass Twenty-six, all references to yours truly, including photographs, dossiers, et cetera, were removed from the Agency files and deleted in the computers."

"Not exactly true," interrupted Leslie. "I was given a limited background on you and so was Ev Bracket."

"The operative word being 'limited,' right?"

"There was enough. I could have picked you out of a crowd, if I had to. Also Toni."

"And what did you do with this limited material, Colonel?"

"What we were ordered to do in each other's presence. Together, Everett and I burned our copies."

"No one else saw them?"

"Of course not. It was restricted data."

"And I presume you haven't been in touch with any of the elusive Matarese."

"Please, Brandon, I'm not a fool, so don't treat me like one."

"I emphatically agree," said Antonia.

"I wouldn't do that," said Scofield, "because you're not a fool, you're a superb officer. My point is that whatever information the Matarese has on me is also limited, very limited and probably very exaggerated. Despite my charm, good looks, and certain abilities in weaponry, I appear to be an average sixty-something-year-old American. A perfectly ordinary fellow."

"When pigs fly over the moon and cows give bourbon," said Pryce softly, slowly shaking his head.

The meeting with the Foreign Office's Leonard Fredericks, second director of European Economic Negotiations, was arranged with all the finesse and secrecy for which Sir Geoffrey Waters was noted within the intelligence community. The arranging began with a perfectly normal request to the Foreign Office. It was to assign a high-level director of European Economic Negotiations to meet with a prominent American banker who had vigorously complained about the FO's policy of accepting Euro-Comm's rates of exchange over those of the World Bank. It was detrimental to U.S. investment and the realization of profits thereof.

It was as foolish an accusation as cows producing

bourbon, but couched in pseudoacademic babble, it was acceptable to the bureaucracy.

"Accommodate me, old chap."

"Just how am I to do that, Geoffrey?"

"Send memoranda all over the place. The banker's name is Andrew Jordan, our target is one Leonard Fredericks. Assign him to Jordan."

"May I ask a question or two?"

"Sorry, it's a major operation."

"A sting then?"

"I told you, no questions."

"I'll have to log this, you understand. We can't be compromised, you know."

"Log whatever you like, just do it, my old friend."

"You wouldn't ask if it weren't major. It's done, Geof."

"Andrew Jordan," a.k.a. Beowulf Agate, was shown into Leonard Fredericks's office by a secretary. The tall, lean occupant rose from his chair, walked around his desk, and enthusiastically greeted the reputedly prominent American banker.

"I'm not sure I like meeting here," said the man called Jordan. "I know all about offices, I have twenty-six in various cities in the U.S. There's a bar, what you call a pub, two blocks from here, the 'Lion' something."

"The Lion of St. George," broke in Leonard Fredericks. "Would you rather we talk there?"

"Yes, I would, if you don't mind," said Jordan-Scofield.

"Then we'll do it," agreed the bureaucrat. "Whatever makes you comfortable. You go on ahead of me, and after I tidy up a few things, I'll meet you there in half an hour."

The Lion of St. George was a typical London pub: thick wood, heavy stools and chairs and tables, with a minimum of light and a maximum of smoke, in short words, an outstanding watering hole for the likes of Brandon Alan Scofield. He sat at a table in the front, nearest the entrance, nursing a draft, and waiting for Fredericks. The Foreign Office's second director arrived carrying an attaché case. He glanced around impatiently in the dim light until he saw the strange American who did not care to talk in the office. He walked between the few tables and sat down opposite Andrew Jordan. He spoke while opening his attaché case.

"I've studied your complaint, Mr. Jordan, and although I find merit in your argument, I'm not sure what we can do."

"Why don't I get you a drink? You're going to need one."

"I beg your pardon?"

"You know the way we work," said Beowulf Agate, signaling a waiter. "What do you drink?"

"A small gin and bitters will be fine, thank you." Scofield gave the order, and Fredericks continued. "What do you mean—the way *who* works?"

"In circuitous ways is the best answer. The complaint is horseshit, I'm bringing you orders from Amsterdam."

"What?"

"Come off it, Leonard, we're on the same side. How do you think I reached you if Amsterdam hadn't set it up?" The waiter returned with Fredericks's drink. The timing was perfect. The Matarese's eyes were wide with doubt and fear. The waiter left, and before the mole could speak, Scofield did. "Damned ingenious, I call it. That complaint may be horseshit, but a lot of bankers across the pond believe it, and I *am* a banker, check your computers. But I'm also something else. I take my instructions from the K-Gracht in Amsterdam."

"The *K*-Gracht? . . ." Fredericks's mouth dropped, the fear overcoming the doubt in his eyes.

"Where else?" said Beowulf Agate casually. "I'm the one who tore apart everything in Atlantic Crown's top offices—our offices—and had it flown to the Netherlands—"

The Matarese mole looked close to panic, his doubt erased, his fear paramount. "What orders do you bring from Amsterdam—from the K-Gracht?"

"To begin with, make no contact whatsoever. I'm your only courier, trust *no* one else. We've created this Foreign Office problem to last a number of days, each day bringing us closer to our objective—"

"Which isn't that far *away*," interrupted Fredericks, as if to emphasize his own importance.

"Now it's my turn to question you, Leonard," said Jordan-Scofield quietly, ominously. "How do you know the date of our objective? It's completely secret, only a very few of us know."

"I've heard—rumors out of Amsterdam, passed to its most-trusted agents."

"*What* rumors?"

"The fires, the fires in the *Mediterranean*."

"Who *told* you this?"

"Guiderone, of course! I walked him through the London labyrinths, showed him everything!"

"*Julian* Guiderone?" Now it was Scofield who was stunned. "He really *is* alive," whispered Brandon, barely audible.

"What did you say?"

"Nothing. . . . What gave *you* the right to seek out Guiderone?"

"*I* didn't seek *him,* he found me through Amsterdam! How could I question him? He's the son of the Shepherd Boy, the leader of our movement!"

"Do you honestly believe he could override Amsterdam with all its resources?"

"*Resources?* Money is a necessary lubricant, a vital one, but commitment comes first. Guiderone could strip Amsterdam of its authority with only a few words, he made that very clear. . . . My God, it's what's happening now, isn't it? If I'm not to make contact, that *tells* me something."

"Julian will be pleased at your perception," said Scofield quietly, locking eyes with Fredericks. "He told me you were good, very good, and very trustworthy."

"My *word*!" The Matarese mole chucked down his gin and bitters, then leaned forward, his voice low, intense, confidential. "I believe I understand," he began, "Mr. Guiderone frequently mentioned that Amsterdam was becoming too self-inflated. He acknowledged its vast wealth, based on the fortunes of the Baron of Matarese, but claimed it was irrelevant without a sound world strategy, workable tactics, and most important, global contacts."

"As usual, Julian was right."

"So, Andrew Jordan, you're not a courier from Amsterdam, you're the messenger from Mr. Guiderone."

"To repeat, you're perceptive, Leonard." Now Scofield leaned forward. "Do you know Swanson and Schwartz?"

"In New York? Certainly, it's Albert Whitehead's brokerage firm. I've traveled there often—for Amsterdam."

"Then you know the attorney Stuart Nichols?"

"He does most of the talking."

"What about Ben Wahlburg and Jamieson Fowler?"

"Banking and utilities—"

"Good," interrupted Scofield. "So you can understand the scope of events. Reach them and tell them what I've told you, but *don't* mention me. Julian would go through the roof, if you did. Explain that through an anonymous source you were instructed to stay away from Amsterdam. Ask if they know anything about it."

Albert Whitehead, chief executive officer of Swanson and Schwartz, hung up the telephone and turned to Stuart Nichols, the brokerage firm's attorney, who simultaneously replaced an extension phone.

"What's going on, Stu? What the *hell* is going on?"

"God knows you tried to probe, Al, I couldn't have done it better myself. Leonard wouldn't move an inch, just simple facts, nothing else."

"One thing more, Stuart. He wasn't lying." The buzzer on Whitehead's console sounded; he touched a button and spoke. "Yes, Janet?"

"It's time for your conference call, sir."

"Oh, yes, I remember, it was scheduled earlier today. Who am I conferring with? I don't think you told me."

"You were late for lunch, I didn't get a chance."

"Well, who is it, Janet?"

"Mr. Benjamin Wahlburg and Mr. Jamieson Fowler."

"Really?" Whitehead looked over at the attorney, his expression frozen.

28

Deputy Director Frank Shields ripped open the sealed *EYES ONLY* envelope with his name on the front and began scanning the contents. Having signed the release for the guard, who acknowledged that the metallic seal was intact, he walked back to his desk. He started reading again from the top, his concentration now absolute.

The six pages were verbatim transcripts of conversations over the private, supposedly nontappable telephones belonging to Albert Whitehead, Stuart Nichols, Benjamin Wahlburg, and Jamieson Fowler. They were the four Mataresans who had convened at the small, isolated restaurant in lower New York after having their shocking meetings with William Clayton, a.k.a. Beowulf Agate, as well as Andrew Jordan and Brandon Alan Scofield. Breaking anti-bug commercial phones was no problem for the intercepting devices of the government.

The language employed by all parties was relatively clear, although not completely. It was as if those speaking had considered the unthinkable: Were their phone lines, which cost thousands, really impregnable?

Regardless, all were stunned at the orders to avoid Amsterdam, which they amateurishly referred to as A.M. There were expressions of dismay mixed with alarmed curiosity, and no little fear about the direction the "enterprise" was taking. Therefore, they all agreed to meet in two days at a small, exclusive hotel in the wealthy township of Bernardsville, New Jersey. The reservations would be made in the name of the Genesis Company, their private planes to land at the Morristown airport, roughly twenty minutes away.

The Directorate of Operations, the CIA's covert branch of infiltration, went to work without knowing what the objectives were, not an unusual situation. The Genesis Company would be assigned four specific minisuites and a conference room. A Directorate team flew up, said as little as possible, and placed bugs in every area.

Frank Shields picked up his scrambler phone and dialed London, Geoffrey Waters's sterile phone at MI-5 headquarters.

"Internal Security," said the voice in England.

"Hello, Geof, it's Frank."

"Have you got something, old boy?"

"Put another feather in Scofield's headdress. His four— now five—candidates paid off. The four possibles over here are now definite. They've arranged a meeting, and it's covered by our DO. Believe me, they're all close to panic."

"How the devil did he *do* it?" exclaimed Sir Geoffrey.

"No doubt, rather simply," replied Shields. "So many of us are inured to the complexities of secrecy and manipulation that we overlook the direct approach. In whatever roles he plays, Brandon disregards the complications of his cover, and goes quickly to the jugular before his target can adjust."

"That strikes me as a quick path to exposing a cover," said Waters.

"I agree, but we're not Beowulf Agate. I'll be in touch."

"Righto, Frank."

Sir Geoffrey glanced at his watch; once again he was late for dinner at home, so he called his wife, Gwyneth. "Sorry, old girl, got a bit tangled down here."

"Same problem, Geof, the one you can't discuss?"

"In a word, yes."

"Then stay as long as is necessary, my dear. Cook has

your dinner on a low oven. Use the pot holders to take out the tray."

"Thank you, Gwyn, and I am sorry."

"Don't be, Geof, just catch the bastards. Clive is a complete wreck, totally depressed. He's here with me now."

"I may be a bit longer—"

"Whatever, I have to take care of Clive. I'll put him in a guest bedroom."

Waters hung up the phone, thinking about where he might have dinner out, thus avoiding his whining brother-in-law at least until morning. He picked up his intercom phone and asked for his SIS guards, the most experienced patrols where assassination attempts were concerned. Don Carlo Paravacini's death sentence would not be tolerated.

The three paramilitary guards arrived, their camouflage dress abetted by the lethal automatic weapons strapped over their shoulders, their berets at the proper angle for total vision.

"Anytime you like, sir," said the leader of the unit, an immense man, whose large, muscular shoulders stretched the fabric of his uniform. "All roofs in the area have been secured. We're up to speed."

"Thank you. Frankly, I think that much of this is unnecessary, but others disagree."

"*We're* the others, sir," said the leader. "A man's life is threatened, no matter by whom, we're here to prevent that threat from being carried out."

"Again, my thanks. Would it be against the rules, however, to stop somewhere, say, Simpsons for dinner? My treat, of course."

"Sorry, sir. Our orders are to take you directly to your home, and wait there until we're relieved."

"I might prefer being shot," mumbled Sir Geoffrey.

"I beg your pardon, sir?"

"Nothing, nothing at all," said Waters, putting on his jacket. "All right, let's go."

The unit opened the right door of the MI-5 entrance on the first floor. Two SIS agents rushed out, instantly taking their positions on the right and the left, their weapons at the ready. The leader nodded to Waters; it was his cue to rush down to the waiting armored vehicle parked at the curb. He ran.

Suddenly, out of the darkness, a black limousine raced around the corner, its left rear windows open. The barrels of automatic weapons were shoved through the dark, open spaces and staccato bursts of gunfire filled the night. The first two SIS guards fell, their chests exploding with blood. The unit's leader crashed his body against Geoffrey Waters, propelling him down the short flight of steps until he was prone on the pavement behind the armored car. The action cost the SIS officer a shattered left shoulder when a semicircle of bullets lodged in his flesh and bone. He raised his right arm, his automatic in his hand, and fired repeatedly at the disappearing limousine. It was to no avail; his wounded shoulder prevented his left arm from supporting him. He collapsed, a part of his body covering Sir Geoffrey.

From inside MI-5 headquarters people rushed out at the sound of gunfire, all carrying weapons. Surveying the blood-drenched scene, a middle-aged officer issued his instructions quietly, firmly. "Call the police, order an ambulance—priority status—and alert Scotland Yard."

Slowly, with assistance, Geoffrey Waters stood up, breathless and trembling but still very much in control. "What's the count?" he asked no one in particular.

"Two SIS dead, the unit leader badly damaged, but we'll put a tourniquet on his left arm," replied the officer nearest in age to Waters.

"The *bastards*!" said Sir Geoffrey softly, in fury, as he pulled out his cellular telephone and touched the numbers of the hotel where Pryce and Montrose were billeted. "Room Six Hundred."

"Hello," said the voice of Cameron Pryce.

"Your Matarese tried to carry out Paravacini's death sentence on me a few minutes ago. The cost was two dead and one severely wounded."

"Jesus *Christ*!" roared Cam. "Are *you* all right?"

"A few bruises on this elderly body and a scratched face from the pavement, otherwise mobile and violently angry."

"I can understand. What can we do? Should we come over?"

"Not on your life!" exclaimed Waters. "The Matarese surely has scouts in the area to assess the damage, and no one knows you're here in London. Stay away!"

"Understood. What are you doing?"

"First, trying to get my thoughts together. Then, since the killers were in a limousine, a black limousine without any rear license plate that I could see, I'm going to tear into every limo rental service in London and its environs."

"It's a place to start, Geof, but it was probably stolen."

"We'll check the police records, naturally. You just stay incognito and incommunicado, except for me and Brandon."

"How's Scofield doing?"

"Very well; we'll fill you in later. In the meantime, he's racking up the largest room-service charges in the Savoy's history, except for several Arabian sheikhs with their multiple wives."

"You can always count on Bray. He has multiple talents."

The small hotel in New Jersey's "hunt country" was conveniently, if distantly, situated between a golf course a half mile down the road on the right, and riding stables a half mile up on the left. Each had memberships going back generations, and family pedigrees of new applicants were studied assiduously. Few ever passed, sons and daughters of members filling the ranks, as was deemed proper. The hotel itself was countrified-quaint, more traditionally New England than New Jersey. The exterior three stories were of white clapboard, the first-floor entrance flanked by colonial pillars below a sloping porch roof with the usual winged brass eagle over the door. Inside was a profusion of dark pine furniture and glistening brass lamps and small chandeliers. Along with the thickly carpeted lobby and the less-than-imposing, even casual, front desk, the small hotel exuded an air of regulated comfort. In the main, the guests seemed to confirm this. They were exclusively white, middle- to late-middle-aged, expensively dressed, and used to authority, both elected and inherited.

There was one addition to the hotel's staff, very much unappreciated by the management. However, since the request was routed through the Federal Bureau of Investigation, the correct authority, it amounted to a demand. On the day before the Matarese quartet arrived, a substitute operator appeared on the switchboard. All taps and calls from the four guests' accommodations were directed through her station, where a triple-layered taping device was kept operative. The woman was in her early forties, well-spoken and attractive, as befitted her environment, and her name was Mrs. Cordell.

She studied her equipment, checked every concealed tap, improving the locations where she felt improvement was needed, and went to bed early. There would be precious little sleep for the next two days, as the operation was considered so secret there could be no relief for Mrs. Cordell. She was the sole CIA agent-technician with instant communication to Deputy Director Frank Shields.

Morning came in New Jersey's hunt country, the fairways and the pastures glistening with the sun and the early dew, and the quartet arrived approximately thirty minutes apart. Cordell had no idea what each man looked like, as there were no television cameras on the entrance; however, their appearances did not concern her. She simply wanted to hear their voices, which would be placed on isometric recorders, sonically identified. The calls began, the first from Jamieson Fowler to the attorney Stuart Nichols's room.

> "Stu, it's Fowler. Let's meet in my place, say in twenty minutes, all right?"
> Kerwish. Voice recorded and identified.
> "Certainly, Jim. I'll call the others."
> Kerwish. Voice recorded and identified.
> "Yes?"
> "Stuart here, Ben. Jamieson's room in twenty minutes, okay?"
> "I may be a little late," replied the banker, Benjamin

Wahlburg. *"There's a transfer glitch between L.A., London, and Brussels. Some idiot punched in a wrong access. We'll catch it soon."*

"Hello?" said Albert Whitehead, CEO of Swanson and Schwartz.

"It's Stu, Al. Fowler wants us to get together at his place in about twenty minutes. I agreed."

"Don't be so quick to agree," interrupted the Wall Street broker harshly. *"Tell him I want an hour!"*

"Why, Al?"

"Let's say I don't trust any of these bastards."

"That's pretty severe, Al—"

"Everything's severe, Counselor! Get your goddamned head out of the law books and look at reality. Several pressure points are eroding, and I don't like it. Como doesn't respond and now Amsterdam is off-limits. What the hell's going on?"

"We don't know, Al, but that's no reason to alienate Fowler and Wahlburg."

"How do you know that, Stuart? We've got millions— no, billions—riding on the enterprise. A breakdown could cost us every cent we have!"

"Fowler and Wahlburg are on our side, Al. They're in as deep as we are. Don't antagonize them."

"All right, but don't give them the decision about timing. A specific time connotes authority, which I will not abdicate. Tell them I'll be there in forty-five minutes, more or less."

Kerwish.

Each voice was recorded on Mrs. Cordell's layered tapes. No matter who spoke on succeeding recordings, he would be instantly identified. Mrs. Cordell was now ready for her electronic surveillance of the Matarese quartet.

The preamble began at precisely 11:02 A.M. in Jamieson Fowler's suite. It was a preamble because the initial dialogue was harsh and contentious between three, not four, men. "Where the hell is Whitehead, Stuart?" Wahlburg said.

"He'll be here as soon as he can."

"What's keeping him?"

"A glitch, not unlike yours, Ben. Lack of communication over the final terms of a merger. He'll straighten it out soon."

"This is far, *far* more important than any goddamn merger!"

"He knows that as well as you do, Jamieson. However, losing your heads over a half hour won't solve anything. Nothing will be gained, only a loss of concentration where it's needed."

"Words! Fucking lawyer."

"Hey, Wahlburg, animus is not our friend right now."

"Sorry, Stu, but you know Whitehead better than any of us. Al plays his little games; he's a control freak."

"How can you leap from one telephone call to control freak?"

"Oh, shut up, both of you! Whitehead's a prick—always was, always will be."

"Now just hold it, Fowler," Stuart Nichols said. "Al's not only my client, he's my friend."

And so it went, back and forth among the trio for twenty-two minutes until Albert Whitehead arrived. By the tone of his voice, he was all contrition. "I'm terribly sorry, fellas, I really am. I had to get a neutral interpreter on my end of the call. Schweizerdeutsch is a hell of a language."

"Schweizerdeutsch," mumbled Fowler in disgust as he threw himself into an easy chair.

"You should try negotiating in it, Jamieson," said Whitehead, standing firm and looking down at the utilities executive. "It's good exercise for the mind."

"I don't exercise my mind over things I can't understand, Al. It's not very good business."

"No, I guess you don't, that's why you need people like us. Men who do exercise their minds, so you can get the financing you need for your mergers and buyouts."

"I'd get it with or without you—"

"Not actually, Fowler," interrupted Whitehead sharply. "Our organization, or enterprise, if you like—"

"Call us who we are, Al," broke in Jamieson Fowler curtly, "or does the name frighten you?"

"Not at all, I use it proudly. . . . The Matarese has specific rules in the funding of capital. Where tracing is possible, only certain channels can be employed, channels that are within the laws of the country of receivership. In the case of a very large transfer, with a firm like mine—usually, *only* my firm, as you well know—"

"Will you two *stop* playing 'who's king of the hill'?" An agitated Benjamin Wahlburg walked between Whitehead and Fowler, looking back and forth at each. "Put your egos back in the stables, we've got much bigger problems!"

The conversation, though no less contentious, zeroed in immediately on the issues. It began with Albert Whitehead's earlier question to his attorney, Stuart Nichols. "What the hell's going *on*?"

The answers came rapidly, on top of one another, and frequently in conflict. They ranged from blaming Amsterdam for a lack of controlling strength to possible defections of individual cells driven by greed and reluctant to give up their fiefdoms. They then considered the role Julian Guiderone was playing relative to the information Leonard Fredericks had supplied from London.

"Where is Guiderone now?" asked Albert Whitehead.

"He has a place somewhere in the east Mediterranean, I'm told," said Wahlburg. "It could be just a rumor, of course. No one seems to know where it is."

"I've a few connections in the intelligence community," added Nichols. "I'll see if they can help."

"Help you find a man who supposedly died twenty or thirty *years* ago?" Fowler grunted a derisive laugh.

"Jamieson," interrupted Whitehead, "you'd be astonished at the number of false deaths that occur, only to be followed by resurrections years later. In point of fact, the recent gossip on the street was that you were Jimmy Hoffa."

"*Funny* man." Fowler turned to Wahlburg. "Say Stu comes up with something, which isn't likely, what can Guiderone do?"

"The answer to that is, anything he likes. And I'd have no

problem flying over and talking to Julian. Regardless of his legend, he's a civilized man, as long as you're honest with him. The Dutchman may *talk* reasonably, but underneath the gloss, he's pathological."

"But what can he *do*?" asked Whitehead. "Jamieson's got a point, a valid one—"

"Why thank you, Al."

"I never said you were stupid, Jamieson, just limited by choice. This time you're not." Whitehead looked at the banker. "I repeat, Ben, what can Guiderone do, if he can even be found? *He* doesn't control Amsterdam."

"And Amsterdam's where the money comes from!" exclaimed the attorney, Nichols.

"Yes, of course, the money," agreed Wahlburg. "And where did that money come from? . . . Never mind, I'll answer that. From his grandfather, the Baron of Matarese's vast fortunes—plural—all over the world. And who is Julian Guiderone? Where does he come from? I'll answer that, too. He's the son of the Shepherd Boy, Nicholas Guiderone, anointed by the Baron to carry out his life's work, his dreams and ideals."

"What the hell are you driving at, Ben?" broke in Fowler. "Get to the point!"

"The point's a subtle one, Jim, but as powerful as all the money the grandson can get his hands on."

"I think you'd better explain that," said Stuart Nichols.

"It's as eternal as the prophets of the Old Testament and their followers, who considered the prophets' words sacred, holy."

"We can do without a Talmudic exercise, Ben," protested Whitehead. "We're dealing with here-and-now reality. Please be clearer."

"That's why it's so real," replied Wahlburg enigmatically. "It goes back to time immemorial. . . . Heaven knows your Jesus had no money, no wealth to spread around to convince people, but within decades after his death by crucifixion, before a half century, the Christian movement began spreading across the then-civilized world. And those converts held the wealth of that world."

"And?" pressed Nichols.

"His ideas, his prophecies—his dreams were accepted by those who believed in him. No money was exchanged."

"And?" roared a frustrated, impatient Fowler.

"Suppose one of the disciples, or even Jesus himself in a death confession, claimed that it was all a hoax? That the whole thing was an ego trip to divide the Jews. What would have happened?"

"Damned if I know!" replied an angry Whitehead.

"The Christian movement would have been at sea, the multitudes of converts lost, their collective commitment all for nothing—"

"For God's *sake,* Ben!" interrupted Fowler, furious and frozen in his chair. "What's all that shit got to do with *us*?"

"Al's partially right, Jim, you do limit your thinking."

"Just clarify, don't preach, you son of a bitch!"

"Exercise your imaginations, gentlemen," said Wahlburg, getting out of his chair and, like the banker he was, lecturing as if to a group of new MBA recruits. He spoke slowly, clearly. "It's both a confluence and a conflict between immediate financial resources and the channels of influence through which those resources must flow. Whereas the Dutchman, the grandson, operates in a vacuum of darkness, distant and unreachable, Julian Guiderone, the son of the anointed Shepherd Boy, travels throughout the world, checking and supporting the troops of the Matarese. Logically, one cannot operate without the other, but realistically, the troops, the converts, trust the one they see and know. Ultimately, influence wins over immediate finance, for no other reason than familiarity with the vision. The stock markets across the globe prove my point, both positively and negatively."

"What you're saying, then," said a pensive Albert Whitehead, "is that Guiderone can either keep everything together, saving our asses, or blow everything apart, and we lose the whole fucking enchilada."

"That's exactly what I'm saying. And don't for an instant think he doesn't know it."

"Find him!" yelled Jamieson Fowler. "Find this damn son of the Shepherd Boy!"

Fearing Bahrain to be dangerous, Julian Guiderone flew to Paris, letting Amsterdam know where he was and how long he expected to stay. As anticipated, Matareisen was cool, his message obvious: The fossil known as the son of the Shepherd Boy was no longer a man to be revered. So be it. The reverence would return later, when the young Turk realized that Amsterdam could not act alone.

It was late afternoon and the fashionable avenue Montaigne was crowded with traffic, in the main, taxies and limousines dropping off their business-executive fares at their elegant, canopied residences. Guiderone stood by a window, staring down at the street. These next few weeks, he mused, would be a preamble to chaos and a prelude to near-global control. Many scurrying out of automobiles in the avenue of wealth below would soon be facing the shocking loss of financial security. High positions would be terminated, boards of directors nullifying extravagant retirements and pensions, preferring to face the courts rather than plunge their corporations into further economic disaster.

Jan van der Meer Matareisen notwithstanding, everything remained on schedule. Van der Meer did not understand how profound was Shakespeare's line, "Between the acting of a dreadful thing and the first motion, all the interim is like a phantasma or a hideous dream." That phantasma, or hideous dream, had to be factored in, calculated, and ultimately rejected. For the "dreadful thing" had to remain constant, neither premature action nor procrastination acceptable. Instant and total coordination was paramount; it was the shock wave that would paralyze the industrial nations. It was that paralysis, however temporary—a few weeks or even a month—that was vital. It was sufficient for the legions of the Matarese to break out and fill the vacuums.

Matareisen had to learn that emotional doubts, however provocative, were intolerable. They were merely potholes in the great boulevard that led to the greater victory of the Matarese. Why couldn't the insolent bastard *see* that?

The telephone rang, startling Julian. No one but Amsterdam knew his number in Paris. No one except several extremely beautiful women who exchanged sexual favors for money or fine jewelry, and none of those knew he was here now. He walked to the table and picked up the phone.

"Yes?"

"It's Eagle, Mr. Guiderone."

"How the *hell* did you get this number? You're to contact only Amsterdam!"

"I got it *through* Amsterdam, sir."

"And what is so extraordinary that Amsterdam gave you this number?"

"I didn't fully explain, I think to your benefit."

"*What?* Not explain to the *Keizersgracht*?"

"Hear me out, sir. I told them—him—that I had to reach you on a matter that did not involve the enterprise. I am a loyal participant and he accepted my word."

"Readily, I suspect. I'm apparently no longer on his list of highest priorities."

"That would be stupid on Amsterdam's part, Mr. Guiderone," broke in Eagle in Washington. "You're the son of the Shepherd—"

"Yes, *yes!*" interrupted Julian. "Why did you contact me? What is so extraordinary?"

"There's a blanket inquiry throughout the intelligence community as to your whereabouts."

"That's *absurd*! Official Washington declared me dead years ago!"

"Someone thinks you're still alive."

"The pig of the *world*!" shouted Guiderone. *"Beowulf Agate!"*

"That would be Brandon Scofield, am I correct?"

"You're goddamned right. Where is he?"

"In London, sir."

"What happened to our *man* in London? He was under orders! Kill the son of a bitch!"

"We don't understand, and neither can Amsterdam. The man in London can't be reached."

"What are you *saying*?"

"It's as though he disappeared."

"What?"

"Every noninvasive avenue to him has been blocked. I've used every access we have here at Langley, all to no avail."

"What the hell is *happening*?"

"I wish I could tell you, Mr. Guiderone."

"It's the *pig* of the world, Eagle," said the son of the Shepherd Boy, his voice guttural. "He's in London and I'm in Paris, a half hour in the air from each other. Which of us will make the first move?"

"If it's you, sir, I'd be terribly cautious. He's guarded around the clock."

"That's his vulnerability, Eagle, because I'm not."

29

Brandon Scofield, in his Savoy robe, paced angrily in front of the windows overlooking the Thames River. Antonia remained at a room-service table, picking on a breakfast tray that she claimed would last her the rest of the week. Beyond the single central room of the minisuite, an armed three-man MI-5 unit patrolled the corridors, their weapons concealed under white floor-stewards' jackets. They were relieved by additional units timed to the schedules of the Savoy's actual employees, and thus were indistinguishable from them.

"Sir *Hog's Butt* has us caged like animals or the lepers of Molokai!" spat out Beowulf Agate. "And not even in a decent-sized suite."

"The larger suites have more entrances; Geof explained that. Why take the chance of diversion and access?"

"And *I* explained that more entrances mean more exits," countered Scofield. "Why eliminate them?"

"It's Geoffrey's call. We're his responsibility."

"And this horseshit that only he can call us but we can't call *him*?"

"Hotel switchboards keep a record of all outgoing telephone numbers for billing purposes, and he's not taking any more risks with cell phones because of scanners. At least not where you're concerned."

"To repeat, we're caged. We might as well be in jail!"

"I doubt that the room service is comparable, to say nothing of the accommodations, Bray."

"I don't like it. I was better than Hog's Butt twenty-some years ago, and I'm still better now."

"However, I trust you'll admit he's extremely good at what he does—"

"I'm better at covering my ass than he is," said Scofield like a pouting, overage adolescent. "There's such a thing as overcomplicating dark operations' security. Does he think the real floor stewards are blind, mute, and morons?"

"I'm sure he's considered that aspect."

A knock on the door sent Bray stalking across the room. "Yes, who is it?"

"Mrs. Downey . . . sir," was the hesitant reply. "Housekeeping."

"Oh, certainly." Scofield opened the door, somewhat startled to see an elderly woman whose tall, slender figure, erect posture, and chiseled aristocratic features hardly seemed compatible with the soft, light blue uniform of the Savoy's maid service, along with the mandatory vacuum cleaner and dust rags. "Come in," Bray added.

"Please don't get up," said Mrs. Downey, walking inside and addressing Antonia, who started to rise from the room-service table.

"No, really," replied Toni, "I couldn't eat another scrap. You may clear it all away."

"I may but I shan't. A steward will take care of it. . . . However, I shall introduce myself. For the time being, my name *is* Downey, Mrs. Dorothy Downey—a fine, solid name, I chose it myself—and I'm duly registered in the Savoy's employment records with splendid credentials, housekeeping division. That, I'm afraid, is absurd; I couldn't properly make a bed to the hotel's standards if my life depended upon it. In point of fact I'm a cryptographer, and at the moment I'm your sole contact with Sir Geoffrey Waters."

"I'll be goddamned—"

"Please, Bray. . . . And how do we reach you, Mrs. Downey?"

"Here's the number," said the MI-5 cryptographer, crossing to Antonia and handing her a small piece of paper. "Please commit to memory and burn it."

"We'll commit and burn after you detail the security of that number," countered Scofield testily.

"An excellent request. . . . It's a direct sterile line that bypasses the switchboard and goes to the small office the Savoy has provided me. I, in turn, have a direct sterile access to Sir Geoffrey Waters. Does that answer you, *sir*?"

"I trust my name is as sterile as your access."

"Bray! . . ."

The extraordinarily efficient "Mrs. Dorothy Downey, Housekeeping" proved to be a perpetual irritant to Scofield and superb at her job. Information flowed back and forth between Waters, Brandon, and Antonia, and Pryce and Leslie Montrose, who were ensconced incognito at the Blakes Hotel in Roland Gardens. Like pieces of a puzzle set in place by unseen hands, the outlines of the next phase of strategy began to emerge.

They would concentrate on Amsterdam, starting with the sparse information found in Myra Symond's flat, which would be reexamined and thoroughly studied. Then there was the equipment stolen from McDowell's office in Wichita and flown as cargo to Amsterdam. Thanks to a faceless executive at Atlantic Crown who felt he might be held responsible if he permitted the expensive items to be removed without an invoice, they knew the KLM flight number. There were airline personnel, ground and cargo crews to be questioned; someone had to know something, have seen something—the people who met the equipment, the vehicle or vehicles that carted it away.

The hunters were down to the stones and the pebbles, for Amsterdam was the key to the first door in Scofield's symbolic maze. It was time to open that door and see what was behind it. The materials were gathered together and fed into a single computer at MI-5. The results were not spectacular, neither were they useless. Correlations led to connections and associations; methods of transport narrowed the field of those who used them; hiring an international cargo aircraft with all the government clearances, inspections, and restrictions was not a task for even the average multimillionaire. They also included every canal that employed the letter *K,* regardless of its position; there were dozens, the hard *K*-sound emphatic in each.

"Get me a list of every resident on every one of them," said Sir Geoffrey to an aide.

"There'll be thousands, sir!"

"Yes, I expect there will be. Incidentally, include the basics, wherever you can. Income, employment, marital status, that'll be enough for starters."

"Good Lord, Sir Geoffrey, such a list could take weeks!"

"It shouldn't, and frankly, I'm not sure we have weeks. Who's our liaison to Dutch intelligence?"

"Alan Poole, Netherlands Division."

"Tell him to go to Situation Black and reach his man in Holland. Explain what we need using the cover of narcotics or diamond smuggling—whatever he's most comfortable with. Telephone companies keep billing records and divide cities into sectors. Our Dutch counterparts can easily gain access and we'll fly a courier over to pick up the material. As I say, it's a place to start."

"Very good, sir," said the aide, crossing to the door. "I'll speak to Poole right away."

The information from Dutch intelligence was voluminous. A team of six MI-5 analysts pored over the material for thirty-eight hours without a break, discarding the obvious noncandidates, retaining even the vaguely possible. The thousands were reduced to several hundred and the process started all over again. Dossiers and police records were gathered wherever they existed, banking practices scrutinized; companies, corporations, and other places of employment were analyzed for dubious transactions, and flight and ground crews at Amsterdam's Schiphol Airport interrogated by Dutch-speaking MI-5 officers regarding the cargo aircraft from Wichita, Kansas, U.S.A. This last provided curious information. According to the agent's notes, the following conversation took place between the MI-5 officer and the ground chief of the cargo crew.

> MI-5: *"You recall that flight?"*
> GC: *"I surely do. We were unloading cartons of unspecified technical equipment with no bills of lading, no breakdown . . . and no one shows up from customs. For God's sake, there could have been all sorts of contraband, even nuclear materials, but nobody with authority bothered to inspect the shipment."*
> *"Can you remember who claimed the shipment, who signed for it?"*
> *"That would be done inside the cargo hangar, at the release counter."*

The release-counter computers had no record of the flight from Wichita. It was as if the aircraft and its arrival did not exist. The MI-5 officer's notes continued during his interrogation of the customs personnel.

> MI-5: *"Who was on duty that night?"*
> Female on computer: *"Let me check. It was a slow night for cargo so most of the crew left early."*
> *"Who remained?"*
> *"According to this, a sub named Arnold Zelft covered."*
> *"A sub?"*
> *"We have a pool of substitutes, usually retired employees."*

"How can I find this Zelft?"

"I'll bring up the pool. . . . That's strange, he's not listed."

There was no Arnold Zelft in any telephone system, published or unpublished, in the Netherlands. He, too, did not exist.

All of the above data reduced the list of several hundred to sixty-three possibles. The reduction was based on dossiers, police records, company and corporate scrutinies, further financial revelations, and incidental information gathered from neighbors, friends, and enemies. The MI-5 analysts kept probing, essentially eliminating possibles based on disqualifying factors that took them out of the running. The names and residences were now down to sixteen, and individual around-the-clock surveillances were mounted.

Within forty-eight hours a number of strange incidents were reported by officers of the surveillance teams. Six couples on the *K* canals flew to Paris, staying at separate hotels but, as reported by the switchboards, keeping in touch with one another. Three husbands left on business trips, two joined in the evenings by women staying the night, one drinking copiously, to the point of unconsciousness after his meetings, only to be picked up by apparent strangers and to disappear in a speeding car out into the countryside. Was he drunk or was it an act?

The rest of the possibles were four couples, one elderly widow, and two unmarried men. Like the others, they were wealthy, influential to the point of having access to high, medium, and low government figures, and the sources of their vast incomes were complex and difficult to define. This was especially true of one of the two unmarried men, a Mr. Jan van der Meer, who lived in an old, elegant mansion on the Keizersgracht. The records described him as an international financier with undisclosed global holdings, the Dutch equivalent of a worldwide venture capitalist.

Breakthrough! Then *another*!

The first came by way of one of the Dutch-speaking MI-5

agents posing as a survey taker for a cosmetics firm. In casual conversations with van der Meer's closest neighbors, it was learned that limousines from a certain company arrived frequently at van der Meer's residence. When questioned, the limousine service denied any knowledge of a Jan van der Meer and had no record of such a person hiring its vehicles. A security-corporation search revealed that the limousine-rental agency was owned by a holding company named Argus Properties. It was one of van der Meer's vast array of business interests, and the deception, although perhaps explainable, was disturbing. Further scrutiny was demanded. Where would it lead?

The second breakthrough was part fluke, part cross-pollinating technology, and buried in the past. Also, it was so significant that it eliminated the necessity for further scrutiny. They had found the house on a *K* canal. Three-ten Keizersgracht, the "canal of the caesars."

A computer at Dutch intelligence picked up a glitch, which often signified a deletion in a past entry. The past in this instance was twenty-four years ago. A computer search was set in motion covering all government and court records going back until that deletion was discovered. Twenty-four years. It turned out to be the Amsterdam Civil Court, Division of Titles and Nomenclature. A second, physical search was mounted in the court's archives, the document unearthed and subjected to spectrographic X-rays. The glitch was found, the words restored.

A nineteen-year-old law student at the University of Utrecht had his name legally changed, or more precisely, altered, his true last name eliminated. From that date forward he was known as Jan van der Meer, no longer Jan van der Meer Matareisen.

Matareisen.

Dutch for *Matarese.*

The final piece of the maddening puzzle was in place.

Julian Guiderone registered under the name of Paravacini at London's Inn on the Park hotel. The better establishments knew the House of Paravacini to be among the wealthiest dynasties in Italy and worthy of their finest efforts. To fulfill the objective of his visit to England—simply put, the death of Brandon Alan Scofield, a.k.a. Beowulf Agate—Julian had to unearth the whereabouts of the Matarese's man in London, one Leonard Fredericks. Apparently, as their mole in Langley phrased it, "It's as though he's disappeared."

However, someone like Fredericks did not just disappear. He might create irrefutable explanations for temporary absences, but he would never vanish. Notwithstanding harsher realities, like his own execution, he was extraordinarily well paid for his services and, like many of his subterranean colleagues, maintained a covert lifestyle that might be the envy of a Saudi prince. Guiderone did not confine himself solely to Matarese conduits, though; he had his own sources and resources. One of these was Leonard Fredericks's wife, trapped in a dreadful marriage from which there was no escape. In the event she was being watched, they agreed to meet in the Islamic exhibition room at the Victoria and Albert Museum, the subject an established interest of hers.

"You know perfectly well that Leonard rarely tells me the details of his trips," said the matronly Marcia Fredericks as they sat on a marble bench in the museum. The exhibition room was half-filled with students and tourists, and Julian's eyes were on the entrance archway; he was prepared to get up and leave the woman at the first inkling of surveillance. "I presume he flew over to his Paris fleshpots, listed, of course, as some trumped-up economic study."

"Did he say when he was coming back?"

"Oh, he was quite specific—tomorrow, to be exact. As usual, I'm on call, which was why he was specific. I'm cooking a roast for a couple from the office."

"Considering the state of your wedded nonbliss, I'd say you were very kind."

"I'm very curious. He's been sleeping with the wife for the last two years."

"He does have nerve, doesn't he?"

"That he does, dearie. If a woman's breath can fog a mirror, he'll nail her."

"Listen to me, Marcia," said Guiderone. "I have to see Leonard, but he mustn't know that we met or that I'm even here in London."

"He won't hear it from me."

"Good. I'm staying at the Inn on the Park, under the name of Paravacini—"

"Yes, you've used that before," interrupted Mrs. Fredericks.

"It's convenient. The family's prominent, and they *are* friends. When Leonard returns, does he call you before coming home?"

"Of course. To give me orders."

"Reach me as soon as he does. He still drives from the office or the airport?"

"Naturally. He may find that he has detours to make, the horny bastard."

"I'll intercept him after your call. He may be late for dinner."

Marcia Fredericks turned slightly and looked imploringly at Julian. "When can I get *out,* Mr. G.? I have no life. I'm in a preconceived hell!"

"You know the rules. Never. . . . I'll amend that—certainly not now."

"But I *don't* know the rules! I just know there *are* rules because Leonard *says* there are, but I don't know what they are or why."

"You certainly understand that they're related to the excessive money your husband brings home—"

"Doesn't do a bloody thing for me!" interrupted the wife. "And I haven't the foggiest what he does to earn it."

Guiderone returned Marcia's gaze, their eyes locked. "No, I'm sure you don't, my dear," he said softly. "Hang in a while longer. Frequently things have a way of righting themselves. You'll do as I ask?"

"The Inn on the Park. Paravacini."

It was early evening on the outskirts of London; the street lamps in this residential section had been recently turned on. The row of neat, pleasant upper-middle-class homes was progressively distinguished by the succession of inside lights filling the windows. Darkness comes quickly in these quasi-suburban areas as the sun disappears rapidly, the close proximity of the houses prohibiting the dying rays from flooding the streets.

On this particular street a nondescript gray sedan was parked at the curb across from Leonard Fredericks's home. Inside, Julian Guiderone sat behind the wheel smoking a cigarette, his left arm slung over the passenger seat, his eyes on the rearview mirror. There they were. The headlights of a slowly moving car angling to the right, sliding into the opposing curb. Leonard Fredericks.

On the oft-confirmed premise that a startled man was verbally careless, Julian turned on the ignition and, timing his move with precision, swung the wheel, lurching the gray sedan directly into the path of the approaching vehicle. Slamming to a stop inches from the car's bonnet, the tires screeching, Guiderone sat immobile, waiting for the reaction. It came instantly as Fredericks leaped out of the driver's side, yelling.

"What the bloody hell do you think you're *doing*?" he roared.

"I think the question should be reversed, Leonard," replied Julian calmly, getting out of the gray car and staring at the Matarese's man-in-London. "What the bloody hell have *you* done?"

"Mr. Guiderone? . . . *Julian?* . . . What in heaven's name are you doing *here*?"

"To repeat, what have you done wherever you were, Leonard? No one's been able to find you; you've answered no sterile calls or coded messages. As Eagle put it, it's as though you had disappeared. That's all very disconcerting."

"Good God, certainly *you* don't have to be told!"

"Told what?"

"It's why I went on a short holiday . . . until things were clarified."

"Told *what,* Leonard?" asked Guiderone sharply.

"Amsterdam's off-limits! Jordan passed the word to me—from *you*."

"From me? . . ."

"Of course. He said you'd particularly appreciate my perceptions. He as much as admitted that he was your messenger."

"He did?"

"Certainly. He knew everything. The K-Gracht, Atlantic Crown, Swanson and Schwartz, even that talkative attorney, Stuart Nichols, as well as Wahlburg and Jamieson Fowler. He knew *everything*!"

"Calm down, Leonard. . . . Now this Jordan—"

"The American *banker,* Julian," interrupted the near-panicked Fredericks. "*Andrew* Jordan. Naturally, I checked his cover out; it was authentic, although, as you know, the complaint he filed with our office wasn't really. And I did as you told me—through Jordan, I explained to the Americans that they were to stay away from Amsterdam."

"Your sources?"

"Anonymous, precisely as you instructed."

"This Andrew Jordan, Leonard, would you describe him to me?"

"Describe him to *you*?" Fredericks was stunned, slipping over the edge.

"Not to worry," reassured Guiderone. "I just want to know if he did what I asked him to do, to change his appearance. After all, I was sending him into the enemy camp."

"Well, he was older than me, about your age, I'd judge. And yes, there was something odd about him. His clothes were a touch too casual for a prominent banker, if you know what I mean. But then, as you say, he was in the enemy camp—"

"The *pig* of the *world*!" spat out the son of the Shepherd Boy under his breath, his suspicion confirmed, his fury absolute.

"I beg your pardon?"

"Never mind. . . . Now, as to the business Amsterdam demanded of you—before it was 'off-limits'—namely, the killing of the American, Brandon Scofield. Did you make any progress?"

"Scant," answered Leonard Fredericks. "He's beyond

reach. The word is that he and his wife are under guard at one of the better hotels, the sort that cooperates with MI-Five. Way beyond reach, I'm afraid."

"Beyond *reach*?" said Julian, his voice ice-cold. "You idiot, you were with him for the better part of an hour! Who the hell do you think *Andrew Jordan* was?"

"That's impossible, Mr. Guiderone! He knew about the fireworks, the *Mediterranean* fireworks."

"Did he know, or did you tell him?"

"Well, it was mutually understood—"

"Get in my car, Leonard, we've other things to discuss."

"I really can't, Julian. Marcia and I are having company. She's cooked a roast—"

"Dinner can wait. Our business can't."

Leonard Fredericks did not return for dinner. When Mrs. Fredericks decided that the meal could no longer be postponed, she and her guests sat down to an excellent roast. What was even more to Marcia's liking, she received a telephone call. Taking it in the parlor, she heard these words.

"I'm afraid your husband has been unavoidably detained, my dear. Since his assignment is apparently confidential, there's no way to determine where or for how long he'll be gone. In the meantime, you've been cleared to have access to his accounts. Instructions will follow. . . . You're free, Marcia."

"I'll never forget you."

"Wrong, my dear. You must forget me. Completely."

Cameron Pryce lurched up from the bed at the harsh sound of the Blakes Hotel phone. He reached over for it on the bedside table, but not before Leslie Montrose sat up. "It's two o'clock in the morning," she mumbled, yawning. "This better be important."

"I'll find out. . . . Hello?"

"Sorry to disturb you, Cam, but I want to keep you up to speed," said Geoffrey Waters.

"Race ahead. What's happened?" asked Pryce anxiously.

"You know that we placed total surveillance on the Fredericks fellow—"

"Leonard Fredericks," interrupted Cameron, "the Matarese contact."

"Exactly. Our lads followed him to Paris, where he engaged in activities best left to the *Kama Sutra,* but otherwise nonproductive."

"You called to tell me that?"

"Hardly. The Paris unit phoned our man at Heathrow with his return flight this evening. The lad picked him up heading for his car and promptly lost him in that damned airport traffic. After driving all over the place checking the exit roads, he finally drove to Fredericks's house. His car was there but he wasn't."

"Was he sure of that?"

"Most definitely. To begin with, Mrs. Fredericks was genuinely stunned at the sight of her husband's car, then she asked our man in. He met a couple from the Foreign Office who told him Fredericks never showed, and there was an empty place setting to confirm it."

"Could the FO people be a setup, a mislead?"

"Highly unlikely, we checked them out. They're young and ambitious, not the sort to trifle in those ways, especially not when we're on the scene. We gather the wife's a bit of a flirt, but that's not an offense these days."

"Never has been. . . . You can kiss our contact good-bye, Geof, another Gerald Henshaw. He had dangerous pastimes and the Matarese plays hardball, as in rolled rocks."

"That's pretty much the conclusion I've reached. I'm sealing off his office; we'll tear it apart."

"Have a good time and keep me up to speed."

"How's Leslie?"

"She's an animal, what can I tell you?"

"Oh, shut up," said Leslie, falling back into the pillow.

When Julian Guiderone walked into the Savoy Court off the Strand, toward the hotel's cul-de-sac entrance, it was eight-twenty in the evening. The wide London street teemed with pedestrians and traffic in combat, the court itself was jammed with taxis, limousines, Jaguars, and two Rolls-Royces. The Savoy Theatre, the original home of Gilbert and Sullivan's D'Oyly Carte company, was flashing the marquee's lights, signifying that its newest production was approaching curtain time. Theatergoers tapped pipes against heels, crushed out cigarettes, and piled through the brass-framed doors. It was a typical night in busy London town.

Julian had been conferring with his sources, basically a disparate group of elderly men and women who had fallen upon hard times and whom he had befriended over his years in the U.K. He called them his small army of observers; none were really sure why they were looking for whatever it was he instructed them to look for, but they were grateful to do it, as he doled out generous bonuses and, frequently, new clothes to replace tattered ones. Apparel was important to this group; it was a remembrance of things past, such as proper employment and self-worth—dignity.

The son of the Shepherd Boy had studied the list of prominent hotels that had records of working with the British authorities; none could really be excluded. So Julian had his small army mill about all of them, looking for an individual or individuals who came around regularly at certain times, and might not appear to be guests, tourists, or part of the staff. Ever anxious to please their mysterious benefactor, the observers relayed numerous "observations," but one in particular caught Guiderone's attention.

A late-middle-aged woman, seen inside the Savoy hotel dressed in the uniform of a senior member of the staff, left every evening between a quarter to seven and eight o'clock, hardly a precise schedule for a working woman. Then, too, every time she emerged she was in an upscale outfit and was met by a waiting taxi in the Strand, not a bus or a spouse's very ordinary vehicle. And not the pattern of a working woman, but easily that of an MI-5 plant.

Julian's plan was laborious and time-consuming; it did not matter, he was after the pig of the world. He would go from floor to floor constantly looking for the unusual; it would be there in one manifestation or another. It had to be.

He found the aberration on the Thames side of the third floor. Whereas floor stewards scurried to various doors with trays and room-service tables, there were more stewards strolling around without trays or tables, their apparent concentration on a single door. Guiderone understood. The pig of the world and his sow wife!

His slight limp intensified by his anxiety, the son of the Shepherd Boy quickly gathered his thoughts, forming a strategy. He had to isolate that door, isolate those inside. He had stayed frequently at the Savoy and remembered the room-service routine. In addition to the service elevators descending to the massive kitchens below, each floor had a good-sized pantry where tea, coffee, hors d'oeuvres, and sandwiches could be prepared for quick deliveries. Casually, although now furious at his pronounced limp, Julian followed a tray-carrying steward and found the location of the Thames-side third-floor pantry. He then remained in the wide carpeted hallway, strolling about as if lost, and counted what he presumed to be the real floor stewards and those who were not.

They were equally divided: three and three, three who delivered, three who merely walked—patrolled, to be more precise. His strategy was evolving, and it would begin in the pantry. He returned to it, waited for a steward to emerge with a tray, and slipped inside. The third-floor kitchen was empty; it would not remain so for long. He checked several doors leading to various dry and fresh foodstuffs, and lastly a toilet. He locked himself in, switched on the light, and withdrew a .32-caliber pistol from his vest pocket and a silencer from his trousers. He attached the cylinder and waited until he heard the hallway door open and close. He stepped out, confronting a startled steward who dropped a silver tray on a counter. Guiderone fired his weapon, the muted spit killing the man. Rapidly, he dragged the body into the toilet and firmly closed the door.

Within moments a second steward arrived, this a strapping young man. At the sight of Julian's weapon, he lunged at the Matarese, hurling an ice bucket at Guiderone's head. It was too late. Two silenced shells sent two bullets into the steward's upper chest and throat, and the son of the Shepherd Boy pulled his second kill into the small lavatory.

The third victim mercifully never knew what happened. A gaunt elderly steward backed a room-service table into the pantry. Julian fired; the old man fell over the table, dead. Soon three corpses were layered on the toilet floor, their shining red blood flowing over the white tiles, and Guiderone prepared for his next encounters, three final steps to the pig who had turned his dreams into a lifelong nightmare.

He limped out into the corridor, turned the corner, and saw the first of the MI-5 guards standing by the elevator within sight of the pig's door. Assuming an air of bewilderment, Julian approached the man, pushed the elevator button, and spoke. "I'm afraid I'm totally confused," he said, half pleading. "I can't find Suite Eight-Zero-Seven."

"You won't on this floor, sir. This is the third floor."

"*Really?* Age dulls the eyesight as well as everything else. I could have sworn I pressed eight."

"No problem, sir, could happen to anybody." The elevator door opened.

"Young man, would you mind pressing number eight for me?"

"Not at all, sir." The guard walked into the elevator and pressed the button. As he did so, Guiderone raised his silenced pistol and pulled the trigger. The elevator door closed, the lift ascending to the eighth floor.

At that moment, a second guard appeared from around the corner of the hallway. It was obvious that he was looking for someone, concerned that he could not spot him. Julian limped toward him. "Excuse me, young fellow, but I'm not sure what to do. There was quite a scuffle here a moment ago. I was talking to a man there by the elevator, someone about your age, when suddenly the doors opened and two other men grabbed him and pulled him inside. He yelled and struggled but to no avail—they were savages. They took him downstairs—"

"*Rafe!*" roared the second MI-5 patrol as another guard appeared from behind one of the glass doors that intermittently divided the corridors. "Reach Downey, code *red*.

Interdiction! Cover while I go after Joseph. I'll use the stairs! Send backup; surround the hotel!"

The third MI-5 officer reached into his belt for his intercom. He was not in time. Guiderone rushed forward, his concealed weapon pulled from under his jacket. He slammed his body into the astonished guard, simultaneously firing, the muted spit further silenced by the man's flesh. The agent fell; the son of the Shepherd Boy instantly bent down and rifled the guard's pockets, knowing what he would find. The key for the suite of the pig of the world!

His leg in agony, Guiderone dragged his fifth kill to the edge of the staircase—staircases were rarely used—and propelled the body down the steps. He returned to the pig's door, his brain on fire. Twenty-five years, a quarter of a century, and vengeance was at last his! The end would come in minutes, the end of the nightmare. He could have been President of the *United States*! And one man had stood in his way. That pig would be dead before the clock struck ten. It was three minutes to ten. Silently, the son of the Shepherd Boy inserted the key.

What followed was a battle of the ancient giants, nothing less. Scofield sat in a chair facing the Thames, Antonia across from him reading the London *Times*. Brandon was writing on a legal pad, as was his wont, analyzing their options. A slight metallic scratch from the door! Barely audible, and Antonia remained oblivious. But in his former life, Beowulf Agate had lived with such indefinite sounds, muffled, minute, nearly inaudible. Often they had been the difference between concealment and discovery—life and death. He glanced over; the door knob was turning slowly, silently.

"*Toni!*" he whispered, "get into the bedroom and lock the door!"

"What, Bray? . . ."

"*Quickly!*" Bewildered, Antonia did as she was told as Scofield grabbed the pole of a heavy floor lamp. Yanking the plug out of the wall, he rose from his chair and gripped the lamp in midsection while walking swiftly to the offending door and stepping to the left of it. When opened, the panel would cover him.

It opened and the limping figure of a man rushed inside, a weapon in his hand. Bray swung the base of the lamp with all his considerable strength at the head of the intruder. The silenced pistol fired twice into the floor as the would-be killer, his skull covered with blood, spun around and fell back, staggering to stay upright. Scofield was stunned to the point of momentary immobility. *Julian Guiderone!* He *was* alive! Far older, the flesh of his face mottled, the face itself contorted, the fury in his eyes maniacal. The son of the Shepherd Boy.

Brandon recovered only an instant before Guiderone found his bearings and raised his weapon. He rammed the base of the floor lamp into the body of the Matarese, sending him back against the window. The blow served only to enrage him further, his pinched, blood-streaked features stretched into pure madness. Guiderone lunged forward, and Bray grabbed the wrist holding the silenced pistol, twisting it clockwise to break the grip. But it was no use. In his frenzy, the son of the Shepherd Boy had the strength of a man half his age and ten times stronger than that.

"Pig of the world!" screamed Guiderone, spit forming at his lips. *"Pig of the world!"*

"I thank you, Senator Appleton," replied Scofield breathlessly, holding back, as best as he could, the Matarese attack. "You wanted the White House, you bastard, and I wouldn't let you *have* it!"

"Augh!" screamed Guiderone, falling on an unbalanced Bray, and clawing at Scofield's face while Brandon held the weapon in his grip. They rolled over and over, crashing into furniture, then getting to their feet, two aging animals in a death struggle, the struggle for life. Glassed wall prints crashed to the floor, crystal vases fell, shattered. Move and countermove; they were the final moments of an epic battle. Brandon fought against the harsh, whipping blows until he was able to grip the cloth around Guiderone's rib cage while holding the weapon away. He spun him around, and with a strength he had not known was left in him, hurled him

toward the Savoy window with such force that the heavy glass splintered into thick fragments, impaling Guiderone's head, severing his throat.

Beowulf Agate collapsed to his knees, his body racked, gasping for breath.

30

"We *move*!" shouted Scofield. "It's got to be *now,* Geof!"

"I agree," added Cameron Pryce as the five of them, Leslie and Antonia included, gathered in the trashed Savoy suite. Guiderone's bloody corpse had been removed, along with the shattered glass and wrecked furniture, by military-intelligence personnel.

"I'm not against you chaps," said MI-5's Geoffrey Waters, "I just want to make certain we've thought everything out."

"I *have* thought everything out," insisted Beowulf Agate. "I know the Matarese, know the way it operates. Each cell is both independent and interdependent. They have certain autonomies, but all are under one global umbrella. You strike when the *umbrella* is vulnerable, when the fabric is torn, and believe me, it's ripped to shreds right now!"

"'Independent yet interdependent,'" broke in Sir Geoffrey. "Let's examine that."

"What's to examine?" asked Pryce. "Look at General Mills and Wheaties, Cheerios, and . . . whatever the hell they are. Different brands, one company."

"What do cereal boxes tell us, Cam?" said Leslie, sitting at a desk undamaged in the fray.

"Don't think of cereal boxes, think of snakes—snake pits, if you like. I said it before—we have to cut off the heads of the snakes, independent and interdependent. Guiderone was one of the two Matarese keys—"

"Scylla to Charybdis," interrupted Scofield.

"Very good, Bray," acknowledged Pryce. "With him gone, the other key is van der Meer in Amsterdam. We take him, isolate him, break him any way we can. We tear his house apart, do what Brandon did at Atlantic Crown. Maybe we'll learn something."

"In the meantime, the independents and the interdependents aren't receiving any instructions," added Scofield. "A number may panic, even going so far as to send emissaries to the Keizersgracht. Should that happen, we'll learn even more."

"Practicality," said Waters. "What's our best scenario?"

"For starters," replied Cameron, "don't involve Dutch intelligence. It's a great organization, but we can't risk Matarese penetration. Our silence mustn't be broken."

"A commando unit in civilian clothes," concluded Sir Geoffrey. "Our personnel, MI-Six, our foreign branch."

"I'll lead it," said Pryce. "Where's Luther Considine? With luck, our flying top gun will be putting in a lot of airtime. Also, Geof, alert Frank Shields in Washington. He may have to move fast on his quartet of snakes, putting them in separate sweat cells."

The night assault on 310 Keizersgracht was a marvel of clandestine operations. Electronic taps confirmed that Jan van der Meer Matareisen was in residence, his only guests two males, one on the first floor, the second on the third, presumably security guards. The architectural plans of the house had been dug out of the turn-of-the-century archives on the pretext of a potential buyer, a Dutch-speaking agent of MI-6. The same intelligence officer walked up to the front door facing the street while two colleagues, along with Pryce, approached the canal entrance, a steel egress within a dark brick archway.

The agent at the front door rang the bell; it was answered in less than ten seconds. A heavyset man stood in the frame. "Yes, what is it?" he asked in Dutch.

"I was instructed to make contact with Jan van der Meer this night, at this hour."

"On whose authority?"

"Four men in New York. Messrs. Whitehead, Wahlburg, Fowler, and Nichols. The circumstances are urgent. Please alert Mr. van der Meer."

"It is very late. He has retired."

"I suggest you inform him of my arrival, or you may be the one retired."

"I don't like threats—"

"It's not a threat, *meneer*. Merely a fact."

"Wait out there. I'm closing the door."

In the darkness of the canal side, the MI-6 commandos had placed two wired plastic disks on the thick, imposing windows flanking the steel door. They were electronic listening devices. In between them, Pryce removed a five-square-inch globule of a claylike substance; he began packing it around the lock and knob area of the door. When fired, it would burn through over an inch of steel.

"The guard's running upstairs," said the commando on the right softly.

"Confirmed," agreed his colleague on the left. "Burn away, mate."

"Which of you has the alarm deactivator?" asked Cameron.

"I do," answered the first commando. "According to the cleaning personnel, each exit has a panel box on the right of the door with a time span of twenty seconds. Mother's milk, old chap. I clamp our little friend over the digits, and he does the rest."

Pryce shoved an electronic torch into the packed globule. Instantly, the substance became a fiery red, then turned a blinding white as it burned, eating through the steel. When the sizzling stopped, Cam took an aerosol canister out of his field jacket and sprayed the burned metal; it turned black, cold. Using thin pincers, Pryce inserted a prong and pulled the jagged steel plate toward him; it fell to the ground. "Let's *go*!" he said.

The three men pushed the heavy door open; the first commando swung around and placed the deactivator over the alarm panel. There was a series of accelerating clicks and abruptly a small red light appeared on the deactivator's casing. "Our little impertinent friend has done his work," whispered the commando. "The place is neutralized. Not much light, is there? Not one bloody lamp in the whole ballroom—if that's what it is."

Footsteps. On the staircase. The guard who had rushed up the steps came racing down, now holding an automatic in his right hand. Pryce and his colleagues knelt in the shadows behind a grand piano, watching as the burly Matareisen employee ran to the door, opened it, and ordered the third commando to come inside.

"Hurry!" he cried. "And look well, I have a gun in my hand, and I'll use it if you do something I don't approve of."

"My business is not with you, *meneer,* so I wouldn't provoke either approval or disapproval from you."

"I think you know what I mean. Come, the great van der Meer is most upset. He'll want to see your credentials."

"He should know better. My credentials are in my head."

"You're insolent."

"He should know better," repeated the MI-6 agent, walking in front of the guard toward the staircase.

Cameron touched the shoulders of the two commandos flanking him. It was the silent signal. As one, and in thick-rubber-soled boots, they rose from behind the piano, inched forward, and as choreographed, Pryce hammerlocked the guard, removing his weapon while he spastically choked. The second MI-6 officer hauled the unconscious man across the wide room, pulled wire and industrial tape from his pockets.

"There's no one on the second floor," said Cam quietly to the other two. "And we can't waste a couple of heartbeats. Matareisen's waiting, no doubt positioning his number two guard. We go up the third flight back-to-back. Are your silencers attached?"

"They've never been unattached," replied the commando

who had used the street entrance. The third man of the assault team returned.

"He's out?" asked Pryce.

"For the duration and then some. I gave him a needle of juice in his neck."

"*Criminy,* you're a sadist—"

"Better that than bloody sorry."

"Shut up. Let's go!"

Starting with the third flight of steps, the unit formed a circle, back-to-back, and glided noiselessly up the staircase. Suddenly, the commando who had manipulated the alarm deactivator fired his weapon; a figure collapsed from out of a dark corner on the third-floor landing, the silenced bullet having found its mark, a skull shot that left no time for human sound.

"There's a door and I'll wager it's our host's."

"Why?" asked the needle-wielding commando.

"He was across from it."

"It works for me," whispered Cameron. "Team effort, fellas?"

"We're with you, sir."

"No 'sirs,' please. This is an equal-opportunity assignment. You know a hell of a lot more about this kind of thing than I do."

"I'd say you were holding your own, old boy. That was a nice hammer you executed."

Shoulders touching, like a human battering ram, the four raced forward. With a thundering crash, the heavy wooden door was literally exploded off its lock and hinges, the result of nearly a ton of sheer strength. A stunned Jan van der Meer Matareisen stood in the center of the room in a blue velvet smoking jacket, his legs encased in loose-fitting white silk pajamas.

"Good *God*!" he roared in Dutch.

And then he took the most improbable action imaginable under the circumstances. Before weapons could be drawn, he *attacked.* His less-than-imposing body instantly became a whirling dervish, legs, feet, and arms thrusting, kicking, and spinning like a dozen rotor blades. Within seconds he had immobilized two of the unprepared, unsuspecting commandos, who lay prone on the floor, trying to shake the agony and the numbness from their heads and spines. The third was squatting in a corner holding his throat.

Eyes on fire, van der Meer focused on Cameron. "You're fortunate, American, I don't really need a gun, or else you'd be dead by now!" he spat out.

"You're good, I'll say that for you."

"More terrible than your worst nightmares, Mr. Pryce."

"You know who I am?"

"We've been tracking you since—what is it called? Brass Twenty-six?"

"The gunboat. The Harrier jet. You killed a lot of fine young men who were simply doing their jobs."

"Too bad you survived the Harrier. You won't *now*!" With these words shrieked and echoing off the walls, Matareisen again became a dervish, the propellers closing in on Cameron. He reached for the weapon in his webbed belt; the instant it was in his hand it flew out, the result of an accurate, brutalizing kick. Pryce recovered from the blow, took a step backward, planted his left foot, and zeroed in on van der Meer's right leg. The kick came; he grabbed the silk, digging his fingers into the flesh beneath, and violently twisted the muscular limb counterclockwise. Matareisen's body, its balance momentarily lost, pivoted in midair as Cam lunged forward, propelling the Dutchman into the wall. A sickening thud accompanied the Hollander's impact, his head taking the punishment, rendering him unconscious. He lay on the floor in a fetal position, a champion of the martial arts reduced to his former unimposing self.

One by one, the commandos revived, bruised but game. "What the hell was *that*?" cried the front-entrance MI-6 officer, staggering to his feet.

"An army of ninjas, if you ask me," replied the alarm expert.

"A bloody maniac in fancy dress," said the agent of needles. "I think I'd better give him a little juice."

"It's safe, isn't it?" asked Pryce. "Too much of that stuff can mess up the head, and we want his intact."

"You just did more to his head than my sweeteners could do with ten syringes."

"Okay, go ahead." Cameron reached into his field jacket and removed a rolled-up set of plans. They were from the early-twentieth-century archives and rendered the architectural details of the house on the Keizersgracht. As the agent administered the needle to Matareisen, Pryce walked out to the hallway landing, followed by the other two. "According to these," he said, "there's a floor above this one, but the staircase ends here."

"You can tell that from the outside," added the alarm deactivator. "There are window frames on the top."

"How do we get up there?" posed the second intelligence officer.

"Probably the elevator, which is undoubtedly programmed," said Cameron, crossing to the locked, brass-grilled elevator shaft. "It's obviously off-limits. That's a false ceiling up there. See the slits? It's movable."

"Why don't we bring up the lift?"

"Why not?" answered Pryce. "We can work from inside, try to break through."

"Easier than falling down three flights in the shaft. We've got tools in the canal boat, should I get them?"

"Please."

A sweat-producing hour later, using battery-driven drills and saws, Pryce and the unit removed the false ceiling. Hand over hand, foot by foot, they scaled the vertically ribbed shaft to the steel door on the top floor. Once again employing a claylike globule packed and fired around the release area, they slid back the steel panel and pulled themselves up and out onto the off-limits fourth floor. What they saw astonished each man.

"It's a ruddy communications center!" exclaimed the alarm expert.

"Like in a nuclear headquarters," said the stunned deliverer of sweeteners.

"It's goddamned scary!" intoned the third commando. "Look at that, the whole wall is a map of the world!"

"Welcome to the inner sanctum of the Matarese," said Cameron softly, breathlessly.

"The what?"

"Never mind. It's what we came for." Pryce took out his powerful military walkie-talkie, tuned in to Luther Considine and Montrose in the Bristol Freighter aircraft at Schiphol Airport. "Luther?"

"What's up, spook?"

"Pay dirt with bonuses."

"That's nice to hear. Can I go home now?"

"You've only just begun, my man. Right now we need Leslie. Tell the Brit patrol to bring her to the target area. Three-ten Keizersgracht, street entrance, unmarked vehicle."

"She's asleep."

"Wake her up."

Lieutenant Colonel Leslie Montrose was, if possible, more astonished than Pryce and the commandos, for she understood the scope of what she was examining. She walked up the aisle between the sets of computers to the elevated console in the center. "These aren't merely world-class, they're world-class-*plus*. Direct satellite transmissions, traffic scramblers, instantaneous alternate routings—good Lord, this whole setup rivals anything at the Strategic Air Command or Langley. It must have cost millions, and considering what's exclusively designed for them in space, probably billions."

"That means a mountain of complexities, right?"

"Several mountains, Cam."

"To make progress in pulling up whatever's in this equipment, you'll need help, also right?"

"All I can get and as quickly as possible."

"Any suggestions?"

"One or two maybe. . . . Aaron Greenwald in Silicon Valley. He's the creative brains behind several major companies, consultant status. Then there's Pierre Campion in Paris. Not well known but he's a wizard, way ahead of the times."

"Do you know them?"

"They were part of the tutorial teams recruited by G-Two. They might remember me, but no guarantees."

"They'll remember you now. Any others?"

"Check with the Army, they were brought in relays."

"Which meant all had maximum-security clearance."

"Most definitely."

Frank Shields went to work in Washington while Geoffrey Waters reached the Deuxième Bureau in Paris. Forty-eight hours passed as Colonel Montrose explored the various computers in the Matarese's communications center. On the morning of the third day, seven of the finest minds in computer science were gathered in London and flown to Amsterdam by Luther Considine. The house on the Keizersgracht had been sealed off, patrolled by a new unit of British MI-6 in civilian clothes. The commandos had returned to the U.K.; van der Meer's residence was now occupied by Cameron, Leslie, the seven computer brains, and a small domestic staff of four, all English and fluent in Dutch.

When one of the former executives who manned the Matarese computers called to speak with *Meneer* van der Meer, he was told that the owner was out of the country on business. Knowing the current circumstances, the man was suspicious. He drove over and saw the bustling activity. He phoned his colleagues.

Stay away from the Keizersgracht. Something's happened!

It was apparent from the first meeting in the downstairs drawing room that the Californian Aaron Greenwald would be the group leader of the computer specialists. He was a slender man, bordering on the gaunt, in his early forties, with a pleasant face and a soft, compelling voice. If there was any hint of brilliance, it was in his eyes. There was a gentleness about them but they were also penetrating, leveled completely on whomever he was addressing, his concentration total. It was as though he were peeling away layers, seeing and understanding things in the other person that someone else might miss. The group was made up of five men, two women, and, of course, Leslie Montrose.

Rooms were assigned, luggage unpacked, and preliminary schedules drawn up. They gathered in the downstairs drawing room and Greenwald spoke.

"We'll take each machine into the progressions from alpha through omega, utilizing all the variations we can create, logging every entry and invasion. I've prepared identical charts with suggestions, but they're only suggestions. Please don't feel constricted by them—it's your inventiveness that's paramount, certainly not mine. Incidentally, we've unscrambled the elevator and wired a top-floor access. Remember, no more than three people per trip. Finally, for maximum efficiency in the workloads, the day and night schedules are posted on the bulletin board in the upstairs dining room."

The labors began, and they *were* labors. Grueling, frustrating, exhausting, and around the clock, for no one wanted to leave the team effort. Schedules went out the proverbial window; sleep came when it *had* to come, meals taken only when hunger pangs interfered with thought and invention. The specialists would temporarily leave their machines and hover over others, encouraging them when near-access progressions were pulled up. There was a growing sense of urgency as each particle of information was revealed, leading to explosive possibilities. But there was far too much that was not revealed, that remained elusive, beyond reach.

"There has to be a commonality," insisted Greenwald from the elevated console. "Or at least a partial, a similar pre-access applicable to all."

"Like an area code, Aaron?" asked Leslie, seated below and to the left of the Californian.

"Yes, an identifying series of symbols branching off to the individual equipment. For efficiency as well as a kind of banner or herald."

"That's certainly consistent with this whole setup," said Pryce, standing by Greenwald, watching his fingers roam over the keyboard. "A powerful ego's behind it all."

"His name is Matareisen, of course," said Aaron, his tone distasteful. "Is Sir Geoffrey making any progress with him in London?"

"No, and it's driving him up the wall. That guy is as impenetrable as Gibraltar. They've tried every serum from the Pentothal to the old scopolamine and nothing works. He's got the mind-set of a robot. He's beaten, but Waters says he acts as if he'd won. They keep him in a lighted cell and won't let him sleep, with minimal food and water . . . nothing fazes him. He's got the constitution of a bull."

"He'll either waste away or break," said Greenwald. "Let us pray it's the latter and in time."

"Why do you say that?"

"Again and again I'm putting up a time frame. Whatever's going to happen is precisely scheduled and widespread."

"And we haven't a clue what it is. The only fragment we've got—Scofield got—is something about 'fires in the Mediterranean.'"

"So it's back to alpha through omega, themes and multiple variations," said Aaron Greenwald, leaning back in his swivel chair, stretching briefly, then pushing forward, hands and fingers flying.

Breakthrough!

It came at 3:51 in the morning of the fourth day. The specialist from Paris, Pierre Campion, burst into Greenwald's room, where the exhausted group leader had retired less than a half hour before.

"*Aaron,* Aaron, wake up, *mon ami!*" cried the Frenchman. "I think we've done it!"

"What . . . *what*?" Greenwald shot up, instantly throwing his long legs over the side of the bed. He was still dressed in his rumpled clothes, his wide, gentle eyes red from fatigue. "When? *How?*"

"Only minutes ago. It was an algebraic combination of your early projections—equations, Aaron! Come, Cameron and Leslie are there with two others. We don't want—don't dare—proceed without you."

"Let me splash some water on my face, then perhaps I can focus. Where are my glasses?"

"You're wearing them."

Upstairs in the vast communications center, the five experts and an outclassed Pryce converged on the elevated console that Campion had taken over from Greenwald. "The *M* and the *B* symbols are factored into a progression that equates them by division," said Aaron pensively.

"The Baron of Matarese," explained Cameron, "the giant and the source of everything they have. He's never far from Matareisen's mind. It's an obsession he has to follow."

"Let's proceed—very cautiously," said Greenwald. "We'll lock in what we have and play with the equation, possibly geometrically, I suspect."

"Really?" asked Campion. "Why?"

"Because cubes and fourth or fifth powers would not be logical. Illogical logic could be the basis of the Matarese's codes."

"You're beyond me, Aaron," said Pryce.

"I'm beyond myself, Cam. I'm fishing."

Twenty-six minutes later, as Greenwald's fingers rapidly accelerated over the keyboard, suddenly the multicolored map of the world on the wall became alive. Scores of flashing red lights appeared to explode all over the place. It was as if the huge map had taken on a life of its own, riveting attention, refusing to be denied. It was frightening, its power hypnotic.

"Good *Lord*!" whispered Leslie, staring at the startling display as Campion and the others took several steps forward in disbelief.

"What is it, Aaron?" said Pryce.

"My guess is that whatever's going to happen will take place in those pulsating centers. . . . We're getting closer. Somewhere in these machines are the answers."

"Keep fishing, please."

"Printout!" shouted Campion, who had returned to his computer. The announcement was as electrifying as it was unexpected. *"Mon Dieu,* the print is self-induced, I did *nothing*!"

"A release trip, Pierre," said Greenwald. "You reached an inload threshold and tripped the printer. For God's sake, what's the data?"

" 'Sector Twenty-six,' " began the Frenchman haltingly, leaning over and reading the printout as it rolled out. " 'Phase One commences. Estimated foreclosures, bankruptcies, suspensions of activity: within thirty business days, forty-one thousand.' "

"Any indication which sector is number twenty-six?"

"I think it's on the map," answered Lieutenant Colonel Montrose, pointing at the illuminated wall. "Of the flashing lights, there's one with a bluish glow on the West Coast of the United States."

"She's right," said Cameron. "It's in the Los Angeles area."

"Any hint as to the date, Pierre?"

"More than a hint. Two weeks and five days from now."

"Wake up the rest of the group!" ordered Greenwald, addressing the two other specialists. "Leslie, you and Pierre go to each machine inserting his codes, everything he's logged. When you've finished I'll cross force-feed."

"You'll *what*?" asked Pryce.

"Vernacular for selectively connecting the equipment. It's really quite simple, if rarely done. Using a master cable, you attach the modems to a central base." Aaron went on to explain that since they had the partial codes, they might save time by interconnecting, in essence locking in additional machines.

A sense of urgency grew quickly as the entire group worked furiously. It was heightened when at first two and three printers became operational, then a few more, and finally the majority were spewing out reams of paper. The hours passed and fatigue turned into euphoria. Had they unlocked the secrets of the Matarese?

At ten minutes past noon, Aaron Greenwald rose from the elevated console and spoke. "Listen up, everybody— quiet, please, and listen. At this juncture, we have more material than we can possibly absorb, but we've got to begin absorbing a large portion of it. I suggest we gather up what we have, collate by source, remove our stiff, bent-over bodies from these savage chairs, and . . . start reading again!"

By three-thirty in the afternoon, nearly twelve hours after the initial breakthrough, the mountain of printouts had been perused, and the group of specialists gathered in the first-floor drawing room for their collective appraisal.

"It is both terrifying and yet tragically incomplete," began Pierre Campion. "A catastrophic financial tidal wave will roll across the industrial nations. Literally millions upon millions of jobs will be lost as companies and corporations collapse."

"It'll make the depression of the late twenties and thirties look like a minor ripple," said an American specialist.

"The problem is that we have no hard specifics," added another.

"But we have *hints,* ladies and gentlemen," pressed Greenwald. "They're in the words! Such as 'media'—newspapers, television; 'consolidating grids'—utilities, power companies; 'act tables'—easily translated as actuarial tables: insurance companies and their derivatives in health care. There are others also, among them quite prominently 'transfers,' 'rollovers.' '*Transfers,*' boys and girls . . . *banks.* Any operation of this magnitude has to involve massive sums of capital unknown in the annals of economics."

"We know a number of the banks that have merged or consolidated," said Pryce. "They're transnational."

"And we've all read about the health organizations that are gobbling up one another," offered Leslie. "Profits first, patients somewhere down the road."

"Certainly, we're aware of many such events," added the Frenchman, Campion, "but our problem is that there are no specific identifications in the voluminous material we've read."

"We must bear in mind," said yet another American, "that the Matarese are not fools—avaricious psychopaths on a global scale, yes, but not fools. They've been at this for a long time, and on the surface we have to assume they have stayed within legal guidelines."

"Naturally," agreed Aaron, "'on the surface' being the operative phrase. So we can't challenge the obvious because, as Pierre says, we *don't* have specifics—"

"No, we don't," interrupted Cameron angrily, "but we have something else and it's enough to work on *now*! We know for certain that the four caballeros Frank Shields has under surveillance are Matarese down to their socks. We'll start with them, *I'll* start with them!"

"By yourself?" Leslie Montrose shot forward in her chair, glaring at Pryce.

"I've done it before. Penetrate and pit individuals against one another. Of all the dumb games in the stupid business, this one has the highest rate of success. Besides, we don't have time for anything else. For Christ's sake, you heard Campion. Two weeks and five days!"

"But you *alone*?" protested Greenwald.

"Slight exaggeration," said Cam. "I'll convince Shields to provide me with all the wizardry we've got, along with a couple of bodies."

"That means you'll be going to the States—"

"As fast as I can, Aaron. Waters will get me there, and I want Luther with me in case there's some fast, quiet flying— no leakable personnel or official requisitions, please."

"I'm going with you, Officer Pryce," said Leslie.

"I figured I'd hear that."

"And we'll keep at it here," said Greenwald. "Please set up instant communications between us so we can feed you whatever additional information we retrieve."

"It's as good as done." Pryce reached into his jacket and pulled out his radio. "Luther, get the bird ready to go. We'll be down there in twenty minutes."

The RAF supersonic jet landed at Dulles International Airport at 7:05 P.M., eastern standard time. An unmarked CIA vehicle took Pryce, Montrose, and Considine to Langley where Frank Shields waited for them in his office. Greetings exchanged and Luther introduced, Frank outlined his proposed scenario.

"Commander Considine—"

"You jumped me one, but Luther's fine, sir."

"Thank you. Luther, we've appropriated a Rockwell jet; it's on a private field in Virginia, less than forty minutes from Washington. Does that meet with your approval?"

"Sure. It's good equipment, depending on the air miles required."

"At the moment, that's not a problem. Jamieson Fowler commutes between Boston, Maryland, and Florida; Stuart Nichols and Albert Whitehead are in New York; and Benjamin Wahlburg is in Philadelphia. No flight is over three and a half hours, including Florida."

"Then there's no problem. May I inspect the aircraft and its security in the morning?"

"We'll all inspect it, Luther. I want to get to New York," interrupted Cameron.

"What do *you* know, spook?"

"I know I want to get to New York."

"Then hear me out before you go off half-cocked," said Shields firmly. "According to Geoffrey Waters, you want to corner Whitehead and the others on a one-to-one basis, correct?"

"Yes. One to one, and one by one."

"We've established that Whitehead leaves his office between five-forty-five and six o'clock each evening, and employs a single limousine service. He makes one stop before going home to his apartment on Fifth Avenue. It's to a bar in Rockefeller Center called Templars. The management reserves a banquette for him. He has exactly two vodka martinis and returns to the waiting car."

"That's very precise."

"That's not all. We've recruited the limo service, very sub rosa, and the driver on the day you choose will be one of our people. Make your contact at the bar, doing whatever you have to do, and escort him back to the car. Can you do that?"

"In spades, aces high."

"I want to go with him," broke in Montrose. "These people are killers and, as I'm sure you're aware, I'm an expert in weapons."

"That's not necessary, Leslie—"

"Yes, it *is*! You made it necessary, my dear."

"No comment," said the deputy director. "We'll position you in a nearby booth."

"What about me?" asked Considine. "Someone should watch their flanks, that's what we do in the air."

"Come *on,* Luther! It'll look like I'm covered, and the driver's one of us."

"Your call, spook, but I'm from the streets, remember? Substitutes can be hired."

"You're overanticipating, my man."

"I happen to agree with Cameron," said Shields. "But if it'll make you feel better, you'll be across the room, all right?"

"I'll feel better," replied the pilot.

"So, Cam, when you're in the car you can talk as long as you like, order the driver to wherever you want to gain time. It'll unnerve our broker that you have control."

"So much for Whitehead. What about Nichols?"

"The next morning. He stops at his club for a thirty-minute workout. It's on Twenty-second Street, and he gets there around seven-fifteen. We've arranged for you to be in the steam room, which Nichols uses after his exercises—"

"Nice touch," Pryce broke in. "How can we be sure that I'll be alone with him?"

"A trainer will take care of that. At that hour it shouldn't be difficult. You'll be inside and once he admits Nichols, he'll stay by the door, telling anybody who shows up that the room is temporarily out of order."

"What explanation did you give him?" asked a concerned Leslie.

"None, Colonel. He's one of us. . . . Now, considering the time change you've experienced, the three of you better get some rest, preferably a good night's sleep. You're in a motel not far from here, it's nearest the private field. Our car will take you there and pick you up in the morning, say eight o'clock?"

"How about seven?" said Pryce.

"Whatever you say."

"I assume we'll be staying at your own private hotel in New York. Bray said it was the Marble something-or-other."

"Wherever we can save the taxpayers' money, we do our best."

"Scofield told me the room service was outstanding."

"He would. He abused it."

31

The flight to New York was uneventful, the traffic in Manhattan horrendous. They had been met at La Guardia Airport by a CIA case officer who drove them to the Hotel Marblethorpe. They used the side entrance and settled into the same suite Scofield and Antonia had occupied when Brandon held his "interviews" with the possible conduits to the Matarese. Luther Considine went into the guest bedroom, Cameron and Leslie into the master; unpacking was rapid, and they emerged as the CIA agent came up for a planning session. His name was Scott Walker, and he looked more like a lean, erect military officer than a member of Central Intelligence. He spoke.

"I'm on a tight need-to-know basis and Director Shields made it plain that the less I knew the better. I'm only here to assist, not actively participate unless an emergency arises."

"Fair enough," said Pryce. "Have you been given the itinerary?"

"Templars bar at Rockefeller Center this evening by six P.M. Each of you will enter separately and sit where you've been instructed. Those seats will be occupied, but when you say the words, 'Oh, I thought I reserved this table,' our people will vacate with apologies."

"I go in last?" asked Cam.

"No, sir, you go in first. When you're all inside, I'll be outside watching the door from the next corridor." Here Walker reached into his vest pocket. "Incidentally, Shields gave me these two photographs. The first is the man you're meeting tonight; the second, the one you're seeing tomorrow morning. I'm afraid I can't leave the photos with you; they can't be on your person. So please study and commit."

"How many times have I heard those words—"

"I'm sure you have, sir. The deputy director allowed that you were top-flight."

"I haven't heard that one—those two. . . . Will you be following me when I get our illustrious Mr.—"

"No names, sir!"

"Sorry. When I get the target into the limousine?"

"Not necessary. Our colleague is your driver and he knows what to do should any problems come up."

"That's comforting," said Montrose. "I think."

The rest of the day was spent with Leslie resting, jet lag catching up with her; Cameron writing on a legal pad, summarizing his thoughts about the meeting with Albert Whitehead; and Luther monopolizing the phone, talking to his girlfriend, the commander, in Pensacola. At four o'clock they ordered an early dinner; no one was sure when he would eat next. At five-fifteen, Scott Walker phoned from the CIA vehicle at the side entrance. It was time to leave for the Templars bar in Rockefeller Center.

Seated in their appointed locations, Pryce at the crowded bar, Luther and Leslie acknowledged each other with mutual glances and slightly nodding heads. At twelve minutes past six, Albert Whitehead walked through Templars' double doors and headed straight for the banquette with a reserved sign on the table. Luther caught Cameron's eye; he nodded as Pryce unobtrusively glanced at the banquette and Whitehead. He acknowledged Considine's message, rose from the bar, and crossed to the broker's table, startling Whitehead as he slid into the small booth.

"I *beg* your pardon," said the offended financial arm of the Matarese. "Can't you see this table is reserved?"

"I don't think you want it to be," replied Cameron softly. "I'm from Amsterdam, ordered by the son of the Shepherd Boy to reach you."

"What?"

"Don't have cardiac arrest, we've got enough problems. You're swimming with sharks."

"Who *are* you?"

"I just told you, I'm from Amsterdam, a courier, if you like. Finish your drink casually—a vodka martini, isn't it. That's what Mr. G. said."

"I haven't the vaguest idea what you're talking about," mumbled the frightened Whitehead.

"You haven't the vaguest idea what's happened. Or whom you're dealing with. Do you have a car outside?"

"Of course."

"Is it secure?"

"Absolutely. I close the chauffeur's partition and we can't be heard. . . . Why am I *talking*? Who the hell *are* you?"

"Let's not go through that again," said Pryce wearily. "I'm here because you need me, not because I want to be."

"Why do I need *you*?" choked the broker, half whispering. "What did you mean, I'm 'swimming with sharks'?"

"A few have fallback positions in case of unforeseen difficulties, surely you're aware of that."

"No, I'm not. We can't fail!"

"We don't expect to. Nevertheless . . ."

"Nevertheless *nothing*. Spell it out!"

"In the event anything short-circuits, your attorney, Nichols, has sheltered himself. Word is that he's filed a deposition under a court seal that he was kept in the dark about your funneling our money."

"I don't believe you!"

"Mr. Guiderone has sources beyond any we possess. It's true. He wants you to keep your distance from Nichols and when you receive instructions, which you will soon, don't relay them to him."

"This is all unbelievable—"

"Believe," said Cameron. "Come on, I'm not comfortable talking here. Let's go out to your car. Shall I get the check?"

"No . . . no. They put everything on my tab." Again, the stunned Whitehead could only mumble.

When they were out on the street, Pryce walked over and

opened the door of the limousine for the broker. "You knew the car," said Whitehead, staring at him.

"Yes, I did." Cam followed the broker into the backseat, leaned forward, and spoke to the CIA agent behind the wheel. "Drive us around Central Park, I'll tell you when to get back on Fifth Avenue. And raise the partition, please."

"The driver," said Albert Whitehead, his eyes wide, glazed. "I don't know him, he's not one of *my* drivers."

"The son of the Shepherd Boy is not only precise, he plans ahead."

By the time the broker reached his Fifth Avenue apartment, he was a wreck. His head was spinning; he was nauseated, his analytical mind—primarily concerned with figures and financial stratagems—was filled with an onslaught of information that had nothing to do with figures and strategies. It had to do with power grabs in Amsterdam, betrayals at the top of the enterprise, conceivable defections of warring cells—above all, with fear. Pure, raw *fear*. It was a storm of negative abstractions, no clean lines of mathematical precision. Stuart Nichols, his lawyer and right-hand man for years, a *traitor*? To *him*?

How many others were there? How many Matarese cells had he illegally furnished with money? Would any of them turn on him? If so, who were they? Some had implied that he skimmed funds from them . . . well, there were certain expenses that went with the transactions. Would those ingrates expose him in case of "unforeseen difficulties"?

Albert Whitehead felt positively ill. Years ago he had marched happily into a sea of great wealth. Now he wondered if he was drowning in it.

Draped in a towel, Pryce sat in a corner of the mist-filled steam bath. There was a single tap on the glass door; it was the signal. The next figure who walked in would be Stuart Nichols, first vice president of Swanson and Schwartz, brokerage firm, and for all intents and purposes, a Matarese attorney. The man walked in, similarly covered, and sat on the slatted bench across from Cameron. Neither could clearly see the other, and that was fine with Pryce. The words would be more emphatic. After a minute passed, Cam spoke.

"Hello, Counselor."

"What? Who's that?"

"My name doesn't matter, my speaking with you does. We're alone."

"I'm not in the habit of speaking with unidentified strangers in the steam room of my club."

"There's always a first time for everything, isn't there?"

"Not this." Nichols rose from the bench.

"I'm from Amsterdam," said Cameron quietly but curtly.

"What?"

"Sit down, Counselor. It's to your benefit that you do, and if you won't take my word for it, take that of Julian Guiderone."

"Guiderone? . . ." Through the layers of mist, the lawyer moved back to the bench.

"It's kind of a password, isn't it? The name of a man presumed dead for years. Remarkable. I mean, the fact that anyone should use it."

"You've made your point, *up* to a point. I want more. What happened to Amsterdam? Why is it on-the-vine unreachable?"

"You already know, but have you tried reaching the Keizersgracht?"

"The Keizersgracht? . . . You impress me. Why should I know?"

"Because Leonard Fredericks, our mole in the Foreign Office, told you. Van der Meer overreached in a power play to reduce Julian's leadership."

"That was patently ridiculous. He's the son—"

"Of the Shepherd Boy," completed Pryce quickly. "If you tried to reach van der Meer, you'd be told he's out of the country on business."

"What does that mean?"

"He's regrouping. He could be anywhere."

"Good *Lord*! This is terrible, potentially *catastrophic*."

"It could be. But my money's on Guiderone, my life as well, I suppose. He's the real power. He's the one we all know—everywhere. From the Mediterranean to the North Sea, from Paris and London to New York and Los Angeles. Van der Meer may create the blueprints, the arrangements, in his tower on the Keizersgracht, but Guiderone implements them. He's trusted; van der Meer is an unknown, the unseen money tree, not a person. He can't operate without the son of the Shepherd Boy."

"Are you saying what I think you're saying? We're in a crisis!"

"Not yet. Everything remains on schedule with Guiderone calling the signals."

"If that's the case," said the attorney, enormously relieved, "I'm not sure why you had to reach me."

"Guiderone wants to make sure of your loyalty."

"Under the circumstances, he has it. Why would he doubt it?"

"Because your employer and close friend, Albert Whitehead, has jumped ship. He's thrown in with van der Meer, staying with the money tree."

"What?"

"He doesn't know how quickly that tree could wither."

"He's never mentioned *any* of this to me," said the astonished Nichols, his voice strained. "It's incredible!"

"And you mustn't mention that we met. This conversation never took place."

"You don't *understand*. We've never had professional secrets between us. Certainly not in this area. It's unthinkable!"

"Not anymore. . . . Mr. Guiderone will handsomely reward you if you keep your eyes and ears open. I'll leave you the number of a phone drop, and if you learn anything, or even if Whitehead displays strange behavior, call it and leave word that . . . the 'attorney' was checking in, that's good enough. I'll reach you and we can meet somewhere."

"I used the word 'unthinkable,' and that's what this is. It's unthinkable that I should be spying on Albert."

"You'll thank me later, and the son of the Shepherd Boy will not forget. You're a damned fine lawyer, perhaps you'll head up our international legal department when we're in control. I'm leaving now. Hold out your hand and I'll give you the number of the phone drop. I've written it out."

Pryce left the steam room, billows of mist sucked briefly through the open door. Remaining inside, a perplexed, terrified Stuart Nichols sat staring at the wet walls, a man in torment, and in conflict with himself.

Cameron changed rapidly, led by the CIA "trainer" into a deserted room where he had left his clothes. Out on the street in the bustling, horn-blowing early-morning traffic, he analyzed his meeting with the Matarese attorney. As with Albert Whitehead, it had gone well. The seeds of dissension had been sown, and into the mix had been added the demand for silence, an intolerable combination. If orthodoxy was conformist, which it usually was, the targets would be under such stress that enormous mistakes could be the result, quickly escalating up the Matarese ladder. That's what they, the good guys, would be monitoring. It was odd, in a way, for according to Frank Shields's transcripts of the conference in the New Jersey countryside, it was all part of the truth. Part of the truth; that was essential.

"I'll be leaving you," said the CIA case officer, Scott Walker, in the Marblethorpe suite, "but we may meet up again in Philadelphia, where the fourth subject is."

"I hope so, Scott," said Leslie, "you've been a great help."

"I haven't done anything, Colonel, and if I did, I don't know what it is. I'm just a facilitator. However, I've given Lieutenant Considine the sealed orders for your flight to Florida, where your third subject is. You'll be met by a colleague, Dale Barclay. He's as much in the dark as I am, but he's tops—"

"As in 'top-flight'?"

"That's a special category, sir. He'll take over my job, following the instructions of the deputy director."

"Don't you fellows ever get curious?" asked Leslie.

"Not when we're told not to, Colonel."

"Good answer," said Pryce.

Jamieson Fowler, utilities tycoon and a major U.S. force in the Matarese, operated out of the Breakers hotel in Palm Beach proper. He was constantly on the phone to Tallahassee, the state's capital, using his own personal scrambler—easily invaded by the CIA—reaching high state officials, pressing his case for a vast network of electrical consolidation, and insinuating enormous bonuses, read bribes, if it came to pass. They certainly would comply. State politics is a losing game financially: a nice office, minor celebrity, and unless you're an attorney with clients petitioning the state government, not a great deal of money. Fowler knew the buttons to press, on his telephone and in person with his guests at the Breakers, flown there on his private jet.

Not unlike Stuart Nichols in New York, he had a habit of exercising in the early morning, the result of a heart bypass several years ago. Not, however, in the hotel's gym, but in the pool, at precisely eight o'clock, twenty laps each morning. Eight A.M. was not a popular time for the majority of the hotel's guests. Frank Shields's CIA "pool manager" made certain it was not. He locked the door after Pryce arrived at three minutes past eight, the outside sign reading, POOL BEING CLEANED, AVAILABLE IN THIRTY MINUTES.

Jamieson Fowler and Cameron Pryce were alone in the luxurious surroundings. Each did several laps, Cam the far better swimmer, timing his fourth lap to coincide with Fowler's reaching the far end and briefly stopping for breath.

"Nice pool," said Cam.

"Yes, it is," replied Fowler.

"Do you swim every day?"

"Absolutely. Eight o'clock sharp. Keeps the body in shape."

"Yes, I'd think so, especially after a bypass."

"What did you say?" Fowler put a pulsating right finger into his ear, as if to make certain what he heard.

"I'm from Amsterdam, and you have to be told. You can't leave here until you listen to me, the door's locked. The son of the Shepherd Boy stays here frequently and has many friends."

"What the fuck *is* this? Who are *you*?"

"Mr. Guiderone claims that obscenity is basically a lack of vocabulary."

"*I* don't! It says what I mean. . . . I'm getting *out* of here!"

"I wouldn't even try, if I were you."

"What?"

"I told you, the door's locked. You might as well listen."

"To what?"

"To me. Let's say I'm talking hypothetically."

"I don't like 'hypothetically,' I like straight talk!"

"All right, straight talk. Amsterdam, specifically the Keizersgracht, has learned that you're very close to Benjamin Wahlburg—"

"I know him, that's all. Generally, I don't like Jews, but he's better than most."

"That's very generous of you, but you should know that the Keizersgracht believes, with considerable evidence, that he's been recruited by the Federal Trade Commission in Washington. He's using you to get himself off the hook if our enterprise somehow fails—which it *won't*. Everything's in place, nothing can stop us."

"Christ, it better not! I've got *billions* riding on it!"

"Stay away from Wahlburg. He's the enemy. . . . Now, *I'm* getting out of here. I've delivered the message, the rest is up to you." With these words, Pryce grabbed the tiled edge and lifted himself out of the pool. He walked to the door, rapped twice, and heard the click of the lock. He glanced back at Jamieson Fowler. The utilities power broker was staring after him, his eyes wide, bulging in shock, his head barely above the water.

Benjamin Wahlburg was a complicated man. In his early years, he had been a dedicated socialist, bordering on the communist agenda. Capitalism, with its vicious economic cycles that oppressed the poor and the lower middle class, was anathema to him. Until he met a man, a professor of sociology from the University of Michigan, and a former socialist. The man had made a 180-degree philosophical turn. The trouble wasn't capitalism, per se, it was the capitalists themselves. They had no sense of social responsibility, individual or corporate. The solution could only be found in changing the outlooks of the corporate rich.

Also a Talmudic scholar, Wahlburg found certain compassionate similarities between this concept and the Hebrew philosophy of the well-off taking care of the less fortunate of the tribe. The core of an idea took hold; the wandering, uncertain socialist made a decision. He would become the ultimate capitalist. Possessed of a brilliant financial mind, he joined a midlevel bank in Philadelphia on the basis of a thesis he submitted about where the bank should go in the bewildering fifties. In two years he became the vice president; in four, the president and the managing partner.

Inflating the bank's assets, he bought other banks in the Pennsylvania area, followed by additional ones in neighboring states. Then, on the strength of paper values, other banks as far west as Ohio and Utah, soon thereafter in Nevada, and finally in California. The times were right, as he predicted; banks were in trouble. Buy low and sell high with the ultimately rising markets. Before he was thirty-five, Benjamin Wahlburg, the former socialist radical, was a force in American banking.

He was ripe for the Matarese. For the appeals of a global economy that would protect the underclasses. Yes, he understood that there *might* be a degree of violence, but the Old Testament was filled with fire, brimstone, and vengeance. That's how the world evolved. It was a sad commentary, but what else was new?

Benjamin Wahlburg was a monumental jerk.

However, he kept reminding himself that the ultimate goal was a far better, far fairer world. So he closed his eyes to the unpleasant, knowing in his heart that it was a justifiable evil, and looked forward to the promised land.

Philadelphia brought Scott Walker back into Pryce's and Leslie's lives, as sharp and as precise as ever. He met them at a private field on the outskirts of Chestnut Hill, handed Shields's sealed instructions to Cameron, and drove them to a small hotel in Bala-Cynwyd, twenty-five minutes from the city. Again registered under false names, Luther Considine joined Pryce and Montrose to hear Cam read Frank Shields's pages.

Wahlburg was a philanthropist, especially where the arts were concerned. He and his banks contributed heavily to the symphony, the opera, and the nonprofit theaters. A side privilege for the few largest contributors was to attend the final dress rehearsal before a specific cultural event took place. Tomorrow evening he was scheduled to attend the rehearsal of the Philadelphia Orchestra, where he was to deliver a speech thanking and encouraging his fellow contributors. He would be alone, as his wife had died four years ago and he had never remarried.

Shields had arranged for the head usher—a CIA officer—to lead Wahlburg to an aisle seat in the sixteenth row, behind the sparse audience; the adjacent seat was to be occupied by Cameron. Once again, the target and Pryce would be alone.

Tomorrow evening came, Leslie and Luther in the back row, and after Wahlburg's speech he sat next to Pryce, as the orchestra swung into the fourth movement of Beethoven's Ninth, the orchestral and choral rendition of the master's "Ode to Joy."

"Your speech was wonderful, Mr. Wahlburg," said Cameron, whispering.

"*Shh, shh,* this is far more wonderful."

"I'm afraid we have to talk—"

"We don't talk, we *listen.*"

"I have it on good authority that you were willing to fly to the eastern Mediterranean to meet with Julian Guiderone if you could locate him. Why not listen to his words? I'm his messenger."

"*What?*" Benjamin Wahlburg snapped his head toward Pryce, his face creased in fear and anxiety. "How could you possibly know such a thing?"

"Mr. Guiderone has sources beyond any we both possess."

"Dear God in heaven!"

"Perhaps we should move to the rear of the theater."

"You're from *Guiderone*?"

"Shall we?" Cam nodded at the aisle on Wahlburg's left.

"Yes, yes, of course."

At the back of the concert hall, while the symphony orchestra segued into the soaring chorale of Beethoven's "Ode to Joy," Benjamin Wahlburg heard the words that would change his life and his world, leaving him to wonder whether his life had been worth living or his world worth saving.

"There's a severe crisis in Amsterdam," began Pryce.

"We assumed something had drastically changed," interrupted the banker. "We were told *not* to contact the Keizersgracht!"

"There'd be no point if you tried. Van der Meer has disappeared. Guiderone is trying to hold things together."

"This is *insane*! Where did van der Meer go? *Why?*"

"We can only speculate. Perhaps he learned that we'd been penetrated, that countermeasures were rapidly being mounted and deployed against us. Who knows? We only know he's vanished."

"My *God* . . ." Wahlburg's hands began to tremble; he brought them to his temples, his face now ashen as the chorus onstage swelled, the myriad voices filling the large concert hall with the intoxicating music of the Ninth Symphony. "The work, the years . . . and now—what have we *done*?"

"If Guiderone has his way, nothing will change."

"*Everything's* changed! Everything came from the Keizersgracht. We're rudderless."

"Julian accepts his responsibilities," said Cameron firmly, with sudden authority. "All instructions will come from him, through me. The schedules remain in force."

"But we don't know what they *are*. Amsterdam hasn't told us."

"You'll know," continued Pryce, trying to recall fragments of the printouts as well as Scofield's summary of his talk with Leonard Fredericks in London. "The Mediterranean, the fires. It will start in the Middle East, and as the sun moves west, so will the chaos. Slowly at first, then gathering momentum, until within a few weeks or months there'll be economic paralysis. Everywhere."

"That's our cue to begin offering solutions. *Everywhere.* Whitehead, Fowler, Nichols, and I understand that, but we don't have the specifics! Van der Meer told us that our moves would be calculated, who to reach in the Senate and the House, even the White House. We don't *have* those instructions!"

"You don't have Jamieson Fowler either."

"What?"

"He's retrenched, if that's the word. Without telling you, he's alerted his associates in the utilities industries to contemplate alternative plans—"

"I don't believe that!" Wahlburg broke in.

"It happens to be true."

"What alternative plans?"

"As near as we can gather, a slowdown, a wait-and-see strategy."

"Preposterous! The electric companies all along the eastern seaboard are prepared to lock into one another, proving the economic feasibility."

"Along with thousands upon thousands of lost jobs," noted Cameron. "Devoutly to be wished."

"A temporary condition, to be eventually rectified."

"Neither will take place if Fowler delays. Everything must be coordinated for maximum effect."

"Why *would* he delay?"

"You tell me, but that's what he's set in motion. Cold feet maybe, last-minute jitters, wanting to see for himself that all the others will participate, and he won't be left holding the bag. . . . Remember, there are still laws; in his mind he could become a pariah, facing years in prison."

"You're wrong, *wrong.* He's as committed as I am, for completely different reasons, I grant you, but he will not turn back!"

"We certainly hope you're right. However, until Mr. Guiderone hears more from his sources, try to avoid Fowler. If he reaches you, we never spoke; and if he acts strangely, saying odd things, leave a message at this number." Pryce reached into his pocket and pulled out a scrap of paper. "It's a drop. Just tell me to call my bank, I'm overdrawn."

Cameron turned and walked toward the doors of the hall as the symphony orchestra and the chorus reached the soaring dramatic climax of Beethoven's Ninth. Benjamin Wahlburg stood immobile, trancelike, hearing nothing and seeing nothing, staring only at a dark red velour wall.

He was a broken man, filled with great sadness, and he knew why. He had listened to the siren's song, a false siren, rationalizing the unpardonable, the ungodly. Yet, in the name of God, for the right reasons! Did they still apply? He would go to temple hoping to find solace, perhaps direction.

32

Back at the small hotel in Bala-Cynwyd, Cam, Leslie, and Luther Considine convened in the couple's suite.

"Man," said Luther. "That cat was on a hot tin roof! He just gazed at the wall like the air had been sucked out of him."

"I think our leader did something akin to that," said Montrose. "Am I right, Obi-Wan Kenobi?"

"Who?"

"I forgot, you don't go to the movies."

"Yes, I rolled over him, but he was different from the others. Hell, he was frightened, but if I read him right, there was something else. There were a few flashes of remorse, genuine remorse. When I told him that the utilities megaboss, Fowler, might be holding back, not ready to deliver—"

"A good tactic," broke in the lieutenant colonel. "Divide, then wait for the panic."

"I think I said as much at the Keizersgracht. The success record is better than most strategies."

"What about the remorse?" asked the pilot. "How could you tell?"

"What he said, just a few words, but also the way he said them. About van der Meer's disappearance, he sort of whispered, 'The years, the work, what have we *done*?' as if what they'd done wasn't kosher. Then later, regarding Fowler, he said, 'He's as committed as I am, for completely different reasons, I grant you that.' . . . 'Completely different reasons,' where does that take us?"

"Different ways of reaching their goals?" offered Leslie.

"I don't think so. The goals themselves, maybe, I just don't know. But I do know that he didn't sound self-serving—trying to protect himself. The others did."

"What do you want to do?"

"Pull rank, as you would say, Colonel. Since I'm in the field, I'm calling Frank Shields and giving *him* orders. I want an in-depth dossier on one Benjamin Wahlburg, and I want it tomorrow morning."

Morning came and the sealed dossier was delivered by Scott Walker at seven-fifteen. "This was flown up at five A.M. You're not the most popular guy in Langley, sir."

"That breaks my heart, Scotty, but I'll just have to live with the pain."

"You look like it. I think you're salivating."

"You've got it, Officer Walker. I am."

"Should I wait for a reply? The pilot's still in town."

"No need to. This is all I need."

"You know where to reach me, sir. I can be here in twenty minutes."

Pryce, in his shorts, tore open the sealed envelope and began reading. Leslie was still asleep; his concentration was absolute. Thirty-six minutes later, when she emerged, yawning, he announced, "Colonel Montrose, we may have found the link in the chain that can be broken."

"What? . . ." She sat down next to him on the couch.

"Wahlburg's dossier. It's a beaut. Our all-powerful banker is a refugee from the radical left. In the late forties, he was on Hoover's un-American list, very vocal and close to the communist fringe. Then he disappeared for a few years and emerged as a bona fide believer of the capitalist system, an advocate of everything he previously denounced."

"He saw the light?"

"Maybe, or maybe he looked for another way, a more realistic way to implement the reforms he sought when he was younger."

"The *Matarese*?" said Leslie, astonished. "How could that be? They're monopolistic, fascist, they want to control everything!"

"The flip side of socialism," interrupted Cam. "An equal playing field for the rich and the poor, which is total bananas because there's no such thing. Kennedy was right when he said it was an unfair world. It is, and the Matarese will make it far worse. Maybe Wahlburg is beginning to understand that."

"What are you going to do?"

"Give him a day to reach me. If he doesn't, I'll reach him."

Scofield and Antonia walked the streets of London in their newfound freedom. Well, not complete freedom, as Geoffrey Waters insisted on a two-man protection unit, one several feet in front, the other behind them. It was early morning and they were strolling down the Mall in St. James's Park when a racing car screeched to a stop at the curb. Instantly, the two MI-5 guards ran toward the street, weapons drawn, placing themselves between the vehicle and the Scofields. Just as quickly, they concealed their guns; they recognized the driver, a colleague.

"Emergency, chaps! Get them in here."

Once hustled into the car, the first guard sitting in the back with Bray and Toni, the second beside the driver, an angry Scofield spoke. "What the hell's going on? Where did *this* come from?"

"You've never been out of my line of sight, sir," answered the driver. "Sir Geoffrey's orders."

"He's kinda overdoing it, isn't he? These two fellas plus an automobile."

"This car is bulletproof, sir."

"That's a happy thought. Who's going to shoot me?"

"Chief Waters is very methodical. He considers everything."

"Where are we going?"

"To MI-Five headquarters."

"Why?"

"I have no idea, sir."

"Golly gee, that's just swell."

"Behave, Bray," said Antonia.

Geoffrey Waters was as upset as anyone could remember during his long years of service. Apoplectic would be a more appropriate description. Scofield and Antonia were ushered into his office, the door firmly closed, while Waters paced furiously behind his desk. "What's eating you?" asked Brandon.

"The last thing you want to hear, old friend. Let's all sit down, I believe it would be easier." They did so, the Scofields in two chairs facing the desk.

"What is it, Geof?" said Toni.

"The unbelievable as well as the unacceptable. Matareisen has escaped."

"What?" roared Brandon, leaping up from his chair. "If this is a bad joke, it's really lousy!"

"It's no joke, I only wish to God it were."

"How the hell could it have *happened*? You had him practically in a glass cage, the guards constant!"

"He wasn't here, Bray."

"Jesus, you gave him a night out on the *town*?"

"Let Geof explain, Brandon."

"Thank you, my dear, this isn't easy for me. At three-forty-five this morning, I received a call from the Matareisen watch. He was coughing up blood; it was literally streaming out of his mouth, according to the doctor, and he was unconscious. Fearing for his life, I ordered him taken to the hospital, the detail to accompany him. Somewhere between here and the emergency entrance, no more than twelve minutes, he regained consciousness, and to my utter astonishment, he overcame two strapping young officers, killing one of them and removing the clothes of the chap nearest his size. He then must have taken billfolds, cash, and

ID cards, for there was nothing left, broke open the rear door, and ran into the traffic."

"Who were your agents, Rebecca of Sunnybrook Farm and Pollyanna?"

"Really, Bray!" said Antonia angrily. "One of those young men was *killed*."

"Sorry, but it's nuts!"

"Cameron Pryce can tell you about Matareisen's extraordinary martial-arts technique—like nothing he'd ever seen. Naturally, we're combing the city for him, using the London police as well, without explanations."

"You won't find him," said Scofield. "He's got to have contacts who'll hide him and get him out of the country."

"So we assume, but that's not my primary concern. You and Antonia are. As we speak, you're being moved from the Savoy to the Ritz."

"Why?" protested Bray. "Van der Meer's not going to stick around London, and Guiderone's dead. I'm not a target."

"We don't *know* that," insisted the MI-5 chief of security. "We have no idea whether Guiderone was in touch with Matareisen, or if he was, what he told the Dutchman. Guiderone was going for his final, most important kill. Perhaps he took out insurance with van der Meer, as you call him."

"Highly unlikely, if not impossible," retorted Scofield. "If I did my job, as I usually do, I split Guiderone from the Keizersgracht."

"In all due respect, old chap, none of us knows what others will do under extreme stress. It's an unpredictable area."

"All right, we're moving to the Ritz."

"Thank you, Bray," said Antonia.

The telephone rang on Waters's desk. "Yes?" he said, quickly picking it up. He listened for a moment or two, hung up, and looked at the Scofields. "A patrol car believes it just spotted Matareisen. They pulled up and he saw the vehicle, then dashed into the underground. They're in full chase now."

"Why do they think it was him?"

"The clothes at first, they were ill-fitting, then the general description based on the photographs we took when we brought him from Amsterdam. We've circulated them."

"Speaking of Amsterdam, could those computers have any data on London? Any references to contacts or conduits?"

"Nothing," replied Sir Geoffrey. "I checked with Greenwald in the Keizersgracht. All he found were vague references to streets and monuments going back months. Meeting grounds long gone." The telephone rang again and Sir Geoffrey pounced on it. "Yes?" He stared at a glass paperweight as he listened. Finally, the caller finished, he briefly closed his eyes and without a word hung up. "They lost him," he said, sitting down.

"Alert all the private airfields," said Bray, "one of them will be his exit."

"Where will he go?" asked Antonia. "Amsterdam's out. Does he own other property, other places than in Holland?"

"If he does, they'd be impossible to find. He operates through holding companies and dummy corporations, like the limousine service and that Argus group. Knowing his resources, he undoubtedly has many other places, but we need a paper trail and we don't have one."

"Does he have any attorneys?" Toni again. "He must use the services of a law firm."

"Probably dozens in as many countries. We traced the Argus group to Marseilles. The offices consist of two rooms, a toilet, and one secretary whose only job is to forward mail and cables to Barcelona, which relays them to a general delivery station in Milan. Are you getting the picture, chaps?"

"In three dimensions," acknowledged Scofield. "Obfuscation, untraceability, and evasion. What's surprising is the Milan relay. It suggests that someone has taken over the Paravacini cell, a very major player."

"I was wondering about that myself," said Waters. "If true, they certainly rebounded in a hurry."

"Too much of a hurry," Brandon interrupted, "which means that somebody was in place to assume the authority." Scofield turned to Antonia. "How'd you like a short vacation to Lake Como, luv? Better grab it now 'cause Sir Hog's Butt's paying, I can't afford it."

"I think we've already paid for Como," said Waters.

"This includes the services of the incomparable Don Silvio Togazzi, who probably owns most of Milano by now, and certainly the postal unions. An upstanding mafioso would never neglect them, unseen communications are too important."

"The general-delivery station?"

"Exactly. I'm sure the transfers are done in relays, one poor soul is paid a few thousand lire to deliver to another poor soul, and then another, until it reaches our major player. We'll be there when the event takes place, and I don't think you care to hear the tactics we intend to employ. They might offend your sensibilities, but we'll bring you a trophy, count on it."

"In this situation, my sensibilities cannot possibly be offended. Just don't bring me a corpse. A corpse can't speak."

Jan van der Meer Matareisen bent his body over in a telephone booth in a crowded Piccadilly Circus. He had wads of cotton in his mouth, which he had punctured with his teeth to create the illusion of hemorrhaging. He removed the cotton, as across the Channel a phone rang in Brussels. "Hello," said the voice in Belgium.

"It is I. Have you the information and, if so, how soon can you make arrangements?"

"I have the information and am prepared to make the arrangements when you tell me."

"The information first."

"The private golf course is called Fleetwood. It is twenty-two miles northwest of London and reached by using the motorways—"

"I know the area and a taxi will get me there. The arrangements?"

"A small plane, a Cessna prop, will land on the fairway between the eleventh hole and the twelfth tee—it's the longest and flattest and farthest away from the clubhouse. He'll arrive around four-forty-five while there's a minimum of light but it's too dark for golfers, not that there are many this time of year. You'll be flown to a field in Scotland where your jet is waiting for you. A flight plan for Marseilles will be filed under one of your corporations, departure open, approval guaranteed. Everything's in place, shall I proceed?"

"At once."

Jan van der Meer killed the time remaining in a motion-picture house. At three o'clock Matareisen hailed a taxi and gave the driver vague instructions to the Fleetwood Golf Club. They arrived at 4:10, the traffic heavy, and van der Meer ordered the man to drive around the outskirts of the course. Fourteen minutes later, the Dutchman spotted the flag of the twelfth hole; he stopped the taxi shortly thereafter, paid the driver, got out, and started walking back when the car disappeared around a curve.

By 4:30 van der Meer lay in the grass of a tree-filled rough midway between the eleventh hole and the twelfth tee. It was twilight but not dark. At 4:39 the muted sound of a distant plane could be heard in the sky. Matareisen crawled to the edge of the forestlike rough, then stood up by a thick trunk of a tree. He peered through the branches; the plane came into view and began circling the area, with each circle dropping lower.

Suddenly, the unexpected, the unwanted. A sprinkler system erupted, cascading sprays arcing everywhere, as a lawnskeeper, flashlight in hand, rode in an electric cart checking the sprinklers in this unusually dry autumn. He zigzagged back and forth over the fairway. He was in the path of the descending plane nearing its final approach! Van der Meer raced out shouting, "You there! Come *over* here. I fell, I'm injured, I've been unconscious!"

The lawnskeeper turned the cart around and accelerated toward Matareisen. They met in the middle of the fairway, the landing stretch, the *runway*! Swiftly, van der Meer grabbed the man's hair and smashed his head down on the front bar, then ripped the flashlight from his hand. He began feverishly waving the beam of light in circles. Seemingly at the last moments before landing, the plane swooped up, swinging to the left for yet another approach. Matareisen yanked the body with its blood-drenched head out of the cart, jumped in, and drove to the edge of the green. Turning off the motor and throwing away the key, he raced back onto the manicured grass, now waving the flashlight in short vertical strokes, indicating a landing. The pilot understood; the small plane came down and taxied toward Matareisen's light.

"Did you bring me a change of clothes as I requested?" asked van der Meer harshly, climbing in the cramped backseat.

"Yes, sir, but I wish you wouldn't change now. I want to get out of here before the place is soaked and we lose traction."

"Then go!"

"Also, the course is loaded with moving carts. I'd hate to crash into one."

"I said *go*!"

Airborne, on their way to the Scottish border, Matareisen returned to the question that had vexed him since his capture. His ego had convinced him he would somehow escape; that was inevitable. The real problem now was where would he operate from, where would he establish the Matarese headquarters? He owned many residences, all well-equipped although not to the technical extent of the Keizersgracht, but certainly computerized for global communications and that was all he needed. Time was so *short*! Only days before the burning of the Mediterranean, the first of the catastrophes, the harbinger of multiple world crises leading to economic chaos!

Suddenly, a calm spread over Jan van der Meer Matareisen. He knew where he would go, where he *had* to go.

It was 3:38 in the afternoon in Philadelphia and Benjamin Wahlburg had made no attempt to reach Pryce. Cam decided the ball was in his court so he called the office of the Matarese conduit.

"I'm sorry, sir, Mr. Wahlburg hasn't come into the office today."

"Do you have his home phone?"

"Sorry again, sir. We're not permitted to give out that information."

Frank Shields in Washington was, both the telephone number and Benjamin Wahlburg's address. Pryce called Scott Walker when no one answered at Wahlburg's mansion and together they drove out to the elegant estate. Repeated rings on the front doorbell brought no response. Finally Cameron said, "I believe it's called breaking and entering, but I think, under the circumstances, we should consider it, don't you?"

"Consider it done," replied the CIA officer. "I carry a national security Invasive Procedures Card."

"What does that mean?"

"Not a great deal, but most of the locals buy it. Under extreme conditions we're allowed extra latitude in completing our assignments, as long as there's no threat to life and we accept responsibility."

"That's pretty loose."

"It has its flaws," conceded Walker. "I really don't have any in-depth knowledge of this operation, but if you tell me national security is involved, well, you're in the loop and there's no one to argue with you."

"National security is involved in ways that would blow your mind."

"The place is no doubt alarmed, so let's break through a patio or a kitchen door and I'll take the heat from whoever shows up. I know what to say and how to say it."

"You've done this before—"

"I've done it before," said the agent quietly, without comment, as the two men started toward the side and the rear of the property. There was a glass-enclosed porch in the back looking over a tennis court. "This is fine," continued Walker, checking the glass-paned door fronted by a screen. He took out his automatic and, holding it by the barrel, broke through the screen, then smashed the windowpane nearest the knob, reached in, and opened the door.

Both were startled by the ensuing silence. "No alarm," said Pryce.

"For a house like this, it's unusual."

"Let's go." Cameron and the CIA man walked through the porch into the interior of the mansion, and it *was* that, a mansion. The downstairs rooms were filled with the finest furniture, recognizable oil paintings on the most expensive wallpaper, and enough glistening silver to dress a showroom at Tiffany's.

The house appeared to be deserted, as Pryce called out, "Federal government, we're here to speak to Benjamin Wahlburg." He did so several times.

"I never heard that name," said Scott. "Bad hearing."

"Sorry, I forgot." They started up the wide, imposing staircase, Pryce calling out his "federal" announcement to no avail. They reached the second floor and checked the various rooms and baths; there was no one. Finally, they came to the master bedroom; the door was locked. Cameron knocked and ended up pounding. "Mr. *Wahlburg,*" he shouted. "It's imperative that we talk!"

"We've gone this far," said Walker, "we might as well try for the bell." With these words, he stepped back, then rushed forward, hurling his muscular body at the door. It splintered but did not open. Several well-placed kicks by the agent and the door collapsed. They walked inside.

There, sprawled across the bed, the satin quilt soaked with blood and human tissue, was the body of Benjamin Wahlburg. The banker had shot himself through the mouth with a .38-caliber pistol, still gripped in his hand.

"You never saw this, Scott," said Pryce. "In fact, you weren't even here."

33

The Villa d'Este resort on Lake Como sent a limousine to the Milan airport for the hotel's latest American guests, Mr. and Mrs. Paul Lambert, a.k.a. Brandon Scofield and

Antonia. Their passports were courtesy of Frank Shields in Washington, who had them jetted across the Atlantic by military courier. The flight landed at ten o'clock in the morning, Milan time, and by noon the exhausted couple were in their suite, "Mr. Lambert" complaining about the long previous night's briefing in London.

"Geoffrey doesn't know how to say something once, he has to say it thirty times."

"Bray, you kept arguing with him."

"Damn right, because I don't *need* him! I have Togazzi."

"Which doesn't thrill Geof, as you know."

"He's anti-Italian."

"No, he's somewhat leery about working with a man reputed to be a powerful mafioso."

"That's horseshit. The Servizio Segreto got some of its best recruits from the Mafia. Besides, Silvio hasn't had anything to do with the Mafia in years. He's honorably retired."

"How respectable of him." The telephone rang and Toni picked it up from the antique leather-topped desk. "Yes?"

"This must be the glorious Antonia, a Mediterranean *signora* whom I have never met, but I spend the moments in great anticipation when I shall have the honor and the privilege to do so."

"Your English is extraordinary . . . Signor Togazzi?"

"Indeed, and much of my English was learned at the feet of a master, your extraordinary companion."

"Yes, I thought as much. Here, I'll turn you over to the . . . master."

"I can hear the lilt of the Mare Nostra in your own speech, great beauty!" pressed Togazzi.

."How nice, I've been trying for years to lose it." She handed the phone to Scofield, who had been shaking his head and pointing to the bed, a nap in his plea. Reluctantly, he accepted it.

"Hi, wop?"

"Ever the endearing Brandon. And how is the Yankee scumball, that is the term, is it not? I gather you've arrived."

"No, I'm a clone who needs a few hours' sleep."

"Not now, old friend, we have work to do. Word from the

Milan post office is that another general delivery from Barcelona has arrived, this to a Signor Del Monte the Fourth, the 'Del Monte' quite a common name in Italy, the 'Fourth' an aberration, the identifying code for the receiver. The next general-delivery truck is due at three o'clock this afternoon. My associate will hold the material, claiming it to be on the last shipment. We must be there."

"I just got *out* of there! Don't you have shadows on your payroll who can follow whoever it is that picks it up?"

"The last communication from Barcelona was six days ago. When will another come?"

"Oh, Jesus, you're right! The Keizersgracht is shut down—"

"What? *Che cosa*?"

"It's been a busy week, I'll fill you in later. But you're right, we won't get another chance to find the Milan connection. How will you pick me up?"

"Walk out the west entrance as if you're about to stroll around the gardens. Then take the path that bypasses the barricade on the road into the villa and start walking up the street to Bellagio. I'll meet you there."

"I'm not armed—goddamned metal detectors—and I want to be armed. Do you have any weapons?"

"Does our Ligurian Sea have water?"

"I figured. See you in fifteen or twenty minutes." Scofield hung up the phone and turned to Antonia. "I guess you heard."

"You guess correctly, and I don't like the need for weapons."

"Probably no need at all, but I'd prefer to have some firepower, since we're behind enemy lines. You do remember the old days, don't you, girl?"

"Yes, dear. I also remember that you were far younger. And Togazzi's older than you. Two old men playing roles they long ago left behind them."

"Why don't you have us mummified while you're at it. Where are my rubber-soled shoes?"

"In the closet."

"Never go to work without rubber soles on your feet."

"You won't be alone, will you? Old men need younger men."

"I'm sure Silvio will find a body or three."

"I hope you know what you're doing."

"We do."

The drive to Milan was made in record time, Scofield and Togazzi refining their tactics of rapid surveillance. Two of the don's guards were in the front seat, a second car with three others behind them; they would meet a block away from Milan's main post office. Togazzi's man inside had provided a floor plan of the general-delivery section; it was intrinsic to the strategy. The don's guards, all with lapel-attached walkie-talkies, would place themselves in receding positions from near the counter to the exit doors, the driver remaining outside, close to Togazzi's vehicle. The don's man would signal the nearest guard when the recipient picked up the Barcelona merchandise; he, in turn, would alert the others, describing the conduit.

Togazzi stayed in his automobile, a high-speed telescopic camera in his hand, while Scofield was a few feet away, watching the door and listening to the guards' transmissions. The words came over the wire.

"The man is in disheveled clothing, a torn jacket and unpressed trousers."

"Got him," said Bray, seeing the Matarese recipient, a short man, walking rapidly out the door of the post office. "You see him, Silvio?"

"Of course. He's heading for the row of bicycles. Quickly, one of you! Get out here and take the motorbike from the trunk. *Follow* him!"

The swiftest of the guards did so, yanking the motorized bike out of its recess, starting the engine, climbing on, and zooming off in pursuit of the bicycling messenger. Minutes later, the pursuer spoke over the radio. "He is in the worst part of the city, *signore*! The bike is new and very expensive. I fear for my life."

"You won't have one if you lose him, my friend," said Don Silvio Togazzi.

"*Dio di Dio,* he's passed it to another beggar!"

"Stay with him," ordered the don.

"He's running down the street to an old church, *signore.* A young priest has come out on the steps! He's giving the envelope to him. It is the Church of the Blessed Sacrament."

"Conceal your motorbike and stay there. If the priest leaves, follow him at a distance, *capisce*?"

"With all my heart and soul, Don Silvio."

"*Grazie.* You will be rewarded."

"*Prego,* my don. . . . He *is* leaving! He's walking up the pavement; he has stopped at an automobile, a very old automobile with much damage on it."

"The safest car in that environment," noted Togazzi. "What make of automobile is it?"

"I cannot tell. There are so many dents and scratches. It is small, the grill half torn off, perhaps a Fiat."

"The license plate?"

"It is too bent, and again the scratches. . . . The priest climbed in and is starting the engine."

"Stay with him as long as you can. The men are in the other car; we'll be in this one. Let us know every turn he makes. . . . Brandon, come inside."

It came as an astonishing surprise, insofar as the Paravacini estate was virtually closed, maintained by a skeleton staff and with its dynastic flag at half-mast, signifying that no one of importance was in residence. The savage and macabre death of Carlo Paravacini had both shocked and electrified the lake community. There were those who prayed for his soul, and those who condemned it to hell, few in between. Yet the small, shabby automobile quickly took the highway to Bellagio and veered off on the road thirty miles north that led to the Paravacini property. Someone was in residence, someone powerful enough to receive the material from Barcelona, a member of the Matarese hierarchy.

"Get back to the house as fast as you can!" ordered Togazzi, turning to Scofield. "There are telescopes on my balcony, perhaps we'll learn something."

They did. The telescope focused on the Paravacini compound revealed the imposing yacht at the dock, behind it deserted lawns with none of the myriad fountains operating.

The estate appeared eerily deserted, as if the elegant grounds cried out for people in their finery, not cold, white statues. Suddenly, two people were there, two men rounding the brick path from the front of the mansion. One was elderly, far older than the younger man, both in dark trousers and loose-fitting sport shirts. "Who are they?" asked Bray, stepping back from the telescope to permit Don Silvio to look. "Do you know them?"

"One I know very well and he's the answer to the question, who's running the Matarese in Italy? The other I don't recognize, but I can suggest a probability; we only saw the back of his head from a distance."

"Who?"

"The driver of the small, shabby car we followed out here."

"The priest?"

"Both are. The older man is Cardinal Rudolfo Paravacini, a prelate with considerable influence in the Vatican."

"He's the head of the Italian *Matarese*?"

"He's the uncle of the late, unlamented Carlo Paravacini, he of the birds."

"But the *Vatican*?"

"I'd suggest that the blood between families is stronger than the blood of Christ. Certainly in this instance."

"Pryce mentioned him, Leslie, too. But there wasn't anything really concrete."

"There is now, Brandon. Here, look. They've walked up onto the yacht, to the aft veranda. Tell me what you see."

"Okay." Scofield returned to the telescope. "Good God, the old guy's opening the stuff from Barcelona. You're *right*!"

"The question is," said Togazzi, "what do we do next?"

"The place doesn't look like it's exactly fortified. Why not move now, before he can relay whatever's in the package, or before he destroys it, which is a distinct possibility."

"I agree."

The guards were called out on the balcony, each taking a turn peering through the telescope. A strategy was rapidly devised and refined, Scofield and Togazzi going back years, recalling the days when together they penetrated hostile areas. Two of the guards left, their instructions understood, the remaining three staying with the don and Brandon.

"You stay here," said Togazzi in Italian, nodding at the guard who manned the barricaded gatehouse of the forest retreat. "Stay in touch with us, and in the unlikely event intruders show up, you know what to do."

"*Sì,* my don. The outer land mines first."

"Land mines?" Scofield leaned forward in his white-wicker chair. "The hills above Portofino?"

"You remembered," confirmed Togazzi. "No one came near our base camps. We'd set off the mines on the perimeters and any who were searching for us would be paralyzed with fear, afraid to walk."

"They'd retrace their steps and get out of the area while we'd find another camp," said Brandon, chuckling. "No casualties, no international incidents, the explosions blamed on undetected mines left over from the partisan wars."

"I've added a touch," explained Don Silvio modestly. "There are now inner mines much closer to the path, and a few under it, also set off from the gatehouse."

"*Va bene,*" said Scofield, laughing.

"You two," continued Togazzi in Italian, addressing the remaining guards, "will accompany us, dropping us off about a hundred meters above the estate. Then proceed to the parking area and take up your positions."

"*Sì.*"

The first car pulled off the road a quarter of a mile away from the Paravacini property. The two guards had changed clothes. Instead of the drab, ordinary suits they had worn in Milan, they were now dressed in what could best be described as rural farmhands' Sunday-church clothing, ill-fitting, old, but clean. Each carried a basket of flowers, the sort grown locally, with care, on small plots of earth, affordable tributes to a great landowner. They walked in the heat of the dusty road down toward the Paravacini mansion, sweat forming on their brows, perspiration stains on their shirts. The road became asphalt, the final two hundred yards to the estate. The gatehouse with its thick glass windows was deserted, the usual barrier raised, signs again that no one of importance was in residence.

They trudged, as if with difficulty, into the circular drive and up the steps of the imposing front entrance. They rang the bell—loud chimes could be heard from the cavernous inside. A male servant opened the door; his shirt was unbuttoned and he had a stubble of a beard. At the sight of the rumpled, crude-looking visitors, he spoke harshly in Italian.

"What do you want? There's nobody home!"

"*Piacere, signore,* we are poor men from the hills of Bellagio," said the guard on the right. "We have come to pay our respects to the memory of the great Don Carlo, who was always most generous to our families at holidays."

"He's been dead for several weeks. You're a little late."

"We did not dare when there were so many dignitaries coming and going," said the guard on the left. "May we bring these baskets in, *signore*? They are quite heavy."

"Leave them out there! There are already too many plants inside to water."

"Open your heart, *signore,*" added the guard on the right, looking beyond the arrogant servant.

"No!"

"Then don't open it." The same guard suddenly leaped forward, grabbing the man by his shoulders, yanking him down and crashing a hard right knee into his face. The man fell to the floor, bleeding and unconscious. Together, Togazzi's men dragged the body into a side room, closed the door, and began their swift but thorough search. They found a maid in the library; she was in uniform, reclining in an armchair, leafing through the pictures of an encyclopedia.

"*Scusi, signori!*" She spoke quickly, jumping up from the chair. "We were told," she continued in Italian, "that as long as we did our chores, we could relax and enjoy ourselves."

"Who told you that?"

"His Eminence, the cardinal, *signore.*"

"Who else is here?"

"Cardinal Paravacini, Signor Rossi, and—"

"Signor Rossi?" interrupted the guard who had assaulted the servant at the door. "Is he a priest?"

"Good Lord, *no, signore*! He brings a different woman here several times a week. He is a *goat*. In deference to the cardinal, he sends them home very early, before it's light."

"Who else'?" asked the second Togazzi man. "You implied there was someone else."

"Yes, Bruno Davino. He's in charge of the estate's security."

"Where is he?"

"He spends much of his time on the roof, sir. There is a section with a cover to protect one from the sun. He says he can see the lake and all the roads from there. He calls it his lookout."

"Let's go up," said the first guard.

"Che cosa?" came the shouted words from the doorway. The guards turned to see a large, heavyset man, his expression conveying his anger. "I saw you two sorry worms coming down the road, but I didn't see you leave! Why are you still here?"

"A spiacente, signore," replied the second guard, his palms upturned, his arms outstretched, as he slowly walked toward the huge man, pleading. "We brought tributes to the memory of the great Don Carlo—" He crossed between his colleague and the Matarese intruder. It was a tactic they had used before, blocking the sight line of two figures. The first guard reached into his pocket and swiftly took out a pistol with an attached silencer. The instant his associate continued walking, revealing the man in the doorframe, he fired twice with deadly accuracy, instantly killing the head of security.

The woman started to scream; the second Togazzi man raced over, lunging, one hand on her mouth, the other pounding her chest with such force that the air was immediately expunged from her lungs, cutting off all sound. Removing a thin rope and a heavy plastic tape from his pockets, he tied her to an upright chair and gagged her. "She's not going anywhere."

"We're clear," said the first guard, "the whole place is clean. Let's go to our next positions."

The second automobile stopped as Scofield and Togazzi got out, walking into the bordering woods as fast as their elderly legs could manage. The car continued down the road, the engine off, and coasted onto the lawn at the left side of the enormous house, unseen by anyone on the yacht. The third and fourth guards stepped out on the grass, silently closed the doors, and crept along the exterior wall of the mansion until they reached the wide expanse of the exposed south lawn. Anybody walking across it would be immediately seen by a person or persons on the deck of the yacht. That could not be permitted, for the targets were *on* the yacht and all means of egress were to be blocked. Which was why the don's guards in the first automobile were on the right side of the huge house, concealed ten feet from the brick path. It was a human pincer attack, all flanks covered.

The reason for this particular strategy was twofold. The first and most vital consideration was the number of defending personnel. There was no way to ascertain how many. The second was the obvious possibility that if the Togazzi unit was spotted, Cardinal Paravacini would instantly destroy the material from Barcelona, undoubtedly by fire. So the key components were preventing the escape of all those in the compound, and equally important, the element of surprise.

To ensure the latter, Scofield and the don removed their clothes in the woods near the shoreline of the lake. Underneath them they wore bathing trunks and they carried small waterproof pouches that held their weapons. In consideration of their ages, each had a snorkeling tube attached to his suit, better to travel farther underwater without surfacing for air. Their objective was the starboard side of the yacht, where there was a chrome ladder for swimmers wishing to climb back to the lower deck. Replaying roles they had played years ago in Italy, Sicily, and the Black Sea, the two former deep-cover operatives slipped into the waters of Lake Como.

Irritated by the awkward breathing but otherwise not much worse for wear, Brandon and Togazzi reached the ladder. The don began to cough softly so Scofield pushed his head underwater. Togazzi reemerged, his eyes furious, but as Bray emphatically put his right finger across his lips, the don understood. This was no time for noise, especially human noise. Scofield opened his waterproof pouch and removed his weapon; Togazzi did the same. Both nodded to each other as Brandon began climbing up the chrome ladder. Halfway to the hull's midpoint, the elderly don could no longer contain his coughing, the result of water seeping into his snorkeling tube.

The excited voices from the deck above erupted in Italian. "What was *that*?"

"Someone's on the ladder! I'll see—"

"Don't waste a moment. Here, take this and run! Go to the house and yell for Bruno."

Scofield pulled himself up the ladder, crawling over the railing, his gun leveled at Cardinal Paravacini. "I wouldn't move if I were you, priest. I might decide your Church would be better off without you." Bray stopped and shouted, "*Stop* him, he's heading for the path! Take the *package*!"

Togazzi came into view, maneuvering his old, gaunt frame over the railing with difficulty, swearing in Italian at the ravages of time. Converting to English, he lamented, "What happens to our bodies? They were so much kinder to us before."

"Don *Silvio*!" exclaimed the cardinal. "You are with this American *pig*?"

"Oh, yes, Your Eminence," replied Togazzi, "very much so. We go back many years, when you were profaning our Church by rising in the Vaticano."

In the distance, on the lawns beyond the port side of the yacht, men raced between the statues, hunters in pursuit of the priest or the false priest who carried the package from Barcelona. Suddenly there were gunshots, with bullets ricocheting off the marble statuary. Scofield ran to the opposite side of the deck. "For Christ's sake, don't *kill* him!" he roared. There was a scream and the gunfire stopped. A voice from the far lawn shouted back in Italian.

"Too late, *signore*. He had a weapon and was firing at us, severely wounding Paolo in the leg. He was exposed; we shot him."

"Bring the package here and take Paolo to a doctor! *Hurry!*" Brandon returned to the silent cardinal, now covered by Togazzi's gun. "I'd like nothing better than to turn you over to the Pope myself. Unfortunately, there are more pressing matters."

"I shall do the honors, old friend," said Don Silvio. "I could use a blessing or two."

A guard raced up the gangplank, the package from Barcelona in his hand. He brought it to Scofield, briefly explaining that he was rushing back to take his wounded colleague to a "private doctor" known personally to his don. Brandon tore apart the thick, padded manila envelope and removed a portion of the pages inside. He sat in a deck chair, reading, aware that Cardinal Paravacini was staring at him.

After several minutes of slowly turning the pages, Scofield put the material on his lap and looked over at the cardinal. "Quite some change, isn't it, priest?"

"I don't know what you're talking about," replied Paravacini. "I never read whatever's there, for it does not belong to me. If you'll notice, the envelope is addressed to a Del Monte and that is not my name. Mail, like the confessional, is confidential."

"Really? Then why was it opened?"

"A courtesy of my late young employee whom you murdered. I shall pray for his soul, even for the souls of those who killed him, as Jesus prayed for the Roman crucifiers."

"That's beautiful. But why did your young employee bring this to you?"

"You'd have to ask him; unfortunately you cannot. I assume it was mistakenly routed to my postal box in Bellagio, which I use when away from Rome."

"Del Monte doesn't remotely resemble Paravacini."

"In haste, mistakes are made, especially when a young man zealously tries to serve his far-older superior."

"He was a priest then?"

"No, he was not. He was a promising youngster who unfortunately strayed from his faith as well as the law—"

"Your *Eminence,*" Togazzi interrupted curtly, "you're wasting your breath, and your lies only add to your sins. I took photographs, from Milan and your first courier to the third driving to Bellagio, where there was no stop at a postal box. Before we veered away I photographed your employee. He was wearing a clerical collar and turning off on the Paravacini road."

"You shock me, Don Silvio. These are things I know nothing about, and the only answers are with a dead man, murdered by this mad American."

"Don't waste *your* time, either, old friend," said Togazzi, addressing Brandon. "We have ways of dealing with such monumental *ipocriti.* What was the change you mentioned a few minutes ago?"

"It's not good news," answered Scofield, picking up the papers in his lap. "They've moved up the schedule—he, Matareisen, has moved it up. . . . Here, listen to this. 'I will announce a new date soon, possibly from another location. I cannot reach our man in London and that concerns me. Was he trapped by MI-Five? If so, did he break? His wife claims to know nothing, but then she never did. It's all very unsettling. In the following pages you will find the coded shortwave transmissions for the sectors as they are triggered. They are only wide areas, your memory must recall the specifics. Use your computer access for deciphering. If I do decide to relocate, it will be one of many possibilities, all sufficiently equipped, and a place where no one will find me. Stay at your post. The moment has come. The world will change.' That's the end of it, no signature, of course, but it's Matareisen. The exquisite irony is that Guiderone, his own man, if not his superior, killed their mole in London, the man he can't find. The only aspect more exquisite is the job I did on Leonard Fredericks, separating the two fuckers. . . . I know you won't be offended by my language, priest, you've symbolically done the same to your Church."

"I'm not only offended," said the handsome, well-spoken

cardinal, his voice icelike, "I'm outraged. I'm not only a prince of that holy Church, I've dedicated my life to her. To associate me with some wild global economic conspiracy is sheer nonsense and the Holy Father will certainly understand. This is just another anti-Catholic diatribe, we suffer from them constantly."

"Oh, boy, Cardinal-baby, you just really blew it. Who said anything about global economics?"

Paravacini's head snapped around toward Bray, his eyes wide. He was trapped and he knew it. "I have nothing more to say."

"Then I'll just have to mess up your face until you do." Scofield put the papers and the envelope on the deck, got up from the chair, and menacingly approached the prince of the Church.

"No need to bruise your frail hands, old friend," broke in Togazzi, walking away from the railing, "I gave the camera to one of my men. For the record, I'm sure he'll take a picture of the body on the lawn, and together with the other photographs, the sequence will be clear. He'll bring the camera to me and you'll hold the Barcelona envelope in front of our errant cardinal. The evidence will be irrefutable."

"Certainly convincing," agreed Brandon.

"Also, I have friends of friends in the curia. This traitor to his faith will be the disgrace of the Church, a pariah in his own world."

Suddenly, without warning, Cardinal Paravacini leaped up from his chair, wrestling the gun from old Togazzi's hand. Before Scofield could react, the priest turned the weapon on himself, the barrel at his temple. He fired, shattering his skull into a thousand fragments.

"Morte prima di disonore," said Don Silvio, looking down at the befouled corpse. "It's an Italian expression, you know, from the sixteenth century."

"'Death before dishonor,'" said Brandon quietly. "The tattoo trade has made it banal, but this is what it's all about. He had power, wealth, and enormous influence in and out of the Church. Stripped of all that, there was nothing."

"Rispetto," offered Togazzi. "He had respect and without respect he lost his manhood. Above all, an Italian male, especially a priest, must keep his manhood."

"So much for the Italian branch of the Matarese. We'd better fly this material to the computer wizards in Amsterdam. Maybe they'll come up with something. It's all we've got." The shipboard telephone rang, startling both men. Five rings echoed throughout the yacht before Brandon found it. *"Buon giorno,"* he said, prepared to hand over the phone to Togazzi if the Italian was spoken too rapidly. Instead, the words were in precise if accented English, the voice that of a woman.

"You have shed the blood of a Paravacini, a man of great honor. You will pay."

Inside the mansion, standing by a library window, the housemaid hung up the phone while putting down binoculars on a nearby table. Tears fell down her cheeks; her lover was gone and with him a way of life she would never know again.

34

"You three have to get back to London," said Frank Shields over the phone to Pryce in Philadelphia. "Right away."

"What about Wahlburg?"

"We're taking care of that. Our people have already been there, removed the body and all signs of the suicide. Nothing will reach the media, he's just disappeared."

"Nobody else lived there?"

"Just a butler or a manservant or whatever you call them who had a room down the hall from Wahlburg. He was a trained male nurse, and Wahlburg was somewhat of a hypo-chondriac. His wife died several years ago, and his two daughters are married and live in Los Angeles and San Antonio. We've got a clear field; the telephone answering machine is covered by an out-of-town message."

"What do you think will happen?"

"I think, and hope, that his three Matarese friends, Fowler, Whitehead, and Nichols, will go out of their minds when they can't reach him. And if you did your job in New York and Palm Beach, they'll assume the worst and start looking for sanctuary. That's when mistakes will be made."

"I did my job, Frank. Now what's this about London?"

"Hold on to your hats or sit down. Matareisen escaped from MI-Five."

"Impossible!" roared Pryce.

"All too possible," replied Shields. "I won't go into the particulars, but he got away and is presumed to be en route to somewhere in Europe."

"Good *Christ*!"

"There's more. Scofield and his friend Togazzi found the Matarese connection in Milan. It was the Cardinal Paravacini you spoke about in your debriefing."

"No surprise," interrupted Cameron. "Have they got him in tow?"

"No, he killed himself, shot himself in the head when they spelled out his involvement."

"They gave him a *gun*?"

"He grabbed it out of old Togazzi's hand. The point is that the cardinal received a multicouriered package sent by Matareisen before you fellows took him. It's all in computer-speak so it's been flown to the Keizersgracht. In essence, the Matarese schedule has been moved up—"

"Moved *up*," yelled Pryce. "There aren't that many days left!"

"That's why Scofield wants you back. He won't even tell me or Geoffrey Waters why. Just that it's a job for you two."

"The elliptical son of a bitch!"

"You're all booked on the Concorde's morning flight at nine-forty-five out of Kennedy. Captain Terence Henderson is the pilot and a good friend of MI-Five. He'll meet you in the lounge and escort you on board."

"That doesn't give us much time."

"A helicopter will pick you up in a field west of the hotel's parking lot and fly you there. We've cleared it; the chopper will arrive in roughly fifty minutes."

"We're going to be jet-lagged out."

"You've only begun. A plane will be ready for you at Heathrow. Lieutenant Considine will fly you directly to Milan, to Brandon and Togazzi."

"As I believe I said once before, you're all heart, Squinty."

"Never pretended to be otherwise, *Camshaft*. Start packing."

The flight to London was uneventful, Captain Henderson the perfect British officer, in the military or out, his modulated speech the essence of understated authority; one did not cross him.

"When we land," said Henderson, "please stay on board until everyone else leaves the cabin. I'll escort you past customs."

"Boy, you're really into this stuff, aren't you, Captain?" said Luther, in the aisle seat across from Pryce and Montrose. "Are you a James Bond type, or something?"

"I have no idea what you're talking about, sir." Henderson smiled; it was a genuine smile, laced with humor. He leaned down and whispered, "But don't pursue it, or I'll switch on the afterburners and blow you out of your seat."

"Hey, man, I'm a flyboy, too—"

"I know that, Commander—"

"Everybody jumps me a grade."

"Why not come up to the flight deck? You might enjoy it."

"I think I will—and watch your moves."

"Be my guest, old chap. Come along now." Luther got out of his seat and followed the captain up the aisle.

Leslie turned to Pryce. "I want to go with you to Milan."

"Not this time," said Cameron. "I called Geof Waters from the Concorde lounge, and he told me that Scofield was sending Antonia back to London."

"That's Antonia, not me," interrupted Lieutenant Colonel Montrose firmly.

"Easy, Army, I haven't finished. Geof also said that Bray requested a truckload of crazy equipment—'positively insane' was the way Waters described it—to be flown to a destination he would name later."

"And Geoffrey agreed?"

"He said a funny thing. He said that when Beowulf Agate behaves this way, he's usually on to something."

"Then I'd say he damn well better share it."

"I said pretty much the same thing; at least he should offer a justification. But Geof disagreed. He wants to give Scofield a day or two to confirm whatever it is he's zeroed in on."

"Shouldn't it be the other way around, confirm first?"

"Maybe not. The Matarese's schedule has been moved up, as I told you, so we could be looking at a week or less. Bray must be damn sure of himself, and if he proves out, we have to move fast."

"It doesn't appear to be sound field strategy to me."

"You mean military strategy, only we're not military and the fields are different."

"I'd still rather go with you."

"Not until I find out what Scofield's got in mind. You have a child, I don't."

The next eight hours were a nonstop whirl of activity. Captain Henderson broke his own record by crossing the Atlantic in two hours and fifty-one minutes. At Heathrow Airport, after being escorted off the plane by the captain, they met Sir Geoffrey Waters, who carried two suitcases, one for Cam, the other for Luther.

"Since we obtained the lieutenant's uniform measurements from the U.S. Navy, and we had a number of Cameron's clothes from the last hotel, we ordered new clothing for each of you. It's in this luggage."

"Why did you do that?" asked Pryce.

"Just a precaution, old man. There are no labels, no common fabrics favored by specific clothiers—in other words, no way to trace your identities through the purchases."

"Holy *shit*!" exclaimed Luther. "What did this cat figure we'd be doing?"

"He didn't say, Lieutenant. But I go back a long time with the man we call Beowulf Agate, much of it at a distance, I grant you. However, I'm aware of his, shall we say, *outré* machinations. Therefore, we must protect the Service."

"What about protecting *us*?" said Considine.

"If it comes down to your clothing, chap, you'll be beyond protection."

"Thanks a lot! I'm a superqualified pilot. Can't NASA send me to the moon or to Mars?"

"Remember Pensacola, Luther," said Pryce. "There's a commander who's waiting for you—Commander."

"That isn't much good if it comes down to the clothing."

"You still have a couple of hours of light, Lieutenant," remarked Waters, "and your Bristol Freighter is on a nearby runway. Your copilot—one of our fellows who only knows he's accompanying you to Milan—has the approved flight plan. You and Cameron had better get started."

"Why can't I fly solo?"

"Two reasons. One, this isn't a small rural airport or a foreign one with which we negotiate, but Heathrow, where the regulations are extraordinarily strict. To disregard them would call attention to your flight, which we don't want. Two, you've just crossed five time zones; that has an effect on your system. Caution dictates a backup."

"Tell that to a couple of thousand fighter pilots from World War Two through Desert Storm."

"Yes, well, that would be rather difficult, wouldn't it?"

"Yassuh, massa."

They landed past nightfall, and Cameron was taken to Togazzi's car while Luther was driven to a preselected hotel, and the MI-5 copilot made arrangements in the terminal to fly back to London.

Inside the familiar vehicle with the distressed exterior and luxurious interior, Pryce found himself of two minds. The first was that he missed Leslie enormously, missed her not being beside him, missed her quick mind and their conversations . . . and, of course, her sexual appetite. He had to face the truth: Cameron Pryce, he of the single persuasion and, except for his job, free of long-range entanglements and the responsibilities therein, was deeply in love. He had come close two or three times since college, but his obsession with academics and later his fascination with the extensive training at the Agency precluded deeper relationships. Those obstacles were eliminated; the fascination would always be there and he understood that with every operation he could learn something, but there was space now and time, as much as there would ever be. And he had found someone he wanted to share those moments with for the rest of his life. It was as simple as that, and he recognized it. Temporary liaisons were simple and gratifying, love was crazy, a topsy-turvy world of longing, exuberance, and impatience.

The other part of Cameron's reflections dwelt on Scofield. What had the legend that was Beowulf Agate uncovered and why was he so secretive? It was no time for grandstanding and Brandon's reality check would tell him that. So what prompted his odd behavior? He would find out within the hour.

They reached Togazzi's wooded sanctuary in the forest above Bellagio, and Pryce was led out to the also-familiar narrow balcony with the row of telescopes overlooking Lake Como. The greetings were brief, as Scofield was anxious to tell his story, anxious and intense. He described the strange telephone call to the yacht, and the woman who said they would pay for Cardinal Paravacini's death.

"That call could only have come from the house, so while Togazzi here was making arrangements to get rid of the corpse and clean things up, I ran to the house and began searching. There was nobody, at least I couldn't find anyone, but I did find a pair of binoculars near a telephone in the library. The sight line was perfect, direct to the yacht. Whoever she was called from there."

"But you couldn't find her?"

"No, but I was curious about that library. It was like no other library I'd ever seen. Oh, there were the usual leatherbound volumes, which meant they were probably never read, and hundreds of regular books, but there was something else. A whole section of what looked like archives. Huge scrapbooks, many with old, thick, yellowed paper, held together with heavy string. I pulled several out and began studying them. That's when I called one of the guards and told him to go down to the yacht and explain to Silvio that I'd be there for a while."

"What did you find?"

"Nothing short of a pictorial history of the Matarese family as far back as the turn of the century. Photographs, daguerreotypes, old newspaper clippings, and maps with specific markings. Not many words, no text as such, only captions in Italian, some short, others longer."

"I translated them for him," Togazzi broke in. "He speaks a little of our language but his reading is practically illiterate."

"I speak French better than you do!"

"A diseased language."

"Did you learn anything new?" asked an exasperated Pryce.

"No, something old, *very* old, and it started me thinking. We've been looking in the wrong direction, trying to anticipate the crises, when and where they'll take place and what they'll be."

"How can we short-circuit them if we don't look for them?"

"That's the point, we'll *never* find them. Only one man knows, the one who gives the orders, Matareisen. He's buried them so deep I suspect he's the only one who has the information we desperately need."

"*So?*"

"I have a hunch so strong it's eating a hole in my gut."

"What do you mean?"

"You see, one of those huge scrapbooks was devoted entirely to the ruins of the old Matarese fortress or castle, as in the *Baron* of Matarese. There were dozens of photographs, from every angle of the inside ruins and the grounds outside. At least thirty big pages, and the pictures weren't old, I mean they weren't grainy or yellowed, but could have been taken yesterday. On the last page, there was a small hand-written note. *Negatives per J.V.M.*"

"Negatives for J.V.M.," said Cameron. "Jan van der Meer Matareisen, the one who gives the orders."

"Exactly. And why would Matareisen want an extensive photographic record of the old place—because they *were* ruins."

"The answer is obvious," Togazzi again interrupted. "For reconstruction."

"That's what I figured," said Scofield. "The genesis of the Matarese, the original seat of power. I'm not much for psychobabble, but we know Matareisen is a fanatic to the core, a brilliant basket case, but certifiable. Where would such a man go but to his roots when he's about to pull off a worldwide catastrophe?"

"But you don't know that, Bray."

"We will tomorrow."

"What?"

"I called Geof in London on one of Silvio's private lines, and got Considine's code name and hotel number. At first light he'll take off from Milan and fly to the unmapped air-strip near Lake Maggiore—he said he knows it because he picked up you and Leslie there."

"He does and he did."

"His tanks will be full and we'll head for the southeast coast of Corsica. It's roughly two hundred forty air miles, four-eighty with a return; that's no problem for his aircraft. We'll fly below Solenzara to Porto Vecchio, north of Boni-facio. Using the coordinates from Paravacini's maps, we'll pass over the Matarese ruins."

"Is that smart?" asked Pryce.

"At twelve thousand feet it is. Among the equipment I asked for was a high-altitude photo-television scope that penetrates cloud cover. With a few passes, we'll be able to determine if there's any activity down there. If there is, we'll go into Phase Two."

"What's that?"

"There's an airfield in Senetosa, about twenty minutes

from the old Matarese fortress. We'll deplane, trek over, and see what we can find."

"Good God, why no backups? Why this *secrecy,* which amounts to a *blackout*?"

"Because I don't trust anybody; we're *all* penetrated. If I'm right, Matareisen will be there in all his simulated glory. But if he has even the inkling of a suspicion that we've centered in on Porto Vecchio, he'll either hightail it out of there or call in enough firepower to blast an army away."

"Reality check, Bray," said Cameron sharply. "Suppose you're wrong and he's not there?"

"So I'm wrong. London's working like hell, Squinty's working, the Keizersgracht is working, they're all working. We're not in this alone, for Christ's sake. All we've lost is our time."

"Suppose he is there and he's already got his guards, his firepower?"

"Hey, young fella, this isn't my first run. I was here when you were sucking tits."

"That's not an answer, Brandon."

"All right, it's in the equipment Geof provided. A Comsat mobile-link phone, direct satellite transmission to London. If what you suggest is the *reality,* as you put it, there's a unit of French commandos at the airport in Marseilles. By jet, they can be in Senetosa in a matter of minutes."

"So your secrecy isn't exactly total—"

"The hell it isn't. Those guys haven't a clue, just that there might be an incursion on an island in the Mediterranean. Once I give Geof the word, he relays it to the Deuxième Bureau and the jet takes off for Senetosa. I'll meet the unit on the road and issue the orders. If I ever call them."

"That would assume you've done some reconnoitering."

"I assume *we* will have. That part's in the equipment, too. Camouflage outfits, binoculars, two machetes, knives, guns with silencers, boots, wire cutters, gas canisters—all the usual stuff."

"The usual '*stuff*'?"

35

They flew down the Corsican coast at eight thousand feet until they reached Solenzara, where Luther ascended to twelve thousand. The sophisticated high-altitude camera was in place, clamped to the floor of the fuselage, the opening part of the Bristol Freighter's multipurpose design.

"Map coordinates coming up two minutes plus," said Considine over the loudspeaker. "Are you prepared?"

"Everything's ready," replied Scofield, hovering over the camera whose ten-inch screen magnified the ground below a thousandfold while photographs were taken roughly every half second.

Two minutes later Luther spoke again. "Start your lead-ins and check for focus. Refine."

"I gather you've done this before, Lieutenant," said Pryce into his throat microphone.

"You gather right, spook. It's called Iraqi flybys. Very relaxing duty, except when the idiots get missile-happy."

"*Rolling,*" cried Brandon, peering down at the screen. "Look at that, Cam! You'd think those trees were only a couple of hundred feet away, not two miles."

"Approaching target," exclaimed Considine. "Good luck, bombardier."

"There it is!" yelled Scofield. "Only it *isn't.* Those aren't ruins—Togazzi and I were right, the whole place has been rebuilt! Turn around and make another pass, Luther."

"Peeling," said the pilot as the aircraft veered to the left.

The second, third, and fourth passes revealed a total of five figures at various times on the grounds of the Matarese estate. Two of the people appeared to be women; one male apparently was a gardener, as he was in the middle of a cluster of flowers, and two other men were climbing into an automobile.

"That's enough for me," said Beowulf Agate, "we go to Phase Two. *Senetosa,* Luther! Can you find it?"

"I found it before we took off, ye elder spook."

On the ground at the Senetosa airfield, Scofield and Pryce opened the crate of supplies, dividing up the equipment among them. Bray threw Considine a camouflage suit complete with a full cartridge belt and a silenced pistol. "What the hell are these for?" asked the pilot. "I've already got new clothes without any labels."

"Just in case we need assistance, and it would only be under extreme circumstances."

"If they're not in the air, I don't like extreme circumstances. I fight in the sky, man."

"I doubt any such thing would be required. However, there's a possibility that a small contingent of French commandos will be arriving—"

"French *commandos*!" exploded Luther. "You white clowns are playing fast and loose with this black ass."

"No, no, Lieutenant, you misunderstand. There's only one road from here to Porto Vecchio and if they're required, I'll meet them halfway and I'll give them their orders. It's just that they'll feel more confident if you're dressed in combat gear."

"*I* won't feel more confident."

"Pensacola, Luther, Pensacola," said Cam quietly.

"I don't know whether that's a promise or an albatross."

"He's a very clever young man," observed Scofield. "Come on, fellas, strip and get into the gear."

Outside the aircraft, Brandon and Pryce, in full guerrilla regalia, and Considine, self-conscious in his camouflage fatigues with the cartridge belt, stood by the plane while the traffic controller from the small tower approached. He spoke in broken English.

"You most welcome to Senetosa, *signori,* although I have never seen you. You are to proceed with your operation. Our crew will cover your plane with nets."

"Is that necessary?" asked Luther.

"Orders from London. Proceed, *piacere,* the airstrip will be closed until we receive additional orders."

"Good enough," said Scofield. "Stay by your radio, Lieutenant. We'll keep in touch."

"You do that."

Bray and Cameron started down the road from the airfield cut out of the hills. It was now late morning and they stayed on the edge of the coarse pavement, prepared to race into bordering woods at the first sight or sound of humans or vehicles. Twice it was necessary to do so; the first time it was the appearance of an old gray Renault coming toward them in the distance. Peering through the trees, they saw it was driven by a couple in their thirties and obviously in the middle of a heated argument. The second was the sound of voices behind them. Startled, they ran for cover. To their relief, the voices belonged to four boisterous teenagers, student-athletes, perhaps, out for a noonday run.

The youngsters out of sight, Scofield and Pryce resumed their positions on the edge of the country road, accelerating their pace. Minutes later they came to a steep, descending section; across the way, on a hill, stood the restored great house of the Baron of Matarese.

"From here on we go solo, agreed?" said Beowulf Agate softly.

"Looks best to me," said Cameron. "I'll take the right flank, you go left."

"Both of us in the woods."

"Certainly not on the road."

"Let's go. We'll check radios in five minutes."

They split, Pryce walking across the road and entering the Porto Vecchio forest, Scofield disappearing into the woods on the left. Each found the steep, ravinelike slope nearly impenetrable, trees and tropical vines intertwined, the ground soft from the Corsican rains. The difficult trudging was matched and overmatched by the subsequent, equally steep climb up the succeeding hill of the brief valley. They had tested the radios, keeping both on open frequencies.

"*Cam,*" came Brandon's whispered voice over Pryce's instrument.

"Yes?"

"Be prepared. If it's the same on your side, you're going to come to a wall of coiled barbed wire rising eight or nine feet high."

"I think I see it," said Pryce. "Up ahead there's a flickering, like filtered sunlight bouncing off metal."

"That's it. Same over here."

"Frankly, I laughed when you mentioned wire cutters. What do you have, precognition?"

"Hell no. From the Paravacini maps we knew the place was surrounded by woods. That eliminated any kind of electrified fence or parameter alarms; small animals and birds would be setting them off every two or three seconds. That left only inhibiting measures, *ergo,* wire."

"I'm glad they taught you Latin at Harvard."

"Ingrate. Remember, start at the bottom, cutting in circles until you make an opening you can crawl through."

"Thank you, Mother."

Inside the borders of the Matarese compound, and staying in touch by radio, the two intruders agreed to meet on the wooded east flank, Cameron's side. Creeping through the foliage, the estate's manicured lawn only feet away, Scofield came into view. Pryce, on his hands and knees, joined him.

"That Italian high-noon sun is hot," whispered Brandon, "even in here."

"Hold it," ordered Cameron quietly. "Look!"

Beyond the profusion of interlocking tree branches in the circular drive that passed the large bronze front door, a man in casual clothes walked out of the entrance. Immediately, he reached into his pocket and took out a pack of cigarettes.

From another pocket he retrieved a lighter, and like a confirmed smoker denied his habit, lit up, drawing heavily. Fifteen seconds later, a uniformed maid emerged, joining him. She, too, removed cigarettes from her laced waist pocket; he lighted one for her as his left hand fondled her breasts. She giggled, reaching down for his crotch.

"Fun and games at Chez Matarese," whispered Pryce.

"More to the point, they had to go outside to smoke."

"I don't follow you."

"Geof's research on Matareisen established that he's a zealous antismoker, pathological about tobacco. You were there, you never saw an ashtray in the Keizersgracht. Pipes, cigars, and cigarettes were banned."

"Seems he's pathological, period."

"In this area, at least he's got a reason. A doctor in Amsterdam, a pulmonary specialist, treated him for severe respiratory problems. . . . He's in there, Cam. My hunch was right."

"We'd better confirm that before we call London and Geof reaches Marseilles."

"*If* we call anybody."

"Bray, this isn't the time or the place for personal heroics!"

"I'm no hero, I hate heroes. They get people killed."

"Then what are you talking about?"

"Why we're here, that's what I'm talking about," replied Scofield, his eyes on the circular drive beyond the trees and the profuse ground cover. "We're here to bring back whatever Matareisen's got that will tell us what he's done and who's involved so we can stop it. If we're not too late."

"How does that preclude Geof and the Deuxième Bureau's commandos?" pressed Cameron.

"I have to go back nearly thirty years," answered Brandon, his whisper flat, pensive, conveying a long-ago memory. "The Appleton mansion outside of Boston. It's true I set off the initial explosions outside the grounds, but after all hell broke loose and bodies were dropping like fireflies in a heavy rain, other explosions took place that started the fires inside. The Matarese chieftains had rigged incendiaries in their inner sanctum guaranteeing the destruction of all their files, contracts, and papers. Eradication by fire is apparently a Matarese standby."

"'The fires in the Mediterranean,'" said Pryce, even his whisper muted, as the two smoking servants began strolling around the circular drive toward Bray and Cam. "I wonder what it means."

"Shhh!" The strollers came within eight feet of them, pawing each other like a couple of hormone-struck teenagers. They rounded the curve in the drive and proceeded up the south leg, by now practically undressing each other. "If this were night," whispered Scofield, "we'd take them both and find out who's inside."

"It's not night, so what do we do?"

"We go back to the airstrip and wait until it is. Night, I mean. I'll use your exit."

"Oh, *Jesus.*"

"Would you rather lie here with the insects and the snakes until it's dark?"

"Let's go," said Pryce.

Back at the airfield in Senetosa, they found Luther in the primitive ground-level "tower." He was dozing in a chair, the radio next to his head, the static low but constant. Across the room the traffic controller was reading a magazine in front of his equipment.

"Luther." Cameron shook Considine's shoulder.

"Yo!" The pilot opened his startled eyes. "You're back. What happened?"

"We'll tell you outside," said Beowulf Agate. "Let's take a walk."

Ambling along the bordering grass of the Senetosa runway, Scofield and Pryce filled Luther in, explaining what they had found in Porto Vecchio and what they still did not know.

"Sounds like you need help," Considine said. "Is it time for those French commandos—"

"No," interrupted Brandon. "Because we *don't* know what security measures they have when it's dark. We're not

going in during daylight, and we're not calling for support. Not yet, perhaps not at all."

"Why not?"

"Because, Lieutenant, the sight of a jet landing up here, especially a jet unloading an armed squad of uniformed commandos, would spread like a brushfire throughout the area. I know the Matarese; they pay the locals for just that sort of information."

"You never *intended* to call for them, did you?" asked Pryce, his anger surfacing.

"Well, it made Waters happy to know that they were there, and if we really need them, I can always make the call. At night, after we're back inside."

"That's just *great!*" exploded Cameron. "After the god-damned horse is stolen, lock the fucking stable door! What is this? A suicide operation, a two-man *kamikaze* run?"

"Come on, young fella, we're better than that."

"You sons of bitches lost me again," said a perplexed Luther. "You've got a bunch of jungle soldiers for the asking and you won't *use* them? For Christ's sake, why *not*?"

"He's afraid we'll miss the pot of gold if we do."

"What pot of *gold*?"

"Information we need, and he's probably right. One stupid move and Matareisen sends out his orders and destroys the data. We don't know what's coming next, or where, or who."

"I couldn't have said it better myself," noted Scofield. "And speaking of truisms, Cam and I had better get some shut-eye. We'll be up all night, and it's been a rough couple of days for him, time-wise."

"Agreed," said Pryce, "but where?"

"There's a cabin on the north side of the runway used by pilots and crews for layovers. That excuse for a controller said we can go there."

"I'm as tired as Cam is, but I'm not going to leave the plane, nets and all."

"You left it when you fell asleep in the shack," disagreed Pryce.

"No, I didn't. I threaded a half dozen heavy tools in the

netting. If anybody tried to lift it, the racket would wake up a family of moles eight feet under the ground. I'd be out of here like a shot and, incidentally, prepared to shoot."

"The lad has possibilities," said Brandon, leading them to the cabin.

"*Goddamn it,* where have you *been*?" yelled Jamieson Fowler into the phone.

"Out of town," answered a cautious Stuart Nichols, attorney for the brokerage firm of Swanson and Schwartz.

"Yeah, well, I don't buy it. All of a sudden I can't reach Whitehead *or* you, and Wahlburg's answering machine says *he's* out of town! What's this 'out of town'? Some place exclusively for you guys?"

"Be reasonable, Jamieson. We all have our personal lives."

"You don't even sound like yourself. Something rotten's going on, and I want to know what the fuck it is! And don't give me that bullshit about obscenity being a lack of vocabulary."

"In your case it wouldn't do any good, and I wouldn't say it."

"Yes, well, somebody else did. Where the hell *is* Wahlburg? Washington, for Christ's sake?"

"He lives in Philadelphia, you know that. Why do you say Washington?"

"Let's put it this way," began Fowler, perspiring in his cool hotel suite. "I heard a rumor, which is why I've—*we've*—got to find the Jew! . . . You know, I've got a lot of friends in Washington, a few on offshore payrolls, actually, and one of them told me—told me . . . told me—"

"Told you *what*?" interrupted Nichols.

"That Ben was seen going into the FTC building."

"The Federal Trade Commission?"

"I didn't say FBI, which is the only thing worse."

"I don't understand."

"Suppose the hebe got yellow and decided to cover his hymie ass? Those people are clever, you know. He could do it in ways that wouldn't implicate himself, like *he* heard rumors, et cetera."

"About our . . . enterprise?"

"It's not about Disney World, you asshole!"

"I don't see how he could. Any deposition he might give to the FTC attorneys, they'd probe, and to be convincing he'd have to implicate himself, even in a minor way."

"That's lawyer talk. The Jew boys are smarter than you."

"God, you're offensive. My daughter is married to a fine lawyer who happens to be Jewish—"

"Yeah, I know all about him. He calls himself Stone, but it's really Stein."

"I suggested that for professional reasons. They live in Boston."

"Now who's offensive? . . . Forget it, back to Wahlburg. What do you figure?"

"I just told you, I question your source. However, we may have a larger problem, and it concerns the schism in Amsterdam."

"What the fuck *is* that? Straight talk, not hypotheticals."

"What?"

"Whaddya know, not whaddya think."

"I'm afraid my source is impeccable. The split in Amsterdam is between the Keizersgracht and Guiderone. The son of the Shepherd Boy will prevail, of course, but it pains me to believe that Albert has conceivably thrown in with van der Meer."

"What the hell are you *talking* about?"

"He's apparently, according to my source, decided to go with the money from Amsterdam."

"Who *told* you this?"

"A rumor, like yours, that's all I will say."

"That's not *good* enough."

"It's all you're going to get, Jamieson."

"Everything's falling apart, for Christ's sake! This is crazy. You're crazy and *I'm* crazy. What the hell is going *on*?"

"I'd like to know," said Stuart Nichols, hanging up the phone.

It was a quarter past five in the afternoon and the offices of Swanson and Schwartz were closed. However, Albert Whitehead remained inside, having said a wary if pleasant good-night to Stuart Nichols. There was a knock on his door. "Come in," called out the chief executive officer.

"Yes, sir." An attractive secretary walked inside. "I did as you suggested, Mr. Whitehead. I waited in the ladies' room until Mr. Nichols left."

"Thank you, Joanne. Sit down, please." The secretary did so and Whitehead continued. "As I briefly mentioned earlier, this meeting is extremely confidential in the highest professional sense. It may turn out to be meaningless, and I pray to the Almighty that it is, but certain information has come to light that might—I emphasize only *might*—concern your boss. Am I clear?"

"Of course."

"Good. How long have you worked for Mr. Nichols?"

"Nearly two years, sir."

"I know he's constantly filing papers, legal briefs, that sort of thing, but can you recall any lengthy statements or depositions directed to be under a court's seal?"

"Not offhand. . . . No, wait a minute. About six or seven months ago there was a *guardian ad litem* situation where the inheritor, a minor, sought the protection of the court to keep the size of the inheritance confidential. Insofar as the taxes were prepaid, the court accepted the seal."

"That was the only one?"

"To the best of my knowledge, yes, sir."

To the best of my knowledge. Whitehead loathed that phrase. It was all too often used as a cop-out, just as secretaries frequently formed bonds of loyalty with their bosses. How many followed them to other and better jobs? Too many to count!

"Joanne, I certainly believe you, my dear, but the few stockholders we have insisted that I make a thorough search. Do you have records of Mr. Nichols's dictation, or the documents he prepared?"

"Every document and every letter, including interoffice

memoranda. . . . I wasn't aware that Swanson and Schwartz had stockholders."

"It's not something we talk about; a small group of investors who helped me purchase the firm. Where are these records?"

"On computer disks, cataloged by date, day, and time of entry."

"Would you mind showing me where they are?"

"Not at all, sir." The secretary rose from the chair, preceding Whitehead out the door and to an office down the hall. Inside, she led him to a huge white file cabinet; she opened it, revealing shelves of disks, the shelves in sections by years and months.

"My word!" said Albert Whitehead. "That's quite a collection."

"Mr. Nichols started it five years ago. He decided it was easier and far more accessible to store things here rather than in the warehouse."

"He was absolutely right. Show me how it works. We all have the same computers, but I could be a little rusty pulling files up." The secretary named Joanne removed a disk, inserted it into the drive, and pressed the appropriate codes. "Oh, yes," said the CEO, "I remember now. It's really very simple, isn't it?"

"Very, Mr. Whitehead. Shall I stay and assist you? I can call my husband—"

"No, no, my dear, you run along. I'll be fine, and remember, our little meeting was just between us, as well as my visit here."

"I understand, sir."

"On behalf of the investors and myself, you'll find an envelope under your blotter in the morning."

"That's not necessary, sir."

"Oh, but it is, it is."

"Well, *thank* you, Mr. Whitehead. . . . And I hope everything is all right. I think Mr. Nichols is a wonderful man, so kind and considerate."

"He's all of that and a dear friend." *And a fucking Judas to boot*!

"Good night, sir."

"Good night, Joanne."

It was close to midnight when Albert Whitehead extracted the last disk. He was exhausted, his eyes bloodshot, his breath short. He had gone back three full years and over four thousand documents. There was nothing! Had Nichols gone outside the office and hired a typist from some sleazy employment agency? Or perhaps from a third-rate newspaper's Help Wanted column? Of course he had. It *had* to be! He couldn't very well indict the head of Swanson and Schwartz in front of an employee—or could he? Secretaries were an unpredictable breed, ranging from stealing petty cash to breaking up marriages.

Shall I stay and assist you? I can call my husband.

Sure, young lady, call your husband and tell him you're working with the owner of the company until midnight! What's next? Rape? Blackmail?

Whitehead dragged himself out of the chair and replaced the final disk in the large white file cabinet. He returned to the desk, picked up Nichols's telephone, and dialed his limousine service.

"Madre di Dio! Il mare Mediterraneo! Mare nostra!" The screams filled the silent night at the airfield in Senetosa, Corsica.

"What the hell is *that*?" shouted Scofield, bolting from the cot in the cabin north of the runway.

"Damned if I know," said Pryce, sitting up on the couch.

The door of the cabin crashed open as Luther Considine ran inside. "For God's sake, will somebody *translate*? Krazy Kat's going nuts out there!"

"What is it?" asked Brandon.

"You tell *me*," replied Luther. "He's running up here."

The air controller burst through the door. *"La radio! Mare nostra. Fuoco, incendio!"*

"Lentamente, lentamente," said Scofield, telling the man to slow down. "English, *piacere*?"

"Over radio," answered the controller in his broken English. "All through *il Mediterraneo*—fires everywhere!

From bay of Muscat to Africa, Israel, *fuochi. Inferno, male-detto! Il diavolo* takes up the world!"

" 'Fires all over,' " said Bray haltingly. " 'The devil takes over the world.' From Oman to Israel to North Africa."

"The Mediterranean fires," said Cameron. "Matareisen's sent it out. It's the signal!"

"Let's *go*!" cried Scofield.

"I'm coming with you," said Luther Considine. "My people came from Africa, and nobody burns our ocean."

36

It was shortly past eleven o'clock, the moon bright, alive in the sky, as Scofield, Pryce, and Considine crawled through the barbed wire into the Matarese compound.

"Luther, you're our rear point," whispered Brandon. "If anyone comes up the road, or even if you see headlights, get on the radio and tell us."

"Gotcha, elder spook. Do you guys do this sort of thing on a regular basis?"

"No," replied Cameron, "usually we're announced."

"Funny man."

"Not at the moment," said Pryce, following Scofield up the steep, wooded incline. They reached the border of the circular drive; the mansion was dark except for a single window on the top floor. Suddenly a figure appeared behind the glass.

"You wanted confirmation?" asked Bray.

"I've got it. It's he."

" 'It's he'? It's *him*."

"Case closed on Harvard. Get *back*! He's looking down here."

"Then stay still, your face down!" Scofield clamped his hand on Pryce's neck. "He's moving away."

"Let's run to the side of the house," whispered Cam.

"*No,* he's come back! He's on the phone."

Matareisen's face in the window appeared angry; he seemed to be shouting. He then walked away again only to reappear, holding what looked like a long computer print-out, his face still twisted in a grimace. Once more he left the window in apparent fury.

"*Now!*" said Brandon, getting up and racing across the drive to the side of the house, Cameron close behind him.

"He's pissed off about something," added Scofield. "We're okay for a couple of moments."

"Then what?"

"I want to look around, study the alarm setup, if I can find it."

"You screw with it, you'll set it off!"

"Maybe, maybe not. Weapons at the ready, as Geof would say, and check your silencer."

"Checked."

"Cover the front door. If I blow it with the alarm, I'll get back as soon as I can, but you be ready. Shoot anyone who comes out—"

"*Hey, spooks!*" It was Luther's whispered voice over both their radios. "Headlights heading straight for that medieval iron gate."

"Let's get out of sight in the back," said Scofield.

"*No,*" countered Pryce firmly. "This could be our way in. No mess, no fuss, no alarms."

"No heartbeats, either!"

"Come on, Bray, we're better than that, aren't we?"

"Explain how."

"Out of sight, yes, but not in the back. Did you see the front door?"

"Three brick steps, a thick, heavy door, carriage lanterns on the right and left," answered the observant Scofield.

"*And?*"

"And what? . . . The *bushes,* tall bushes flanking the

porch! Whoever it is goes inside while the alarm is off and we—"

"We're wasting time. I'll take the far side, you take this one."

"Spooks!" Considine again. "The gate opened and they're driving through."

"They?"

"Two gorillas, I'd say."

"Get off the radio," ordered Cameron, turning to Brandon. "Hurry *up*. Get in there and crouch!"

"Easy for you."

The large black sedan, its headlights blinding, rounded the curving drive and stopped in front of the wide brick porch. Two men got out, the driver medium-sized with long, light brown hair, the other much larger, barrel-chested, his head topped by a receding crew cut. Instead of walking up the steps to the entrance, they opened the rear doors and began carrying out grocery bags and small cartons, the labels and logos indicating that they had been purchased in the port city of Bonifacio. They piled the merchandise on the porch, speaking in the patois of Corsica, an odd mix of French and Italian.

"In the name of God, such delicacies!" said the driver. "The *padrone* must be planning a celebration."

"For whom? Us and the three servants? I doubt it."

"Certainly for the whore. He likes her, you know."

"I'm not sure she's a whore, I think she's a nymphomaniac. As for his liking her, wait'll he finds out she's slept with all of us! It would offend his aristocratic dignity. He looks down on us, I trust you know that."

"I know that, and I don't give a shit if he considers us worms. The pay is good—more than good—far better than the Sicilians."

"Same rotten jobs, my friend. Frankly, I cannot go to the confessional any longer."

"Do not worry. Our God sent us here to do what we do. Everything is preordained."

"Ring the chimes, tell the idiots to shut off the alarm and open the door."

The driver did as the larger man told him. Moments later there were lights in the downstairs windows and a female voice over the porch intercom. "Yes, who is it?" she asked in the Corsican dialect.

"Two of your most experienced lovers, Rosa."

"*You're* certainly the heaviest!"

"Open up," said the driver. "We need help out here. Quickly!"

"Not until I turn off the alarm, unless you care to be blown out of the hills."

The two Corsicans looked at each other, their expressions conveying weary disgust. "Loud bells would have been sufficient," muttered the large, heavyset man. "Why the explosives? A true idiot inside could blow us to hell, along with the porch."

"The *padrone* takes no risks. He's safe and we take our chances."

The door opened and the voluptuous maid, who had previously strolled in the driveway with a guard, appeared. Her revealing negligee emphasized the swells of her generous breasts and the curvature of her hips.

"Mother of God!" cried the woman. "What are all these?"

"The *padrone* must be having a party," replied the driver.

"*That* explains things," said the scantily clad maid.

"What things?"

"We're running around like headless chickens! The rooms must be spotless, the sheets washed and softened, the silver polished, the banquet hall set up, and the cook is going crazy. The butcher and the greengrocer were here this afternoon delivering enough meat and produce to feed a houseful of Sicilian mamas!"

"What does the *padrone* say?"

"Nothing himself. He's locked on the top floor and sends down messages in the air tube. Besides the ones I just told you, he tells us that guests will be arriving shortly past dawn. Shortly past *dawn*! Can you imagine?"

"With the *padrone* I can imagine most anything," said

the large man, picking up a case of wine. "I'll take this into the kitchen."

"I'll follow with two of these cartons. They're too heavy for our delicate Rosa."

"Delicate, my ass!"

"That isn't, Rosa."

The two Corsicans disappeared into the house as the maid bent over, sorting through the packages. Suddenly, Pryce broke through the bushes and leaped up on the porch, grabbing the woman by the neck, yanking her head back, his left hand clamped over her mouth. "Your *gas*!" he whispered to Scofield, who was climbing up the front steps, the low brick side too difficult for him to negotiate. Swiftly, he reached into the pocket of his camouflage fatigues and pulled out his canister of aerosoled chloroform. He rapidly administered two sprays into her face, concentrating on her nostrils; she collapsed instantly. Cameron dragged her off the porch and placed her unconscious body to the right of the foliage, out of sight. Both men raced back behind the bushes.

The two Corsicans returned, confused by the absence of the maid. "Rosa, where the hell *are* you?" called out the driver, walking down the brick steps. This time it was Scofield who walked out of the thick foliage, his silenced pistol in the porch's light.

"You raise your voice, young man, you won't have any vocal cords. I'll blow them out of your throat."

"What *is* this?" roared the huge man, lunging across the porch. "Who *are* you?"

Again, Cameron ran out, his pistol in hand. *"Silenzio!"* he said in his limited Italian. "One move and you are *morto*."

"I understand English, *signore,* and I do not care to die." The large Corsican backed up the steps. "We are merely servants of the house, our possessions are insignificant."

"We're not interested in your possessions," said Pryce, "only information. We know the owner of this house, as you call it, is upstairs. How do you reach the top floor?"

"The stairs, *signore,* how else?"

"The front stairs *and* the back stairs?"

"Both. You know the house?"

"I'm trying to. Where are the back stairs?"

"In the kitchen. The staff must use them."

"How many floors?"

"Four, *signore.*"

"Are there any exits to the outside from the back stairs?"

"Not directly."

"Fire escapes, where and how many?"

"Che?"

"I know that one," interrupted Scofield. *"Scala di sicurezza."*

"Ah, *sì,*" acknowledged the Corsican. "There are two, *signore.* West and east sides, the first for guests, the second for the staff."

"How are they reached?"

"Each floor has a locked emergency door in the corridor that opens on the *scala.* It is released by a concealed button in the wall or by a master switch in the kitchen."

"Besides the owner, your *padrone,* who else is inside and where are they?"

"The cook and a second maid—where is *Rosa?*"

"She's resting."

"You *killed* her?"

"I said resting, not dead. Now where are the cook and the second maid?"

"The cook has a bedroom on the second floor above the kitchen, the girl on the third."

"I think that does it, don't you, Bray?"

"Short, sweet, and complete," agreed Scofield.

"Now!" cried Pryce. Operating in tandem, the Americans shoved their weapons into the stomachs of the two Corsicans while yanking out their gas canisters. Holding their breaths, they sprayed each at close range and, as each started to collapse, they propelled the body into the interior lawn of the circular drive. The men would be unconscious for at least an hour, and maybe as long as three hours. "Use the radio and get Luther up here," continued Cameron.

"The second fire escape, right, youngster?" Scofield pulled out his radio and spoke into it.

"You've got it. When Luther gets here, you two cover the fire escapes, and I'll go in for the cook and the maid."

"*Here* I am, spooks." Considine raced out of the Porto Vecchio woods. "What do I do?"

"Come over here," said Pryce as the pilot ran to his side. "Around the corner of the house, on the west side, there's a fire escape. If anyone tries to come down, fire your gun, but *away* from the body. We don't want anyone wounded, much less dead."

"Gotcha, brother," whispered Luther.

"So do I," said Brandon, removing his weapon. He turned, walking rapidly to the east side of the estate.

"Unless there are interruptions, we'll meet back here in ten minutes," was Cameron's last instruction before heading into the house.

Inside, he bore to the left, the east section, where the Corsicans had carried the cartons from Bonifacio. The kitchen was immense, worthy of any upscale restaurant, the back staircase narrow and poorly lighted, as apparently befitted the staff, in their employer's view. Pryce crept up to the second floor, his body nearly prone, his camouflage fatigues giving rise to the image of a giant lizard approaching its prey. He stood up in the hallway, judging which door on the right was above the kitchen. It was obvious, so he sidestepped toward it, his gun and the gas canister in his hands. Awkwardly, he shoved the canister under his left arm and silently tried to twist the doorknob; it did not move, it was locked.

He studied the door, stepped back across the hallway, shifted the canister to his right hand, and bolted forward with all his weight and strength. With an enormous crack, the door burst open, and Cam rushed in, holding his breath and spraying the bed with the immobilizing gas. The slender, stunned chef opened his eyes in panic, started to scream, then collapsed back into the pillows.

Pryce returned to the back stairs, checking his watch; he had four minutes to go. He climbed to the third floor and rounded the corner into the narrow, dark corridor. The first thing that caught his eye was the strip of light at the bottom of the second door on the right. Shoving his weapon into his belt, the canister in his left hand, he reached for the knob. The door opened and Cam quickly stepped inside. The room was deserted but on the wall above the bed was a small glass panel, a red light blinking in the center accompanied by a low humming sound akin to a soft but constantly ringing alarm clock. Apparently the room belonged to the arousable Rosa. Obviously, it was her night to cover the doors and the alarms.

He had barely two minutes left, not that the time was written in cement, but time spans were important and he did not want Scofield and Considine to think that something had gone wrong and do something foolish like rushing in to search for him. He returned to the dark, narrow hallway, looking to the right and the left. There were three more doors, four in all. A modicum of propriety would dictate that the floors be divided by gender, the proper way for servants' quarters regardless of improper visiting rights.

Taking his chances, based only on a vague perception that Rosa was the sturdier of the women, Pryce crossed to the first door nearest the staircase and the emergency exit. Oddly enough—and something he had not noticed in the very dim light—the door was open, only an inch perhaps, but definitely open. He slowly pushed it back when he heard the words spoken from within the darkness.

"Padrone? Mi amore?"

One did not have to be a linguist to catch the lady's meaning. *"Sì,"* replied Cameron, approaching the bed. The rest took less than fifteen seconds and Pryce was back by the front porch with twenty-odd seconds to spare.

"I gather your incursion was not only successful but silent," said Beowulf Agate, his voice low.

"It was," answered Cam. "Now comes the delicate part."

"Time for the Gallic commandos, right, fellas?" said Luther.

"Not right," replied Scofield. "A jet landing—*very* cautiously, I might add—on that not exactly state-of-the-art airstrip, and word goes out about how *crazy* it is. The same jet unloading a commando unit, and emergency sirens aren't out of the question."

"However," interrupted the pilot, "not any telephone calls."

"What do you mean?" asked Pryce.

"Well, before we left Senetosa, I took a pair of pliers out of the nets on the plane, ran into that so-called tower, and cut the telephone wire that came down from the roof."

"This young man *really* has possibilities," said Bray. "You should recruit him."

"No thanks, elder spook. I like it in the sky."

"Don't minimize your contribution, Luther," Pryce broke in firmly. "You may have given us the few extra moments we need."

"Why? Because of the telephone?"

"Exactly."

"But if that controller was going to call here, why didn't he call before?"

"Good question," said Scofield, "and I'll answer it. Because the French authorities told Senetosa that we're gathering evidence of drug couriers sailing in to the port of Solenzara. This is the nearest airfield, and no French officials will interfere with drug interdictions. They could spend twenty to thirty years in prison if they did."

"So they don't know anything about *this* place?"

"That's the way it's been planned, Lieutenant"

"What do you suggest, Bray? You've been here before, we haven't," Cameron said.

"Matareisen's isolated, no guards, no servants, right?"

"Right."

"Total surprise, shock. The fire escape on the top floor has a short lateral walk that passes the right window. One of us breaks through the door from the front stairs, the other stays by the side of the window and crashes the glass. Timed right, he's cornered."

"I can climb on your shoulders, Cam," said Luther. "I'll be able to reach the bottom rung of the ladder."

"You could also be in the first line of fire."

"I can't support *you*, you big white gorilla, so in for a dime, in for a dollar."

"Remind me to call a naval commander in Pensacola."

"Not with my obituary, you dirty dog."

"I hope not, but I want you to know what you're doing."

"I want to do it. Enough said."

"Enough said."

"Let's synchronize our watches, as all those dumb movies say," said Scofield. "What do you figure, Pryce?"

"Give us three minutes to get Luther on the ladder, another one for me to rejoin you, and thirty seconds for you to go out and cover our pilot on the fire escape. If Matareisen walks to a window, he could spot him. Then allowing for me to find out where I'm going and how to get there without any noise, add five minutes. Altogether that's nine minutes, thirty. It's now midnight plus seven. *Mark*. . . . Let's go, Luther."

The pilot climbed to the lowest tier and sat motionless, his eyes on his watch. He would creep up to the top floor during the last thirty seconds of the time span. Cameron slid along the side of the house, judging the line of sight that would be the most feasible for Scofield to protect Considine. Once that was determined, he ran back to Brandon.

"Take your position at the edge of the woods, Bray."

"Why so far?"

"It'll have the best sight line to the window. The other angles would either show you on the lawn or are too tough to shoot from."

"Thanks, kid, I might have recruited you myself."

"Gosh, thank *you*, Mother."

"You've got roughly five minutes."

Pryce ran up the porch steps and into the house. The front staircase was at the end of the long foyer of rose marble, the railings gold-plated and glistening under the dim glow of a distant chandelier. He approached the steps, looking for concealed wire trips. His fingers caressed the underside of the railing that curved around to the first landing leading to the second floor; there were none that he could find. He then tested the staircase runner for slight bulges that could indicate alarms; again there were none that he could feel. He found the rheostat for the chandelier and turned up the lights.

Silently, he began climbing, reaching the second floor, his eyes searching every inch below him, looking for the abnormal, a trap. Cam glanced at his watch; his caution was costing him time. He had ninety-eight seconds left and two more floors to go; he hastened his pace.

Stop! On the steps to the fourth floor, there was a slight discoloration in the runner caused by a minuscule elevation. Pryce took out his knife and swiftly carved around one-half of the circular bulge. Carefully, he peeled the carpeting back. Beneath was a flat metal disc with two wires leading up the staircase. It was either an alarm trip or a land mine, and considering the monstrous agenda of Matareisen, the mine was a distinct possibility. What's a servant or two?

Sixty-one seconds!

Cameron took the steps two at a time, his eyes now red with strain, knowing that each planted foot could cost him his life. *Thirty-nine seconds!* And he had to be ready, weapon in place, his concentration absolute, his breathing steady. He had been in too many similar situations where a calm, still attitude was as vital as firepower. Without it, operations could easily fail or be aborted. *No more time!*

Breathing deeply, Pryce stood five feet from the door, his arm outstretched, his gun aimed at the wood around the knob. Several shots would weaken the lock, his shoulder doing the rest. *Four seconds, three, two, one—now!* He fired three bullets, splintering the wood, simultaneously hearing the loud crash of shattered glass from within. He rushed forward, and with all his strength crashed through the door, instantly lunging to the floor, rolling away from his point of impact.

Jan van der Meer Matareisen, in shock, recovered enough to race to a stack of computer printouts. He picked it up and dashed to a shredder clamped over a large iron receptacle, the glow from which indicated burning coals at the bottom.

"Don't do it!" roared Pryce, his weapon aimed.

"There's no way you can *stop* me!" screamed Matareisen. "You can't kill me, I'm worthless to you dead!"

"You've got a point," agreed Cameron, firing. Not, however, into any life-threatening part of his body; instead, at his legs, specifically his kneecaps. Shrieks of agony filled the room as the Baron of Matarese's descendant fell to the floor, the printouts flying everywhere but into the shredder. "Break the rest of the window and get in here, Luther!" yelled Pryce, taking out his canister and going over to the writhing, screaming Matareisen. "I'm going to do you a favor, you *bastard*," said Cam, bending over and spraying the wounded monster's face. "Unpleasant dreams," he added.

Considine leaped through the destroyed window and rushed over to Pryce. "Piece of cake, spook," noted the pilot. "You know, I'm getting to be pretty good at this sort of thing. I mean, when you consider the nets on the plane, the Senetosa telephone, and now this, well, I'm not too shabby."

"You're a goddamned hero, Luther."

"Why, thank you, Cam."

"I haven't finished. I agree with Scofield, I hate heroes. They get people killed."

"Hey, what kind of remark is that?"

"An extremely truthful one. Come on, we're not finished."

"What's to do?"

"First, go downstairs to the kitchen, it's on the ground floor to the right. Tear the place apart and try to find a first-aid kit. There should be one; people cut themselves in kitchens. We have to bind and tourniquet Matareisen's legs."

"Why so kind?"

"Because he was right. He's no good to us dead. On the staircase, stay off the carpet, the runner, it's tripped."

"It's *what*?"

"Never mind, just stay on the marble. Hurry up, get *going*!" Luther ran out, leaping over the fallen door as Cameron scooped up the computer printouts, shuffling them, and staring at the contents. Two sheets appeared to be some sort of key codes in columns, but they were beyond his expertise. The rest, twenty-odd pages, were again coded, perhaps decipherable with the columned two sheets. Pryce walked rapidly to the damaged window and shouted, "*Bray, are you down there?*"

Silence. A disturbing silence.

Suddenly, an ear-shattering bell echoed throughout the entire mansion, so loud and startling that it produced instant paralysis. Putting down the printouts, Cameron raced over the demolished door into the hallway. Below on the staircase stood a bewildered. Scofield; he had stepped on the alarm trip. Pryce ran down the steps, pulling out his knife and shoving the vaunted Beowulf Agate aside. He knelt down, lifted the cut circle of carpeting, and severed the wires. The deafening bell stopped. "You're lucky it wasn't a bomb," said Cam.

"Why the hell didn't you *tell* me about it?"

"I thought you were still outside. Come on, I want to show you what we've got up here." They returned to Matareisen's lair.

"His legs are bleeding," observed Scofield, seeing the unconscious figure of the Matarese leader.

"It's his knees, actually. Luther's looking for some bandages."

"Bandages, hell. Put a bullet in his head."

"Counterproductive," said Pryce, picking up the printouts. "He tried to get rid of these."

"What are they?"

"Unless I'm grossly mistaken, they're the signals he was sending out. They're coded and I'm not that much of a computer whiz."

"Send them to Amsterdam. With all this equipment, there must be a fax machine."

"There's one over there, but I don't know the fax number at the Keizersgracht."

"I have it," said Beowulf Agate, reaching for an inside pocket. "You should learn to be prepared, youngster."

While the fax did its work, Cameron phoned Greenwald in Amsterdam, explaining the circumstances and the material he was sending to the Keizersgracht. The computer scientist made it clear that all other work would cease, the unit's concentration fixed solely on the pages from Corsica. "Do you have a number where I can call you back?"

"Whatever you learn, call Waters in London and Frank Shields at Langley. I can't do anything here and we'll be damn busy. I'll reach you later this morning." Pryce hung up and turned to Scofield. "You've got the Comsat mobile-link phone on you?"

"Of course. Direct to MI-Five on scrambler."

"Call Geof. Tell him to reach the Deuxième in Marseilles and fly those commandos here."

"Here? *Now?* What in God's name *for?*"

"We're going to a banquet."

It was shortly past dawn and one by one the six limousines arrived at the estate in the hills of Porto Vecchio above the waters of the Ligurian Sea. A seventh vehicle was missing, for no one could locate the final guest, a Cardinal Paravacini of Rome. Under threats of exposure and severe punishment, the two revived Corsicans met each car and escorted each guest to the banquet hall. Upon entering, the guests were met by the armed Pryce and Considine, who proceeded to strap them to the chairs and gag them with silver duct tape, the ropes and the tape found in the gardener's shack. Once everyone—five well-attired men and one fashionably dressed woman—was in place, Cameron and Luther briefly disappeared through a door in the left wall only to return moments later. Between them they carried a dining-room chair; in it sat the wounded Jan van der Meer Matareisen, his legs bulging from the bandages under his trousers. Like the guests, ropes bound him to the chair and two layers of tightly wound duct tape secured his mouth.

The leader of the Matarese was placed at the head of the table, his maniacal gaze darting back and forth at the others in fury. Suddenly, Scofield, in civilian clothes, walked through the door and stood behind Matareisen.

"Gentlemen," he began, "and, of course, the lady, I'm here because I probably know more about your organization than anyone else alive. To call it a monstrous horror would be a vast understatement. The good side is that it's finished, *you're* finished. Your brilliant gaucho here blew it. He was caught with the whole computerized ball of wax right in his avaricious little hands. Some brilliance, huh? Fortunately for our side, we put together a team of the best brains in the world and broke his computer codes. . . . As I stand here, government agents, the police, and military personnel in several dozen cities in the industrial nations are fanning out, taking people into custody, including an *Eagle* at Langley, caught dialing too many numbers for a call made from a pay phone. It's called sterile access; he's toast. Also, not incidentally, courts and legislatures everywhere are being convened in emergency sessions to take measures against a potentially destructive global economic virus. As for the fires in the Mediterranean, the maestro in this chair has managed to do what few diplomats and statesmen have been able to accomplish. Hostile countries and warring factions have come together to put those fires out.

"Speaking of chairs, you'll note that your seating arrangements are identical to those of your mentor. That's not merely to provide you a level playing field with the man who has destroyed you, it's for your own safety. You see, some men have arrived to escort you away from Corsica, away from the land of the Matarese. Should any of you have been tempted to run or display firearms, you would have been shot. We wanted to spare you that embarrassing and egregious possibility."

"Egregious?" mumbled Pryce to Considine. "Harvard lace."

"Tuskegee bullshit," whispered Luther.

"Gentlemen!" called out Beowulf Agate in a loud voice. "You may come in now."

The double doors in the north wall opened and the squad of uniformed French commandos walked in in single file. They took up their positions surrounding the enormous banquet table as the bound and gagged guests writhed in their chairs, their heads whipping back and forth, their eyes fired in panic.

"I declare this conference closed," said Scofield in

exaggerated formality. "Gentlemen, untie your prisoners and take them to your plane. If any offers you a bribe, I'd suggest you *whack* 'em!"

It was ten o'clock in the morning, the sky dark, heavy rain imminent. The two Corsican servants had been promised leniency in return for their cooperation and were led away by the Bonifacio police. It remained for the three Americans, the two maids, and the chef to complete the task insisted upon oddly enough by Scofield. All portable valuables in the mansion, along with the cartons of food, many packed in ice, were to be placed in the gardener's large shack. It took nearly four hours and enough sweat to fill up a small pool.

"*Okay,* Bray," said a perspiring Pryce. "Now what the *hell* is this all about?"

"Closure, my young friend, simply closure," replied Scofield, picking up a five-gallon can as he ran into the mansion.

Three minutes later the fires started, instantly billowing up from the drapes and the furniture. Within five minutes the flames began enveloping the house, accentuated by the progressively blackening sky. Cameron was alarmed— where was Scofield? He had not come out!

"*Bray!*" he yelled as he and Luther ran toward the engulfing fires. Suddenly, there was an enormous explosion. Pryce and Considine threw themselves on the ground as the entire front porch was blown away, fragmented marble, concrete, and glass flying in all directions. The rains then came, torrential, unrelenting, but still the flames continued to erupt as if challenging the storm, nature against nature, fire and water in combat. "*Scofield!*" roared Cameron, getting up unsteadily, as did Luther.

"Where did the son of a bitch *go*?" screamed Considine. "If he's pulling some self-sacrificing crap, I'll break his face!"

"What are you guys *doing* out here?" shouted Beowulf Agate, rounding the west wing of the estate, running as fast as he could. "You're too damned close, you idiots!"

"What are *you* doing?" asked Pryce as the three walked rapidly away from the burning building. "What have you *done*?"

"What I should have done nearly thirty years ago in Boston. Reduced the Matarese's seat of power to ashes."

"What difference does it make? This isn't Boston, it's Porto Vecchio, Corsica!"

"I'm not sure. A symbol maybe, a memory, a relic of destruction, *total* destruction. Hell, I don't *know*! I just had to do it—for Taleniekov, perhaps. Anyway, I talked to the girls, the maids, first. I put them on notice."

"About what, the fire?"

"Let's say they'll spread the word. First come, first served at the gardener's stall. Some of that stuff will keep a number of families high on the hog for years at today's market prices. Why should it be impounded as evidence? It'd be stolen anyway." Scofield's Comsat phone buzzed inside his jacket pocket. He removed it and spoke. "Sir Hog's Butt, I presume."

"I can't even get angry at your provocative insolence, Brandon. Well done, my old friend, a splendid show."

"Spare me your British kudos, just send money."

"Actually, I expect you to submit certain expenses, but please, don't be *too* creative."

"I may want to buy a new island, or maybe a small country."

"Antonia wants to know when you're returning to London," said Waters, overlooking Scofield's reply.

"Within an hour or so. I want to sleep for a week."

"We'll check Heathrow, an auxiliary runway, and meet the plane. I'll call Leslie as well. Incidentally, Frank Shields phoned. You're to report to Washington as soon as possible."

"I'm 'to *report*'?" shouted Beowulf Agate. "*He* doesn't give me orders!"

"Come, old chap, we're going to require a debriefing as well. Official records, y'know."

"That's for *employees,* I'm a consultant! Let Pryce do it."

"Do what?" interrupted Cameron.

"A debriefing, you jerk."

"It's standard, Bray. No big deal."

"Then you and our lieutenant do it."

"Your 'lieutenant' is now a commander, Brandon," broke in Sir Geoffrey from London. "The papers from the Department of the Navy came through. And if Frank Shields and I had extolled his abilities much further, they'd probably have made him a rear admiral."

"You're a commander, Luther," said Scofield, turning to the pilot. "Or maybe a rear admiral."

"Pensacola, here I come!"

"One last thing, old friend," added Sir Geoffrey. "Frank said the President asked for a personal meeting with you. He's not only fascinated, but you'll be highly decorated."

"Why? I haven't voted in years. Besides, young Cameron had as much to do with this enchilada as I did. Let the President talk to him."

"That can't be done, Brandon. Officer Pryce remains in deep cover. He can't be part of any mop-ups."

"Goddamn it, I want to go *home*. Our island's probably grown over with every weed known to the Caribbean."

"As I understand it, your Army Corps of Engineers has that problem under control."

"I should be there to supervise!"

"Send Officer Pryce. He and Colonel Montrose certainly have some leave coming."

"I'm being *sandbagged*!"

epilogue

Sundown, Outer Brass 26, twenty-four nautical miles south of Tortola in the Caribbean Sea. Cameron and Leslie were in lounge chairs by the lagoon, Leslie on the portable satellite phone. "All right, dear, as long as you've thoroughly thought it out," she was saying. "I wouldn't want you to lose your place in Connecticut."

"Not a problem, Mom," came the young man's voice from London. "The headmaster knows Roger's school and spoke to the admissions proctor. I can enter as an exchange student at midterm, that's next month. I'll get full credit and the people I've spoken to both here and in Connecticut think it'll be a great experience for me."

"It will if you apply yourself, Jamie. The Brit schools can be tougher than ours."

"Roger's told me all about it. But I'll be going into the grade he already finished, so he can help me through the rough spots."

"That's not exactly the solution I was hoping for. By the way, how *are* Roger and Angela?"

"Terrific! We really get along, even though Coleman moved into the house with us. He can be pretty strict."

"That's the most comforting thing you've said."

"Gotta go, Mom. Coley's taking us on another excursion. He says if I'm going to go to an English school, and since I don't really speak the language, I should learn as much as I can about the U.K. Say hello to Cam for me. I really like him."

"It's my turn to say *'Cam?'* Do you mean *Mr.* Pryce?"

"Oh, get off it, beautiful lady, I'm not that young."

"You're a twit, as the British say."

"Would you believe I have hormones?"

"Jamie!"

"Bye, Mom. Love you." The line from London went dead.

"The little, big bastard," mumbled Leslie, pressing the button that cut off the phone. "He said to say hello to you and that he really likes you."

"I like him, too. Why did you yell at him?"

"He had the temerity to tell me that he had hormones."

"He's what? Fifteen? I can assure you, it's true, and they're racing around like crazy."

"I'm his *mother*!"

"Does that disqualify you from knowing the truth?"

"No, but certain realities are best treated with taste."

"I gather he's staying in London, going to school in England."

"Yes, but while they're in Belgravia, Coleman's moved into the house."

"Not a bad idea."

"A glorious one."

"Now what about us?" asked Pryce, sitting up and reaching for his drink on the Lucite table next to his chair. "We haven't really faced that, have we?"

"Does anything have to change? I'm comfortable, you're comfortable."

"I want more, if I can have it, Leslie. I've always known there was a void in my life. I identified it and could live with it, but I don't think I can any longer. I don't want to live alone anymore, I want to live with the woman I love very much."

"Why, Officer Pryce, are you asking me to marry you?"

"I am, Colonel Montrose."

"I'm touched, Cam, really I am," said Leslie, reaching for his hand and holding it gently. "But I think you're forgetting, I'm carrying a fair amount of baggage. I'm career Army, and it can post me wherever and whenever it likes. I'm not ready to give up that career, I've worked and studied too long and too hard to get where I am. Then there's my son; he could be a responsibility you may not care to assume."

"Why not? I think he's a wonderful boy—hell, I don't have to think it, he's proved it! You said he likes me and I like him, that's a pretty good beginning."

"What about the Army?"

"I'm a career intelligence officer and Frank Shields can send me to Outer Mongolia and I'd have to go. Just think how great our reunions would be. . . . Look, Leslie, considering our backgrounds, neither one of us would be ecstatic in sedentary jobs. Jets can fly people from Tokyo to New York over the pole in thirteen hours, from Beijing in seventeen. Traveling salesmen have to travel, women executives, too; actors, actresses, and models go everywhere for work. It simply depends on the work you do. I think we can handle it."

"You're very persuasive, my darling."

"Score points for the lady," said Pryce enthusiastically. "Scofield says that if a woman uses the term 'my darling,' keep her around."

"How generous of him. . . . But you *are* persuasive and I'm being rather shortsighted."

"Am I gaining ground?"

"Yes, I believe you are."

Suddenly, from the sky, came the roar of approaching rotors. A helicopter was arriving from downwind, accounting for the abrupt thunderous sound. They looked up through the palms; a pontooned chopper was circling to land on the beach beyond the photoelectric cells. Together, Cam and Leslie, hand in hand, got up and ran down the path toward the sandy cove. As delicately as possible, considering its mass and the tonnage, the enormous helicopter touched down on the edge of the beach, the palms in an uproar at the intrusion.

The door of the chopper opened and the first to step out was Scofield. He turned, helping Antonia into the knee-deep water. They waded to shore as the clattering rotors came to a stop, and as women tend to do, Leslie and Toni embraced.

"Antonia, this place is paradise!" exclaimed Montrose. "No wonder you adore it so."

"It has its points, my dear. Good heavens, the Corps of Engineers did a wonderful pruning job. The palms have been cut back beautifully."

"They also upgraded your generator system," said Pryce.

"Who *asked* them to?" argued a petulant Scofield. "It was working fine."

"I believe the orders came from the White House," answered Cameron. "Your capacity has been tripled, and the major in charge was instructed to tell you that it was a gift from a grateful nation."

"The President didn't say anything, and I was with the kid for over an hour."

"The *kid*?" said Antonia disapprovingly. "Really, Bray . . ."

"I didn't say I didn't like him. Actually, I think he's a very bright young fella, very conscientious. Also, quite generous. I explained that my pension barely covered my needs, due to the fact that my reputation forced me to live incognito out of the country, so right before my eyes and ears, he called the Agency and had them double it."

"That's the *second* President you've conned!" cried Pryce. "I read your unexpurgated dossier, remember?"

"I don't remember anything, youngster. It's one of the blessings of advanced age. . . . Now, let me be clear, these two chopper pilots have a schedule to keep and you're part of it. We'd love to have you stay for a while, but I'm afraid it's not possible. Get your things together and climb on board. You've got about ten minutes."

Scofield and Antonia sat in the two lounge chairs by their lagoon. "How does it feel, luv?"

"We're home, my darling. I couldn't ask for anything more."

"Any vittles around?"

"A new walk-in refrigerator with enough food to last a year."

"They didn't have to do that."

"Oh yes, they did, my . . . *dearest* darling. You're remarkable."

"Hey, this could be a terrific night, you know what I mean?"

"At our age? . . . Yes, yes, I do."

Aboard the Navy helicopter, on its way to Puerto Rico, where Officer Pryce and Lieutenant Colonel Montrose would be flown by jet to Washington, Cameron spoke. "We were interrupted," he said. "Have you thought about my proposition?"

"Your proposal, is that what you mean?"

"It certainly is."

"I have. Briefly but deeply. In your later years, do you think you'll be like Brandon Scofield, also known as Beowulf Agate?"

"I suppose it's possible. We're alike in many ways."

"With an Antonia?"

"You're my Antonia . . . my *Leslie*."

"Then yes, my darling. I wouldn't miss the ride for anything on earth."